# SINS
## OF THE HOUSE OF
# BORGIA

## SARAH BOWER

sourcebooks
landmark

*For Kairo*

Published by Sourcebooks Landmark, an imprint of Sourcebooks, Inc.
P.O. Box 4410, Naperville, Illinois 60567-4410
(630) 961-3900
Fax: (630) 961-2168
www.sourcebooks.com

Originally published as *The Book of Love* in the UK in 2008 by Snowbooks.

Library of Congress Cataloging-in-Publication Data

Bower, Sarah.
Sins of the House of Borgia / by Sarah Bower.
    p. cm.
    1. Young women—Italy—Fiction. 2. Household employees—Fiction. 3. Borgia,
Lucrezia, 1480-1519—Fiction. 4. Borgia, Cesare, 1476?-1507—Fiction. 5. Alexander VI,
Pope, 1431-1503—Fiction. 6. Italy—History—1492-1559—Fiction. 7. Nobility—Papal
States—Fiction. 8. Popes—Fiction. I. Title.
    PR6102.O944S56 2011
    823'.92--dc22

2010048515

Printed and bound in the United States of America.
VP 10 9 8 7 6 5 4 3 2 1

# The Estense Territories

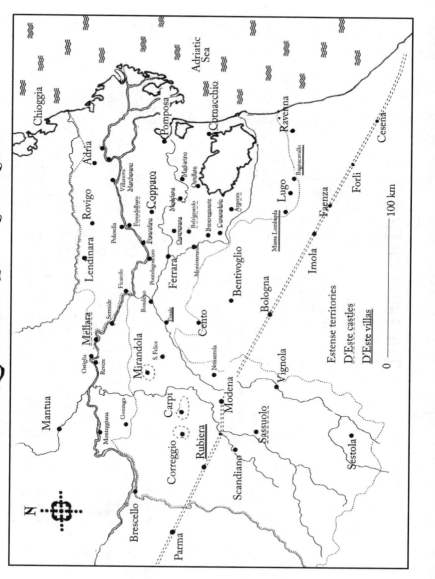

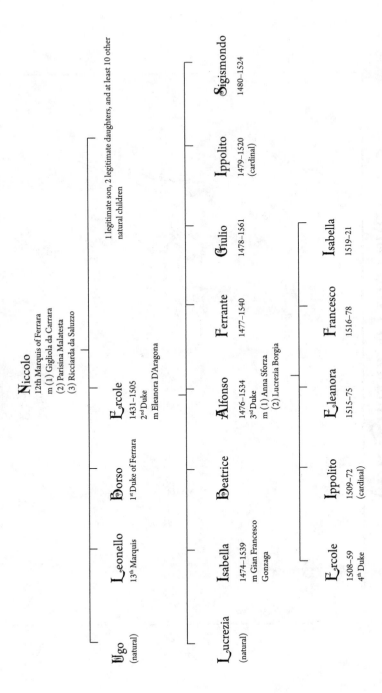

# The Family of Rodrigo Borgia

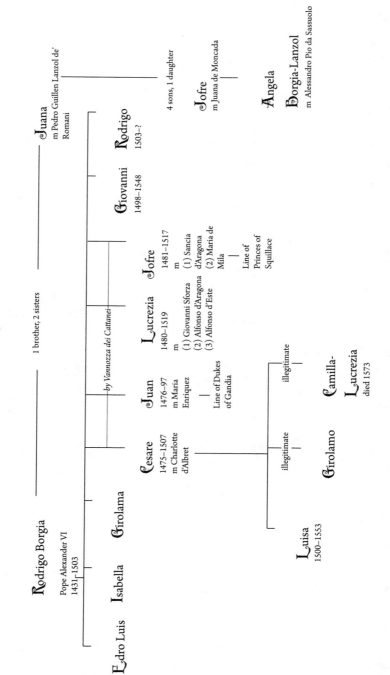

**Rodrigo Borgia**
Pope Alexander VI
1431–1503

1 brother, 2 sisters — **Juana**
m Pedro Guillen Lanzol de'
Romani

Edro Luis   Isabella   Girolama

*by Vannozza dei Cattanei*

**Cesare**
1475–1507
m Charlotte
d'Albret

**Juan**
1476–97
m Maria
Enriquez

Line of Dukes
of Gandia

**Lucrezia**
1480–1519
m
(1) Giovanni Sforza
(2) Alfonso d'Aragona
(3) Alfonso d'Este

**Jofre**
1481–1517
m
(1) Sancia
d'Aragona
(2) Maria de
Mila

Line of
Princes of
Squillace

**Giovanni**
1498–1548

**Rodrigo**
1503–?

4 sons, 1 daughter

**Jofre**
m Juana de Moncada

**Angela**

**Borgia-Lanzol**
m Alessandro Pio da Sassuolo

illegitimate

illegitimate

**Girolamo**

**Camilla-
Lucrezia**
died 1573

**Luisa**
1500–1553

*The past doesn't change, of course; it lies behind you, petrified, immutable. What changes is the way you see it. Perception is everything. It turns villains into heroes and victims into collaborators.*

Hilary Mantel, *A Change of Climate*

*Now Love has bent the pathway of my life.*

Pietro Bembo, *Gli Asolani*

# PROLOGUE

*Sometimes I dance, alone, to music no one can hear but me. When I dance I feel the beat of the earth's own heart rise through my feet and legs, through my loins and belly and into my chest, until my own heart beats in time with the earth's. Then I wonder if you feel it too, beneath that portion of the earth's crust where you stand, or walk, or lie, or dance too. Because always, when I am dancing, I am dancing with you.*

The end of the vanilla harvest always attracts a lot of visitors. There are the merchants, of course, and the queen's representatives who come to set the price, but there are also those who come to see the flying men. The tree has been chosen, felled, and set up in the town square, and priests of all denominations have chanted their prayers over it, sprinkled it with incense, and daubed it with chicken blood. The ropes have been tested and the finishing touches put to the feathered capes and headdresses. I sleep poorly these days, and I was awake before dawn this morning, haunted by the brave, lonely music of the *caporal*, high up on his platform, where he is bent by the wind and the weight of the sky, practising on his flute.

So I was already up when Gideon arrived back from Villa Rica with a traveller from Ferrara. The floor was swept and the maize pot on the boil. Gideon went straight in to Xanat and the baby, perhaps out of tact, perhaps because he had missed them, leaving me alone with the traveller. I say alone, but four or five of the older children were about, also up early because today was the day of the flying men. I shooed them all outside while I asked the traveller for news. Silly, really. None of them understands

Italian and even if they did, I have nothing to conceal from them. But I did not want them to hear our conversation. I do not want to live with anyone who is contaminated by my past.

The traveller told me the duchess was dead. My first thought was to wonder what she had done with the letters from Spain, but I made no mention of them to the traveller. I hope she had time to destroy them.

She had died last summer, the traveller said, after a difficult childbearing. The duchess's pregnancies were always difficult, for one reason or another. I do not mourn her because I know she has longed to leave this life for the past twelve years. And I am too close to death myself for mourning. The orange tree is four years old now. It has blossomed this year for the first time, which seems to me like a sign. My body is as sere and twisted as an autumn leaf; it curls ever tighter as though it longs to return to the womb, to be a bud again, a little fist of life. In Toledo, where I was a child.

# THE BOOK OF ESTHER

*Then said the king's servants that ministered unto him, Let there be fair young virgins sought for the king.*

The Book of Esther, 2:2

# CHAPTER 1

*There are days when I believe I have given up hope of ever seeing you again, of ever being free, or master of my own fate. Then I find that the heart and guts keep their own stubborn vigil. When we say we have given up hope, all we are really doing is challenging Madam Fortune to prove us wrong.*

When I was a little girl in the city of my birth, when my mother was still alive, she would take me to the synagogue, to sit behind the screen with the other women and girls and listen to the men sing the prayers for Shabbat. Sometimes, out of sight of the menfolk, while they were preoccupied by the solemnity of their duty, the women would not behave as their husbands and brothers and fathers liked to think. There would be giggling and whispering, shifting of seats, gossip exchanged by mouthing words and raising eyebrows. Fans would flutter, raising perfumed dust to dance in sunbeams fractured by the fine stone trellis which shielded us from the men. And around me was a continuous eddy of women, touching my hair and face, murmuring and sighing the way I have since heard people do before great works of art or wonders of nature.

This attention scared me, but when I looked to my mother for reassurance, she was always smiling. When I pressed myself to her side, fitting the round of my cheek into the curve of her waist, she too would stroke my hair as she received the compliments of the other women. Such a beautiful child, so fair, such fine bones. If I hadn't been there for her birth, added my Grand Aunt Sophia, I would say she was a changeling, possessed by a *dybbuk*. And several of the other children my age, the girls and little boys who had not yet had their *bar mitzvah*, would fix solemn, dark eyes on my blue ones as if, whatever Aunt Sophia said, I was indeed a *dybbuk*, a malign spirit, an outsider. Trouble. Rachel Abravanel used to pull my hair, winding it tight around her fingers and applying a steady pressure until I was forced to tip back my head as far as it would go to avoid crying out and drawing the attention of the men. Rachel never seemed to care that my hair bit into her flesh and cut off the blood to her finger ends; the reward of seeing me in pain made it worthwhile.

A year after the time I am thinking of, when Rachel had died on the ship crossing from Sardinia to Naples, Señora Abravanel told my mother, as she tried to cool her fever with a rag dipped in seawater, how much her daughter had loved me. Many years later still, I finally managed to unravel that puzzle, that strange compulsion we have to hurt the ones we love.

As it was, from before the beginning of knowledge, I knew I was different, and in the month of Omer in the year 5252, which Christians call May, 1492, I became convinced I was to blame for the misfortunes of the Jews. It was a hot night and I could not sleep. My room overlooked the central courtyard of our house in Toledo, and, mingling with the song of water in the fountain, were the voices of my parents engaged in conversation.

"No!" my mother shouted suddenly, and the sound sent a cold trickle of fear through my body, like when Little Haim dropped ice down my back during the Purim feast. I do not think I had ever heard my mother shout before; even when we displeased her, her response was always cool and rational, as though she had anticipated just such an incidence of naughtiness and had already devised the most suitable punishment. Besides, it was not anger that gave her voice its stridency, but panic.

"But Leah, be reasonable. With Esther, you can pass, stay here until I've found somewhere safe and can send for you."

"Forgive me, Haim, but I will not consider it. If we have to go, we go together, as a family. We take our chances as a family."

"The king and queen have given us three months, till Shavuot. Till then, we are under royal protection."

My mother gave a harsh laugh, quite uncharacteristic of her. "Then we can complete Passover before we go. How ironic."

"It is their Easter. It is a very holy time for them. Perhaps their majesties have a little conscience after all." I could hear the shrug in my father's voice. It was his business voice, the way he spoke when negotiating terms for loans with customers he hoped would be reliable, but for whom he set repayment terms which would minimise his risk.

"King Ferdinand's conscience does not extend beyond the worshippers of the false messiah as the Moors found out. For hundreds of years they pave roads, make water systems, light the streets, and he destroys them on a whim of his wife."

"And you would destroy us on a whim of yours? We have three months before the edict comes into force. I will go now, with the boys, and you and Esther will follow, before the three months is up, so you will be perfectly safe. Besides, I need you here to oversee the sale of all our property. Who else can I trust?"

"Here, then." I heard a scrape of wood on stone as my mother leapt up from her chair. I dared not move from my bed to look out of the window in case the beam of her rage should focus on me. "Here is your plate. I will fill it and take it to the beggars in the street. If you go, you will die."

"Leah, Leah." My father's conciliatory rumble. China smashing.

"Don't move. If you tread the marzipan into the tiles I will never get them clean." Then my mother burst into tears and the trickle of fear turned to a torrent of cold sweat, so when my nurse came in to see why I was crying, she thought I had a fever beginning and forced me to drink one of her foul tasting tisanes.

"I'm sorry, Haim," I heard my mother say before the infusion took effect and sent me to sleep. My father made no response and I heard nothing more but clothes rustling against each other and the small, wet sound of kissing that made me cover my ears with my pillow.

❧

A week later, my father and my three brothers, Eli, Simeon, and Little Haim, together with several other men from our community, left Toledo to make the journey to Italy, where many of the rulers of that land's multitude of tyrannies and city states were known to tolerate the Jews and to be wary of King Ferdinand and Queen Isabella, whose approach to statecraft was not pragmatic enough for them. Even the Kingdom of

Naples, which was ruled by relatives of the king, was said to be content to receive refugees from among the exiles of Jerusalem. My father, however, intended to go to Rome. The pope is dying, he explained, and there is a Spanish cardinal prepared to spend a lot of money to buy the office when the time comes. This Cardinal Borja will be needing a reliable banker. We were unsure what a pope was, or a cardinal, and Borja sounded more like a Catalan name than a Spanish one to us, and a Catalan is as trustworthy as a gypsy, but my father's smile was so confident, his teeth so brilliant amid the black brush of his beard, that we had no option but to nod our agreement, bite back our tears, and tell him we would see him in Rome.

⤛⥊⤜

The days of Omer passed, and no news reached us. We heard rumours of ships taken by pirates in the Tyrrhenian Sea, of the legendary Corsair of Genoa who liked to cut off the ears of his victims and have them stitched into belts by his sailmaker. Some Jews attempting to leave Spain had been robbed and beaten to death by over-zealous subjects of King Ferdinand and Queen Isabella, particularly those who owed them money; some had died in the mountains, denied shelter or sustenance by the villagers. We heard of synagogues turned into warehouses and farmers grazing their pigs in our cemeteries.

Yet, as my mother repeatedly reminded me, there was no proof. Who had encountered a pig in our graveyard at the foot of the Cerro de Palomarejos? Had I noticed any bolts of cloth or barrels of salt herrings in the synagogue? Who had seen the Corsair wearing a sash of Jews' ears? Who had seen the smashed bodies on the beaches or the frozen bones beside the mountain passes? No one, of course, because there was nothing to see. The king and queen had declared an amnesty until the end of Omer, and until then the Jews were as safe in Spain as they had ever been, and Papa and the boys were in Rome by now preparing a new home for us with brighter tapestries on the walls and a bigger fountain in the courtyard.

Our house seemed empty and silent, especially at night when I lay in my bed listening to the crickets and my mother's soft footfalls as she paced the corridors waiting for my father's summons, willing it to come, fearful of encountering ghosts, perhaps, as she passed by the places where her sons used to play: the stables of their favourite horses, the

8

long chamber where they all slept and which still smelled faintly of boys' sweat and flatulence. Then, late one afternoon, while I was still drowsy from siesta, my mother told me to get up and to put on as many of my clothes as I could, and never mind the heat. When I balked at my good winter cloak, she herself bundled me into it and fastened the clasp under my chin. Then we went to the stables behind the house, where I watched in astonishment as my mother saddled a horse, her fingers moving with rapid assurance among buckles and straps. I had no idea she was capable of such a thing. She slung a couple of saddlebags over the animal's back then lifted me up also, then led it around to our front door, where she paused to remove the *mezuzah* from the doorpost. She wrapped it, together with the key to our house, in her *ketubah*, and placed the package in one of the saddlebags.

It was growing dusk by this time, and the link boys had long since stopped coming to light the street lamps in our district, so those who joined us as we rode towards the city gates seemed like shade fragments broken off from the deepening mass of twilight, walking or riding beside us with hoofbeats and footfalls muffled and breath held in that strange, portentous hour of everything turning into something else. Buildings looked like dreams, random glints of mosaic tiles or brass door fittings floating in a pool of dark. Faces occasionally emerged into clarity long enough for me to recognise people I knew, then disappeared again so I could not be sure whether I had seen them or dreamed them. Especially when Rachel Abravanel smiled at me; that must have been a dream.

Once outside the Jewish quarter, our party bunched together, the men forming a protective cordon around the women and children. We had heard talk of Jews being stoned in the street, being pushed into middens, or having chamberpots emptied over their heads. My mother and her friends spoke in whispers of a Jewish woman forced into some humiliation involving a pig though, strain my ears as I might, I could never find out what. We, however, were ignored, although I imagined I could sense eyes watching us through chinks in shutters, our old neighbours too ashamed to look us in the face as they calculated the value of our abandoned houses, our vineyards, and metal works and shops.

I felt, rather than heard, my mother speak from time to time, the vibrations of her voice running through my body pressed to hers, the comfortable contours of her breasts and belly cushioning my back.

"May the All Merciful forgive me," she was saying to someone walking beside us, "but I should never have listened to Haim." She paused, checking, I think, to see if I had fallen asleep. I stayed still and kept my eyes closed, so she went on, "At least, if they had to die, I could have gone with them."

"Now Leah, what about your daughter?" came a voice from the darkness. I hardly dared breathe. Dead? Had my mother had news? Was that the reason for our sudden flight? Were they all dead, or just some of them? Please Lord, if any of my brothers had to be dead let it be Little Haim so I would not have to put up with his torments any more. How had they died? Where? What was going to happen to us now? I was suffocating beneath a shower of questions pouring like sand through a funnel.

"If it hadn't been for my daughter, I would have gone with Haim. He said we could pass, with Esther being so fair and dainty. And now the amnesty's run out, I've waited and waited and nothing. No money. Nothing. How is a woman on her own with a little girl supposed to get to Rome? And what if he isn't there? Then what?" My mother too, it seemed, was foundering beneath questions.

I remember little more of that journey, only dark, then light, then dark again, I don't know how many times. I remember dropping out of the saddle like a stone, and waking almost too stiff to stand from the bruises on the insides of my legs and my backside, and the knobbly earth I had slept on impressed on my skin and bones. To begin with, there were picnics, bread and apricots and little meatballs seasoned with cinnamon. Then hunger and thirst until I thought I could not bear it any longer and an angel of indifference came and took them away so I wondered if I had died and if paradise was just this nothing. We exchanged land for sea, the ridges of the earth for stumbling waves, the sway of the horse for the slant of a deck and the slop of ballast water. And always, like the chorus in a play, those words: *if it wasn't for my daughter.*

My mother's behaviour towards me did not change. She remained, if not cheerful, then steadily optimistic. She oversaw my prayers at the correct times of day; she taught me songs and made me practise the fingerings for the dulcimer on patches of flat earth or a strip of decking marked out with chalk. She saw to it I had plenty of needlework to do, though now it was more patching and darning than embroidery, and reassured me my ears were so small the Corsair of Genoa would be sure to spare me, to throw me back into the sea like a fish too little for eating. When, at the beginning of our sea voyage, before I had my sea legs, I was sick, she hid her own failing health long enough to hold my head while I vomited over the ship's rail and make me gargle seawater. The best cure, she said. I was sure she had no idea I now knew what she truly thought of me.

❧

As my mother's exodus had begun between light and dark, so it ended in the margin between land and sea, on the beach at Nettuno. It was hot, the sun at its summer zenith, a ball of white fire in a sky scoured of everything but the tense silhouettes of buzzards describing their waiting circles. The beach was striated with shrivelled bladderwrack; the dry white sand kept falling away beneath our feet as we struggled away from the sea with our bags and boxes. There was no shade. So many were sick the captain had panicked and put us ashore at the first sight of land, and his boats, as we rigged makeshift canopies over those too ill to go any further, were nothing more than giant insects crawling across the sparkling face of the sea.

I sat miserably beside my mother, waiting for her to get better and chide me for my bare feet and the tear in my dress which I had picked at until it was beyond repair. Nobody spoke to me or took care of me; they were all too busy checking over their possessions or looking after their own sick. Some boys were sent to look for fresh water, or a village where help might be obtainable, and I longed to go with them but I dared not. What would my mother say if she woke up and found I had gone roaming around the countryside with a group of boys? I wiggled my toes in the sand; I held my mother's hand and imagined I felt an answering pressure; I believed the rasp and rattle of her breathing were attempts at speech.

After a while, with no daughter of her own to care for any longer, Señora Abravanel came to sit with me. She took a comb from her girdle and combed my hair. She talked to me about Rachel, which I found embarrassing, and I wondered why she did nothing for my mother, to help her get better.

Suddenly, my mother's lips began to move, and she jerked her head feebly from side to side, as though trying to shake off a fly.

"Esther?" Her voice was as dry and powdery as the sand.

"Yes, mama?"

"Where are you?" She pawed at the sand until her fingers touched my bare calf, then she smiled, stretching the purplish cracks in her lips.

"I don't think she can see you," said Señora Abravanel.

"Why not?"

Señora Abravanel was spared the need to reply when my mother spoke again. "I lived for you, my darling, I was so proud. I'm sorry."

Sorry? Sorry for what? Surely it was I who had to be sorry, because I had brought all these misfortunes down on us.

Señora Abravanel tugged gently at my hand. "Come along, Esther, there's nothing more to be done here. Señor Abravanel and I will take care of you."

Nobody ever actually told me my mother had died, and so I did not believe she was dead. Even when I saw the men say the prayers for the dead over her, and pass a coin over her eyes, even though she made no attempt at resistance when they cut her nails and pulled out a few strands of her hair and wrapped them in a cloth and gave it to me. They apologised that there was no bread to conduct the rites of food with, and wondered aloud if the casting out of water could be done with saltwater as well as sweet, but she did not seem to mind.

When the boys came back and reported they had found a village, and everyone was preparing to leave, I dragged behind so mama could catch up with me when she felt better. At the next bend in the track, I told myself, or the next time I saw a cow, or a seagull, or a lizard on a rock, I would turn round and see her striding towards us. So it was I left my mother on the beach with the tide nibbling her toes by stages, each backward look more despairing than the last, but bearable, taken one at a time. Señora Abravanel clung to my hand and in Nettuno they believed I was her daughter. She received their compliments on my fair hair without demur.

The people of Nettuno, fearful of disease, gave us food and water, and mules to speed us on our way to Rome. I sat up in front of Señor Abravanel, in a cradle of shifting bones, the mule's and Señor Abravanel's, hugging to my chest the leather satchel Señora Abravanel had given me, which smelled faintly of home. She said it contained our *mezuzah* and the key to our house, and my mother's book of recipes which I would need one day, when I was married. Surely, I thought, Mama would have caught up with us by then.

We remained unmolested on the road, perhaps because He whom we cannot name is in the habit of keeping an eye on His people as they move from place to place, perhaps because the people on this coast had grown used to parties of homeless Jews, stinking of saltwater and rejection and riddled with the contagion of defeat.

Though Rome might consider itself the centre of the civilised world, it was then a smaller city than Toledo, and my father, whose Valencian Cardinal Borja had, with the aid of his own fortune and my father's financial judgement, made himself pope, was not difficult to find in the Jewish quarter close to the Campo de' Fiori. His was one of the largest houses, newly built and surrounded by gardens, just as he had promised my mother and I before he left Toledo.

I expect he was happy to see me, and I him, and that he was distressed by the death of my mother, whom I believe he cared for in his fashion, but I cannot remember. Somewhere on the road from Nettuno, swaying and jolting on the back of a mule, I had lost myself, and it would be a long time until that self would be rediscovered. To begin with, Eli, who was six years older than me, so almost a man, and should have known better, used to pester me. Where's your fight, Esther? You're such a pushover. Come on, hit me back.

I didn't. I became a model of maidenly virtue. I caused my father no shame and gave him everything to be proud of as his star rose in the heavens commanded by Pope Alexander VI. Along with several well-born young Roman women, I practised music and embroidery under the supervision of the nuns of the Convent of Santa Clara, who seemed to see nothing odd in educating a Jewish girl. From the rabbi I learned Torah and from a young Greek scholar with hungry eyes and a tubercular bloom, my brothers and I learned Greek and Latin and geometry. And from the girls at Santa Clara I learned how to dress my hair, pinch a flush into my cheeks, and drop rosewater in my eyes to make them sparkle, and that the hunger in the young scholar's eyes probably didn't arise in his belly.

Though my father faithfully performed the proper rituals on what he calculated to be the anniversary of my mother's death, and lit candles in her memory on Yom Kippur, he never spoke to me about her, nor I to him.

⟨•⟩

My father called me into his study one afternoon early in the month I had learned to call September, in the year after the Jubilee, when he had returned from doing business at the Vatican. The day meal had been eaten and cleared away, and the house was still, sleeping away the heat of the afternoon. Even the house slaves were resting, in their wooden dormitory opposite the stable block. Simeon was probably not in his own bed, and probably not resting, but this was just one of many pieces of intelligence my father and I shared yet did not talk about. He ran a successful bank; I kept an orderly house for him. The rooms were swept away from the door; we had separate kitchens for meat and dairy; we observed the fasts and feasts with their proper rituals, lit candles for Shabbat, and kept the *mezuzah* my mother had carried from Toledo and I from Nettuno fastened to our doorpost. It would be dishonest to say we loved one another; neither of us would admit an emotion as messy as love to our well ordered universe. We kept one another in balance, like finely calibrated scales.

My father was sitting at his desk when I entered, staring at a space somewhere between the table's edge and the doorway where I stood, fiddling a ring around one broad finger. I waited for him to speak, noting with annoyance that his copy of the *padron real* hung slightly crooked on the wall behind him. I had warned Mariam repeatedly about dusting that map. She was to leave it to me; the map was far too valuable to be handled by a slave. My father would have been better advised to keep it locked in a chest rather than exposed to air and dust and the covetous eyes of others.

"Shut the door, daughter, there's a draught."

I pushed the heavy, panelled door to, then dropped my father a curtsey.

"Sit down, Esther. No, here." He rose from his desk and came to join me in the pair of cushioned chairs which stood either side of the porphyry fireplace. He gave a half-hearted slap at a mosquito which had landed on his cheek. "You are aware Donna Lucrezia is to marry again?" he asked. Had I but known it, the scales were about to tip.

"I would have to be deaf and blind not to be. The cannonade from

Sant'Angelo when the news was announced nearly shook my teeth out."
Nor had the cannonade been enough for the jubilant pontiff, the upstart
Catalan whose bastard daughter was about to marry into one of the
foremost families of Italy, the Este of Ferrara. He had also caused the
Capitoline bell to be tolled for most of the night and had bonfires lit in
the grounds of the castle, laced with explosive charges which threatened
to ignite the Sant'Angelo bridge. The following day, Donna Lucrezia had
processed to the church of Santa Maria by the Porta del Popolo in the
company of three hundred horsemen and four bishops, which must have
felt more like three thousand and forty to anyone trying to go about his
daily business in the cramped streets. When the Holy Father's children
had something to celebrate, the Holy Father made sure his spiritual
children had no option but to celebrate too. There had even been a display
of two clowns dressed in Donna Lucrezia's cast off gowns, sashaying
around the town proclaiming, "Long live the most illustrious Duchess of
Ferrara!" Actually, they had been really funny, pursing their carmined lips
and squawking in falsetto voices.

"Three husbands before she's one and twenty. That's quite a record." I
was fifteen, and my friends at Santa Clara and I were women of the world.
We knew all the gossip, and much of it concerned Donna Lucrezia, the
pope's favourite daughter.

I did not wonder at the pope's having a daughter. Our rabbi had nine
sons, and it struck me as unnatural—if I thought about it at all, which I
rarely did—for a priest not to have a family. A priest's congregation is a
kind of family, so surely he can minister to them better if he knows how
families work. Nor did my Christian friends remark on Donna Lucrezia's
parentage; one or two of them were cardinals' daughters.

"She has been unlucky in her husbands, it's true," said my father carefully.

I struggled to keep the smirk from my face. Even by Roman standards,
Donna Lucrezia's life was sensational. To begin with, she lived with her
father's mistress, the gorgeous Giulia Farnese, who was only three years
older than Donna Lucrezia herself and married to one of her cousins.
Donna Lucrezia had married her first husband at thirteen and divorced
him four years later on grounds of impotence. Though according to
Battista Farignola, whose older sister was being pursued by Donna

Lucrezia's brother, Don Juan, at the time, she was six months gone when she testified to her continuing virginity. No baby ever appeared, so who could know?

"His Holiness says she is much chastened since her widowhood," my father persisted, staring at me until I stopped smiling.

Donna Lucrezia's second husband, Alfonso of Bisceglie, who was a distant relation of King Ferdinand, and, said Lucia de Mantova, absolutely divinely good looking, had been murdered about a year previously, some said by Donna Lucrezia's oldest brother, the Duke Valentino. The girls kept quiet about that; keeping quiet was the wisest thing to do where the Duke was concerned.

Only a week before, Little Haim had told me he had seen a man's severed hand, with his tongue stitched to his little finger, hanging from a window of the Savelli prison, and that Duke Valentino had put it there because the man had written a public letter accusing the duke of living like a Turk with a harem of prostitutes. I had screamed and stopped my ears and thought, though I could scarce admit it to myself, of the Corsair of Genoa.

"And you should consider your betters with more respect," my father added. As for being my better, Donna Lucrezia's father might be pope but everyone said her mother was just an innkeeper, albeit a wealthy one, who had done well out of last year's Jubilee, when the city was packed with pilgrims from all over the world.

"Yes, Papa." I could see my father was struggling with whatever it was he had to tell me and had no wish to make it harder for him.

"Duke Ercole of Ferrara, her new father-in-law, drives a hard bargain by all accounts," he continued, "and has put a high price on the hand of his son and heir. I am to help His Holiness with the dowry."

What had this to do with me? I waited. My father cleared his throat. He looked at me, his hands steepled in front of his mouth, then seemed to come to a decision. "His Holiness very graciously suggested, Esther, that you might be considered as a lady-in-waiting to Donna Lucrezia, should she find you pleasing."

"Me, Papa? Go to Ferrara? That's right at the other end of Italy. I might never see you again. I can't." I was leaning towards him, fists clenched in my lap, shoulders hunched. My eyes raked his face to see if he really meant it. Perhaps this was some elaborate test of my loyalty.

"You would have to be baptised, of course."

Once again I felt that fear of the unknown that had trickled between my shoulder blades almost ten years ago in Toledo, as I listened to my parents arguing about the Edict of Expulsion. I had not, I realised, ever been afraid since, not truly afraid. Until now, and now I was too old simply to pull my pillow over my ears.

"How could you even say such a thing?" My voice surprised me, so calm and steady despite the anger beginning to seethe inside me. I sounded like my mother. My father's eyes told me he had noticed it too.

"Now before you fly into a temper, listen to me, daughter. You are fifteen years old. If we were still in Toledo, you would likely be married by now. But we aren't, we are here and our people are scattered. I have to consider your future. There is no one else to do it."

"Señora Abravanel will find me a husband, Papa," I interrupted, though I, too, was not saying what I really meant. "She is a good matchmaker. You let her choose for Eli, why not me?"

"Eli will not marry for years. Josepha is still a child. And a son...well, it's different. If you go with Donna Lucrezia, she will be able to find you a husband among the nobility, a man of standing and good fortune who will keep you...safe," he finished lamely. "Duke Ercole apparently approves the idea that his daughter-in-law should have a reformed Jewess among her ladies to whom she can give religious guidance and instruction. He is a very pious man."

Now I laughed, though my laughter was harsh and humourless. "Me? Receive religious instruction from Lucrezia Borgia? Have you any idea how absurd that sounds?"

"She takes communion every day, I'm told, since the death of the Duke of Bisceglie, and has taught their son his catechism herself."

I was breaking myself against a wall. "My mother died because she was Jewish. How do you think such talk would make her feel?" I held my breath. I waited for the roof to cave in. I could not look at my father, but I heard the wincing intake of breath, as though he had cut his finger or stubbed his toe.

"Do you think it has been easy for me, all these years," he asked quietly, "watching you grow up, becoming more and more like her? Because you are, you know, despite your fair hair and blue eyes. The way you looked at the *padron real* when you came in. Just like her. And if you're thinking Mariam has been at it with her dustcloths again, she hasn't. I brushed against it when I came to my desk. You say your mother died because she was Jewish. If that's true, do you think she'd want the same to happen to you? Because we're never safe, you know, among Christians. They believe we gave up their messiah for crucifixion. Having done that, we're no longer necessary to their salvation so they feel at liberty to take their revenge. The pope is nearly seventy. Who's to say his successor will be as amenable as he is? Who's to say there might not be another expulsion? Believe me, Esther, your mother would support me in this. Use your advantage; get away from us while you can."

A war raged inside me. On the one hand, my father was asking me to betray my culture, my upbringing, the people I had known all my life. On the other, though I was conscientious in observing our rites and rituals, I had never paused to consider whether I actually had faith in the beliefs which lay behind them. They were marks on the calendar, historical remembrances, occasions for feast or fast, parties or vigils. It would not be that difficult to exchange one set for another, especially as many, like Christmas and Easter, fell close to our own festivals. My mother's passion and my father's pragmatism were doing battle for my soul.

"You may take the rest of the day to think, if you wish," my father conceded with a tight smile.

"I will do as you ask, Papa." I was suddenly certain, almost as though someone had whispered it in my ear, that I was not destined to die on a beach somewhere, barefoot and fever blind with a ragged child squatting beside me in the sand. I stood and awaited his permission to leave.

"I did send for you, you know," he said, kneading his forehead with his fingers, "but by the time I learned the ship carrying my letter had been wrecked off Corsica it was too late. You had already left. I have tried to tell her but I don't know if she hears me."

"I expect the Christians would say she does." I stooped to kiss his cheek and tasted salt. Closing the door softly behind me, I left him to his tears.

# CHAPTER 2

*On the ship from Ostia, at first I did not mind being kept below decks in chains, because there was no choice. I was too tired for choice; I wanted nothing but to be relieved of the responsibility of thinking. I was, I suppose, content, though I do not know because I have never understood what contentment is, except an absence—of joy, or sorrow, or ambition, or imagination.*

I met Donna Lucrezia only once before my baptism, when my father took me to the great Orsini palace at the foot of Saint Peter's steps where she lived with her aunt, Adriana da Mila Orsini and Giulia Farnese, who was Donna Adriana's daughter-in-law but also the pope's favourite. I was secretly disappointed La Bella Giulia was not present at our meeting, for I was as curious to see her as I was to meet Donna Lucrezia. They said she was as beautiful as Helen of Troy.

We were received in the piano nobile, a room so vast that even a fire big enough to roast an ox, burning in a fireplace of Carrara marble, failed to penetrate its icy elegance. I watched my breath cloud in front of my face as a liveried slave noiselessly closed the double doors behind us and Adriana da Mila beckoned us forward.

She and Donna Lucrezia were seated either side of the fire in upholstered chairs. Donna Lucrezia's baby son, Rodrigo of Bisceglie, who was then just over a year old, sat between them on a fur rug, playing with a set of wooden dolls dressed as janissaries; the turban of one was unravelling and the baby was chewing its loose end. A black slave girl stood behind Donna Lucrezia's chair, so still I wondered if she was a statue. Her cheeks were marked with pounce work circles, though she was richly dressed in a proper gown of mulberry silk.

"Perhaps you would not mind waiting there, Ser Sarfati," said Donna

Adriana, waving a jewelled, liver-spotted hand at a bench set about halfway down the length of the room, "while we talk to your daughter." My father bowed, gave me a little push in the small of my back, and seated himself on the bench. Its leather upholstery creaked; my new kidskin shoes, wet from the puddles in the palace courtyard, squelched softly as I approached the fireplace. I was so nervous I was beginning to sweat despite the cold, and kept my arms pressed tight to my sides and my teeth clenched to stop them chattering. You were so stiff you looked like a puppet, Donna Lucrezia would recall, years later, with a catch of laughter in her voice.

Her expression that morning was stern and rather tired, her high-bridged nose and large, grey eyes red-rimmed as though she had a cold or had been crying. The hand she extended towards me was plump and languid. I took it briefly in mine and bowed, as my father had told me was the custom among well-bred Christians. Her skin was so soft I could hardly feel it, and her extraordinarily white knuckles were dimpled, like a child's. I then turned to curtsey to Donna Adriana, who inclined her coiffure in my direction with a soft clicking of pearls.

"Well," said Donna Lucrezia, "but you really are fair, aren't you. Tell me, is it entirely natural?"

"Yes, madonna."

She sighed, touching a hand to her own hair, which was caught up in a green silk net scattered with tiny rubies. "Mine used to be that colour. Then it fell out in handfuls when I had Rodrigo, and grew back a shade darker. I have to spend hours with it spread out in the sun now. I have a splendid contraption like a sunhat without a crown, made of copper to speed up the bleaching process. Caterina Sforza gave me a recipe for a concoction of saffron, cinnabar, and sulphur she swears by, when she was Duke Valentino's…guest last year, but it makes the head stink foul, as you can imagine. You may sit. Catherinella, a stool."

I realised the slave was not an ornament as she turned to pick up a low firestool and placed it just behind me. The lining of my nose began to tingle. I fancied I could hear Mariam's insistent whisper: "Sneeze, child, to ward off the devil." I cannot sneeze in front of these ladies, I told myself. Better the devil than to be rejected by Donna Lucrezia and have to face my father's disappointment. With a discreet sniff, I sat, folding my hands in my lap, fixing my gaze on them to avoid staring at the two women in their silks and furs and glittering jewels.

"Tell me how your instruction progresses," Donna Lucrezia resumed. "I find it particularly gratifying when one of your race comes to Christ, for after all, He was a Jew."

"I hope I am a good student, madonna. I have learned the Apostles' Creed and the sacraments, and of course my...the Jews also have the commandments of Moses."

"And can you recite Our Lord's Prayer?"

"Yes, madonna. *Pater noster qui es in caelis, sanctificetur nomen tuum...*"

"Excellent. You have some Latin."

"And also a little Greek, madonna."

"And Spanish, I suppose?"

"I'm sorry, madonna. I was six years old when we left Spain. I no longer remember the language." Though sometimes, still, I dream in it, in the Castilian of a six-year-old child, doubly distant from who I am today.

"I was born here, but we have always spoken our own language among ourselves. My family is of the Valencian nobility."

A note of reproof in her voice made me feel the need to justify myself. "My father thought it important for us to practice our Italian, to blend into our new surroundings. And I do not think we would understand one another in Spanish anyway, madonna, for my family is from Toledo, so you are Catalan and we Castilian."

"Is that so? I am afraid I am not very clear on the geography of the Spains, especially as they now seem to be everywhere, since the discoveries of Ser Colon." Her tone was chilly. Donna Adriana's pearls clicked. A slight creaking of the leather bench where my father sat told me I had overstepped the bounds of propriety, but though the thought made my heart beat faster, in my mind I did not care. I was there because my father wanted it, not for myself.

"You know the Romans call us *marrano* whenever we do something which displeases them? That is ironic, is it not, that we, the family of the Holy Father, should be branded secret Jews? Perhaps we might speak to one another in Hebrew, eh girl?"

There seemed to be no reply I could make that would not be offensive either to Donna Lucrezia's family or my own. Then, suddenly, she smiled. Her smile transformed her; it seemed to light her from the inside rather than hang on her face like a picture put up to hide a crack in the wall. It made you believe in the goodness of her heart.

"Tell me," she said. "Do you know Petrarch?"

From bad to worse. I did know Petrarch, a little, from the much-thumbed copies of some of his verses handed round in secret among the girls at Santa Clara, but with my father sitting behind me, I was wary of admitting it. On the other hand, if I failed to give the lady an honest reply, she would never consider me suitable for her household, and I would disappoint all my father's plans for me.

"And Dante, of course." That was a relief. Dante was far more worthy, if not to be recommended too soon before bed. I opened my mouth to reiterate one of my teachers' comments on the religious symbolism of the poet's love for Beatrice, but before I could speak, she continued, "*Lasciate ogne speranza, voi ch'intrate,*" with a tight little laugh which drew me to glance at her face. She intercepted my look as she raised her eyes to her aunt, who gave a little cough which sounded more like a warning than an obstruction of the throat. I felt my cheeks burn. My father's disapproval seemed to bore into my back. On no account, he had told me, must you look so great a lady as Donna Lucrezia in the eye; it will be accounted the height of rudeness.

But as soon as Donna Lucrezia's gaze met mine, I knew my impropriety did not matter. A spark kindled in her grey eyes. She smiled. She liked me. I had given her no particular reason to, but she had obviously seen something in me, some like-mindedness to which she could respond.

Just then, the baby, bored by his dolls, started to grizzle. The slave, Catherinella, stepped forward, but Donna Lucrezia waved her away and took the child into her lap, where he grabbed happily at her necklace, gnawing on an emerald pendant the size of a duck egg.

"He has some teeth coming, at the back," Donna Lucrezia told me.

"Madonna," I said, emboldened by what I had seen in her eyes. Another cough from Donna Adriana. A sharp intake of breath from my father. I ploughed on. "May I ask you a question?"

"Shall we let this bold young woman ask us a question?" she asked her son. "Why not? Rodrigo says you may, Signorina Esther."

"What are the duties of a lady-in-waiting, madonna?"

"Why, child, she waits, like any other woman. For a husband, for childbirth, for…"

"You will attend Donna Lucrezia at her will, girl, that is all," interrupted Donna Adriana.

Believing our interview to be over, I waited to be dismissed, but before any more could be said, the double doors to the room were flung open, ushering in a blast of even colder air which set the flames dancing in the hearth. A messenger wearing a livery quartered in crimson velvet and gold satin strode down the length of the piano nobile as though he owned it. He bowed to the ladies, then handed Donna Lucrezia a parchment, folded and sealed. Her pale face flushed a delicate pink as she tore open the seal and read her letter.

"It is an invitation to dine this afternoon," she said to her aunt, though her flushed cheeks and shining eyes made it seem like something more. "Of course, we accept," she told the messenger, who bowed again, and retreated. On his back, as he turned, I saw the letters C E S A R emblazoned in gold thread.

Donna Lucrezia rose and handed her son to Catherinella. "Take him to the nursery. I must go and dress."

I stood also and waited to be dismissed.

"Your father will hear from us," Donna Adriana told me.

"No, wait." Donna Lucrezia turned to me. She looked quite feverish. "Esther, when is your baptism to be?"

"I'm not sure yet, madonna."

"Then I will have my secretary speak to the dean at Santa Maria del Popolo to set a date. You will receive instruction from my chaplain from now on, and I will stand godmother to you. I should like you to take the name…Donata. Donata Spagnola."

"Yes, madonna. Thank you, madonna." I made a deep curtsey, but she waved me away. As I rejoined my beaming father and we were escorted from the room, I heard Donna Lucrezia discussing gowns with her aunt.

I should be ashamed to admit this, but dress, rather than the condition of my soul, was the matter which most vexed me as the date set for my baptism grew closer.

Though I had not seen her since that first meeting a month previously, Donna Lucrezia was as good as her word. Her chaplain came daily to our house, edging his way through the courtyard door on the side farthest from the *mezuzah,* crossing himself and mumbling his prayers as he did so. Little Haim and I used to run up to the loggia on the roof to spy on these furtive arrivals, and my sides would still be aching with laughter when I was summoned to meet Fra Tommaso in the small sitting room where I received my instruction. He was a timid man, more afraid of the Almighty, it seemed, than joyful in His service. But I tried to be a good student, for my father's sake, and because I could not forget that spark of understanding in Donna Lucrezia's eyes when she looked at me.

The day before the service was due to take place, the black slave, Catherinella, arrived at our gate, attended by a footman carrying a parcel of yellow silk fastened with ribbons. I could not wait to see what was inside. As soon as the slave had gone, I opened it, there in the vestibule, spreading the silk wrapping over the polished stone floor. I took out a beautiful missal, bound in red leather with silver corners and filigree clasps, then a white lawn baptismal gown, its wide sleeves and hem decorated with gold embroidery a foot deep, its lace collar as fine as cobwebs. To go with the gown was a cloak of white velvet, lined with the fur of winter foxes and with a clasp set with pearls at the neck. Mariam, loitering out of curiosity after she had answered the knock at the gate, gasped at the richness of the gown as I lifted it clear of its wrapping and held it up to the light of the lamps in their bronze wall sconces.

"Be careful, miss. You don't want to get smoke on it."

What concerned me, however, was the way the lamplight shone right through the fine lawn. Whatever Donna Lucrezia's reputation, surely she did not expect me to stand in the church, in full view of clergy and congregation, in a gown as transparent as one of Salome's veils?

I took the cloak and gown up to my chamber and summoned Mariam to help me, for I had no regular maid of my own. After emptying out the press in which my shifts and underclothes were stored, scattering the rug at my bedside with powdery sprigs of rosemary and lavender so poor Mariam would have to give it an extra beating, I tried on every combination of undergarments I could devise, standing in front of a lamp with my arms stretched out to either side while Mariam scrutinised me for any evidence of the body beneath the clothes. Eventually we settled on two linen shifts and a wool underskirt. I looked rather bulky, but at least I would be warm and my modesty remain unimpeached.

For a long time after Mariam had left me, I remained in my room, studying the different images of myself I could achieve by holding my hand mirror at different angles. My father was right; I had grown like my mother. It was not that I could clearly remember her face after so many years, or the mannerisms my father identified as hers, a way of tugging my hair at the temple and winding it around my finger, or standing with my hands on my hips which Donna Lucrezia would no doubt school me out of. But when I took inventory of my features, my sharp cheekbones and small, straight nose, my jaw that was slightly square and my eyes which were round, though deep set so they did not give the same impression as my brothers', who looked like a row of staring owls when they were all together, I saw my mother. No, saw is the wrong word. It was more that I recalled her. She hovered behind the reflection in the glass, mouthing words I could not quite read because my own expression of doubt and stubbornness veiled her.

Was Papa right to say she would have approved of what I was doing, or had he lied to convince me? Or perhaps never understood his wife? Well, it was too late now for such speculations. Tomorrow, at morning Mass, the daughter of the pope would take my bird-boned hand in her plump one and lead me into subjection to her father. Tomorrow, Donna Lucrezia would become my mother in the sight of God. I would be washed clean of my sins and the sins of my people; I would become a *tabula rasa*.

As I was about to begin changing, a gentle, almost shy knock came at my door.

"Who is it?"

"Papa."

"Come in. I was just…getting changed," I finished lamely, seeing his expression as he took in the sight of his daughter in her baptismal gown.

"I...er...," he cleared his throat, "have to dine out this evening, with Fugger's man. Something to do with rising port duties on pepper coming into Venice. Important, when you think how much pepper we consume. I shall be back late, I expect."

"You can wake me." We both knew it would be a long time until we saw one another again. He and my brothers could not come to the church tomorrow, nor could they make social calls to Santa Maria in Portico, and I had no idea how much time or liberty my new duties would leave me, if any.

"I'd rather not." Coming towards me, he placed his great hands on my shoulders. "You'll want to look your best tomorrow, no rings under your eyes."

"It's not..." my wedding, I almost said.

"It's good that Donna Lucrezia favours you so. Good for your future. Your mother would be so proud," he finished, all in a rush as though plunging into a cold bath or swallowing bitter medicine, and before I could reply he had turned on his heel and was gone, leaving nothing behind but a light scent of the ambergris he used to keep his beard glossy.

I took off my christening garments and laid them on top of the travel chest which would be carried in the morning to the palace of Santa Maria. It was a fine chest, new for the occasion, covered with red Spanish leather and bound with brass. It contained special, cedar-lined compartments for small linen, hair brushes, girdles and shoes, and two trays for gowns. Somewhere in this mix of practical planning and careful craftsmanship lay the soul of Donata Spagnola.

❧

Christian baptism is a strange rite. We Jews place a great emphasis on food in the celebration of our faith. We eat our roast lamb with garlic and rosemary and *matzoh* cakes at Passover, our red eggs and saffron rice on the eve of Shabbat and—my favourite, these, because of their association with Queen Esther—the syrupy *orejas de Haman* at Purim, their sweetness almost unbearably intense after the three days of fasting. But we do know they are simply made of dough, rolled and curled to resemble a human ear; we do not believe they are somehow magically transformed into Haman's ears as we eat them. How many ears can one man have, even if he is the most devious and scheming of courtiers who ever listened outside a king's chamber?

Yet here I was, dizzy from the thick scent of incense and the sickly soprano voices of the boy choristers, washed, oiled, and salted as though ready for the spit. Garish, bleeding saints were everywhere, on walls and ceilings, atop plinths or looming from alcoves. Kneeling before the altar, flanked by Donna Lucrezia and a bishop whose name I cannot now remember, acting as proxy for my other sponsor, Donna Lucrezia's brother-in-law, Cardinal Ippolito d'Este, I was now expected to consume bread and wine and believe they had been transformed into the body and blood of Christ by some sleight of hand of the priest. I, a Jewess, who had only ever consumed flesh from which all the blood had been washed, who was forbidden even to eat an egg which had blood spots in it. I prayed, not for the Holy Spirit, but that my throat would not contract and cause me to choke.

It was a morning of driving rain and bitter wind, so Cardinal Vera, who was to preside over the service, was content for the ceremony to be held inside the church door rather than outside as laid down. Perhaps that is why the Holy Spirit decided to stay away. Once the Cardinal had pronounced the exorcism and placed the veil on my head, all I knew as I approached the altar, Donna Lucrezia and the nameless bishop each holding me by the hand, was that the salt on my tongue was making my stomach cry out for its breakfast. Water dripped from the ends of my loose hair, soaking through my clothes on to the backs of my thighs. I shivered. Donna Lucrezia squeezed my hand and smiled in the direction of the altar; perhaps she thought my shivering was a sign of divine intervention, the wings of the dove fluttering across my skin.

I knelt, on a white silk cushion. I recited the Creed and the Lord's Prayer, then Cardinal Vera himself, the cords in his weathered neck reminding me of well-hung venison, administered the Sacrament. Bread and wine I told myself, just bread and wine, and neither of them very good at that, as I swallowed the little disc which tasted like paper and the wine which left a fiery aftertaste in my throat. How did Donna Lucrezia manage this every morning on an empty stomach? I wondered. I glanced at her, kneeling beside me, head bowed, lips moving in silent and seemingly impassioned prayer, then took my cue from her to rise and process back towards the door as the clergy pronounced various blessings and graces.

I noticed Battista Farignola and Isotta de Mantova among the congregation, but they were too busy trying to catch the eye of a group of fashionably dressed young men lounging against a pillar and chatting in loud whispers to return my smile. This seemed to me to be thrillingly wicked. At synagogue, girls and boys only met after the services, under the watchful, calculating eyes of parents and matchmakers. The Christians, however, appeared to think nothing of the sexes mingling in church, so whole courtships of looks and gestures, of fans fluttered and kisses blown, could take place over the bowed heads of devout patriarchs and their pious spouses. If they thought Eve was the mother of all sin, they had only themselves to blame.

I also could not help but notice Giulia Farnese. She was the loveliest woman I had ever seen, with her eyes as warm as roast sugar and her honey coloured hair twisted with ropes of huge pearls beneath a veil of gold tissue. She held the hand of a plump little boy about four years of age whom I presumed to be her son, Giovanni, known as the Child of Rome though less grandly presumed by most people to be the child of Pope Alexander. He was as plain as his mother was beautiful and his imposing title seemed to sit ill on his round little shoulders. La Bella Giulia inclined her head to me, which caused a flurry among a group of ladies standing behind her, mostly young, with watchful eyes. Only one of them seemed unconcerned with the social adjustments which needed to be made to admit me to the favour of the pope's mistress. Covering her mouth with a sable muff, she yawned then winked at me. I thought I must be imagining it, but I soon found out I wasn't.

A reception was to be held for me at the palace. This makes me sound very important but, of course, I was not. That household needed little excuse to throw a party, and it was only a small party, a day meal followed by dancing, to introduce me to the rest of Donna Lucrezia's ladies, with Giulia Farnese as guest of honour. On my arrival at the palace, the slave, Catherinella, whisked me away through a maze of corridors and showed me into a small room on one of the upper floors.

"You change clothes," she said, in her slow, precisely enunciated Italian, "I help you."

My travelling trunk stood at the foot of the bed which, along with a nightstand and a simple wooden chair, constituted all the furniture in the room. I saw that it had been opened and my best gown, of dark blue velvet, had been laid out on the bed. Next to it were a *camorra* of a bright, emerald green brocade, lined in silver silk, and a necklace of pearls with a sapphire pendant.

"From my lady," said Catherinella.

I was as puffed up with pride as a courting dove that Madonna Lucrezia should give me such presents. Surely it was a sign of special favour. I did not realise, then, that among people whose wealth is as fabulous and careless as that of the Borgia family in those years, it is the small presents which count, not the lavish ones. A bracelet of plaited hair, an empty casket which once contained a poem. I was certain that, the moment I entered the salon where the meal was laid, every head would turn and all conversation cease as Donna Lucrezia's ladies struggled to contain their envy of the new favourite, the rising star, Donata Spagnola arising like the phoenix from the ashes of Esther Sarfati. Oh how thoroughly she was erased, that girl from Toledo on the remote edges of the Christian world, and how thoroughly Roman was Donata in her velvet and pearls.

As it was, only one person detached herself from the peacock throng milling about the room, the girl with the sable muff, a little older than me, I now saw, and unmistakably a Borgia, with the same high-bridged nose and large eyes, slightly too close together, as Donna Lucrezia.

"I'm Angela," she said, holding out her hand. She had a firm, dry grip and a candid stare. "Lucrezia's cousin. Well, one of them. There's Geronima too, but she's terribly…Spanish. Wears black, always in church, you know the sort. Oh lord, I mean, I'm sorry, you're Spanish. But then, Jews are Jews, aren't they? So you're not really Spanish."

Not really Jewish either, I thought, trying to feel insulted but disarmed by Angela's frankness and the warmth of her smile. "Are Catalans really Spanish?" I asked.

"Oh God."

I winced. How carelessly these Christians invoked the Holy Name.

"We Borgias are something and nothing, really," Angela went on, and I found myself wondering if Duke Valentino had ever heard her talk this way, and how long her tongue might stay in her head if he did. "The Romans say we're *marrano* and they're probably right."

"Then we're the same."

Angela was still holding my hand. Now she pumped it merrily up and down. "And we shall be friends. I've arranged for us to share a room. I hope you don't mind." I could not say I minded, but it gave me pause. Having no close female relatives, I was unused to sharing a bed. What if Angela snored, or ground her teeth, or kicked out in her sleep? What if I were guilty of any of these?

If Angela noticed my reservations, she certainly did not let them bother her. "Now," she prattled on, "who is that tall creature admiring her reflection in the silver? One of your friends? Can you perform a *moresca*? My cousin Cesare likes to see ladies dance it rather than gentlemen." Tucking my hand beneath her arm, she kept up her bombardment of questions except when she interrupted herself to introduce me to somebody or pass comment on a hairstyle, or the width of a sleeve, or the heaviness of someone's makeup. If Angela said we would be friends, I thought, then there seemed to be little point in arguing with her.

Donna Lucrezia sat at the head of the table, with Giulia Farnese to her right and Angela to her left. I sat next to Angela, though the honour of sitting only one place removed from Donna Lucrezia was lost on me now, and I longed to be as far from the high table as possible, with my friends from Santa Clara, where nobody was watching me. No one could eat until we at high table had taken our first mouthful of each dish. There were crayfish; there was veal in a cream sauce and suckling pig stuffed with figs. Repeatedly I reminded myself that it was no longer a sin for me to eat these dishes, but it was as though my body and mind had become disjointed from one another; my brain commanded my body to eat, but my gullet squeezed shut and forbade me to swallow. With the aid of copious swigs of wine, I managed to force down a few mouthfuls, then, glancing down the length of the salon to where Isotta and Battista were seated, saw everything double and realised I must be drunk. I remembered Simeon listing double vision as one of the symptoms.

I longed for water but dare not ask. The liveried pages who stood behind each of us were as stiff and solemn as the effigies on tombs; I could not believe they would deign to hear me even if I could summon the courage to speak. So I drank more wine and, when the meats were cleared and bowls of fruit brought in, accompanied by dishes of sweetened curd cheese, found myself suddenly ravenous. My plate was indecently heaped with pomegranate skins and stones from bottled peaches in pools of syrup when Donna Lucrezia clapped her hands and announced that we should remove to a larger room on the ground floor where the musicians awaited us.

I tried to stand, but felt as though I were once again at sea, in a squall, the deck rolling and slipping beneath my feet. Sugar water filled my mouth and nose with its sickly sweetness. Certain now I was about to vomit, I stumbled over the bench, pushing one of the solemn little pages out of my way, and fled the salon with Angela's "Donata? Are you all right?" cutting through the buzz in my ears.

Air. I needed air. I had to find a way out, but we were on the first floor and I had no idea where the stairs were. A window. Anything. I ran, turned, ran in another direction, tripped over the edges of rugs, caught my sleeve on a wall sconce. My mouth flooded with bile. Too late. Retching till I believed my throat would tear, I fell to my knees and threw up my dinner all over a rather fine silk runner laid down the centre of the marble floor. Without the strength to rise, I crawled away from the stinking mess I had made and lay on the floor, my forehead pressed to the cool marble. All I wanted was to sleep, but I had no idea how to find my bed, in that small room buried at the old heart of the sprawling palazzo. Besides, if I closed my eyes, my head began to spin and I feared I would be sick again.

How long I had lain this way when I heard footsteps approaching, I have no idea. At first I hoped it might be Angela, or one of Donna Lucrezia's slaves sent to find me. I would be disgraced, of course. Perhaps I might even be sent back home. The prospect made me feel slightly better, then I heard men's voices, a murmured exchange followed by a sudden bark of laughter. A shuffling of soft shoes accompanied by the smart clank of spurred boots. I squeezed my eyes tight shut, my drunken brain convincing me that, if I could not see them, they would not see me.

Silence. Torchlight illuminating the filigree of veins in my eyelids. Winy breath on my cheek, a faint perfume of jasmine oil. The toe of one of those boots in my ribs, but gently, cautiously, levering me on to my side. Then the fear I would vomit again as a blast of foul breath hit my face followed by the warm slick of a tongue licking my nose.

"Drunk," pronounced the voice of the boot wearer, rich with suppressed mirth. "Let her alone, Tiresias. If she tastes as good as a truffle, she's mine, you damned dog."

"Can't see a mark on her," said the other, his voice softer, almost whispering in my ear. His accent was not Roman. "Stinks like an inn parlour, though."

"Must be one of Lucrezia's girls," said the boot wearer. "Page, go to the Hall of the Zodiac and inform Donna Lucrezia one of her lambs has gone astray."

"My lord." A boy's treble, followed by scurrying footsteps and darkness, no, a shift in the light. The boy must have taken the torch, but lit one of the wall lamps before he did so. I opened my eyes.

Kneeling beside me was a young man in cardinal's robes, one arm draped companionably around the shoulders of a battered hound whose albino eyes were milky blue with cataracts. The cardinal seemed to me all red and black, with his dark beard and his red gown and full, glistening lips.

"She's woken up," he said, smiling at me. The hound grinned too, tongue lolling over brown stubs of teeth.

Shadows shifted as the boot wearer squatted down behind his dog to take a closer look at me. This man was masked, and dressed entirely in black; even his hands, resting loosely on his knees, were gloved in black velvet and a black cap covered his hair. The light from the wall sconce haloed him, making it difficult to discern the details of his dress or mask.

"Well," he said, "I hope all my sister's women are not in the same state as you. Cardinal Ippolito and I were on our way to watch the dancing and it will be a pretty muddle if you're all falling down drunk."

Duke Valentino. I thought of the hand and the tongue. I closed my eyes again and clenched my teeth, and hoped so skilful a killer would be able to dispatch me without pain, the way the kosher butchers do.

Nothing happened. I opened my eyes again, wishing it would. For by now my befuddled mind had registered that, not only had the duke found me lying drunk on the floor, but also Cardinal Ippolito d'Este, the man appointed to be my godfather.

"Try to sit," the cardinal was saying. "You'll feel dizzy at first, but it's best to be upright then all that wine running in your veins can drain from the head."

"I'm so sorry, forgive me, I…"

"Never mind all that. Cesare, take her other arm and let's get her to her feet. She needs some air."

Each man placed a hand beneath my elbow, the cardinal's a well-manicured paw, the duke's fingers hard and lean under his glove. While he was briefly preoccupied with extricating his spur from the hem of my *camorra*, I stole a look at his face. The handsomest man in Italy, the girls at Santa Clara used to say, though I do not know if any of them had actually seen him close to, yet because of his mask only his neatly trimmed, auburn beard was visible, and pale lips which had a certain muscular mobility about them. It struck me that he wore his mask, a winged confection of black velvet, gold braid and pearls, because in him, even beauty was dangerous. Did he, perhaps, fear to look at his own face?

The blood seemed to rush from my head as I stood, and pool in my feet, weighing them down as I stumbled and swayed, with further profuse apologies, against the cardinal.

"Please," he said roguishly, "the pleasure is all mine." He slipped an arm around my waist as the duke released his grip on my elbow. I thought of my father and his good intentions, and felt tears pricking my eyes.

"Donata!" Angela. Oh, praise the Holy Name.

"Donata?" repeated the cardinal.

"Yes, your eminence." Was that the right form of address? I hoped so.

"Forgive me. My lord cardinal, cousin Cesare." Arresting her flight towards me, Angela dropped into a deep curtsey. The cardinal offered his free hand and she kissed his ring then, though the duke raised her to her feet and brushed her cheek with his lips, she continued to gaze at the cardinal through her eyelashes, with a charming affectation of modesty.

"Donna Angela," reproached the cardinal, "I shall require you to take better care of my goddaughter in future."

"Perhaps your grace should give me guidance in the matter."

Horribly aware of my soiled and crumpled clothes, the wisps of hair matted to my forehead, my foul breath, I felt more inadequate and out of place than ever.

"Take a cup with me when you have attended to Signorina Donata," said the cardinal, "and we will make a lesson plan."

"Come, Ippolito," said the duke, "we have done our good deed for today." Though he said no more, I could feel the deeds he now contemplated hanging in the cold air of the corridor, and a curious thrill ran through me.

Seeing me shiver, Angela put her arm around me. "Bed for you, young lady. You have partied quite enough for one night."

"Will Donna Lucrezia banish me?" I whined, both dreading and longing for her reply.

She laughed. "Good lord no. At worst, you'll get a ticking off from Donna Adriana; at best, Lucrezia will just be amused. Elisabetta Senese once mistook the Holy Father for a chair cushion and sat on him. He was delighted. He gave her a great store of silk floor cushions that used to be in Prince Djem's apartments. Her room looks like a harem now."

"Who is Prince Djem?"

"Oh, he died years ago. He was the Sultan's brother, but the Sultan paid for him to stay here so he wouldn't have to murder him. Apparently that's how the Ottomans secure the succession. They murder their brothers. We all loved Djem, especially Cesare, but Djem loved Juan the best." She paused. I felt a calculating glance upon me, though we were far from the new, well-lit parts of the palace now, back in the maze of narrow, rickety passages where Madonna Lucrezia's ladies-in-waiting had their rooms. "And I do mean loved. Juan was as pretty as a girl. Here we are."

Angela led me into the room, feeling for the edge of the bed and pushing me down on to it while she groped in a little niche in the wall for the flint box she kept there at the foot of the wooden crucifix.

Emboldened by the fact that I could not see her face, I asked, "What did happen to Don Juan?" Though I was still quite a little girl when he died, all Rome had been abuzz with the gossip when his mutilated corpse was pulled from the Tiber by a fisherman, and the name Valentino was never far from people's lips. The brothers had argued over the favours of their sister-in-law, the princess Sancia of Aragon, it was said, or over the fact that Juan, though inept as a soldier, had been made gonfalonier of the Church whereas Cesare, then cardinal of Valencia, was destined to follow his father up the steps of Saint Peter's throne. No one had ever been convicted of the murder of the pope's favourite son, so the rumours festered like an untreated sore.

Angela struck her flints and light flared from the candle on the nightstand. Bending towards me, eyes wide and earnest, shadowed by an exhaustion I had not noticed before, she took my hands and pressed them against my knees. "Donata, I want to be your friend. You are pretty and quick-witted and you can do well here. But there are some questions you must not ask, and some things you may see which you must keep to yourself. As for Juan," she added, straightening up and admitting a lighter note to her voice, as though no mystery at all attached to his murder, "it was the Orsini. They have had it in for us ever since Uncle Rodrigo imprisoned Virginio Orsini for going over to the French in '93 and then he died in prison. They were sure Uncle Rodrigo had had him killed, so they went after Juan for revenge. Honours are even now, so there's an end to it."

Honours were not even, of course; the cycle of the vendetta never ends, and I wonder if Angela really believed a word she was saying or was simply trying to protect me. As it turned out, in a roundabout way, the bad blood between Borgia and Orsini would transform my life, but not yet. Not yet.

Angela helped me to undress then tucked me into bed. The pallet stuffed with wool and horsehair felt as soft as a featherbed to my raw stomach and spinning head. Dabbing rosewater behind her ears from a small flask on the nightstand, Angela said she was returning to the dance and bade me goodnight.

"I'm taking the candle," she said, and with the sudden descent of total darkness on the small room which had now become my home, I fell into a profound and dreamless sleep. I was unaware of Angela coming to bed.

❦

I was excused attendance on Donna Lucrezia when she rose next morning, but summoned before her after the day meal in the small salon overlooking Saint Peter's steps where she held her private audiences. Donna Lucrezia looked as though she had slept little; hectic spots of colour highlighted her cheeks like badly applied rouge and her eyes glowed like moonlight at the bottom of a lake. Though swathed in a cape of fur, she shivered intermittently, and I feared she had caught a fever. Donna Adriana was with her, and opened our interview, jowls atremble with indignation.

"My daughter-in-law, Donna Giulia, was disappointed that you could not be presented to her last evening."

I bowed my head for fear the ladies would see me blushing.

"As was His Beatitude, my father," added Donna Lucrezia in a tone that might splinter glass, "who surprised and honoured us with his presence."

"Have you nothing to say, girl?"

"I am truly sorry. I am unused to wine, and such rich food, and the emotions of the day…It will not happen again," I finished lamely.

A silence ensued. The cries of hawkers vending pasties and medallions of the saints on the basilica steps came to us, muffled by the glass in the windows. Donna Lucrezia glanced out, her carefully plucked brows drawn together briefly in a frown. I remembered that the Duke of Bisceglie, the father of little Rodrigo, had received the wounds which ultimately killed him on those steps, and wondered why, if she had loved her second husband as much as the *avvisi* said she did, she had chosen this room for her own.

I was surprised in this train of thought by Donna Lucrezia's distinctive laugh. "You met my dear brother, Cesar, though," she said, using the Catalan form of his name even though she spoke to me in Italian. I wondered if perhaps it would be better for me to leap from the window and meet my own fate on Saint Peter's steps. If, perhaps, the duke was this very moment, hidden behind a tapestry covering a secret doorway, drawing a dagger from his belt with which to finish me.

"I was inclined to be severe with you, but both he and Cardinal Ippolito interceded for you, so I shall be merciful. I had intended that you should have three new gowns for my wedding celebrations, but now it must be two, to offset the cost of replacing the rug you ruined. Still, I dare say, with the *camorra* I gave you for your baptism, and the white velvet cloak, you will manage not to disgrace me."

"But…"

Donna Adriana's eyebrows arched alarmingly. "I told you you should have interviewed this girl more closely," she said to Donna Lucrezia in a stage whisper. "Now she is answering back."

"My decision does not please you?" Donna Lucrezia asked.

"No, madonna, I mean…you are very generous. I thought you would send me back to my father."

"And that is what you wanted." It was not a question, but a statement, delivered in a low, compassionate tone. "Oh, my dear." Donna Adriana placed a warning hand on her niece's arm, but Donna Lucrezia continued regardless. "We have to learn to want what our fathers want."

༺৶৶༻

The next few weeks sped by in a whirl of dress fittings and beauty treatments, petty, exquisite agonies of pins and hair plucking. Nor did Donna Lucrezia, conscious, no doubt, of the eyes of Duke Ercole's envoys upon her, neglect her duties as godmother to me. She had been appointed regent at the Vatican, while the pope and Duke Valentino made a tour of inspection of the fortifications at Nepi and Civita Castellana, but nevertheless found time to accompany me to Mass every morning and to direct me in the correct ways to genuflect or cross myself or take the dry wafer these cannibals called the body of Christ, in my mouth. She supervised my needlework and singing, and graciously relented over the third gown when particularly pleased by my composition of a Petrarchan sonnet. Serene, smiling, and capable, she appeared to entertain no doubts that she would be happy with the homely man whose miniature she carried everywhere, suspended from her girdle by a gold chain.

Only on our weekly visits to the bathhouse did she relax and admit a little good natured teasing about Don Alfonso's broken nose and unfashionably short hair. Of the more serious rumours about him, that he had been driven mad by the French disease and was prone to violent depressions during which he raged around the streets of Ferrara as naked as the day he was born, or that he kept a string of mistresses, she would hear no mention.

"I know all I need to about the French disease," she once snapped at Angela, when the rest of us put her up to mention it. "You of all people should know better."

"Forgive me, madonna," whispered Angela, and I felt for a moment as though I had thrown my friend to a pack of stag hounds.

We would troop across the garden to the bathhouse in nothing but our Neapolitan wraps, loose, diaphanous garments made fashionable by the Princess Sancia. Every time I put mine on I felt more naked than if I had been wearing nothing at all, and I could see the look of disapproval on Mariam's face as clearly as though she were watching me from behind the fig tree which shaded the garden door and dropped sticky fruit in splashes of pink on the path. Sometimes I had a fleeting sense of other eyes upon us, of looks that made me blush and feel cold all at once, and tied knots in my stomach.

The bathhouse was fashionably disguised to look like a ruined temple, with broken marble columns and statues of plump Venuses whose noses had been deliberately knocked off, but inside it was absolutely modern. A hypocaust running under the floor kept the water warm in the deep marble tub where we lounged on steps covered by towels. Catherinella and another black slave kept a second, smaller chamber filled with fragrant steam by pouring buckets of water onto a bed of hot charcoal mixed with sandalwood and lavender. Screened from the palace by a trellis of hibiscus, emboldened by the veil of steam, we giggled and gossiped and exchanged confidences.

In this perfumed confessional one might admit that her belly was too prominent or her breasts too flat, while others debated the difficulty of persuading a lover to use his tongue where he would prefer to insert another part. I used to sit close to Angela, who would whisper explanations.

"You can't get pregnant from a man's tongue, nor can it pierce the hymen. And besides, it gives much greater pleasure."

This was not, perhaps, the carnal education my mother would have planned for me, but my mother was long dead and I had grown up in a household of men with only the taciturn Mariam for female companionship, and the uninformed speculations of the girls at Santa Clara. It shames me now to say I felt no shame then, only a hungry curiosity that seemed to lodge as much in my growing breasts and the untouchable place between my legs as in my mind. This was something my new, dear friend seemed to understand, as she drew me through the steam to her own voluptuous, golden-skinned body, stroking my arm or my thigh.

A small mirror hung on the wall of our chamber, an oblong in a plain silver frame just large enough to show us our faces. Angela would command me to take this down from time to time and hold it at the right height for her to trim her private hair with a nail parer. There she would stand, brazen in her nakedness, her skin glowing in the light of a brazier now the weather was growing colder, telling me to move the mirror a little to the right, or up a bit, or could I prop it up on the commode and hold the candle higher so she could see better. For a time, I performed this duty without query, too proud to admit that, to me, it seemed strange and indecent. If Donna Lucrezia's cousin thought nothing of it, then this was obviously what ladies of fashion did and I would not humiliate myself by revealing my ignorance.

Then, one evening when she had plucked out a stray hair with her tweezers and drawn blood from her groin, and we were already late to help Donna Lucrezia dress for a reception in the Vatican, I asked, "Why do you do this?"

"For my sins?" she retorted with a quick laugh, then became almost serious, except for the telltale dimples in her cheeks, impressions left by her smile the way a head leaves its indent in a pillow. "Ippolito likes it."

"Ippolito? *Cardinal* Ippolito? You mean you're...?" She had spent some nights away from her own bed recently, but had told me she was attending Donna Lucrezia, who was unwell. Donna Lucrezia was often unwell, so I had thought nothing of it.

"You did me a favour, getting sick like that."

"And you let him..? I mean, you're not married."

"He is very skilled." She ran her hands over her unfashionably full breasts, down her flanks, and over the rise of her belly. "Very skilled," she repeated. "And once his pious father dies, which can't be long—he's as old as Methuselah—cousin Lucrezia can find me a compliant husband, just like those men her mother has been married to. Most men are content to be cuckolded for a decent price. I swear old Della Croce used to count it an honour to have his wife poked by Uncle Rodrigo."

I marvelled. From the moment Angela's eyes met those of the cardinal over my prostrate form, it seemed, she had begun planning a future for herself.

"Don't say anything," said Angela. "Not before we get our feet under the table in Ferrara."

"I won't. But Angela?"

"What?"

"Think of Monna Vannozza."

"I am. Four children with Uncle Rodrigo and she still enjoys his protection, even though she's old and ugly now. She's set up for life."

"But Lucrezia loathes her, Juan's dead, and Jofre…"

"Cesare adores her. That has to count for something."

I wondered what that something might be, though felt it safer to say nothing, even to Angela. Though she was my friend, she was Cesare's blood.

"Oh, don't look so po-faced," Angela went on. "If you purse your lips that way you'll get wrinkles. You don't want to end up with a mouth like a dog's bum like cousin Geronima."

The image banished my pain and sent me into fits of giggles. Angela started to laugh too, bent double so the little pearl of blood at the edge of her garden smeared her belly.

"Let me clean that," I gasped, trying to recover myself, "or would your lover like you better for torturing yourself to please him?" I sat up, spat on my kerchief, and leaned towards Angela, but before I could attend to her wound, she gathered me up in her arms and kissed me full on the mouth, the tip of her tongue flickering over my lips.

"You need a lover of your own," she told me, stepping back, putting her finger to my closed mouth.

"I shall be lucky even to get a husband if we don't make haste to wait on madonna," I said, hoping she would not detect the tremor in my voice.

"Come on, then, help me dress," and she began to whirl about the small room, picking up shift and hose in time to wild dance steps, her small, brown feet stamping down the rug beside the bed and the sprigs of dried rosemary which had fallen from among our bedding. She was the most beautiful creature I had ever seen. I would have died for her then.

# Chapter 3

ROME, OCTOBER 1501

*I can feel your body as truly as if we were still dancing for Papa, when your waist was tiny and my bones did not ache as they do today in the mountain wind. Listen to me. I sound like an old man getting sentimental over his first sweetheart—which you were, of course, and are.*

We lay side by side on Angela's bed, pressed together for warmth. It was the end of October and, while sunlight rarely found its way into our room, which faced on to an inner courtyard at the old heart of the palace, the autumn winds off the marshes surrounding the city seemed to poke their fingers everywhere. Angela lay on her back, her face smeared with a foul smelling paste of pigeons' blood and fresh cheese ground with peach stones and pebbles steeped in milk which she swore kept her skin fair. I lay with my head beside her feet and my own feet propped on her pillows in an attempt to reduce the swelling in my ankles brought on by too much dancing in unsuitable shoes the night before.

As the date of our departure drew closer, the celebrations for Donna Lucrezia's marriage grew more hectic. Every day there were spectacles in the city's squares, races, tableaux, performances by troupes of clowns and actors, and poets declaiming the virtues of Donna Lucrezia and Don Alfonso and their houses. Remorseless cannonades from the Castel Sant'Angelo shook the air. The Holy Father, who loved to sail, could not be deterred from a river excursion to Ostia, despite warnings from his astrologer and Duke Valentino's plain observation that it was pouring with rain and looked set to do so all day. Of the musicians who accompanied us, two singers caught chills and had to be replaced and a mandolin player slipped on the wet deck of the papal barge, fell overboard, and drowned. Baby Rodrigo was sick and madonna was beside herself in case he had caught a chill too.

Every evening, after long and elaborate dinners punctuated by theatrical or musical interludes, his indefatigable Beatitude would command the ladies to dance, so dance we did, until our feet were bleeding and the musicians' heads nodded over their instruments. Then he would order us all outside to watch firework displays from the Belvedere or the ramparts of Sant'Angelo before, with chattering teeth and blinded eyes, we were permitted to retire. I was thankful the pope's eye never alighted upon me with anything more than his customary, general benevolence. How any of Donna Lucrezia's ladies found the energy to resist, then graciously submit, to his advances, I cannot imagine. Perhaps it came from contemplating how well the Farnese family had done out of Giulia, or even Donna Lucrezia herself, the bastard daughter of a Spanish upstart and an innkeeper, about to marry into the House of Este.

Tonight, Duke Valentino was to throw a party for his sister in his private apartments. At least, Angela had remarked when the summons came, we were more likely to get a good meal. The duke, unlike his father, was famous for his appreciation of good food and wine. And we were honoured to have been asked; not all Donna Lucrezia's ladies were to attend, as this would be an intimate function with only about fifty guests.

"How you can think of food with the stench of that paste in your nostrils I don't know." It was doubly offensive to me, the mixture of blood and cheese; my senses were proving slow students of Christianity.

"Don't be so serious, Donata. And don't make me talk any more; it's all cracking round my mouth." We lay for a while in silence, nothing but the soft hiss of tallow from our candles and, once, a crash followed by raised voices from across the courtyard in the direction of the palace kitchens. Then Angela suddenly said, "Donata. It's such a pompous name, so... pious. You need a nickname."

"And Angela isn't? Pious, I mean."

"Not at all. Angels simply are; gifts must be given and received and thanks made and all that. It's too complicated. Besides, Lucifer was an angel. Angels have some side to them."

"So what are you going to call me? Lucifer?"

"I don't know. It will come to me. Now, help me wash this off. We had better not be late for cousin Cesare. I'm dying to see what La Fiammetta is wearing."

I tried to focus my mind on the notorious Fiammetta, the flame-haired Florentine courtesan who was the duke's current mistress, as I helped Angela wipe the beauty treatment from her face. Yet I found myself wondering what our rabbi would think if he could see me now, irredeemably unclean of body and mind. Then realised I didn't care; outcast I might be, but with Angela's newly clean skin beneath my fingers, I felt a sense of belonging I believed I had left behind in Toledo.

◆◆◆

I should have known; I should have realised what the duke must think of me, that his invitation was not a compliment, nor even an insult. He had simply selected those he thought suitable to participate in the entertainment he had in mind, and of course, given the circumstances of our first encounter, he would think me suitable.

Insofar as he lived anywhere, the duke lived, not in his palace of San Clemente in the old Borgo which, for as long as I knew it, was in a continuous state of reconstruction, but in a suite of rooms directly above his father's in the Vatican. These rooms had once belonged to Prince Djem and, despite the Holy Father's ironic gift to Elisabetta Senese, retained much of the oriental opulence with which the prince of the Turks had surrounded himself. We dined at low tables, reclining on cushions like the ancients. Candles scented with vanilla and sandalwood sparkled in ornate brass stands, and the drowsy, sensual air was trapped by heavy curtains in some dark velvet.

Men and women dined together, young gentlemen of the duke's household, some of whom I recognised, a handful of the younger cardinals, solid blocks of scarlet among the shifting, shimmering silks and brocades of the ladies, a great many of whom, though they seemed perfectly at home here, I had never seen before. Donna Lucrezia lounged beside her father who, in consideration of his age and exalted status, sat in an ornately carved chair with one foot resting on a cushion and the other, in which he had the gout, propped on the shoulder of a small black boy who knelt before him.

But the duke himself was nowhere to be seen. All through dinner he failed to appear until, just as the servants were clearing the fruit course and the musicians were shuffling the music on their stands to find the dances, the great double doors to the room swung open and he entered, preceded by two men in his red and gold livery, a tall, red-haired woman on his arm whom I took to be La Fiammetta. Beside her, the duke, clad as always in plain black and wearing very little jewellery, seemed almost to disappear among the shadows beyond the light of the scented candles. She was magnificent, with creamy skin and an erect bearing that made me think of the classical marble statues decorating the new facades of the great palaces such as our own Santa Maria. Except for the depth of her décolleté and the boldness of her makeup, you might easily mistake her for a great lady rather than a courtesan. She was, apparently, a skilled musician and could recite most of Ovid from memory, though some said that was because she put so many of the recommendations of the *Ars Amatoria* into practice with her lovers.

We rose and bowed, a somewhat ragged obeisance as those who had already drunk more wine than was good for them stumbled over cushions. La Fiammetta knelt to His Holiness and kissed his ring, and bowed over Donna Lucrezia's hand, but surveyed the rest of us with imperious disdain. Duke Valentino's wife and daughter remained at the French court, hostages, some said, for her husband's good behaviour. La Fiammetta was queen of Rome. The duke handed her into a cushioned space beside Donna Lucrezia; Donna Lucrezia moved readily enough to make room for her, but the air between them seemed jagged and frosty, as though the light and warmth of the perfumed candles could not penetrate there. Clearly they were not friends.

The duke himself went to stand behind his father's chair and was soon deep in discussion with the Holy Father, their heads bent together, the duke's arm stretched along the back of his father's chair while His Holiness' pet monkey raced up and down it as far as its gold chain would extend. The girl who had somehow insinuated herself into the blessed lap was swatted away like a tiresome insect when she tried to nibble the pope's ear. Then, with a sudden, loud laugh, the duke knocked the monkey aside, straightened up and, business at an end, began to survey the room as he planned his assault upon his guests. I realised, with a sensation of trapped birds struggling behind my ribs, that his face was set in my direction.

Perhaps he wished only to greet his cousin, who was sitting beside me. But no. He had crossed the room in a few long, light-footed strides, and his body now inclined towards me in a shallow bow. I struggled to my feet and managed a tolerable curtsey despite being entangled in cushions and Angela's skirts. I bit my lip as my shin struck the low table edge.

"Well, Signorina Donata, you are steadier on your feet than the last time I saw you."

I felt the flush bloom on my cheeks as though my head had been thrust into a pan of boiling water. Cardinal Ippolito, seated at Angela's other side, sniggered. I could think of nothing to say, but I had to say something or the duke would think me rude.

"It had been a very emotional day for me, your grace. I regret my...lack of control."

"Holy Mother Church can have that effect on some people," he replied, with a savage disdain that made me forget myself and glance up at his face.

I had never seen the duke unmasked before. Angela said he kept his face covered because it was marred by the scars of the French disease and he was absurdly vain. I could not have told you if this was the case or not, could not have told you what he looked like, except that he seemed younger than I had expected. And that I knew, in less than the space of a breath, his face was the prism through which I would see the whole world from now on, the yardstick by which I would measure the beauty of every face. And that he understood my feelings, and that for this moment, if for no other, his beauty was a gift reserved only for me.

Don Cesare took my hand in his and brushed my palm with his lips. He was not wearing gloves and I noticed he had a powder burn on the back of his right hand, a smudged grey tattoo just behind the middle knuckle. Of all the memories of him I carry in my heart, this is one of the tenderest. It showed me he was a man, who could be damaged. Who could be loved.

"Will you dance with me, Donata?"

"If my lady permits it, your grace."

"Oh, she will permit it. And she will permit you to call me Cesare."

I was aware of Angela looking at me, her expression blended of amusement, curiosity, and a trace of anxiety. My eyes were drawn to her, but they were held by Cesare as firmly as he now held my hand, with a slight, delicious crush.

Emboldened, I said, "If you wish me to dance, sir…Cesare, you must let me go. I fear the table stands between me and the dance floor."

"Step up. It's surely not too high for you." He smiled, a boy's smile, showing very white teeth. "Or are you less good at physical gymnastics than spiritual ones?"

Uncertain what he was talking about, I said, "The reverse, I think," and stepped up on to the table in response to his light tug on my arm. A shout of laughter and a burst of applause came from the direction of the pope's chair as Cesare placed his hands either side of my waist and lifted me down. A bowl of marzipan roses crashed to the floor, dislodged by the hem of my skirt. Various dogs crept out from beneath the tables and snaffled the sweets, among them the same old blind hound I recognised from my last, humiliating encounter with its master, its scrawny neck now weighed down by a gem-encrusted collar. For a moment, Cesare paused, watching the dogs, then hailed one of the slaves and gave him some instructions I did not hear because just then, seeing the duke step out on to the floor, the musicians struck up a pavane. The French dances were all the fashion since the duke had taken a French wife.

Couples formed behind us as we led the dance. The pavane, my dancing master taught me, should be performed with a stately grace, the couples always two arms' lengths apart and no more than palms touching. Clearly, Cesare and I had not shared the same dancing master; the pavane as he performed it had grace, certainly, but little in the way of stateliness. When I offered my palm, he interlaced my fingers with his own; when I attempted to walk through a turn, he seized me by my waist, whispering to me how he marvelled at its smallness, and whirled me around, holding me so close I could smell wine and cloves on his breath and feel his heartbeat, the flex of the muscles in his thighs, his arousal which thrilled me then made me feel ashamed of myself. All the time we danced his dark gaze held mine, and though I could not mistake the desire in his eyes, I was unnerved by a sense that this was just what he wanted me to see, that he could control those vital spirits that originate in the heart and show themselves in the eyes with the same easy competence that made him disdain the proper rules of the dance.

"You perform the pavane most...originally, my lord," I said, trying to restore our communion to a proper level of decency.

"You have a quarrel with my style?" He paused for the space of a heartbeat, his brows arched in surprise. No one else could possibly have noticed, so quickly did he rediscover his rhythm.

"If we do not dance according to the rules, surely we disrespect the music, and music is the voice given us by the Almighty with which to worship Him, is it not? Ficino says..."

"Ficino, is it? So you are an educated girl." He pinched my waist. "Good. My illustrious sister should have intelligent women about her, or she is as a princess clothed in rags."

"In which her beauty would shine all the brighter by contrast."

"And now will you quote me your drawing master? Much more of this sparring and I shall lose my footing utterly and," lowering his voice to a whisper so I felt the words rather than heard them, a hot breath against my ear, "fall helpless into your arms. Did anyone ever tell you your earlobes are just the colour of *lokum*? I am very good at making *lokum*, you know, one day I will show you." He grazed one of my rose candy lobes with his even teeth.

It dawned on me now that those women whom I had not recognised were other honest prostitutes, courtesans like La Fiammetta who pursued their trade discreetly, in houses set up for them by their wealthy lovers. Perhaps I was no better, but I did not care. Dizzy from the dance, ecstatic with longing, I thought no further than the next moment he would put his arms around me and press his body to mine. La Fiammetta could go and count her gold. Cesare was mine. Surely he must love me more than her. I, after all, was a virgin, and had he not once rounded up all the virgins in Capua and had them locked in a tower for his pleasure?

And then I was alone. The music ended and, though the world was still spinning about me, I stood still in the middle of it, abandoned, the impression of Cesare fading from my flesh as it cooled. As quickly as he had sought me out, he had left me, back across the room to sit between his mistress and Donna Lucrezia, one hand on La Fiammetta's knee, his head resting against his sister's shoulder. Servants were removing the candelabra from the tables and placing them at intervals around the floor. Angela was beckoning me back to my seat, as some of the prostitutes formed up, somewhat raggedly among the lamp stands, for another dance, chattering parrots in a forest of lights. I made my way back to her side as the band struck up a sarabande. Turning her back momentarily on Ippolito, she gripped my hand and looked at me with concern, but I felt only Cesare's fingers pressed into my flesh. Though I was close enough to her to feel the race of her heart as Ippolito stroked her thigh, I was already, fatally, beyond her.

On the dance floor, as the women came together in formation, they were not so much pressing hands as fondling one another, unlacing bodices and unhooking skirts, shrugging and stepping out of their clothes in time to the music. This was like no sarabande I had ever seen, and I averted my eyes. I looked, or so I told myself, to Donna Lucrezia for guidance. Surely she could not consider such a display suitable for mixed company, especially for a lady about to marry, even if it was for the third time. The gaze that met mine, however, was not Donna Lucrezia's but her brother's. Of course. What else had I intended?

Boldly, I smiled. With a peremptory nod in the direction of the dancing prostitutes, he made it plain I should watch them, not him. My smile froze and dropped. That was his pleasure, then, not to make love to me but to humiliate me with this spectacle of naked flesh. Or perhaps his interest did not extend even that far; as I dragged my gaze from him to the dance floor, I saw him turn away, giving all his attention to La Fiammetta as he slipped the hand with the powder burn inside the neck of her gown. Through the shimmer of my tears, I stared at the dancers' undulating flesh, pink and brown, bare nipples staring back at me as though they were those creatures described in the Letter of Prester John that have no heads but whose faces are located on their torsos with eyes where the nipples should be.

More servants now entered, all in Cesare's quartered livery with his name emblazoned across the backs of their tunics. They bore wide, flat dishes of roast chestnuts, which they scattered about the floor like farmers casting seed. Dropping to their hands and knees, the prostitutes began to scavenge for these, crawling among the lamp stands so buttocks and thighs and hanging bellies loomed in and out of the candlelight. Some simply picked the nuts up in handfuls and crammed them into their mouths; some scooped them up with lascivious tongues. Yet others, balancing the nuts on the very edges of the tables, managed to clench them in the openings to their women's parts, then, squatting before the young men of Cesare's household, invited them to help themselves. This they did, with hands or mouths as the fancy took them, eliciting enthusiastic applause from Cesare and his father.

Though the musicians played imperturbably on, an intense stillness settled on the spectators which felt like silence. Men and women alike watched with faces carefully composed to mask their excitement as Cesare's gentlemen, replete with chestnuts, began to copulate with the prostitutes on the dance floor, the Holy Father shouting instruction and encouragement the way the owners of prize fighters do from the edges of the *piazze* on festival days. The watchers began to shift in their seats, hands disappeared beneath folds of linen and silk, conversation dwindled to rustles, low moans, an occasional grunt as a disturbing, intimate musk began to mingle with stale sweat, camphor from disturbed clothing, and the exotic perfume of the candles. Appalled and fascinated by turns, I wondered if I was the only one in the room whose hands still lay in her own lap.

I glanced at Angela, slack-jawed and lazy-eyed, stroking Ippolito's crotch while his fingers scrabbled in her cleavage. I shifted my gaze cautiously in Donna Lucrezia's direction, fearful of what I might see, yet hoping she would be too preoccupied to notice if I slipped away. She was sitting bolt upright, her knees still tucked under her but her body as straight as if she had been laced too tight and could not breathe. Next to her, Cesare and his mistress were sunk in a long kiss. As though she sensed me looking at her, she turned her head in my direction and bestowed on me a look of such misery it branded itself there and then in my memory, though it would be a long time before I understood it.

Cesare, disentangling himself from La Fiammetta's creamy limbs, signed the musicians to cease playing. The couples on the dance floor began to separate, Cesare's young men straightening their clothes sheepishly, flushed as if they had been caught with a maidservant by the family priest. The prostitutes dressed themselves more languorously, lacing one another and tidying each other's hair, exchanging secret jokes and low laughter as they did so. I imagined this was how they behaved when the men left and they could relax, and that they were not much different from Angela and me, curled up together for warmth in her bed or mine, gossiping about our fellow ladies-in-waiting, their clothes, their beaux, their courtly accomplishments or lack of them.

A knock came at the doors and Master Burchard, the papal master of ceremonies, sidled into the room, bowed, and said something to Cesare. Seeing him in his sober robes, his grey beard spread over his chest, was like seeing my father. Though we were exempt from the rules about Jewish dress because of my father's relationship with the Vatican, he always dressed modestly, in long, dark-coloured gowns with, perhaps, a little squirrel trim in winter. A sullen ember gathered in my chest, anger with myself for caving in to my father's suggestions for my advancement so thoroughly I now yearned more for a look from Cesare's black eyes than I did for a pure heart or a clear conscience. But anger also against my father's ambition. For deserting my mother and me to build himself a fortune in Rome. It was his fault. All this.

Servants were carrying silver bound chests into the room, which they placed before Cesare, Donna Lucrezia, and His Holiness, then opened the lids and knelt beside them. Cesare announced that prizes would be given to the men who, in the opinion of himself, his illustrious sister, and the Holy Father, had displayed the greatest prowess with the prostitutes. In the event of disagreement, he added, with something between a smirk and a sneer, La Fiammetta would, with her great experience, be the final arbiter. Applause and whistles greeted the prize winners, who received silken doublets, hats, Spanish leather shoes, and embroidered shirts. We had been busy embroidering shirts lately. We had thought they were for Don Alfonso d'Este, or for the squires and pages who were to accompany Donna Lucrezia to Ferrara. Well, perhaps they were; it was impossible to tell in the smoky light.

After the prize giving, though the party looked set to continue into the daylight hours, Donna Lucrezia rose to leave and we filed out behind her, each dropping our curtsey to the pope and Cesare. He will give me some sign, I thought, he is bound to acknowledge what we shared on the dance floor. But many other couples had shared much more on that dance floor since we performed the pavane together, and Cesare was far more concerned with the setting of tables for cards than with bidding his sister's waiting women a good night. So engrossed was I in my disappointment, I did not notice Angela slip away until I found myself, once again, alone in our room, struggling with my laces by the light of a single candle, shivering under the covers in my shift to which the perfume of vanilla and sandalwood, and something else, feral and sharp, still clung.

❦

The nights were worst. During the hours of daylight, as the date set for our departure grew closer and the wedding celebrations intensified, there was no time for thought or remembering. In the mornings, after Mass, we sat with Donna Lucrezia in her private apartments and did our needlework, taking turns to read, sometimes from the Lives of the Saints or the letters of Saint Catherine, of whom madonna was particularly fond, sometimes poetry or romances teeming with lovelorn knights and cold-hearted ladies. What was wrong with me, I wondered, that I identified more with the knights than the ladies? Then, more often than not, there were engagements for the day meal followed by spectacles and entertainments laid on for the visiting Ferrarese. Cardinal Ippolito had now been joined in Rome by his brother, Don Ferrante. The Holy Father's desire to impress his new in-laws was unremitting; even Cesare, it was rumoured, had taken to receiving embassies while lying in bed, so exhausted was he by the old man's pace.

But though we tumbled into bed each night worn out from dancing and marvelling at the tableaux, the banquets, the feats of acrobats and castrati, I could not sleep. My throbbing head and aching feet were as nothing to the lust that burned in my belly like the fires I imagined Cesare's sappers might set below the walls of a fortress. Often it made me cry. I believed I was going mad. How was it possible so to miss something you had never had?

I was frequently alone. Angela would touch my hand in farewell and slip silently away to meet her lover as soon as we had prepared Donna Lucrezia for bed. If I had not been so absorbed in my own longings, I would have noticed that their affair had developed to a dangerous intensity. Angela had become reckless, sometimes going to him even in the middle of the day, should Donna Lucrezia be writing letters or seeing petitioners and have more need of her secretary than of us. If she had not been so wrapped up in Ippolito, she would have noticed sooner than she did what was happening to me.

"What is it?" she demanded crossly, one night when her monthly courses had condemned her to chastity. "Are you still homesick or something?"

I thought of how Cesare had admired my hair. So fair, he had murmured. As a maid, I wore my hair loose, then, with only a narrow silver circlet to keep it off my face. So like…then he broke off, as though he could not think of an appropriate likeness, or wondered if a soldier should pay a lady so personal a compliment, or leave it to the poets. "No," I said. "Angela, is it true about the virgins of Capua?"

"Ah," she said as enlightenment dawned. "I suppose it had to happen." She laughed. "I think it's more likely cousin Cesare had to lock himself in a tower to protect himself from the voracious virgins than the other way around."

"Oh. I suppose so."

In the dark, I heard her sigh, then a rustling of bed-clothes and the click and rasp of flints striking. I looked across at her, acutely aware in the sudden flare of candlelight of my swollen eyelids and red nose.

"Come here," said Angela, holding out her hand. I climbed into bed beside her and sat hugging my knees. Angela put an arm around my shoulders. "Don't do this to yourself. He isn't worth it."

She lied.

Earlier that day, Cesare had given a display of bullfighting in Saint Peter's Square, and we had watched from the loggia above the front door of Santa Maria. A cold, needling rain was driven against our faces by a wind from the river, but the weather had failed to deter the crowds who jostled the barricades set up around the square and warmed themselves with little hot pasties stamped with the arms of Este and Borgia. The vendors were specially licensed by His Holiness, in exchange for a cut of the proceeds. The Romans tend to see little difference between a Spaniard and a Jew, and they may be right. And though they are quick to blame either for all their misfortunes, two Spanish customs they cannot resist are bullfights and gambling with cards.

The square was pitted and churned by the wheeling of bulls and horses. Flags and banners snapped in the wind, compounding the fury of the bulls already roused to foaming, snorting rage by the work of picadors and *banderilleros*. Cesare dispatched each bull alone, on foot, using only a light sword. He relied solely on his own quickness and accuracy to triumph over the power and cunning of the animals. He danced with the bulls, twisting, sidestepping; he flirted, luring them on to the point of his sword whose fine blade he sunk deep into the place between the shoulder blades where the straight path to the heart begins.

He killed four bulls that way, with grace, precision, and perfect ruthlessness, and when he had made his final kill, he cut off the ear of the bull and presented it to his sister. A dwarf brought it, a black velvet purse of gristle on a small gold salver, up to our balcony, while Cesare stood below and bowed to madonna, his hair, bound with black ribbon into a thick braid, falling over one shoulder. He was naked to the waist, his skin glistening with sweat and rain, patterned with mud and blood as though he were one of the painted savages of the New World.

All the women leaned towards him like flowers turning their heads to the sun, including Angela, even cousin Geronima, whose corset of boiled leather creaked slightly like a new saddle, even Catherinella, her black, tattooed face shining, and the plump, sensible woman who had charge of the two little boys, Rodrigo and Giovanni, the Infant of Rome, who pressed his tearful face even more firmly into her bosom as she shifted her position.

Though I do not think anyone other than me went on looking once Donna Lucrezia had acknowledged the gift of the ear and he had turned away. I do not think anyone else noticed the way he squared his shoulders, bringing the shoulder blades up and together as though he longed to have wings, to be able to take off and be somewhere else.

"He is. I love him; I'm sure I do."

She gave a snort of laughter. "No you don't. You've had one dance with him, that's all."

"And how long had you known Ippolito when..?"

"That's not love, you silly goose; that's scratching an itch."

"Well I have more than an itch; I have a terrible pain."

"Tell me, where does it hurt?" She touched my breast. "Here?" I clutched at the neck of my nightgown; my body was Cesare's and his alone. But Angela pushed me back against the pillows, her palm flat against my breastbone, then slid her hand down my body, pausing at the base of my belly, the warmth without meeting the warmth within. "Here?" she whispered, moving her hand lower, prospecting with her knowing fingers. I tried to press my legs together, but instead they parted. She lifted my nightgown and stroked me, my belly and thighs, the folds and pleats of my private flesh, exclaiming in a low voice at the darkness of the hair.

"There you are a Jew," she said.

Then her fingers found a place which felt like the seat of my pain, for as she stroked it hurt so exquisitely I was forced to arch my back and would have cried out had Angela not silenced me with her tongue in my mouth. Yet hurt is not the right word for it because it would have hurt more if she had stopped what she was doing, until the point came where I felt as if not only my clothes but my skin had been peeled from my body leaving my nerve ends singing in the air warmed by Angela's breath, fragrant with her sweat and her favourite tuberose perfume. I wanted to beg her to stop, but only animal noises came out of my mouth. She seemed to understand, though, because she straightened my nightgown and lay quietly beside me, her big, dark, Borgia eyes gazing into mine, her hair with the red lights in it entangled with mine on the pillow.

"Now what do you feel?" she asked softly.

"Free," I said, without knowing that was what I was going to say.

"You see?"

But the second I had said the word, it had escaped me, and the space it left filled with embarrassment, guilt, and a yearning for Cesare which felt like a hunger for whatever had happened to happen again, or maybe for marzipan. I was so tired I could no longer distinguish between my senses.

"Go to sleep, little goose," murmured Angela, kissing my forehead, "the world is such a big, bad place."

I remembered, as I sank into sleep, that today was the 10th of Tevet, when Jews fast in memory of the siege of Jerusalem by King Nebuchadnezzar. A day of solemn repentance, marking the beginning of our wanderings, which will not cease until God thinks we have suffered enough to assuage His disappointment. How glad I was to have gone to bed on a full belly, I thought, burrowing into the bedclothes which smelled, oddly, of salt and iron and onions, and reminded me of the night of the chestnut feast.

# CHAPTER 4

ROME, DECEMBER 1501

*I could have used her any way I chose, she was so passive, though I did not. There would have been no joy in it.*

One morning shortly after Christmas, as I was helping Donna Lucrezia to dress for a ride out to Tivoli, a messenger came to the door with a note for me. Santa Maria in Portico is a huge palace, its miles of passages leading to hundreds of rooms so convoluted I doubt even Donna Adriana, who had lived there most of her life, could have known them all. The only people who did were the messengers, old men mostly, or those who had been maimed in battle, or were too ugly to attend on us in our salons or dining halls. From their headquarters in a room behind the main kitchen, whose walls were lined with partitioned shelves to serve their arcane system of sorting mail, they carried notes to all quarters of the palace and beyond. Invitations to tryst or summonses to appear before the steward to explain a broken glass or a chip in the fresco of Cupid and Psyche in the Hall of Lovers, small gifts of thanks or appreciation, promissory notes for losses at cards, mislaid gloves or call outs to duels, all flowed around Santa Maria in the messengers' battered leather pouches, and out into the city, or down the river to Ostia, or out of Rome's great gates to Naples or Romagna, our lifeblood and the web anchoring us to our place in the world.

So a note in itself was nothing remarkable. What set madonna's ladies abuzz, as madonna's riding boots were buttoned and her hair coiled into a net of dark blue velvet, was the unprecedented fact that the note was for me.

"Well, well," said madonna, snatching the note from the messenger before he could hand it to me, "our little Donata has a beau after all. You are a dark horse, Donata, and treacherous, keeping secrets from your godmother."

"I assure you, madonna, it is as much a mystery to me as to your grace."

"Maybe it's one of the Ferrarese who has been admiring you from a distance and thinks this morning might be his lucky chance," said Elisabetta Senese, she who had once mistaken the Holy Father for a cushion.

"No," said Donna Lucrezia, in a tone calculated to shatter crystal, "there is no mystery after all. This is the duke's hand."

The other women fell silent. I stretched out my hand for the note. It was as though I were the only person moving, breathing even, as though the palace had fallen under the enchantment of the sleeping beauty of Perceforest, and I had somehow, miraculously, escaped. Even Donna Lucrezia did not move, but held the note, on creamy vellum, between her thumb and forefinger, just out of my reach.

"May I see it, please, madonna?" Oh, how emboldened we can be by passion. Donna Lucrezia blinked several times, the way my father would if roused too suddenly from his afternoon nap.

"Of course," she said, in a faint voice. "It is yours."

The vellum felt crisp and smooth to my touch. I unfolded it, running my thumb over Cesare's arms embossed at the head of the page. The cunning bull of the Borgias, the keys of Saint Peter, the lilies of France. My thumb paused over the lilies, the emblem of his French wife. Did he care for her? Did he miss her? Had he tried everything in his power to prise her from the clutches of King Louis?

"Well? What does he say?"

"He…asks if his jockey may wear my colours at the races tomorrow, madonna. And if I will watch them with him." I blushed fierce enough to warm the room without a fire.

"Well we shall all be watching. The finishing post is here, in the square."

"Yes, madonna."

"That is settled, then. You will reply accordingly."

"Yes, madonna." Though nothing seemed to me to be settled at all. I glanced at Angela, who was brushing madonna's short cape. She shrugged. I picked up a tray of gloves and held them for madonna to select those she wished to wear.

⋘✣⋙

"You made me no reply." He was waiting in the stable yard as we returned from our excursion towards midday, muffled against the cold in a cloak lined with sable drawn up over his mouth and his black velvet cap pulled well down over his forehead, though this, I suspected, had more to do with concealing a cut he had acquired during the bullfight than warding off the weather. It was mild for the time of year now the sun had reached its zenith. He held my horse while I dismounted, careful to avoid stepping on Tiresias who was, as usual, milling about his master's feet.

"Madonna says we shall be watching the races anyway, as they are to finish at the obelisk. I was to write to you, but there was no time."

Cesare glanced across to where his sister stood chatting with Don Ferrante and, almost as if he had called her name, she cut short what she was saying and looked back at him.

"And does madonna say if my jockey may carry your colours?" he asked, his eyes still locked to Donna Lucrezia's.

"She did not say, my lord."

"Then give me something now, before she does. This will do." I had been riding with a veil pinned to my cap, to protect my face from the darkening effects of sun and wind. Deftly, he unpinned it and tucked the pale gauze into his sleeve. "And this." He brushed my lips with his own, so quick and light I wondered if I had imagined it. Except that my imagination, tutored by Angela, would have imagined nothing so chaste.

Then Don Ferrante said hot wine and cakes awaited us in his apartments, so off we trooped behind Donna Lucrezia to make the necessary adjustments to our costumes for this next stage of the day.

Angela told me later that Don Ferrante had paid me special attention, even refilling my cup personally rather than letting one of his slaves perform the duty. I had not noticed. It astonished me to realise I had drunk anything, for fear the wine would wash away the impression of Cesare's kiss. I should be courteous to Don Ferrante; he was unmarried and second in line after Don Alfonso to one of the oldest and most powerful duchies

59

in Italy. But I was dancing on the starting line of my life, the way Cesare's horse would dance in the Campo di Fiori tomorrow.

"You are tottering on the brink of an abyss," retorted Angela, "and I am going to see Ippolito, and tell him his brother has taken a fancy to my best friend. Ippolito has Donna Lucrezia's ear."

Donna Lucrezia. I remembered her icy response to Cesare's note, her cool, grey gaze on us as he kissed me. "No!" I shouted at Angela as she dabbed carmine paste on her lips. "She will seize any opportunity to keep me away from Cesare. Please, Angela, say nothing." Our eyes met in the mirror.

"I am trying to help you, Donata. We are friends, more than friends. But I will not go down with you. I can be no use to you that way."

"I don't know what you mean."

"You will, I fear. Now, how do I look?" She straightened up and turned to face me. She had loosened the ribbons at the neck of her chemise to reveal the beginnings of her breasts and had let down her hair. Her lips were as scarlet as the cardinal's robes.

"You will please your lover," I said.

She smiled and made to leave, but paused with her hand on the door catch. "I hope you will please yours," she said. "Believe me, I hope it more than anything else in the world. I would pray for it if it were a fitting matter for prayer. I will say nothing to Ippolito, for now."

⁂

The morning of the races dawned fair. As I unfastened our shutters, and inhaled the steam of the kitchens which this morning smelled of chicken broth and reminded me of home, Angela groaned and turned her back on even this pale light, muted by the high walls surrounding the inner courtyard. Once again, she had crept back into our room in the early hours. But the city's sparrows were in full voice, our square of sky was cloudless, and this was no day for hangovers or homesickness. Quite another sickness tied my stomach in knots so I could not touch my breakfast and felt as though I were floating somewhere up near the ceiling, watching myself as I sat on the edge of Donna Lucrezia's bed, straining my eyes under the shade of its brocade canopy to make a small repair to the bodice she had chosen, from which the topaz eye of a bird had come loose. He would send for me, of course he would; he was not a man to bow meekly to his sister's whims.

"Donata," said Donna Lucrezia, as I put the finishing touches to her coiffure, fastening a square cut emerald the size of a miniature portrait around her forehead with a silk ribbon, "I should like you to stay behind with me awhile. I have a commission to discharge for my father-in-law this morning. I'm afraid it means we shall miss the horse racing, but I believe the duke has more races planned so we shall not have to miss all the fun."

"Yes, madonna."

Donna Lucrezia drew in her breath sharply between her teeth. "That is a little too tight, Donata."

"Sorry, madonna. The stone is so heavy I feared it might slip."

"Loosen it."

"Yes, madonna."

"Good, that's better. Now, the rest of you may go. Donata, accompany me to the Sala delle Donne. This will interest you, I am sure."

The Sala delle Donne, so called because its walls were decorated with painted panels depicting the lives of virtuous women, adjoined the piano nobile where I had had my first meeting with madonna. I had been such a different girl then. Glancing at the panel to the left of the great double doors, which depicted Queen Esther kneeling before King Ahasuerus, I no longer felt the tug of recognition I used to experience when I still thought of myself as Esther Sarfati. This morning, in fact, I would have identified myself far more strongly with the mutinous Queen Vashti, but I kept my counsel, carefully lifting madonna's train as she seated herself in the gilded, throne-like chair she used for public audiences and dispatched Catherinella to "fetch the nun."

"You may sit," said Donna Lucrezia, indicating a low stool at the foot of her chair.

The nun arrived accompanied by a priest, her abbess, and two other nuns, all clad in the black and white habit of the Dominicans. I shuddered, hoping madonna had not noticed. I could not help myself; there is nothing more terrifying to a Spanish Jew, even one who fled the country as a small child, than the sight of the magpies of the Inquisition. But the nun was small and frail, supported on either side by one of her attendant sisters, as though she could not stand unaided. I feared she might be a leper, for her hands and bare feet were bound in dingy bandages. As she approached us, Donna Lucrezia slipped from her chair and knelt, signalling Catherinella and I to do likewise. It took all my self control not to flinch when the nun laid her bandaged hands on my bowed head in blessing.

"You do us great honour, Sister Osanna," said madonna as she rose. "I hope your journey was not too onerous and you are comfortable at Santa Maria."

"I would be more comfortable if the church were not built on the foundations of a heathen temple," retorted Sister Osanna in a surprisingly strong voice.

Donna Lucrezia bowed her head reverently. "Will you take some refreshment?"

"A little water only. I am fasting until I return to my sisters at Mantua."

At this, Donna Lucrezia's expression filled with consternation. "But has nobody told you..? Do you not know why you are here?"

"I listen only to God, daughter."

"We have tried to explain, but…" The abbess shrugged, appealing with her eyes to the priest, who merely shook his head.

"I see." Donna Lucrezia sat forward in her chair. A hardness came over her face, almost as though its soft mouldings of flesh had been fired in a kiln. White patches appeared either side of her fine nose and her eyes glittered. "Do you know who I am, sister?"

Instead of a response, Sister Osanna let out a wail which reverberated around the room, bouncing off the smooth, white brows of the virtuous women on the walls. She fell to her knees, doubled over as if in pain, clutching her side with her bandaged hands. Her two escorts knelt beside her, plucking at her sleeves and making cooing noises like concerned doves.

Donna Lucrezia seemed unfazed. "I am the daughter of your Holy Father, Pope Alexander who, of his benevolence, purged your order of the heresies of Fra Girolamo in Florence. So you can listen to me, can't you?" Her tone was sweet, but firm, one of those gelid confections which put you in danger of breaking a tooth on an ice crystal.

Moaning and rocking back and forth on her knees, Sister Osanna now clawed at her ears as though she wished to pull them off. "The devil tempts me," she whined, "oh how he tempts me!" Then, still kneeling, but still now and straight backed, she said in calm, ringing tones, "but he cannot triumph. 'And out of his mouth goeth a sharp sword, that with it he should smite the nations.' I will listen to the voice of God, daughter."

Donna Lucrezia looked relieved. "I have brought you to Rome so that you might accompany me to Ferrara, sister. My illustrious father-in-law, Duke Ercole, has long appreciated your great saintliness, for you bear the marks of Our Lord's Passion and are blessed with the gift of prophecy, and wishes you join Sister Lucia of Narni in the house he has built for her." She paused for the effect of her words to sink in; Sister Lucia of Narni was famous for her prophecies and Duke Ercole had gone to great lengths, some more orthodox than others, to have her spirited away to Ferrara from her convent in Viterbo. "Mother Abbess and your priest, Father Eustasius, are in agreement that you should thus spread your word out from Mantua."

A certain set of the Abbess's thin lips and a certain glow in Father Eustasius's rheumy eyes told me their agreement had not been cheaply bought. I realised now the meaning of the bandages. Sister Osanna must carry the stigmata, the mysterious wounds in her hands and feet and side that were supposed to replicate the injuries done to Christ by the Romans. Or perhaps the Jews.

Sister Osanna nodded, all mild obedience since Donna Lucrezia's reminder of the fate of Girolamo Savonarola.

"Then we understand one another," said Donna Lucrezia.

"God moves in mysterious ways, madama."

"Indeed he does, sister, indeed he does. Rise now, and come closer." I saw the priest and the abbess exchange questioning looks as Sister Osanna did as she was bidden and Donna Lucrezia continued, "You see this girl at my side? She was born a Jew but by the mercy of Our Saviour and the intercession of the saints has come to Christ. Would it not be a great demonstration of His compassion for a sinner if you were to let her witness the marks?"

I was horrified, but when I glanced at Donna Lucrezia, the words of protest died in my mouth. Her expression was just that of our old neighbour, Señor Perdoniel, the cloth merchant, when he rubbed a piece of wool or linen between thumb and forefinger to assess its quality. Donna Lucrezia was a genuinely pious woman but, like her father, even when her heart was among the angels, her feet remained firmly on the ground, particularly that narrow, pitted stretch of it running between the stalls on the street of the *bancherotti*, the traders in foreign coins and pawned trinkets, where my father had started out on his arrival in Rome, while awaiting an audience with Cardinal Borgia. So she did have some reason for bringing me here other than to keep the humble *conversa* away from her magnificent brother.

At a nod from the abbess, the two other nuns stepped forward and began to remove the bandages from Sister Osanna's hands and feet. Sister Osanna stood, docile as a child, with her eyes cast down, lifting her feet or turning her hands this way and that to make the nuns' task easier for them. Both anxious and detached, she was like an artist unveiling his work before a patron in the knowledge that it is both his and not his, executed by him with materials paid for by his patron and the inspiration of the Holy Name. I wanted to look away, but could not, as the bandages became bloodier and a stench of putrefaction caused Donna Lucrezia to pull a kerchief from her sleeve and hold it to her nose and mouth. I swallowed repeatedly, trying not to gag. Then the nuns started work on Sister Osanna's side, unfastening a row of hooks concealed in the seam of her habit.

Suddenly, we were all distracted by a commotion outside the doors. Raised voices, followed by a scuffling and scrabbling of soft shoes on the polished floor and a thud as something hit the doors, rattling the catch. Only Sister Osanna seemed oblivious, still and poised as the women on the wall panels as the rest of us looked in alarm towards the doors.

Cesare burst into the room, closely followed by another man whose head scarcely reached his shoulder, though he was powerfully built, with a face as pocked as a pomegranate and hard, glittery eyes like sparkles of marcasite in a broken rock. As the double doors crashed open, one handle chipping a lump of plaster from Queen Esther's bare feet, I caught a glimpse of one of the doormen on his knees, a hand clutched to his bleeding nose.

"Here you are, you treacherous little hussy," shouted Cesare, staring at me. Tiresias barked in support and stared at me too, for all that he was completely blind. Flinging my veil to the floor, Cesare went on, "Well, I hope it will gladden your hard heart to know we won anyway. Mantua's horse led all the way, but threw its jockey somewhere around the pyramid in the Borgo."

"Startled by something in the crowd," growled pomegranate face. I wondered who he could be, a man who could interrupt Duke Valentino with impunity.

"Doubtless," said Cesare with a nasty smile.

"My lord duke, Don Michele, what is the meaning of this interruption? Have you no piety in your souls? Look at this woman." Donna Lucrezia gestured towards Sister Osanna. Don Michele dropped to his knees as if felled and crossed himself extravagantly. Cesare merely glared at his sister.

"You knew of my invitation to Signorina Donata. What possessed you to cross me in this?"

Donna Lucrezia had scarcely opened her mouth to reply when Sister Osanna turned away from us to face Cesare, who was standing a little way behind her. I saw the flush of anger drain from Cesare's cheeks and his skin turn as white as Sister Osanna's wimple. His dog cringed, laid its face on its paws, and began to whimper.

"The kingdoms of men are but as a straw fire," said Sister Osanna in her strange, strong voice. "How bright you burn, how utterly you will be snuffed out. Beware, little duke, beware the hand of the Great Avenger."

Cesare swayed. I thought he would faint. I started from my stool to run to his aid, but Sister Osanna, even though she had her back to me, raised her hand in a stalling gesture, the bandages falling away to reveal a blood-crusted puncture wound. I stood, stunned, as though I had run into an invisible wall. The room felt suddenly colder, even the portraits on the walls seemed to shiver. I saw Father Eustasius chafe his upper arms as though he, too, felt a draught. Whatever script he and the abbess had written for Sister Osanna, the lines she had just spoken were not part of it.

Cesare's lips moved, but no sound came from them. He tried again. "Twenty eight," he said eventually, in a hoarse whisper.

"Twenty," replied Sister Osanna, and for some reason, that made him laugh.

"You flatter me there, sister," he said, and the spell was broken. Sister Osanna turned her back on Cesare, almost with contempt, it seemed to me.

"My bandages," she commanded her attendants, though they paused, glancing from their abbess to Donna Lucrezia for direction. Donna Lucrezia nodded and they began to re-bind Sister Osanna's wounds. Catherinella returned with the water, inscrutable in her blackness, or perhaps in her experience of serving Donna Lucrezia.

"Come on," said Cesare, holding out his hand to me. "They have held up the boar racing until my return. You will miss nothing more." I fancied Don Michele's hand moved a fraction closer to the hilt of one of the daggers in his belt.

"Madonna...?"

"You may go, Donata. As Sister Osanna is to accompany us to Ferrara, you will have plenty more opportunities to benefit from her sanctity."

I looked to see what effect this news might have on Cesare, but it was as though Sister Osanna was of no more consequence than any other nun he might encounter in the street or the public audience chambers of the Vatican. Tucking my hand under his arm, he began to trade odds with Don Michele, leaving me to luxuriate in the warmth from his body as he guided me through doorways, along passages, down staircases, until we reached a small, plain door I had never seen before. Don Michele unlocked this with a key Cesare gave him and stood aside to let us through. Cesare ducked to avoid hitting his head on the lintel. From one of the low, winding passages in the oldest part of the palace of Santa Maria, we stepped out into the cavernous, incensed space of the basilica, cool and silent save for the whispering footsteps of the priests making ready for the next service of the day. And now the spurred boots of Cesare and Don Michele, and my own shoes, as we crossed the nave and passed behind the altar to a second small door concealed behind a screen bearing a triptych of the martyrdom of Saint Peter.

"The hours I've spent on my knees in this place," remarked Cesare as he hunted in the purse on his belt for another key. "It makes them ache just to remember it. You know I was a cardinal once?"

I did know. All Rome had buzzed with the scandal, and nowhere more than the schoolroom at Santa Clara, when, shortly after the murder of Don Juan, Cesare renounced his religious calling to take up his brother's post at the head of the papal armies.

"Such a waste of time," he added, shaking his head. But before I could ask him what he meant, the second door opened on to another series of stairs and passages, better lit than those in Santa Maria, with marble floors and walls hung with tapestries. I guessed we must be in the Vatican, and sure enough, within seconds we emerged from a first floor window on to a short bridge leading to the stand set up in front of the palace for the pope and his guests.

As we stepped on to the stand, beside the pope's chair, the noise of the crowd seemed to slam into my chest, almost knocking the breath out of me. The spectators were packed behind wooden barriers, waiting for the races to begin. A surge opposite the stand caused planks to begin to buckle and splinter and guards in Cesare's livery to ready their halberds to prevent a break out. Their blades glittered in the hard winter sun. The great square was ablaze with banners bearing the arms of Borgia and Este, hanging from every window and fastened to every roof cornice, silk bulls on the rampage, white eagles hovering over their prey. Above our heads the scarlet and gold striped canopy of the stand snapped and rustled in a stiff breeze, and I rued the fact I had not had time to fetch my cloak.

Cesare paused to acknowledge the crowd, gripping my hand so I was obliged to remain at his side, aware also of Don Michele standing close behind me, the smell of his garlic breath mingled with the sharp scent of new wood and the perfumes the guests wore to mask their sweat: attar of roses, sandalwood, bergamot, and lavender. I felt awkward and exposed; I had not even kissed the Holy Father's ring; surely even he would register such a slight, despite his tolerance of all the laxity of the household of Santa Maria in Portico.

Cesare did not smile or wave or bow, merely stood, his features as composed as the masks he favoured, waiting for the silence he knew would come. I found myself wondering how the bulls had felt, a few days before, when the barrier was lifted and they were goaded into the ring which had now become a race track, and they had come face to face with that potent stillness amid the contrived chaos of his *cuadrilla*.

The hubbub died in seconds, only the cries of the hawkers of miracles and roast chickens on little wooden spits still unravelling loose threads of sound across the piazza. Cesare turned to Don Michele and said, "How long to the Campo at a gallop, Michelotto?"

I did not hear his reply. Michelotto. Of course, I should have guessed. To whom else would Cesare entrust the keys to secret doors than to Michelotto, the Navarrese *condottiere* known as his left hand, because when Cesare hatched a sinister scheme, it always fell to Michelotto to carry it out? Not least among his victims had been the Duke of Bisceglie, it was said. Even the pope feared Michelotto, because he could not bring himself to fear his son.

"The boar race will commence in twenty minutes," announced Cesare, his voice not loud, but pitched to carry across the square, "and in the meantime, to atone for the delay, my servants will come among you with cakes and wine." At once the crowd began to whirl and eddy around gold and scarlet liveried figures bearing great trays of cakes and earthenware jugs, who seemed to have popped out of the very ground itself, like Jason's skeletons.

Only now did Cesare take his place on the cushioned bench beside his father's chair, a mighty piece of carved Spanish oak upholstered in red leather; the stand beneath it creaked ominously every time His Holiness shifted his bulk. Seated to the right of Cesare, with Michelotto at my other side, still breathing hard from his dash to the Campo di Fiori to start the race, this was the closest I had ever been to Pope Alexander. Leaning forward on the pretext of straightening my skirt, I stole a glance at him.

His face, framed by a close-fitting cap of white velvet and the ermine collar of his cloak, was full of the contradictions that seemed to define his life and exasperate all who had dealings with him. His mouth, settled between opulent, smooth-shaven jowls, was full and sensual, but he had the eyes of a wealthy peasant set deep under fleshy brows and the swarthy complexion of a man of action rather than the pallor of prayer and contemplation.

I had heard tell that in his bedchamber was a painting by his favourite artist, the little painter from Mantua, of himself kneeling in adoration before the Virgin Mary. The model for the virgin had been Giulia Farnese. Thus it was with him, the sacred and the profane jumbled together. Devout in his calling, he believed the temporal power of his office should match its spiritual gravity and, head of this church of celibate priests, saw no objection to using his son's sword arm and his daughter's womb to achieve his ambition. I noticed the pope had taken Cesare's hand and that Cesare's head was inclined towards his father's as the pope spoke to him rapidly and emphatically in Catalan, all the time pressing his son's hand hard against the carved arm of his chair. From across the square, where Donna Lucrezia had now joined the rest of her ladies in the loggia above the front door to Santa Maria, they must have looked a picture of mutual affection.

A distant rumble began to vibrate the air. The crowd fell silent and turned as one towards the southern end of the square from where the boars would race to the finishing post beside Caligula's obelisk. The watchers in the stand leaned forward, releasing a sweat of excitement into the stale air under the canopy. Suddenly I realised I was the only woman among men, that the other ladies, apart from Donna Lucrezia's household, were collected on the other side of a gangway bordered by rope handrails. I pressed my hands together in my lap and stared at them, fancying all the men's eyes on me, although I knew they were watching the point where the race would debouch into the square, betting slips crumpled in clenched fists as the rumbling grew louder, as though a storm were rolling through the narrow streets.

"Up there," murmured Cesare, close to my ear, or perhaps I would not have heard him, "are Julius Caesar's ashes. Is his spirit there also, do you think? Does he laugh at our games?"

As I looked up at the golden sphere on top of the obelisk, clouds of brown dust bloomed above the ancient tiled roofs of the Borgo and belched into the piazza, making the crowd at that end start to cough and wipe their eyes. The hinges holding the wooden barriers together began to rattle. Guards vaulted to safety, flinging their halberds over before them. Then the first of the boars charged into the square, squealing and tossing its head as it tried to rid itself of the dwarf on its back, who clung on with the aid of powerful, bandy legs and a rein fastened to a ring in the boar's nose. The furious beast veered away towards the barrier just below Donna Lucrezia's vantage point. The crowd fell back with a collective gasp like the sighing of the sea. Plunging its tusks into the planks, the boar catapulted its jockey over the barrier, where he was caught by several spectators and tossed back again.

By now, several more boars had entered the square, some with their dwarf jockeys still clinging on, some bareback. One, with a bloody rag caught on its tusk, foaming with sweat, eyes red with terror, charged the unfortunate jockey whom the crowd had thrown back on to the track and gored him. The man fell beneath the hooves of the rest, and the race ended in barbarous confusion as the boars stopped short of the finish and began to eat their victim.

"Well I never," said the pope, leaning back in his chair. The stand emitted a soft shriek. A high-pitched, manic laugh was coming from Michelotto's barrel chest.

"Look," said Cesare, digging him in the ribs. "See those two with the leg. Five hundred *scudi* says the brindle one gets it."

"Done," Michelotto replied. "Shall we have the winner for supper? A boar with a man's leg in its belly, now there's a novelty."

"I have plans for this evening." Though he did not look at me, his hand was gripping my knee and it was clear what he meant. I felt as though my skull had cracked like an egg boiled too fast, letting in all kinds of conflicting emotions. Disgust at the spectacle of the pig killing the dwarf vied with the fascination of the living for death and dying. The humiliation of sitting unchaperoned among men, of a man with his hand on my knee in a public place, was overwhelmed by a sense of reckless excitement, of being caught up in Cesare's own aura of invincibility.

From deep within me, perhaps in the place Angela could touch with her knowing, loving fingers, I felt a force of yearning that moved my leg fractionally closer to his and did not resist when he slid his hand a little higher up my thigh, one of his rings catching a loose thread in my green *camorra*. I closed my eyes to shut out the clamour in my head, my cheeks burning and my heart crashing against my ribs. My senses were filled with the scent of the jasmine oil he used to perfume his beard and a dangerous, feral musk it did not quite conceal.

"You should watch this," he said, his voice laced with a languid menace that cut through my dream. I opened my eyes and glanced at him, but he was looking straight ahead, his mouth curled in an enigmatic smile. Someone was looking at me, though, drawing my gaze. A beardless boy richly dressed in dark red velvet, a large gold ornament pinned to his cap, had turned to face me from a lower rung of the tiered seating. Fine, chestnut brown eyes above smooth, creamy cheeks appraised my body with bold curiosity. I dropped my gaze just as Cesare nodded a curt greeting to the boy and he turned abruptly back to face the square.

To half-hearted cheers from the crowd, for whom the debacle of the boars was clearly a hard act to follow, a group of men dressed in black was stumbling rather than running towards the finish post. One fell, wiping his palms down his sides as he struggled to his feet. At first, through my jasmine haze, I wondered only how anyone had been able to round up the boars before they went on the rampage, and which had been declared the winner. Then, as my senses cleared, I felt a chill settle around my heart, a bitter pool of guilt and foolishness.

The men were Jews. I could see now, with appalling clarity, the yellow stars stitched to the fronts of their robes and worse, that there were faces I recognised through the masks of dust and the distortions of exhaustion. Daniel Cohen, son of the cobbler who had made my trunk, Isaac ibn David, whose violin playing could reduce my undemonstrative father to tears. Worst of all, on his knees now, grovelling in the dust for the eye-glasses he had to wear to be able to see anything at all, bowed beneath the jeers of the spectators at the finishing post, my own brother, Eli.

Images whirled past me, as though I too were running, faster and faster, in ever decreasing circles. I saw my mother, dying on the beach at Nettuno, and my father's shuttered expression as he told me of his plans for me. Myself in white, floating like a ghost towards my baptism. Sister Osanna's wounded hand, Angela's pink, laughing mouth, the misery of Donna Lucrezia at the supper of the chestnuts, the set of Cesare's naked shoulders as he walked away from the bull ring. Queen Esther kneeling to King Ahasuerus, but that was only a painting on a wall. I was running, and something was eluding me, running, but all my veins would burst before I found it. All this light and noise, so many people. How could I find anything?

I tried to rise, to get away, but Cesare's hand merely gripped my knee more firmly, his fingers digging into my flesh through the layers of my clothes. On my other side, Michelotto quietly took hold of my upper arm.

"Not enjoying yourself?" Cesare enquired. Leaning closer to me, he hissed in my ear, "Little Esther Sarfati, did you think I was as sentimental as King...whatever his name was? You see that crowd? They'd tear you to pieces as surely as those damn pigs with their dwarf. And me. We're both *marrani*. But they tolerate me because I keep them amused, and I keep their enemies away from the gates. And they rather like you at the moment because you're pretty and you're sitting next to me. Something for them to gossip about in their greasy taverns and round their nasty little hearths. I know your father helped us buy all this, but now we have it, the tables are turned, you see. Now you need me."

Someone had started to scream. A woman's voice. *Let me go! Let me go!* People turning to look. The smooth-skinned boy with the brooch in his cap, a grin spreading like a wound across his face. Screams rising to the canopy, ripping through the striped silk, soaring up into the pale blue sky, one, then another, and another. A flock of screams. My screams.

"Let her go, Michelotto; she's beginning to bore me." And I was floating after my screams, drawn by the threads of my voice, my arm throbbing, my legs light as air in their sudden freedom, lifting me over the bench, along the gangway into the Vatican, through the secret door which Michelotto must have left unlocked, back into the basilica whose ponderous serenity finally brought me to a halt. I fell to my knees and tried to pray to any god prepared to hear me, to show me a way out of the mess I was in. Strike me with a plague, I begged, send a stray boar to eat me, or Michelotto with a dagger. I was not afraid; I was already plagued, torn, pierced to the heart.

"Duke Valentino has a...unique sense of humour," said God, in a voice rich with innuendo, yet still unbroken. I looked up into a woman's secret mouth, though made of gold, not flesh, and clinging with little gold frogs' legs to the flanks of a golden horse. Two tiny arms held aloft a bow primed with an arrow. I blinked, and the curious ornament was replaced by the chestnut eyes of the youth from the stand. No youth, I realised, turning clammy with mortification, but La Fiammetta, her long, shapely legs set off to perfection in doublet and hose, her velvet cap pulled to a seductive angle by the weight of the gold pussy-goes-a-hunting pinned to it. She slid the tips of her gloved fingers along the shaft of a dainty dagger at her waist and laughed.

❧

I remembered nothing more until I awoke in my own bed, with Angela sitting beside me holding in her lap a bowl of something steaming that smelled like rotting leaves.

"Drink this," she said.

"No."

"You fainted. Your bleeding has started. This will help."

"Nothing that smells that bad can help." I remembered Eli's crushed eyeglasses, the dwarf's leg in its breeches like a joint of meat wrapped for boiling, the exquisite savagery of Cesare's little speech, La Fiammetta... he was probably with her now, enjoying some joke at my expense as he unlaced her hose and peeled them slowly over her perfect legs, his fingertips brushing the skin of her white thighs... "Nothing can help."

With a sigh, Angela picked up a folded parchment from the night stand. "This came." She watched with her mouth compressed into an exasperated line as I opened the note and ran my thumb over the embossed insignia. Bull, keys, lilies.

*You will forgive me,* he had written. *I was not myself. As you know, I was somewhat upset by my sister's nun. Sometimes I am ill. You will understand; you are not yourself either.*

*Valentino*

"You know what he is calling you now?" asked Angela, taking the note from me and reading it with a shake of her head. "La Violante, the breaker of promises."

"Is he?" This pleased me, this pretty word with its ugly meaning. "I have my nickname, then. You said I should."

# CHAPTER 5

ROME, EPIPHANY 1502

*I have always known I could not live without you. It is a constant, just as the sun rising in the east is a constant, or the fact that I have five fingers on each hand.*

S hall I lay the trail of moon pebbles for you, Lucrezia, so you can find your way home?"

Donna Lucrezia gave the Infant of Rome a wan smile and stroked his cheek with the tips of her fingers. Her nails gleamed pearl pink against his putty-coloured flesh. We had spent a good hour on her manicure the previous night, soaking her hands in a distillation of nettle root, massaging them with a rose-scented lotion, buffing her nails with fine glass cloths. Anyone would have thought, grumbled Angela, rubbing her stiff knees, that she was arriving in Ferrara tomorrow rather than merely setting out on a journey liable to take several weeks.

"Ferrara will be her home, Giovanni," remonstrated the Holy Father, his voice breaking with sentiment, "but we shall all go to visit her there, have no fear."

I saw Cesare swallow. Oh, I had become adept at watching him. I could sense when he entered a room even when my back was turned, by some brightening of candles or sweetening of the air. I was drawn to him as the Platonists say the soul is drawn to Beauty. Or so I told myself. Even the jump of his Adam's apple above the neck of his shirt was an enchantment to me.

Then he exhaled sharply, raked his fingers through his hair, and pushed himself away from the wall where he had been leaning, apart from the family group around the fire in madonna's little sitting room overlooking Saint Peter's Steps. He stalked across to the window and peered out. I wondered what he thought when he saw the steps where his assassins had attacked his sister's last husband, but I could no more read him than I could the script of the Moors whom, they say, write backwards. All his demeanour registered now was impatience.

Standing behind madonna's chair, I could not look out of the window myself, but I could hear the din, even through the glass panes. The new Duchess of Ferrara's entourage was too big to be assembled in the courtyard of Santa Maria and was gathering instead in the great square before the basilica. A continuous rumble and clatter was shot through from time to time by men's shouts, the whinnying of horses, and the lowing of bullocks.

"Right," said Cesare, "we need to get on."

"Oh but…"

"Papa, if someone doesn't go down there and set things in order, it will be nightfall before we leave, and it's already beginning to snow. Violante, take the children to their nurse, if you please, and do not return. We have family matters to discuss." He took Giovanni by the hand and led him to me. For a moment he was standing so close to me I could pick out every stitch of the gold embroidery on his black velvet doublet and inhale the scent of jasmine. I ached to look at his face but I dare not, so fixed my gaze on his hand, on the smudge of the powder burn and the tips of his sinewy fingers resting in the soft curl of his little brother's fist .

"I want to stay," whined Giovanni. "I'm family. Let me stay, Cesare."

"Do as you're told and I promise I'll take you to see Bella's pups later."

"When later?" He pulled Cesare's fingers. When later? Was Cesare not coming with us to Ferrara? Had he not spoken only moments before of "we" leaving before nightfall?

"When I say. It's a promise between gentlemen so I would not dishonour myself by breaking it, would I?"

No, I thought, and a little worm of anxiety began to burrow into me.

"No. All right then." He transferred his hand from Cesare's to mine, his skin still warm with the warmth of Cesare's, but I had to let him go to lift Rodrigo from his mother's lap.

A thread of Rodrigo's gown had become entangled in the pearls sewn on to madonna's bodice.

"Give me a moment," she said, though it was clear she was not in the least concerned about the pearls coming loose. She stroked her son's back, kissed his hair, pressed his nose with her fingertip which made him laugh. Her hands hovered and flapped around the entangled threads as if she half knew what they should be doing but could not quite remember. Cesare moved around behind her chair and placed a hand on her shoulder. I saw his knuckles flex and whiten as he began to squeeze. She turned to him, eyes raised in supplication. He nodded, then they both looked directly at me, their eyes moving in such unison you would think they had rehearsed it, their expressions so alike the one might have been copied from the other. There was a moment when I felt they were trying to tell me something, then Giovanni tugged at my arm and said, "Come on, or it'll be too late for the puppies by the time the grown-ups have finished talking," and the spell was broken, whatever I had glimpsed hidden from view before I could discern the true shape of it.

Of the ladies who accompanied Donna Lucrezia, only I had ever been outside Italy, and that hardly counted because I was too young to remember it. Most had never been further than Tivoli, or the baths at Stigliano. But if anyone was apprehensive, she put a brave face on it. We were, after all, a wedding party, though such a large one we were more like a city on the move, with our cooks and tailors, our locksmith, our saddler, and Alonso, the goldsmith, who never washed his hands for fear of sluicing away a few grains of gold. Three bishops accompanied us, not to mention Donna Lucrezia's two chaplains. Two, said the gossips, because one was not enough to bear the weight of Donna Lucrezia's sins. We had our aristocracy, our share of gallants to swagger and gamble, drink too much, flatter us ladies-in-waiting, and seduce our maids. We were accompanied by scions of the Orsini and the Colonna, prepared to remain on speaking terms so long as they were living at the pope's expense, and by more than thirty of Cesare's gentlemen.

A hundred and fifty carriages had been bought, built, or requisitioned from the wealthier Roman families to transport this household, not to mention the horses, mules, and oxen which numbered far more than I had been taught to count. By the time Don Ferrante's household was joined to our party, we numbered, I am told, more than a thousand people. Even in the slushy vastness of Saint Peter's Square we jostled for space, the mules nipping one another's necks, grooms' feet broken by restless hooves, those who should have known better elbowing one another out of the best positions below the windows of the Vatican where the pope stood to wave his beloved daughter farewell. As Angela remarked, the makers of shovels must have done well out of Donna Lucrezia's marriage. The stable boys were going to have a devil of a lot of shit to clear before this journey was through. Like all her family, Angela was a peasant at heart; even her words must be made to have more than one meaning, like the bones of today's joint made into a broth for tomorrow.

When we finally began to file out of the square into the old, narrow streets of the Borgo, the men at arms provided for our escort by Cesare were forced to use the shafts of their halberds to knock onlookers aside to make way for us. Long before we reached the gate, we in the vanguard, riding immediately behind Donna Lucrezia, who was escorted on either side by Ippolito and Cesare, were separated from the rest of our party when an ox cart became jammed on the Sant'Angelo bridge. Cesare despatched a man at arms to see what had happened, then, as the delay lengthened and the snow began to fall more heavily from a darkening sky, went back himself to investigate. I tried to catch his eye as he rode past me, but he continued to look straight ahead, eyes straining in the murky light to see the cause of the delay, his mouth set in a snarl of frustration. I shivered, wound my reins around the pommel of my saddle, and thrust my hands deep into my lynx muff. What if he really was not coming with us? What then?

"They're dismantling the bloody parapet to get it through," he called to Ippolito on his return. So we all dismounted and milled about, fretful and cold, with wet feet and a sense of awkwardness, like guests who had outstayed our welcome. Cesare and Ippolito escorted Donna Lucrezia under the shelter of a nearby stall selling sweetmeats, and we looked on enviously as the astonished proprietor, hands shaking, served dishes of sugared almonds and preserved ginger to his unexpected guests.

Finally, the cart was freed and, as it creaked into view in a haze of animal breath and steam rising from the coats of the straining oxen, we remounted and set off once again towards the gate. There we paused a second time. Ippolito bowed over Donna Lucrezia's hand and wished her Godspeed, then rode off to talk to his brother. Cesare leaned from his saddle, took both madonna's hands in his, and kissed her cheeks.

Still holding her hands, her little crimson gloves so bright against his black ones, he said, "Scatter the moon pebbles, cara mia, so I can find you." They laughed, then Cesare and Ippolito wheeled their horses back to face the city. I glanced at Angela. Tears were running down her cheeks but she did not seem surprised. She must have known all along that Ippolito was not to accompany us, but not Cesare. Surely she would have told me. Perhaps nobody had known. Perhaps the decision had only been made that morning, when he had promised to take Giovanni to see the puppies.

Perhaps, seeing me near at hand, he had chosen to speak to madonna in Italian to be sure I would hear and understand his words. That was it. There was some message there for me to, if only I could decipher it.

As the two men passed us, Ippolito reined back almost imperceptibly and nodded to Angela, who dipped her chin a fraction in acknowledgement. All I saw Cesare do was lift one black gloved hand from his reins to wipe the snow from his eyes, then put the spur to his horse's flanks and ride on, weaving back through the procession towards the broken bridge and the Vatican. Not a word to me, not even a glance.

But he had joked with madonna about the moon pebbles. Like the resourceful child in the fairy tale, he wanted to be sure of finding his way back to the treasure.

⁂

Two weeks after leaving Rome, we reached Urbino, where we took over the ducal palace, compelling Duke Guidobaldo and his wife to lodge in a convent outside the walls. Even though we were packed in like a cargo of slaves, we ladies forced to sleep on the floor of Donna Lucrezia's ante chamber with only our own cloaks for bed linen, I thought the palace the closest thing to heaven I was ever likely to see on this earth. After the rigours of the journey, perhaps anywhere we had the prospect of staying more than a single night would have seemed like heaven. The mountain roads had been treacherous with mud and snow, often blocked by landslides. Sometimes there were rushing streams where our maps showed none, and we had had to make lengthy detours to find fords. One night, unable to reach our planned destination before nightfall, we had been forced to camp in the open, ringed about by our wagons like gipsies, and I had fallen asleep to the wild sorrowing of wolves, and imagined myself a soldier in Cesare's army.

The evening of our arrival in Urbino, the walls of the palace glowed rose in the light of thousands of torches as we wound up the hill from the town. Poised on a sheer cliff, invisible in the darkness, it shimmered as though suspended in air. The following morning, the sun made one of its rare appearances, and the marble cloisters around the main courtyard glittered as though studded with diamonds. Whereas the palace of Santa Maria was stuffed with art works and antiquities simply because someone had told Donna Adriana such and such a painter or *tapissier* or vendor of Cupids with chipped noses was the fashion, everything about Urbino was a testament to good taste and thoughtfulness. If Santa Maria was like an old tart whose mouth was crammed with sweetmeats, the palace at Urbino was like philosophy made concrete, designed to nourish the spirit. There were breathing spaces between the paintings, box-edged walks or avenues of pleached limes between the statues in the gardens.

Following the duchess on a tour of halls and salons hung with rich tapestries which had been freshly beaten for our visit, so they glowed even in the grey, winter light, I began to understand why my father had made me learn geometry. It will show you your place in the world, he used to say. I thought he was referring to the matter of calculating a position by the stars, and wondered what use that could ever be to me. Then I wondered if it was something to do with comparing myself to my brothers, who would very probably go to sea in pursuit of the family business. Now, admiring the marquetry *trompe l'oeil* panels in the old duke's *studiolo*, how cleverly they depicted his armour hanging in a cupboard and his favourite books piled on a shelf, I wished I could tell my father I knew what he meant; I wished I could thank him. What geometry shows us is how to measure proportion, how to build and paint and plan gardens which do not oppress us by being cramped or overawe us by being on too great a scale, but make us aware that we truly are made in the image of the Holy Name.

⟨⟨⟩⟩

A ball was to be held in Donna Lucrezia's honour but I looked forward to it with mixed emotions. Perhaps Cesare would attend. None of us knew where he was; he might have been in Naples or Milan, or conferring with Duke Guidobaldo in his convent only yards from the city walls. On the other hand, I had been sleeping badly in our various makeshift accommodations. My bones ached from hard floors, lumpy pallets, and long hours on horseback. My monthly course had begun the previous day; I felt pot-bellied and foul tempered, and had a spot on my chin which pulsed like a drum. There was no doubting my power to curdle milk or tarnish mirrors. If Cesare did turn up, I would just have to be laced an inch tighter and keep my mask on my face all night, even if it suffocated me.

My head ringing with the hen-house clamour of women getting ready for a party in a confined space, I took myself off out of doors. I was bound for a telling-off if Donna Lucrezia discovered I had been roaming about without a chaperone, but in the mood I was in, she was likely to get as good as she gave. Besides, I doubted she would notice I was missing until the time came for her to dress, which would not be for hours yet. Madonna made a fine art of being late for everything.

Duchess Elisabetta had a sunken rose garden, a circle sliced into five segments symbolising the five parts of the madrigal. They converged at the centre on a dainty, pillared rotunda, a trysting place deliberately hidden from the eyes of the house. I walked for a while, listening to the crunch of my footsteps on the gravel paths between the beds and the song of a solitary robin perched among the gnarled knuckles of the pruned rose bushes. Then I sat in the rotunda, simply enjoying my solitude and the cold air seeping through my clothes to calm the rash of fleabites I had acquired during our travels, resting my aching back against the cool marble bench.

Time passed, and I became aware of the sky darkening, the pillars of the rotunda and the rich, red earth of the rose beds taking on an ethereal glow as though they had captured and held the last of the day's light. I must have been outside longer than I thought. I had better go in now, before madonna started asking for me. But I could not rise. A sensation that began like the feeling of hands on my shoulders sank through me to rest in the bowl of my pelvis, a hot stone weighing me down on the bench. The sweetness of jasmine stung my nostrils and made me dizzy. He was close, I knew it. At any moment I would hear his brisk footfall on the gravel, and walk into his arms here, in this secret place at the heart of a madrigal.

"Look at the great lady."

"How pretty her face ith."

"How exthellently she danceth."

"No, no, no, you pig's arth. Exthellently'th my line. You thay, how well she dances and I thay…"

"Rawly but elephantly."

"Rarely but exthellently."

The trumpet of a loud fart. "Ath rare and exthellent athat? I think not. Oopth…thorry, milady, we thought no one wath here."

"No one is," I said as the light cleared. "Just me."

Gatto and Perro, madonna's Spanish dwarves.

"We were rehearthing," explained Perro who was, confusingly, with his yellow eyes and a certain sinuous grace despite his stunted form, the more feline of the two.

"For madonna'th danth at the ball," added Gatto, still speaking Italian with a Castilian lisp. "We are to follow her and praith her danthing."

"Is madonna ready to dress, do you know," I asked, stepping out of the rotunda, "or is Don Cesare still with her?"

"Don Cesar? He wouldn't dare show his face here."

"Not after the incident with Dorotea Caracciolo." The jesters had reverted to Spanish.

"Speak slowly. What incident?"

"Donna Dorotea was a lady of Duchess Elisabetta's. A stunner by all accounts. Don Cesar was supposed to give her a safe conduct through the Romagna on her way to join her husband in Venice, but he kidnapped her instead."

Perro snapped his fingers. "Just like that."

"Spirited her away." Gatto bent to pick a stone from the path, placed it on the flat of his right palm, and passed his left hand over it. The stone vanished.

"Never been seen since," added Perro.

Gatto scooped the stone from his left ear. "Probably f…"

Perro dug his partner in the ribs.

"To death," finished Gatto lamely.

"Nice," said Perro, who liked boys. "Now look, you naughty cat, you've upset Violante."

"It's nothing," I said, trying to stop my voice shaking, keeping my eyes fixed open so the tears would not spill over and give me away. "I'd better go. You won't tell you found me on my own, will you? Or…"

"Or what?" Gatto jammed his hands on to his hips and stuck out his protuberant belly in a gesture of defiance. The sight was funny enough to ease my heart.

"Or I'll tell madonna you think she dances like an elephant." I hoisted up my skirts and ran, the two jesters in mock pursuit, though they stopped short at the foot of the staircase leading up to Donna Lucrezia's rooms, and bowed to Angela, who was waiting for me there.

"I was just about to come looking for you. Where have you been? She can't find the necklace Don Ferrante gave her and she's on the war path."

"I think it's in the black jewel case. You know, the one her father gave her." Gripping her upper arms I turned her to face me. "Angela, has Cesare been here?"

Angela sighed. "No, dear. As far as I know, he's still in Rome trying to raise an army for his next campaign. Borrowing money from your father probably. The wedding must have cleaned out Uncle Rodrigo until he can sell a few more cardinals' hats. Why?" Angela demanded, twisting out of my grasp and rubbing her arms.

"Because I'm sure he was in the rose garden."

"When?" Angela looked doubtful. Cesare kept relays of the fastest horses in stables all over the Romagna so he could travel more quickly than most; and he loved surprises, from impromptu parties to military coups.

"Just now." We stared at each other, then Angela shook her head.

"I have been with Lucrezia all afternoon, rubbing her temples. She has one of her headaches. He would not have come here without seeing her. You're bleeding, aren't you? That must be it. It sometimes causes visions."

"But…" Everything which had seemed so clear a moment before was crumbling into confusion. What had I seen? Just a shadow, a cloud across the sun. Yet the scent of jasmine was still in my nostrils, still lingering on my skin.

"You're tired, dear, we all are. You must try to stop thinking about him. Has he given you any sign of favour? Has he even written to you since we left Rome? No. There isn't a woman born who could hold him, except Dame Fortune, if that's any consolation." Poor Angela. She spoke plain sense, but where Cesare was concerned, I had no use for sense. Every time couriers found us, bearing letters under his seal, I hoped, and every time those letters proved to be for Donna Lucrezia, or Don Ferrante, or the gentlemen of his household who were escorting us, I would console myself with the two notes I had received from him in Rome, not so much reading them as caressing the lines and loops of his handwriting with my fingers and eyes.

"Has Ippolito written to you?" I snapped, and immediately regretted it as a brief, pained frown passed across her face.

"I told him not to. You know I don't want anything to upset the apple cart before we're settled in Ferrara."

I started up the stairs ahead of her. "The trouble is, you don't know what it's like to really be in love. If you did, you'd understand we don't need letters. We…he…he's just *here*, that's all."

"Oh, so that's why you keep that note he sent you tucked into your corset. Wait a minute. Let me brush your skirt. There are petals all over it." She breathed in deeply and made a little hum of appreciation in the back of her throat. "I love winter jasmine, the way it puts out all its perfume just as the sun goes down. It's such a hopeful flower."

From Urbino, we headed east towards Pesaro, in Cesare's territory, and from then on, until we came to Bologna, his presence was everywhere. All the roads had been levelled and repaired, and in every one of his cities we visited, we were extravagantly greeted by crowds of children in his livery, waving olive branches and shouting "Duca, Duca, Lucrezia, Lucrezia!" The palaces in which we stayed had had their artillery damage plastered over and the smoke stains scrubbed from their walls. New tapestries hung in their halls, many depicting the triumphs of Caesar, and new duckdown mattresses graced the beds in which Cesare had slept off the exhaustion of battle and where his sister would now lie awake, staring up at the brocade canopies or painted *alcove,* speculating about Don Alfonso.

At Cesena, Don Ferrante doubled the guard on his new sister-in-law, having heard rumours that Dorotea Caracciolo's husband was planning a raid to kidnap Donna Lucrezia and hold her to ransom for his wife. Don Ferrante rode close beside her litter, though sometimes he dropped back to inspect the guard, spending long periods in close conference with their officer, who looked to me far too young for the responsibility. We moved as rapidly as he could make us to Forli, Faenza, and finally Imola, where Donna Lucrezia insisted on spending an extra day to wash her hair and give us all a chance to recover before we entered Bologna and finally left behind any semblance of what madonna might call home. She was, I thought, like an athlete pausing to gather her strength for the final push to the finish, focused on her own centre, withdrawn from all that surrounded her. Angela said it was as though she had passed through a veil, the way some people do on the eve of Ognissanti, crossing to the other side and unable to find their way back again.

Hair washing days were usually like our sessions in the bathhouse in the gardens of Santa Maria in Portico. The steam rising from the great coppers of hot water as we dipped our jugs to wet madonna's hair created the same confessional atmosphere. Unable to see one another clearly through the mist, we were encouraged to divulge our secrets. Absorbed in the careful task of thoroughly soaking the hair without wetting madonna's scalp, or of ensuring the lightening paste of saffron pounded with egg white and lemon juice coated every strand evenly, we could avoid looking one another in the eye. We talked to water, or the floating, golden tangle of hair, or our own fingers, pungent, sticky, and orange stained.

At Imola, however, it was nothing like that. Madonna was mainly silent, except when she was being tetchy, complaining that the water was too hot or too cold, or that someone had pulled her hair, or wet her shift. We went about our task with sullen efficiency, aware of our damp clothes clinging to us and the wet earth smell of the saffron, like a graveyard in the rain. We had completed the shampooing, once with the plain white soap from Venice, once with soap scented with rose oil, and were towelling madonna's hair before applying the bleach, when madonna jerked up her head and glared at the dish of glutinous orange paste as though it had insulted her.

"There isn't enough egg white in that," she said.

"But madonna, it is the same number of eggs as usual." As usual, Elisabetta Senese did not know when to keep her mouth shut. Cousin Geronima, who had been reading aloud from the "Life of Saint Sebastian," perhaps in the forlorn hope of marshalling his arrows in an assault on madonna's vanity, fell silent and folded her hands in her lap. Angela rolled her eyes at me, for which I was grateful; things had been strained between us since our conversation about letters in Urbino.

"Then they must be small eggs," replied madonna. "Violante."

"Yes, madonna."

"Go to the kitchens. Fetch more eggs, and two bowls, for the separating." Donna Lucrezia had her domestic side.

Why me, I thought, rinsing my hands in the copper and wiping away the scum of suds on the old sheet I had fastened around myself to protect my gown. How should I know where the kitchens were in the *rocca* of Imola? And were there kitchens attached to the ducal apartments, where we were lodged, or would I have to find the main kitchen block, no doubt at some distance from the keep itself, where arms and gunpowder were kept?

"Yes, madonna." As no offer of guidance or directions was forthcoming, I bowed and set out on my quest. Only once I had closed the door to Donna Lucrezia's chamber behind me did it occur to me that Donna Lucrezia had never been here before either. Somehow, the fact of Imola being her brother's city made me feel she had.

I do not know how long I had been wandering along stone passages whose thick, rough-hewn walls had been hastily and imperfectly disguised with carpets and tapestries, when light falling through an open doorway led me into a high room with a tall, arched window at one end. Hearing voices, I went in. I seemed to be in some kind of armoury, though more for display than practical use. Torches were lit against the early dark of a winter's afternoon, and their flickering reflections bounced off suits of armour ranked on stands around the edges of the room. On the limewashed walls spears, javelins, halberds, and battle axes hung sheaved like corn stoops. Ranged down the centre of the room were open chests full of swords and daggers in ornamented scabbards.

There were two people in the room, a man and a woman. Though they had their backs to me, it was clear from their easy manner together, the way their heads were bent close and their elbows touched, that they were more to one another than mere acquaintances, and my immediate impulse was to withdraw. But it was too late; my presence had been noted.

"Monna Violante," said Don Ferrante, turning towards me. "I am surprised to find you here. Have you an interest in arms?"

"I am lost, your grace," I replied miserably. "I am looking for the kitchen."

"Ah," he said. "Can we help? You have been here before, haven't you?" Though he addressed himself to the woman, she made no reply but continued to gaze in great absorption at a peculiar suit of armour given pride of place directly under the window. I thought her demeanour rude, and her gown was made of some cheap looking stuff, a gaudy purple more fitting for a whore than a lady. I felt awkward, and a little insulted, so I stared at the armour too.

It was beautifully made, ornamented with climbing roses chased in gilt, every petal and leaf and thorn in minutest detail, but looked, nevertheless, as though it had been made for a knight who suffered some deformity. The pieces were very small, as though made for a boy rather than a grown man, and the upper breastplate ballooned curiously before the plackart cinched into a tiny waist.

Don Ferrante caught my line of vision. "Very fine, isn't it?" He placed his hand lightly in the small of his companion's back. "We have been admiring it."

Still the woman made no move to acknowledge me, nor did Don Ferrante offer to introduce me to her, leaving me no option but to carry on as though she did not exist, which was difficult as long as Don Ferrante's hand rested with such familiarity on her narrow waist. I concentrated on the armour.

"Very," I admitted, "but such an odd shape. For whom was it made? Do you know?"

To my surprise, Ferrante laughed. "Of course I do. It is La Sforza's.

She wore it at the siege of Forli. You see the little hooks there, around the upper lame?" He pointed to a strip of steel just below the plackart. "Apparently they were designed so she could hook a skirt on to them if she wanted to."

I had glimpsed Caterina Sforza once when, as Cesare's prisoner, she rode in his victory parade through Rome in the Jubilee year. I remember how the noise of the crowd had swelled as Cesare himself entered the Porta del Popolo, and how it had died, leaving a puzzled echo of itself, when the people saw the young man, who had left for France eighteen months earlier in a blaze of gold and jewels, now dressed all in black, without an ornament to his name. Caterina Sforza rode close behind her captor, swathed in a long, dark cloak with a hood, and closely flanked by two mounted men who led her horse. Her wrists and ankles were bound with gold chains, like Zenobia. Her image stayed with me, her small, shrouded figure riding in chains behind the serious young general like the embodiment of his conscience or, perhaps, a statement of his intent.

It came into my mind again now, as Ferrante remarked quietly, "She's the only one ever to have forced him into a fair fight."

I glanced at him, unsure if I was supposed to have heard his remark, but the lady with him seemed to have no such uncertainty.

"He directed the artillery barrage himself," she said. I wondered if she was well; her voice had something of a croak in it. "A whole day and night without rest. He refused to retire even when a gun backfired on him and burned his hand. It was a marvellous thing to see. I will never forget him, eyes streaming from the smoke, his shirt stuck to him like a second skin and torn where he'd cut a strip of it to bind his hand. He was like, he was like...Hephaestus."

"Oh, a lame comparison," quipped Ferrante.

"I am surprised there were ladies present," I said, and as soon as I took in Ferrante's flaming cheeks, and his companion's wild eyes and Adam's apple bobbing furiously above his pearl choker as he tried to swallow his words, I wished I could do the same. Ferrante shuffled his feet and cleared his throat.

"Vittorio knows where the kitchen is," he said. "As you will have gathered, he has been here before."

Vittorio? Now I recognised the young officer of the guard with whom Ferrante had conferred so closely during our journey, the dark beginnings of his beard thickly coated in white lead powder, his cheeks rouged and lips carmined, his dress, I could now see, ballooning awkwardly from the angles of his boy's body.

"But you have been paying me so much attention all this time," I blurted, all restraint shocked out of me by the sight of Vittorio in his gaudy purple, a necklet of something cheap and sparkling bent over his prominent collarbones. "Am I some sort of..." I waved an angry hand at the arms and armour displayed around us, "...diversionary tactic?"

To my astonishment, Ferrante began to laugh. Even Vittorio's bony features softened in a bashful smile, as he slipped his hand into Ferrante's.

"I hardly need one," said Ferrante. "My tastes are common knowledge in Ferrara, and as long as I am discreet, no one is going to report me to the authorities. You will just have to accept that the gossips of Rome don't know everything, my dear."

"But why..?"

"Because I like you; I should like to be your friend. Because in many ways we are the same, you a Jew, me a sodomite, both tolerated but not quite accepted. And such convenient scapegoats in the event of poisoned wells or plague or the failure of the harvest. We outsiders should stick together; our lives can be very precarious."

I was speechless. How could Ferrante, always able to find exactly the right phrase or gesture to put people at their ease, to charm them and make them laugh, make so graceless and offensive a comparison? "You forget, my lord, that I am baptised."

"Yet I have seen how your hand hesitates to make the sign of the Cross at Mass. Why, girl, you mumble your Credo as if you were being made to eat a blood sausage."

I could not deny it. But that still did not justify his remark. "My people are the Chosen of God, my lord, whereas your sort..."

"Take our example from the Greeks." It was thrown out as a light challenge, but a defensive note in his voice made me realise I had hurt him, and that I regretted it. At a loss what to say, I dropped my gaze and found myself staring at his great, bear claw hands, the fingers with their scattering of freckles and sandy hairs interlaced with Vittorio's, bony and not very well manicured.

"What I mean to say," continued Ferrante more gently, "is that we cannot help the way others see us, and that is what we have in common. A basis for understanding, I hope."

"Forgive me, Ferrante. The Bible speaks against your...practices. But in speaking against them, at least it acknowledges their existence. I must believe we are all God's people, I suppose. Your offer of friendship..."

"Would do you more honour if I could help you find the kitchen." We all laughed.

"Madonna's temper will certainly not improve if I do not return soon with her eggs," I admitted.

"This must be very hard for her."

"For all of us."

Ferrante nodded. Vittorio explained to me in his hoarse, boy's voice the whereabouts of the kitchen, and I was relieved he did not offer to accompany me.

I acquired the eggs and the two basins from a thin, dour woman with blood under her fingernails and small feathers sticking to her wrists, and returned to my mistress to finish the hair washing.

❦

The following morning we left Cesare's frontier behind us and moved on to Bologna, then Bentivoglio, from where it was planned to sail to Torre del Fossa, where madonna would be met by Don Alfonso. But in Bentivoglio, our plans changed; now I look back on it, everything changed.

We arrived in the town towards dusk, the bells in all the *campanile* clanging the evening Angelus as rooks cawed their way to roost, black scraps against a sky of sullen, windblown cloud. Ploughing had begun in the *campagna*, and as we rode towards the gates, our route was lined by squat, grimy-faced peasants, pushed aside by our guards to let us pass. I was tired and longed for nothing more than to ease my bruised backside out of the saddle and on to a pallet or cushioned bench. I hoped our accommodation would not be too spartan and that madonna would not keep us too long before she herself retired. The Bentivoglio family had entertained her with a ball in Bologna, and nothing on the same scale was planned for this stop, where the old family castle was much smaller. As for food, I had long since given up hope of ever eating a palatable meal again, and was trying to accustom myself to the bland, stodgy northern fare which lay in the belly like so much lead shot.

We had scarcely helped madonna off with her outdoor clothes, however, when our host, Annibale Bentivoglio himself, burst into her chamber, scattering the little pages who were stationed outside and, with the briefest of apologies for his poor manners, stammered that horses had been seen approaching from the north, and it was believed they belonged to Don Alfonso d'Este.

"Coming here?" What little colour remained in Donna Lucrezia's face after a long day on the road concentrated itself in two hectic spots on her cheeks and her eyes shone. It would be hard to say if she was angered by Don Alfonso's importunity, or exhilarated by the challenge, or perhaps just plain feverish from exhaustion. "He can't," she said, as though that was an end to it. "Look at me."

Summoning all the gallantry at his disposal, Don Annibale made a deep bow and said, "I see nothing to displease Don Alfonso or any man, madama." Little though I knew of men then, I agreed.

Those who have called Donna Lucrezia beautiful have generally been poets, or ambassadors with masters to impress, or petitioners grateful for her fair-mindedness. And, of course, the one man who truly loved her blindly. But she was charming and quick-witted; she had a way of smiling at a man and looking at him from beneath lowered lids that could make him believe she could rival Helen of Troy. She was naturally very graceful, walking as if she glided and dancing as though stepping on clouds. Of course she dressed exquisitely, with the same innate sense of style she shared with all her family, though her figure and bearing were such that she could impress even in the bleakest mourning. Even now, with mud on the hem of her gown, with damp hair plastered to her forehead and circles like bruises under her eyes, I felt Don Alfonso would find little to complain of.

"If he is coming, he is coming," said Angela, whose relationship to Donna Lucrezia gave her more freedom to speak plainly than the rest of us. "He is your husband. We had better make the best of it."

Donna Lucrezia took a deep breath. "Of course," she said, stooping to lift a hand mirror from its travelling case on the floor. "Where is it best that I receive him, do you think, Don Annibale?" She began to pat her hair, which tended to frizziness in damp weather.

Don Annibale shrugged. "My house is a small one, madama. There is only the hall."

"Very well. You may tell Don Alfonso I will attend him directly, in the hall."

Don Annibale bowed and retreated, and the small tower chamber became a flurry of activity as boxes were torn open, gowns, *camorre*, shifts, caps, and veils tossed on to the bed, jewels and cosmetics spilled on to the dressing stand. Eventually, Donna Lucrezia dismissed all her ladies except Angela and me, and the slave, Catherinella. Why she kept me I had no idea; I was one of the least experienced of her waiting women, and the challenge before us was great. Donna Lucrezia thought she could probably keep Don Alfonso waiting an hour, which seemed an alarmingly short time in which to dress her for her first meeting with her new husband.

Mercifully, she chose a simple gown in the deep, mulberry brown she favoured, with plain laced sleeves. Under it she wore a clean shift of white linen, fastened high at the neck with a pearl brooch from among the Este wedding gifts presented to her by Ippolito at the proxy marriage, when Ferrante, of all people, had stood in for his eldest brother. With her hair combed loose, rippling over her shoulders and down her back in tight waves caused by the plaits in which she had been wearing it since we left Imola, she looked every inch the demure, virgin bride. Don Annibale sent a page to escort us, but before she would leave her chamber, Donna Lucrezia asked for Sister Osanna to be sent for. No one knew whether she had been lodged in the castle or the town, but when she did eventually appear, madonna banished us to the passage and spent a few minutes alone with the nun.

Finally, we made our way to the hall, Catherinella following close behind and holding her mistress's skirt clear of the dusty floor. No one here was under orders from Cesare to make ready for us as they had been in the Romagna, and a veneer of neglect covered the surfaces of the house;

a faint smell of mildew hung in its air. In the hall, though, an effort had been belatedly made in honour of the Duke of Ferrara's heir. Lamps and candles were lit, platters of bread and cheese, cured hams and fruit set out on the long, tallow-spattered table for the travellers' refreshment. They themselves were clustered around the fire at the far end of the long room, a gaggle of large men in rough clothes, with dogs at their feet and pages weaving among them bearing wine jugs.

Our page announced us, and one man detached himself from the group around the fire, crossing the hall towards us with long, heavy strides and a couple of brindle hounds at his heels. His right hand lay across his heart in a romantic gesture ill-suited to his burly form and plain dress.

"May I present Don Alfonso d'Este," said Don Annibale, hurrying towards us. Don Alfonso bowed. I noticed that his short, tightly waved hair was thinning at the crown. Donna Lucrezia, whose eyes remained dutifully cast down, made a deep curtsey.

"Donna Lucrezia Borgia," said Don Annibale as Donna Lucrezia offered her hand for her husband to kiss.

For what seemed like an eternity, Don Alfonso did not move but remained as he was, frowning at the top of Donna Lucrezia's head. The smells of tallow and wet hound stuck in the back of my throat, making me hold my breath until I felt dizzy. For some reason she did not please him. We would be sent back to Rome, all that way in the winter weather, retracing our steps weighed down by humiliation as well as our baggage. I would see Cesare at last. He would not want to see me. I tried to imagine his anger but could not, felt relieved, then mortified that he could already have faded so much in my memory.

With an awkward movement, Don Alfonso shifted his left hand over his heart, freeing the right to take Donna Lucrezia's and raise her from her curtsey. He remained slightly stooped, as a man does when he has been winded, or is trying to protect a wound in his midriff. Don Alfonso looked healthy enough, with his broad shoulders and choleric complexion, but perhaps that was only an outward appearance and the pox was eating him from within. I tried to catch Angela's eye, but she seemed oblivious to the pantomime and was gazing intently towards the group by the fire; perhaps she hoped to see Ippolito among them.

"Your servant, madonna," said Don Alfonso. He had a gruff voice and spoke with a pronounced northern accent.

"On the contrary, sir, I think it is I who am yours, if the contract exchanged between our families stands." Donna Lucrezia looked her husband directly in his shrewd, blue eyes and smiled. It was clear he understood everything implied by her response, but he looked uncertain what to do with it. Suddenly, he doubled over, clutching at his chest with both hands. Donna Lucrezia gave a little gasp. A strange whimper escaped Don Alfonso. I feared he had suffered a seizure and took a step towards him to help him; it was an instinctive gesture, and one not missed by madonna, who gave me a reproving stare.

Don Alfonso straightened up, grasping in both hands a squirming bundle of white fluff. Extending his arms stiffly towards Donna Lucrezia, he said, "I brought you a present."

My heart sank; once again, I tried to gain Angela's attention, but she was still gazing off towards the fireplace. Despite growing up among men who loved hunting, Donna Lucrezia disliked dogs; she said they were noisy, messy, and their fleas made her sneeze.

"A lap dog," prompted Don Alfonso, confirming my fears, as Donna Lucrezia remained rooted to the spot, her smile set like a mask. "Got its mother from an Indian I met in Venice."

"It's very…"

"Here, take it; let it get used to you, then it'll sit quiet. Dogs like to have a leader. Wolves, you see."

Donna Lucrezia looked as though she did not see, but she knew her duty and took the little dog from Don Alfonso, holding it cautiously under the front legs. It looked bigger dangling from her hands, its legs stouter, its snub face more fully formed.

"Giulio said you'd like it," Don Alfonso ploughed on. "Said women like that sort of thing." He nodded towards the group of men around the fire. "My brother. Giulio."

One of the men nodded back, and now I understood why Angela was paying no attention to her mistress or Don Alfonso. You could see they were brothers; they had the same long noses, bent at the bridge as though they had been broken and imperfectly set, but there the resemblance ceased. Where Don Alfonso's mid brown hair was cropped close to his head, Don Giulio's was a tumble of blond curls. While Don Alfonso's eyes were the washed out blue of a fine winter's day, his brother's were violet, with lashes thick enough to be the envy of any girl. He was clean shaven and his cheeks had the downy bloom of a peach. Instead of Don Alfonso's thin lips, with their prudish downward curve, Don Giulio had a mouth like Ippolito's, full and sensual and made for kissing. In other circumstances, I too might have found myself captivated.

"Thank you, my lord. Your brother is indeed thoughtful. I think you are fortunate in all your brothers. Don Ferrante, especially, has been a tower of strength to us on our journey. And Monsignor Ippolito, of course, is a good friend of my brother, the duke." She must have known about Angela and Ippolito, yet she gave no hint of it, and Angela seemed unaware her lover's name had even been spoken.

"They were made cardinal at the same consistory, I think," said Don Alfonso, sounding slightly puzzled, then, solving the puzzle to his own satisfaction, went on, "Suppose that sets up some sort of camaraderie. Bit like the men you get your spurs with, that sort of thing. Eh?"

"I'm sure you're right," replied madonna warmly.

"Well, wife, will you sit with me a while? I dare say once we reach Ferrara, the celebrations will leave us little time to get to know one another." He moved to place his hand beneath Donna Lucrezia's elbow. Donna Lucrezia juggled the lapdog ineptly. They looked like a couple uncertain about a set of new dance steps, until I stepped forward and took the animal. Don Alfonso seemed to notice me then for the first time.

"By Jove," he said, and for a dreadful moment I thought I had acted too boldly by Ferrarese standards; you could see Donna Lucrezia feared as much too. Then Don Alfonso continued, "You're as like as two peas in a pod."

Donna Lucrezia looked, not only relieved, but genuinely delighted. I was, after all, some six years younger than her, and my face was a better shape; poor madonna struggled with the receding chin she had inherited from her father. It was really only the hair we had in common, and mine was not bleached.

"This is Monna Violante," she said. "She has not been with me long, but I favour her. She and my cousin, Donna Angela, are inseparable." The seconds stretched out as Angela registered madonna's attention upon her, dragging her eyes from the fireplace to cast them down in a perfect parody of modesty and drop Don Alfonso a curtsey. I felt a sigh of relief escape me and was sure Don Alfonso must have heard, though he made no sign of it.

"Rum sort of name," he commented.

"A nickname. Given by my brother," countered Donna Lucrezia, and I saw the same mixture of impotence and resentment cross Don Alfonso's face that I had often seen on Ferrante's whenever Cesare was mentioned. Rearranging his expression into a smile, he addressed himself to me.

"Well, it would be ungallant of me to ask how you got it, but I trust you will do no more to deserve it in Ferrara."

"She did nothing to deserve it in the first place," said Donna Lucrezia smoothly. "It is an irony, that is all, an acknowledgement of Monna Violante's integrity." Then, offering Don Alfonso her arm, she allowed herself to be led down the hall towards the fire. At a signal from Don Alfonso, the rest of the men retreated to give him and his bride some privacy.

Angela and I sat down side by side on a bench drawn up to the table. I managed the occasional glance at Donna Lucrezia and Don Alfonso, though mostly I was occupied trying to prevent the little dog jumping on to the table in pursuit of food; it was not very strong but it wriggled prodigiously.

"They look all right, don't they?" I said to Angela, seeking confirmation of my impression that, despite the dog, Donna Lucrezia appreciated her husband's romantic gesture in coming to meet her this way, ahead of all the official ceremonies in Ferrara; and that Don Alfonso, whatever might have been reported to him, had been pleasantly surprised by madonna's discreet bearing and modest attire.

"Fine," she replied, glancing briefly in their direction before her gaze returned to Don Giulio as iron does to a lodestone. "Oh my God," she whispered, clutching my sleeve so I was forced to let go of the dog which pranced off among the dinner plates, "they're coming over."

Sure enough, the ground between us and the group of men was shrinking as they shifted towards us, still chatting among themselves, not looking in our direction, trying to ensure that neither their lord nor Donna Lucrezia would notice the impropriety. I thought of Cesare's chestnut supper, and told myself life in Ferrara was going to be very different.

Unnoticed by us, Ferrante had joined his brother's party and now presented us, taking up a position between us and Don Alfonso's men as though he were our chaperone. They bowed, we curtseyed, then we stood in an awkward circle, chatting about our journey, the weather, the relative merits of travelling on to Ferrara by road or water, the imminence of Carnival and how it was celebrated in Rome and Ferrara. Few of them knew much about the former. I was not much excited by prospects of the latter, where throwing eggs at prostitutes seemed to be the main source of entertainment.

Angela said nothing. My worldly and accomplished friend, who had conducted her campaign to win Ippolito with such finesse, stood beside me like a gawky girl, winding her skirt in her fingers and staring at the ground, the wall hangings, the dog cavorting among the dishes on the table, anything other than what she longed to look at, the beautiful violet eyes of Don Giulio.

# Chapter 6

*Never simple, simply happy...*

As Duke Ercole was a widower, his daughter Isabella, Marchioness of Mantua was to welcome madonna to Ferrara. It was clear from the outset that Donna Isabella undertook her task with an ill grace. Her court had given shelter to many of those exiled from the Romagna by Cesare, including madonna's first husband, Giovanni Sforza. She made no secret of her deep disapproval of her brother's choice of bride and her resentment that madonna, as Duchess of Ferrara, now outranked her on her own home ground.

Although Don Alfonso and Donna Lucrezia had decided to complete the journey to Ferrara by road, when Donna Isabella, accompanied by Don Giulio, met us in Malalbergo, she insisted we travel by boat.

"It will make us late," protested Don Alfonso, glowering at his sister.

"But I rose at dawn to bring a bucentaur especially," Donna Isabella countered, making a great play of raising weary eyes to her brother's face. Donna Isabella was plump, with reddish hair, whose unfashionable curliness she disguised with coiffures almost as elaborate as Donna Adriana's. She had a small, mean mouth and a crude, fleshy nose, but her eyes were very fine, and she knew how to deploy her forces to best advantage.

Though she kept up her determined cheerfulness in public, those of us close to Donna Lucrezia knew how she had been dreading this encounter. Donna Lucrezia could handle men but the friendship of other women did not come easily to her.

"I would rather she had sent her husband on this errand," she muttered as Angela, Geronima, and I helped her dress. There was a general murmur of agreement. We had all met Don Francesco Gonzaga in Rome, and had been delighted with him, despite his thick lips and a nose which looked as though it had been squashed by a mis-kicked ball in Florentine *calcio*. He tended to wear a permanent frown, because he was vain, and believed frowning made his somewhat bulbous eyes look less prominent, but this could not disguise his love of pleasure. He was rumoured to loathe Donna Isabella, because she had a brain and liked to use it, and to enjoy many mistresses as well as some of his prettier pages.

"Unlikely in the circumstances," said Geronima, and even she sounded regretful.

"Perhaps," said madonna, raising her arms and turning her back so Angela could lace her corset, "we should find some opportunity to comment on his absence. As a reminder of the sort of thing that tends to happen to my husbands. If they displease my father. Or my brother." Her tone contained just the slightest hint of irony, as though she had tried, and failed, to keep it out. "Good God, girl, not so tight. Do you want me to fall in a faint at Isabella Gonzaga's feet? Let me out a little. It's not as though there's any danger of my looking fat in comparison to her."

"She looks like an overdressed toad," Angela whispered to me later, as the two women smiled and embraced one another on the muddy shore and we stood to one side, Angela trying both to attract and evade the violet gaze of Don Giulio. Sleet drove into our faces before an icy wind. The countryside looked flat and brown and sad. As Donna Isabella temporarily forgot herself and attempted to board the little ship ahead of Donna Lucrezia, one of the horses waiting on the towpath raised its tail and defecated. I saw Don Giulio glance at the steaming turds, at his sister and madonna in a tussle of satin and sable, at Angela hiding her face in the fox edged hood of her cloak, and smirk.

At Torre del Fossa we disembarked while the horses were unharnessed and the oars broken out for the final leg of our journey. Here Duke Ercole and all his court awaited us on the canal bank. The Este arms snapped from the top of the watch tower which gave the village its name. Snatches of music and conversation came to us on the wind from the deck of the duke's own bucentaur, its prow almost as high as the tower and fantastically carved with the twin-headed eagle of the Este. A row of squat, homespun peasants blinked the sleet from their eyes as their new duchess, in her gown of drawn gold with crimson satin sleeves, her hair sparkling with diamonds and snowflakes, a pearl the size of a small pear rising and falling at her bosom, knelt in the mud to kiss her father-in-law's hand. We held our breath. Duke Ercole raised madonna and kissed her on both cheeks then, stretching his thin lips in a smile, waved Catherinella forward to dust the mud from her mistress's skirts. We exhaled shakily.

Donna Lucrezia now joined the duke's barge, leaving the rest of us to follow on. They were entertained by the court musicians and poets declaiming eulogies of the Este and the Borgia. We in the second barge were left to our own devices. We sipped hot, spiced wine and watched the dreary country slip by on either side to the creak and splash of the oars, flat fields crossed by irrigation ditches lying like strips of lead under the wintry sky, black vines and bony poplars, low buildings the same dun colour as the people who lived in them and the soil they tilled. My Spanish heart ached for colour. Glancing across at Angela, I wondered if she felt the same, but she looked so withdrawn I doubted she had noticed our surroundings. I looked away again, drawn to a concentration of shadow on the horizon, beyond the lattice of poplar branches lining the canal bank. As I looked, the blur resolved itself into a block from which four square towers emerged, and I had my first sight of the castle of the Este which was to become my home. It looked bleak, forbidding, and horribly cold.

"You can almost hear Parisina Malatesta weeping from here," said Angela with a shudder. Parisina and her lover, Ugo d'Este, who was her stepson and had been Duke Ercole's eldest brother, were nearly as famous in those days as Dante's Paolo Malatesta and Francesca di Rimini, but today, the dungeon where they were held and executed by Duke Niccolo, is famous for holding other prisoners and Ugo and Parisina almost forgotten.

❦

"You know the first thing he will show you is where the block was set up for the executions." Triumph mixed with bitterness in Donna Isabella's tone as she stared down at the diamond and ruby necklace which had once belonged to her mother and now adorned madonna's slender neck. We were standing on the long staircase leading up from the main courtyard of the Corte Vecchio to where the head of the Savi and other civic dignitaries were waiting to make their speeches of welcome. Donna Isabella commanded the top step so Donna Lucrezia was obliged to look up to meet her eye.

She had refused to come down the stairs to greet her sister-in-law in the courtyard. Too crowded, she said, surveying the melee of people, horses and mules, baggage carts, oxen, the litter the Holy Father had given to madonna for the journey angled like a stranded boat, its curtains dragging in the mud. But I think she was hoping madonna might trip on the worn, slippery marble, hoping she might break that pretty neck or at least dislodge the tiara of diamonds and sapphires and enormous pearls which had also once belonged to the Duchess Eleanora.

She must have heard how madonna's horse, startled by a sudden loud noise during the procession into the town, had reared up and thrown her. No doubt she was infuriated by the way madonna had turned the mishap to her advantage, once she had been helped to her feet and remounted, calling out to the crowd in halting Ferrarese, "You see, I have fallen in love with all Ferrara."

There had been much clapping and cheering and waving of little pennants in Don Alfonso's colours of red and white. Then someone let off an arquebus, and the duke insisted madonna abandon her mount for something more placid or he feared she might fall again.

If Donna Isabella was hoping Donna Lucrezia had exhausted her stock of charm and good fortune in extricating herself so graciously from the incident, she was destined for another disappointment as madonna said smoothly, "I believe the lady's husband imprisoned Ugo and Parisina below the Torre Marchesana, where I am to be lodged. My husband has already warned me his father will wish to show me the place and that the doors to the prisons are very low." She laughed her mischievous laugh as Donna Isabella straightened up and madonna drew her into a sisterly embrace. "Perhaps he thinks I am particularly accident prone and am in danger of striking my head." She dabbed artlessly at the tiara.

Duke Ercole suggested madonna's Roman ladies might like to accompany her on her visit to the execution site, where dark stains on one of the flagstones might have been damp or might have been the mingled blood of the ill-fated lovers. Though not generally considered an imaginative man, Duke Ercole entertained some lurid notions concerning the morals of young Roman women and felt bound to make it clear to all of us that the ladies of Ferrara were expected to adhere to higher standards.

We began our excursion in high spirits. It was three nights since our arrival and, though she had said nothing to us, Donna Lucrezia seemed content with her husband. Whatever his reputation for drinking and whoring and spending long hours in his foundry or his pottery kiln, one or other of which was frequently setting fire to the northern end of the castle gardens, he had been punctilious in his attentions to his wife. Each evening he made the short walk along the gallery linking the Corte Vecchio to the castle where he joined her for a private supper, and he did not return to his own rooms until first light. From madonna's languid smile as we dressed her, and the dark shadows under her eyes which we concealed with lead powder and oil of violets, we deduced Don Alfonso had learned a pleasing trick or two from his whores. She had even conceived enough affection for her little dog to give it a name. She called it Alfonsino, Fonsi for short.

In defiance of Duke Ercole's purpose in bringing us to Ugo and Parisina's place of execution, there was much giggling and flirting as we hitched up our skirts to climb down the ladders to the dungeons, displaying ankles and calves and even knees to the young men who waited at the bottom to catch us. Many of them had travelled with us from Rome and were pursuing flirtations which had developed on the road. But the hilarity flickered and died as we made our way through a mouldering wicket gate, along a narrow passage whose walls oozed slime, to stand outside the cell, not much wider than the sluices which controlled the water level in the moat, where Ugo d'Este had defied his father, rejected his confessor, and sacrificed his life for love.

"Good source of food during a siege anyway," joked one of the young men, scraping a snail from the back of the iron-bound door, but nobody laughed. I felt Angela shift and sigh at my side and reached for her hand, which felt clammy in mine. Though the duke offered madonna his arm, she gave a slight shake of her head, took a torch from one of the link boys, and, stooping under the lintel, stepped alone into the cell.

When she re-emerged, her face was white and beaded with perspiration which sparkled on her forehead in the torchlight, her expression serious and inscrutable. Like a mask, it drew attention to her eyes where I almost fancied I could see the ghosts of the martyred lovers reflected on her dark, dilated pupils.

Then the moment passed, the dank air stirred by polite laughter as she remarked, "It is as well neither of them had to suffer imprisonment in such a place for long. Your father's anger and compassion were as happily blended as the traitors' blood, your grace."

I have often wondered if she remembered her words in the years to come. Whether she came to regret them or not, they served their purpose that day with Duke Ercole. To Donna Isabella's chagrin, he now conferred on Donna Lucrezia the family jewels which had not been given by Ippolito at her proxy wedding. He was captivated, not only by her wit, but by her success in bringing Sister Osanna to Ferrara and her excellent understanding of falconry. Angela saw the duke's generosity as evidence of Donna Lucrezia's way with men, though I, being my father's daughter, I suppose, reasoned that the jewels were merely on loan whereas madonna's dowry, the money to pay the expenses of her household, and still in a strong box in Duke Ercole's treasury, was not. I was sure the jewels were a sop, and a certain ironical twist to Donna Lucrezia's mouth when she admired herself in them made me certain she thought so too.

"Such a hypocrite, that Isabella," Angela remarked in the privacy of our room. "You know her eldest boy is to be betrothed to Luisa?"

"Luisa?" What was she talking about? I had hoped, as we were yet again on the subject of the Este and their shortcomings, to lead the conversation around to Giulio, but instead she veered off in this new, and surely irrelevant, direction. Isabella's son could not be more than a baby.

"Yes, Luisa. Cesare's daughter."

Of course she must have a name. Doubtless I had heard it before, but I did not want to know it, neither the name of his daughter, nor of his wife. The gentlemen of Cesare's household who had accompanied us to Ferrara had stayed on, for Carnival, I had convinced myself, just for Carnival. But if that were the case, the duke would have sent them packing, to put up at inns or the houses of the better-off citizens. Duke Ercole was parsimonious about household expenses, unless they related to his orchestra or his nuns, or his pack of long-haired, blue-eyed cats from Persia, who had their own grooms and their own little doors cut into the bases of all the doors in the Corte Vecchio. Even though his frescoes were permanently threatened by damp and eruptions of fungi, he forbade fires to be lit before nightfall.

Cesare's young men remained in the ducal palace because they were awaiting the arrival of his wife, the Princess Charlotte, and her daughter, and because, in Ferrara, if you were not nodding and smiling at the Venetians, or keeping a weather eye on the Emperor, you were allying your interests with those of France. Whether Cesare himself would then come to Ferrara, or whether he would meet his wife in Rome, or somewhere in the Romagna, was not known.

"Oh," I said. Charlotte d'Albret was reputed to be one of the most beautiful women in France, a cousin of the queen, virtuous and devoted to her husband, even though he had spent scarcely four months of their marriage at her side. What else could I say?

"I wonder when she'll turn up? Charlotte, that is. Maybe for carnival. All foreigners love to see an Italian carnival."

❧

The Princess Charlotte did not come for Carnival, prevented, it was said, by the weather in the Alps.

"She could have sailed," said Angela. "I wanted to meet her."

"Perhaps Cesare will come anyway," I replied.

"Perhaps."

But he did not; only his wife, it seemed, might have lured him to Ferrara.

So I had to make do with watching the antics of his gentlemen from the loggia over the great arch that gave on to the piazza from the Corte Vecchio. We wore masks and threw eggs, tiny works of art exquisitely decorated by Don Alfonso with the paints and enamels he prepared for his majolica. It was rumoured the whores gathered up the broken shells to display in the shop fronts whose storerooms and back parlours they used to ply their trade, as a mark of Don Alfonso's favour. As Don Alfonso was known to be something of a connoisseur in that area, they found it good for business to have his seal of approval.

If we leaned out far enough over the balustrade, we could just see the bronze statue of Duke Borso flanking one side of the arch, sporting a conical paper hat with a horsehair plume. By craning our necks the other way, we could see his father, Duke Niccolo, his stern face covered by a cuckold's mask adorned with rough-hewn wooden horns. No one knew who climbed the columns supporting the bronzes to mock Borso's sagacity with a dunce's cap or remind the city how Niccolo was deceived by his wife, but it happened every year, and Duke Ercole, though a proud man, never attempted to find the culprits or remove the decorations, and the people loved him for it.

❦

The privations of Lent were exaggerated for us by Duke Ercole's continuing refusal to hand over madonna's bride money. Several of her Spanish musicians had been forced to return to Rome when she ran out of funds for their keep, though the singers seemed glad to go because, they said, the marsh air was ruining their voices. Now her goldsmith, her candlemaker, and assorted grooms were obliged to follow. Perhaps madonna hoped, when the Holy Father saw how his daughter was impelled to reduce her circumstances, he would threaten the old duke with excommunication if he did not take the padlocks off the coffers. Whatever her belief, she continued resolutely to smile and charm and acquiesce in all the new arrangements, and if she cried herself to sleep at night, we did not know it because she spent every night with Don Alfonso. As they were newlyweds, a papal dispensation had been granted from that aspect of the Lenten fast.

Our days were marked by attendances at Mass, followed by visits to Sister Osanna in her new quarters in the convent of Santa Caterina.

"I expect it will make Sister Osanna feel more at home, to see a familiar face," remarked Donna Isabella, who accompanied us on one of our visits. "Of course, all Mantua is honoured by your highness's interest in her, but I always doubted she would travel well."

"She seemed perfectly content all the way here," said Donna Lucrezia as we waited for our carriage door to be opened in the convent courtyard. "Do you not think, Violante?" Once again, I had been chosen to be madonna's companion on this visit in the interests of my Christian education, and as custodian of Fonsi, who now went everywhere with her.

"No doubt she caught the mood of us all, madonna."

Donna Lucrezia gave a faint, but grateful smile. She looked pale, and the flesh had fallen somewhat from the bones of her face, making her so like Cesare I could hardly bear to look at her and was relieved my situation obliged me to keep my eyes cast down for most of the time. If I ever forgot him, it was only the way we forget the world of nature surrounding us, merely to be drawn back into consciousness of it by the exquisiteness of a frost-furred cobweb or the sharp, lonely bark of a fox in the depths of the night.

"All the same," countered Donna Isabella, popping a crystallised mint leaf into her mouth, "I had the feeling she was about to begin prophesying and the upheaval was bound to set her back. I would have counselled leaving it a little longer, had anyone asked my opinion."

A glint in Donna Lucrezia's eyes conveyed the impression that she, like me, found it hard to believe Donna Isabella would wait to be asked her opinion before giving it freely.

"I know it's Lent," Donna Isabella went on, her plump fingers scrabbling for a second mint leaf in the gold and enamel thread box hanging from her girdle, "but I can't get the taste of that pike we had at the day meal out of my mouth. I'm sure it had gone off. You'll have to take firm charge of the kitchens here, my dear. There has been nothing but men running the house for far too long."

"You should try cardamoms, Isabella. They have more power over the breath than mint, and no need of sugar to preserve them."

The coachman's boy placed a step beside the carriage door and I carried Fonsi down into the courtyard to relieve himself before helping Donna Lucrezia from her seat while Catherinella arranged her train. She had had no appetite for two or three weeks and seemed weak. A chill, she insisted, brought on by the change of season, but we were all certain she must be pregnant. After all, Don Alfonso had not missed a night in her bed and, as Angela put it, her voice tinged with envy, they obviously weren't whiling away the midnight hours playing cards. Bets had been laid and we ladies were counting the days until madonna's next course was due as carefully as those who had lovers but no husbands counted their own.

A novice led us to the nuns' parlour, which was divided by a wrought iron screen. On our side were upholstered chairs, a jug of wine, and a plate of unsweetened oatcakes held for us by Catherinella, whose ability to stand perfectly still for hours at a time continued to amaze me, though Angela said it was in the blood of Africans, to help conceal them from lions and elephants in the jungle. Donna Isabella also seemed to marvel at Catherinella, for I noticed she kept touching the slave, on her cheek or hand, almost as though trying to provoke her into movement. On the other side of the grille, Sister Osanna perched on a stool and drank water from an earthenware beaker to dull the sharper edges of her Lenten hunger. She was accompanied by Sister Lucia da Narni, who also bore the stigmata and had been wooed from Viterbo by Duke Ercole with the promise of this grand new convent.

"She looks peaky," said Donna Isabella. At first I thought she was referring to Donna Lucrezia, and was astonished at her bluntness, then realised she was peering through the screen at Sister Osanna.

"Do the wounds look infected? Can you see, Lucrezia?" Donna Isabella craned her neck to one side, her string of pearls disappearing into a gully of flesh between neck and shoulder. "Bandages look clean anyway. I would have expected no less. Sister Lucia sets the highest standards. Spends every night sweeping the church herself, you know, except when she has her trances. Don't you, sister?" Donna Isabella raised her voice to ensure she could be heard through the screen; the effect was as if she were trying to make herself understood by an imbecile.

I felt the hairs rise on the back of my neck; my scalp prickled. I was certain that, somehow, Sister Lucia had looked into my heart and put there the image of Mariam sweeping out our house in preparation for Shabbat, and myself trimming the candles in the *menorah*, always with one eye on the square of dimming light beyond the open shutters where soon the evening star would appear to mark the beginning of our holy day.

Donna Isabella, whose plump fingers had been creeping once more towards her box of mint leaves, redirected her hand to the oatcakes as Sister Osanna, fixing Donna Lucrezia with her gaze, said, in that loud, flat voice of hers, "You must look to the foundations, daughter. Fires may be set there. Do not give them air to breathe."

I was afraid of how madonna might react in her present frail state, but she merely frowned, as though presented with a puzzle to which she did not have the key.

"Perhaps her words are meant for me," said Donna Isabella hopefully, through a spray of crumbs which attracted close attention from the little dog in my lap. But Sister Osanna seemed scarcely aware of her existence. Her eyes, I noticed, were set very shallow in their sockets; they lay on the surface of her face like puddles of silvery water.

A hectic flush appeared on Donna Lucrezia's cheeks and an angry glitter in her eyes. "I think not," she said, "for Sister Osanna prophesied in my presence in Rome." Her phrasing was careful, but if she lost her temper she might reveal more than she intended.

As Donna Isabella's brows rose in interrogative arches, I felt compelled to speak, whatever the consequences. "She assured my lady that her marriage to Don Alfonso would be happy and fruitful, madonna." Well, it was done now, and what would follow, would follow, but at least Cesare would be safe from any divulgence of the curious scene I had witnessed between him and Sister Osanna in Rome. Though I had no idea of its meaning, some instinct told me he would not welcome its being bandied around the salons and dining halls and bathhouses of the fashionable set in the Veneto.

After waiting for Donna Lucrezia to reproach me for my boldness, which she failed to do, Donna Isabella arched her eyebrows a notch higher and said, with a scornful snort, "You could scarcely call that a prophecy."

"Given your family's antipathy to the match I would call it little short of miraculous," Donna Lucrezia came back, as fast and hard as if she were hitting a French tennis ball.

Donna Isabella retreated. "All the same, I am surprised you allow your ladies so much liberty. You should not have spoken for your mistress that way, girl."

"Monna Violante and I are of a single mind in this and many other matters." Donna Lucrezia turned the full force of her gaze on me, the candour of her wide, grey eyes having the effect of letting daylight into a long darkened room. Of course she had understood from the beginning about Cesare and me. How could she not? If she had said nothing it was because nothing needed to be said.

That night, though she dined with Don Alfonso as usual, Donna Lucrezia slept alone. There was much speculation among us ladies as to what excuse she had made to her husband, and whether or not it might be the truth. Certainly, said Elisabetta Senese, he was smiling as he called for a torch bearer to accompany him into the town.

In the depths of the night I awoke, thinking at first I had been disturbed by the ringing of the Matins bell from one of the city's monasteries. Then the sound of a woman's anguished weeping reached my ears, so heartbroken it had pierced my dreams. Parisina, I thought, and held my breath. My lungs shrivelled and froze in my chest. I dare not wake Angela because if I moved, Parisina would hear me and come looking for me, cradling her weeping head in her arms. I do not know how long I remained listening, rigid as a corpse under my bedclothes, before nature compelled me to take a deep breath and with air came common sense. The sound was coming from the direction of Donna Lucrezia's dressing room, which was separated from the chamber I shared with Angela only by a set of double doors.

I wrapped myself in my robe, lit a candle from the embers of our fire, and went to attend my mistress. She was sitting at the table where she normally kept her cosmetics and perfumes, but all these had been swept to the floor. Glass vials with their stoppers dislodged released scents of rose and lavender, bergamot and clove oil into the chilly night air; the marble tiles were patterned with lead powder and cochineal. Her head was in her hands, her elbows either side of a small, ornate casket worked in gold filigree and velvet lined, which might once have contained a piece of jewellery. So intently did she seem to be peering into it, I wondered if she had lost something, or feared it stolen.

"Madonna?"

She did not appear surprised to see me. "I was dreaming," she said, turning to me. Her eyes were puffy and snot trickled unheeded from her nose. "About Ugo and Parisina." Her teeth chattered, her words squeezed between cold stiffened jaws. I removed my robe and put it around her shoulders.

"When I heard you crying, I thought for a minute it was Parisina's ghost." I gave a sheepish smile but she did not seem to notice.

"I can't do this, Violante. I thought I could but I can't." Dropping her head into her hands once again, she clenched her fists around hanks of loose hair and let her tears fall into the empty box. "Everywhere I am watched. D'you know why I came in here? Because I have discovered there is a loose panel in my bedroom ceiling."

"Just something in need of repair, I expect, madonna."

She recovered herself slightly, more indignant now than distressed. "And what is above my bedroom? The roof. Where my husband has his lenses set up for looking at the stars. Or so I thought." She wiped her nose on the back of her hand. I began to pick up some of the bottles and jars from the floor. I was cold and needed to do something to warm myself. But when I tried to move the casket to one side she grabbed it fiercely and held it to her chest, though it contained nothing more precious than her tears. I wondered what made her so fearful of being seen with it, yet so reluctant to give it up. Had it contained a gift from Don Alfonso?

"What do you think Sister Osanna meant by her words this afternoon?" she demanded.

"I don't know, madonna. Perhaps that you must do your best to make sure your marriage is established on strong foundations."

"I fear it was both less simple and more perspicacious," she said, looking away into the darkness beyond the intersecting circles of light cast by our candles. Snapping the lid of the casket shut, she turned back to me with the air of someone who has come to a decision. "And if I am right, then she is right; I must always have regard to the foundations. It is what…it is…Violante…" Still clutching the box to her breast with one hand, she reached out to me with the other and grasped the sleeve of my nightgown. "Whatever happens in the future, we must remember that underneath all this, the new decorations, the fine furniture, the music and what have you, in that dungeon, there are those two lovers."

I shivered.

"No, no, no, I don't mean it that way. Not ghosts. Love. The power of love. Do you understand?"

I nodded. I understood nothing; when I look back now, I can scarcely credit my ignorance, nor imagine what I would have done with the burden of understanding. My head ached with cold and bewilderment. All I wanted was for this interview to be over so I could climb into bed beside Angela and warm my feet between her smooth calves. "Let me help you back to bed, madonna."

"Very well, but blow out the candles. In case he's having me watched."

"Shall I take this? Where would you like me to put it?" I placed a hand on the casket, but she merely tightened her grip upon it.

"It's all right; I'll see to it myself. But Violante?"

"Yes, madonna."

"If anything should happen to me, you must be sure and give this to Cesare. He will know why." She paused, her mouth working as if she could not decide whether to speak or keep the words dammed up inside. "My whole life is in this little box," she said eventually, then yawned as though saying these words had cost her all the energy she had left. I did not know how to reply, so blew out the candles as she had insisted, and led her back to her bed chamber, barking my shins and elbows on door jambs, chair legs, the corners of tables. It was as though the room had completely rearranged itself under cover of darkness.

Suddenly she let go of my hand and said, "Catherinella will take care of me now. She can see in the dark." Only then was I aware of the slave's presence, her steady, regular breathing, the whites of her eyes gleaming in some light whose source I could not determine, the whisper of her bare feet as she moved across the room towards her mistress, sure as a cat.

Unable even to find my candle where I had left it in the dressing room, I blundered back to bed. I did not get into Angela's bed because I did not want to wake her and have to tell her about my conversation with Donna Lucrezia. Instead, I lay shivering, wondering if she had fallen prey to some sickness of the mind, yet even more afraid that she had not. I never mentioned our exchange to anyone, and when we went in to dress her next morning, and, over our wine and hot water and fresh white rolls, to gossip about the day to come, we both behaved as though it had never taken place.

Just before the beginning of Holy Week, Ippolito arrived from Rome with a baggage train almost as long as that which had accompanied us to Ferrara. Watching with me from the balcony of the Camera Dal Pozzolo where we were accustomed to sew and gossip when Donna Lucrezia had no official function to perform, Angela sprang up and down on the balls of her feet like a little girl, clapping her hands and squealing with delight at the prospect of presents from Ippolito. It took nearly an hour for his procession of mules, carriages, ox-carts, and boxes balanced like tabernacles on carrying poles, to make its way through the piazza.

By this time, Ippolito had joined us on our balcony, having been told his father was out hunting in the Barco, and preferring our company to that of his brothers. Angela rushed across the room with the force of a small tornado as he was announced, flinging herself into his arms so he staggered a little, a dazed smile spreading across his face. Angela had obviously decided that, having survived the latest cull of madonna's household, which had seen both Cousin Geronima and Donna Adriana return to Rome in the company of Cesare's gentlemen, her position in Ferrara was now strong enough to throw discretion to the winds.

Or perhaps she had some other reason for her display of affection. Her silence on the subject of Giulio was not, I was certain, a result of any lack of interest on his part. Though I had never seen them alone together, I had noticed how often he contrived to sit near her at Mass, how he always seemed to be on hand to tighten a girth for her, or pick up a dropped book, or re-string her lute when she complained her fingers were too sore from playing. Their conversation was never more than ordinarily polite, but the discourse between their two bodies struck a different note entirely. But if they had not reached any understanding, Angela would not want to forfeit her cardinal's affection.

"Well," said Ippolito, "what a welcome. Tell me, where is your lady? I must chide her instantly for the lack of decorum among her women." His voice trembled slightly with surprise and delight, and I was sorry for him. More than that, I felt a sense of foreboding, an urge to warn him of something though I had no idea what. It was as though time stopped for a second, and the way certain things become visible at dawn or dusk, in unaccustomed guises, I saw behind the decorated walls, below the rich rugs and polished floor, the savagery of this old castle. Trapped in its red stones was the pain of all the tortured prisoners, abused slaves, humiliated opponents, discarded lovers, the wives dead in childbirth, infants taken by fevers, the soldiers and fratricides and faithful retainers whose bodies bent to the service of the Este as a tree bends to the prevailing wind.

"My dear goddaughter. Are you well? You look a little…absent. Not the wine again, I trust?" I was condemned to be embarrassed afresh every time Ippolito and I met, but I concealed my irritation. He meant no unkindness by it; on the contrary, he made a joke of it so I would understand I was pardoned.

"Oh, it is her heart that is sick, not her stomach," teased Angela, her arm through Ippolito's, her skirt entwined in the folds of his soutane.

"Still? Well, I may have a remedy for that," he said, patting a leather scrip which hung from his belt, "but first, I must see my sister, Donna Lucrezia. Where is she? Don't tell me she's out hunting too."

"No this morning, she's in bed. She could not keep her breakfast down. We think she's…" Angela made a little dome over her belly with her free hand and, putting her mouth close to Ippolito's ear, whispered, "*enceinte.*"

"Well, that is good news. And so quickly. Clearly my brother has been assiduous in his duty."

"Oh, assiduous," Angela repeated, spinning out the vowels and sibilants as though the word were Eve's serpent uncoiling from her lovely mouth.

A remedy, I thought, staring at Ippolito's scrip. A letter, it must be, a letter from Cesare. But why not give it to me? Why must he see Lucrezia first? I could not bear to wait while he loitered with his mistress, sharing her lascivious jokes and teasing me about my poor head for wine.

"I will go and see if she is fit to receive you," I said, rising in such haste the collar I was embroidering slipped from my lap in a tangle of needles and different coloured threads. I could hear Angela laughing as I hurried towards the door.

There was something instantly calming about the bed chamber, despite the faint odour of vomit and stale bedlinen hanging in the air. The bed curtains had been drawn back, though the windows remained covered, giving the light which filtered through the green silk drapery a cool, underwater quality. I thought Donna Lucrezia, her hair unbound and spread over her pillows, looked like a mermaid. Catherinella stood at the bedside, fanning her mistress with slow sweeps of a paddle-shaped palm fan. Fonsi lay in the crook of Donna Lucrezia's arm, snoring gently.

"How are you feeling, madonna?"

She waved a limp hand and Catherinella stopped fanning.

"Would you like me to uncover the windows? The air is rather stale in here and it's a lovely morning outside."

Frowning, she shook her head. "I have such a headache, Violante." Her voice was plaintive and girlish.

"Madam is sick so often it strains her here." Catherinella put her free hand to the back of her neck.

I made a sympathetic hum in the back of my throat, but persisted. "I have news I hope may cheer you, madonna. Cardinal Ippolito has arrived with letters from Rome. He would like to see you." My hearty tone reminded me of Sister Beatrice who used to supervise us playing ball games at Santa Clara.

"I wondered what the commotion was." Donna Lucrezia smiled, and I fancied her cheeks began to show a little better colour. "I suppose he has travelled as light as ever?"

"I imagine the end of his train is not yet through the city gate, madonna." We laughed. Fonsi awoke and began to wag his tiny plume of a tail.

"Well," said Donna Lucrezia, pulling herself up a little against the pillows, "I'm sure I cannot be sick again this morning. There is not even a drop of water left in my stomach, I'm certain."

"It is a good sign, though." I took my cue from her hint that her sickness was confined to mornings.

"Let us hope so, my dear." Clearly that was all she would have to say on the matter for now. "Catherinella, fetch me fresh water for washing, and inform Monsignor the cardinal I will be ready to see him in half an hour." I raised my eyebrows; madonna was notoriously slow about her toilette.

"Make that an hour, Catherinella. I'm sure he can find enough to occupy himself until then."

An hour, another hour. "Shall I take the dog out, madonna?"

"No, stay with me and help me get ready. Let in some light. I shall need more than this to make myself respectable. And read my letters."

It was easier to speak frankly with my back to her. As I tied back the drapery, letting my gaze follow the swoop and dart of a swallow in the clear, pale sky above the glitter of the moat in the light breeze, I said, "His Eminence gave me to believe he might have a letter for me also." I heard the rustle of linen and the swish of silk, and a soft thud as madonna shifted her position and the dog jumped to the floor.

"From Duke Valentino?" Her voice was warm with affection, whether for him or me I could not tell. Donna Lucrezia pushed back the bedclothes and swung her legs to the floor. Her calves, I noticed, were in need of depilation, but I doubted she would be able to stand the pain of the hot wax in her present condition. Besides, if she truly were pregnant, Don Alfonso would be obliged to seek his pleasures elsewhere until his wife was delivered and churched, so her intimate appearance would not matter so much.

"Yes." My father and brothers did not write to me, my father believing I could only hope for complete assimilation into a Christian household by severing all my ties with my origins. My friends, Battista and Isotta, had promised to write in the extravagant grief of parting, and perhaps they would.

"I hope he has written," said Donna Lucrezia, patting my hand as I approached her to help her to her feet.

She decided she had not the energy to dress, but received Ippolito sitting in a chair in a wrap of violet velvet, her bare feet thrust into matching slippers in the Turkish style, her hair arranged in a loose plait over one shoulder. I waited in such tension while they exchanged pleasantries about madonna's health and Ippolito's journey I could hardly keep my feet still. What a waste of time the high art of conversation can sometimes seem.

Finally, madonna had mercy on me and said, "You have letters for me?"

"Yes." Ippolito unfastened his satchel and withdrew a bundle of parchments, their seals dangling like clusters of bright, wax fruit. "From His Holiness, who is still prone to weep every time your name is mentioned and chides you for not writing to him every day. And this from Madonna Giulia. From your noble mother."

Madonna frowned at her mother's letter and put it down on the floor beside her chair.

"And these from your illustrious brother."

The bundle contained three letters. Donna Lucrezia fanned them out as if they were a hand at cards, withdrew one, and held it out to me. "I think this is what you have been waiting for, Violante."

"Thank you, madonna." It took all my will to prevent myself from snatching it up and running from the room. I slipped it into a pocket in my skirt where one stiff corner of the parchment grazed my leg each time I moved.

"You may read it," said madonna.

"Thank you, madonna, but I...I would like to wait."

"I think Fonsi would like to be taken out now." The dog was indeed snuffling about the edges of the room as though looking for somewhere to relieve itself. "Perhaps you had better take him before he disgraces himself in front of the cardinal. Send Donna Angela to me on your way out."

"Thank you, madonna." Gathering Fonsi in my arms and forgetting to curtsey, I fairly flew from the room, feet slipping on the stair edges as I whirled down to the floor below, stuck my head through the door of the Camera Dal Pozzolo to summon Angela to wait on madonna, then continued down to the garden.

Even here, however, there was little peace to be had. Don Alfonso had begun a renovation of the bathhouse originally built for his mother, and everywhere there were workmen, whistling and calling to one another as they barrowed loads of stone along catwalks or mixed their sharp smelling quicklime in great leather buckets. Ignoring their teasing, I hurried on to the vine walk, where I sat on one of the marble benches arranged at intervals along it.

As I drew the letter from my pocket, I watched the play of sunlight and shade on my hand, on the stiff parchment, and the seal hanging from the scarlet ribbon which bound the letter. My fingers traced the address, pausing on a smudge where "l" looped over towards "a," worrying a stray blob of sealing wax with the tip of a nail. Not the neatest of writers, I thought, with a surge of love which made me smile at a gardener shovelling up behind Fonsi.

I broke the seal with sweating fingers. Cesare had kept his silence so long, and his silences were generally held to precede the anonymous glint of steel in moonlight or the whisper of poison slipping into a glass. What, now, had he to say to me?

*Madam*

Well, it was hardly the way a hot-blooded lover would begin a letter to his mistress.

*My illustrious sister, the Duchess Lucrezia, to whom I defer in all things, insisted that I write to you, to put an end to your misery. Doubtless she flatters me to think that I should have such power over your peace of mind. I am certain that any unhappiness you have suffered since quitting Rome must have been a consequence of leaving behind friends and family, and of the rigours of travel in the middle of winter. But now you have, God be thanked, reached Ferrara in safety, I do not doubt your spirits have lifted in that lovely and prosperous city and this letter will be forgotten as soon as read.*

Here there was a space between the lines, a pause to draw breath. Perhaps he had laid his writing aside at that point to do something else and had come back to it later.

*Violante, my sister admonishes me to tell you the truth about myself. She says your steadfastness deserves it. Let us begin with a truth about my sister. Perhaps one reason why she and my noble mother do not see eye to eye is that they are both as stubborn as mules and not to be gainsaid in anything. I am a busy man, without the resources to do battle against Donna Lucrezia, so I shall endeavour to obey her command. How Ser Castiglione would approve, for he has often accused me of using the ruse of charm to conceal the scandalous fact that I am not a true courtier whose heart and sword arm are consecrated to the service of the fairer sex. I allow him to get away with this because he also praises my ingenuity in devising practical jokes.*

*Perhaps the task your mistress has set me is not so daunting as I had anticipated. There, already, are two truths. That I prize certain things higher than the love of women, and that I am a trickster. I can give you a list, Violante. I can tell you I am the Church's general and the ruler of a state founded on practical, secular principles, that my mother's family were painters in Mantua and my father's descended from the royal house of Aragon. That I once wore priest's robes but was never ordained, that no confession I have ever* heard was freely given, and that absolution is not in the gift of priests, but in the judgement of posterity. I can tell you, in the sure and certain knowledge you will never be able to distinguish one from the other, that I keep my friends close and my enemies closer. My soldiers adore me, my subjects pay their taxes on time, but my father fears me. I can straighten a horseshoe with my bare hands, and you have seen me kill bulls, but I am sick. Sickness smoulders in me like fire at the heart of a damp haystack; it ticks in the night like a death clock in the rafters.

I could tell you I was lonely, which would soften your heart towards this confession, but that would not be true, so I will tell you how I see my heart as an island in a cold lake. When the lake freezes over, you may approach it, but you risk being stranded, and the island is a hostile desert where basilisks live, not a sylvan glade where unicorns roam. I cannot be bothered with enticing virgins, Violante.

But Galen says the heart is just a kind of bellows, squirting blood around the body, and Galen was a soldiers' physician. If this is so, I ask myself, who pumps the bellows? God? My own will? Or whatever force, blind, deaf, mute and without wits, makes basilisks basilisks and unicorns unicorns and keeps the planets on their treadmill. Now there is a truth it would be worth knowing.

There are so many matters a man might pursue if he grew old and still. Do you know there was a German at the university in Bologna two years ago who taught that the earth revolved around the sun? It is an interesting proposition. If we are not at the centre of God's universe, then what are we here for? Perhaps we are just a random accident, a throw of the celestial dice. As Caesar said on the banks of the Rubicon, alea iacta est. Our fate is what we make it.

It is a disappointing little stream these days, the Rubicon; I expect you did not notice when you crossed it on your journey north. But cross it you did, so you too have cast your die.

I fear this letter will not have achieved what my sister hoped, but I cannot tell you more. I dislike writing. Look at it, tangled like ill-kept harness, as muddled as a badly drawn map. I am only comfortable with actions, which cannot be misconstrued. I urge you to consider more the act of my writing than the words I have pinned to the page like so many insects collected by a natural philosopher.

The truest truth I know is that I cannot tell you the truth. All I can say to you *is this, with as much honesty as I am capable of, as Donna Lucrezia says you deserve, that I am not free to love a woman, but if I were, perhaps that woman might be you. One day, I fear, you will know why.*

*Your servant in those things I can be.*

*Valentino*

I could make no sense of the letter. Was he drunk when he wrote it? Or ill, as he suggested? Certainly the hand changed, after the opening passage, after the space between the lines where, I suspected, most of the answers lay. The writing leaned forward, was less careful, with letters missing and some words unfinished, as though his hand were racing to keep up with his thoughts.

I looked up, resting my eyes on the dappled sunlight falling through spring green vine leaves. I breathed in the clean, medicinal perfume of blue-starred rosemary, waiting for tears, but all that came to me was a line from Dante.

*There is no other penalty*
*Than to live here without hope, but with desire.*

This is the fate the poet consigns to the unbaptised, to my people.

But I had been baptised, and I was young, in love, and alive. In this life, desire can no more live without hope than a candle flame without air. Surely he had honoured me with words written from the heart, sincerely and without artifice. And had he not said he would love me if he could? Just because he was not free to love at the moment, surely this could change. Perhaps he merely wished to spare me the pain of losing him while he was still obliged to fight for the security of his state; perhaps, if I remained patient and steadfast, he would come to me in the end. I presented a smiling countenance to Donna Lucrezia's questioning glance when I returned to her chamber, which seemed to set her mind at rest; she had much greater concerns than her brother's dalliance with one of her ladies-in-waiting.

Angela questioned me more closely later in the day, when we were in our own room dressing for a dinner to be given by madonna for her father-in-law.

"So?" she began, breaking off briefly to ask me if I thought her neckline was high enough; Duke Ercole disapproved of Roman fashion, which had plunged us into a flurry of stitching collars and fichus into the necks of our gowns, though it was a relief not to have to lace oneself so tight to push up the breasts. "What did he say?"

"Who?"

"Don't tease, you know perfectly well who. You'd hardly go running off into the garden with a face as pink as a pomegranate to read a letter from those school friends of yours."

"He said…" What had he said? I glanced at my travelling chest, where I had hidden his letter beneath one of the loose compartments. "He said he would love me if he could."

Angela frowned. "Really? He wrote that?"

"Why shouldn't he?"

"Frankly I'm surprised he can even spell the word love. It's just not something he ever…"

"Well you're just his little cousin. I don't suppose he would speak to you of love." I felt myself beginning to flush, a defensive sweat prickling between my breasts and under my arms.

"Violante…"

"Yes?"

"Oh…nothing. What do you think about La Fertella? Isn't he just the funniest thing? How clever of Ippolito to find him." Ippolito had brought La Fertella as a gift to Donna Lucrezia. A small, dainty man with the dark, darting eyes of a bird and a narrow jaw almost completely filled by his pale, mobile lips, his strength as a clown lay not in banter or practical jokes, like Gatto and Perro, but in conjuring and mime. Donna Lucrezia was delighted with him.

"Are you pleased to see Ippolito?" I was standing with my back to Angela, rummaging in my jewel case for the necklace Donna Lucrezia had given me at my baptism. When she did not reply immediately, I turned to look over her shoulder at her reflection in the mirror she held. In the brief moment she remained unaware of being watched, I read the panic and confusion of a lost child in her expression, and realised things must have gone much further with Don Giulio than I had imagined. Then her reflected gaze met mine and she smiled.

"What are you going to do when Cesare comes? Will you give yourself to him?"

"Is he coming, then? He has not said so."

"He never says what he intends to do. You know how he is. I doubt he even tells his valet what time to bring his shaving water, he's so secretive. But he's bound to come before long, and you need to be clear in your mind what you intend before he's nibbling your ear in some dark corner and you're wetting yourself."

The very thought drew my nipples tight and brought the familiar pressure between my thighs that Angela's clever fingers were so skilled at relieving. Coming close behind her, I slid my arms around her waist and laid my cheek against her back, feeling the cross hatching of the laces tying her bodice against my flesh. Pressing my hands flat against the curve of her belly, I felt her hesitate, yield for a moment, then stiffen and whirl to face me, dashing my arms away.

"Stop it," she said, "we're not children any more. It's not a game."

"This is to do with Giulio, isn't it?" I asked, once more busying myself with my jewel case.

"This is to do with you and Cesare," she replied firmly. "I know my cousin and he will not tolerate a tease. It seems the more devious a man is in his own ways, the more he appreciates direct dealing in others. If he has written to you of love, be sure it means something more to him than exchanging sonnets and nosegays. Be sure you understand him, or…well, who knows what may happen." A vision of the tongue and little finger hanging from the window of the Savelli prison flashed into my mind, yet it no longer appeared as real or terrible as when Little Haim had described it to me, making sure my father was well out of earshot before giving me every grizzly detail. It did not seem to be the act of the man who had written that odd, ambiguous, introspective letter.

Whom, it seemed, I must now take seriously as my lover. This realisation did not bring me the joy you might expect; there was a problem.

"But what if I am not virgin when I marry?" It was different for Angela, I assumed, whose close relationship to the Holy Father would make her a desirable catch under any circumstances. Cut off from my own family, I would have no dowry but what Donna Lucrezia could provide for me and no worth but my virtue.

"First," said Angela, sitting on the edge of her bed and patting a space beside her, "all sorts of things might break the hymen other than a man."

I thought of her fingers, strong and slender and knowing, though I had never bled during our games.

"Horse riding, for one," she went on, her voice warm with laughter, her eyes dancing as I sat beside her, our knees touching, forgiven now she had managed to deflect the conversation yet again from Don Giulio. "And anyway, there are all sorts of things you can do. A little chicken blood on the sheets. There's even a paste I've heard of, which you smear inside and it sets to create a likeness good enough to fool most men, but I don't know what it's made of, though I'd bet a gold ducat Aunt Adriana does. What you have to remember about a husband is, he wants to believe you're virtuous, and beautiful, and good at everything from brewing to sketching in perspective. Otherwise he looks like a fool who's struck a bad bargain. You see?" She kissed the tip of my nose. "You're such an anxious little goose. Relax. When Cesare takes you to his bed, enjoy it. Most women do, I'm told. Learn from him. Perhaps, by the time you marry, you'll know some tricks to keep your husband's mind off how and where you learned them."

"You're so wise." I remained sitting a moment after Angela had risen, saying we must hurry to dress madonna as Duke Ercole could not sleep if he ate dinner any later than the twenty-second hour. I tried to imagine the bruising passion of Cesare's kisses, how his body must look beneath the layers of black velvet and white linen, what scars were written on it, what stories it would tell, how it would feel when...

"Come on," said Angela, taking my hands and pulling me to my feet. As she dragged me from the room, I took a last look over my shoulder at my travelling case where his letter lay, crisp vellum next to pleats of dark red satin.

I still have that letter; it is the second most important letter I have ever received. Sometimes, when I am alone in the house, I remove it from the bottom of the tin-lined sea chest where I keep it, and hold it between my flattened palms, warming his memory with my hands. Faded now, dog-eared and torn along one of its folds, the seal crumbled and its ribbon frayed and brown, stained with the water of an ocean Cesare never saw, it lies alongside the most important letter ever sent me. That letter drove me to action, Cesare's to dreams. I wonder how differently my life might have turned out if it had been the other way round? If I, too, would not have lived to see the ocean?

What a blessing it is we cannot see our futures.

# CHAPTER 7

*Love is plain and deep, like the sea when no one is looking at it.*

Madonna fainted during a performance of the Passion in the cathedral on Good Friday, just as Christ was descending into hell through the maw of a papier mache serpent. After that, there could no longer be any doubt about her condition. Naturally, we expected to see less of Don Alfonso once the duke's physician and madonna's physician had conferred, and declared a child would be born at Christmas time. He had done his duty and would return to the life of travel and debauchery he had enjoyed before his marriage.

Yet to my surprise, he took to spending the first hour of the afternoon with his wife, keeping her company as she rested on a daybed set up for her in the Camera Dal Pozzolo, beside the windows overlooking the gardens. Sitting next to her, her plump, impossibly white hand lying in his great paw, he would talk to her, in that jerky, awkward way of his, attempting to interest her in the varying proportions of copper and tin in the gun-metal from which he cast his cannon.

"Got to be at least nine parts copper, you see, twice as rich as bell metal."

And Donna Lucrezia would nod gravely, with a faint smile which said she was interested, nay fascinated, but so tired just now. So he would move on to his other passion, which was pottery making. All the chamber pots, and the majolica plates from which we ate on Fridays and fast days had been made by Don Alfonso, intricately decorated with birds and flowers, tiny hunting scenes, miniature figures engaged in domestic pursuits such as brewing or baking or spreading laundry to dry on bushes beside a river bank. It was one of the Creator's mysteries how a man with such broad hands, with fingers fat as sausages and gouty joints, could paint such careful, dainty designs.

Sometimes Don Alfonso's visits were shared by one or other of his brothers, though never Don Sigismondo, who had the pox on his brain and was too busy preparing a military campaign against the rats which lived in the earth banks of the castle moat and were, he said, planning to stage a coup against the Este. We had the most fun when Ferrante came. Though Duke Ercole despaired of his second son who, he said, was nothing but a damned fop of a courtier, he made us laugh. He was cruelly funny, though his sharp cuts were delivered with such languor they sounded like courtly flattery, a style which reminded us Romans of the society we had left; though Ferrara was a cultivated court, famed especially for its music, it was also formal and cold. Since the death of Don Alfonso's mother and his first wife, a severe and solitary masculinity had settled upon it.

Ferrante could do conjuring tricks and vied with La Fertella to produce trinkets from behind ladies' ears or streams of coloured ribbons from the neck of Don Alfonso's shirt. Even Perro and Gatto were drawn to him, laughing madly at his jokes even when they could not understand them. Fonsi, who was rapidly growing fat from hours spent lying across Donna Lucrezia's belly while she fed him marzipan and sugared fruits, would balance on his short legs like a small barrel on a stand and yap in a frenzy of delight when Ferrante visited. Ferrante's determination to keep his sister-in-law amused in her enforced inactivity endeared him to me especially, for I knew Vittorio had returned to Rome with the rest of Cesare's men, and understood perfectly how lonely Ferrante must be without him. I would have spoken to him of it, but the opportunity never arose.

Cardinal Ippolito brought us the gossip from Rome, both secular and ecclesiastical, though it all amounted to much the same thing: who was giving the best dinners, spending most on their collection of art and antiquities, attending the salons of La Fiammetta or her great rival, Imperia, what were the funniest, most scurrilous of the *avvisi* pinned to the Pasquino. The social season looked set to extend well beyond Easter, he said, darting a look at Donna Lucrezia, as Duke Valentino remained in town, even though the weather was improving all the time and the troops he had encamped outside Rome were growing restless. Spain and France were quarrelling over Naples again, a situation Cesare and his father no doubt intended to exploit one way or another, but how? Even the pope did not know, it seemed, for he complained as much as the next man of the difficulty of communicating with his son, who went to bed at dawn and slept through the day, only venturing out of his apartments after dark and in disguise. The gossips said it was the French disease again, disfiguring his face, but others looked at growing unrest in Florence, and wondered.

Almost as an afterthought, Ippolito told me he had seen my father in the Vatican several times, and that he sent me his respects.

To all this, Donna Lucrezia listened intently, with her little dog in her lap and her husband at her side. "How unfair of you to make me worry about my brother's health when I am so weak myself," she complained when Ippolito finished. "He wrote me nothing of this in his letters, which are all cheerful and full of praise for my dear husband." She turned a doting smile on Don Alfonso, who responded by scratching the dog behind its ears. Paying close attention to this talk of Cesare, I did not miss the quick look which flashed between him and Ippolito. As if to say, whatever she knows we shan't get it out of her this way.

When Don Giulio visited, Don Alfonso always brought his viola. All the brothers were fine musicians, but Giulio was best of all; he could play any instrument and sang like an angel. If he had been unable to hide behind the screen of music, I do not think he would have come. Whenever he and Angela were in a room together they behaved like a pair of moonstruck calves, alternately blushing and pale, staring at one another for long, enraptured minutes only to look away almost in panic if their eyes should happen to meet. Donna Lucrezia was teaching Don Giulio some Spanish songs, and liked to accompany him on her guitar, her stockinged feet tapping out dance steps against the raised end of her daybed. When she grew tired, she would hand the guitar to Angela, who was a competent player herself, though you would never know it from the way her fingers fumbled over the strings while Don Giulio's pure tenor voice soared ahead. He sang with his eyes closed; perhaps that was his secret, though I doubted it; not being able to see your lover does not make your heart beat any slower or your mind pay any closer attention to reason.

I watched this pantomime intently, not only because Angela was my friend and I feared for her caught between the Scylla and Charybdis of the two brothers, but because it gave me something to think about other than the music. Even now, the sound of a Spanish guitar can carry me all the way back to Toledo. Now I can simply close my eyes and enjoy it, the memory of sitting on my father's shoulders as we watched a comedy performed by street players in the square near our house, the evening sky deep indigo beyond the light of torches flickering across the players' painted faces and setting the shadows of the shade trees dancing. I let my thoughts linger on the smell of sweet dough balls frying in oil until my saliva begins to run. I feel the strength of my father's shoulders under my skinny child's legs with a love at last freed from regret. But then, such memories would have made me cry, and my tears would have been a betrayal of my father's concern for my future, and of Donna Lucrezia's generosity towards me, so I shut the music out of my heart and concentrated instead on my friend and her new admirer.

One afternoon towards the end of April, Duke Ercole himself paid a visit and said he would speak with madonna privately. She might keep the black slave in attendance to see to her comfort, but he would have the rest of us dismissed. I went straight to Angela's and my chamber, where Angela lay curled on her bed, her knees drawn up almost to her chin, shivering despite the close warmth of the day. The air in the room smelled fetid and sung with the high whine of mosquitoes.

She had begun to complain the previous day of stomach cramps and feverishness. I had made little of it, thinking it was probably something she had eaten; a shellfish sauce had been served the evening before which smelled off to me, though my Jewish nose tended to be oversensitive to foods I had been brought up to believe forbidden. I had made her up an emetic of wine mixed with antimony powder begged from Don Alfonso's founding master then, once she had vomited, we accompanied Donna Lucrezia to watch the Saint George's Day races in the Barco. Angela remained uncharacteristically quiet, her face pale and pinched, taking no part in the betting of pennies and hairpins which madonna allowed because she could not see how betting with tokens of little value could be sinful. Even when a fight broke out between the winning jockey, in Donna Lucrezia's colours, of course, and the man whose horse had finished first, but riderless, she remained miserable and withdrawn, rocking back and forth where she sat, with her hands crossed over her belly. By evening, she could no longer conceal her distress and was excused by an anxious Donna Lucrezia.

"Go with her, Violante," she ordered me. "You have some knowledge of physick, I'm sure. It is customary in the education of your people, I think?" I had learned a little practical wisdom from Mariam, though probably no more than Donna Lucrezia herself, but the Gentiles tend to believe all Jews are doctors because doctors are usually the only Jews they will allow into their houses.

"Yes, madonna," I replied, and hurried to Angela's side.

We had a disturbed night, with Angela often groaning and writhing in pain, getting up frequently to relieve herself, saying she believed that would make her better, though it never did. Daylight brought no change; the little serving girl who brought our wine and biscuits and washing water looked shocked by Angela's grey, drawn face against the sweat-soaked pillow and carried out the chamberpot at arm's length as though it were contaminated. I was certain some poison was to blame, either from bad food or some more sinister source. Had Ippolito realised her feelings for Giulio? I wondered. But she insisted the pain felt more like that which heralded the onset of her monthlies, though worse, and the time was wrong.

"Could you be pregnant?" I asked, sitting on the edge of her bed in my wrapper, trying to coax her to take a little wine. If possible, her cheeks turned a shade paler.

She nodded miserably. "I've tried to be careful but mistakes happen."

"Angela, you haven't done something reckless, have you?" She screwed up her face to protest but I held up my hand to silence her. "I'm not going to give you a lecture. It's just that if you've taken something, you need to tell me so I can find an antidote."

"I'm such a fool. What am I going to do, Violante?" Wracked by another cramp, she curled up on her side and bit into her pillow.

"You must tell me what you've taken."

"I don't know. I got it from a woman in the Via dei Volte. Some dried leaves."

"Do you still have the packet? Is there any left?"

Angela shook her head, drawing her knees into her chest and squeezing her eyes shut in pain. "I burnt it. No one must know."

"That you're pregnant, or that you've tried to make yourself miscarry?"

"I don't know."

I was puzzled. "You used to say you wouldn't mind a child, once we were settled in Ferrara."

"But it's different now."

"Because of Giulio."

She nodded. "I love him, Violante; I want to marry him. When he looks at me he makes me feel…clean, pure, at the beginning of things. How could he look at me that way if I were lumbering around with Ippolito's child in my belly?"

"He must know. The feeling is all yours, Angela, not his. It's just what you imagine."

"Yes, well, you'd know plenty about love and imagination," she snapped back, her pain forgotten for the moment. "For you it exists entirely in the world of make believe."

I thought of Cesare's letter in the bottom of my trunk and drew strength from remembering his words. My pity for Angela helped me to answer calmly. "We aren't talking about me. The difficulty is yours. Have you and Giulio spoken? Have you a plan to extricate yourself from this affair with Ippolito?"

Again she shook her head. "I have told Lucrezia how I feel. It's impossible to speak privately to Giulio because he's so concerned to treat me honourably." At this she gave a wry laugh, before another wave of pain screwed her features into a frown. "And Ippolito is jealous. I am afraid of him, to tell the truth, and of the influence he has with Don Alfonso. They are the closest of all the brothers."

"And what does Lucrezia say?"

"That I should aim higher than the bastard and marry Ferrante."

"But Ferrante has no interest in the duties of a husband."

"Quite. Marry Ferrante and be Giulio's mistress, she says. That way Giulio's bastards become Ferrante's rightful heirs and everyone's happy."

"But she has no view about Ippolito?"

"I have never spoken to her about him, so she chooses to pretend she doesn't know about us."

"Perhaps you should take her advice and let her arrange a marriage with Ferrante. He would protect you from Ippolito, if it came to that."

"But it's not what I want. I want to start again. Giulio…he's like an angel, with those great violet eyes of his, and his voice. How could I think of dragging him into such a murky compromise?"

Before I could reply, Angela groaned and her face turned, if possible, even paler. When the pain eased, she pushed a hand between her thighs then held it out to me. Her fingers were smeared with blood. She gave a weak smile. "At least it's working."

Just then a soft knock came at our door; opening it, I found Catherinella standing outside, slightly breathless.

"You come," she said.

I felt cold and sweaty all at once, my bowels griped. What had happened? All this talk of miscarriages with Angela made me fear the worst. "What is it, Catherinella?"

"Chief summon you." By "chief," I assumed she meant the duke.

"But Donna Angela is unwell. She cannot come."

"Just you. The Jewess, he say, then my lady say, Monna Violante. Sound angry." She shrugged and muttered something in her own tongue.

"Angela," I said as I fished my shoes from under my bed. "Tell me where this woman is. Maybe I can get help."

"Somewhere near San Paolo."

"I'll go as soon as I can get away from Lucrezia."

"Say nothing to her."

"Not unless I have to," I promised. Because if Angela died, I could not let madonna believe her cousin had been poisoned. We were none of us secure until madonna was safely delivered of a son.

❦

A young woman I had not seen before was standing beside Duke Ercole when I entered the Camera Dal Pozzolo. As I dropped my curtsey to him, I noticed the uncomfortable shift of her feet beneath her none-too-rich skirt of scarlet wool. She had large feet, so it did not surprise me as I raised my eyes to see that she was tall, almost as tall, indeed, as the duke himself.

Duke Ercole, though powerfully built, had short, somewhat bowed legs and all his sons towered over him.

"This is Fidelma," said Donna Lucrezia, though she made no attempt to raise herself from the cushions supporting her back, and her tone was peevish and reluctant.

"She is to replace Donna Angela," added the duke. "You will take her under your wing, Monna Violante. She is a baptised Jewess like you."

How I managed to make sense of anything the duke said I do not know. Replace Angela? What was he thinking of? How could he? Angela was irreplaceable. Had the Este poisoned her after all, and whatever she had been sold by the crone on the Via dei Volte was merely masking the true cause of her sickness? But why? Perhaps Duke Ercole had decided the only way to turn the Borgia parvenue with her doubtful reputation into a wife worthy of his heir was to cut her off completely from her family. Donna Adriana and Cousin Geronima had already left; now it was Angela's turn.

Lovely, laughing Angela, who had so easily and generously filled my empty heart when I first joined Donna Lucrezia's household, who had listened with such patience to my lovelorn rantings about Cesare... Cesare. Would the duke try to keep him from Ferrara also? Surely his sister's marriage to Don Alfonso had drawn his teeth as far as the duke was concerned; he was unlikely to invade the duchy as long as his beloved Lucrezia presided over it. For a moment, I breathed easier until, mortified by my heart's selfishness, I recollected Angela as she had looked when I left her, curled tight around her pain, her belly cramped up with the effort of expelling her unwanted child.

If she lived, how could she return to Rome, disgraced, cast out from Donna Lucrezia's protection? If she lost the child, Ippolito would be under no obligation to her; even if she kept it, his father's hostility to her would make it difficult for him to acknowledge his bastard. As for Giulio, or Ferrante... Suddenly I saw what Duke Ercole was about, and that it had far more to do with the welfare of his sons than with asserting his authority over Donna Lucrezia.

I turned an appraising gaze on Fidelma. Thin, flat chested, with a pronounced bridge to her nose and a sallow complexion, she was certainly unlikely to replace Angela in the affections of Ippolito or Giulio. Or me. I looked away from her without so much as a smile, and tried to catch Donna Lucrezia's eye, but she and Catherinella were absorbed in re-arranging her cushions. I knew I must acknowledge the duke's instructions but I could not bring myself to do so; my head refused to bow, my mouth to form words of obedience.

All my life I had been obedient to the men who exercised authority over me. Staying behind in Toledo at my father's insistence, until it was too late to travel safely and I was forced to witness my mother's lonely, unnecessary death on the beach at Nettuno. Renouncing my own faith and family in favour of these Borgias with their dangerous charm, their plausible lies, and their inhumane religion. Even taking my vicious nickname because it was bestowed on me by a man.

My name. My real name.

I dropped to my knees in front of Duke Ercole; I bowed my head to the floor; I would have kissed the toe of his boot had he not hurriedly stepped back out of my reach.

"My lord duke," I began, straightening up. The duke gave a strangled cough; his face had turned the colour of *melanzana*. Perhaps my behaviour had brought on an apoplexy. So much the better. In the chaos that would ensue, I could slip away unnoticed to find the woman on the Via dei Volte. If Don Alfonso were duke, he would not banish Angela; he was too fond of his wife to treat her so cruelly.

But nothing happened so I was compelled to continue. "You know Violante is not my name, merely a jest whose origins do not matter here. My given name is Esther. I know you to be a devout man, so I do not have to remind you of Esther's story. I humble myself before you now as Queen Esther did before King Ahasuerus, to beg you to reconsider."

I was aware of Donna Lucrezia and Catherinella falling still behind me. The songs of birds, the cries of market traders, and the rattle of cartwheels over cobbles in the street below, all seemed muted by an immeasurable distance. In the silence of the room I could hear the whisper of the blood in my veins, the rasp of Duke Ercole's nail as he scratched his jaw with one crooked finger.

"Go on," said the duke, a note of mild amusement in his voice almost undermining my resolve.

I tried desperately to remember the instruction of my teacher of rhetoric. No time for *dispositio* or *elocutio* or *pronuntiatio*. I had to proceed straight to *actio* and hope to carry the day on the sincerity of my feelings. "I cannot offer you a banquet, or any other service a queen might offer her king. All the riches I can place at your feet, my lord, is my love for my mistress which emboldens me to seek her happiness. Donna Angela is her sister in all but birth, her closest kin and confidante. Your grace, you were blessed with so many brothers and sisters it is not possible to count them all. They are as the stars of the heavens and the sand upon the shore." I hoped he would appreciate the biblical allusion, even though it was from one of our books rather than one of the Christians'. "But my lady had only three brothers, and one of them is already dead, so I beseech you, do not take Donna Angela from her also."

I stole a glance at Duke Ercole, to see what impression I was making. He wore an expression of dispassionate tolerance, like an adult forced to sit through the party piece of a child for whom he does not much care. Then I must hope his ambitions for his line in the long term would outweigh his immediate concerns about his sons. "Especially in her present condition. At least wait until she is safely delivered of a son and heir for Don Alfonso." I was aware of some movement from Donna Lucrezia, a sigh, a rustle of silk as she shifted her position, but I dared not look round and kept my gaze fixed on the toes of Duke Ercole's black boots and my thoughts on Angela and the life bleeding from between her thighs.

"I fear Donna Lucrezia is more likely to be upset if Donna Angela stays in Ferrara than if she goes," said the duke, with a candour I had not expected.

"Honoured father…" began Donna Lucrezia, but I gestured to her to keep silent. If the duke were sufficiently rattled to disclose his hand, I must press home my advantage before he recovered his composure. Donna Lucrezia might discipline me for my lack of respect, but I doubted my punishment would be very harsh if I succeeded in pleading Angela's case.

"I cannot imagine anything calculated to upset madonna more than to be separated from her dear cousin, your grace, but if I cannot persuade you by that argument, consider this. Here before you you see the miracle of not one, but two, Jewesses brought to Christ, exulting in the opportunity to atone for the wickedness of their race. No doubt you have made many gifts to the Church in thanksgiving, but the truest and most valuable gift would be to exercise compassion in your heart for your daughter-in-law to whom you have entrusted the grave responsibility of overseeing Fidelma's and my journey towards salvation. Remember, my lord, that the Almighty sees beyond altar cloths and reliquaries, right into a man's soul, and that He values no gift, however rare or beautiful, if it is not given with a true heart."

I fell silent. My own heart thudded in my throat; I felt sick and shaky, so when the duke bade me rise, in a voice unsteady with emotion, I feared I was more likely to fall. Slowly, carefully, wobbling like an acrobat on a tightrope, I stood up.

"Look at me, girl." I lifted my eyes to his, pale and prominent, the whites yellowed and thickened with age. What had those eyes not seen? What thoughts and calculations, plans and dreams had they concealed or revealed over the long years of his life? For more than half of it he had lived abroad, passed over by his father, watching and waiting for his opportunity. Though no one spoke of it, everyone knew the exact spot in the *cortile* of the old Castello where he had had the block set up and his nephew, Niccolo, the chosen heir, beheaded. He might despatch a mere Jewess, a money lender's daughter, with no more care than he would slap away a mosquito. Thinking the worst calmed me; I waited with a dignity which would not have shamed a Christian martyr for my sentence to be pronounced.

"You have spoken well," he said, "and wisely. You are right. I have allowed matters which are immediate, and probably frivolous, to distract me from what is most important. Donna Angela may stay in Ferrara and in the meantime, I will entrust Fidelma to your particular care, for I think there is much you can teach her about being a Christian, and," he added, with a twist of his thin lips I took for a smile, "a courtier." Then he bowed to madonna and left the room, his page scurrying in front of him to open the door.

"Brava, brava," exclaimed Donna Lucrezia, clapping her hands, as soon as the door had closed behind him. "Oh, Violante, come here and let me kiss you." Bending over the daybed, I submitted to her embrace. I thought of Cesare as her lips brushed my cheek and her arms encircled my shoulders, about how often she must have kissed his cheek this way, how her lips carried the imprint of his skin, his beard, the fine bones beneath, and now her mouth carried the memory of my face to plant on his, and if she ever kissed me again, the whole cycle would start over.

"I hoped you would win him over," she said as she released me. "He is not such an ogre as he likes to think he is. Remember how thoughtful he was when my horse threw me during the welcome procession when we first arrived? And he had a mule brought straight away? He is a considerate old soul at bottom."

Oh yes, the duke was certainly considerate; once he had beheaded his nephew, he had ordered the head stitched back on and the corpse dressed for burial in gold brocade. "I am glad I managed to appeal to his soft side, madonna. I think we would both miss Donna Angela very much."

"Fidelma, stand a little way off. I would have some private words with Monna Violante."

Fidelma took a step back, trod on the hem of her skirt, and almost overbalanced. Madonna and I exchanged a look, then madonna rolled her eyes heavenward. "We shall have our work cut out with that one," she whispered. "Now, dear, tell me how Angela does?" After a short hesitation, she added, "Is she pregnant?"

"Madonna, I…"

"Come, girl, do you think I know nothing? She was lying with Ippolito long before we left Rome and I suppose it has started up again since he arrived in Ferrara. Or is it the other one? The beautiful bastard. I wouldn't blame her. He really is quite exquisite. I could be tempted myself if he weren't my brother-in-law. What about you, Violante? Could Don Giulio lead you astray, or do you still hold a candle for my brother?"

"You know I do, madonna," I confessed. She had never before spoken to me with such candour, and surely I owed it to her to be equally frank.

"His letter…encouraged you?"

"It did not discourage me."

"Well, that is…" She seemed to be casting about in her mind for the right word. "Good," she said eventually, though with a doubtful expression about her mouth and eyes. "But we were talking about Angela," she went on, with a little movement of her head as though to shake off rain. "Am I right about the cause of her indisposition?"

"Yes, madonna and, if you please..."

"And the father?"

"Cardinal Ippolito, she says."

"Do you believe her?"

"Yes, I do."

"Not that it matters. Either way, it is all a mess."

"I think it likely she will miscarry, madonna. I suppose that would make matters a little less messy."

Donna Lucrezia considered me with her grave, grey eyes. "You have an odd turn of phrase sometimes," she said, "for a young girl."

"I should return to her, madonna; she is really very unwell."

Again, she hesitated, her gaze raking my face as though she might find the solution to the problem of Angela there. "This is what will happen," she said finally. "Shortly I am to travel to Duke Ercole's country estate at Belriguardo. The air will be healthier there, now it is getting so warm. Don Giulio is to escort us, on his way to visit Donna Isabella in Mantua. Angela will not be fit to travel so I shall leave her behind, in your care. Do I make myself clear? My husband is going away on an embassy to the court of France. Ippolito will accompany him. That leaves only Ferrante, and Sigismondo, of course, in Ferrara. You have some influence with Ferrante, I think; he is fond of you. By the time we return, let us hope Angela's situation will look a little rosier."

She looked at me with eyebrows raised, as though awaiting my confirmation that her plan was a good one. Even while Angela lay suffering not more than twenty steps away, Donna Lucrezia was thinking of her own survival.

"I will do my best for her, madonna." We understood one another, Donna Lucrezia and I; we were both becoming adept at living cut off from our roots, like roses in bowls of sugar water.

❧

The Via dei Volte was so called because many of its tall, stooping houses had their upper floors built out to join one another, forming vaults over the street. Originally the main street of the merchants' quarter, it used to be kept lit night and day; there were still sconces fastened to many of the house fronts, though most were buckled and rusty. When Duke Ercole razed the old north walls to make room for the new quarter, the wealthier merchants moved out of their cramped, dark houses into modern palazzi bordering the Barco. The Via dei Volte, more a tunnel than a street in places, was now a run-down warren of cutthroats and cut-purses, cheap whores and old witches who helped them stay in business with their aphrodisiacs and abortifacients. It was no place for an unescorted lady, and I wondered at the desperation which had driven Angela there, and at my own foolhardiness.

I longed for Mariam as, with my hood drawn across my face as if I were one of the veiled women of the Mohametmen, and my torch held aloft like a sword, I hurried towards the church of San Paolo which backed on to the Via dei Volte. I had not put on pattens, because it was impossible to run, or even walk quickly, on the ungainly little stilts, and my shoes quickly became soaked in the foul porridge of piss and turds and rotting vegetables which overflowed the gutters. Squelching past an empty gong cart whose driver seemed to be engaged in placing bets on a couple of scrawny hounds fighting over what I hoped was an animal bone, I was tempted to berate the man for his idleness, but knew I had to avoid drawing attention to myself. Even my oldest cloak was attracting covetous looks.

Reaching the church, I was forced to slow down, to look for signs that might indicate the house of a cunning woman, though what these might be I could not imagine. Bunches of herbs pinned to the doorpost, perhaps? Arcane carvings on lintels, charmed stones? Mariam's image came to me as vividly as if one of the witches I was looking for had conjured her. I could hear her voice, prickly with scorn, see the pursing of her lips, the lines deep as scars beneath the dark down over her upper lip, listing remedies for fever. Wormwood, borage, marigold flowers, laburnum leaf. Laburnum leaf. Guaranteed to induce miscarriage, I had once been assured by Isotta de Mantova. So useful to know, she had said, with a world weary air, just in case. I would look for laburnum, or a picture of laburnum, or...what? The situation was hopeless.

Suddenly overcome with weariness, my wet feet frozen, I leaned against the high, blind wall of the church, heedless of dust from its peeling plaster sticking to my cloak, my hood slipping back as I raised my face towards the narrow strip of light between the buildings. My limbs shook so hard I feared I was coming down with some dreadful sickness breathed in from the fetid air. The stink of death and failure filled my nostrils. Angela had probably bled to death by now, alone, afraid, in terrible pain. After all she had done for me, what sort of friend had I turned out to be to her? What use my pretty speech to Duke Ercole? By the time I returned to the castle, I would probably find her bloody bed sheets had been stripped and burned and Fidelma's things laid out in place of her Venetian glass perfume bottle, her tortoiseshell hairbrush, the little silver tweezers I had used to pluck out her hair to please Ippolito.

I plunged my torch upside down into a misshapen sconce beside a rotting doorway. The rusty ironwork came away, leaving the torch to fizz and splutter in the drain, its heat intensifying the stench until it made me retch and spit bile. A rat scurried over my foot. As I straightened up from my bout of retching, what little light filtered down between the deep, dank arches was abruptly blocked out and I felt a hand on my shoulder, heavy and broad, with a firm grip. A man's hand. And suddenly I was not afraid any more, I was furious. I would be raped, probably murdered. The treasure I had been saving for Cesare, for my lover, would be stolen from me and I might die without ever knowing what it felt like to lie with him.

"Get away from me," I yelled, kicking out at the stranger's shins, twisting to loosen his grip on my shoulder. "I'm not alone, you know. There are people with me. Beware." I heard a sharp hiss of pain as my kick found its target. The man removed his hand from my shoulder, though the skin continued to burn where my struggles had chafed it.

"Violante?"

I knew that voice. As I pulled up my hood and straightened my cloak, I found myself looking into the incredulous eyes of Don Giulio.

"What on earth are you doing here?" he asked. He sounded angry, but his gaze was dark with worry. "This is no place for a young lady. I shudder to think what might have happened to you had I not found you. What can your mistress be thinking of to let you go roaming about like this without an escort?"

"She doesn't know," I said miserably.

"Ah, I see, you have come in search of the purveyors of love charms.

Something to try on Duke Valentino perhaps? I can see how you might want to keep that secret from Donna Lucrezia." He gave me a sympathetic smile as he stepped aside to make way for a donkey laden with firewood. To my astonishment, the urchin driving it saluted Don Giulio with his stick and Don Giulio nodded in return. "I have an interest in the chemical science," he explained. "That boy's father, being a woodsman, knows a great deal about the chemic properties of plants. It is for my garden," he added. "That is why I come here."

"And I…for Angela." There was something about Don Giulio, some air of candour in his broad, open face that made it impossible to lie to him. Perhaps his woodsman could help. Better for Angela to be disgraced in his eyes than dead through my neglect.

"I need not ask why, I suppose." A bitter twist briefly disfigured his beautiful mouth.

"She…she got something from a cunning woman near San Paolo, she said. And now…oh Giulio, she is terribly sick. I'm afraid she will die. I wanted to find the woman, to find out what she had given her and if there was any antidote."

"Take me to her." Turning to the servant who had accompanied him, he said, "Go to my house and tell Ser Pandolfo to come to the castle immediately. He will find me in the Torre Marchesana, in the duchess's apartments. Ser Pandolfo is my physician," he explained.

"You are very kind, my lord."

"It's quite simple, Violante. I love her. Nothing she has done could cause me as much pain as the thought of continuing to live in the world if she had left it."

❧

I thought she looked a little better when Giulio and I entered the room, and she had enough energy to protest at my bringing Giulio to her unannounced. Catherinella was sitting with her. The bed was made with clean linen, her hair had been brushed and her face washed. Though I realised all this must have been done at Donna Lucrezia's bidding, I was still somehow left with the impression that the power of Giulio's devotion had been at work. I could see they had much to say to one another, so dismissed Catherinella and went myself to wait in the courtyard for the arrival of Ser Pandolfo. By the time I returned, accompanied by the doctor and a servant bearing his case of cups and fleams, Angela appeared to be asleep, a faint smile on her lips and her fingers entwined in Giulio's.

"I think the worst is over," Giulio whispered as we entered the room, "but I will not leave her. I have sent word to Ferrante requesting him to take my place on the trip to Belriguardo. I will go to Mantua direct as soon as I can."

The following day, she was well enough to sit up and take a little chicken broth while Giulio read to her. In the afternoon, she even joined in when he and I sang part songs to while away the time. Now that Donna Lucrezia had left Ferrara, Giulio decided he would take Angela to his own palace to recuperate, with me to chaperone her. Giulio lived on the Corso degli Angeli, in the heart of the new city, where the roads were wide and a proliferation of parks and gardens sweetened the air. We were trying the life out of one of the household slaves, chopping and changing our minds about what gowns to take with us, when Angela suddenly complained of a headache and begged me to close the window shutters for she found the light unbearable. Brushing her hair back from her face, I felt her forehead, which was burning with a dry heat.

"I'll send the slave for water," I said. Angela had lost so much blood her body was struggling, in the summer heat, to restore itself to the cold, damp humour which Aristotle tells us is natural to women. "And send a messenger to me," I instructed the slave. "I will write to Giulio and tell him you're not fit to travel today after all. Perhaps tomorrow."

But we were not destined to travel the next day.

"The marsh fever," Giulio pronounced the minute he arrived, with Ser Pandolfo and his case of instruments in tow. His tone was bleak; he seemed to age before my eyes as he slumped against the doorpost and emptied his lungs in a long sigh. "Do what you can," he said to the doctor, though both of us knew there was little to be done but wait and hope.

"Do you pray for her?" Giulio asked me, on the third or fourth day of our vigil. She had fallen quiet by this time, exhausted almost into unconsciousness by bouts of vomiting and fits of fevered dementia during which her body thrashed, her eyes rolled into her head, and she yowled and shrieked like a cat in heat.

"Who to? I was taught that the God of the Christians is merciful and forgiving. Is this merciful and forgiving of him, what he has done to Angela?"

She had lost control of her bowels and the room stank, however frequently I changed her linen or lit fresh candles scented with ambergris and liquorice root to purge the air. Nobody else attended her but we two and Ser Pandolfo. The servants would not come near her for fear of infection, and many in the castle were sick already.

"You have spent too much time in the company of Valentino." Giulio gave a strained laugh which did nothing to lighten the atmosphere. "I hope you don't speak this way in my father's hearing."

Wishing I could bite back my words, so glib, so thoughtless, I fussed over Angela's covers to avoid having to look Giulio in the eye. He caught my hand, curled his fingers under my palm as I smoothed her quilt. "Pray for her," he pleaded. "The hardest won prayers mean the most to God."

How could he know that? I wondered. But the gentle directness of his nature made me want to please him, so I promised I would pray. I would not go to madonna's chapel in the Torre Marchesana, a cramped, claustrophobic little room without outside walls, where the perfume of incense and the gilded leer of the saints overpowered the spirit. I would go to the Lady Chapel in the cathedral, and contemplate the image I called to myself the Madonna of Strangers.

It was Catherinella who had first drawn my attention to her. Donna Lucrezia liked to attend services in the Lady Chapel; she shared with her father a particular devotion to the Virgin. And she liked to surround herself with her little clutch of heathens whom she was bringing to God. Fidelma would make a great show of her piety, word perfect in her prayers, anticipating faultlessly when to stand or kneel. Catherinella would stand behind madonna as always, straight and still as the pillars supporting the roof arches, her eyes fixed on some point in the middle distance, not even seeming to blink. I was generally distracted, watching the other people in the cathedral out of the corner of my eye. I know of no better place for watching people than a big Christian church, whose nave and transept are like a crossroads where men of affairs strike deals, mothers show off their marriageable daughters, and beggars play on the consciences of the rich.

But one morning during Lent, when the cathedral was uncharacteristically quiet, perhaps on account of the foul weather keeping people at home, their doors and windows shuttered against wind and rain, I had decided to amuse myself by trying to spot Catherinella moving. I made bets with myself, mostly to do with food for we had not yet broken our fast. If I saw her breathing, Donna Lucrezia would weaken and allow us morello preserves with our bread. If she blinked, the bread would be rye and moistened with nothing but a little oil. Thus it was, as I watched the bluish gleam of the whites of Catherinella's eyes in the weak, dusty light, my own gaze drew a bead along hers to fix on the framed image of the Madonna and Child. The Madonna wore an ornate crown and mantle of beaten gold, and her face, as well as that of the child in her arms, was black. Only then had I noticed Catherinella's faint smile, the expression of furtive recognition with which she regarded the black queen in her golden robe.

I do not know what made her black. Some fault in the pigment, perhaps, or smoke staining from the banks of candles which usually burnt before her, though not during Lent, blinding us to her true appearance. Perhaps, in the past, the faithful had been able to touch her and her face had been darkened by palmers' sweat, coin grime, the rank breath of beggars. For in the sight of our Father, we are all beggars. Her blackness comforted me, though; it made me feel there was a place after all in the house of the Christian God for oddities like Catherinella and me. It reminded me that Mary was a Jewish mother like mine, sometimes beatific in her selflessness and sometimes, no doubt, on preserving days or when the laundry refused to dry, a scold. She might tell me off for having knots in my hair or a hole in my stocking, but I could talk to her.

I would go now and talk to her about Angela. Except that I did not. With Giulio's remark still fresh in my mind, I stood before the little icon in its deep frame and thought about Cesare. So perhaps everything that happened next was my fault, because I prayed the wrong prayers and the black Madonna heard them and chose to answer them.

⟐

Angela grew weaker. When he could no longer find a vein to bleed, Ser Pandolfo applied his cups to her back. When the cup burns began to fester, Giulio threw him out. Angela slipped in and out of lucidity, her fevered brain careering along a switchback we struggled to follow. She would ask for water then accuse us of feeding her scorpions which stung her lips. She saw prison bars in the sunlight which seeped through the shutters and striped her bed, the ghosts of her long dead parents in the shadows which danced up the walls when we lit candles. She had drunk her mother's perfume, she said, she could smell it in her throat, and now her mother was angry, was reaching skeleton fingers down into her daughter's belly to get the perfume back. Her mother was screaming as the baby in Angela's belly bit off her finger end.

"She is dying," whispered Giulio, tears glazing his cheeks.

"We should send word to Donna Lucrezia," I said.

The torchbearer pushed open the door and stood aside with his head turned away from the room and his expression puckered in distaste. Donna Lucrezia marched past him without even slowing her pace, bringing into our stinking darkness the smells of fresh air and horses and warm dust. I noticed with alarm that she was dressed in Venetian breeches, with spurs buckled to her stout boots and a short whip still in her gloved hand. Surely she was mad to ride, with her child due in less than five months, and so fast. It was less than twenty-four hours since Giulio's messenger had left for Belriguardo. At least Don Alfonso was still abroad and need not hear of it.

"Thank God you came so quickly." Giulio jumped to his feet to greet her so his face was immediately plunged into shadow and only his hands reaching out to grasp Donna Lucrezia's, the nails bitten to the quick, showed in the jaundiced glow of the lantern on Angela's nightstand.

"How long has she been like this?" Donna Lucrezia made a brave attempt to sound calm, but a tremor in her voice made it plain how badly she was shaken, and how angry that she had not been called back sooner.

"She has had the best care we could give her. But many of the household are sick, the doctors too."

"Of course you have been wonderful," said Donna Lucrezia more gently, as though soothing a fretful child. She sat down beside Giulio on Angela's bed and stroked her cousin's matted hair back from her forehead. "But now you must rest, so she can see your smiling face as soon as she comes round. Violante and I will take care of her for you." Ladies-in-waiting are only servants in fancy gowns, after all; they do not need sleep.

Giulio rose, but looked at a loss as to what to do next. He started for the door, then hesitated. "I love her, Lucrezia. If she pulls through this, I would like very much your permission to marry her."

"Even though..?"

"She lost the child."

"Was it yours?"

He shook his head miserably. "I never wanted her for my mistress. But I would have cared for it. Everything that is Angela is precious to me. Everything." The love in his eyes as he looked down at the bed filled me with affection for him, yet sharpened by jealousy the way vinegar can bring out the sweetness of strawberries.

Was this how my lover would think and speak of me? When he came to Ferrara. As he surely must. And for a brief moment, in the tired, uncertain light, I saw his eyes, guarded and black, in place of Giulio's, the spare angles of his face superimposed on Giulio's cherubic oval, that dense, red river of hair flooding Giulio's soft, fair curls. I blinked, and there was Giulio, his hand resting on the door catch as he shouted for a link boy.

We had scarcely finished changing the sheets when we heard footsteps in the passage. Thinking it might be Giulio returning, I opened the door. Pushing me aside with such force I fell to my knees, Duke Ercole strode into the room. Donna Lucrezia had already begun to blow out the candles as the sky brightened from grey to aquamarine and the first birdsong wound its way into our hearing, and in the flat, ashy light the duke's face looked ancient, his cheeks yellow and sagging, his tortoise neck above the fur collar of his dressing robe crazed with lines and folds.

"When I woke and asked what the disturbance was, I hoped my servant had got it wrong," he said, his pale eyes fixed on Donna Lucrezia, absorbing every detail of her stained clothes, her dishevelled hair and delicate features pinched with exhaustion. He had spoken quietly, but now his voice became louder, harsh with indignation. "How could you act so irresponsibly? You are not a stupid woman. You must know there is one reason and one reason only why we tolerate you in this house and that is because you have proven your ability to bear healthy sons."

I saw madonna wince, stabbed, no doubt, by the memory of her beloved Rodrigo, hundreds of miles away in Naples, in the house of his aunt, the Princess Sancia. But all she said was, "I had thought there was another." She spoke softly.

"Eh?" said the duke, pulling at his ear.

"I had thought," madonna repeated, raising her voice, "that my father's son was as much a factor in my marriage as any possible sons of my own."

I felt my heart lurch and looked away. It was like being forced to witness some ritual of torture, where victim and torturer kept changing places in a kind of macabre dance. My eye was caught by a silver mirror hanging on the wall, in whose uneven surface I glimpsed, not my own reflection, but that of Donna Lucrezia, though so pared down to patterns of light and shade that it seemed more like a preliminary sketch of her face than the face itself, a silverpoint scribble dominated by cavernous eyes and a jaw set rigid with defiance. Her face? Or Cesare's? A scent of jasmine threaded its way through the stench of sickness, drawing me back to the palace garden in Urbino.

"You think we need protection from some hobbyhorse general like your brother, madam? We, the Este, who have been soldiers for two hundred years?"

Donna Lucrezia shrugged. "There are women of nobler birth than I who might have given Don Alfonso sons, though few as wealthy, I admit. Yet you were gracious enough to agree to my father's suit. And though I have tried my best to be a good wife to him and a good daughter to you, you have made it very clear to me you were not moved by any affection for my person." A lesser woman might have tried tears at this point, or spelled out the threat from Cesare more clearly, but Donna Lucrezia did neither. She merely left her words in the air, for the duke to make of them what he would. Released from the spell of the mirror, I watched him twisting this way and that, caught between greed and fear and his grudging admiration for his daughter-in-law. Then he seemed to spot a way out of the trap she had set him.

"If you would only be a little more yielding in certain matters." His tone was wheedling now, his anger suppressed. "Your household, for example, the suitability of your companions." His gaze slid lizard-like towards

Angela, whose teeth had begun to chatter convulsively despite the warmth of the morning and the bedclothes piled over her. I climbed cautiously to my feet, hoping the duke would not notice me. I needed to fetch warming pans, and more quilts, to sweat out the fever. But with a backward cutting motion of his flattened palm he commanded me to stay where I was.

Donna Lucrezia lifted her chin and smoothed her hair back from her forehead. "She was carrying your grandchild too, your grace."

I closed my eyes. Perhaps if I could not see what was happening, it would not happen. Madonna's disembodied voice, ringing like skates on ice, cut through Angela's moans and the silly cooing of doves in the gardens. "I had as much thought for the Este as for my dear cousin in wishing to help her."

Opening my eyes again, I watched Duke Ercole's fist, opening and closing as though he were trying to strangle a snake.

"Do you remember when you first came here?"

"It is not so long ago, your grace."

"I showed you the place where the Duchess Parisina was executed for her infidelity with her stepson. That was not for your entertainment, madam, but your edification and that of your…ladies." He spat the word, heavily seasoned with sarcasm, at Angela. Her half-open eyes rolled back in her head, though I am certain she had not heard a word he said.

"And with whom, exactly, is my cousin supposed to have been unfaithful? Neither Don Giulio nor his reverence the cardinal is married, though the cardinal, I grant you, should know better."

The duke snorted. "That's rich, coming from the pope's daughter."

I hoped she would say nothing of Giulio's honourable intentions or Angela's true feelings for him. Something told me the duke's humour would not be improved by the prospect of a second Borgia daughter-in-law. I need not have worried.

"But good enough for your son and heir, your grace. Perhaps his moral welfare matters less to you than that of the cardinal. Through the one you will ensure your position on earth, and through the other buy your seat among the saints." She glanced down at her belly with a resigned smile and spoke as if to the child inside her. "Well, we are all made use of by our fathers. It is the way of things. But sometimes I think we are more like the cards than the money they are played for. We have our own fate, independent of the players. You, little one, have your own fate, separate from mine, even before the cord is cut between us. What do you think, your grace?"

The duke cleared his throat and stared at his feet. Perhaps he even blushed, though it was no more than the natural colour of flesh creeping back into his grey cheeks and might have been more on account of the rising sun than any discomfiture on his part. But Donna Lucrezia had played a trump and she still held the ace in her womb. Who else, after all, could give the duke an heir but Don Alfonso? Ippolito, the bridegroom of the Church? Pox-brained Sigismondo or Ferrante with his harem of boys? Only Giulio, and he was not of the legitimate line.

"What do you need?" he growled, swivelling his head to include me in his question. "I will send help. Someone to watch Donna Angela while you get some rest. You must rest," he insisted, glaring at Donna Lucrezia.

"You're right, father, but perhaps later you would consent to accompany me to see Sister Osanna. My astrologer assures me I shall have a boy, but I should like to have the sister's opinion." Her smile was as sweet as must on a grape.

Duke Ercole smiled back, and only I saw how Donna Lucrezia's shoulders sagged as he closed the door behind him.

"Go to your room now," I said. "I will stay with Angela."

She yawned and nodded like a child made docile by fatigue. At the door she paused, reaching behind her back for the lacing of her bodice.

"I can't..."

"Let me loosen the top, madonna, then you can do the rest."

"Violante?" she asked over her shoulder while I worked at the laces.

"Yes, madonna?"

"What language do you dream in?"

"I...don't know, madonna. None that I can think of."

"I dream in Catalan. Strange, isn't it, considering I was born in Italy? Angela's the only person still close to me who does the same. Living close to me, I mean." So I would know there was another.

When she had gone, I closed the shutters against the foul air rising from the marshes with the sun. Pausing to tuck the bedclothes closer around the shivering Angela, I went in search of a servant to fetch the things I needed. I found a boy sleeping late beneath the stair foot at the base of the Torre Marchesana, kicked him awake, and told him I needed incense, and warming pans filled with olive pits from the heap Don Alfonso used to fire his kiln. Olive pits hold their heat longer than wood ash. His blank, sleepy stare inspired me with little confidence that he would fulfil my order. Then I remembered Mariam had packed what she called "a few necessaries" in the bottom of my trunk when I first left home for Santa Maria in Portico. Creams and suspensions in little blue glass jars, dried herbs in linen envelopes, they had remained where she had put them for, though I might look frail with my fine bones and fair complexion, my health was robust and I had never had need of them. There was bound to be something among them for breaking a fever.

But I was so tired my mind was blank, and the deeper into my memory I pursued their uses, the more elusive they became. I could do no more than identify lavender and spread some crushed leaves on Angela's pillow to aid peaceful sleep. Impatient to pack the rest of Mariam's mysteries away, so they would not remain in my sight to remind me of my inadequacy, I knocked one of the glass jars over, dislodging the stopper so the contents spilled in the base of my trunk. I lunged for Cesare's letter, though the jar held some viscous substance which crept only slowly over the red silk lining. Clove oil, I thought, inhaling its woody, spicy vapour as I righted the jar, good for toothache, and wondered, with the letter crushed in my other hand, if Mariam had provided a balm for a sore heart.

Though it was daylight, and the life of the castle in full spate beyond the bedchamber door and shuttered window, my body was telling me it was night and my mind responded with that bare truthfulness which can keep us awake during the hours of darkness. It was nearly half a year now since I had seen Cesare, and then he had ridden past me without a glance as our party waited to ride out of the Porta Pinciana. I should admit to myself I meant nothing to him, no more than any other pretty girl addled by his good looks and high station. I saw maidens like tall grass, and Cesare striding through them with a scythe, cutting some down, crushing others beneath the soles of his high black boots.

Yet I had his letter, in which he clearly said if he were to love anyone, it would be me. I did not question myself too closely about why he was not free, but satisfied myself with vague notions to do with the fact that he was married and also a soldier, liable at any moment to death or maiming. A true mistress must understand these things. She must have patience and forbearance and not badger her lover with demands nor seek to tie him down. And, if he were not free to love me, neither was he free to love anyone else. La Fiammetta, or the kidnapped Dorotea Caracciolo. So, drawing up a stool to Angela's bedside, with the letter in my hand, smoothing my thumb over the crumpled sheet, feeling the creases, and the sweeping indentations of his nib in the vellum, I composed myself to wait for my fortunes to change.

I must have slept, for the next thing I remember is a voice, low and hoarse, rasping against my ear with the insistence of a file.

"Violante? Violante?"

I lurched into wakefulness and stared at Angela. Was it a death rattle that had cut through my exhausted half-sleep? Darkness had descended beyond the shutters, and my eyes strained to see her.

"Why aren't you at Belriguardo?" she demanded, her voice, though weak, sounding perfectly lucid. "Or are you in disgrace too now, by association?" She attempted a smile, then frowned as her dry lips cracked with the effort. For a moment I could not speak, just sat there with tears of relief and self-pity sliding down my face and Cesare's letter clutched in my hand.

"What is it?" Angela persisted, looking from my wet cheeks to the letter and back again. "Has he written again? Has he said something to upset you?"

"You've been ill. That's why I'm here. Giulio sent a message to say you were dying. Donna Lucrezia came back...yesterday, I think. I'm supposed to take care of you and look at me just..." I could not say any more. I must light candles, give the patient water for her parched throat, check the warming pans, the bedding, her pads...But where to begin?

"Is there some water?" she asked, as though prompting me. "My mouth tastes like the floor of a piggery."

I poured water and held it to her lips. "The awful contemplation of death has done nothing to clean up your tongue, then."

She sipped from the cup then fell back against her pillows. "You say Giulio was here?" she asked, with a smile that seemed to seep into every corner of her thin, pale face. "You know, I remember almost nothing, except being able to see his face, all the time. I had dreams the colour of his eyes, in daylight, candlelight, and he smelled like honey."

I have heard tell of those who have come as close to death as a man's razor to the skin of his cheeks, and how they have seen the light of heaven at the end of a long tunnel, and inhaled the perfume of the land of milk and honey.

"He watched you without ceasing until madonna arrived. She packed him off to bed. He was worn out. Shall I send someone to let him know the crisis has passed?"

"Not yet. I must look a fright."

"You know that won't matter to Giulio."

"I can't see him," she said, as though that were the end of it, then added, "but I miss him."

"Do you think he has not seen you worse, while you were in your delirium? He has nursed you as tenderly as a mother." Even as I said it, I thought what a stupid, meaningless phrase it was. Mothers are fierce and angry, frustrated because they cannot live their children's lives for them and make their mistakes for them. Mothers die. "And he will not take it kindly if you refuse to see him. He will think you have rebuffed him."

"How can you be so wise and ingenious about the life of my heart when you crash about like a moth in a lantern when it comes to your own?"

I didn't know. How could I?

⟨⟩

Angela recovered quickly once her fever had broken, and plans were laid for madonna's court to remove to Belfiore. Madonna had hoped to return to Belriguardo, or to go to the summer villa at Medelana, but, although Ippolito's physicians believed either would be ideal for Angela's recovery, Giulio's doctors favoured less of a journey. Belfiore, standing on an island in the Barco, within the confines of the city but away from the heat and foul air of the old quarter surrounding the castle, was their preferred option. Besides, the duke had just told Pietro Bembo he could go to Belriguardo to be able to work on his verses in peace, and the muse of so great a poet must not be frightened off by a gaggle of chattering women and their attendants.

The white marble façade of Belfiore was so perfectly mirrored in the still waters of the lake on the afternoon of our crossing that it seemed like a drowned twin of itself, a replica built by meticulous Nereids. But madonna was ill-disposed towards it even before we arrived on account of a series of rooms decorated with frescoes celebrating the accomplishments of her husband's mother, the Duchess Eleanora. It was all very well, she snapped, to remind her the duchess had been a Spaniard like herself and, like herself, a member of the royal house of Aragon, but it would curdle her stomach and addle her brain to live among constant reminders of the duchess's excellence at chess, at music, at dancing. Then she laughed. And at feasting; apparently the duchess had been very fat, like her daughter, Donna Isabella.

"Do you suppose," she whispered, dropping back level with me as we walked though these rooms, which ran along the west side of the palace and glowed now in the last glory of the sun before it sank into the lake, "old Ercole had to mount her doggy fashion? Or d'you think he's enough of a man to have reached round that belly?" She had become flatteringly familiar with me since Angela's illness, in the belief that I had somehow cured her.

I laughed.

"What's the joke?" demanded Angela, twisting round in the wheeled chair in which I was pushing her. "Oh I do so hate being stuck down here with the dogs and the midgets!"

I leaned down and told her, adding, "You and madonna would know more about the Este men and their capabilities than I would, my dear."

Angela launched into a vigorous defence of her virtue where Giulio was concerned, at which her cousin scoffed merrily, dropping nuggets of intimate information about Don Alfonso designed to trap Angela into her own revelations. Our laughter bounced off rotund Duchess Eleanora and her court. A spirit of scurrilous mockery scampered ahead of us along the gallery, only to be brought up short by the appearance of a procession of servants carrying our luggage in from the flotilla of barges moored to the palace jetty. Angela shrieked, but Donna Lucrezia told her to calm down before she made herself ill again. Servants had no more consequence than walls, nor any better hearing neither. A disingenuous statement, I thought, from a woman who had grown up among the labyrinthine intrigues of the Vatican.

⬥⬥⬥

Spring turned to summer and we became well settled at Belfiore. As the child swelled in her belly, Donna Lucrezia grew stronger, more confident of carrying the baby to term and giving Don Alfonso the son who would cement her position as the proper heir to the ubiquitous Duchess Eleanora. She joked that she was even beginning to acquire a girth to match her mother-in-law's, or perhaps that of the elephant whose visit to Ferrara was commemorated on the walls of the Sala del'Elefante.

Angela too began to regain her health, though it was a slow process, so weakened was her blood by the fever following hard on her miscarriage. She remained thin and feeble, unable to take more than broths and syllabubs and in need of a great deal of rest. Our routine was relaxed. We took picnics out on the lake, listened to music in the garden in the evenings, the notes floating on air heavy with the scent of night stocks and heliotropes, and the incense candles we burned to ward off mosquitoes. We played cards, devised masques, and traded jokes with Gatto, Perro, and La Fertella. Being a household of women, except for the clowns, our chaplains, and Fonsi the dog, we spent most of our time drifting about informally in loose clothes, arming ourselves in our corsetry for only a very few formal events.

Don Alfonso remained at the French court, so our only regular gentleman visitor was Giulio, who would have stayed, I am sure, had his father permitted it. As it was, he was rarely accompanied by even so much as oarsmen to row him, slipping discreetly from the old landing stage on the city side where the game carcasses were landed after hunts in the Barco. Angela was convinced his little craft would be capsized by the slightest breeze and he would either drown or be eaten by descendants of the great worms with which Duke Niccolo had stocked the lake in the days when it stood outside the city boundary and formed part of its defences. Angela believed in the worms with an unshakeable conviction, despite the many and various fish the lake offered up for our table on fast days. Her illness had left her credulous, and the hostility she and Giulio had aroused by falling in love had convinced her the whole world was conspiring to do him harm.

There is a certain kind of febrile, adulatory love which sees its object as impossibly fragile, not made to withstand the rough and tumble of life and the everyday living of it. Such a love was as much abroad as the marsh fever that summer.

Seated in the loggia on the roof one morning, working at my corner of an altar cloth Donna Lucrezia had promised for the cathedral in gratitude for Angela's recovery, I turned aside to rest my eyes from the close work for a moment, and caught sight of Angela and Giulio in the garden. The loggia faced north and east, away from Ferrara, so we could not have seen his boat crossing the lake from its vantage point. She lay on a cushioned marble bench beneath the shade of a chestnut tree. Her face was fitfully veiled as its leaves shuffled and slid over one another in the morning breeze from the lake. Giulio perched beside her on an arm of the bench, with a book open in his lap. The jewels in its binding flashed from time to time as he picked it up and, I suppose, read to her from it. Perhaps that was why the scene had caught my eye.

I envied her her simple good fortune in being able to sit in a sunny garden and listen to her lover read, to smell the sunlight in his hair and feel the warmth of his body filling the small, complicated space between them, to savour the unique cadences of his voice. With a sensation that felt like an infidelity, I realised I could no longer hear Cesare's voice. And the more I tried to conjure it, the more the memory of it fell apart, crumbling the way the old Moorish brick in Toledo used to if you brushed against it, staining your hand or your skirt desert red, the ancient buildings eaten away by the homesickness of the men who built them.

"Leave your work awhile, Violante. Rest your eyes." It was not until Donna Lucrezia spoke to me, and the musicians who had been entertaining us with lute and theorbo suspended their playing, I realised my eyes were full of tears and madonna must have noticed me rubbing them. The back of the hand in which I held my needle was slick with moisture; I might have put out my eye, or left the stain of my tears on the altar cloth.

"Yes, madonna." Her slight, kind smile swam in my vision.

"Go and fetch cousin Angela. Her convalescence is making her lazy."

Polite laughter from the rest of the women, a jagged, butterfly flight from one to the next.

"Yes, madonna."

By the time I had made my way down four flights of stairs to the garden, hotly pursued by a wheezing Fonsi, Angela and Giulio were no longer alone. Cardinal Ippolito had joined them, his robes fairly pulsing scarlet in the sun's glare. Giulio had discarded his book and risen to face his brother. It was obvious the two men were arguing. Not wishing to trespass on a family squabble, I scooped up the little dog and withdrew behind a trellis of honeysuckle bordering the knot garden. I did not mean to eavesdrop, but it was impossible not to hear their raised voices.

"I haven't crossed the lake in this heat to be ignored," yelled Ippolito, sounding, I imagined, much as he must have done in the nursery when thwarted by his brothers and sisters. "Our father summons you back to Ferrara."

"Oh, he's always trying to draw me away from here. He doesn't mean it." Giulio sounded unconcerned; nothing mattered to him that summer but Angela and her restoration to health.

"He does this time. An embassy has come from Florence. There is to be a family council."

"Well I am not family as such, am I? It is your council he wants, and Ferrante's, probably even Sigismondo's before he would consult me."

Ippolito's soutane hissed against the gravel path as he paced. "Stop being petulant, Giulio. You know he loves you."

"Of course he loves me. He loved my mother, which is more than he did yours, I dare say. But that doesn't mean he values my opinion. No royal blood of Aragon runs in my veins."

"Giulio, I must speak with you privately."

Giulio laughed, a harsh, uncharacteristic sound which made Fonsi whimper and wriggle in my arms. "Surely we three have no secrets from one another."

"Giulio…" Angela's voice sounded weak and plaintive.

"I mean it. Anything you have to say to me you can say to Donna Angela."

"Angela…my dear." The term of endearment seemed to fit awkwardly in

Ippolito's mouth. I was surprised, for it did not seem to me this argument was really about whether or not Duke Ercole required all his sons to meet an emissary from Florence. "It is not that I wish to have secrets from you...after all we've...suffered together." His words sounded as though he had plucked them from thorny bushes. Once again that laugh from Giulio and the dog squirming in my arms. "It is not you," Ippolito ploughed on, "so much as your...family."

Now it was Angela's turn to laugh, her voice sounding stronger, I thought, than it had in many weeks. "Ah, I see," she said, her tone as warm as the sun on my back. "What's he done this time, then, that cousin of mine? Invaded Florence?"

I heard scuffling, effortful grunts from the two men and a quickly curtailed shriek from Angela, but I dared not look out from my hiding place. This talk had gone too far for my eavesdropping to be construed as accidental or innocent.

"What do you know?" demanded Ippolito. "What has he told you?"

"Take your hands off her," shouted Giulio.

"Nothing," said Angela. "You're more of a fool than I gave you credit for if you believe Cesare confides in me. He's as close with his thinking as a Jew with his purse."

I winced.

"You see?" mocked Ippolito. "She likes a bit of rough handling. It merely serves to taper her wit."

A sharp smack followed by a silence which lasted just a little too long. I clamped my hand over the dog's nose to quiet his whimpering.

"Dammit, that's a tooth," said Ippolito, slurring his words like an old man who has suffered a seizure.

"Oh Giulio, now how will you play your lute for me. Look at your knuckles. You must let me bathe them."

"Ask our new duchess, Ippolito; she has more letters from her brother than she does from ours. He must say something of his plans in them, for what else has he in his life but this hunger to devour Italy?"

"You think he would move while Alfonso and our brother-in-law Gonzaga are at the French court? You're a fool. He depends on Louis for half his army and the money to pay them with."

"Even if Alfonso and Francesco have Louis's ear, they say Valentino is prepared to tickle more persuasive parts."

"Oh really, what nonsense. My late cousin Juan, possibly, but not Cesare."

"Do they?" persisted Ippolito, taking no notice of Angela's defence of Cesare's virtue. "And who are they? Ferrante's kitchen maids?"

Like a plump, fur-coated trout, Fonsi twisted out of my arms and flopped to the ground, galloping as fast as his stubby legs would carry him towards Angela and Giulio. There was nothing for it but to follow him and hope they did not realise I had heard the entire exchange. Angela crouched to pet the dog, but looked up at me. Though her eyes were shadowed by the broad brim of her sun hat, I could tell immediately, from a slight deepening of the lines bracketing her mouth which had developed since her illness, that she knew I had heard everything.

"Sorry," she whispered. "For the Jew joke," she elaborated, seeing my frown of incomprehension.

I stooped to retrieve the dog. In the moment when her face and mine were as close as the brim of her hat would allow, I asked, "Why should that offend me?" I straightened up, to see Giulio glowering at me, cradling his bruised knuckles in the palm of his other hand.

"She must have heard everything," he said to his brother, who came up beside him rubbing his jaw, which was already so swollen it had pulled his neat beard out of shape. Blood from his mouth made a splash of darker red against the scarlet breast of his soutane. Walking straight past Giulio without a glance, Ippolito put himself so close to me I could smell the blood on his breath.

"Are you Valentino's spy, girl?" His words came slurred as a drunk's from his misshapen mouth. Afraid he would lay hands on me, I clutched Fonsi in front of me like a shield; if nothing else, his teeth were sharp and his temperament possessive. On cue, the little dog gave a high-pitched snarl, a sound like rice rattling into a metal dish, and I saw laughter welling in Ippolito's dark eyes. His lips twitched; he winced and turned from me. "Be assured I shall be watching you from now on. And if you were thinking of getting word to him, remember how easy it is for a messenger to miss his way among our marshes. You would do well to remind your mistress the same. Giulio, the boat will leave in ten minutes. Be there."

I turned towards the house but Giulio, taking no notice of his brother's command, brought a hard hand down on my shoulder and twisted me around to face him. Fonsi fell into a frenzy of yapping. Angela took him from me, stroking his head and making cooing sounds over him until he quietened and nestled, snuffling in her arms.

"Is it true?"

"That I am Duke Valentino's spy? No, Giulio, it is not." Until now I had been buoyed up on some spurious elation, flattered that Ippolito should imagine Cesare would trust me enough to spy for him. Now, as Giulio raised the possibility for examination, it was bitterly clear to me how absurd a suggestion it was. "He could invade Ferrara this afternoon and I most likely wouldn't know until next week," I added, feeling a tide of black bile spread through my body. The concern in Angela's eyes, her Borgia eyes, made me feel worse.

"But you see his letters to the duchess?" he persisted.

"She sees as much of them as the rest of us," snapped Angela. "She sees rolled vellum and a red seal dangling from a purple ribbon. What transpires between my lady and her brother is anybody's guess." I thought she was lying, but about what I had no idea, and I was grateful for her intervention, for making me look less of a fool. I nodded my agreement.

"Now we must see to your hand before it stiffens up completely."

With some unworthy pun on stiffening extremities, Giulio allowed himself to be led away, leaving me to return to my needlework, an abandoned Fonsi trailing on my heels. As Angela and Giulio were swallowed up by the dense shade of the cloistered arcade running along outside the Sala del' Elefante, the garden seemed suddenly, shockingly empty. Not even the creak of a wheelbarrow or the oiled snip of shears interrupted the heavy silence. There was no breeze to tickle the lake into laughter or set the chestnut whispering, no music from the birds roosting through the heat of the day. From this side of the house I could not even hear the racket from the kitchen as the day meal was prepared. I was sunk in a bright dungeon of heat, the sun hammering on my head and scalding my lungs as I breathed, the edges of my corset chafing under my arms where my sweat-soaked shift had bunched into a swab of wet linen.

I didn't care if Cesare invaded Florence, or Milan, or Venice, or the

Holy Roman Empire itself. I just wished he would get whatever he had planned over and done with and come here, and fill this dull Ferrarese court with jokes, intrigue, Spanish music, and all-night card games. I would personally climb that damned chestnut tree to pick its spiny fruit for a chance to watch him throw back his head and laugh at the sight of naked whores crawling among lamp stands in pursuit of it. Closing my eyes I could glimpse the point of his tongue caught between his white teeth, smell the perfume released by his hair as it tumbled down his back. Jasmine, olives, the salt air from Ostia when the wind blew from the west, and something secret and feral that was unique to him, the truth of him, perhaps. Or perhaps my famished memory suffering the delusions of hunger.

Well, my wish was granted, but, as is the case with all the best wishes, not in quite the way I had imagined when I made it.

⨒

Though we all retired to our rooms during the hottest part of the day, Angela did not join me in our chamber. She was, I suppose, giving Giulio's bruised knuckles her undivided attention. It did not occur to me for one moment that Giulio might actually have taken up Ippolito's instruction to return to the city; his status as the bastard of a much loved mistress made him a slippery eel to catch. By rights Fidelma should also have had her bed in our room, but whatever differences had emerged between Angela and I since we came to Ferrara, we were of exactly the same mind about Fidelma. She was humourless, pious, and not to be trusted. Any confidence shared with Fidelma would bounce off her like water off hot steel, to land heaven knew where and in what misconstruable fragments. We made sure there was no room for her in our chamber.

Was it Angela's urgent whisper, her hand rattling my shoulder as though it were a stuck lock, that woke me? Or had I come to my senses seconds before, roused by the cacophony of screaming, cursing, breaking glass, and wood splintering.

"Violante. Wake up. I need your help with Lucrezia."

"What's happened?" My eyes felt swollen and gritty, my head full of furry mould that had leaked into my mouth.

"She's had a letter from Cesare."

My heart seemed to squeeze shut like a fist. "Is he dead?"

"Oh God give me strength. I said from him, not about him."

"Sorry, sorry." I shook my head, rubbed my eyes. A torrent of Donna Lucrezia's Catalan reached my ears from somewhere along the passage outside.

"He's taken Urbino."

"Urbino?"

"Exactly," said Angela, utterly misinterpreting the shock I could not keep out of my voice. "He's totally overstepped the mark. Guidobaldo's a popular ruler. Good God, he was even Uncle Rodrigo's Gonfalonier himself at one time. And his wife is Donna Isabella's sister-in-law. Lucrezia's raging. If we can't do something to calm her, I'm afraid for the baby."

But, though I went through the motions of tightening my bodice, pushing my feet into my shoes, hurrying after Angela, my thoughts were all centred on myself and my curious experience in the palace garden at Urbino. Had I known all along? Should I have told what I knew? No one would have believed me. I would have been dismissed as Angela dismissed me, as a moonstruck girl, sick with unrequited passion. Besides, what would I have had to tell? A mere whispered nonsense, a wraith of perfume, a breath which might have been no more than the winter breeze.

We found Donna Lucrezia stalking the broad, arcaded walkway before the door to her private apartments. The sinking sun cast long bars of shadow which she crossed and re-crossed, a prisoner of the fury that shook her body as though it were possessed of a demon. Her hair hung in her eyes, her clothes were torn, the backs of her hands scored with bloody scratches. Her stockinged feet crunched heedlessly over shards of glass and pottery, splinters of wood from a broken stool whose leather upholstered seat now balanced precariously on the balustrade running along the open side of the passage.

"She is mad," I muttered to Angela. "There is nothing we can do. We must fetch her doctor. Or a priest," I added, feeling myself blush.

Angela shook her head. "We must just calm her down. Take her arm one side and I'll take the other. If we can just get her to stand still long enough to listen to reason."

I doubted mere reason could make any impression on her, but lunged towards madonna as her steps turned in my direction, in an attempt to grab hold of one of her flailing arms. Seeing me, she stopped dead in her tracks.

"You," she growled, in the eerie voice of a fighting cat. She brought her arm down and pointed at me, jabbing at my chest with a finger whose nail was as ragged as a scullery maid's. "Come with me."

I looked at Angela. She shrugged. Terrified, I followed Donna Lucrezia into her apartments.

The rooms looked as though they had been sacked. Curtains had been torn down from the windows and lay strewn across the floor among clothes, jewels, and more broken glass and pottery. Bloody footprints marked everything like an angry skin rash.

"Do you know what he's done?" she demanded, turning on me before I had any chance to close the door to the little antechamber into which I had followed her. Neither Catherinella nor any of the other servants was anywhere to be seen. I could hear Fonsi whimpering somewhere, but I could not see him and did not dare call out to him.

"N…no, madonna." Why was she asking me? Did she know what had happened in Urbino, or was her question merely a rhetorical device?

She seemed not to have heard my reply. "He promised," she went on, speaking now almost in a whisper, shaking her head with a terrible, weary sadness. Then, "You promised!" she shrieked, her gaze fixed on me so for a moment I was scouring my memory for some promise I had made and failed to fulfil, until I realised she did not see me at all.

"At Nepi. You promised, you swore you wouldn't interfere." She began pacing again, printing more blood spatters over the ones already drying on the torn curtains, clawing at her ears and tangled hair as though some foreign body were lodged in her head and she was trying to tear it out. Her fingers were soon bound as fast in long strands of pale hair as silk worms in their cocoons. I feared for her eyes. "Why won't you leave me alone? Leave me, let me get on with it, I can do it. Trust me. Is it the boy? Is that why?"

At the mention of the boy she became suddenly calm. So, I realised with relief, she was not so deranged by the news from Urbino she had forgotten her responsibility to her unborn child. "It's too soon," she said, staring directly at me, hands folded over the rise of her belly.

"Are you in pain, madonna? Perhaps you should lie down." Though if her bed chamber was in anything like the same mess as this, God alone knew where she could lie. "I will send for the physician." I stepped forward and tried to take her arm, but she shook me free with a grunt of impatience.

Casting her eyes around the room as though she were seeing the chaos for the first time, she said, "I want you to see something." She lifted a torn-down wall hanging to reveal the bureau where she kept her correspondence; balanced now on three good legs, it wobbled as the weight of the hanging was shifted from it and a half folded parchment slid to the floor. With an effort, Donna Lucrezia stooped to pick it up and handed it to me.

"Read," she commanded.

The document was in a hand I did not recognise, though measured and careful, the hand of a scribe.

"Read," Donna Lucrezia repeated, "out loud."

"'This lord,'" I read, "'is truly splendid and magnificent, and in war there is no enterprise so great that it does not appear small to him; in the pursuit of glory and lands he never rests nor recognises fatigue or danger. He arrives in one place before it is known...'"

"Yes, yes, that's enough. He sent it as a joke, you see."

I frowned. I did not see. Donna Lucrezia sighed, and explained. "It is a report from the Florentine embassy which came to him at Urbino. He had the messenger intercepted and the report copied. He sent it, he says, for my amusement, that I might see how easily he had charmed the 'maidenly republicans,' he called them. You see, he takes nothing seriously, Violante. What am I to do?"

"You must write and tell him your mind, madonna. If he understands how he has hurt you, he will withdraw from Urbino; I am certain of it."

Though tears were sliding down her face, carving salt channels through the scratches on her cheeks so I marvelled they did not seem to sting her, she laughed at this. "If he had any consideration for me, he would not have taken it in the first place. The Montefeltri are my family now, and they were forced to flee with nothing but the clothes on their backs, according to Donna Isabella, who has taken them in."

"Cesare is your family also, madonna," I ventured.

"Cesare is..." Now she began to cry in earnest, greedy, gulping sobs that threatened to use up all the air in the darkening room. "The very devil," she wailed, stringing out the syllables of the word as though making a sound picture of the devil's own tail. She began once again her pantomime of pacing, scratching, tearing at her hair, and muttering about Nepi, and, without waiting to be dismissed, I fled to get help.

"Why does she keep talking about Nepi?" I asked Angela as we hurried in search of madonna's cowering servants and shooed them back to restore order.

"Nepi?" Angela looked puzzled. "You, there, find madonna's chaplain. And the physician. Go!" she roared at a scrawny boy I thought I might have seen with Ferrante. "Nepi," she repeated, in a tone of dawning understanding. "Lucrezia fled there with Rodrigo after his father was murdered. He was only a baby, and everyone knew Cesare had killed Alfonso of Bisceglie. Not with his own hands, but as good as. Michelotto," she mouthed, not quite prepared to release the feared name into the balmy evening air of Belfiore. "Lucrezia was heartbroken. She swore she would never speak to Cesare again. A few weeks later, Cesare stopped over at Nepi on his way to Cesena to join his army. No one knows what happened, except that Lucrezia returned to Rome all sweetness and light and life carried on as though Alfonso had never existed." She shrugged. "That's all I can think of."

❧

Though Donna Lucrezia ceased her ravings, and waited with the docility of a child who knows she has been naughty and strives to make amends while her servants made good the damage to her rooms, restoring upset furniture and torn down hangings where they could, consigning the rest to a bonfire beside the muck heap at the back of the stable yard, she was clearly not herself. She fainted while making confession in the ducal chapel. Her physician pronounced that she was running a fever, for which he bled her, and recommended complete bed rest for at least a week. Madonna, however, was having none of it, insisting upon an immediate return to Ferrara. No doubt Angela had reported to her the uneasiness of Ippolito and Giulio and, with her husband in Milan with the French court, and Duke Ercole said to be on his way there in response to Cesare's invasion of Urbino, she was determined to secure her position as duchess.

"What if the journey puts the child at risk, madonna?" I remonstrated with her as I supervised the packing of her wardrobe and she lay on her bed, her swollen feet, clad in purple silk stockings, as round and shiny as *melanzane*.

"If I am to lose the child, it must be in Ferrara," she replied. "I am far enough advanced now for it to be seen to have been a boy." The weather had turned. A flat, grey light filtered through fine drizzle, in harmony with her pallor and the determined lines drawing her mouth down towards her jaw. I had rarely seen her father without a smile on his face, yet in repose, this is what he looked like, fleshy and ruthless, sentimental and without conscience. I determined to say no more. For one reason or another, God was bound to be watching Donna Lucrezia.

# CHAPTER 8

*You are my first and last and only love.*

It began with a member of the duke's chapel choir. We were attending a service to celebrate one of the innumerable saints' days which claimed our obligation. If I had known what would result from this particular Mass, perhaps I would have remembered which it was, and burned candles, or named a child in his honour.

But all I knew was that the day was hot, and the incense-laden air of the chapel stifling almost beyond endurance. My fan seemed to raise the temperature rather than reduce the stuffiness, the way stirring a cauldron serves to release clouds of steam. How Donna Lucrezia could breathe through the heavy veil covering her scarred face, I could not imagine. I tried to concentrate on the service, but found my attention fixed instead on the dark patches of sweat beneath the choir master's arms, rhythmically appearing and disappearing as he conducted the singers; on a single dust mote standing in the hard stream of light from the chapel windows.

Suddenly there was a commotion in the choir. A boy, his sweat-shining face like polished ivory, dropped to his knees and slumped sideways. The music faltered, stumbled. With a series of rapid, emphatic hand movements the master steered them back on track. A couple of acolytes, feet tangled in their lace-trimmed albs, hauled the boy off through the door to the baptistry. Our worship continued unabated, and I felt sharper now, as though the faintness I had been experiencing had engulfed the choir boy instead. When we heard later that he had died, an irrational and unexpected sense of guilt overcame me, almost as if his death had been meant for me.

We began to hear of more deaths. The fever started like marsh fever, with sweating and shaking and aches in the joints, but within hours the victims were seized with vomiting so severe it tore their vitals and left them bleeding from every orifice. Though the quarters in the Corte Vecchio set aside for the choir were thoroughly cleaned with hot water, and pomanders of ambergris and camphor hung from the roof beams, two more boys fell ill. The passage linking the castle to the Corte Vecchio was locked, and incense set to burn before the gate, but even so, Donna Lucrezia's doctors stepped up their campaign to persuade her to leave the city once again. Don Alfonso was sent for from Milan, however, and she was determined to see him and take his advice.

He and his father reached Ferrara about two weeks after the death of the choir boy, by which time the dead carts were collecting bodies from outside most of the humbler doors of the city each morning, and an intrepid group of Franciscan friars had begun to hold mass funerals on the edges of the lime pits which had been dug outside the Porta degli Angeli to receive the dead. The lay clergy had retreated within the walls of the cathedral, where masses were sung continually and those who could came to beseech San Giorgio to fight off the dragon of infection and San Maurelio to absolve them of whatever sins had brought this calamity upon them.

Don Alfonso let it be known he would see his wife once he had met with the city council to see what might be done to alleviate the people's suffering and slow down the rate of infection. That gave us three or four hours' grace to devise some means of disguising the scratches which still scarred madonna's face. Lead powder was Angela's solution, but not too thick, I warned, or Don Alfonso would think madonna sick of the fever also. Elisabetta Senese set to work with pestle and mortar to concoct a paste of lead powder, carmine, and rose oil which would match madonna's own complexion. Madonna, meanwhile, to my unease, spent an hour closeted with Fidelma.

When Don Alfonso arrived in madonna's apartments, he was still in his travel clothes, though he had made a cursory attempt at washing his face and hands and had beaten the worst of the dust from his cloak and boots. Like an artist's sketch half erased, he wore a smudged, unfinished air, his eyes distracted and unfocused, his mouth working with anxiety. When madonna, accompanied by Fidelma, came through from her dressing chamber to the Camera Dal Pozzolo, her face was unveiled and bare of makeup. I heard Angela, beside me, catch her breath, sensed her draw her hood closer over her head. Don Alfonso stared at his wife, the hand he had lifted to kiss stranded in his great paw with its grimy fingernails. Recollecting himself, he bowed, let his beard brush the back of madonna's hand, then straightened up and glared around the room at us as though he wished we would melt into the walls.

He said nothing, however, so we remained where we were.

"What the devil have you done to your face, wife?" he demanded. "Looks as though you've been in a tavern brawl. Or got at by Sigismondo's rats." He gave an uncertain laugh. Donna Lucrezia smiled a holy virgin's smile, but said nothing.

"Well?" said Don Alfonso. Madonna's gaze flicked nervously towards Fidelma. Whatever they had planned was clearly not equal to the occasion. There was nothing for it, I thought, stepping forward, but to rely on my status as Angela's saviour and Cesare's inamorata, and erect a truth on this foundation of lies and wishful thinking.

"My lady was so mortified by the Duke of Romagna's actions towards your family in Urbino, she inflicted these wounds on herself out of grief." Let him draw his own conclusions as to her reasons for that grief; the grief itself was genuine enough.

"I did not give you leave to speak, Violante. But what she says is true, husband." She knelt, leaning on Fidelma for support. "Forgive me. I should have thought of your displeasure at seeing me so."

"Get up, woman." It relieved me to hear how his gruff tone wavered towards sentimental tearfulness, and warmed my heart to see how he batted away Fidelma's hand to help madonna to her feet himself. We can keep her feet hidden, I thought, my mind racing ahead, for he will not be bedding her again until the child is born. Though the low bawdy houses he preferred were bound to be full of the sickness so we would have to ensure the right kinds of girls, plump and on the coarse side, capable of gutting a capon or tickling the master's cock with the same cheerful competence, were put in his way as a line of defence for our lady.

Husband and wife dined together that evening, but then Don Alfonso went straight into conference with his father, Ferrante, and Giulio to plan their campaign against the fever. The city was placed under siege. No one was allowed in for fear of bringing in further contagion, nor were the able-bodied permitted to leave for they were needed to bake the bread and butcher the meat, and drive the dead carts to the sulphur pits where the corpses were burned. Although Jews were usually allowed to live and work freely among the Christian population of Ferrara, now the duke ordered them into the old quarter surrounding the synagogue. For their safety and the security of their property, he said, because the Jews might be blamed for the outbreak and attacked.

"That's what Queen Isabella said," I remarked to Fidelma, as the voice of the duke's officer, hoarse and punctuated by phlegmy coughs, rose from the square to the loggia of the Corte Vecchio where we had gone to hear the announcement, "in the Edict of Expulsion." Or so my father used to say, in the same tough, ironical tone I now found myself using with Fidelma, a tone at odds with his words, as though there was something else he was trying to tell me.

"It's a sensible precaution," she said. "And compassionate not to expose Christian souls to temptation when they are in danger of dying unshriven." The priests were refusing to enter the houses of the sick for fear of infection; Ippolito had been quick to offer to travel to Rome to request a papal dispensation for the granting of absolution by lay people, and doubtless it would be granted, but it had not yet arrived.

"Why are you here? In service with Donna Lucrezia, I mean? If you are so sincere in your conversion, would not convent life have suited you better?"

"I struck a bargain with my father. He is a goldsmith. He said, if I wanted to be a Christian, I might at least be some use to him. He has done some work for Donna Isabella Gonzaga in Mantua, and she recommended him to Donna Lucrezia, but because those two dislike each other, he thought to increase his chances by sending me to Ferrara. We cannot choose our destiny. Look at Saint Paul, or Christ himself. We must do God's work where we find it."

Night and day the city squatted under a pall of dirty yellow smoke that reeked of rotten eggs; it was hard to believe this was intended to purify the air. It clung to our hair, caught in our throats and lurked in the folds of our clothes, coated the bright buildings in soot and turned our skin the colour of butter. The crop of red crosses which bloomed on street doors was no respecter of rank, fresh paint dripping like blood from the carved bronze gates of the nobility, the stout iron bound doors of the city's merchants, and the ragged hides covering the entrances to the lowest hovels alike. The taverns were full morning, noon, and night of the sick, the dying and the grief stricken, seeking oblivion. The duke ordered them closed, but that only led to trouble in the streets, when gangs of drunks encountered processions of hymn-singing flagellants, so they were re-opened. The carcasses of animals which had starved to death when there was no one left to feed them littered the streets and were scavenged by packs of dogs run wild as their masters sweated out their lives on straw pallets or feather beds. At least the smoke kept the flies away.

The connecting walk between the Corte and the castle remained closed. The kitchen door through which food and drink were brought on to the premises was washed every day, and the staff handling grain sacks and wine barrels, jars of olives and boxes of salt fish were ordered to wear gauze masks over their mouths and noses. We were forbidden fresh meat or fruit and vegetables ripened in the contaminated air; even milk and eggs were denied us, so we learned to subsist on little more than the same *polenta* the peasants ate. No one was allowed in or out of the ducal residences; even letters were burned. Yet the fever was cunning, and beat us at every end and turn, and, at the end of July, one of madonna's ladies, Giuliana Cecharella, a demure girl with a talent for close work, was found dead in her bed, her back arched and her private parts fully displayed where she had kicked away her bedding and her night-clothes in her final paroxysms. As both madonna's physicians were also sick, she had died unattended.

In the evening, madonna complained of pains in her abdomen.

"Where my waist used to be," she said ruefully, attempting to dismiss her symptoms as nothing more than wind brought on by the enforced diet of grain porridge. But I feared for her. I could see the humours at war in her, her depression at the death of Giuliana, alone and unshriven, her body tossed into the sulphur pits with every kind of labourer and street urchin, and at the same time the deep joy of a woman close to her term. Whenever the child in her belly moved, the dull absence was banished from her eyes and her whole face was animated by delight and excitement. There seemed to be some imbalance between the elements of her own blood and that of her child's. I thought the child must be born to save her, yet the child was not due until the beginning of Advent.

I said I would stay in madonna's room that night, seeing that her doctors were themselves laid up in their sickbeds, and she did not protest. Though I settled comfortably enough on my makeshift bed of quilts piled on madonna's floor, I slept little. Night was the best time during the fever, when the air cooled and the fires died down and it became possible to breathe properly again. I was content to lie awake, cocooned among feathers, listening to the purr of nightjars and the mewing of owls, and the rustle of mice under the floorboards. It comforted me to think of the wild creatures continuing their lives oblivious of us and our sufferings. I felt secure in my insignificance; if I mattered so little, perhaps the pain in my heart mattered even less and would, given time, become bearable.

Or disappear completely. That thought jolted me out of my drowse. I could no more live without that pain than without air to breathe or water to quench my thirst. If I succumbed to contentment, the love that lodged inside me would soften and dim and I would be ordinary again, just one more young woman of good birth and little fortune to be deployed by my mistress in building the web of influence that would fasten her securely in her new life. Loving Cesare was my distinction; it singled me out. My family, my faith, even my language, had all been taken from me, and I had filled the spaces they left with this love. If I allowed it to seep away, who knew what might take its place and make me unrecognisable to myself?

With my will bent to nurturing my necessary pain, I was fully awake when the sound of Donna Lucrezia retching banished Cesare from my thoughts. Disentangling my limbs from the pile of quilts, I hurried to her side, whisking back the bed curtain and crouching to hold her head until the fit of vomiting had passed. The moonlight filtered through the window shutters catching the sheen on her black skin, Catherinella detached herself silently from the darkness and squatted beside me, cradling a basin in her arms. When Donna Lucrezia recovered from her spasm, I lit the candle at her bedside and together the three of us examined the contents of the basin for the black blood of the fever.

"The light is poor," I said.

"There was blood pudding at dinner," said madonna, the memory making her retch again. Only Catherinella remained silent; perhaps, despite the fever, she was incapable of seeing a threat in the colour black.

Donna Lucrezia lay back against her pillows; wisps of damp hair escaped from her lace nightcap plastered to her forehead.

"I will send Catherinella to find a doctor," I said. "They are not all sick surely."

"She would do better to fetch a priest." Tears began to slide down madonna's pale, puffy cheeks. "That it should all come to this," she complained, her voice a frail whine.

This was Cesare's fault, I thought furiously, then, anger rising like bile in my throat, wondered why everything must always come back to him. If he had not invaded Urbino, we would still be at Belfiore, out of harm's way. I did not know, as I removed the basin and offered madonna a sip of water, which she immediately brought back up, if I loved him or hated him, or if there was any difference.

"Go," I shouted at Catherinella. "Fetch a doctor."

"But madam say…"

"She has no need of a priest. Not everybody dies."

Though when the slave had gone, her bare feet whispering across the polished wood floor, madonna said, "It's all up with me, isn't it, Violante?"

"No, madonna, of course no…" But, confronted by her hard and hopeless stare, my voice trailed to nothing. "I don't know," I admitted.

"Look under my bed. There's a chest. Fetch it out."

I knew the chest she meant, a small box of scuffed leather bound with brass and locked with a key which madonna wore on a chain around her neck. I drew it out from beneath the bed and placed it gently in madonna's lap. The key chain became entangled in her hair but she refused my assistance; no one but she ever touched that key. No one but she could go wherever it was she was going. With a small gasp of triumph she released the chain, drew it over her head, and unlocked the box. I hoped the mask of indifference we ladies-in-waiting were obliged to perfect had not slipped, but inside I was seething with indecent curiosity. What was in the case? Love letters? A secret hoard of gold or diamonds? A phial of poison as a last resort?

At first I thought it was empty, then, as the candlelight found its way under the arched lid, I saw that it contained the little filigree casket I had seen her with that night shortly after our visit to the dungeon of Ugo and Parisina. Quickly, instinctively, I glanced at the ceiling, looking for the false panel, but, if it were truly there, it was closed. Lifting the casket out of the chest, madonna held it for a moment in her cupped hands, smiling at it as though it held in its web of kinked and buckled wires some exquisite memory.

"Remember what I told you, Violante. If I should die, you are to give it to Cesare with my..." Her voice faltered, she blinked several times, rapidly, then went on, "with my sisterly duty and affection."

I tried to think of some excuse to ask why it was so important to her, but nothing came to mind before Catherinella returned with one of Don Alfonso's physicians, drowsy, dishevelled, and looking terrified. Familiar with nothing but the pox, I thought, hating him for frustrating my curiosity. Hating myself for having it.

It seemed that Donna Lucrezia, already weakened by her pregnancy and the exigencies of caring for Angela, could not possibly survive this latest blow to her health, but Don Alfonso was determined that every effort should be made to save her. Having acquired a reputation as a healer, and, I imagine, being considered dispensable, a mere *conversa*, I was commanded to remain with madonna day and night. Don Alfonso himself had a bed made up in her dressing room, from where he could be quickly summoned if her condition changed in the night. During the day, he was with her as much as his duties permitted, and always when she took food; even though I myself prepared her sick dishes of chicken broth and barley porridge over a brazier in the dressing room, and anyway she could keep nothing down other than a little water, Don Alfonso remained suspicious of poison. It was wishful thinking on his part; even poison was preferable to the fever.

As the news spread through the palace, the vultures began to gather, the ambassadors of other powers with their sharp eyes and enigmatic smiles, the painters and poets and musicians who enjoyed madonna's patronage and had families to feed, the merchants who overcharged her for satin or soap, the priests and doctors who eyed one another up from opposite sides of the room, each profession secure in its own convictions and contemptuous of the other. Here was Gian Luca Pozzi, who had been Duke Ercole's envoy to Rome for madonna's proxy marriage and had been sniffing around her ever since in the hope of gaining her support for a cardinal's hat in exchange for the positive—or at least, not hostile—reports he had sent of her to his master. And there, in a secluded corner, his eyes gleaming like a cat's in the dark, lurked Francesco Troche, the man known as the pope's fixer. From time to time he addressed a whispered remark out of the corner of his mouth to his fellow Catalan, Francesc Remolins, who had come from Urbino with news of the fall of Camerino to Cesare's forces. The lords of Camerino were related to the Este too.

The family came, the duke accompanied by Sister Osanna and a bevy of his own pet nuns who wept and tore their clothes and assured His Grace of a miracle to protect his unborn grandson. Ferrante brought gossip and books of verse, and wept briefly on my shoulder. Even Sigismondo came to see his sister-in-law, to assure her the fever was yet another conspiracy of the rats and he had the matter well in hand. He even brought the corpse of one of the offenders which he had embalmed in pickling spice and wound in butter muslin to prove to her that victory was nigh. I shooed him out with his prize, relieved we had our own kitchen at the base of the Torre Marchesana.

The bishop of Venosa, His Holiness's favourite doctor, scythed through the crowd like Moses parting the Red Sea on his way to and from the bed chamber, assistants bearing covered basins and trays of cups and fleams, scurrying in his wake. Every time he emerged from the bed chamber, and the waiting faces, patient, anxious, curious, speculative, turned towards him, his expression was more solemn and portentous. Every time the door closed once more behind him, the murmured surmisings and conspirings resumed. The sigh of voices was like the whisperings of the daemons who live in the ether.

Then, one afternoon, when madonna seemed a little better and I had gone to my own room to rest and change my clothes, I returned to her apartments to find the crowd swept away and Michelotto da Corella, in the garb of a knight of Saint John, standing guard at her bedroom door.

"Well, well," he said, plastering the nearest expression he had to a smile over his pitted features. "The little Jewess. There's a nice bonus for my lord."

"He is here?" I felt breathless. The floor began to lurch and slide under my feet like the deck of a ship. Michelotto nodded. I was afraid I might kiss him, though he reeked of garlic and rancid butter and had teeth like an old horse.

"But he is not to be disturbed." He squared his shoulders and let his right hand hover conspicuously over the hilt of his sword.

"Donna Lucrezia will be looking for me." I commanded my heart to remain steady, but it took no notice. "I am her special nurse, you know."

"Not right now you're not," said Michelotto with a revolting leer. "You'll wait here till you're sent for. But I'll have some wine before you make yourself too comfortable. And food. We were bloody nearly in Milan before he made up his mind to come here and we never even stopped to change horses."

"We have very little. We have been besieged in the city by this fever. You did well to get through the gates."

"Ah, but we are Hospitallers, see?" He pointed to the white cross emblazoned across the breast of his tabard. "We come to help the sick."

Cesare, I thought, feeling I might explode with joy, could make a joke out of anything. "I will see what I can find in our own kitchen. I will go no further, mind."

"Afraid he's going to light out on you again? You'll have to get used to that, girl."

"Anxious to be close to my lady should she need me."

"Fetch Torella, Michelotto. Quickly." Cesare's voice, light and strong as sunlight, with its little Spanish inflection. I was not ready; this was not how I had dreamed it. But at least my chemise was clean and my hair combed. I dropped a curtsey and waited, my gaze fixed to the floor, for him to address me.

"Violante. Thank God. Come with me." No greeting, no surprise; we might have seen one another only yesterday.

"My lord." Now, at last, I could look at him. His face was plaster white and rigid as a mask; even his lips were white, compressed, and his beard grey with the dust of the road. Fear flickered in his eyes, though whether he was afraid of what he had seen in madonna's room, or that his expression might break and give him away, I could not tell. Turning his back on me he returned to the bedchamber, holding the door open behind him with the flat of his palm. He wore no gloves and crescents of grime edged his fingernails. His hand trembled slightly and I ached to touch it, to feel its human warmth and trace the fan of bones from wrist to fingertips.

The low, bestial growling and gargling entered my consciousness only gradually through the dizzy distraction of Cesare's sudden closeness after the months of yearning. I hurried after him, almost collided with him as he stopped short just inside the door, pushed past him to madonna's bedside, felt my flank and shoulder grazed by every fibre of his Hospitaller's tabard, burned by the heat of his body as we touched.

Though she had been in bed when I left her, madonna was now lying on top of the covers, wrapped in her dressing gown, which had slipped from her shoulder and fallen open to leave one leg exposed. Her back was arched to a degree where I feared her spine must snap, her eyes had rolled up into her head, a foam of saliva slicked her chin, and the unearthly growling came from deep in her stretched throat. Fonsi, who was, as usual, sitting beside her on the bed, set up a frenzied yapping

"We were just talking and…"

"What? I can't hear."

He tried again, but could not make himself heard above the dog's ear-piercing racket. He grabbed the dog by the scruff of its neck. It whimpered; I winced. "Shut up," he told it, and rapped its nose before replacing it at the foot of the bed, where it remained, snout on paws, perfectly silent. I wanted to be Cesare's dog, I thought, lying at his feet, secure in the smell of him, to be kicked or kissed at his whim and grateful for his attention.

"I can't deal with this," I said. "She needs a doctor."

"I brought Torella. She seemed quite well, so I sent him to rest. He's not used to hard riding like Michelotto and I. Michelotto!" This in the direction of the door. "Where the devil is Torella? How long can it take to find someone in this bloody hutch?"

No reply.

"Now you must help me," I told him; this was no time for deference, and if he thought me impertinent he could deal with me as he saw fit once the crisis was over. One way or the other. "We must put her on her side. There. You hold her steady while I pile the pillows behind her so she can't roll back. And her tongue. In the falling sickness, they say people bite off their tongues."

Cesare remained with his hands clamped over his sister's flank as though his flesh was fused to hers by the heat of her fever. "She doesn't have the falling sickness," he said, while I hunted about the room for some strap or stick to wedge over her tongue.

"The fever can do it sometimes. I have seen it in others."

Nothing. Perfume bottles, hair brushes, tubs of cochineal paste, jewelled girdles, and hat pins. What was needed was…

"Your sword belt. Give me your sword belt." The sword was already unclipped from it and propped in a corner. But he stayed frozen, unable to move. "The sword belt," I shrieked, leaning across the bed, only inches from his face. He started, straightened up, tried to unbuckle the belt but failed, his fingers all of a tangle. Racing around to his side of the bed, I squeezed myself between him and it, our thighs and bellies pressed together in a parody of lust of which we were neither wholly aware nor unaware. I unfastened the belt, clambered on to the bed, and, kneeling behind Donna Lucrezia, pushed it into her mouth. She tossed back her head and bucked like a stubborn horse resisting the bit. Attempting to soothe her, I rubbed her back. It was then I realised the bedding bunched and rucked beneath her was sodden.

"Her waters have broken," I told Cesare, twisting round on the bed to face him.

"It's two months too soon." We stared at one another with the calm of complete hopelessness; even Donna Lucrezia fell quiet, coming out of her fit with a long, shuddering sigh then lying as if asleep, spared the pains of labour as though the child too knew there was nothing to be done. Then Cesare blinked and shook his head as though shaking off a dream.

"Torella!" he roared. "Name of Christ, where are you, man?"

The arrival of Gaspare Torella, still clutching a lump of bread and cheese, was immediately consoling. I had met Cesare's physician on several occasions in Rome, for he was a man as well versed in the social graces as in the profession of healing, and I liked him. He came from Valencia and he used to make me laugh. Cesare, I knew, held him in great trust since Torella had cured him of the pox by a complicated regime of purgings, blood lettings, and mercury sudations which were the talk of the spa at Stigliano while Cesare was enduring them. Torella had then written a treatise on the cure, with the patient's enthusiastic connivance, and had, from the proceeds of his growing fame, presented his young patron with a gold and enamel pill box in which to keep the pills of celandine and aloe he was supposed to take each day with meals to prevent a recurrence of his illness.

Cesare fairly pounced on him as he entered the room, knocking the remains of his meal out of his hand. As the food hit the floor, I expected Fonsi to rouse himself and go scavenging for it, for he loved cheese, but he stayed where Cesare had put him, though his nose quivered optimistically.

"Thank Christ. We were just talking and then she had this…this fit and now…"

"Yes, yes, your grace. If you would be so good as to sit quietly while I make my examination. Monna Donata? Will you assist me?" Torella was not a man for nicknames. I suppose it is a physician's business to look behind masks.

As I removed the pillows and turned madonna on to her back, she woke from her sleep with a groan of pain and clutched at her abdomen.

"No," she whispered, turning her grey, pleading gaze on me. "Please, no."

"Your waters have broken, madonna."

Hearing her speak, Cesare leapt out of the chair where he had been perched, fiddling with his sword, whose loose buckles made an irritating rattle against the scabbard. He knelt beside the bed and took her hand, obliging Torella to abandon his attempt to take the pulse of that wrist and move to her other side. This he did with almost paternal forbearance, as Cesare spoke low and passionately, in rapid Catalan, to his sister. She nodded and smiled, then another contraction gripped her and she turned from him, frowning, squeezing her eyes shut. "You must go now," she whispered in Italian. "You will just be in the way. You can come and see your new nephew when it is all over."

He tried to resist but she was adamant.

"It will only distress her further if she thinks you are witness to her suffering," I said. "Go to Don Alfonso. He will be in need of company." And I touched his cheek with the tips of my fingers, as though it was the most natural thing in the world to me.

"Yes. Thank you."

Finding Don Alfonso was not difficult. He was already pacing around outside the bed chamber like a performing bear chained to a pole. Catherinella and two girls bearing armfuls of clean bedlinen cowered against the walls, though I think they were more afraid of Michelotto's bloodshot, appraising eye than Don Alfonso's impotent distress for his wife. Michelotto was seated beside a small table, a large wine jug at his elbow which, by the ease with which he lifted it, I determined to be nearly empty. Leaving madonna's husband and her brother locked in a tearful embrace, I returned to her bedside.

❧

The child was born towards evening, when the sky outside the bedroom window was suspended between light and dark, and birds going to roost were beginning to be indistinguishable from the ash floating up from the plague pyres. At the final moment Donna Lucrezia suffered another fit, arching her back and growling like a dog as her daughter slid into the world in a pool of blood and mucus. Now she lay unconscious as I struggled to clean her and bind strips of linen between her inert legs to absorb her blood. Half of me waited for the baby's thin, new cries to cut through the tolling of the evening Angelus; half of me knew she was dead. Prodding and turning the little corpse laid out in a silver dish, holding it up to the fading light, Torella pronounced the child to have been dead for several days at least.

"Skin brownish, wrinkled, chest sunk, no vernix." He peered into her ear, parting the whorls of gristle and skin like a gardener looking for a worm at the heart of a rose, then nodded, as though the ear had somehow confirmed his diagnosis. "Nothing to be done," he said, handing the dish to me. He had not covered it; that was not his job. "I will speak to Don Alfonso if you will bring me to him."

There I stood, nodding like an idiot, cradling the dish against my ribs. "I will call the girls to change the bed, and Catherinella to comb her hair before…she must look her best for him."

"Monna Donata," said Torella more gently, "she is dying. There is not much time, I believe. Find Don Alfonso. And her priest."

"And Don Cesare?"

Torella gave a resigned smile. "And Don Cesare," he agreed. "Cover the dish," he added, causing me to pause in my flight towards the door.

I set the dish down on a table and looked at the dead child who, for all the months of careful anxiety and elaborate preparation, had slithered into the world as easily as a rabbit stripped of her skin. She was perfect, from the damp spikes of lashes fringing her eyelids to the bare cleft of her sex to the dawn grey nails at the tips of her toes. And suddenly I was glad she was dead, so she could never be changed the way I had been changed, or her mother, or any other woman in this man's world.

"Tell one of the servants to get rid of it," said Ser Torella, then, mistaking the reason for my hesitation, added, "It's nothing, it was not baptised, no need for ceremony."

But something, surely, to mark her passing, this tiny girl whose arrival in the world had been so keenly and lovingly anticipated. Some words, a smile, a touch. "I will do it myself. Best not to let the news get out among the servants before Don Alfonso learns of it. I will do it, and then go to find him."

Ser Torella nodded. "Sensible girl."

I would give her to the fever carts. That way, at least she would have some words said over her by the poor Franciscans with their streaming eyes and smoke-hoarsened voices who prayed beside the lime pits and sometimes, stricken themselves, fell in among their congregation and burned. I would go now, carrying my basin as if it were no more than a full chamber pot or an empty dinner plate, across the courtyard and out into the piazza. There was always a cart near the cathedral, waiting outside the Porta di Guidizio from where the dead are carried out of the church for burial. I knew there would be another close by, at the locked gate to the Jewish quarter on Via San Romano, but I would not go there. People were saying it was Duke Ercole's tolerance towards the Jews that had brought God's wrath down on the heads of the Ferrarese, and it was not only the fever they had tried to shut out when they locked the gates.

I had not even begun to think how I would persuade the porter to let down the drawbridge for me, when I heard my name called out of the abnormal silence of the closed and shuttered courtyard.

"Violante!"

In the deepening twilight, thickened by the smoke from the last of the day's pyres, the voice was eerie, disembodied, coming from everywhere and nowhere. Was it the voice of my conscience? No. I had done no wrong. I wanted nothing more than that the child should be able to rest peacefully.

"What are you doing out here all alone?" Cesare. Oh God, no, not yet. I gripped the basin tighter, drawing it close as though I could hide it under my clothes. What could I say if he asked? Though as he emerged from the gloom and I saw his face, the furrows pinched between his brows, the strained, almost pleading expression in his dark-circled eyes, I realised there was nothing to say. "Why are you not with your mistress?" he demanded, his tone veering between hope and dread. "Is the child born?"

The lip of the basin dug into my ribs. Perhaps, if I pressed hard enough, the bones might part and swallow the child. "Yes, my lord. I was looking for you…and Don Alfonso, of course."

"Out here? Alfonso is bird watching. On the roof with his lenses and a wine jug." I thought of the loose panel in madonna's ceiling. He knows already, then, I thought, relieved.

"You are here," I said in my defence.

"Needed some air." He gave an ironic cough, but there was no humour in it. "Tell me, have I a nephew? How is my sister?"

"My lord…Cesare…"

"Tell me. Do not mince your words." He grasped me by my shoulders and shook me. I clung to the basin. The smell of wine and sleeplessness was heavy on his breath.

"The child was stillborn."

His hands dropped to his sides. My glance flickered over the basin. Seeing where I looked, he lifted the corner of the cloth. I cringed from him, hugging my burden to my belly, but I could not stop him.

"A girl," he said, covering the bowl again with careful deliberation. "Good. If she had lost a son at this stage, it could have been catastrophic for us."

How could he be so cool? Had he not looked, had he not seen? Her tiny fingers, splayed like frogs' feet, her mouth that had been made to suckle and chatter and one day kiss her lover? Inside me, something broke. "Her daughter," I yelled, "your niece. Dead." In that moment, I hated him. "If it hadn't been for you, she might have carried a child of either sex safely to term. If you hadn't invaded Urbino, she never would have become ill. Tell me, are you here out of concern for her or your own ambition?"

"They are one and the same," he said, then paused, looking at me as though he had only just recognised me. "Torella should never have asked you to dispose of it." Even through my tears, I was aware of something in his tone which made me anxious for Ser Torella. "Give it to me."

My grip tightened. "What will you do with her?"

"Just give it to me." He wrenched the bowl from me and, stepping up on to the ravelin alongside the drawbridge, emptied its contents into the moat, the little corpse slipping from beneath the linen cloth just the way the dead slide off the shrouded board when they are buried at sea. He stood for a moment, a dark silhouette, staring down into the water, and when the body did not sink, he stooped to pick up a loose stone from the walkway and threw it after it. As the stone hit its mark, and Donna Lucrezia's daughter sank from view, something snagged at my memory.

Don Juan. There had been a witness, I recalled, a watchman guarding a consignment of logs on the riverbank overnight, who had seen Don Juan's body slipped into the Tiber from the rump of a horse. The horseman, a well-dressed man wearing gloves with jewelled cuffs, had been obliged to spend some time throwing stones at the dead man's billowing cloak until the corpse sank. The body, they say, is lightened by three pounds when the soul leaves it. The watchman had thought nothing of it; bodies were dumped in the Tiber every night.

Then Cesare stepped down from the ravelin, out of the shadow of its salient, and he was merely a man in his shirtsleeves, his hands bare, his expression tired and shuttered and sad.

"Did you make a wish?" I asked him. He looked puzzled. "When you threw the stone," I added.

"Ah." He paused. I was certain he was only now thinking of a wish, and wondered why he would bother, why he would not simply lie to me. "Yes," he said, "but before I tell you what it is, you must tell me what you meant. Concerning Urbino." It was not a request, though his tone was light enough.

"You would know if you'd seen her. Crying and screaming. Tearing at her hair and face. She even ripped the curtains down and broke most of the furniture at Belfiore."

To my utter confusion, Cesare started to laugh. "Did she indeed, the little cat? Well, she must learn to trust me better."

Sweat was breaking on my brow and upper lip. I wiped my palms on my skirt and felt the damp flesh between my breasts prickle in the breeze which had risen with the coming of evening. He took a step towards me, pressing his body, clad now in nothing but his shirt and breeches, against mine.

"Now you know my wish," he whispered. I felt short of breath, my heart was hurling itself against my ribs like a madman in a cage. I lifted my face, inhaled jasmine and sweat and stone dust, let my eyes graze the lean curve of his mouth. I was opening, wide as a pond lily, a blown rose...

"You must go to her. Ser Torella says it will not be long." Shaking as if I, too, were coming down with the fever, I turned away. Now was not the time.

"She is dying? She will not die, Violante; you will prevent it." He took my arm, though more like a gaoler than a lover, and turned me towards the Torre Marchesana. "Tell her...tell her Guidobaldo of Urbino was planning to go to the defence of Camerino."

I could feel through my sleeve and my skin the frailty of his bones against mine, and it came to me suddenly that this great physical strength of his, this wrestling with peasants and bending horseshoes and beheading bulls, was just another performance, another mask. This thought gave me confidence. Donna Lucrezia would not die; I would save her. "Tell her yourself," I said.

❦

When we entered her bedchamber, it seemed at first that Donna Lucrezia was completely unattended. Clean linen had been put on the bed, and madonna's breasts had been bound to stop her milk, but she was still unconscious, her cheeks sallow, her eyelids tinged with blue, her mouth bruised from my ramming Cesare's sword belt under her tongue. Cesare went straight to her side. He lay beside her on the bed, his head close to hers, and spoke softly to her. Taking strands of their hair, where it mingled on the pillow, he began to plait it together, the dark red and pale gold. It seemed too intimate a scene for me to witness, so I began to busy myself about the room, tidying away the detritus of Ser Torella's trade. Where was he? Had he simply given up on her and gone away? It was then I noticed Catherinella. She was seated at madonna's dressing table. This was behind the door, which explained why I had not seen her before. A gold circlet set with jewels sparkled in her springy hair, necklaces covered her breast.

"What do you think you're doing?" I shouted.

"Madonna dyin'," she replied. I raised my hand to hit her, then, catching a glance at her reflection in the polished silver mirror, lit by candles burning on the dressing table, I saw, not the slave taking advantage of her mistress's incapacity but my Madonna of Strangers.

"Are you praying for her, Catherinella?" I asked, more gently, but before she could reply, Cesare was upon her, wrenching the circlet from her head. A few strands of hair, curled tight around the gold band, came away with it, causing the slave to cry out.

"Where is Ser Torella?" he demanded, thrusting his face so close to hers she flinched as though his breath had scorched her.

"Gone."

"Gone where?" He grabbed her by her hair and bent her head back until I heard the bones crack in her neck.

"Find Don Alfonso," she whined.

"And he left you to watch over your mistress. And this is how you repay her. By stealing what belongs to her." His voice was barely above a whisper. He hauled the slave to her feet, turned her to face him, and yanked the necklaces from her neck. They slid through his fingers and clattered on to the dressing table. Catherinella began to jabber in her own tongue. As Cesare dragged her from the room, her embroidered satin slippers fell off and her broad black toes scrabbled at the rugs.

"Michelotto!" he roared at the door. "Come here."

The thud of running footsteps, the jangle of sword and spurs.

"Don Cesar?" He sounded breathless.

"Put that somewhere secure until I have time to deal with it."

"Yes, Don Cesar."

⁂

By the time Ser Torella reappeared, accompanied by a dishevelled, red-eyed Don Alfonso, Donna Lucrezia had regained consciousness and I had persuaded her to take a little chicken broth, which she had managed to keep down, though it stung her bruised lips. In calm, matter-of-fact tones, Cesare told her about the baby. "Your womb was made to carry sons," he concluded, and bowed to kiss her hand so he missed the sad smile with which she greeted his speech. I thought nothing, then, of her docility, putting it down to her weakness, and relief that she had not given birth to a dead boy.

Towards morning, Ser Torella decided madonna was strong enough to endure a bleeding. "It's a miracle," he said, glancing in my direction as he made his selection from his case of fleams. "You have the gift, Monna Donata; there is no doubt about it."

"You are a good doctor, messer." It said much for Ser Torella's medical skill that he had the confidence and breadth of mind to admit the existence of natural healers, even though I thought it unlikely I was one of them. Most doctors dismissed such gifts as witchcraft or old wives' tales. "And I believe the devotion of her husband and Duke Valentino must also have helped to restore madonna to strength."

Madonna nodded and smiled her agreement, though her gaze flicked uneasily towards the blade Ser Torella was now holding up to the light as he tested its sharpness on the ball of his thumb.

"Is it absolutely necessary to bleed her, man?" asked Cesare, as though reading her mind.

"The sooner the bad blood retained during her pregnancy can be drawn off, the sooner she will be restored to health and her husband's bed. Otherwise the womb can suffocate."

"Let Ser Torella do his work," Donna Lucrezia admonished gently, slurring her words a little through her damaged lips.

The doctor elected to bleed her from her right foot, the moon being now in Virgo, and Virgo an occidental sign, cold and feminine like Pisces, which governs the feet. Though, he sighed, Virgo is dry and melancholic, while Pisces is wet and phlegmatic, but beggars can't be choosers. He had me set up a low stool at the side of the bed, upon which madonna could rest her foot at a lower level than the rest of her body to aid the flow of blood, but still he had difficulty in finding a responsive vein. Eventually, he let Cesare hold her foot, and all the while he told jokes, and did wicked impressions of people we had known in Rome—dour Master Burchard, Cardinal Piccolomini who was nearing ninety and prone to snoring through Mass, Don Diego Lopez de Haro, the Spanish ambassador whose nose Juan Borgia had broken in a wrestling bout and who now always spoke as though he had a cold.

He gave us Prince Djem.

"Dear Djem," madonna sighed. "Do you remember the times we had with him? How mercilessly Juan used to tease him. He adored Juan, you know, and Juan was the most fearful flirt." Though her remark was evidently addressed to me, her gaze kept shifting uncomfortably towards Cesare. I remembered she had once said Cesare loved Djem, yet he was showing little respect for his friend's memory now as he puffed out his cheeks and tucked his chin into his neck to emulate the prince's portliness.

"Sip the poppy juice, my dears," he said in a sibilant wheeze, "so much more efficacious than a tisane."

"He grew some special poppies in a corner of the garden near the Belvedere," explained Donna Lucrezia, "from seeds sent him by his brother the Sultan. The juice made you see..." Her voice tailed off briefly, then she asked, "What did you see, Cesar?"

"The future," he replied with a dismissive laugh, and moved on to the Holy Father's Greek secretary, Podocario, who had become somewhat deaf in his old age.

When Don Alfonso excused himself to answer a call of nature, for excessive drinking was always prone to loosen his bowels, he extended his repertoire to include Donna Isabella, so that by the time Don Alfonso returned, we were all, including Ser Torella, weeping with laughter, Donna Lucrezia clutching her bound breasts and begging her brother to stop for she could not bear the pain of laughing with them so engorged. The pain of the bloodletting she scarcely noticed.

"Now," said Ser Torella, setting aside the basin of blood for examination and cleaning his blade with a soft cloth, "you must rest, madonna. Perhaps you would like Don Alfonso to remain with you until you fall asleep?" It was a subtle choice. Ser Torella clearly understood that Cesare would be her choice, but also, perhaps, that I might persuade him away from her side. Cesare hesitated.

"We will not go far," I promised him. "Come, my lord, walk with me in the orange garden." The orange trees grew in lead and terracotta pots on a roof terrace overlooking the moat from the Torre Leone. From madonna's apartments you reached it along a cloistered walk running the short distance between the two towers.

"Stop 'my lording' me," Cesare ordered, slipping his arm through mine in comradely fashion as we stepped out on to the walk. "You and I have been through something of a campaign together this night. It makes equals of us."

"That is very republican—for a duke," I teased, emboldened by his familiarity. Bushes of lavender and rosemary lined the walk, clipped and trained into the chalices, swords, money, and batons of a pack of playing cards. Cesare snapped a stalk of rosemary from the tip of a sword, rubbed it between his fingers, and held it to my nose. I breathed in, the sharp, hot fragrance filling my lungs and making my nerves tingle with new energy.

"Government by the people has much to commend it," said Cesare. "My cities in the Romagna all have their own council of elders. They appoint their own judges and suchlike. They are even permitted to raise their own militias, within certain limits. I have found men fight far better if it is their own homes and families they are protecting."

"They are still your cities, though."

"You know, Violante, I have acquired some great reputation as a soldier. It is because my father likes to arrange triumphs. He wants the Romans to see me as some kind of latterday Caesar. But truth to tell, most of those cities surrendered to me of their own free will, happy to escape tyrants who ruled by whim. I negotiated with them. That's what the best generals do; they avoid battles if they can. They remain loyal to me because my taxes are systematic, my justice predictable, and my capacity to buy grain when harvests fail almost unlimited. Money and good management. If you read Caesar, which I don't suppose my father has since he was a boy, you will find he says the same. The rest is putting on a show. The people like that too."

Something did not ring quite true about this practical Utopia he was describing. "What will you do about Catherinella?" I asked.

"Who?"

"The slave."

"Why? Does it matter to you?" He turned to me with a slow, lascivious smile. "Is that your price, then, the slave's life? Nothing more?"

"I do not know what you mean."

"Of course you do. Everyone has their price. I will spare her, if you like."

I felt humiliated, and angry that he should try to make Catherinella's fate my responsibility. Part of me knew that was his way, but part of me struggled to deny it. I wanted him to be worthy of my love. "You should spare her for your sister," I said. "For myself, I love you anyway." There. The words were out. Not as I had imagined, with tears and maidenly tremblings. Not syrupy with lust, but strident with indignation. If he were worthy, I realised, if he were noble and forgiving, fair-minded and unselfish, he would hold no fascination for me at all. The store of love inside me shifted a little, away from myself and towards Cesare.

He leaned over the parapet of the walk and gazed towards the cathedral. A light, warm breeze was blowing, carrying the warbling of the doves which nested among its friezes and statues. Its pink marble façade glowed like flesh in the rose-tinged early sunlight. "Leon Battista Alberti," he announced. "Built the campanile," he added, seeing me look puzzled. "The man who says there are no rules. None to break and none to guide us, just each of us alone with his own ingenuity."

I placed the flat of my hand against his back. The tips of his red curls licked my fingertips like flames.

No smoke, no sulphur. No fires were burning. The air was perfectly clear. Both of us realised at the same instant. We turned towards one another, each about to speak, but neither of us said a word. And this is where time slows, then stops, and my life's direction changes forever.

❧

Lips parted for speech meet in a kiss. Tongues which have teased and flirted, reproached, defended, or explained now speak only the dumb language of attraction. Perhaps because I am so tired, I am both engaged in the kiss yet watching myself, floating outside myself somewhere in this new, clean air which shows me my intentions without any obfuscation. At base, beneath our silk and linen, we are not so different from the dogs that copulate in the gutters, I think, and with that thought comes a surge of dirty lust, driving my body against Cesare's, sluicing from me reason, propriety, and common sense. My eyes close with the weight of it; my breath quits my lungs and enters his.

And just when I believe my rapture will drown me, when all my organs seem to have turned to syrup, he saves me.

"Thank you," he says, pulling out of the kiss, though he continues to hold me, so close I am still lost in the landscape of his face. This near, it is a geometer's landscape, all planes and angles, and I see it still, despite the years and the ocean, with the eyes of the heart that knows nothing of the passing of time.

"For what?" I ask, in the now of then, when I was a girl.

"For saving Lucrezia's life."

"I did nothing. It was your Ser Torella who saved her. You must thank him."

Removing one hand from my waist, he makes a dismissive gesture. "He will be rewarded. I have a pair of fine carriage mules to give him. The best. From Poitou. In France," he adds, seeing I do not know where Poitou is.

"Where your wife is." As I hear myself saying it I wish I could snatch back the words.

He gives an exasperated sigh. "Violante, did I not tell you once I had no time for wooing virgins? Your conscience is your own affair, not mine."

"And yours?"

"I have none. Didn't you know?" He grins suddenly and hugs me close, grazing the lobe of my ear with his teeth. "I am a monster," he growls, softly, in the back of his throat. "I turn into a wolf when the moon is full and feast on the hearts of all those unwise enough to fall in love with me. Roasted, with *trompetti de morte*."

"Mine you must have with rosemary," I tell him, my breath hot against his neck. For rosemary is the herb of the sun, which eases the heart and cleanses the mind. Lest there be any doubt in me about what I am doing.

"And oranges." He takes my hand and leads me into the orange garden, weaving a path between the trees in their pots and the little braziers where fires are lit to keep them warm during the winters. The fruit all ripen at different times, so the air is rich with the mingled scents of the fruit and its blossom, with hot stone and the drone of bees nosing among the waxy white flowers. A loggia runs along the back wall of the garden. Deep in its recess is a broad stone bench beneath a brocade canopy, piled with cushions of satin and velvet, plump and glossy as fruits on a market stall.

Cesare leads me under the white marble arcade, into the blue shade of the loggia. His magic blinds the eyes at the castle windows and bridles the tongues of gossips in the piazza. Nothing matters but the sinuous curl of his fingers and the heat of his palm pressed against mine. I watch as he takes the cushions from where they are stacked and spreads them over the bench. Apparently careless, his actions are fastidious, considered. I am fascinated by the way in which his grace of form can transform even such domestic commonplaces into a kind of physical poetry, each cushion picked up, each twist and stoop at the waist a stanza. The cushions, I think, are line endings, and this thought makes me smile, and my smile makes him pause to intercept it with his own.

He holds out his hand, the one with the powder burn. I take a step towards him and begin to slide my arms around his waist, but he takes my hands and presses the flat of my palms against his chest. His shirt has come unlaced so we are flesh to flesh and the sweat dampened hair on his chest coils around my fingers, knots us together. The hair is dark, it has no red in it, and his heart beats so steadily compared with mine, which is dashing itself in a frenzy against my breastbone.

I am suddenly rigid with anticipation and uncertainty. I feel my palms begin to sweat and pray he will not notice. But he does.

"What is it?" he asks.

My cheeks burn in the fire of his eyes. "I…I am not La Fiammetta, or the Princess Sancia…"

He presses two fingers to my lips. I smell the camphor used to preserve the cushions from moth. "You are more precious to me than either. You know that, don't you?"

I nod. I do know it, though I do not understand why, when I have no city, no land, no name or titles nor any amatory skills other than what Angela has taught me. Knowledge without understanding is not enough to make me relax. With a wry little smile he scoops me up, one arm under my shoulders, the other beneath the backs of my knees, and lays me gently down on the cushions.

"Then what are you afraid of?" he asks, pulling his shirt over his head. His chest hair makes a pattern the shape of a goblet, the bowl narrowing to a stem just under his ribs. "What are you thinking?" he tries, when I do not reply. I tell him. He laughs and sits beside me. "Show me."

I raise my hand to a point next to his left nipple, dark as a mulberry. I watch my hand as though it belongs to somebody else; it is stained violet by the light filtering through the canopy. As I trace the outline of the goblet with the tip of one finger, following the ridges of his ribs to the muscular flat of his belly, Cesare flinches and laughs. He is ticklish, I realise, and my heart somersaults. But he is deadly serious again as my finger comes to a halt where the stem of the goblet extends below his navel.

"Don't stop," he says, loosening his breeches. Freed from constraint, his sex seems to yearn towards my hand. "You see, you are the lodestone of desire," he murmurs, but my hand is paralysed, as though it has its own sense of modesty quite apart from anything my brain might try to impose upon it, and my whole body trembles in the grip of this war between them.

And Cesare, who understands war, sits back, tugs off his boots, then stretches himself out beside me on the cushions and begins, with slow, assured fingers, to unlace my bodice. Dressed in haste for nursing, I am not wearing a corset. I lie with my arms stiff at my sides, fists clenched, nails dug into my palms, aware of nothing but his sex pressed into the dip between my belly and my Venus' mound. He loosens the neck of my shift and kisses my breasts, one after the other, making a circle around each nipple with the point of his tongue. I think of Angela.

"Did you know," he murmurs, "that Don Cristobal Colon, the governor of the Indies, once wrote to Queen Isabella that the earth is the shape of a woman's breast and the Garden of Eden is on the very nipple of it."

I do not ask myself how he knows this. Desire washes from my throat to the parts of me that have been secret until now, waiting for my conquistador with his wise hands and his smile that dares the devil. Shifting his position slightly, he slides one hand beneath my skirts, pressing my thighs apart, seeking out this new world.

"You don't believe in the Garden of Eden," I remind him.

"Oh but I do," he assures me, and I think of Don Cristobal, and of how I am the whole earth cupped in my lover's hand.

His fingers stroke and probe, but they do not find their mark, and I want to tell him, to reach down and guide his touch, but I do not know how. I want to make him happy; I want him to love me, so I pretend, squirming and sighing, and I believe he is deceived. Abruptly, he twists free of me and rises to his feet. Removing the rest of his clothes, he stands over me, and I am suddenly seized by a desire to laugh.

He looks so foolish, foolish and vulnerable with his sex stuck out in front of him, thick and coarse, the dark flesh ridged with gristle. It seems not to belong to the rest of his fine-boned, long-sinewed body, his skin unblemished except for a small, red scar the shape of a sunburst just above the line of his private hair. Nothing is written on his body; even in his nakedness he is an enigma. I bite my lips and hunt for something serious to think about. Kneeling between my legs, he bundles my skirts around my waist, opens me with two fingers, and pushes himself inside.

This is impossible. He is too big. I will tear; everything inside me will be ripped and ragged. The pain is deep and sharp, sudden, focused, but where, I cannot tell. I moan, I shake my head, I squeeze my eyes shut. Again I am misunderstood as he drives further into me. Now something changes. My thighs strain apart, my hips arch up to meet his; I am all greed, nothing but a mouth, sucking and salivating. He shudders, gives a muffled groan which I feel against my neck, and lies still. I feel his skin cooling against mine; I feel like a child who has been offered a sweet, only to have it snatched away as she reaches out to take it. I breathe in deeply, willing my blood to slow, my heart to steady, my legs, which are clasped around Cesare's waist, to relax their grip, to let him go.

After a while he raises himself on one elbow and gives me a searching look. "What's wrong?" He waits, but I do not know how to reply so he comes to his own conclusions. "Only now do you think of the consequences, eh?" he teases, tickling my belly.

"It's not that. Angela says no one ever gets pregnant their first time."

He looks sceptical at that, but all he says is, "What then?" I see realisation dawn. "I didn't please you, did I? Well, well. What can I say in my defence? I wanted you so much, you see, have wanted you for so long, and I am overwrought with my sister's illness...But excuses are not what you want, are they?" He strokes my private hair, prospects again for what it hides.

"It doesn't matter." Truly, it doesn't. Because his need has given me a glimpse of what it is to have power. I gaze up at his face, at the frown which has scored two lines of uneven length between his brows and the air of hesitancy flickering about his mouth and tell myself that, for this moment if no other, we are equals. More than equals.

"Don't lie to me." He raises his hand from between my legs and licks his fingers. "Mistress Quim doesn't."

I push a tangle of his hair back over his shoulder and, as I touch his damp skin, I have an unearthly, fleeting sense that we are fused, that I can understand. "Really," I say, "it doesn't matter."

Apparently satisfied I am telling the truth, he makes himself comfortable once again on our bed of cushions. Drawing me close, until I am lying with my head on his chest, my ear to his heart, his voice a tremor through the bones of my skull, he says, "I will tell you about Urbino, then. And by the time I have done that, we will be ready to make love again. And I will do better next time, I promise." I wonder if he can feel me smile.

As he speaks, he strokes my hair, in long sweeping movements down my back, ending just at the rise of my buttocks where he lets his hand rest for a moment before beginning again.

"Do you remember," he begins, which has almost the same magic power as once upon a time, "when the French occupied Rome in '94?"

"Only vaguely. I was just a little girl. And the Jews had their own militia. It was quite efficient. The French left us alone mostly, I think."

"Well I was nineteen. I had just been made a cardinal. I had a doctorate in canon law but no sword. Juan was in Spain, Lucrezia with her Sforza husband in Pesaro, Jofre...oh, I can't even remember where he was; he was only a child still anyway. So it was just Papa and me and a handful of old churchmen. We had to take refuge in Sant'Angelo. Papa also brought along Giulia Farnese and my mother." He laughs, and his tone changes to that of the gossip-mongering courtier who charms the visitors to

La Fiammetta's salons. "Can you imagine? Poor Master Burchard, who refused to leave Papa's side, come what may, was terribly vexed by the order of precedence at dinner. Giulia was the current favourite but Mama, on the other hand, was the mother of the pope's favourite children.

"But that's not the point. The point is this. While the women bitched and my father and the other cardinals planned how they would negotiate with Charles, I watched his army. It was the biggest army ever seen in Italy; it took them till long after dark to get through the Porta del Popolo, and I never saw so much as one foot soldier out of step. They had cannon with a bore the size of a man's head. With an army like that at his back, even that slobbering little cripple could do anything he wanted. You know, Violante, it made my arms and legs tingle, cooped up in those horrible, thick-walled rooms in Sant'Angelo, thinking about what I could do with an army like that. It made me fall over my shiny new cardinal's robes, so my mother would snap at me for being clumsy."

Moved by a surge of affection for this awkward, out-of-place boy he is describing, I lift my head from his breast and kiss him.

"What was that for?" he asks, amused.

"Nothing. Go on. You haven't mentioned Urbino yet."

"You're too impatient. There's no hurry."

"People will be looking for us soon. What hour do you think it is?"

He assesses the angle of the shadows fading across the brick patio. "Thirteenth, fourteenth. Sun's going in, though. Where was I?"

"Being told off by your mother."

"*Plus ça change*," he says ruefully. "Yes, well, perhaps you know because it is one of those apocryphal stories they tell about me, that one of the conditions my father negotiated with Charles for his departure was that he could have me and Djem as hostages for everyone's good behaviour. Considering what his men had already done in Rome, and elsewhere, you might say it was shutting the stable door after the horse had bolted, but anyway, it was done. I escaped almost immediately. Papa and I had hatched a plan…"

"I know. We used to talk about it at my school. We used to talk about you quite a lot at school. The main reason my friends came to my baptism was in the hope of getting a look at you. But you weren't there."

"Ah, well, I didn't know how beautiful you were then. I might have been prepared to enter a church for you." He lifts my hair between his fingers and puts it to his lips. Then his fist tightens; he begins to pull, only stopping when my hiss of pain makes him realise he is hurting me. "But they killed Djem," he says, in a voice as flat and dangerous as ill-tempered steel.

"Donna Lucrezia says he died of a fever."

"He was poisoned, for sure. Charles realised how my father and I had planned my escape when he discovered my baggage train contained nothing but rocks and empty boxes, so he thought to spite Papa by depriving him of the money he received from the Sultan for Djem's keep. Djem was as strong as an elephant; he would not have succumbed to a fever that easily."

"You were very fond of him, weren't you?"

"He let us be ourselves. You have no idea how rare a thing that is for people like us."

I think of myself, of my fair looks and three names and the language I sometimes dream in but no longer understand, but I keep silent because I want to find out who Cesare is when he is himself.

"Entering his apartments was like walking into a dream. He lived in a sort of tent, with bright silk hangings rigged up like sails from the ceiling, and floors covered with cushions and silver trays on little curly legs, full of sweets."

I glance up at the canopy above us, feel the textures of silk and velvet against my skin, the tiny, random pricks of loose feathers. Perhaps Djem is watching us, from wherever the Mussulmen go when they die.

"He burned incense because he liked the smell, not to ingratiate himself with some deity that didn't give a damn about him. He taught us to cook *lokum* in a bronze pot hung over his fire, and encouraged us to drink poppy because he said there were all kinds of secrets locked up in a poppy seed that only the heat of our bellies could release. Lucrezia could never understand why you couldn't just inhale the perfume of the flowers, but of course, they have none. I will never forgive the French for Djem."

"But they are your allies. Your wife is French."

"Why must you keep harping on my wife? She is my wife, and the

French are not my allies; they are my tools, them and Spain. I will tell you one thing about my time in France and one thing only."

My heart begins a heavy, wet thudding, as though someone is pounding laundry inside my chest. I am not sure I want him to tell me anything about France.

"While I was there, I realised something. It was, I suppose, the effect of distance, a kind of mental perspective if you will. I realised that if Italy were ever to be anything more than a playground for the kings of France and Spain, then she must become a state herself, with a king of her own."

"You?"

He shrugs. "That does not matter. What matters is this." He turns to face me, burrowing deeper among the cushions, and I know he has nearly reached the end of his story because I can feel he is ready for love again. With my arms around his waist, I draw him against me.

"I took Urbino because I could," he whispers, "because I wanted it, because I'm never going to be anyone's prisoner ever again. I'm never going to do anyone's will but my own." He is on top of me now, his hair veiling our faces as we kiss, and I am opening to the sweet pressure of his desire...

"Don Cesar?"

In seconds he is on his feet, pulling his shirt over his head, shaking his hair out of his eyes. "Michelotto."

Time starts to move again.

⌘

Michelotto stood, legs crossed, leaning against one of the white marble pillars of the arcade with the air of a man who had seen all this before. Cesare's sword belt was slung over his shoulder, his spurs hanging from it as well as the sword, and the black tabard of the Knights of Saint John, in which Cesare had arrived in Ferrara in another lifetime, folded over his arm.

As I scrabbled among the cushions for my discarded clothes he said, "Salvatore's here. Says he's intercepted a summons from Cardinal Orsini to Vitellozzo. And he's got the assessment of fortifications at San Leo you asked Leonardo for."

"It begins, then. Good. Let's lance the boil once and for all."

Michelotto cast me a suspicious glance as Cesare hauled on his hose and breeches. "Not a problem," he said, in answer to his lieutenant's unspoken query. No problem indeed; I had no idea what Michelotto was talking about, though soon all Italy would be talking about it too.

Michelotto tossed him the tabard. He pulled it over his head and stepped out of the loggia. As he buckled on his sword he turned to me and said, "Bid my sister farewell for me. Tell her... tell her we will spend Christmas together."

And grinned, and blew me a kiss, and was gone, my last impression of him the clanking of his spurs overlaid by some choice remark about the state of the road to Milan. A saying of Plotinus came to me, one which had been a favourite of my father's, that the life of every practical man is a bewitchment.

⤬

I do not know how long I remained as I was, lying half naked in the loggia. My body ached with frustrated desire, yet my limbs, as I stretched them, felt impeded by a kind of heavy languor, as though I were under water. The air I breathed had become oppressively hot, yet my sweat was clammy and the damp patch where Cesare's seed had trickled out of me made a cold brand on my right buttock. It was that which roused me, the thought of my maiden's blood staining Donna Lucrezia's cushions. What would become of me if it were discovered? Shame burned my cheeks. Rolling on to my side, I looked over my shoulder. Thank God, neither my skin nor the cushions showed any marks, and I remembered what Angela had said about horse riding, and some of the things we had done together. My virginity had slipped away from me like a thief in the night, leaving no trace of itself.

I gathered up my clothes and began to dress, smoothing my rumpled shift and lacing my bodice as best I could with fingers that seemed reluctant to obey me. I rushed, I fumbled, both panicked by my nakedness in this place I had no right to be and thrilled by it because it marked my transition to womanhood in the arms of this man I so adored, who could—and did—have any woman he wanted and had chosen me, filling me with his intimacies until I thought I might burst with excitement.

Thunder rumbled. The gods, it seemed, were sceptical. I smiled defiance as I fastened my shoes and the first drops of rain smacked on to the leathery leaves of the orange trees and spread dark stains on the patio. No mere summer storm could threaten me, for I was the mistress of Cesare Borgia, the man the Roman gossips called the son of God. When people looked at me from now on, they would see the imprint of his passion on my body, the fever in his eyes reflected in mine. Anyone who brushed past me in the street might inhale the scent of jasmine clinging to my hair.

I could hardly wait to tell Angela everything, yet not everything. There are some transactions between lovers which, like the ancient paintings on the walls of the catacombs hollowed out beneath the streets of Rome, fall to dust on exposure to the air. How could I explain to Angela that the true change in me had been wrought, not by the physical act of penetration but by the power of words? It was like the powder burn all over again, to hear the terrible Valentino describe himself as a clumsy boy who got on his mother's nerves and had a weakness for Turkish sweets. The child in the man had made a woman of me.

Dragging and dawdling like the idiot girl with the wall eye who sold violets by the Porta Mare in the spring, I made my way back to the Torre Marchesana. The rain sluiced down now, veiling the empty piazza, streaming from the cloisters. I began to be aware of unfamiliar pains in my body, muscles stretched in my thighs, my lips bruised and chin stinging from the abrasion of Cesare's beard, a burning in my cunny that could not be described as purely pain. He had gone, he had made no promises, and my body was teaching me how loss feels.

Then a whiff of rosemary came to me through the dank smells of old, wet walls and moss-choked guttering. I stopped beside the bush clipped in the shape of a sword to breathe in its scent. Rosemary for remembrance. I glanced down at the moat, pocked by the rain until its surface resembled that of a battered pan, and thought of the baby, sleeping in the soft mud, among the quiet fishes. How right it was that she should be there, this child who had rejected the medium of air even before she had been pushed out into it. How far wide of the mark my own instincts had been, and how perfect Cesare's. How he humbled me, how lucky I was to have been chosen to bear the stigmata of his passion.

A crack of thunder which must have been directly overhead, putting up a pair of swans from the moat, brought me to my senses and the realisation that my feet were sodden, my shoes probably ruined. Even worse, I was sure to have been missed by now. I must try to sneak back to my quarters to change my clothes without being seen. With any luck, everyone would still be too busy attending Donna Lucrezia to notice me. Though I hoped Angela might be in our room to wrap me in a towel and hear my confession.

"Well, my dear, this is fine weather for mooching among the oranges." Ferrante, holding open the door at the end of the walkway. "I went to condole with your lady, and found her very peevish for want of her ministering angel. She said Duke Valentino had unaccountably left without bidding her farewell and you had disappeared. I did try to suggest you might be resting, but you were seen. Gossip and the smell of boiled cabbage—both can somehow get into every corner of the building. I must say you look...well, perhaps try to wipe that smile off your face before you enter the presence. She has just lost a child.

"And there is another thing you should know before you go up to her. Another loss. The slave, Catherinella."

With all that had happened, I had quite forgotten Catherinella.

"She is hanging from the Torre Leone in a cage," Ferrante continued, his tone flat, without emotion. "There is a wooden plaque around her neck. It says, 'Catherinella, slave, displayed at the command of the illustrious Don Alfonso for showing disrespect to his noble wife, the Duchess Lucrezia.'" We stared at one another; we both knew whose command lay behind that of Don Alfonso. "It is an unfathomable love they bear one another, your inamorato and his sister," said Ferrante, and I looked away.

"How long must she hang there?"

"Until she dies. It will not be long in this heat, without water. For that we must thank God."

Everyone has a price, he had said.

"But it's raining. We must get her down."

Ferrante looked at me as though I had proposed dislodging the moon from her orbit or asking the sun to shine at midnight. "How? And what could we do with her? Alfonso would never let your mistress take her back, even if she wanted to after she had shown such dishonesty."

"She wasn't stealing, Ferrante, she was...oh, never mind. But she wasn't stealing, I know. How are the cages hung? We must just do the same in reverse."

"The gaoler's men just throw them over the parapet. They fasten the chains into rings set into the roof and throw them over."

I thought of the cage, spinning and smashing into the wall of the tower, bouncing over pediments and window frames. "Well it wouldn't take much to haul it back. Catherinella doesn't weigh heavily; she's only small, not much more than a child I think, though it's hard to tell." Sometimes she seemed as ancient as Africa itself.

"Violante, be reasonable. It cannot be done. We would be discovered. Alfonso would surely have the slave killed and we would be punished also."

"What can he do to us? He is not duke yet, remember. Besides, we both know it wasn't him who imposed the sentence, whatever the plaque may say. We will do it. You must find someone to help. What about Vittorio?"

Ferrante sighed. "Vittorio is Cesare's creature, Violante. I tolerate it because he has certain…attributes I find irresistible. Cesare knows that. That is why he chose him to escort Donna Lucrezia to Ferrara."

"God, Ferrante, you're such a…such a woman! I will find someone and do it myself. A couple of madonna's footmen. That's it. She will protect us—even from Cesare."

"You think so?" he asked quietly. "What about Urbino?" His question surprised me. Somehow, I had never considered the possibility that Ferrante interested himself in politics. He waited a moment then, when I made no reply, went on, "There is something. A shoddy compromise, I'm afraid, but Alfonso would tell you that is my forte."

"What?" I demanded.

"Don't ask, child."

I'm not a child, not any longer, I wanted to point out, but Ferrante's tone had been sympathetic, not patronising, so I held my tongue. I had to trust him.

"Now go to your mistress. I am sure the distraction of your…adventures will aid her recovery."

I stood at the door a moment longer, watching Ferrante trudge back along the walk towards the orange garden, his shoulders braced against the echo of himself Cesare left everywhere like a malign and charming sprite. Why did I love him? I might as well ask why my heart beat or my lungs breathed.

The following morning, as a company of us were crossing the square to attend Mass in the cathedral to give thanks for madonna's recovery, we were distracted by a commotion among the knot of onlookers gawping up at the slave in her cage. People pointed and muttered. Instead of standing still, the small crowd whirled and shifted in agitation. Even the street hawkers, who rarely took much notice of prisoners hanging from the tower, had paused beneath Catherinella's cage with their necks craned upwards, regardless of light-fingered beggar boys making off with apples or apricots or hot pumpkin tarts from their trays. I looked up, but could see nothing other than the plank floor of the cage which emitted fine points of yellow light through its cracks. I glanced at Ferrante, standing beside Don Alfonso with his missal clutched across his chest. He refused to meet my eye. I saw him pluck at his brother's sleeve and try to urge him on, but Don Alfonso was already despatching one of his gentlemen to find out what had happened.

Word came just as the choir concluded the Te Deum, passing from mouth to mouth like fire jumping between buildings. The slave was dead. Somehow, she had acquired a length of rope, by which she had hanged herself from the great bolt in the roof of the cage that held the chain in place. Don Alfonso's thick neck was flushed beneath the line of his short hair. Next to him, Ferrante's head was bowed as if deep in prayer. I hope the All Merciful forgave him for what he did, risking his immortal soul for the dignity of a slave.

# THE BOOK OF
# BROKEN PROMISES

*She does know the earth
is run by mothers, this much
is certain. She also knows
she is not what is called
a girl any longer. Regarding
incarceration, she believes
she has been a prisoner since she has been a daughter.*

Louise Glück, "Persephone the Wanderer"

# CHAPTER 1

FERRARA, SEPTEMBER 1502

*I gave you nothing but an empty casket and a borrowed verse.*

Angela told me I was lucky.

"At least your face is clear," she said, straightening up and blowing out the candle by whose flame she had been examining my private parts. I had believed it was just a severe chill, hardly surprising considering I had become soaked to the skin during the storm and had been obliged by Donna Lucrezia to sit with her for as long as it took to explain, so far as I was able, why her brother the duke had left Ferrara with nothing but some futile promise to return at Christmas. That, she railed, with a renewed vigour I was too tired and cold to feel grateful for, was no use to her. It was now she needed him, now when she had to face up to the Este having not only miscarried but miscarried a daughter. She made no mention of Catherinella, though the body was left hanging for a fortnight, until the crows had had her eyes and much of her flesh and people passing by in the square below marvelled that her bones were as white as theirs.

Then Angela noticed me scratching. I cannot tell you which was worse, the shooting pains in my arms and legs which kept me tossing and turning all night in search of relief, or the itching and burning between my thighs which drove me into dark corners, behind screens or doors or garden trellises, anywhere I could scratch myself in private. I dreamed of sitting on ice blocks; I drank as little as I was able to avoid having to piss knife blades.

"It's just a chill on the kidneys," I said, levering myself on to my elbows.

"See for yourself," replied Angela, handing me a small mirror which I angled between my legs until I could see the reflection of my privities. A small ulcer filled with yellowish pus perched on the lip of them, hard and painless to my touch. "He has definitely left you a little *memento amoris.*"

"I thought he was cured." My voice sounded plaintive.

"Surely you don't imagine he has been a model of monkish virtue since Torella's famous mercury baths, you little goose. I suppose he has caught another dose himself." *Sickness smoulders in me like fire at the heart of a damp haystack; it ticks in the night like a death clock in the rafters.*

"I wish Torella was still here."

"Oh, we'll manage. We need a frog. Or a chicken. That would be easier. The main thing is to keep it from Lucrezia. It will not help her marriage plans for you if she cannot pass you off as clean and virgin." Since her recovery, this was madonna's great project, to find good husbands for us all, good Ferrarese husbands to help repair the damage done to her standing by her miscarriage. Angela was supporting her cousin enthusiastically in her endeavours as Donna Lucrezia was now championing her own prospects of marriage to Giulio.

"A frog?"

"A live frog, split in two and applied to the sore. Or a chicken."

"In the same way?"

"Yes. It's one of Ippolito's remedies," she confided, "and it must work because I am clean."

"But how long is it since you lay with him?" Ippolito had not been in Ferrara since before the fever, and even before that, it was my understanding Angela had begun to decline his attentions. She blushed; she fiddled with the mirror which I had handed back to her while I straightened my clothes.

"It's difficult," was all she would say.

❧

Though we made several attempts at catching a frog by means of flower pots and small keeping nets, pretending in front of madonna and the rest of her ladies that it was a game we had devised to ward off the chill of the autumn afternoons when we walked in the gardens, our efforts failed and a chicken had to be acquired. It was a messy process, for the bird had to be split and applied to the affected area while still alive. Lying flat on the floor, to save soiling my bedding and raising questions among the laundresses, with my legs spread and my skirts bunched around my waist, there was little I could do to help Angela keep a firm grasp on the protesting bird, a task made harder for her by her decision to wear a hawking glove to save her hands from its pecking and scratching.

Nor was she certain how long the dying fowl should be kept pressed against the ulcer. Until it's cold, was the suggestion of Ferrante, who had procured the gauntlet and kept watch outside our door; it was impossible to trust any of the rest of Donna Lucrezia's women, for Angela and I were more resented than loved for being her favourites and the pious Fidelma had made herself a focus of hostility towards us, believing we led madonna astray and were probably responsible for her miscarriage by encouraging her to dance and keep late hours. We compromised. Angela kept the squirming, blood-pulsing mound of flesh and feathers braced against my privates until it fell still and its blood stopped flowing and it was clearly dead. Then she threw it on the fire and the stink of burning feathers made me cough as I stepped out of my soiled petticoats and sponged my thighs.

"Perhaps we should have made a broth of it, for good measure," I said.

"I swear I will never eat anything made of a fowl again." Angela flung the washing water after the fowl in an attempt to damp down the bitter smoke, but only made matters worse.

"Well now we shall stink of giblets. You'll have to lend me your perfume."

"Only if I can wear your rubies. Giulio says they bring out the colour of my hair."

That evening, there was to be a new play devised by Ercole Strozzi, and madonna was entertaining him to dinner beforehand. Despite his twisted leg and the receding forehead that seemed to thrust his eyes and nose forward like those of a large ferret, we all adored Strozzi because he made us laugh. Madonna's friend, Barbara Torelli, was much given to intellectualising about the erotic power of laughter, and she should have known for she was sleeping with Strozzi; it was an open secret.

❧

Whether by luck or Angela's healing skill, the chicken remedy worked and, as the autumn progressed and we began to look forward to the short season of Carnival before Advent, I felt wonderfully well. My appetite, which had tended to be modest since I joined Donna Lucrezia's household with its Christian eating habits, grew ravenous. I devoured everything, from creamy risottos seasoned with juniper broth to crayfish we grilled ourselves over small braziers and ate straight from the shells when we "picnicked" in Donna Lucrezia's apartments before donning our carnival masks and venturing out to join the revels in the town. One day, watching acrobats perform in the piazza, I ate so many sugared almonds and sweet cheeses Angela muttered she was afraid our stand would collapse and Fidelma permitted herself to wonder if I were fattening myself up in anticipation of the Advent fast, like a camel contemplating a desert journey.

Though hunting and hawking were duties I previously undertook solely at my lady's command, that autumn I rode out at every opportunity, savouring the meaty warmth of fresh-killed game mingled with the smells of horses and saddle soap and frost on water. I loved to watch Don Alfonso's truffle hounds at work in the woods and to eat fine slivers of the pungent, earth-scented fungus fried in butter over woodsmen's fires. The truffles were the colour of long-buried bones, and I wondered if this was why the hounds were attracted to them.

When the dressmaker came to fit us for the new gowns madonna was to give us for Christmas, he consulted his notes and found my waist had grown by half a hand's width. My breasts, too, had acquired a more womanly gravity and, said Angela, with an unreadable look, I was developing a little pad of fat beneath my chin identical to that Donna Lucrezia had inherited from her father. She spent half an hour every morning with her chin raised and neck extended, massaging the flesh in an attempt to dissipate it.

"I shall change your name," announced Angela. "From now on you will be La Bolognese, because we all know how they enjoy their oral pleasures."

Something drew up tight in my gut in response to her innuendo and her casual dismissal of the name Cesare had given me. "My name isn't yours to change," I spat back, and tipped my platter of bread with oil and anchovy paste on to the floor where Fonsi snaffled it.

Sometimes, we behave in certain ways only because we do not know why we are doing it. Once I realised I was eating to fill the empty place left by Cesare, though I was often still hungry at odd times of the day and night, the ache in my belly became confused with that in my heart as I waited for word from him which never came. I consoled myself with endless rehearsals to Angela of my small stock of memories, until her eyes became glazed, her smile fixed, and she nodded at me like an automaton. I made excuses for him. To begin with, he was with the French court in Milan. Perhaps his wife was there; even if she was not, as she was a cousin of the queen, perhaps it was difficult for him to get a letter to me without his infidelity being discovered. Then, once his letters to his sister and Don Alfonso informed us he was back in the Romagna, well, he was a busy man, with much to secure before he could return to Ferrara for Christmas.

Yet scarcely a day passed without a letter for madonna. Sometimes she would share passages with Angela and me. The woman's brazenness was scarcely credible, she told us one day, but Donna Isabella had written to Duke Valentino requesting an antique Cupid from the gardens at Urbino, "knowing that Your Excellency does not take much pleasure in antiques." And this while the erstwhile duke and duchess were still in exile in Mantua. He had sent the Cupid, and an accompanying Venus, by special messenger; the gift had given him particular pleasure, he added, as the statues were not antiques but fakes, mocked up by the Florentine, Michelangelo. He had recognised the work immediately, because the Florentine had made some similar pieces for the vestibule of his palace in Rome. He had also, he added, sent Guidobaldo the *De Consolatione Philosophiae* from his father's library, before having the rest of the books boxed up and dispatched to the *rocca* at Forli for safekeeping until he had decided what to with them. Though we all laughed, I felt only my laughter came close to the same bleak and mordant tone of the letter.

Only once did I receive a message from him. Enclosed in a letter to madonna sent from Imola was a small sketch on a rough palimpsest. It showed Cesare's head and shoulders, the expression on his face characteristically self-contained, his mouth drawn down at the corners, his eyes shielded by their long, thick lashes. Ghosts of a cramped, crooked handwriting shadowed his cheeks and had become entangled in his beard.

*Give this to Violante*, madonna read. *My engineer, Leonardo, did it while I was looking at a map he has made me of Imola, just as if he had flown over the city on the back of a great bird. He has made me look like an Old Testament prophet so our little Israelite should appreciate it. This Leonardo does me many services. The other day, as a group of us had dined together and were being treated to Sperulo's latest panegyric on my achievements, he let loose on the table a small lizard with paper wings fastened to its back, each quartered red and yellow in my livery. Chaos ensued, most of the women screaming and running from the room, and Ramiro stabbed Torrigiano in the hand trying to spear the lizard to the board. When I asked Leonardo later if he was pleased his rival sculptor would be out of commission for some weeks, he simply said he had noticed I was falling asleep—the room was crowded, the fire banked high, the wine heavy and, to be honest, Sperulo's version of the fall of this fine city somewhat tame for my taste—and so had devised this joke to wake me up.*

Madonna continued to read, though silently, now smiling, now frowning, leaving me to torture myself with thoughts of the women Cesare mentioned so casually. Who were they? The wives and mistresses of his dinner guests, or his own? Was Dorotea Caracciolo among them? Was she truly so beautiful Cesare had risked the wrath of Venice to have her? I stared miserably at the drawing clutched in my hand, this substitute of parchment for my lover's own, warm skin, this reduction of the fires running in his veins to lines of charcoal.

Donna Lucrezia, I thought, did not need even a picture of her brother, for his words conjured him up for her. His letters were the start of long, internal conversations between them as though they remained somehow physically present to one another despite the distance of miles and the worsening weather as winter set in and the Advent fast imposed itself upon us. My loneliness would have been incomprehensible to her, even if she had noticed it.

But she did not. She was too busy repairing the damage done to her position by the loss of her daughter, passing her evenings and nights with her husband and her days in the company of his brothers. She would even, from time to time, listen gravely to Sigismondo as he expounded his plan for poisoning the rat king with the blood of a pig held upside down and beaten to death. Though she warmed, as always, to Ferrante's wit and Giulio's singing, it was Ippolito, now returned from Rome and full of news from the Vatican, who commanded most of her attention.

The two little boys, Rodrigo and Giovanni, had looked enchanting in the velvet caps she had sent them and were thrilled with the parrot. The Holy Father remained, God be praised, in robust health and as sharp in his mind as ever. His pride in his children was undiminished, though he grieved for Lucrezia's loss and was currently exasperated by Duke Valentino's mysterious silence and inertia. Overhearing Ippolito's conversations with Lucrezia, I learned that the fortress of San Leo, in the Duchy of Urbino, had rebelled against Cesare in October and a league of his enemies had been signed against him at the Orsini stronghold of La Magione. Yet Cesare, apparently, did nothing but go hunting around Imola and trade jokes with Leonardo. *The ground is burning beneath their feet,* he had told the Florentine orator, *and there is not enough piss in any of their maidens' bladders to put it out.*

I was afraid for him. I longed to confide my fear in Donna Lucrezia, to hear her tell me she knew he was in control, always a step ahead of his enemies. But it was clear from her tense and doubtful smile that she was as much in the dark as her father. Then I remembered Michelotto mentioning San Leo when he found us in the orange garden, and I realised that the balance had tipped. For once, I knew more about Cesare's plans than his beloved sister or even the pope. I hugged my knowledge to me as if it was a lover, a comforter, a shield, but I said nothing to Donna Lucrezia. If I shared what I knew, its power would dissipate. She would ask me questions I could not answer. She might come to believe me capable of betraying Cesare and warn him away from me. So I kept my counsel, and told myself there was nothing to fear.

On Saturdays madonna, accompanied by Duke Ercole, was in the habit of visiting Sister Osanna. She took me with her only once, but the holy clairvoyant's reaction to my presence was so curious and unnerving that, without anything being said, the decision was taken to leave me behind in future. The very moment I entered the visitors' half of the parlour, a few steps behind madonna and carrying her ermine wrap, Sister Osanna fell into a kind of fit, toppling sideways from her chair, her back arched and rigid, legs twitching, a foam bubbling between her lips and dribbling down her chin. Her left hand remained raised, the index finger pointing crookedly in my direction, until Sister Lucia, who was accompanying her, suggested to madonna that she send me away.

Doubts were expressed about the authenticity of my conversion and I was sent to see Father Tommaso. Fidelma took my place on the Saturday visits, though I do not think this pleased the duke as well as my presence did. Fidelma's Christianity held so much more conviction than mine, she did not need the exposure to the holy sisters to ensure her place in heaven. And I was more attractive to the old man's eye than the scrawny Mantuan, especially since my gowns had been altered to show off my new, womanly shape. He no longer kept a mistress, but he was inclined to pinch my buttocks occasionally when he had drunk a cup too many, and on several occasions sought me out to try jewels on me which he was thinking of giving to madonna. As our colouring was so similar, he explained.

Father Tommaso set me meditations on the Holy Martyrs and prayed over me in Donna Lucrezia's chapel until my head was spinning like Saint Catherine's wheel and my unchristian stomach growled for something cooked on Saint Lawrence's gridiron. Secretly I meditated on the coming of Christmas, and my own saint, my Saint Valentine. Perhaps he would stay until Epiphany. As an honoured guest of the family he would no doubt be given rooms close to madonna's, to which he could invite me. I saw him standing at the door to his bedchamber, clad only in a fur-lined robe, a blazing fire and the corner of the bed visible behind him. I felt him envelop me in his arms, the two of us skin to skin, tented in fur. We would have entire nights in which to perfect our lovemaking and mornings jewelled with frost on which to ride out hawking. Perhaps the lake would freeze over and there would be skating parties. Beyond the range of the lanterns we would glide together where the ice threw back a perfect reflection of the star-spangled sky so it would be as though we were flying through the heavens themselves, the ring of our skates echoing the music of the spheres.

❧

Christmas morning brought a light sprinkling of slushy snow from a dirty yellow sky, just enough to mute the city's colours but not to gladden the eye with a blanket of sparkling white. Although, much to the delight of Ferrante, Cesare's young officer Vittorio had arrived in Ferrara on Christmas Eve, there was no sign of his master.

We attended Mass in the cathedral where Ippolito preached on the iniquities of the census which had taken the Holy Family to Bethlehem. His meaning was not lost on any of us; it was common knowledge that the pope had recently imposed new taxes on the clergy to pay, it was said, for a new levy of troops for Cesare. We stole apprehensive glances at madonna, who sat beside her husband beneath a white silk canopy, holding his hand and wearing an expression of enigmatic gravity. We had to fight our way back across the piazza through a crowd which had gathered to hear a mendicant friar's rant about the humility of the baby in the manger. Some appeared to be listening seriously, but as many were pelting him with cabbage leaves and doffed their caps reverently as we passed by, tall and stately in our pattens, our slaves holding skirts and cape hems clear of the slush of snow and crushed fruit.

Halfway across the square, Fidelma hesitated and turned back towards the friar, who was mounted on the back of a flatbed cart. Elisabetta Senese walked into the back of her and lost her balance. Helped to her feet by a giggling Vittorio and a moon-faced youth who followed Elisabetta about like a pet dog but later died of smallpox, she slapped Fidelma across the face for causing the ruin of her new Christmas gown. The friar's congregation was quickly distracted by the prospect of a fight. The friar looked across to see what was happening. Fidelma, apparently oblivious to Elisabetta's slap and the red welt beginning to rise on her sallow cheek, lifted her chin to look over the top of the rabble; she was so tall in her pattens it was easy for her. It was as though her gaze was joined to that of the mendicant in his mud-spattered woollen robe and threadbare black cloak, by a taut, invisible string. I looked around for Angela.

"Angela," I whispered, tugging on her arm to distract her from dusting down the flushed and trembling Elisabetta, "*Angela*."

"What?"

"I think that must be Fidelma's Fra Raffaello. You know, the hedge preacher she thanks for her conversion. Look at them."

She turned. I noticed the gash of blood darkening the lapis blue of her skirt. "You're bleeding," I whispered. "I'll walk behind you." Due to the complexities of her love life, Angela had lost track of her cycle. She swore at me, then smiled and thanked me, but her change of mood was lost on me, Fidelma, and her friar forgotten. With a sick clenching of my bowels, and a flush rising up my neck as I contemplated what an utter fool I had been, I realised I myself had not bled for months.

Not since Cesare left.

My face burned. Cold sweat trickled down my sides, making me shiver. It couldn't be... Angela had said... Perhaps it was just some lingering side effect of the pox. But oh God, what if it had made me barren? What hope of a good marriage then? "Come on," I said, giving Angela a sharp shove in the back. "Madonna and Don Alfonso are almost at the Corte. We'll be missed." She cast me an irritated look but set off obediently to catch up to Donna Lucrezia, with me close behind as though I were helping to keep her skirts clear of the snow.

❧

"We'll have to talk about this later," she said as she bound on a pad and stepped into a fresh petticoat, and I dabbed at the stain on her brocaded overskirt with a damp towel. "We can't do anything in a hurry and there'll be trouble if we miss present giving."

"D'you think he might be there by now? In the Sala Grande?"

"Dearest Violante," she shook her head in a kind of benevolent exasperation, "he's not coming. I doubt he ever was. It was just his get out strategy. I've known Cesare all my life and I've never yet known him do what he said he'd do. Deceit is like a drug with him. He has no idea when to stop using it."

I blinked furiously. I refused to cry and smudge the shading I had so carefully applied to my eyelids with a burnt stick. Whatever Angela said, Cesare might still arrive, and what would he think of me if my skin were blotched and my eyes swollen with weeping for him? What competition would I be then for the bewitching Dorotea Caracciolo?

❧

The present giving in the Sala Grande seemed interminable. The duke and his family were seated on a dais at the head of the hall, with the ladies and gentlemen of the household obliged to stand in packed ranks, gentlemen down one side, ladies down the other, leaving room for all the stewards, secretaries, treasurers, cooks, grooms, the head of Don Alfonso's foundry and his chief potter, the tiny, bow-legged man who trained Duke Ercole's racehorses, the poets and musicians and court painters, to process down the middle of the hall to receive their gifts. Slaves wearing new red and green tunics and chamois leather gloves carried the gifts from a long table set out below the dais, up to the duke and his family in the order in which they were to be presented.

I tried to distract myself from my aching back and pinching slippers, and the odour of unwashed bodies inadequately masked by clashing perfumes, by wondering how much drill the slaves had been put through by the duke's chief steward in order to ensure the under falconer's wife received her jar of candied fruits and Sigismondo's personal valet his set of embroidered handkerchiefs and not the other way around. I played a game with myself. If the groom responsible for Don Alfonso's racing pigeons received his gift before the keeper of Ferrante's peacocks, Cesare would arrive in the next five minutes. If I could count to fifty before the head brewer's small daughter could cover the ground from the hall door to the dais, he would not come until dinner time. If more than three of the candles in the great bronze stands flanking the dais burnt out before Duke Ercole's speech of thanks to his staff for their year's service was complete, it would be tomorrow. Whatever Angela said, my stubborn heart refused to entertain the notion he would not come at all.

Though I worried about the weather. By the time we were finally released to prepare for the evening's entertainment, and were crossing the courtyard towards the Torre Marchesana, the snow had begun to fall more thickly. Straw strewn cobbles were transformed into a blue-grey carpet, splashed with sparkling apricot where the torches fastened to the gate towers caught it. Fat, silent flakes whirled out of the darkening sky, catching in our eyelashes. Angela turned up her face and stuck out her tongue. Her skin glowed; snow-stars glittered briefly among her curls before melting in her warmth. Swooping groundward, she gathered a handful of snow, moulded it into a ball, and threw it at me. It caught me on the side of my neck and slid down towards my shoulder, a slick of ice, melting, dripping from my hair, soaking my shift and bodice.

The tears were hot; that was how I knew the difference.

"Please, Violante, please." Angela flung her arms around me and pulled me close, smoothing my hair, pressing her cold cheek to my wet one. "I'm sorry. Don't cry. It doesn't mean anything, Cesare not coming. You know what men are. Take Ippolito. Dear Ippolito has been sharing a bed with Sancia all the time he was in Rome, but it doesn't mean he isn't just as hot for me now he's come back. Men have short memories. We may not like it, but we have no option but to accept it. It's just the way the world turns."

I wondered if she would be so cool if it were Giulio who had been sleeping with Princess Sancia, but it would have been spiteful to say such a thing, and she was trying to cheer me up. But even if she was right, even if, when Cesare was with me, I had the power to drive all thoughts of other women from his head, I still had something to cry about.

"What about the other thing?"

"God, there you are." Elisabetta Senese, the water mark still visible like the outline of a map on her yellow Venetian velvet. "Angela, you'll have to talk some sense into her. She's decided she wants a bath, it's so cold. She's already ordered the bathhouse prepared, but it will take hours to heat the water, and we shall be late, then the duke will fume and Don Alfonso will sulk and…"

"Well, I can't go to the baths; I'm bleeding. Besides, Don Giulio told me he and all his brothers are performing a new work by Tromboncino tonight. For six violas. Tromboncino will play the sixth. God knows what Sigismondo will do, but we had better not delay."

Tromboncino's concerto for six violas notwithstanding, madonna insisted on her bath, but as Angela was indisposed, excused me to keep her company. We should wait in her apartments, she said, in order to oversee the new slave. The new slave had been sent by Cesare, and wore a gold collar embossed with his coat of arms. She was Dalmatian, he thought, washed up on the beach at Porto Cesenatico following the destruction of a pirate vessel by the guns guarding the port. A striking child, with high, sharp cheekbones, pale skin, and hair the blue black of crow's feathers, she spoke no language any of us could understand and Donna Lucrezia had not yet given her a name.

As I watched her moving silently around madonna's dressing chamber, laying out her clothes, smoothing the nap of her crimson velvet bodice with tiny, deft fingers, polishing a jewel on her sleeve, despite myself I began to remember the beach at Nettuno. I told myself that part of my life was over, irrelevant, exorcised along with my Jewishness by the priest who had baptised me. But the human mind cannot, it seems, be made to cease its work; it continues scrabbling about among its old records like a tenacious scholar, seeking out connections. How could my mother's pathetic end be without purpose, if the thought of it was what had spurred my father to make his decision, and the memory of it was what drove me to accept? If the road which began at Nettuno would end with my becoming a mother myself?

"You can get rid of it, you know. I know lots of ways. From Sancia. No, you stupid girl, not like that! Two drops of musk in the rosewater. God, Violante, why did that lover of yours have to go and hang Catherinella?"

He didn't, I thought, but I kept the thought to myself. "W…what? Get rid..? Sancia? But you said it wasn't possible to get pregnant the first time."

"Did he only enter you once?"

"You know he did. I've told you often enough. Michelotto turned up."

She shrugged. "Well there is always an exception to prove the rule. And as I said, I know how you can get rid of it."

"As Princess Sancia did."

"Yes, darling, Sancia. I helped her ever so many times. Juniper's the least painful but a needle is probably the most reliable."

I sat down abruptly on madonna's dressing stool before my legs buckled under me. "Was it…were they…Cesare's?"

Angela shrugged. "Who knows? The only thing you can be certain of is they weren't Jofre's. All he ever did was watch."

"Watch. I see."

"You don't, do you?" She squatted in front of me, taking my hands in hers. Hers were so warm. "But if you want to have this baby, well, that makes you family. So you might as well know what kind of family we are. Jofre's impotent. He just likes to watch."

"And Cesare…?"

"Well I don't think her other lovers knew. But Cesare, well, you give him a stage and he'll perform."

I twisted my hands out of her grasp. "I know what you're trying to do, Angela, but it won't work. I don't care about those things. I love him. My baby is part of him. I'm not going to let you kill it." I tried to stand, but Angela laid her head in my lap, its weight pinioning me to the stool. Her arms slid around my waist and I felt the warm vibration of her laughter through the layers of my clothes.

"You've got quite a little belly there already," she said, sitting back on her heels. "You're going to have to tell Lucrezia. Sooner rather than later."

"Do you think she'll be less angry if she knows it's Cesare's?"

"I'm not sure," said Angela, dropping her gaze. For a moment, she looked so like him it made my throat ache.

I meant to tell Donna Lucrezia the following day, the Feast of Saint Stephen, but she rose very late and then only to receive a messenger from her brother. The man had struggled through blizzards to bring secret dispatches to the duke, Don Alfonso, and Ippolito, and a note for madonna whose brevity was chilling. Sitting up in bed swathed in a fur wrap, sipping her hot water and lemon juice, she turned the single sheet, folded and sealed, over and over in her hand, examining it from every angle before demanding a knife with which to cut the seal. I had made sure I brought her her morning drink alone, to give me the opportunity of asking for a private audience in order to tell her my news. Now I made to excuse myself from her presence while she read her brother's letter but she commanded me to stay.

"I have an anxious feeling about this," she said. "Do not leave me alone with it."

I stood at her side, my hands folded into my sleeves for warmth, arms resting on the little rise of my belly, brushing against the sideways swell of my growing breasts. She read the entire letter aloud.

*Illustrious lady,* she began, then paused to sip her drink and grimaced at its sharpness, *and beloved sister, we beg to inform you that this morning, the Feast of the Nativity, we have had executed Ramiro da Lorqua, formerly governor of the Romagna, for the crime of embezzlement.*

Madonna gasped. "Ramiro? Ramiro has been with him…oh, I can't remember how long. Longer than Michelotto even. It is impossible."

Ramiro, I thought, though I said nothing, that same Ramiro of whom he had written fondly only weeks ago when describing the incident with the winged lizard. Madonna read on, her tone weighed down with doubt and dread.

*On Saint Stephen's Day we shall leave here for Senigallia, to receive the surrender, and we would request your prayers for our safe journey.*

*Your devoted brother, who loves you as himself,*

*Caesar Valentinus*

*Given at Cesena the 25th day of December, the year of Our Lord 1502.*

The letter was in the hand of Cesare's confidential secretary, Agapito Geraldini, and countersigned by him.

"Prayers?" demanded Donna Lucrezia, frowning at me. "Since when did Cesare ask for prayers?" She shivered. "Send word to my husband and ask him if he will see me, then come back and dress me right away. Call the Dalmatian. Where is Angela?"

"I will fetch her immediately, madonna." Angela, I knew, was waiting in our room for news of my meeting with madonna.

"And Violante, perhaps we had better pray…"

"Yes, madonna."

For the rest of that day and most of the next, we ladies were left to our own devices while madonna consulted with her husband and his family over the contents of Cesare's despatches. Though we passed our time mainly in the Camera Dal Pozzolo, where our small looms and embroidery frames were set up and we kept a good supply of poetry books, song sheets, and a couple of old lutes, even there the frisson of nervous excitement pervading the Corte reached us. Every time we heard voices in the gardens, or hooves in the courtyard, someone rushed to a window or out into the stairwell to look and listen. Around the middle of the second day, a disconsolate Strozzi called on us in our tower, but though he did his best with rhymes and jokes and banter with madonna's clowns, even the Ferrarese girls, to whom Cesare was little more than a name, a cold breath on the back of the neck, a ghost in the guise of a knight of Saint John, remained distracted and serious.

I was in agony. I tried to pray, but my prayers came back to me, useless as echoes. To what god could I pray, a *conversa* asked to pray for an atheist? What did he mean by his request anyway? Was it some kind of code? If so, clearly madonna did not understand it. Or had something occurred which was enough to frighten Cesare into a reliance on religion? Had Lady Fortune deserted him? Was he dead? Surely I would feel it if he were, now his seed was growing inside me.

Then it happened. The message came. I dropped a ball of yarn I had been winding with Fidelma and, as I bent to pick it up, my eye picked out a tiny lion in the design of the rug beneath my chair. San Leo. All this had begun with the rebellion at San Leo. I forced my mind to go back over Michelotto's rude interruption of my tryst with his lord. What had he said? What exactly? *He's got the assessment of fortifications at San Leo you asked Leonardo for.* He had asked his engineer to undertake a survey. As if he already knew, as if he were planning something of his own.

I handed the yarn to one of the others, saying I needed to answer a call of nature. Angela threw me a meaningful look, a frequent need to urinate being, she assured me, one of the certain signs of pregnancy. Closing the door quietly behind me, I raced to the duke's apartments in the Corte. Needless to say, I had never entered them before. But as I stood outside the door to his solar, waiting for his doorman to find out if Donna Lucrezia was there, I felt no nervousness, just a consuming desperation to reassure madonna that her brother was not in danger.

I could hear voices behind the door, the rumble of the men's, the occasional, lighter interjection from madonna, but I could not discern what they were saying. Suddenly Fonsi started yapping and a hound growled in reply, and there were murmurs of strained laughter. One of the duke's exotic cats shot through the flap in the base of the door, its tail puffed up like a flue brush. Then I heard the footman's voice, a brief, gruff response from the duke and the footman's soft shoes whispering back towards the door. I took a deep breath, squared my shoulders, and stepped into the room.

The hunting scenes on the wall hangings seemed alive in the light from the fire and the ranks of candles in brass stands, hounds baying after fleeing stags, huntsmen's spears plunged into the flanks of spotted boar. The Este and Donna Lucrezia were seated around a deep fireplace, Ferrante and Don Alfonso side by side on a settle, Giulio on the floor with the spaniel in his lap, Donna Lucrezia on a low faldstool. Sigismondo was not there. The duke leaned forward in his high-backed chair as I walked towards the family group, his thin lips compressed to nothing, eyes as blank as a snake's. He held a small silver hammer in his right hand, the sort used for cracking nuts, and tapped it steadily against the palm of his left. He favoured me, I kept reminding myself as I approached; he had often shown it.

"You have something you wish to say to the duchess?" he asked, his tone dangerously quiet. As Donna Lucrezia turned towards me I noticed the patches of hectic colour on her cheeks that told me how angry she was beneath her calm exterior. I hesitated.

"Whatever you have to say you may say in front of my family," she said, shifting almost imperceptibly closer to Don Alfonso. I looked from her faint and inscrutable smile around the faces of the Este turned expectantly towards me, from Don Alfonso's small, hard eyes, blue and bloodshot, to Don Giulio, his gaze open and violet as a summer evening sky. How could I speak in front of them, every one still outraged, however discreetly, by Cesare's treatment of the Duke and Duchess of Urbino? Yet what excuse could I make for my intrusion? My mind whirled; I could no longer think.

"I'm sorry," I mumbled, feeling my cheeks begin to flame, the sound of the duke's hammer cracking a nut going off like a shot inside my head. I turned and fled, aware at the edge of consciousness of Ferrante rising from the settle and taking a step towards me.

I ran back to the Torre Marchesana, heedless of the snow now turning to ice beneath my feet, shut myself in Angela's and my room and waited for the world to fall in on me. Madonna's summons was not long in coming. Angela was her messenger, her face white as a goose egg as she peered around our door and told me I was wanted.

I went immediately; though delay could not make matters any worse, I decided it was best to confront my fate head on, before I had time to think about it. As I entered the room I dropped madonna a deep curtsey. With a swish of velvet, the thud of her small feet pounding the floor, she was close enough to grasp me by the ear and pull me to my feet. Then she slapped my face so hard I felt the bones of my jaw jar together and saw a heaven of exploding stars before my eyes.

"God's blood and balls, girl, what did you mean by such behaviour?" she yelled, inches from my face, her breath, smelling of cloves, in my nostrils. "As if it were not enough that my brother, 'who loves me as himself,'" she quoted with a sneer, "seems set on jeopardising everything we...I...Do you imagine playing mares and stallions with him gives you the right to meddle in matters of state? If that were the case half the women in Italy would be queuing up to advise me. You believed I didn't know?" she went on, pausing only long enough to read the question that must have formed itself on my face. "You think when I ask Michelotto where my brother is and he says the duke is not to be found we don't both know perfectly well what he means? Oh, grow up, Violante."

Not knowing my true compulsion to tell her what I knew, or thought I knew, or had conjured out of a few words, half understood, she meant to humiliate me. Instead, she made me angry. My eyes felt hot and dry; a tiny muscle began to tick in my bruised cheek; my belly clenched with rage until I feared the baby might be crushed.

"I have every right," I shouted back, rushing on before Donna Lucrezia could recover from her astonishment. "My only misjudgement was in thinking I could say what I had to say in front of the duke and Don Alfonso."

"What are you talking about, girl?"

"I am pregnant, madonna. With Cesare's child. I think that gives me at least as much right to be concerned for his welfare as you."

Silence. A log settled in the fire with a soft crackle. I heard the foolish, monotonous cooing of a wood pigeon from beyond the casement. Donna Lucrezia stared at me, fists clenched at her sides, breast heaving beneath the lace fichu she had put on to appear modest in front of her father-in-law. A smile forced its way on to her lips, though her eyes seemed magnified by unshed tears. "Of course," she said. Her face assumed an inward expression, brows drawn together in a slight frown, as though she were searching for something. "The eating."

"Eating?"

"Yes. Surely you have noticed how Cesare eats? He is always ravenous."

"I have not really had the opportunity, madonna."

She looked surprised at this, then said, "No, I suppose you haven't. When he was born, he was very poorly, you see, not expected to live. He was ill nearly all the time until he was five. He had to spend every afternoon resting. Can you imagine it?"

I could not. Cesare was notorious for the hours he kept, holding audiences in the middle of the night with bleary-eyed ambassadors, hunting at dawn with companions who frequently nodded off to sleep on horseback while he watched his pet leopards pit their cunning and agility against swift stags and bad-tempered boar. Perhaps he had accumulated a lifetime's rest in five years of afternoon naps. Perhaps he had been born knowing the time would come when he would be forced to race against his father's advancing years to build a state strong enough to withstand the old pope's death when it came.

"Anyway," continued madonna, "having spent five years living on little more than bread and goats' milk, once he grew strong enough he developed an enormous appetite. It seems this little one," and she nodded towards my belly, "is going to be just the same."

I felt lightheaded with relief at the good natured way she seemed to be taking my news, so much so I feared I might faint and had to ask for permission to sit. Madonna herself drew up a stool for me, asked me if I needed water. We sat either side of the fire, madonna in her high-cushioned chair, the tips of her toes scarcely grazing the floor, me on my stool, trying to ignore my aching back. Seeing me reach for a log and the poker, she immediately admonished me and rang for her slave.

Once the girl had mended the fire and left, she asked me, "Well? What was it you had to tell me?"

"I don't know exactly. It's just that, whatever is going on now seems to have begun with the rebellion of San Leo."

Madonna nodded, as though approving my analysis. "Go on."

"Well, when Michelotto discovered us, Cesare and me..."

"Yes, yes, stop your simpering and get on with it."

"He said a messenger had come, then something to do with Vitelozzo, and that Leonardo had prepared the plans of San Leo Cesare had asked for. It made me wonder if Cesare organised the rebellion himself. To flush out the Magione conspirators."

Donna Lucrezia nodded. "So you think there is nothing to worry about? That he is in control and his plea for our prayers is some kind of double bluff? You are either very naïve, or the only woman I have ever met who thinks as deviously as he does. All we can do now, I suppose, is wait and see which it is, but at least your news gives us something to occupy ourselves."

"Yes, madonna." Though it seemed to me that my pregnancy was also a matter of waiting and seeing.

"You must be found a husband. And it will be even less easy now than before. You know the duke is still withholding payment of some of my bride money, so I have little enough to endow you with and you, my dear, are a pill that needs a great deal of sweetening. A *conversa*, and now pregnant. On the other hand," she mused, seeming to carry on the conversation more with herself than with me, "Cesare will own the child and he will be generous, so if we can find a man prepared to tolerate a well-fledged cuckoo in the nest…Yes, well, leave it with me. And look after yourself. You must rest, and avoid shocks. No dancing, no…well, that is unlikely, I imagine. You must stay out of the wind but not sit too close to the fire…"

"Madonna?"

"Yes?"

"May I ask a question?"

"Of course."

"Where is Senigallia?"

"It is a little south of Pesaro. Why?" My expression must have given her all the answer she needed. Leaning forward to close her hand over mine where they lay knotted in my lap she said, "I'm sorry, Violante. It doesn't look as though he will be coming this way again soon, whatever he said to you."

"Then I must write and tell him about the baby." I must look forward, not back.

"No," said madonna quickly, "let me do that. It will carry more authority, coming from me. He will not think you are trying to deceive him."

"Why would I do that?"

"Women do. He is wealthy and powerful, and because he can be gentle and charming when he pleases, they think they can make him believe sentimental lies. They think they know him. Do not make that mistake, Violante. You might make him a lifetime's study and you would not know him."

She had hit near enough the mark to embarrass me. A flush began in my cheeks but seemed to grow and spread until I felt as though a brazier had been lit in my belly. Mindful of Donna Lucrezia's instructions, I shifted my stool back from the fire. "But you will tell him soon, madonna? I would not wish my condition to become known and my baby's parentage remain unacknowledged."

"When the time is right, I promise. Do not worry. Your child carries my blood too, remember. I will see it properly cared for. On that you have my word."

"Thank you, madonna."

"You may go. I will rest now. We have a long evening ahead of us at the Roverella ball, and I have promised the volta to Ferrante. He tells me Roverella's musicians have practised nothing else for a week so it will not do if I am too tired to perform it." I was relieved to hear her say she would dance with Ferrante, for I felt he had been out of favour somewhat since Catherinella's death, almost as if Don Alfonso knew...

It was a season of balls. Almost every night, it seemed, we gathered in the castle courtyard after supper to walk or ride to the home of one of Ferrara's foremost citizens to dance and listen to intermezzi and eat fairy palaces made of spun sugar and almond paste. It was nearly a year, now, since madonna's marriage to Don Alfonso and the initial coolness of Ferrarese society had been replaced by, if not affection for their new duchess, at least a cautious acceptance of her. The dour Castello Estense had fallen prey to no orgies, there had been no poisonings or bodies found floating in the moat, nothing more sensational, in fact, than some redecoration and re-arrangement of the gardens. Glancing over their shoulders at the plight of the Duke of Urbino, still in exile in Mantua, some of the Ferrarese quietly thanked God for Donna Lucrezia, who stood between them and Duke Valentino a good deal more effectively than their old city walls which would have been no match for his French artillery.

Some days after Epiphany, Ercole Strozzi gave a ball in Donna Lucrezia's honour. Though Strozzi's family, who were successful bankers, moved in the highest society of Ferrara, Ercole himself, being a poet and a man famed for intense and hopeless love affairs, was different. As Donna Lucrezia put it when she received his invitation, "at least in that house we shall be treated as guests rather than entertainers." Strozzi was attached to madonna more for herself than who she was. They shared a passion for poetry and extravagant clothes, and each carried a colourful past in their wake like the train of a magic cloak; the truth of each was largely invisible to anyone outside the charmed circle they had drawn around themselves.

I should have been looking forward to the Strozzi ball but I could not rid myself of a nagging discontent. None of my clothes fitted properly any more, yet I must appear corseted as usual as madonna did not yet wish my condition to be known. As far as I knew, she had made no move to tell Cesare and no doubt felt he should know before anybody else. I could understand her delay; we had had no further word from him since his Delphic note about da Lorqua and his march on Senigallia. But I was anxious. If he were in danger, if he were at risk of his life, I wanted him to know about the child in case…before…but I could not put my fears into words. If madonna were serenely concerned with no more than which shoes would look best with her white tabi ballgown, and how soon the yellow velvet would arrive from Venice to make up the tabards she had promised for Cesare's lutenists, I could only follow her lead and keep my worries to myself.

I missed him. Whatever the feelings proper to my condition, I wanted him. His seed was growing in my womb, yet he had left an ache of emptiness inside me that the physical changes in my body seemed to make only more acute. Madonna recommended a paste of fig kernels mixed with oil to soothe the tenderness in my breasts, but when I applied it I felt only a longing for the balm of my lover's tongue circling my nipples. Angela said I should also anoint my women's parts regularly with oil, for this would make the delivery easier and ensure they did not remain stretched afterwards. Men, she said, might enjoy a moment's sentimentality about the birth of a baby, but it could quickly turn to resentment if it led to a dulling of their pleasure. I could not apply the oil without succumbing to the ecstasy of my memories of Cesare's touch, and then I feared the child would be tainted by my lust and arrive in the world already sick with love.

So, although the night sky was thick with stars and the light from our torches sparkled on a crust of ice over fresh snow as we crunched up the long carriage drive to Strozzi's house, and ice broke from the frozen fountain with the tinkle of fairy laughter, I felt out of sorts and irritable. My corset dug into the pads of flesh which had developed just below my armpits and chafed the welts already there from the day before and, despite the cold, my feet had swollen so my shoes pinched my toes as much as the frost did. When madonna was pregnant, I thought savagely, she would have had herself carried this distance. She would not have walked as I was obliged to, every step jarring my aching back and sore breasts. It would serve her right if I miscarried and Cesare was angry with her.

Yet she had lent me a sapphire diadem, which matched my eyes, she said, to complement my sleeves slashed with blue satin. And she had made me raspberry leaf tea with her own hands after the evening meal. My foul temper was graceless and unjustified. Oh, if only Cesare were here, everything would be all right. He would work his enchantment and I would be floating over the snow instead of trudging through it. But I would be forced to watch him dance with other girls while I sat aside among the matrons and granddams and flat chested little girls. Watch him smile and flirt and juggle their hearts like a masked mountebank. If only he would send word he was safe. That would be enough.

After the first intermezzo, Strozzi himself passed the flame to madonna to begin the torch dance. Dutifully, she executed the opening steps then carried her light to Don Alfonso.

"No surprises there then," remarked our host, easing himself into a chair at my side. He propped his crutch between us and began to massage his stiff knee. "Damn cold. I should go and live in the south. Or Outremer, perhaps. What do you think, Monna Violante?"

"I think we would all miss you very much if you left Ferrara, Ser Ercole."

"Nonsense. Your mistress is the very image of uxoriousness. See now, how she whispers sweet nothings in Don Alfonso's ear."

"I expect she is telling him to be sure and choose Donna Angela next, so she can hold the torch for Don Giulio."

"I hope so. Those two make a fine couple on the dance floor, though I doubt the Cardinal would agree with me." He paused as we both glanced in the direction of Ippolito, conspicuous in his scarlet and the air of isolation surrounding him, even though he was locked deep in a game of dice with the Hungarian ambassador. "But speaking of fine couples," Strozzi resumed, "are you not dancing? Should I flatter myself you are staying out to keep an old cripple company?" He gave me a questioning look, although I am certain he had already guessed why I was not dancing and sought merely to confirm his suspicion. Strozzi was like that, quick to solve a mystery but quite unable to leave it alone if it had potential for creating gossip.

"I do not know the Spanish steps, sir."

"Strange. And you the chosen dancing partner of Valentino by all accounts."

"He is a good leader. One does not need to know the steps to follow him."

Strozzi laughed, slapped his thigh, and winced as one of his rings struck the weak knee. "I like you, Violante, I like you very much. But I must deprive myself of your company now, for there is someone here who wishes to meet you."

My heart rocked on its moorings. For one second I thought, it's him; they are playing a trick on me. I looked up, expecting a tall figure in black, wearing a mask, feathered and jewelled, wearing a white smile and a beard the colour of blood and sunlight. I saw a man of middle years, powerfully built, with the broad shoulders and squat stature which marked out the men of the Padano. He was prosperously dressed, his knee-length gown of sober blue velvet trimmed with sable and his cap set with a substantial pearl.

"Monna Violante, allow me to present Ser Taddeo di Occhiobello."

I held out my hand. Taddeo di Occhiobello bowed over it. His eyes were not beautiful; they were small and shrewd and coloured the greenish brown of an under-ripe chestnut. He was, perhaps, the age of my father. Without a word being said, I knew exactly why he desired to meet me, and the knowledge seemed to shrivel me. My tongue stuck to the roof of my dry mouth; my lips felt as though they would crack if I smiled. My hand, in Ser Taddeo's, was a winter leaf. I looked for Strozzi, hoping for some witticism to carry me over this impossible barrier, but he had melted away among the crowd gathered around the dancers and now, to an audible intake of breath from their audience, and even applause from some who had left their inhibitions at the bottom of a wine jug, Giulio and Angela took to the floor.

"Aren't they beautiful?" I could not help myself. Like everyone else I was swept into the race of their passion. So close they danced that Angela seemed to have stepped right inside the filigree of fire made by Giulio's swooping, circling torch. She moved like a flame herself, sinuous, effortless, so perfectly in time with the music you could not hear the beat of her footsteps and she seemed to be dancing above the ground, on an invisible cushion of desire. Then their figure ended, and Giulio spun her off into a knot of young women simpering and giggling among their chaperones like a flock of chickens behind a fence. He handed the torch to Fidelma, who held it stiff and straight in front of her as she plodded through the steps on her great, flat feet, and Giulio became like water flowing around a rock. Only then did I realise I had been holding my breath; only when I began to relax did I feel the ache in my shoulders which had been tensed as if for flight.

I turned to Ser Taddeo. "Forgive me. I am very fond of dancing but I have...sprained my ankle. It is most frustrating."

"I am not much of a dancer myself," he replied. He sounded defensive, prickly. I became aware of Donna Lucrezia's eyes upon me from the opposite side of the room. Who else was watching me? Cesare had his spies everywhere; probably Donna Lucrezia had not written to him about me because she had no need to; probably the girl who could count to four, and ensured the piles of clean cloths appeared in my clothes chest each week I was due to bleed, was in his pay; possibly even Ser Taddeo, already. I had made my choice when I fell in love with Cesare; there was no other.

"I am sure a man of affairs such as yourself has far more serious things to think about." I smiled, and my lips did not crack, though perhaps my heart did, a little. He responded to my invitation by telling me he was, indeed, a busy man, dividing his time between his estate on the banks of the Po, where he grew vines and nurtured ponds full of pike, and his duties as secretary to the Savi, the governing council of Ferrara, of which his good friend, Ser Strozzi, was a member. He was, he was quick to inform me, a widower with three grown children, a daughter of twenty years and two younger sons. The youngest of these enjoyed the patronage of Cardinal Ippolito and was destined for a career in the Church.

He was perfect in every way, I could not deny it. He could give me a good name and a comfortable home. With two grown sons and a marriageable daughter he had no need to importune me for an heir, but would appreciate whatever dowry madonna might settle on me to provide a marriage portion for his own girl. Doubtless, also, putting a roof over the head of the pope's grandchild would not hinder his younger boy's ecclesiastical ambitions. As for my lover, Occhiobello would turn a blind eye, unless he wished to be left with nothing but blind eyes to turn. I smiled and nodded, nodded and smiled, and Donna Lucrezia turned away, satisfied, to watch the gentlemen perform a galliard.

After the galliard and before supper was served, Strozzi announced a second intermezzo. Ser Taddeo fell silent and we waited. My stomach grumbled. I hoped Ser Taddeo would not notice it. My lover's hunger seemed to be growing in me apace with his child. We waited for a chorus, for the musicians to shuffle their places, to make way for virtuosi, for actors, for an ingenious machine which would represent the movement of the heavenly bodies, or Leda turning into a swan. Nothing. Nothing but a small man dressed in scholar's black, stepping into the centre of our expectant circle with a whisper of soft shoes on the polished floor.

A murmur of excitement began to buzz about the room. Bembo. It's Bembo. Is it Bembo? Question answering affirmation responding to question as though a dance of words echoed the dances of music and feet. Strozzi hobbled to the centre of the circle of onlookers and raised his free hand for silence.

"Dear friends," he began, "it is my unique honour to present Ser Pietro Bembo, the finest poet of his generation. Ser Pietro has been shut away for many months, as my guest or that of his grace," and here Strozzi executed a bow in the direction of Duke Ercole, "working on his dialectical verses on love which he titles *Gli Asolani*. Finally, he assures me, he feels some parts are fit to be heard by an audience and has graciously agreed to favour us with a recitation this evening."

We applauded as Strozzi stumped off to sit beside Donna Lucrezia and Bembo cleared his throat, pale and slender as a lily. Good, I thought. However great a poet, Bembo was just one small, softly spoken man. His recital would give me time to think about my new situation without the distractions of music or dancing or mechanical ingenuities. I knew Donna Lucrezia would seek my opinion of Ser Taddeo as soon as she called us to prepare her for bed, and I must find a way to show my appreciation for her choice. I wanted to talk to Angela, to rehearse with her a suitable form of words.

I looked up, seeking her out among Bembo's audience. Tall candelabra had been drawn forward to light him, so my eyes were dazzled by banks of tiny flames reflected almost to infinity in mirrors and goblets and jewels, but I picked her out eventually. She still stood among the group of women where Giulio had left her at the end of their torch dance, but now he was close to her once more, standing just behind her. Her head seemed to be resting against his shoulder, her throat extended, lips apart. A silver punch cup was poised halfway to her mouth. She was as still as the frozen fountain in Strozzi's courtyard, unblinking, scarcely seeming to breathe, her attention fixed on the poet.

I began to listen.

> *Now Love has bent the pathway of my life;*
> *That happy time and those unclouded days*
> *Which never knew the bitter taste of tears*
> *Have faded into black, tormented nights…*

No Ovid or Petrarch, this Pietro Bembo, but there was a quality in the way he delivered his lines, in a quiet yet lucid voice which carried clearly above the background scuffle of silks and shoes, the chinking of cups, the whispered laughter of the few inattentive listeners. I felt as though he had reached into my heart and ordered its confusions into Petrarchan *rime*. And, just as you might find a lost letter or forgotten pair of shoes when you tidy out a deep chest, he had discovered a truth, not new, but long buried. I could see Angela felt the same, and shifted my gaze.

❧

Madonna did not ask me about Ser Taddeo that night, though she talked much of Bembo and the excellence of his verses.

"Though I think it is in the delivery more than the construction," she told us as we prepared her for bed. "One cannot believe anything less than perfection could issue from such pretty lips. The great Platonic deception." She looked very pretty herself, her eyes shining and cheeks flushed even after she had removed her cochineal paste.

Neither she nor Don Alfonso had yet risen when the messenger arrived from Senigallia, full of breathless apologies for his lateness, his yellow and scarlet quartered livery barely distinguishable beneath the mud of the road. Hardly aware what I was doing, I led him straight to the door of madonna's bedchamber where I gave a loud cough, though I could scarcely hear it myself above the hammering of the blood in my ears, before entering the room to announce the messenger's arrival. Only bad news travels fast, I told myself, only bad news travels fast.

"He is outside now?" asked madonna in some amazement. Her hair was loose, her breath a little short, the sheet she clutched barely covering her breasts. Beside her, Don Alfonso looked like some great farm boy, the skin of his chest and arms ruddy from the hours he spent stripped to the waist in kiln or foundry, the backs of his hands blotched with burns in various stages of healing.

He scowled at me, but madonna spoke with gentle exasperation when she said, "I cannot receive him until I am somewhat clothed, Violante. Perhaps you will return to dress me in a few minutes, to give my husband time to retire."

"Yes, madonna. I'm sorry, madonna." I curtsied and retreated, my cheeks scalded with shame as I closed the doors on a sudden burst of laughter from Don Alfonso and his wife.

Yet I had not even had time to find a slave to take the messenger to the kitchens to wash and refresh himself before the Dalmatian came padding after me to let me know, by a combination of signs and the guttural grunts that passed for language with her, that madonna wished me to return.

"Where is he?" she demanded as soon as I entered the bedchamber. She was still in bed, but wearing a chaste nightgown with a high neck and long sleeves, and a cap on her head into which she had bundled most of her hair. The covers were smooth, the pillows where Don Alfonso had rested plumped. The Dalmatian crouched in front of the fireplace with flint and pine spills.

"Waiting outside, madonna."

"Well fetch him, then. I am decent enough, aren't I?"

"I suppose so, madonna." Our eyes met. He will report everything, they told one another, it must all be just as Cesare wishes it to be. Donna Lucrezia stuffed a few more stray hairs beneath her cap. I arched my spine, so my belly protruded just a little more than usual. Madonna gave a small frown, then shrugged, then smiled. "Enter," she called to the messenger.

He brought in with him the smells of mud and snow and horses. As he knelt to madonna, and I watched the letters C E S A R stretch and contract across his bent back as he breathed, I wondered if he would take back with him in his report the scents of tuberose and lavender, of conjugal bed linen and hot pine resin. At first I thought it was the odd conjunction of smells turning my stomach. I had not yet broken my fast, and hunger made me queasy. I put my hand over my belly to quell its fluttering.

"Yes, yes," said madonna testily, waving at the man to rise. "Get on with it. What have you for me from my lord duke?"

"He sends you his compliments, madam."

"Oh for heaven's sake, hand me the letter."

The fluttering persisted. My belly felt as though it was full of butterflies, that if I opened my mouth they might fly out. I watched the letter, wrapped in an oil cloth, pass from the messenger's leather glove to madonna's plump, white fingers. She slid one neat nail under the seal binding the cloth and broke the wax. The butterflies had folded their wings now, and were trampling my bowels in lead-soled boots. Only bad news travels fast.

The letter ran to several pages. How long must it take her to read it? How could I bear to wait? Unable to stay still, I fidgeted with perfume bottles and cosmetic jars, jewel cases and underlinen, telling myself I was tidying up. Just tidying up.

"Stand still, girl. How can I concentrate?" Madonna peeled off three of the pages and lay them on the bed beside her. "For Duke Ercole. For my husband. And Ippolito." Only one page was hers. I felt shaky with relief.

"Yes, madonna." I stood beside the bed, my hands folded in my sleeves, gripped to my forearms to prevent their trembling. The messenger waited on his knees, in case there should be any reply. The butterflies fell still.

Madonna gasped. "Oh my God," she exclaimed, then again, "dear God." Then she smiled, then gave a muted laugh, a mere forcing of air through her throat and down her nose, then, finally, she handed the letter to me. "Well, Violante. It seems you were right."

*Most Excellent Lady,* I read, *dearest sister,*

*Well, the snake is scotched, the Magione conspirators no more. Now, at last, I can tell it. You must forgive my closeness, but absolute secrecy has been of the essence. I did not even divulge my plan to our father until the day of its completion, for you know how, whatever dissembling words he may use, his face and demeanour give him away. He has been calling me all sorts of names unfitting for a lady's ear, I am told, because I have written him no letters, spent all his money and—he says—done nothing but pass my time playing* calcio, *and other games involving balls (forgive my indelicacy—I merely quote His Holiness) at Cesena. As always, this is true and not true.*

*It goes back to Ramiro, no, further, to the rebellion of San Leo, for that gave the traitors the confidence to show their hand. They thought it would distract me, but in actual fact, it served only to focus my attention. As I told the grovelling castellan when he arrived in Venice to report his failure, by losing San Leo he had already made sure of its recovery.*

*Ramiro I had long suspected of complicity with the Orsini and the rest of the Magione curs. Three months ago I had to deprive him of his position as governor of the Romagna because his corrupt administration was undermining my authority there. I spoke to him at great length on the night before his execution (thereby denying myself the favours of Marescotti's wife, who had been put in my way at a ball hosted by her husband, and she is a pretty enough girl). I reminded him how he had been in my service since I was fourteen and sent to school in Perugia, how we had been friends as well as master and man, fellow Spaniards far from home, who should stick by one another in our exile. We both wept, though he with more passion than I, and finally, he told me what the conspirators had planned for me. That they intended to entrap me at Senigallia, making sure Doria, its castellan, would only surrender the* rocca *to me in person, then turning on me once I was in the town, surrounded by the troops they had billeted there.*

*God grant me cleverer enemies, beloved sister! It was the simplest, most beautiful deception in the world. I sent away all my French officers and their men. This served a dual purpose, both giving notice to Louis that I no longer need him and will go my own way in future, and lulling the conspirators into a false sense of security. Just to make certain of the latter, I dispersed my troops south from Cesena in small groups, by varying routes, and made believe they had been released for the holiday. I then waited for the message I knew was coming from Doria. You might have seen I was nervous but I would defy anyone else to detect it, until, at any rate, I set out for Senigallia wearing full battle armour, even though I was, on the face of it, merely going to formally accept a surrender already given, from a man surrounded on all sides by my loyal troops. I debated the wisdom of this briefly, but quickly decided it made no sense to risk the very skin I was setting out to save by going unarmed.*

*My army met me near Fano, and I sent word ahead to my* condottieri *to have them evacuate the town so I would be able to billet my own troops there. I wish you could have seen their faces by the time I arrived, dearest sister. Each was the image of panic, pale as the corpses they were destined to become, sweating freely despite the cold. Paolo Orsini could not speak except in a squawk like a parrot, but Vitelozzo was the best. He was so sick of the pox he could not ride unaided, and wore a green cloak which made him look even more bilious. For myself, I was the embodiment of charm. I kissed them all; if I lick my lips now, while writing this, I fancy I can taste the salt of their fear, and God, is it sweet.*

*As we entered the town, its single gate was locked behind us, shutting my troops in and theirs outside. I bade them accompany me to a house Michelotto had found for me, where a meal was laid in a room perfect for its purpose, on an upper floor, with but one door and the windows barred. A last supper of sorts. But I can see you shaking your head and clucking your tongue with disapproval for fear I should blaspheme, so I will take the analogy no further.*

*I talked to my guests for a while, feeding them a great deal of nonsense about how much I must rely on them now King Louis had recalled his troops, and how I rejoiced in that because they were the loyalist and bravest captains a man might find this side of the Alps. Oliverotto da Fermo even laughed once, and Vitelozzo took a little wine, though I feared he would vomit it back up again.*

*Then I excused myself to answer a call of nature, and Michelotto barred the door behind me. I heard a few screams, the scraping of furniture and a clatter of overturned tableware. Oliverotto and Vitelozzo, after generously giving details of the extent of the conspiracy to my attentive Michelotto, were garrotted next morning, blaming each other to the last for their unchivalrous conduct and calling upon our Holy Father for his absolution. The three Orsini I have sent to Rome. I shall be on my way back there myself before long; I allowed my soldiers some licence in Senigallia and it quickly ceased to be a comfortable place to stay.*

*I shall enjoy Carnival all the more for the thought of those three sons of whores locked in Sant'Angelo awaiting whatever fate our illustrious father will devise finally to avenge the murder of Juan.*

*You see, dear sister, given the occasion, I knew well how to use it. Our brother can rest easy now, and I have, I hope, finally proven myself a worthy successor to his title as gonfalonier of the Church. My only regret is Vitelozzo. He was the finest gunner in Italy in his day.*

*From your brother who loves you as himself,*

*Cesar*

My eyes devoured the familiar, cursive script, marking the transition from conscientiousness to chaos as his thoughts began to race ahead of his pen. As I read the butterflies started up again. By letting me see this letter in its entirety, I felt Donna Lucrezia had admitted me to the very heart of her family. Noticing me press my free hand to my midriff, she asked me if I was quite well.

"A little unsettled, madonna, that is all. So much excitement before breakfast."

"Come closer." I stepped forward and she laid her palm against my belly and gave a little squeal of delight. "It's our baby, Violante. Dancing for his clever papa."

The butterflies seemed to rise in a cloud from my belly to my throat. Surely now she would tell him; now there could be no doubt the child was real and growing strong. Surely soon he would come to lay claim to it.

"I feel Dame Fortune is about to begin smiling on us at last," she said.

# CHAPTER 2

*My life isn't over, is it? So soon?*

Perhaps Dame Fortune had no option than to smile on us, with Cesare twisting her arm up her back, but, whether sincere or otherwise, her smiles all have the same effect. Within days of receiving the news of Cesare's "beautiful deception," Duke Ercole finally relented over the last of madonna's bride money. This meant my marriage to Ser Taddeo could go ahead and my pregnancy be acknowledged. I could put off my corset so my baby need no longer dance in a cage of boiled leather and wooden stays.

A greater cause for private rejoicing, however, was Angela's happiness. She was convinced the duke must now acquiesce in her marriage to Giulio. It was the final dose of physick she needed to restore her completely after her fever of the previous summer, putting the bloom back in her cheeks and igniting the old spark of mischief in her smile. Her nocturnal disappearances resumed, and this time, I was certain, it was not Ippolito's bed she was going to.

Kept awake by my child, who seemed to be as active during the hours of night as his father, I would lie in the winter dark, made deeper by the absence of Angela's breathing or the rustle of her bedclothes as she turned in her sleep, and speculate. Did she go to Giulio's house, or did he meet her somewhere in the castle? I liked to think of her going to his house, masked, treading silently over the snow in her pattens, accompanied only by a link boy, their shadows long and blue and sparkling in the empty streets. I envisaged her stepping into his embrace in the dark vestibule, trembling as they climbed the stairs in a servantless hush, stretching her lovely body against his with a sigh of ecstatic release, because this was what she had been looking for all her life and now she had found it.

The pope wrote to his daughter that Cesare would spend Carnival in Rome, where, he cheerfully anticipated, *he will do a thousand follies and throw away several thousands of ducats.*

"If my father is so equable about Cesare wasting money, then he has indeed achieved the impossible," madonna joked as she read the passage aloud to us while we decorated masks with gold wire embroidery and peacock feathers stolen from the birds in Duke Ercole's garden. Cesare, the Holy Father went on, was to give the city of Camerino to his little brother, Giovanni, and I wondered what present he would make to our child. Urbino, perhaps. That would be fitting.

We were shortly to be graced with a visit from Donna Isabella, who had written that nothing would please her more than to spend Carnival with her dear sister-in-law and celebrate with her her family's great good fortune. She had sent her noble brother, Duke Valentino, a gift of one hundred carnival masks, twenty of them made of gold and patterned with pearls and precious stones, twenty of silver, and the rest of the finest silks and velvets. *After the strains and fatigues which you have undergone in these your glorious undertakings,* she had told him, *you should also find time to amuse yourself.* Cesare wrote to madonna that he was delighted with the masks, one of which was adorned with curling horsehair moustaches and a turban of cloth of gold, and reminded him of Prince Djem.

He wrote to her, as ever, almost every day. I used to wonder, sometimes, how many calfskins, oak galls, and pots of gum Arabic were invested in their relationship over the years, whether it owed more to ink and vellum than flesh and blood. So, when she summoned me, one morning close to the Feast of Saint Valentine, and I found her seated at her writing bureau with a folded parchment in her hand I thought, at last, she had composed a letter to Cesare telling him about the child and wished to show it to me before it was despatched.

"How are you?" she asked, rubbing her eyes. The February light from the deep window was poor, stifled between low cloud and muddied snow, and no lamps were lit; writing must have been difficult.

"Well, thank you, madonna. The child is very lively, and growing, I think."

She smiled, but her gaze slid away from me and I could see she had not really listened to my response. "I have favoured you, have I not?" she asked.

"Yes, madonna." I was puzzled. I stared at the letter in her hand, wishing I could see through the dense, creamy surface of the vellum to the words folded inside.

"I command your loyalty."

"Of course, madonna."

"I have chosen you, you see, because we stand in a special relationship to one another now."

"Chosen me for what, madonna?" Perhaps I was a little abrupt. I was annoyed by her slowness in coming to the point, but mostly because it was clear from the way she was talking that the letter in her hand had nothing to do with Cesare or me or our child. I noticed now that it carried no seal; had it been intended for Cesare it would certainly have been sealed by madonna in person.

"To deliver this." She held the parchment out to me and I grasped it, but she did not immediately let it go; as we remained in this impasse, the rectangle of creamy vellum stretched between us like a flimsy bridge, I saw the letter did not even carry the name of an addressee. Blank, blind, and virgin was the skin it presented to the world. "And you must follow my instructions exactly, mind," she admonished as she finally released the letter into my care.

"Of course, madonna."

"At the back of the bathhouse, where the gardeners come to collect the waste water. Strozzi will be waiting there, from the fifteenth hour. You will give him the letter, and anything he gives to you, you will bring straight to me." She paused. "It would be best if you were not seen."

"Yes, madonna. I understand."

"Do not say that, Violante. Do not try to understand. Take Fonsi," she added. "Then, if you are seen, you may say you are exercising him."

Were she and Strozzi lovers? I wondered as I made my way to the bathhouse with the little dog trotting at my heel. Certainly they were close, but I had always thought their friendship more like that of two women, founded on gossip and Strozzi's skill at acquiring cameos, fine fabrics or rare perfumes at good prices through his connections in Venice.

Then again, what about my friendship with Angela, before Cesare, and then Giulio, changed the balance of it?

⟨❦⟩

"The setting is appropriate, don't you think? On the one hand, a Judas tree, on the other, a tank of dirty water." Strozzi stepped out from behind the bathhouse, his cane crunching on the gravel path encircling its arcaded rotunda. He looked cold, his face pinched and bluish above the fur collar of his cloak. I wondered how long he had been waiting. Fonsi leapt up at him, tongue lolling, claws scrabbling at his boot.

"I do not know, Ser Ercole. I only know I am to deliver this letter."

"She was wise to choose you. You keep your curiosity on a short leash. Good girl."

"I do not wish to know anything which might endanger my child."

"And how fares Saint Valentine's little acolyte?" He patted my belly. The baby gave a kick and he withdrew his hand abruptly, though he smiled at me as if we had just shared an intimate joke. "Are you taking proper care of yourself? You have no cloak. You must not catch a chill."

"I no longer feel the cold. The child is like a little furnace in my belly."

"A sort of personal hypocaust." We laughed.

"He is growing very strong. He will be born in May, I think."

"And seems likely to be a good at *calcio*."

"As is his father."

"You see, Violante," and I could read in his expression the way he saw me, a young girl made foolish by love, "how passion can take us out of ourselves. Be kind to your mistress. Do not judge her. Do you imagine for one moment she would willingly jeopardise her brother's child? She trusts you because of him; she honours you, and if she is not thinking as clearly as she might, have sympathy. We can none of us choose whom we love." He spoke with authority; he had lived for ten years in the shadow of a hopeless attachment to a woman married to a man so powerful his name was never mentioned.

I thought of my brother, Eli, scrabbling in the mud for his eyeglasses, of La Fiammetta's pitying laugh, and Catherinella, broken-necked in her cage, and I understood Strozzi with my heart. Love is random and entirely mischievous. "Do you have anything for me to take back with me?" I asked meekly. Strozzi handed me a folded parchment, anonymously sealed and addressed to Donna Nicola. I must have looked puzzled.

"It is a name he favours, that is all," said Strozzi with a shrug. Who, I wondered, but I would not ask. I felt the solidity of the Torre Marchesana at my back, weighing down upon the prison of Ugo and Parisina. I felt eyes in all its windows. And suddenly, for no reason I could think of, the words Sister Osanna had spoken during last year's Lent came into my mind. *You must look to the foundations, daughter. Fires may be set there. Do not give them air to breathe.*

I opened my mouth to bid Strozzi farewell, but he had vanished, as insubstantial, it seemed, as the wisps of steam coming off the tank of used water from the baths. Nor could I find Fonsi, though I called him several times. Strozzi's footprints, unevenly spaced and punctuated by the full stop of his cane, were unmistakable in the gravel. I could not afford to loiter where we had met. I would simply have to hope the dog had gone back indoors without me. Besides, if madonna were expecting me to return with a note from a lover, concern for her dog was not likely to be uppermost in her mind.

Then I heard him yapping, persistently, as though he were trapped somehow and trying to draw attention to his plight. The sound seemed to be coming from the direction of a walk of trellised peach trees which led away from the bathhouse in the direction of the old palace. As I stepped under its first arch, I saw Fidelma, the little dog wriggling in her arms, trying to clamp her hand around his muzzle to silence him. She looked as guilty as if it were she who had been keeping an illicit tryst, and the thought of that gave genuine warmth to the smile with which I greeted her.

"I thought he was lost," she said, her gaze sliding away from my face to settle on the rise of my belly. I once remarked to Angela I feared Fidelma's disapproval would curdle my milk. Jealous, pronounced Angela, a good fucking is just what she needs and she isn't going to get it from that whey-faced Fra Raffaello of hers.

"I was just walking him." Now it was my turn not to look at her. She had followed me, I was sure of it, but why? And what had she seen? And with whom would she share her knowledge? I felt the letter in the bodice of my gown where I had concealed it, the stiff parchment digging into one tender breast. Surely Fidelma must know it was there. I could not take it straight to madonna. I must throw Fidelma off the trail first.

"Look," I said, "I absolutely have to go to the privy. This young man," I patted my belly, feeling like a great, overblown rose beside tall, skinny Fidelma, "is sitting right on my bladder. You take Fonsi back, and make sure nobody else hogs that chair I like for sewing in, you know, the one with the high back."

She hurried away without another word, struck dumb by my brazenness, the little dog still squirming in her arms, looking back at me beseechingly out of his black button eyes.

I went to Angela's and my room, though by a circuitous route, entering the castle at the Torre Leone and through a series of rooms linking it to the Torre Marchesana which were currently being redecorated and visited by no one but the workmen. Once there, I dragged out my trunk from beneath my bed with the aim of hiding the letter at the bottom of it, but as I lifted out the loose compartments, my attention was distracted. There, at the top of the slim pile of my letters from Cesare, was the sketch done by Leonardo which he had sent me. I gazed at the likeness which was both his and not his, which captured perfectly a particular look he had when thinking or reading, his eyes veiled and lips in a loose pout of concentration, yet sacrificed so much else. How many expressions, I wondered, actually crossed that agile, intelligent, beautiful face in the time it took Leonardo to make the sketch? I put it back in the trunk and hid it beneath his letters, because there was a danger in committing that one image to memory. I might forget all the rest, all the humour, impatience, affection, sadness, passion, and anger that change the shape of a mouth, the light in an eye, the hue of a cheek, which both mask and reveal the ultimate mystery of the faces we present to the world.

What expression would he wear, I wondered, when, eventually, he found out about our child?

"Here you are." Angela. "Fidelma said you'd gone to the privy, then Lucrezia said you'd been far too long and she was worried and sent me to find you. What are you doing?" She crouched beside me on the floor. "Not mooning over cousin Cesare? Still?" Her tone was gentle, but more exasperated than sympathetic. "You know it will not matter to him; that's how men are. They sow the seed and leave us women to tend it."

I believed she was wrong but I could not say why. "But it matters to madonna," I said in my defence.

"That's because…" but she never finished her sentence. Her attention was distracted by the letter Strozzi had given me. "What's this?" She picked it up, testing the quality of the parchment, fingering the dog-eared corners from where it had been crushed against my breast. "Who's Nicola?"

"No one."

Angela looked briefly puzzled, then gave a shout of laughter as revelation dawned. "I know that hand," she said, "it's Bembo's. Nicola. Of course. He has a favourite sister or cousin or…God, could be his housekeeper. Anyway, I know there's a Nicola in his life. It's a *nom de guerre*, isn't it? That's why Lucrezia's prowling about like a cat on hot bricks. It's nothing to do with you having a miscarriage; it's that letter. From Bembo. To her."

"Bembo and madonna?"

"Of course. It's no surprise really; she's been going on about his pretty mouth and beautifully rounded vowels ever since Strozzi's party. If you weren't so wrapped up in your own affairs you'd have noticed."

Angela could talk, I thought. She had not spent a night in her own bed for weeks. "If you were ever here we might have talked about it."

"Violante," she sat back on her heels, her wide, grey eyes fixed on mine, "if Cesare were here, living in a palace half a mile up the road, alone, and he wanted you, how many nights would you sleep in this room? What is it about people in love that they always think they're the only ones? Darling, it's not that I don't understand, probably more that I understand only too well. I don't crow over your pain; so don't you deny me my pleasure."

"Sorry. I just feel in limbo, you know, waiting. For the baby. For her to tell Cesare so everything can be out in the open. As things stand, everyone knows it's Cesare's child, yet everyone pretends they think it's Taddeo's and he and I have to play up to the improbable notion that we couldn't keep our hands off each other until after the marriage. And when will that be? He won't even commit himself to a betrothal ring until he sees what Cesare is going to do for the child and how it might benefit him."

"She should have told him by now."

"Can you speak to her?"

"Not about that. No one can ever speak to either of those two about the other. You know how they are. They play by their own rules."

"I hate your family. One minute you're all smiles, including everybody, the next, up go the shutters and no one's good enough."

"Aren't all families like that?"

"How would I know? Mine bartered me away. I was just part of the package my father put together to help your Uncle Rodrigo buy Saint Peter's keys."

"And has it never occurred to you that Lucrezia, and I, even Cesare, were also part of that package? Though perhaps, since Senigallia, Cesare has enough credit to pay the piper himself." We remained for a moment in silence, each thinking her own thoughts, then Angela said, "Come on, let's not argue. If you want to continue in Lucrezia's favour, you had better deliver that letter, or baby or no baby, you will find yourself banished to Occhiobello with no one but Ser Taddeo's prize pike to talk to." She rose and gave me her arm to help me to my feet.

"Fidelma saw me collect it; I'm sure of it. That's why I brought it in here. To hide it until I could find a better time."

"Give it to me. She has a jewel case with a false bottom. We've used it before."

"Before?" I was surprised. Donna Lucrezia somehow gave the impression of having a constant heart, but she was a good actress. She had to be.

"Lucrezia has always had lovers, you silly goose. This is nothing new. I'm only surprised it's taken her so long to choose someone. It's the longest she's been faithful to anyone except poor little Bisceglie."

⋘∙⋙

The following week, Donna Isabella arrived from Mantua, plunging our household into a chaos mirrored by the city's preparations for Carnival. Donna Isabella and her retinue occupied Duke Ercole's apartments in the old palace, the duke moved into Don Alfonso's rooms, and Alfonso went to stay in a hunting lodge in the Barco which belonged to Ippolito, who was in Rome. With Cesare, perhaps.

Except for Donna Isabella's old Spanish duenna, who had been with her since she was a child growing up in the Castel Estense, none of her

Mantuan staff knew where anything was and were perpetually getting lost; if Donna Isabella wanted hot water, it would be cold by the time it reached her; if she asked for candied lemons she might well be offered writing paper by some bewildered maid who feared to return from a mission empty-handed. In this topsy turvy atmosphere, nobody noticed my furtive trips to the bathhouse to meet Ercole Strozzi beneath the Judas tree.

Whatever Bembo wrote in his letters to madonna, it seemed to please her. I had never known her so light-hearted and girlish, though Angela said this was the truest she had been to her real self since her return from her self-imposed exile at Nepi and the announcement of her betrothal to Don Alfonso. Her energy seemed inexhaustible. This year she did not merely watch the Battle of the Eggs from the loggia over the palace gate, but went down among the crowd, cloaked and masked, and joined in. She took to rising early to go hunting with the men, riding out among her hounds and falconers while the morning mist still clung to the bases of trees and scenting was at its best. Every evening she devised entertainments for Donna Isabella. She choreographed wild Spanish dances with castanets and tambourines, in which she and Angela were the principal performers, tossing their long, loose hair and drumming their heels like gypsies.

Donna Isabella lacked the agility to do more than spectate at these events. She was a poor horsewoman and too heavy to dance well, and even if the Duchess of Ferrara was content to have her cloak pelted with eggs and her fine, kidskin boots caked in mud and horse shit, the Marchioness of Mantua had her dignity to think of. I kept her company when she was not with her father, or making visits to the homes of her friends in Ferrara. She talked incessantly of the betrothal of her son, Federigo, to Cesare's daughter, Luisa. I wondered if she feared he might have greater ambitions for Luisa since the success of Senigallia. I wondered if she knew he was the father of my child also. It was impossible to tell with Donna Isabella; picking out what was important in her conversation was like looking for a safe channel in a perilous stream. She could shift from the balance of power between France and Spain, to the uses of allegory in painting, to how I could best impose my authority on Ser Taddeo's household when I married, to the latest fashions in Milan, without drawing breath.

One morning, when I had been accompanying her on a walk through the rose garden which had been planted by her mother and was now in Donna Lucrezia's care, she broke off in the middle of a tirade about greenfly to ask me what had happened to the black slave.

"Which black slave?" I asked, though I already knew the answer.

"The one your mistress brought from Rome, of course. Surely she cannot have sold her or exchanged her for this." She gestured behind her, at the sallow, sharp-boned Dalmatian, who was following us with an armful of rugs. "She told me once how attached she was to the girl. A gift from her last husband, I believe."

I had not known this before. "She died, alas," I said, hoping Donna Isabella would not ask me how.

"What a shame. She was so striking, such a dense, shiny black. I was going to ask Lucrezia to lend her to me to model for the servant in a *Judith with the Head of Holofernes* I am commissioning from Squarcione."

"I am sorry, madonna." Her voice was like a wire passing through my brain from ear to ear. What does it matter, I wanted to ask, what difference is there to you between a Jew and a black? What is this false hierarchy you have set up to make Judith into one of your own, a great lady with lapdogs and slaves and her lover's head in a silk purse?

"No matter. It happens all the time. They look strong then succumb to the merest sniffle. It all goes to prove we are the superior race. Now tell me, who will win the Battagliuola this year?"

"Madonna says the Ferrarese, Don Alfonso the papal force."

"Ah, they are being kind to one another. Tell me who you think will win?"

"The side whose mothers get to market earliest, madonna, and buy up the biggest vegetables."

The Battagliuola was an uproarious affair in which teams of children fought one another in the Campo Franco beside the convent of Corpus Domini with fruit and vegetables fired from slings. It commemorated an ancient victory of the Este over a papal army. For Donna Lucrezia, it was a point of honour that she should attend, so the people could see she was an Este now and owed her allegiance to Ferrara, not Rome.

We walked the short distance from the castle, Donna Lucrezia and Don Alfonso arm in arm at our head, servants following behind with chairs and rugs and braziers and two chests containing prizes for the winners and runners up. With the heir to the duchy now married to the pope's daughter, there could be no losers. Don Giulio, masked as Spavente, his black ostrich feathers bobbing tall above his blond head, walked beside Angela in the guise of Columbine.

"I wish you could have seen the masks I sent to dear Cesare," remarked Donna Isabella, more to Ser Taddeo than to me, I supposed, as I had heard them described in minute detail several times already. "The gold and silver particularly. The young sculptor who did them for me is a marvel, such a find. He understands just what I mean when I say all art must have a beautiful meaning." Her voice was muffled by her own mask of black velvet trimmed with ermine tails which bobbed either side of her plump cheeks as she walked.

Ser Taddeo gave the smile of a benevolent lion. "Doubtless he was grateful to find so sensitive and understanding a patron, madonna," he said. Donna Isabella lifted her chin, and her shoulders settled into an attitude of great self-satisfaction.

As we waited in the square for our chairs to be set up, and a servant went round with jugs of hot, spiced wine and little cakes, Ser Taddeo asked her for the man's name. "I am such a poor suitor," he said. "I have not even given my intended a betrothal ring yet. He sounds like just the man for the job, to invest our marriage with a beautiful meaning." He squeezed my elbow.

Had madonna finally told Cesare about the baby, then? Had she heard from him? His intentions towards the child? There must be a letter for me.

"He is called Gideon. Gideon da Quieto d'Arzenta."

There must be. Cesare would not let such news go unacknowledged.

"That is my brother, madonna." Who was speaking? Whose brother? The wine. It was too strong.

A sudden shriek from Donna Isabella brought me to my senses. Donna Isabella was embracing Fidelma. She looked like a great spinnaker sail draped around Fidelma's mast-like straightness.

"Gideon is your brother!" exclaimed Donna Isabella, her voice soaring to such a pitch on the word brother that people stopped what they were doing and turned towards her.

"Yes, madonna," said Fidelma, staggering discreetly beneath Donna Isabella's weight. "Before I came to Christ I was Juditha da Quieto d'Arzenta."

It was the first time I had ever heard Fidelma make reference to her family or her life before her conversion. I remembered the bargain she had struck with her father, and thought her well named, for she was faithful. She did not break her promises. A gust of wind blew dust into my eyes and made them water. My baby kicked and somersaulted as though he wished he could join the excited combatants, now jostling around men in the papal and Este liveries who were handing out ammunition and last-minute tactical advice. What would he be, I wondered, pressing my hands to my belly to calm him, this child of the oath breaker and the victor of Senigallia?

"Oh look," said Taddeo, pointing towards the ducal party who were arranging themselves in the chairs set up by the servants. "There's our poet." It was a gallant conceit of Taddeo's to refer to Bembo as "our poet," because his recital at Strozzi's party had been the occasion of our first meeting. I looked. Bembo, conspicuous in his scholar's black, was making his way directly towards Donna Lucrezia. I glanced around for Strozzi, who was nowhere to be seen, but I did intercept a hard look from Donna Isabella, who had disengaged herself from Fidelma and was watching the poet's progress across the crowded square with as close concentration as if she had placed a bet on the time of his arrival.

"Excuse me, messer," I said to Taddeo. "I must make sure they give madonna the right cushions. She is a martyr to her back since her miscarriage last summer."

Just as Pythagoras tells us, two straight lines moving towards one another must intersect at an apex. Using my great belly to forge a path through the melee of shrieking children and their scolding mothers, piles of wizened winter oranges and misshapen parsnips, and servants clustered around the braziers they had set up to mull wine and roast chestnuts, I managed to cut off Bembo a few feet from madonna's chair.

"Monna Violante." He bowed, and as he straightened up I saw he was blushing. So he knew, then, that I was the letter bearer. "I was just...The duchess asked me to declaim a eulogy for the winners." He withdrew a folded parchment from a satchel he had fastened across his chest like an arquebusier's ammunition belt.

I had not got my breath back enough to speak before Donna Lucrezia exclaimed from behind me, "Ah, Messer Pietro, there you are at last. I had begun to think we must start without you."

Bembo craned his neck to see her around my bulk. "I am guilty of leaving your commission to the last minute, duchesa. Forgive me. Perhaps you would like to cast your eye over the work, to make sure it meets with your approval."

I glanced behind me to see her reaction. Don Alfonso looked interested, but madonna made a dismissive gesture with one gloved hand. At the same time, I was aware out of the corner of my eye of Bembo thrusting the parchment towards me with some insistence. I took it. Only then did I realise a second parchment was tucked inside the folds of the first. What was I to do? Don Alfonso was already reaching out his hand to take the verses from me. In my haste to prevent him, I lunged for the parchments and they slipped from my grasp. Unable to bend and pick them up, I stared in horror at the corner of the secret enclosure poking out from the folds of its outer wrapping. Bembo stooped swiftly to rescue them, but not as quickly as Vittorio, whom I had not noticed until now.

"Allow me, Monna Violante," he said, handing me the parchments with a look that said, I know what this is; my master knows; he will do nothing for now, but beware.

"Thank you, Ser Vittorio, my mistress is grateful for your gallantry." He nodded and melted back into the crowd. I believed we understood one another. Somehow, with my back to Don Alfonso, I managed to slip the second parchment into my sleeve before handing Bembo's eulogy to Donna Lucrezia for her approval. My heartbeat was just beginning to return to normal when she rose from her chair. "Messer Pietro," she said, "come closer." Oh God, what now? What had they been writing in the letters I carried to make her so indiscreet?

Don Alfonso frowned. "Sit down, woman, and let the game begin before these children are all crying for their mothers."

Donna Isabella, acutely sensitive to any hint of discord between her brother and his Borgia wife, had discarded Fidelma and was watching Don Alfonso and Donna Lucrezia as though they were combatants in a close fought game of tennis. Donna Lucrezia served her ace.

"I wished to ask Ser Pietro to cast his eye over some verses I have written. I fear they are too poor for their subject." She bestowed a meaningful smile on her husband. "I hope Ser Pietro can help me make them more worthy."

"Ah." Don Alfonso cleared his throat; he shifted about in his chair and his naturally high colour deepened a little. "Well, well, wife. I am certain anything you would write would honour so unworthy a subject." He took her hand and patted it. He picked up Fonsi, who had slid from her lap as she rose and was now scrabbling at Don Alfonso's knee, and while his attention was distracted, Donna Lucrezia handed her "verses" to Bembo and a look passed between them which I envied to the core of my being.

Only some time later, when the Battagliuola was in full swing, did I consider the significance of Vittorio. The din of screaming children and cheering adults, of squashes smashing into the convent doors and cabbages clattering against braziers was keeping my baby wakeful. As he turned somersaults and pummelled my belly, and a small pumpkin hurtled past within inches of my nose, I began to wonder if, in years to come, he would take part in Battagliuole, and if he would have brothers to fight alongside him.

How soon after the birth could I return to my lover's bed to begin making those brothers? What was the ruling of the Church on such matters? Was it true that breast feeding prevented pregnancy? When would it be safe to lie with him again? I had never stopped wanting Cesare, though whenever I saw myself in a mirror, I wondered where the I was who had been desirable to him. I longed for him to know about his child and come to Ferrara and lay his palm against my belly and feel our baby reach out towards its warmth, but I feared his reaction should he see my extroverted navel and the skin stretched taut and shiny over my leaking breasts.

Then I thought of Vittorio, of the look he gave me as he handed me Bembo's papers. Cesare must know, of course he must. He was far from depending only on letters from his sister for his intelligence at the court of

Ferrara. Perhaps his silence meant he suspected the child was not his. He had given me my name because I had once broken a promise I had made him. Why should he believe I would be a faithful mistress? So I must tell him. If madonna would not write to him, then I must.

I could no longer give my attention to the spectacle. The letter I had to write clamoured to be let out on to the page. I could almost feel the pen in my hand, the feather tickling my palm, the yield and spring of the nib as I pressed it into clean vellum and formed the words. What words? Should I give the bare facts of the matter or dress them in declarations of love? Dwell on the practicalities or write of our child as the embodiment of our passion, a tie which bound us for life? Should I leaven my news with humour, or would that make him believe me too frivolous to make a fitting mother for his son? The more I thought about it, the more impossible the task became.

Then I remembered the letter tucked into my sleeve, the poet's letter to his mistress. Surely there could be no better example for me to follow. But if I were to have an opportunity to read it before handing it over to Donna Lucrezia, I must leave the Battagliuola before her; I must leave now. Turning to Ser Taddeo, who was standing behind my chair, I touched his sleeve to gain his attention.

"I feel a little unwell, my dear," I told him. "I think I would like to rest awhile, if you would be kind enough to escort me back to the castle."

"Will the duchess permit it?" he asked, casting a doubtful glance towards madonna, who was absorbed in feeding sweets to her little dog while Don Alfonso cheered on a sortie by the Ferrarese forces from behind a barricade of green and yellow striped marrows.

"As you know, the welfare of this child concerns her closely. She will excuse me if you explain the reason, and come straight back yourself."

"Should I ask Donna Angela to accompany you?"

"I would prefer it to be you." I squeezed his wrist and gave him a smile I hoped conveyed both warmth and vulnerability.

He picked his way cautiously across ground made treacherous by squashed fruit and vegetables, dodging missiles as he went, wincing at the high-pitched screams of over-excited children. I watched him bow to madonna and Don Alfonso, madonna cocking one ear towards him to hear what he had to say above the din of battle. She cast me a troubled glance, I frowned and clenched my hands over my belly, she nodded and waved Ser Taddeo away impatiently as he attempted a second bow.

❧

I overdid the delicacy of my condition a little on the way back to the castle, so that it took me some time to persuade Taddeo it was safe to leave me and no, I had no need of a physician. As soon as I had shut the door of my chamber on his bowing figure and anxious expression, I slid Bembo's letter out of my sleeve. Seated on the edge of my bed, I unfolded it, careful to avoid leaving any trace of my subterfuge in the way of tears or creases or ink smudges. I wondered that so sensitive a piece of correspondence should be unsealed, then immediately realised that dollops of wax and ribbons would only make it more conspicuous. Far from being made reckless by their passion, these two were well versed in the skills of illicit courtship. They knew the rules of the game.

As I opened the letter, hot with shame at my disloyalty and anticipation of what I might find, yet another, smaller parchment fell out of it. It would have landed in my lap had I still got one. As it was, it slid over the mound of my belly on to the floor. I squatted to retrieve it then levered myself back up on to the bed. Bright spots danced before my eyes from the effort and I could not immediately catch my breath. I feared I was to be punished for lying to Taddeo by my lie coming true. Forcing myself to breathe steadily, willing my heartbeat to slow, I read the larger of the two parchments. It contained only a few words.

*How could I better this? I return your lines to you, sweet lady, as the only possible expression of my sentiments, the perfect mirror to your perfect loveliness.* I unfolded the smaller page, where a verse was inscribed in Donna Lucrezia's hand. I committed it to memory. I remember it still, though my reasons are more complicated than you might expect. It read thus:

*I think were I to die*
*And with my wealth of pain*
*Cease longing,*
*Such great love to deny*
*Could make the world remain*
*Unloving.*

*When I consider this,*
*Death's long delay is all*
*I must desire,*
*Since reason tells me bliss*
*Is felt by one in thrall*
*To such a fire.*

Were these truly madonna's words? She was a competent versifier, but no better than the rest of us when we composed sonnets or *maccheroni* to pass the time on wet days. We invented patterns of words and meanings with less thought than we embroidered shirts or altar cloths. I found it difficult to believe her capable of writing so plain and full of feeling. But if the poem was hers, dare I make use of it? Surely Cesare would recognise it. Then again, why should he? Why should he be interested in the lines madonna composed for her lovers? He was happier poring over Vitruvius or Caesar's Gallic Wars than reading poetry of any kind. Besides, Vittorio could not have had sight of this letter; he had handed it straight to me after Bembo had dropped it. Unless he had eyes in Bembo's inkwell, or a spy lodged in the poet's heart, Cesare could not know what it contained.

I read it through again. I thought of how I would wake up sometimes, terrified, in the middle of the night. Convinced my baby was dead, I would press my palms against my belly and will him to kick. Then, feeling as though my body filled the whole dark space of the bedroom, squeezing out lamps and linen chests, even Angela's usually empty bed, I was certain I would die giving birth to some monster, my womb torn and bleeding, my heart burst from the effort. Fear jangled the nerves in my arms and legs until I was forced to get out of bed and walk about, though the joints in my knees tended to grow stiff and painful during the night. How could I bear to die while Cesare still lived? What good could heaven do me while he remained on earth? *Such great love to deny, could make the world remain unloving.*

My decision was made. I would send him the poem, and it would assure him far better than my own poor words that I was a faithful mistress and the child I was carrying was his. His son, God willing, his firstborn son.

With Carnival at an end, madonna distracted herself from the dreary privations of Lent by throwing herself into the preparations for my lying-in, which would begin after Easter. Perhaps taking vicarious pleasure in the fact that my condition excused me from the Lenten fast, she supervised my diet closely. If the child were to be a boy, I must eat only warm foods. She had all my dishes prepared in her own kitchens, usually under her personal supervision, or that of Angela, who made no secret of her resentment of this enforced time away from Giulio. You should not be thinking of love at this time, admonished madonna. Nor of beef with peppers or red fruit puddings, retorted Angela, putting in front of me a compote of figs in ginger syrup in a bowl decorated with a picture of a robust baby boy pissing an arc of golden urine into a stream. Eat, said madonna. I felt like a goose being fattened for *pate di fegato*.

The dish was one of a set Don Alfonso had made for Donna Lucrezia's use during her ill-fated pregnancy of the summer before. It made me remember the shrivelled bundle of flesh and bones Cesare had cast into the moat, the grim cast of his mouth, and the way he dropped his eyelids so nothing could be read in his face of grief, or frustration, or anything else. I feared these thoughts would harm my child, but I could say nothing. It was a sign of madonna's special favour that she was allowing me to use the dishes, and of Don Alfonso's indulgence of her generosity towards me in my predicament. So I ate, but madonna must have read some reluctance in my face, spotted some hesitation so minute even I was unaware of it, as I put the spoon to my lips. Drawing her chair close to mine, so we would not be overheard, she murmured, "You see, if I had not been so ill, he would not have come when he did. Your baby was made from the loss of mine. Perhaps her soul may enter your child and live."

Once Easter had passed, I moved out of the room I shared with Angela, into an inner chamber on the floor below madonna's apartments where there was no risk of draughts from windows. There I would have to stay until my churching, six weeks after the birth of my child. Even sitting among the braziers in the orange garden was no longer advised by Donna Lucrezia's doctors and the midwife she had engaged to attend me, if we were to be sure of the baby's sex. I wondered, briefly, how madonna proposed to pursue her correspondence with Bembo, but I had not the energy to care much as my body swelled and my heart grew indolent.

To make absolutely certain I would not be exposed to cold, for it was a chilly spring, with damp, salt winds blowing off the Adriatic, madonna had the walls of my room hung with several layers of rugs and tapestries and the bottom of the door padded with a sort of fabric salami, a linen tube stuffed with wool and fastened at either end with a drawstring. Red brocade curtains surrounded my bed, which was piled with soft blankets made only from the wool of young rams. The fire was lit day and night, fed and stoked by the Dalmatian slave, whom madonna had lent me with misgiving because her sallow complexion indicated an excess of cold yellow bile in her nature. A male slave would have been better, but males could not enter a lying-in chamber.

I was glad of her silence, and Cesare's arms stamped on her collar. It made me feel a part of him was there with me, muffled in my woollen gowns and choking in the fragrant smoke of the fire, in which handfuls of coriander seeds popped and spat to ensure a quick and easy delivery.

I was never alone. Madonna herself spent as much time in the lying-in chamber as her duties permitted, almost as though pregnancy were a contagion she hoped to catch from me. We women played at *biribissi* and cards, read to one another, or sang to pass the time. Fidelma read passages from the *De regimine praegnantium* of Michele Savonarola, the grandfather of Fra Girolamo, whose example had inspired her beloved Fra Raffaello. To my surprise, madonna tolerated the readings, and even praised the soundness of Ser Michele's advice; the Savonaroli were a respected family in Ferrara, doctors and teachers at the university. Madonna's Ferrarese women, many of whom were already married, told tales of their own confinements, tales which became darker and more lurid whenever madonna was absent. I knew they resented being obliged to attend the upstart Valentino's concubine, and that they wanted to frighten me, perhaps even precipitate an early birth. But I was beyond their reach, inviolably content to sit and do nothing, to watch my companions sewing baby clothes or gambling their jewellery on a hand at *cacho*, to listen to Angela singing Giulio's songs, her voice cracked as a broken heart in the smoky atmosphere.

One morning, after she had heard Mass, Donna Lucrezia came to my chamber in the company of a couple I had never seen before, country people from their dress, which was plain, though of good quality, clean and not patched. In her arms the woman held a baby, pink cheeked and solemn eyed beneath a coarse lace bonnet. My mind filled with the image of my child, curled in my womb, coiled like a spring, awaiting the signal to begin his life in the world. Was this what he would look like, this swaddled doll with its oddly expressionless face? I put my hand over my belly and felt him kick, sharp and angry.

"Leave us," madonna ordered my companions. "All of you," she added as Angela made as if to stay. Then, smiling first at the woman with the baby, then at me, she said, "This is Giuseffa. She is from Medelana." The Este had a summer house at Medelana, not far from Ostellato, where Pietro Bembo was a frequent guest at the Strozzi villa. Giuseffa bobbed a curtsey. Her husband, who was less tall than her, snatched his cap from his sparse hair and made me a bow.

"I have seen several women," madonna went on, "and I believe Giuseffa is the most suitable. She has raised four children as healthy as this one. I have inspected them all, and they have straight limbs, clear eyes, and sound wind. The eldest can even read a little, I believe."

Giuseffa's husband smiled and nodded his confirmation. His upper front teeth were missing.

"Suitable for what, madonna?" I asked.

"A wet nurse, child." She spoke as though it were obvious. Yet I knew she had suckled Rodrigo herself. The Roman gossips had made much of it, so unusual was it for a lady of madonna's rank. Did she do it out of love for the Duke of Bisceglie and his child, or to keep him from her bed a few months longer?

Forgetting my manners I stared at her, then recollected myself and stared instead at Giuseffa, at her chapped cheeks and rough, red hands and the placid, vacuous baby in her arms. "But…"

"Yes?" She gave me a look hard enough to cut diamonds, but this was my child we were talking about, not a torn gown or a misplaced glove.

"I'm sure I have no need of a wet nurse, madonna. My milk is coming in well already."

"You are very young, Violante. Giuseffa tells me she is thirty years old. At that age her milk will have gained in richness."

I opened my mouth to protest, but before I could say anything madonna added, "My own mother was in her thirties when she nursed me."

And when she nursed Cesare, so weak he was not expected to live beyond infancy. "Like your respected mother," I began cautiously, "I am not of noble birth and am unaccustomed to the ways of those who are. Giuseffa, how old is your eldest child?"

"She is coming up fifteen, your grace. She is to be married as soon as… that is…" Her gaze wandered doubtfully in madonna's direction.

"I have agreed to provide a dowry for the girl."

And a wet nurse for her first child? I wondered. "So you were sixteen when your daughter was born?"

"If you say so, ladyship."

"And she thrived on your milk?"

"Oh yes, she's been a bonny lass all her life." Giuseffa beamed at me. I beamed back.

"The cases are not comparable, Violante," said madonna, "and well you know it. There is the matter of your health for a start."

"My health, madonna?"

"Yes, girl." She drew me aside and spoke in a whisper. "I know my brother left you with more than just a child in your belly, and Torella counsels that the pox may be passed through mother's milk."

"But I am cured, madonna. I have been perfectly well for months. I am more afraid I might become ill if I don't feed my baby. The wife of one of my father's friends went mad because her child died and her milk soaked her brain."

"You do not think, perhaps, it was the death of her child that sent her mad? I believe the loss of a child must be the hardest blow God in His mercy can inflict on a woman." Her eyes did not fill with tears; her lips did not tremble. She merely fixed me with a gaze from which I could not look away. "Be warned," she went on, "be prepared. Even a Jew is a woman."

"That's it, isn't it?" It was not my youth, not even my health, but my Jewishness that would make my milk unpalatable to her beloved brother's child. That was the contagion his son might suck from my breasts. I laughed, though my laughter sounded mirthless in my ears. Giuseffa stared at me in alarm and clutched her own child tighter. "How little you must value yourself as my godmother, then, if you are afraid I am still a Hebrew in the blood."

Donna Lucrezia turned to Giuseffa and her husband. "Go," she said. "Wait for me outside, and make sure the door is well shut behind you." They bowed and shuffled out. A sense of triumph kindled inside me, but was snuffed out as soon as I turned from the door to look at Donna Lucrezia. Shoulders bowed, face creased with misery, she looked suddenly ten years older. With a deep sigh she sank on to a stool and leaned her head on one hand.

"Sit down," she ordered me.

I perched myself on the edge of my high bed. "Are you well, madonna?"

She raised her head; the pressure of her fingertips had left three white coins on her forehead. "Sometimes," she said, "the heart will speak what the mind will not acknowledge. Perhaps I have not acted as conscientiously as I should towards you. I dare say, in the circumstances, many people would say I had not, letting you become…ensnared by my brother in such a way."

"But that was not your fault, madonna. You were ill and he was anxious for you and I…"

She held up a hand to stop me before I went any further. "Yes, yes, I know Cesare's ways. There is no need to spell it out for me."

Yet for me, every need to relive it, as I did a thousand times a day. "Sorry, madonna."

"No, it is I who am sorry. I spoke like a coward and a bigot. I showed you discourtesy and betrayed my faith." She rose and stood in front of me, taking my hands in her own, squeezing them so her rings dug into my flesh. "My only excuse is that…this baby matters a great deal to me, do you see?"

Once again I had the feeling she was trying to tell me something more than she was saying, the same feeling I had had on the morning of our departure from Rome when Cesare had ordered me to take the children to their nurse, and he and she had turned the same gaze on me, like a pair of hawks fixed on the same prey.

"Then I am grateful, madonna, and I regret I have given you cause to doubt me."

⟨❧⟩

Though our conversation had seemed inconclusive, the matter of the wet nurse was quietly dropped. New dishes began to appear on my menu, barley broths and wine warmed with fennel seeds to promote lactation. Every Wednesday, Friday, and Saturday, madonna sent one of her chaplains to my room to give me communion, and from Duke Ercole's library she brought a Life of Saint Margaret of Antioch who, having been safely delivered by God from the belly of a serpent, became the patron of Christian women in labour.

And she decided I should have Fidelma for my most constant companion, day and night. She ordered a featherbed to be brought into my already crowded chamber and placed on the floor beside my own bed so I could neither climb into bed nor step out of it during the night without stubbing my toes on Fidelma's bony form.

"The Dalmatian is not reliable," madonna said. "We must have someone we can understand, if anything happens during the night."

We must have a guard dog, I thought, for my Christian morals, and what better than a sincerely reformed Jew? There is none more pious than the convert, though madonna would have been horrified if she had known the course Fidelma's and my conversations began to take.

I took a small, mean pleasure in the fact that Fidelma was obliged to sleep on the floor like a servant, and to be kept awake at night by my growing insomnia. Unable to make myself comfortable, no matter how many pillows Fidelma dutifully piled at my back, or beneath the sag of my belly if I lay on my side, I would frequently get up, light all the candles and, by their crackling light, read and re-read Cesare's letters. I kept them under my pillows now, because I could no longer bend to retrieve my travelling chest from beneath the bed.

"He has written to you again, then?" Fidelma sat up, rubbing her eyes, pushing stray hanks of hair back under her sleeping cap. I always pretended they were new letters, imagining I could pass off their worn appearance as travel staining. But in truth I had heard nothing from Cesare, not even a reply to the letter I had sent with Bembo's poem in it.

Perhaps Donna Lucrezia had intercepted it. I believed I had taken every precaution to keep it secret, choosing a messenger who was trusted by Angela and Giulio, and whom I had never seen speaking to Vittorio, so I thought it unlikely he was in Cesare's pay. And I had placed Bembo's letter to madonna in the false bottomed jewel case as was customary. But it was impossible to know for certain.

"What does he say?" asked Fidelma.

*...there was a German at the university in Bologna... If we are not at the centre of God's universe, then what are we here for?* What indeed did he say? What was this world into which I was about to bring a child?

"Oh, he tells me his little brother Giovanni has just been invested with the Duchy of Camerino and that he is very pleased with the coronet and staff of office he was given because he can play hoopla with them." This much I had learned from Donna Lucrezia.

"You know it cannot go on, this abuse of office by the popes."

"What are you talking about?" Wrenching my gaze from Cesare's handwriting, my mind from its interrogation of his thoughts, I looked down at her, hugging her sharp knees through the featherbed, her expression keen and glowing with something more than the candlelight. It was an intelligent face, but still ugly, so ugly.

"Fra Raffaello says..." I gave a contemptuous snort, but she was not to be deterred. "Fra Raffaello says there is a backlash. It began with Fra Girolamo, but he made the mistake of trying to keep the link between the spiritual and the temporal. The two must be separate. God's servants must not be corrupted by the owning of property or the wielding of earthly power. The Church must reconnect with the old principles of poverty and chastity and the power of prayer."

"And so I am sure Cesare believes. Never forget, he chose to quit the Church because he could not keep his vows. At least he is not a hypocrite."

"Yet he seems to be no better at keeping his marriage vows."

I flushed. I felt as though someone had lit a brazier in my belly and was fanning the flames. But this was nothing unusual; it happened several times a day, the sweat prickling my skin, stinging the rash which had lately flared up behind my knees and under my arms. All my companions insisted I must endure it with joy, for it surely meant I was carrying a son.

"He does keep his vow to the Church. As captain general of its army. No other has been as successful at bringing the papal states under control."

"Under whose control? Not the pope's, I think."

Though nothing was openly acknowledged, it was accepted now that Cesare had turned his attention beyond the Romagna, to Bologna, even to Florence and Venice. With France and Spain once again bickering over Naples, some murmured, he would make himself king of Italy while their backs were turned.

And, I thought, he would need an heir.

"So he is doing exactly what you and your Fra Raffaello want to see done. He is taking the state from the Church."

Fidelma's eyes, which were dark and actually, I decided, rather fine, if a little prominent, shot hunted glances around the room. "It's as well for you these walls are muffled," she said. "I cannot think of a single person who would want to hear you say that. I doubt your…paramour would even put it so baldly."

I felt foolish, I, the favourite from Rome, Valentino's mistress, duped by this raw-boned provincial girl. "Of course he is doing nothing of the sort. I am tired. You have confused me with such serious talk at this time of night."

"Then put out the lights and go to sleep."

I blew out the candles and clambered back into bed, but I could not sleep and nor, it seemed, could Fidelma.

After a short silence broken only by the rustling of bedclothes as I tried to come to an accommodation with my belly and Fidelma to cushion her bones against the floor, she said, "My father says the pope has levied a tax on the Jews in Rome to pay for Cesare's war games. He says Saint Peter's coffers can't keep pace with his demands to rebuild his cities and then buy new guns from Burgundy to knock them down again." Fidelma, unlike me, kept in regular touch with her family.

But I gave no credence to what Fidelma's father had told her. The pope would do what he had always done. He would borrow from men like my father, fellow Spaniards even before they were Jews, and they would be glad to lend. Elderly cardinals were always dying and leaving their fortunes to the Holy See, and the men appointed to replace them paid handsomely for their scarlet hats. There was always money to pay back loans, and though the pope did not pay interest, he did give generous gifts.

As my time drew closer, the waiting itself seemed to absorb all my energy. Even when madonna came to the lying-in chamber one day clutching a pouch of cypress green velvet embroidered in gold with Cesare's coat of arms, I could not summon more than an idle curiosity. My back ached, my breasts were hot and sore, my feet so swollen I had to lean on Angela to keep my balance while I made my bow to madonna. The rash had spread to the crooks of my elbows and itched unbearably. I longed to bathe in cool water but this was out of the question as the innate coldness of water might affect my chances of giving birth to a boy. By now, to be honest, the memory of Cesare and the brief, interrupted pleasure he had given me, was more likely to make me irritable than sentimental.

"The carpenters have delivered the crib," said madonna, testing the stuffing in the draft excluder under the door with the toe of her shoe. "I wish you could see it, but it's too big to get in here comfortably. The door would be open for too long. The posts are all carved with cherubs and the canopy is painted to look like a spring sky with birds and fluffy white clouds. And there is a cunning mechanism so it can be rocked with the foot with hardly any exertion. We tried Fonsi in it. He's about the weight of a newborn. There is enough swansdown cured now for two quilts so, ladies, there must be less gambling and more embroidery." Murmurs of assent accompanied the soft slap of cards against the table top.

"I have something for you," she continued, handing me the little velvet bag. "Open it," she commanded, as I stroked and probed it with my fingers, hoping against all the logic of my senses there might be a letter inside it. I opened it, loosing the golden strings with my nails. Delving inside, my hand closed around a stone, not large, perhaps the size of a lark's egg, and mounted on a dainty stand of worked gold set with diamonds. As I drew it out, a faint fizzing sound came from it, like the sound of the tide running over fine shingle in the far distance.

"It is the eagle stone," said madonna as I held up the milk and water crystal to the candlelight and dimly discerned in its hollow centre tiny fragments which spangled and whispered as I tipped and turned it. "You see, it is like a tiny womb full of sparkling seeds. Its properties are beneficial in reducing the pain of labour and easing the birth. My brother sent it. It will make your child shine. You must keep it always on your right side."

And as soon as she said this, I knew it was her own contrivance. She had found the stone, perhaps from some quack on the Via dei Volte, and she had had the pouch embroidered with Cesare's arms. I felt trapped, caught fast in the web that bound the two of them, gagging on all the words and thoughts that passed between them. I had to escape. I struggled to my feet and lunged for the door. My sleeve caught on a candle flame. As I turned to pat out the fire with my free hand, I caught my foot in the hem of my *cioppa* and fell.

There was no pain as madonna and Angela and the rest rushed to help me to my feet and back on to the bed. Only once they had stopped fussing about me, plumping pillows, straightening the red velvet coverlet, trimming the singed edge of my sleeve, did a curious sensation begin at the base of my spine, a heaviness spreading between my thighs where it rested like sorrow until driven out by a desperate desire to urinate. The pot was brought. I lifted my skirts and squatted, supported under my arms by two of madonna's ladies. In seconds, the pot was overflowing and the turkey rug it stood on saturated.

"My waters," I said. My voice sounded weak and plaintive, though I felt quite calm. As madonna bustled about, barking orders like one of her brother's serjeants at arms, the first pain came. I felt as though a hand had reached into my belly and was squeezing my womb like an orange. Then its grip relaxed long enough for me to smile at the aptness of the image and the midwife, a thin-lipped woman with great, raw hands like rusty shovels, to remark that the smirk would soon be wiped off my face. No use in soft-hearted midwives, madonna had remarked when she first engaged the woman. I wondered how she had arrived so suddenly. I had the crazy notion that madonna had been keeping her in a press, and had fetched her out like a clean chemise or a change of bedlinen.

Full of an energy that felt too big for my body to contain, I paced my little room, bumping into furniture, shaking off the anxious pawing of my attendants, railing at madonna that I must have fresh air, that if I could not escape those four muffled walls I would explode like a rotten melon.

"Deep breaths," ordered the midwife as the next pain came.

"Of what? Smoke?" I shouted, doubling over a low chair whose back came away in my hands. I flung it at the midwife. She dodged it with a practised air. "Good job the father isn't here," she remarked to Donna Lucrezia. Donna Lucrezia pressed the eagle stone into my right hand.

Later I felt tired, my back and legs ached, so I lay on the bed. I must have slept, because when I awoke the rugs had been cleared from the floor and the birthing stool squatted in the centre of the room. I had been talking to my mother. A cockerel's head, she had reminded me; there must be a cockerel's head nailed above the door to the birthing chamber to ward off the spirits waiting to snatch the baby. As I opened my eyes, Angela crouched beside me, dabbing at my forehead and temples with a cloth soaked in rosewater. I grabbed her wrist. The cool liquid dribbled into my ear, making my voice sound as though it could not escape from inside my head.

"I need a cockerel's head," I told her.

"What for?"

"It's a Jewish custom," said Fidelma.

"Then it has no place here," said madonna.

"Get that scrawny cow out of here," I told Angela through gritted teeth as another pain came. I was aware of Donna Lucrezia's grey, speculative gaze.

"Send to my kitchen for the cock's head, Angela. But let us tie the prayer to Saint Margaret about her left thigh also. We must do everything we can."

I felt reassured. For a while, it made the pains easier to bear. Some hours flew by, some dragged. When madonna said she must go to dine because the Imperial ambassador was visiting and had brought his wife, I thought she must already have missed one dinner and her concern for me made me cry, loud, coarse sobs that turned to groans and screams as the pains crushed my abdomen and forced the air out of my lungs.

"I can't do this," I whimpered to Angela while the monster in my belly was drawing breath. "I want to die."

"No you don't." Her own face was pale and sweaty, hair hanging in her eyes and plastered to her cheeks. "Think..." Her gaze darted about the room, as though what I should think of were hanging among the cobwebs in the corners or dancing in the lamp smoke. "Think how soon you'll be slim again, and have pretty gowns. And see Cesare."

I believe I hit her. I wanted to hurt her the way I was hurting. Most of all, looking at her long, grave face with its large eyes and high-bridged nose, and the red in her hair, I wanted to hurt Cesare. All those months of placid acceptance, of making excuses and building hopes. Castles in the air. Castles in Spain. I laughed, or screamed. He didn't care. He had handed me over to Taddeo and moved on. I was like some small town he had conquered on his way to somewhere else, breeched and battered, stripped of its resources and left in the care of a meek, wage-serving governor.

"You think I'd let that bastard stick his cock in me again? After this?"

A silence, a stillness, as though the room itself were stunned with shock. A voice from somewhere among the shifting shadows, just a voice which could have belonged to any of madonna's ladies. "You can't talk about the duke like that."

"On the contrary, I seem to recall speaking of the Duke of Bisceglie in much the same terms when our son was born. All cats are black in the dark." So madonna had returned. "How is she progressing?"

The midwife grasped my ankles and pulled me down the bed until my buttocks were balanced on its edge, then rolled up my skirts and told me to part my legs and bend my knees. Her hand thrust inside me seemed to draw out memories of other hands, of my mother's hand shielding the taper from draughts as she lit the Shabbat candles, of Mariam's blunt fingers pressed into my scalp as she washed my hair at my first *mikveh*, of Angela's wise fingers and the pads of Cesare's thumbs grazing my nipples as he told me how Don Cristoforo had described the shape of the earth to his beloved queen.

"The head is well down, duchesa, and the birth canal wide open. Time for the stool, I suggest."

My attendants helped me from the bed to the birthing stool and held me there, for it was nothing more than a simple v-shaped structure with a low back and no arms. Finally, with the wooden slats digging into the backs of my thighs and the midwife kneeling in front of me with her coarse, scrubbed hands cupped to receive the child, with a surge of panic inextricable from the next contraction of my womb, my situation became real to me. I was sixteen years old, unmarried, and about to become a mother. How could I bring up a child? I was too young, too tired. I had no mother to guide me. This had to stop now; it could not happen.

"Stop it," I pleaded, but no one seemed to hear me.

"One more push," said the midwife.

"Now," said madonna, and I felt her breath on my neck. She was kneeling behind me, her arms braced beneath my breasts. Angela and one of the Ferrarese ladies seized hold of either arm. "Push. As hard as you can. I won't let you slip. The stone is there beside you and we have invoked Saint Margaret. All will be well."

I pushed because I could not help it, then because all that mattered in the world was to expel this incubus from my body. Suddenly, after the long months of being no more than the host of this new life, valued for nothing more than my body's dumb, blind capacity to grow a child as nature grows trees or nettles or rain clouds, the beginning was in sight and I fought my way towards it. The blood pounded in my temples, my bones cracked. I inhaled salt and iron, beeswax, camphor, and stale perfume. I held my breath and pushed again, and then I was floating on the scent of lavender water, born up by angels' wings fashioned from starched linen. The notion that I was dead drifted across my mind and I examined it with indifference.

"A boy!" Donna Lucrezia's face appeared above me, flushed and shining, hair dishevelled. I must do her hair, I thought, but I was so tired.

"You have a perfect little son, Violante. Look. He even has red hair. Oh…"

"What? What is it?" I struggled to sit up, feeling the sickly squelch of blood soaking into the bandages between my legs. Something in her tone brought the world back into sharp, fearful focus.

"He is…marked." She placed my son in my arms. Still unwashed, he squirmed on his blanket slick as a skinned rabbit and gave me a long, steady look out of dark blue eyes. His carroty hair stuck to his scalp in whorls like flattened snail shells and his long fingers made complicated gestures in the air as though they had yet to learn the limitations of human hands. On his left thigh, just where the medal bearing the prayer to Saint Margaret had left its outline in the flesh of my own thigh, was a smudge of bruise-blue skin. This mark, I noted, had the shape of Spain on my father's maps. The smile inside me broke out into laughter.

"It is the *mancha mongolica*. All my family are born with it but it fades to nothing by the seventh year of life."

"But what does it mean? Is it a curse, or good fortune?"

"It shows he is a Jew," I said, but madonna did not seem to hear me. Turning to Elisabetta Senese she said, "Have the clerk bring my household book. We must record the time of the birth and have his horoscope cast." From the midwife she demanded, "Did you note the hour from the candle when you cut the cord? It was a little after the eighteenth, I think."

"Yes, duchesa, about half way between the eighteenth and the nineteenth. And you will see I left a good long tail so he will be man enough when he grows." A few giggles rippled around the room; a few coarse jokes were exchanged. In this room, in our womb-fug, we had long since abandoned any show of treating our menfolk respectfully. Let the world praise them for making sons. We knew better.

Then something began to nag at my complacency, something I had to do, something prompted by talk of tails and cutting.

"What will you call him?" madonna asked, as one of the women prized my baby from my arms to wash and swaddle him. *Bris mila*, that was it; I could call him nothing before his circumcision on the eighth day.

"Have you not decided?" madonna prompted.

"Girolamo," I said quickly, feeling the shining eyes and expectant smiles of all these Christian women upon me, "for my father." I surprised myself by saying this. It was true I had not thought about names. I had, I supposed, somewhere very deep within myself, expected to have those seven days of the Creation in which to find his name. And even then, I had not expected to find my father's name.

"Good. Very suitable. And you will add Cesare, of course."

I looked at my son, lying in Angela's lap as she began to bind him, straightening his arms before wrapping the linen band around his shoulders. My eyes devoured the vanishing perfection of his nakedness, just as the Creator had made him, as He had made his father.

"And Giulio," said Angela. "Giulio must be one of his godfathers. Girolamo Giulio Cesare. How does that sound?"

"Almost as long as he is."

"He'll grow to master it."

And he would grow complete, with no part of what Cesare and I had given him taken away. He could not be improved by pain. "Will you be his godmother?" I asked her. "I can think of none better."

Angela glanced doubtfully at Donna Lucrezia, who waved her glance away. "I am his aunt," she said. "Best to share the honours, give him as many protectors as possible."

"And presents," added Angela. "What will you have for your baptism, baby boy? Silver spoons? A damask bonnet? A hobby horse?" None of her suggestions seemed to impress Girolamo. He had begun to grizzle at the imprisoning of his limbs, a thin, fractious, magical sound which drew the milk tingling into my breasts.

"Let me have him," I pleaded. "I think he must be hungry."

As I put him to my breast and felt the sturdy pull of his mouth on my nipple, a kind of calm strength spread through me, a rich sense of well-being that banished the griping in my belly and the discomfort of the bloody cloths wadded between my thighs. Bending to kiss his fuzzy scalp, I was overwhelmed by the miracle of his existence. Gazing into his unblinking eyes I wondered what thoughts he had brought with him from the dark waters of the womb, and if they were mine, or Cesare's, or all his own.

⟨≈⟩

An outbreak of fever in the town made madonna determined Girolamo should be baptised immediately, long before my churching. As I would be unable to attend the ceremony, it became even more important to me to choose the right man to stand as his other godfather, and I wanted to choose Ferrante. Yet, since the death of Catherinella, I had found it difficult to be in his company. His presence was like my guilty conscience made flesh, and it soured my precious memories of Cesare, but I knew what he had done had shown the kind of courage and compassion I would wish for my son and could not, apparently, find within myself. I wanted Girolamo's new life to atone for the cutting off of Catherinella's.

Ferrante was not permitted to visit me during my confinement as he was not a relation, though he did send presents, a tiny taffeta cap and mantle for Girolamo, sunshine yellow with deep scarlet fringes, and a porcelain box of sugar-coated sweets and *pane bianchi* to help me build up my strength. I tried to write to him, but each time I tried to put pen to paper, the lines on the page seemed to transform themselves into the tattooed circles on Catherinella's cheeks. Then I would find myself in tears, my tears dropping on to the page and smudging out my words.

Of the men at court, only Taddeo, as my betrothed husband, was allowed into the lying-in chamber. So, in the end, I asked him to be Girolamo's other godfather. He blushed with pleasure, and could not look me in the eye, and stretched his mouth in the smile of a foolish suitor as he agreed, but I was not deluded. I saw where his gaze alighted as he told me how honoured he was and how this would cement his bond with my son and how he would be a father to him in all but blood.

Earlier that same day, a boat had arrived from Cesenatico. It had taken six mules to carry its cargo from the dock to the castle, so Angela told me, her tone mixed between excitement, teasing, and a kind of wary admiration. All this cargo was destined for me, or rather, Girolamo and me, and came under the supervision of a steward of Cesare's household. My already cluttered room was now piled high with his gifts and I sat in my bed, with my infant in my arms, as though I were presiding over some Turkish bazaar.

There were lengths of fabrics of all kinds, from Egyptian cotton and Brussels lace for swaddling bands to heavy, figured velvets and brocades to make fitting gowns for the mother of the Duke of Romagna's heir. Folded beside his crib were hangings of white damask, embroidered in gold with the signs of the zodiac, waiting to be pinned to the newell posts. A set of silver spoons sprouted from an ivory and enamel *cuchiaiera*. Standing in a corner of the room, hemmed in by a wooden fort festooned with tiny flags bearing Cesare's arms, was a flautist in his master's red and gold quartered livery. He seemed to speak no Italian. I think he was French, or possibly from somewhere in the Empire, but by means of signs he gave me to understand he was charged with playing the baby to sleep.

Gold coins were scattered over my bed like a map of Cesare's campaigns, Venetian ducats and Medici florins, *louis d'or* and Spanish *doblons*, coins from the mints of Urbino and Pesaro and some bearing Saint Peter's keys. They fascinated Girolamo, who gazed without blinking at the pattern of bright discs on my crimson coverlet. Taddeo stared at them too, as he helped himself to Ferrante's sweets. "I think we shall be content," he said.

"I'm sure we shall, my dear, but now, if you will forgive me, Girolamo will soon need feeding."

There was a letter to accompany the gifts from Cesenatico, which I had tucked under my pillows, and I ached in my bones to read it. As soon as Taddeo had made his farewells, and edged out of the room around the bolts of cloth and boxes of perfumed wax, I drew it out and tore open the seal.

The hand was not Cesare's own but that of his secretary, Agapito.

*To the worthy and virtuous Monna Violante,* the letter began, and I blushed fiercely to think how the secretary and his lord might have sniggered at the choice of address. I read on with a chill in my heart, as though all the warm blood in my body had rushed into my cheeks.

*We offer our most hearty congratulations and thankful prayers on the safe delivery of your son...* "Your" son, he had written; not "our" son, not "my" son, but "your" son. Well, he was just being cautious, choosing his words with half a mind to the powerful interests of his wife's family. Surely the extravagance of his gifts proved he acknowledged Girolamo as his, even if he thought it wiser not to say so. I scanned the lines hungrily for some sign, some coded phrase that would make his pride and pleasure and love plain to me.

There was nothing, a mere half page of formal platitudes concluding with his official signature, *Dux Valentinus.* Struggling against the weight of a sudden, awful loneliness, I left my bed, crossed the room to the fire, and flung the letter into it. I watched the wax seal bubble and smoke, the bull and the keys and the lilies melt away. Very well, I thought, very well. It is just Girolamo and me, then, Girolamo and me against the world.

❧

"Lucrezia tells me she is thinking about your wedding." Angela lay beside me reading her letter as I suckled Girolamo. I seemed to spend most of my time with him either latched to my breast or stretched across my knees for winding. He was a very hungry child. Like his father, madonna said, and I clung to her remark. However cold Cesare had become towards me, at least he had not denied Girolamo's parentage to his sister. "She wants you married and back at court. She misses you and your... special services."

"You mean my courier services. We can speak freely here, Angela. We are in the outer reaches of the universe."

We were at Taddeo's house in Occhiobello, a full day's journey from

Ferrara for a new mother and her child travelling in a litter. The August afternoon was hot, and we had taken ourselves into the shade of a walled orchard which grew on the north side of the house, facing away from the river and the miasma which hovered over its sluggish waters. Bees droned and a fountain splashed in the formal garden on the other side of the brick walls. We had spread an old rug and sprawled on it to enjoy a picnic of strawberries and frascati wine cold from the cellar. Angela had stripped to her chemise, and I had unbound Girolamo from his clouts and swaddling bands so he could kick and wave his arms freely. I had no fear for the straightness of his limbs. He was quickly becoming sturdy and was, to my eye at least, as beautifully made as his father.

Donna Lucrezia had persuaded Angela to accompany me to my new home because, she said, it would add weight to the argument she intended to put to Duke Ercole in favour of a marriage between her cousin and Giulio if Angela could be seen to be capable of demure conduct and restraint, and loyalty to her friend. Besides, the duke was sending Giulio on a mission to Venice to try to woo the fashionable singer, Gian de Artigianova, away from service with the doge.

As I transferred Girolamo to my other breast, Angela sat up and kissed my cheek.

"What was that for?"

"Because you look so beautiful. It suits you, all this—babies, the country. I begin to believe you might be happy." In the absence of Giulio, and with Taddeo gone for much of every day on estate business, Angela and I had resumed much of our old intimacy. "Cousin Cesare will be well pleased with you."

"Oh, I don't think he will care much either way." I had not believed I could say such words and yet, there they hung, in the air between us, among the butterflies and dancing dust motes, and I was no different, just in a different place upon the road. "He does not acknowledge Girolamo, you know."

"Not in so many words, perhaps. That is not his way. He does strange, reckless things, but deep down he's as cautious and wily as any Catalan peasant, just like Uncle Rodrigo. He never makes a bet without hedging it."

"I suppose." I had reached the same conclusion myself, but still the fear lingered that he did not believe Girolamo was his child and I was loathe to let it go because it might yet serve to cushion me against any more disappointments. I could not afford to think well of Cesare; I could not waste my store of love on him now I had my child to think of.

"What presents do you think Giulio will bring me back from Venice? I asked only for a box of vanilla wax for I know he was snowed under with demands from Lucrezia and tips on where best to buy from Strozzi. But he will bring more, surely."

I laughed, but she was serious. Though Cesare's gifts proved nothing to me, Giulio's were everything to Angela because they were honestly given.

"Oh Violante, I wish we could have been married before he went, then we could have had our honeymoon in Venice. Wouldn't that be grand? I long to go there."

"We will. Madonna says we all will, in the autumn, because Don Alfonso wishes her to accompany him there. I expect by then you and Giulio will be married, so you will get your honeymoon." I winded Girolamo and lay him on the rug to sleep. He grizzled a bit, until Angela tickled his belly with a feather and made him laugh. Then Angela turned the feather on me, tracing a fine line down my throat and between my breasts, staying my hands as I attempted to refasten my bodice. I put my arms around her and kissed her mouth and could make believe, with my vision blurred by closeness, that her fair, fine-boned face was that of my lover.

◈

We were still lying on the rug, drowsing in one another's arms, Girolamo asleep at my side, when I heard Taddeo calling my name. Lifting Angela's arm from across my shoulder, I struggled to my feet, straightening my clothes and smoothing my hair out of my eyes. Angela mumbled something, rolled over, and went back to sleep.

"Get up," I hissed, picking up her bodice and throwing it at her. "Taddeo's back." Girolamo began to whimper as Angela sat up, rubbing her eyes. She took the baby in her lap and began to dress him. He always resisted swaddling, and his whimpers soon turned to a fully fledged bawling.

"Give him to me. You'd better make yourself decent." Our eyes met and we giggled like a couple of schoolgirls caught out in a prank.

"Here you are." I could see Taddeo was trying to smile at the image I presented with my loose hair and dishevelled clothes and my naked baby in my arms. The pastoral Madonna. But he seemed unable to arrange his features quite right. His mouth stretched more in a grimace than a smile. He would neither hold my gaze nor look directly at Angela. With a sudden, furious flushing of my face and neck, I wondered if he had been in the orchard longer than we thought, if he had seen Angela and I together. Well, it was not a sin; only between men could such a thing be sinful because women had no bodily means of penetration. I tilted my chin defiantly.

"We have been picnicking," I told him. "Would you like a cup of wine?"

"What..? No...I...I have news." His tone filled me with foreboding. His words fell like drops of ice water into the drowsy heat of the afternoon. Angela finished lacing her bodice and stood up and stepped into her skirt. I held Girolamo against my chest, like a shield.

"You will have to go. Both of you. Immediately. The pope is dead," Taddeo blurted out.

"Uncle Rodrigo? He can't be," said Angela, but of course he could be. He was more than seventy years of age. Angela began to shake; her fingers fumbled at the laces of her skirt. Low, keening sobs forced themselves down her nose, between her compressed lips, then she opened her mouth and started to scream. I tried to put my hand on her shoulder to calm her, but Girolamo was squirming and crying so hard I needed both arms to prevent him slipping from my grasp. Above the noise I scarcely heard Taddeo's next remark.

"Poison," he said. "They say the duke will die too."

"The duke? You mean..?" My brain felt slow and sodden, like a wet sponge. It absorbed his words but could make no sense of them.

"Cesare," said Taddeo, coughing with embarrassment at his unaccustomed use of Cesare's given name. "He is probably dead already."

I clutched my baby so fiercely I fancied the tiny cage of his ribs might fuse to the curve of my clawed hands. He gasped and fell abruptly silent. I braced myself for the onslaught of grief, but it did not come. Instead I felt angry, a cold, clear-headed fury which both urged me to hit Taddeo and cautioned me this was not my best course of action. "He is not dead. I would know if he were dead. He is not going to die."

Perhaps infected by my own ruthless calm, Taddeo finally managed to look me in the eye. "As far as you and I are concerned, madam, he might as well be dead. What power is left him without his father? How long before those he usurped come creeping back into their cities and he is flung into the Tiber one dark night like so much rubbish? Or his brother Gandia?"

"You would be well advised to take back those words if you don't want to wind up drowned yourself, sir. My lord's eyes and ears are everywhere." Angela, a Borgia from her dark red hair to her toes which curled in on themselves because she favoured sharp-pointed shoes, squared her shoulders and wiped her nose on the back of her hand. "As are those who love him," she added, putting an arm around my waist and fixing Taddeo with a look of grim impassivity which made me think of how Cesare might have looked as he listened at the door to the upstairs dining room in Senigallia.

"Love," said Taddeo, in the tone, both regretful and resentful, of a man who has discovered the antique Venus he had set his heart on is nothing but a modern fake, "is somewhat like my pike. Introduce a little salt into their pools and they all die."

"Did you never mean to marry me, then? You knew the duke's father was an old man and might have died at any time."

"Do me the honour of not doubting my word, madam. Have I not kept my promise to you, even though your duke has failed to acknowledge his bastard?"

Now I felt the tears behind my eyes, the grief squeezing my throat, but I leaned closer to Angela and fought it.

"So what has changed?"

"Poison, madam, poison. That says to me the duke has got too big for his boots. He has become careless. Careless men will lose their states as easily as they might lose a pair of stockings or a throw of the dice."

"We will see what Donna Lucrezia has to say about this," said Angela.

"I dare say she will do as her husband requires of her, at last."

"Come, Violante, we will return to Ferrara." She pushed me in front of her, turning away from Taddeo with a haughty toss of her head. "You will allow us horses, Ser Taddeo, if only to hasten the hour when we are out of your sight."

He did not reply immediately and though I refused to look back at him, I could sense some struggle taking place within him; it seemed to disturb the thick, peach scented air as we passed through it. Then he said, more gently, "You may have my coach, Violante, and whatever supplies you need for the journey."

Even a fake may have some value, if it is good enough.

On arriving at Ferrara, we found the castle deserted and the court removed to Medelana. We sent the carriage back to Occhiobello and set out on horseback to make the journey into the mountains, riding astride, with stirrups, like a couple of camp followers, said Angela, and I think we both wondered if something of the sort was what our suddenly terrifying and empty future might hold for us. We had no escort, and it was very likely our future held nothing more than a band of brigands with long knives and a sharp eye for expensive horse furniture. But the road was quiet and the air grew clearer as we left the city behind us and climbed away from the river plain. We even sang from time to time, to humour Girolamo, who lay in a reed basket lashed to my pommel. Angela called him Moses.

There was an inn, we knew, at Quartexana, where parties travelling from Ferrara to Medelana would usually break their journey. I was all for stopping there only to change our horses but Angela insisted we stay the night. It would be madness to travel after dark.

In the inn parlour, rumour was rife. Though we sat in a private booth to eat our evening meal, the conversations of our fellow guests were clearly audible through the drawn curtains, hot words turning the food to ashes in our mouths.

"They say the Holy Father was heard making a pact with the devil with his dying breath."

"By his confessor, of all people."

"Pleading for a few more years, I heard."

"And the devil there beside him in the guise of a black monkey."

"I heard the old sot was so bloated they couldn't ram his corpse into its coffin."

"And the duke's men looted his apartments so thoroughly there weren't even the vestments left to bury him in."

Attempting to force the innkeeper's wife's stringy mutton down my throat with a gulp of thin wine, I stared at Angela, and saw my own wretchedness reflected in her miserable expression. How long had the pope been dead? I wondered. Even rumour can only travel at the speed of a fast horse. Even if Cesare had still been alive when these myths of his father's end fled Rome, he might well be dead by now, suspended like a daemon between his final breath and the first whisperings of the tales that would become his legend. I imagined our fellow guests were talking this way solely for our benefit. I was certain they knew who we were. The curtain shielding us was somehow transparent to them if not to us. We were mocked, degraded, defenceless.

"We should travel on tonight," I muttered to Angela, half choked by a gobbet of gristle. "We're not safe here."

"Nobody knows who we are, sweetheart; how could they? And I swear, any more of that road tonight will shake out all my teeth." She flashed me a wide smile. "Imagine if I were to present myself to Giulio transformed into a toothless crone."

"Do you think Cesare is dead too?"

"Cesare? He has the constitution of an ox and a digestion to match. I doubt there's a poison invented that could kill Cesare."

I thought of the sick child madonna had conjured for me, living on bread sops and goats' milk, gasping for air on hot afternoons, his lips and fingernails blue as sloes. "But if someone has tried once, they will try again. With something a little more certain. A blade, or the *garotta*." His own favourite.

"If they have tried—and remember, we do not know that for sure—they will not get a second chance. Come now, we're exhausted. It will all look less bleak in the morning."

She was right. It was impossible, even after the landlady's execrable breakfast of rye bread fit to sole shoes and a cheese so salty it stung the tongue, not to feel optimistic. The verges were studded with tiny flowers, fragrant cushions of saxifrage and juniper, gentians like flakes of virgin blue chipped from the face of the sky. Pale grey stones crunched like sugar under our horses' hooves, and when we stopped to drink, the water in the swift running streams tasted of the clean air of the hills. But as we clattered through the gate into Medelana and looked up at the villa which dominated the slope above the town, I shivered to see how its high, blind curtain wall cut into a sky the fragile blue of a robin's egg.

❧

We were met by Ippolito. Standing in the courtyard, his soutane blowing against his legs in the dusty breeze, he banished the groom and held our horses himself as we dismounted. Though he gave Girolamo, whom he had not yet seen, a perfunctory smile as I gathered him up out of the basket, it did nothing to dispel his grim, preoccupied demeanour. He did not kiss either of us; he made no comment on our arrival, unescorted, hatless and sunburned as a couple of peasants.

"I had to tell her," he said. "Dear God, I wish you two had been here. It was dreadful. I thought she had run quite mad." Remembering the scenes at Belfiore when she had heard the news of Cesare's invasion of Urbino, I could well believe it. "And the best I could find to deal with her were Fidelma and that empty-headed Elisabetta Senese."

"You will take us straight to her?" asked Angela. Was no one ever going to get to the point?

"What news of Cesare?" I demanded. Ippolito shook his head. My legs, still shaky from long hours of hard riding, threatened to give out completely. Tripping over a loose thread in my skirt, I longed to fall, to rest my cheek against the cool, worn flagstones and never rise again.

"She had a letter from Cosenza this morning. Cesare's hanging on, but only just, by all accounts. He has the Vatican under siege. No one goes in or out, not even for His Holiness' funeral. Michelotto's in charge. Cesare is raving most of the time, they say. Cosenza does his best to be encouraging, but reading between the lines, it sounds like Dante's inferno in there."

"Was it poison?" asked Angela.

"Cosenza doesn't think so. The physicians all agree it's the tertian fever. It's been a particularly bad summer for it, apparently. The trouble is, with Cesare keeping them shut in the palace, in his very bed-chamber, Cosenza says, there's no one to make an announcement so the rumour-mongers are having a field day."

"He has lost his judgement then," said Angela, a flat note of finality in her voice. Cardinal Cosenza was a reliable reporter, an old and loyal friend of the household at Santa Maria in Portico and a palace cardinal of long standing.

"But he can get well. Many survive the tertian fever, and he is young and strong."

"Oh Violante, if your love were medicine, he would be well already." Angela gave a little laugh and squeezed my arm, but Ippolito looked dark and preoccupied. The hearts of women were clearly far from his thoughts.

"Who is here?" asked Angela, trying to sound casual, as we climbed the wide, shallow stairs from the courtyard to the first floor whose arcade was smothered in dusty bourgainvillea leaves. The flowers were all gone this late in the summer.

"Giulio is at Belriguardo with our father. Alfonso and Ferrante are there too. I am only here because I had to bring her the news about her father." He gave a gallows laugh. "Being the priest in the family, I suppose they thought I was best placed to bring her comfort."

"And have you?" asked Angela, arch with disappointment.

"See for yourself." He stopped before a closed door and knocked. We waited. He knocked again with greater insistence. The door opened a little way and the wan face of the Dalmatian emerged from the shadows.

"Tell your mistress her cousin and Monna Violante are here," said Ippolito, speaking loudly and deliberately, as if that would make him understood. The Dalmatian's inability to speak or understand Italian had, it seemed to me, developed into a positive act of will, a way to deny the collar around her neck and keep the road home clear in her mind's eye. Her face disappeared again, a sallow moon swallowed by cloud. Ippolito pushed the door wider and stood aside to let us pass.

All the window shutters were fast, and at first I could see nothing. As my eyes adjusted to the gloom I realised there was, in fact, almost nothing to see. The room was bare of furnishings except for a pallet on the floor, up against one wall. There madonna sat, hugging her knees, her hair hanging lank and loose to either side of her face. Her gown was coarse black linen, her chemise frayed where the lace had been torn from it. She wore no jewellery but her wedding ring, and the ash cross of mourning was marked on her forehead. I was not sure she had noticed our entrance, then I saw the whites of her eyes gleam briefly in a bar of afternoon sunlight shining through a gap in the shutters as she glanced at us and looked away again.

We curtseyed.

"Angela," said madonna. Her voice was hoarse from weeping. Her words sounded like sobs, as though the grief inside her could not help but spill out when she opened her mouth. "I will speak to you later. For now, I have matters I must discuss with Violante. Alone."

"But..."

"Later. Refresh yourself. Change your clothes. All this way on horseback must have worn you out." How could she know the details of our journey? Angela threw me a look of helpless puzzlement and withdrew. Gesturing to me to sit beside her on the pallet, madonna went on,

"I can't face her just yet. She will ask me about Giulio and, oh, Violante, I have done everything wrong."

"Wrong, madonna?"

"When Alfonso came to offer his condolences, I shouldn't have let him go; I should have hung on to him. Now they will all be plotting my downfall at Belriguardo. You know there are already murmurings that my marriage is not lawful because I was not properly divorced from Giovanni Sforza."

"Oh madonna, that is old gossip. You cannot imagine Duke Ercole would take any notice of it. No one can prove now one way or the other whether or not that marriage was consummated."

"There is always Giovanni's word. While my father lived, no one took him seriously. Now, however...Oh God, I wish I could talk to Cesar, I wish...Do you think he still lives, Violante?" She had begun to rock back and forth like a madwoman. An earthenware pitcher and cup stood beside her. I poured water and offered it to her, as much to distract her from her morbid speculations as to quench a thirst. She looked at the cup and shook her head. Just then, Girolamo, who had slept sweetly while rocking in his basket on the back of my horse, woke up and began to grizzle.

"Oh, let me see him," exclaimed madonna. "I expect he has grown a good deal in the country."

"I thank the Creator he is strong, madonna."

"Give him to me, let me hold him."

I passed him into her outstretched arms and immediately his grizzling gave way to a full-throated bawling. "I'm sorry, he must be hungry," I said.

"In him at any rate his father lives." She kissed his forehead and handed him back to me. "Feed him," she said with a smile both warm and wistful. "If I had only been able to give Alfonso a son, things would be very different, for me and Angela."

"So you do not expect the duke to give his permission for Giulio to marry her?"

Donna Lucrezia shook her head. "Even if Cesar recovers, how much ground will he have lost? What if we get a hostile pope who will not reappoint him gonfalonier? Della Rovere wants Saint Peter's throne, and he has many supporters and no love for Cesar."

"Cesare also has supporters. Surely there must be enough cardinals whose votes he can influence to keep Cardinal Della Rovere at bay?"

"He has always tried to ensure that. We...he tried to be prepared for Papa dying. He was an old man, though he never behaved like one, did he? But who would have thought Cesar might be close to death himself when it happened? That was a trick Dame Fortune kept well hidden in her sleeve. And Della Rovere is clever, as clever as Cesar probably, and has friends in France."

I shifted Girolamo to my other breast, wincing for I was suffering from sores on my nipples. My child had a strong suck and little regard for his mother's comfort.

"Cabbage leaves," said madonna.

"I have tried them," I replied, though my mind was on other matters. "Della Rovere does not have blood ties in France as Cesare has. His daughter has French royal blood in her veins." I had tried to keep my tone neutral but it was clear from the look of understanding madonna gave me I had not succeeded. We sat in silence for a moment, the light leaking between the window shutters mellowing to the colour of old gold and apricots, the only sound in the room the tiny, wet sucking noises made by Girolamo as he fed. Then Donna Lucrezia sighed, and reached out to touch the baby's downy red curls with the tips of her fingers.

"There is something you must do for me," she said. "It will be dangerous, but you are better placed than anyone else. You must go to Rome."

"Rome? Me?"

"You must go to my brother in my stead, Violante." She gave a brief, bitter laugh. "You know, just before we came up here from Ferrara, dear Messer Pietro fell sick of a fever. Alfonso was away, and I went to see him. I sat on the edge of his bed and administered a decoction of willowbark to bring down his temperature. I mopped his chin and stroked his hair, and he held my hand and told me he would die of love for me if nothing else. Simple things, though risky."

"Yes, madonna, very." Yet I had already been so shocked by her telling me I must go to Rome I could not really feel the impact of her candour about her affair with Bembo.

"And now the world has turned, and it is safer for me to minister to my lover than to my own sweet brother. I cannot endanger my position here even further by going to him. If…when he gets well he will need friends like the Este. So you must go in my stead. He has an affection for you…"

"And for many women, madonna."

"I cannot think of another he has watched save his sister from a fit, though. That is an experience which is apt to give him confidence in you as a healer, which matters more now than…well…other things. And Violante…"

"Yes, madonna?"

"You must not return."

"I swear to you you will not see me in Ferrara until Cesare is well again. Madonna, I am honoured by your faith in me…"

"I mean, Violante, that you must not return, not even when my brother is restored. It will not help my position if I am thought to be harbouring my brother's bastard."

"Oh…yes…I see."

"Go to your family. He will be safe there."

"No one will think to look for the Duke of Romagna's son in the household of a Jew, you mean."

"Before you let your sharp tongue run away with you, girl, consider that you would not be the mother of the Duke of Romagna's son if it were not for the favour I have shown you. Must everything we Borgias say have a double meaning? Might it not simply be that, with my own family bereft and scattered, I appreciate the value of families?"

"I am sorry, madonna."

"You must leave at first light, and there are arrangements to be made. Send Sancho to me. I will have him prepare you a safe conduct for your journey. Choose a good horse, and I can spare you one of my personal men at arms. Oh, and one other thing…"

"Yes, madonna?"

"Try to send me word of Giovanni."

"Surely his mother's family will have taken him, madonna."

"He is a Borgia. Who but we will want him now?"

"I still want Girolamo."

"You are different."

"I am merely a mother, like Donna Giulia. She would not let her child come to any harm."

"Yes, well. I hope he is with Cesare." For some reason the image came into my mind of Giovanni's plump fist curled around Cesare's fingers as he handed the little boy into my custody on the day of our departure from Rome.

"Then I hope so too, madonna."

"I will not see you again before you leave, Violante. I wish you godspeed."

"And I pray all will be well with you."

"I had better see Angela now."

"Yes, madonna."

Only as I closed the door behind me and stood for a moment, looking down into the courtyard, a patch of sun-yellowed stone, the corner of a water trough framed by bourgainvillea leaves, did I think of the pope. And how a certain flatness in the light, as though the world I knew were suddenly just a picture of itself, marked his leaving of it.

# CHAPTER 3

## ALPE DI SAN BENEDETTO, AUGUST 1503

*My life has taken on the quality of a dream, but I do not know which is real, this, or the other, where you still live.*

*He is wearing fine, soft gloves with lace cuffs, and his face is pale, so pale, hollowed out like a skull, though not a skull. His eyes shine with quicksilver tears, which makes me realise it is not him I am looking at but his reflection in a glass mirror. I reach out to touch him and my fingers pass through the mirror as if through water. The image ripples, breaks, dissolves, and turns the water in the mirror the same whey-blue as his skin. I cup my hands and he drinks from them, lapping up the milky liquid like a cat, his tongue tickling my palm…*

Don't bother with this one. Look at her hand. You'd get a dose more than you bargained for."

It was true, however much I had tried to tell myself otherwise. The rash had appeared on my palms just after we left Medelana, and nothing could account for it other than a recurrence of the French pox. I lay still, listening to the men's retreating footsteps, their boots scuffing the brittle rock and splashing in puddles. Two pairs, it sounded like. I suppose that was what saved me, though saving myself was the last thing on my mind as I lay there, feeling the cold seep of water through my clothes and blanket. An outcrop of rock had provided shelter the previous evening, but the wind must have changed during the night, blowing the rain straight on to the ledge where we had pitched our camp.

I wanted to die. My bones ached and my teeth chattered with fever. I could not return to Ferrara, yet how could I present myself to Cesare sick and disfigured with the pox? How was that going to help me convince him Girolamo was his responsibility? Yet convince him I must, if Angela's antics with dead chickens had failed to cure me. I thought of Sigismondo prosecuting his war against the rat king, and of the old whore who used to beg for alms from mourners carrying their dead out of the Porta di Guidizio. She had protected what was left of her nose with a battered leather sheath, prompting a great many jokes about what she might have done better to sheath in the first place. My body had betrayed me; it was no longer subject to my will but to the random fortunes of disease.

"Take the horses. They look as though they'll fetch a decent price," said the other man, the one who had not turned my palm to the light of his torch before deeming me unfit even for rape. His voice grated like a squeaking cart wheel. Where was Beppo? I wondered. He would stop them taking the horses. I ought to rouse myself, but I was so stiff and tired and the weight of the wet blanket was pinning me down, pressing me into the mud, the dark, the grave-cold. I did not care about the horses.

"She might have some money on her."

"Well I'm not going to search her. I'm not going to touch her."

"Let's kill her, then."

"No point. She's seen nothing. She looks half dead anyway. Too cheap a price to sell our souls to the devil for." They laughed and their footsteps squelched away.

A thin wailing sliced through me like a hot wire. I wanted to stop my ears but I could not move my hands. My hands were bound by the wire, bound around Girolamo's tiny, warm body. Like Talia in the old tale, I was roused from my stupor by the needs of my child. Shrugging off the blanket, I sat up and looked around, my sore breasts throbbing as the baby's cries brought in my morning's milk.

"Wait a minute," I told him. Something was wrong. Everything was wrong. A few early birds were singing, attempting to conjure a dawn from the lowering, rain-filled sky. The swollen stream roared and rattled its way through the gorge where we had sheltered last night and out down the mountainside. But it was quiet, too quiet. No hooves crunched the rock-strewn pasture, no harness jingled, no fire crackled. I could not hear Beppo singing. I would not have thought I could miss so tuneless a noise so much, but I had grown used to it. Every morning of our journey I had woken to Beppo's singing and the smell of something roasting over a fire. Girolamo's crying grew louder and more insistent, as though he too missed Beppo's songs and was trying to fill the space left by their absence.

"Beppo!" No reply but the echo of my voice bouncing back at me off the walls of the gorge. I called again, but I knew in my bones he was not going to reply. Panic swelled in me like a djinn in a lantern, but I struggled to contain it. I had to feed Girolamo. I bit back the urge to scream and burst into tears, and crept to the back of the ledge where the overhang still afforded a little protection from the rain. I could scarcely remember when it had not been raining, when there had been August sunshine to fill my bones with hope and blind my eyes to the bleak truth of my situation.

It took me a little time to settle Girolamo. Covered by layers of permanently damp clothing, the cracks in my nipples had no chance to heal, which made feeding an ordeal for both of us, but there was a toughness about my son, a certain set of his tiny, pointed chin and an unblinking steadiness in his gaze that made me certain he was meant to live, whatever might happen to me. I wonder sometimes if my own mother saw the same quality in me, on the beach at Nettuno. Once he stopped bobbing his head about and struggling against his swaddling, his rhythmic sucking calmed me, and I began to try to take stock of my situation.

We had been travelling alone, keeping away from the main roads. Beppo said it was wisest. To begin with, I had protested. I had money sewn into my clothing and Donna Lucrezia's letter of recommendation to the governors of her brother's cities and the castellans of their forts. Exactly, said Beppo, who had been soldiering in the Romagna when Cesare was still learning Greek declensions and fighting with a wooden sword. Its cities had changed hands so often the citizens had mistrust of their rulers running in their blood. He did not think either madonna's money or her recommendation would count for much with them. He had been proven right at Imola, where the gatekeeper would not even summon the governor without Cesare's personal countersigns. At Forli, we found a group of flagellants outside the gates, chanting anti-papal slogans and lashing themselves with bundles of thorn twigs under the eye of a phalanx of archers with very twitchy fingers. Beppo thought it wiser to move on than to reveal ourselves in earshot of either the flagellants or the archers.

So we took to the mountains, the bony spine of land dividing Cesare's duchy from the Florentine Republic.

"They'll shoot before asking questions up there," said Beppo, "but we don't want to answer questions, do we? And I'm a good shot myself."

Where was he? I rushed Girolamo through his feed, did what I could to clean and change him, and scrambled down towards the track carved into the gorge beside the stream which Beppo said would lead us to Arezzo. Beppo had a cousin in Arezzo. I resumed calling his name. I told myself he had gone hunting for our breakfast, or had chased the thieves and was even now making his way back up the gorge with our horses, or had simply taken himself off behind a rock somewhere to move his bowels. This thought set my belly griping with one of its periodic bouts of flux; without time to conceal myself, I squatted over the stream to relieve myself, my groans bouncing back at me off the walls of the gorge as though the mountains themselves were sick.

We had been riding down the gorge, following the flow of the stream, before stopping the previous night, so this was the direction in which I continued. I knew Arezzo was somewhere to the south, but as long as the sun remained hidden, I had no means of navigation other than to trust that Beppo had known where he was going. As the morning wore on, my empty stomach yearned for his reappearance, though my head kept telling me I was on my own now, and listing in a remorseless litany everything I had lost to the thieves. All my dry clothes, clean clouts, and swaddling for Girolamo had been packed in my horse's saddlebags. My good shoes, I remembered as I stubbed my toe against a rock, had been among the things packed on Beppo's horse. I had no tinderbox to strike a fire, nor any means of getting meat to roast over it if Beppo were gone. All I had were the gold coins madonna had given me, sewn into my corset, and her letter of recommendation wrapped in an oil cloth and tied into my underskirt.

My situation was so hopeless there seemed to be nothing to do but laugh. So I laughed, and some idiot locked inside the mountains laughed back, and perhaps there were hyenas laughing, and jackdaws, and all manner of the Creator's holy fools, laughing fit to spill their empty guts at the fall of Duke Valentino, his Jewish whore, and their little orange-headed bastard. I laughed so hard I lost my footing and slipped a way down loose scree, the small stones chuckling under the weight of my body. Something complicated broke my fall, both hard and yielding, and oddly shaped.

A body. I stopped laughing and wiped the tears from my eyes with the grubby corner of my shawl. Beppo's body. They must have caught him unawares, for there were no signs of struggle, no cuts or bruises or torn clothes, just a clean, almost bloodless wound through the left side of his chest. Wedging Girolamo against a rock, I scavenged the body like a practised grave robber, all the time watching myself, interrogating myself. Had I learned this ruthless practicality so quickly out of necessity, or had it always been there, in my Jewish blood, passed down from Moses, whose compromise with the enemy had marked him out as just the kind of man the Lord of Hosts needed to lick His people into shape?

Not that there was much to find. The thieves had taken Beppo's sword and bow, his leather corselet, boots, and gloves. They had, however, overlooked his meat knife, perhaps because of the way he had fallen, concealing it from view, or perhaps because it possessed only domestic virtues, its blade carved from bone and ineffective against most flesh unless it were well cooked. I took it anyway, and his padded doublet which remained serviceable thanks to the neatness of the fatal wound. I could not bury him here, where the mountains' bones were only thinly covered with earth, so I piled a cairn of stones over him to keep off the buzzards and said some lines from the songs of David.

*Some trust in chariots, and some in horses; but we will remember the name of Yhwh Elohim.*

*They are brought down and fallen; but we are risen, and stand upright.*

I did not know the Christian prayers for the dead, and, being a woman, I could not say *kaddish* and besides, the words seemed somehow fitting for both of us.

❦

My instinct was to travel down from the mountains and try to regain the main thoroughfares. I could not hunt or easily build fires. I would have to risk the company of other travellers and spend some of Donna Lucrezia's money on food and shelter if I were to survive. If my luck held, my sickness would keep others at bay as it had done Beppo's murderers. Almost as though giving approval to my plan, the sun came out as I walked, at first casting a weak, primrose light and laying dusty shadows across my path, then growing in strength until its warmth on my back made me feel like singing and I tried to remember the words to Beppo's marching songs as I tossed my baby in my arms and made him laugh.

"We sacrificed Beppo to the sun and the sun is happy," I shouted, then was suddenly, terrifyingly certain I was no longer alone. No matter. Look at me, listen to me. A mad woman with the pox. No one would come near me.

"I don't know who Beppo was, but I'm mighty grateful for his influence with the sun." A voice both gruff and light in its pitch, a boy trying to sound like a man. An accent I did not recognise, guttural, full of tiny stones. "Are you alone?"

"Except for my child."

"And Beppo was...your husband?" He hesitated, fearful, perhaps, of a woman who had apparently sacrificed her husband to the sun. I shook my head. A relieved smile spread across his beardless face. "Strange times," he said.

"Strange indeed."

We passed through a deserted hamlet, its silence imposing itself on us. A thin dog fixed us with a hopeful gaze and we both looked away.

"How do dogs do that?" asked the youth. He wore a sword too long for him, and a corselet of overlapping leather plates which made him look like a skinny tortoise. A deserter, perhaps? But from whom, from what conflict? What was going on in the world down there? I lengthened my stride. The youth paused to peer into the village bakehouse, but the oven was cold, empty as my belly.

"Come on," I said, "there's nothing to be had here. We should try to find an inn before nightfall."

"You have money? Or something to trade?" He sounded curiously disapproving for a soldier, but I had no chance to think about this before his gaze slipped from my face to a point somewhere behind me and a new sound reached my ears. A rhythmic rattle and squeak. Cartwheels, in need of greasing. My companion's hand went to the hilt of his sword, but then he cracked a broad grin, gave a shout of laughter, and ran past me, arms outstretched towards the approaching cart.

"Felice?" The man pushing the cart, which was more of a barrow, really, sounded as though he was habitually suspicious of good fortune.

"Of course it's Felice," confirmed the old man in the barrow, his head supported by a pile of folded sacks, his wasted legs hanging like broken branches over the front lip of his conveyance, "for all she's chopped off her hair and put on breeches."

I thought of Ferrante and Vittorio. I wondered if we were anywhere near Imola, and realised that, even if we were, I was not. I cast about and could not even find a shade of myself, an echo of the smooth-skinned, untrodden virgin who had become lost in the castle and had discovered a truth much pricklier than merely the way to the kitchens. As the two men and the youth who was apparently a girl greeted one another, I stayed apart, struggling with a second, older set of images, assailed by the memory of men and boys running and jostling, slipping and sweating, of eyeglasses trampled in mud and long, beautiful legs sheathed in silken hose. Fiammetta, Cesare's boy-woman, receptacle for the love of a misfit.

All this meant something, it had to. Such motifs do not repeat themselves accidentally in life any more than they do in art. But what? Girolamo began to cry and nuzzle at my breast. Felice and the two men looked at me. The outline of Felice's figure was so clear to me now I wondered I had not noticed before the way the overlapping plates of her corselet lay not quite flat over her bosom.

"We might as well stay here the night," said the younger man. "The buildings will give some shelter. Felice, help me with grandpapa then you can take the cart and collect firewood."

"What can I do?" I asked, wanting to banish my memories, to feel less apart. As Felice and the man I assumed must be her father lifted the old cripple from the cart and propped him against a crumbled dry stone wall, I felt I no longer belonged even to myself.

"Feed your child, or we'll none of us be able to hear ourselves think," he replied, his tone full of warmth and normality. I was so grateful, so desperately grateful, to realise he looked at me and saw no more than a young mother with a hungry child, that my legs almost gave way beneath me and I sat down so abruptly beside the crippled grandfather, I felt the bones in my spine all jolt against each other.

I travelled with my new companions for several days. I learned that Felice had run away with a Swiss pikeman a year before, and had carried on soldiering in his place when he had been killed in the service of a Tyrolean count by an exploding gun barrel. As his death had been an accident, the count had provided no pension, leaving Felice with little other option.

"You could have come home," her father said.

Felice shrugged. "You say that now."

"Things have changed." He seemed to direct his words more at me than Felice, but I must have been imagining it. I had told none of them anything about myself, not even that Rome was my destination, though I knew theirs was Citta di Castello, from where I hoped to travel on by river.

Just outside Sansepolcro we hitched a ride on a half empty grain wagon. The weather, grumbled the woman driving it, hot as hell and then the rain, not to mention the fact that, since the Holy Father's death, all the men were running about brandishing swords at one another instead of bringing in what harvest there was. She wished the duke a speedy recovery; he might sup with the devil, but at least he made sure the granaries were filled and the *campesini* got a fair price for their wares.

"A fair man, the duke," commented Felice's father.

"How can you say that after what he did to us?"

"Hold your tongue, girl."

"So much for things having changed." Felice sighed, folded her arms, and lapsed into a sulky silence. My curiosity burned.

"If I bear the duke no malice, why should you?" demanded Felice's grandfather.

"Let us speak no more of him," said her father, exasperated.

"Very wise," agreed our driver, nodding at me where I sat beside her on the cross bench, "for here's a girl with no wedding band and an orange haired child."

I pulled my shawl closer around Girolamo as my cheeks flared, making the rash itch. I felt the eyes of my travelling companions fixed upon me, the warm afternoon air suddenly thick with their unspoken questions.

"Let's ask her, then," said Felice. "If that's the duke's bastard, let's see what she thinks."

"Felice…"

But she was not to be stopped. "I'll tell you a story. Once upon a time, when the duke was besieging Imola, and the town was half flattened by his guns and we couldn't retrieve the bodies from the streets because he went on firing at us all night as well as all day, a respectable man, a carpenter by trade, went up to the *rocca* with a delegation of other respectable men to plead with Donna Caterina to surrender before there was no town left. Donna Caterina threatened them with an arquebus and sent them packing.

"So, after night fell a second time, the carpenter crept out of the city and presented himself at the duke's camp. The duke's men would have cut him to pieces there and then, but the duke was curious to hear what he had to say. The carpenter had worked on the fortifications of the *rocca*, he explained, and he knew a weak corner where they might be breached. He would give the duke this information in exchange for his word that his men would neither loot the town nor rape its women, and the duke would make good the damage his guns had done out of his own pocket. The duke gave his word and the carpenter made him a little drawing. Sure enough, the *rocca* fell not long afterwards.

"The duke was as good as his word. On the whole, his men behaved themselves and those who did not were hanged in the town square. The town was rebuilt at little cost to its citizens. Then one day, the duke sent for the carpenter, who went gladly, believing the duke would offer him some reward. The duke, however, explained to him that he could not be seen to condone treachery and must therefore, with great regret, punish the carpenter. He did not have him executed, as that would have seemed unjust to him. Instead, he had him tied to tail of an unbroken colt and watched while the colt galloped six times around the town square, dragging the carpenter behind him. After that, even though the duke's own physician attended him, the carpenter's body was too broken to heal and he was condemned to be a cripple for the rest of his days.

"How do you like that?"

"I…I could not say." I had tears in my eyes, but not for the carpenter. It was rather that Felice's story had for a moment made Cesare so vivid to me, so immediate I could not believe he might actually be dead and wept with relief.

"Leave her be," said the old man gently. "I did what I had to and so did the duke. We understood one another. I would not have it different."

"Well I would have a republic, like they do in the Swiss cantons. There are no wars in Switzerland."

"Aye, and they are a colourless lot who make cheese that tastes like tallow."

Everybody laughed and the tension relaxed, but at the gate to Sansepolcro, while they were arguing with the tax collector about how much was due on the grain, I left them one of Donna Lucrezia's gold pieces and slipped away. They had been good to me and I did not want to put them in danger. I have thought of them often since, and wondered if the scars left on them by Cesare healed any better than mine did.

❧

I bought myself passage to Rome on a barge carrying tufa and Carrara marble. The river traffic passing through Sansepolcro was brisk, and I could have found myself a quicker boat, but the bargee was travelling with his wife and children, which made me feel more secure. And the marble blocks, showing gashes of glittering white through their waxed linen wrappings, reassured me. Rome was still building. The world had not come to an end. Who knew, perhaps some of the stone was destined for Cesare's own palace. Perhaps he was even now poring over plans with his architects or chivvying his workmen, because he would have to move out of the Vatican once a new pope was elected. He would have, finally, to come to a decision about the siting of his mews and whether or not to build a loggia on the roof. The thought made me smile, and the bargee's wife smiled too. She worried about me, she said, a young woman so solemn and sickly looking, and with a child to raise.

Perhaps it was the quiet way she cherished me, as if I were just another of her flock of grubby children, or being able to spread my clothes over the great stone blocks to dry, or simply the chance to rest, to sit with my back to the warm, rough-textured tufa and my face to the sun, but by the time we passed under the city walls of Rome, nothing remained of my illness but a slight dryness of the skin of my hands and face. I felt strong and lean from my days of riding and walking in the mountains, well rested and calm. If he were dead, I could cope, but he was not dead. If he were dead, I would not feel this lightheartedness, this bubble of happiness swelling up in me like a song. Soon I would see him, perhaps as soon as today. We would tie up at the Campo Marzio dock, and it was only a short walk from there through the Borgo to the Vatican. I determined to pass by San Clemente, in case he was already there.

Although we were all compelled to remain aboard the barge for some time after mooring, what transpired gave me hope, and hope made me patient. Almost before we had tied up, armed men approached us, one staying ashore to hold the barge horse's head, two more boarding the vessel. They were not the regular tax collectors, so the bargee, with his wife at his elbow, challenged them. The shorter of the two drew a dagger and held the point to the bargee's chin.

"We're Borgia's men," he said. He had a thick Spanish accent. "He's not done yet." His words fell on my ears with the rhythm of a dance.

"And I owe duty to the city, not Borgia," growled the bargee. His horse tossed its head, almost swinging the man holding it off his feet.

"We just want to make sure you're only carrying what's on your manifest," said the taller boarder with a cold, conciliatory smile. "Let's say we want to make sure the city gets its dues on everything you've brought in."

The bargee cast an unhappy glance in my direction. His wife dug him in the ribs.

"Family," he mumbled, which had a range of possible meanings in the circumstances.

The taller one laughed. "Mine is in Naples and I make sure they stay there. Have a look," he ordered the Spaniard who swaggered the length of the deck lifting the covers from the stone with the point of his dagger and grinning a pirate's grin at the bargee's children; one of his upper front teeth had been replaced with a plug of gold.

"*Nada*," said the Spaniard, sounding disappointed.

"Thank you," said the other to the bargee, and handed him back his manifest with a slight bow. "We can't be too careful. There's a French army to the north of us and a Spanish one to the south, and Don Cesare would rather parley with their generals than their spies."

I pressed my lips together and willed myself to swallow the questions bubbling up in me. Was Cesare well again, or bluffing? Where was he? Who was with him? Did he hold the city, or just the Borgo?

"Any news of a new pope?" asked the bargee conversationally. The taller man turned, one foot on the gunwale of the barge.

"Not yet. Their eminences are all shut up in Sopra Minerva like hens in a coop."

"Sopra Minerva? What's wrong with Saint Peter's?"

"You'd have to ask Don Cesare that."

As soon as the guards had gone, I left the barge with hugs and tears and prayers for good luck from the bargee's wife, and set out for the Vatican through the old, winding streets that netted the Campo Marzio. This was normally the most crowded quarter of the city, where people had lived, said the historians, since before the days of Aeneas. And some of the houses looked at least that old, retorted the wags. But today it was virtually empty, the narrow, rutted walks and slipshod tiled roofs left to the cats and dogs and pigeons. The lower reaches of the walls still carried tidelines of dried salt from recent flooding. Split rice sacks and broken down log piles littered back yards and passages between buildings. When the Tiber flooded, the people here usually sought shelter in the Castel Sant'Angelo, whose raised aspect and curtain walls afforded protection from the river.

But they usually came out again as soon as the water began to fall. Where were they now? What had happened here? I shivered and Girolamo, catching my mood, started to grizzle. I sat down to feed him leaning against the parapet of a well, where I washed my face and feet, though did not drink for fear the water had been spoiled by the flood. I knew San Clemente was just around the next corner, bordering one side of the *piazzale* which gave the palace its name.

All the street windows were shuttered, and sunk in late afternoon shadow, giving my lover's home an aspect both hostile and forlorn. I felt instantly he could not be there, though a gaggle of men milled about in front of the barred street door and four bronze mortars were drawn up in the *piazzale*, mouths gaping at the row of arcaded shops opposite. As I paused, hesitating whether to speak to the guards or simply make my way to the Vatican, one of them detached himself from the group. Though he walked in my direction, I was clearly not the object of his attention for he did not see me until I thought I would have to step out of the way to let him pass. He was a tall man, with curling, red-tinged hair and a face dominated by a narrow, aquiline nose. His neat beard disguised a somewhat weak chin. He was extravagantly dressed, in padded hose, slashed sleeves, and gloves with jewelled cuffs. When he caught sight of me, his large, protuberant eyes widened and his already pale complexion blanched as though he had seen a ghost.

"Lucrezia?"

"My name is…" and while I was debating which of my names to call myself, it dawned on me who he was. "Don Jofre," I said.

He looked suspicious. "Who are you?" His right hand hovered over the hilt of his sword.

"I am a friend of your brother, Don Cesare."

His eyes flicked over me, taking in my worn dress over which I still wore Beppo's doublet, though more as a keepsake than because I needed it now the sun had reappeared, my undressed hair, Girolamo swaddled in my dirty shawl. "Another one," he said wearily. "I wonder he had the energy left to govern his state he spent so much on getting bastards to populate it. Don't waste my time, woman."

He would have walked on but I stepped into his path. "I am here at the behest of the Duchess of Ferrara. Wait. Here." I thrust my son into his arms and he waited, looking amazed and awkward with the baby balanced across his forearms, while I rummaged among my petticoats for madonna's letter of recommendation. "You know her seal?" I asked as I took back Girolamo and handed it to him. He nodded, broke the seal, and read the letter.

"So what happened to you?" he asked when he had finished.

"It's a long story. Where is Cesare?"

"Still in his apartments in the Vatican. Violante…I may call you that?" He touched my arm with his gloved fingertips. "He is still terribly ill. I am far from sure he will live."

"Take me to him. I am a good nurse. He knows that. He will believe I can make him well."

"Why?"

I told Don Jofre about Donna Lucrezia's fever the previous summer, and what Ser Torella had said about me. He thought for a moment, then said, "My sister's letter says you have family in Rome."

"Yes."

"Then go to them for tonight. I will tell Cesare you are here and send for you in the morning. He must not suffer anything unexpected. He is not strong enough. I will let you have one of my men to escort you, then I will know where you are to be found."

Though tomorrow seemed impossibly far off, though nothing I had ever heard of Don Jofre led me to think him trustworthy, what he said made sense. His concern for his brother seemed genuine, even if it was prompted by a fear for his own skin should Cesare die. And he was not dead. Everything was still possible. I would see him tomorrow. He would get well. He would ensure the election of a friendly face to Saint Peter's chair and we would all awake from the nightmare.

Don Jofre found me a mule and made a mounting step for me with his own hands. As his man at arms took the reins and led me away, he called after me, "My sister is a cunning little vixen, you know. Never underestimate her." I scarcely heard him. My mind was filled with Cesare and tomorrow.

"Where do you want to go?" asked my escort as we turned into Saint Peter's Square. I glanced at Santa Maria in Portico, which looked shabby and neglected, the window shutters sun-warped, the street door bereft of the smart footmen who had always stood there, overseeing our comings and goings with deep impassivity. Then, as I shifted my gaze across the square to the Vatican, something gleamed in the corner of my eye, the flat, bluish glint of broken glass reflecting the summer afternoon sky, and instead of the palace walls, its barred windows and guards in Cesare's quartered red and gold, I saw a wooden stand decked with banners and packed with courtiers in all their finery. In the midst of it all sat the old pope, and I swear I could hear him laughing and his laughter did not sound as though it came from beyond the grave.

A little to his right a girl in an emerald green camorra struggled against the grip of a handsome man whose fingers dug into the flesh of her thigh as he held her down, imprinting bruises there she would keep for weeks. Though I did not notice her until she escaped the man's clutches and fled, screaming, in the direction of the basilica. Even then I could not see her clearly. I had lost my magnifying spectacles, you see; they had fallen off as I ran and been trampled into the mud by my fellow competitors. I could not see she was my sister; I could not see the bruises left on her by Valentino.

"Mistress?" Don Jofre's man was saying. "Where to?"

"Leave me. I have the mule; I can manage."

"Don Jofre will want the mule back," said the man doubtfully.

"I will send it. Please, let me go; I will be quite safe, and you will know I have arrived at my destination by the return of the mule. Tell Don Jofre I dismissed you. I'm sure he has too much on his plate to bother being angry with you about me." He seemed to see the reason in this and turned back towards San Clemente. From the set of his shoulders, I would say he was as relieved to be rid of me as I of him.

To this day I cannot say for certain what happened to me that afternoon in Saint Peter's Square. Looking back, I am inclined to think it was simply the trick of a mind exhausted by travel and ill health. At the time, however, that memory of recognising Eli racing with the other Jews, scrabbling in the mud for his broken lenses, that strange sense of being him rather than myself, seemed to be telling me to go home, just as I was, with my son and a mule. Tonight I would sit at my father's table. I would wash and change, and light the candles as if I had never been away. My family would embrace me and call me Esther, and I would lie in my old bed and I would soothe my child to sleep with stories of all my names.

Discarding the planchette with which Don Jofre had provided me, I got astride the mule and kicked it into a smart trot. There is a clock inside me which rings a bell in my brain about an hour before sunset. It is a Jewish thing, a need to be indoors before the rising of the evening star which marks the beginning of Shabbat. Some men stopped me on the Sant'Angelo bridge, but let me pass after I showed them Donna Lucrezia's seal, and from then on my short journey was uneventful. I passed a few people on the road, but they hurried by, closed in on themselves, shoulders hunched and eyes fixed on the little patch of ground just in front of their feet.

Ambassadors and *avvisi* write in apocalyptic terms about society breaking apart whenever there are riots about the price of bread or more plague deaths than there were last year or the Turk begins to rattle his sabre in our ear. But this, I thought, as the blue shadows lengthened across the Tiber and my mule's hooves struck small, sharp echoes from the blind walls of shops and houses, was how it truly showed itself, in this fragmentation, each man withdrawn into his own shell, looking no further than a foot's length into the future.

The Jewish quarter looked shabbier than I remembered it, the streets meaner, the dogs thinner. I became aware of people turning to stare at me, and could almost entertain the illusion that I was as fine as the red leather harness on my mule. As long as I kept looking ahead, as long as my chapped hands and broken nails were out of my line of vision, as long as I avoided thinking about the holes in my shoes and the frayed hem of my skirt. I had to detour around a collapsed building which had completely blocked Via di Sant'Ambrogio, so by the time I dismounted and knocked on the street door of my father's house it was almost dark and the evening star showed very bright in the alley of purple sky between the roofs.

The door looked unkempt. Some of the timbers were splintered, almost as if an axe had been taken to them, though halfheartedly. The *mezuzah* my mother and I had carried from Toledo was still fastened to the doorframe, but at a crazy angle and swinging slightly in the breeze which had arisen with the sunset. I reached up to straighten it, though I could not really see what I was doing. No lamps appeared to be lit in the courtyard. I knocked a second time and was rewarded with the whisper of soft shoes on the courtyard tiles and a shrieking of unoiled hinges which made the mule waggle its ears in distress as the wicket was opened from within.

"I'm sorry," said an old woman's voice, "I can't lift the bar; it's that bent. You'll have to come in by this door."

"Mariam!" She was more bent than I remembered her, and fatter, and the light of her torch found out the pleats and creases of flesh around her eyes and mouth without mercy. For the second time that day I was confronted by someone who looked as though she had seen a ghost. "Mariam, don't you know me? It's Esther." My voice sounded thin and wheedling, like that of a complaining child.

"You can't stay here," she said, darting a glance over her shoulder.

"What?"

Before she had a chance to explain herself I heard Eli's voice from across the courtyard. "Who is it, Mariam?" He sounded both fearful and resigned, as though he had plenty of evening visitors and none of them welcome. Where was my father? Mariam appeared at a loss for a reply. I stepped past her into our courtyard, clutching my sleeping baby before me like a shield.

"Good God," said Eli, then muttered a quick prayer to ask forgiveness of the Lord for calling Him by name. "I am astonished you have the nerve to come here."

"What do you mean? Where is Papa?" Mary's welcome at the inn at Bethlehem might have been warmer than this.

"As if you didn't know," thundered Eli, his ear locks quivering, his open mouth an angry gash among the black curls of his beard. Ear locks? When had he started to wear those? Papa always kept his beard and sideburns neatly trimmed.

"I don't know," I said. My voice shook. Eli's coldness, and then this sudden rage, had frightened me.

"Ser Eli, perhaps…" began Mariam.

"You are forbidden to speak. What are you doing outside the women's quarter anyway?"

Women's quarter? What was going on here?

"There was no one else to answer the door."

"It would have been better not to answer it."

With an exasperated sigh, Mariam stumped off towards the kitchens, though the set of her shoulders was anything but acquiescent.

"Eli, what is going on here? Call my father. He will not shout at me this way."

"Our father is dead, Esther. Will you pretend you did not know?"

The courtyard seemed to lurch beneath my feet like the deck of a ship. I staggered, or perhaps I only imagined I did, because no hand reached out to steady me. I tried to take a step towards Eli, but he held arm across his face as though to protect himself from me.

"I did not know," I whispered, bowing to kiss my baby's head, feeling my only comfort in the warmth of his skin beneath his bonnet. "When? How did it happen?"

"Look around you." Eli flung out his arm. I looked at my surroundings. The fountain, I now saw, was clogged with broken bricks from its supporting basin, which looked as though a giant, angry child had taken a stick to it. Many of the courtyard tiles were cracked or splintered. Tethering rings had been torn from the walls, bringing down clumps of stucco. The wisteria around the door to the vestibule, which had been my father's great pride, though still living, now lay on the ground, smashed trellis-work poking out from among clumps of foliage and gnarled branches. "This is your lover's work," said Eli, spitting out the word "lover" with utter contempt. "All Rome knows it, and all Rome knows why. And you have the gall to come here, pretending innocence, asking for our father. You disgust me." His gaze flicked over the baby in my arms, his eyes behind their lenses hard as pebbles. "That is his, I suppose. Oh, don't try to deny it. I saw you, you know, sitting with his hand on your knee. I do not need my eyeglasses for everything."

I sensed other eyes watching me from the house, flitting between half-closed shutters, gleaming in the arched shadows of the arcade. I felt small and shabby and foolish. What could I say? That I had my lover's child but not his confidence? I kept silent.

"Now get out. Go to him. Share his fate if you have a single loyal bone in your body. May the Judge of Men have pity on you for I cannot. I no longer have a sister." He turned his back on me and was swallowed up in the dusk gathering beneath the porch, the skirt of his dark robe catching on a twisted finger of wisteria as he went inside and the door banged shut behind him. At a loss what to do next, I simply stood where I was. Despite Don Jofre's warning, I supposed I must go to the Vatican. I had nowhere else. Donna Adriana might receive me, perhaps, but the palace of Santa Maria had appeared to be empty when I had passed it earlier in the day. Besides, Donna Adriana was married into the Orsini and had very likely decided it was wiser to throw in her lot with them than with her Borgia relatives now Alexander was dead and Cesare so desperately ill. I would have to go to Cesare, whatever the risk. He could not refuse Girolamo now. He needed a son. If he were to die, what use to him was an infant daughter in France? Night was falling fast. I must make haste.

"Miss Esther."

"Mariam?" I found myself whispering also, straining my eyes to see where Mariam was hidden.

"This way. Towards the kitchens."

As I approached the arch in the courtyard wall which led through to the kitchen block behind the house, a hand shot out and grabbed my arm. "Quickly," said Mariam. "Come to my room. No one will think to look for you there." I realised the truth of this with some shame; I had never been to Mariam's room, had never even considered how and where, in the warren of buildings behind the main house, she lived. I resolved to do better, when Cesare was well again, and everything returned to normal, and he set Girolamo and I up in our own house in Rome.

Mariam half dragged me, stumbling along dark, unfamiliar paths, under a lintel so low even I had to duck to avoid hitting my head. While Mariam busied herself lighting a lamp, I stood listening to the roar of my blood in my ears and the comfortable rustle of roosting chickens somewhere nearby. A taper flared, then warm light spilled from a lantern with waxed paper shutters, revealing a homely room. The beaten earth floor was covered with a bright rag rug. Sturdy, well-polished stools flanked the hearth and a chest crudely painted with a pastoral scene of shepherds and shepherdesses doubled as a table in the centre of the room.

"You can have my bed tonight," said Mariam, setting the lamp down on the chest. "You look dead on your feet."

"I have walked a lot of the way."

"From Ferrara?"

"My horse was stolen, then..."

"Shhh. Sit down." She took a stub of candle on an iron dish and lit it from the lamp. "I'm going to the kitchen for hot water and some food. If anyone comes near, you blow out the lantern and you hardly even breathe."

"I'll go. I don't want to get you into trouble. I have my mule. I can get to the Vatican in no time."

"And what do you suppose you would find there? You're going nowhere till you've had a bath, a supper, and a good night's sleep. Your brother should be ashamed of himself. Calls himself a righteous Jew and won't even open his house to his own sister when she needs him. Your parents would turn in their graves."

"Mariam, what has happened here?"

Understanding my need to know was greater even than my need for food and rest, she sat down opposite me, resting the candle on the floor beside her stool. "Last spring the pope levied new taxes on the Jews. It was supposed to pay for a new public well. As you know, the only one we have is the one in the Piazza Giudecca and that almost dried up last summer. But we soon discovered the money was going to pay for troops for your...for the Duke Valentino. So a lot of people refused to pay. Beatings of Jews increased. There were groups of young louts hanging around the synagogue on Saturdays, shouting, pushing us around. Nobody actually said they were the duke's men but everyone knew it. Your father negotiated a meeting with the pope to try and sort things out. I don't know what happened but he came back bulging with rage like an angry toad, and that night the duke ordered raids on the homes of all the leading Jewish families. They stole money and jewels, even our *menorahs*. When they came here, your father tried to reason with them, but one of them hit him with his pike handle. He died three days later." She reached across to pat my knee, to comfort me, though I felt no grief, not then, just a cold fury which seemed to turn my vital organs to ice, one by one, brittle and sharp.

"He never regained consciousness. He suffered very little, thanks be. The pope sent a message of condolence and promised Eli the duke would see his men suitably punished."

Oh, he is very good at suitable punishment, I thought. Mariam waited for me to say something, but what I had to say was not to her. With a sort of embarrassed clucking in the back of her throat, she rose, picked up her candle and went to the kitchens for food and hot water.

I submitted to her kindness, allowing her to strip me of my worn and travel-stained clothes and sponge warm water gently over my shoulders as I sat hunched before the fire in a small laundry copper. She tutted at my sore nipples and went off to rummage for some salve or other among her simples. While I dried myself, she unpicked the rest of Donna Lucrezia's gold from my bodice and piled the coins carefully on top of her chest before dumping all my old clothes on her fire, even Beppo's doublet, though its wool padding threatened to stifle the blaze. Then she gave me underclothes, and a gown to put on which I recognised.

"This is one of my old ones," I exclaimed. "It'll never fit me now."

But it did, it fitted me passably well, though it was a little short in the hem and tight in the bodice, and I realised how brief a time I had been away.

"Have you kept all my clothes?" I asked, as Mariam thrust a dish of artichokes fried with oil and garlic into my lap.

"You never know when things might come in handy. Now, eat up while I see to the baby."

The artichokes were one of Mariam's own specialities, but they tasted bitter and metallic, as though they had been left too long in the skillet, and the sliminess of the oil made me nauseous. My skin glowed from the bath but my blood still felt cold, my tears for my father frozen. I set the food aside and tried to take pleasure in watching my son luxuriate in the warm water, wriggling his stout legs and arms and squealing with glee as Mariam splashed his belly and tickled him with the corner of the wash cloth. She showed great confidence with him for a childless woman. For as long as I had known her, since I was handed into her care by Señora Abravanel at the end of our journey from Toledo, Mariam had been old, with no family but ours. Perhaps by now Eli and Josefa had children. I thought of asking her, then decided I didn't want to know. It didn't matter anyway. Mariam dried Girolamo then laid him on the rug and set about applying goose grease to his thighs and bottom to ease his sore skin.

"Not circumcised, then," she observed, with a slight pursing of her lips.

"Neither is his father," I said, and saw how she was about to say more, and how something in my expression stopped her. I wondered if she had ever been with a man, ever even seen a grown man naked, and felt suddenly far older than her.

"How little I know about you, Mariam."

She shrugged. "Nothing much to know," she said, beginning to wind Girolamo in clean bands.

"Leave him. He likes to play." I remembered him lying on the rug in

Taddeo's orchard while Angela and I ate strawberries and drank frascati. I had not thought of Angela once, I realised, since leaving Medelana. Guiltily, I tried to imagine how she must be feeling, now that she no longer had any prospect of marrying Giulio, but any emotion other than my anger at Cesare was beyond my grasp. I was filled with it, lying like a rich meal in my belly, the taste of it in my mouth, its colours in the shadows which wavered across Mariam's walls.

"I have thought too little of my family's honour for too long, Mariam."

"You were obedient to your father. What more can be expected of a girl? If you ask me…"

"My father wished me to serve Donna Lucrezia and make a good marriage." We both gazed at the baby, who smiled and gurgled and stretched his long fingers like the petals of a lily opening to the sun.

"He knows he's the centre of attention."

"Yes." Like father, like son. I scooped him up and held him close, wrapped in the clean shawl Mariam had found for me. He fixed me with that unblinking stare of his. Madonna used to say babies look like that because they are born blind, but even if that were so, Girolamo was not blind now. He was hungry for the world and all it had to tantalise and enchant his senses.

"Keep him for me, Mariam. Have him circumcised. Have him taught Torah. Bring him up a Jew. Keep the gold, that should cover much of the cost of him and I have no need of it." Now I knew what I wanted to say to her the words were falling over themselves to escape my mouth.

"You know I can't. You know Ser Eli would forbid it utterly. You can stay here tonight and be gone before dawn. That's the best I can do for you, for your mother's memory."

"Please, Mariam. It's me Eli's repudiated, not Girolamo. He's a baby. You can make anything of him. He doesn't have to be a Borgia. He can be a Sarfati, grow up with Josefa's children, go into business with my brothers. I named him for my father, you know."

"You think you can give your child away just like that?" Mariam did not raise her voice, but spoke to me in a furious hiss, like an angry goose. "You think your poor mother dragged you all the way from Toledo and died doing it just so you could go giving away babies as if they grew on trees? He it is who gives us children and only He can decide to take them away. You lie with the son of a pope and believe yourself greater than the Almighty?"

"I just want him to be safe." I sounded like a plaintive child myself.

"Safe? There is no safe in this world, but Esther..."

"Yes?"

"There is love. You follow love."

"And duty?"

"You follow love." Her eyes shone among the soft creases of her face and her liver-spotted hands plucked at her skirt. She made it sound so simple, yet what if love tore you two ways? Mariam, it seemed, had no more to say on the matter. She bossed me to bed, just as she had done when I was a child, tucking my son into the crook of my arm. I had only the vaguest memory of her climbing in beside me, the dip of the mattress beneath her weight. My sleep was profound and dreamless, and when Mariam woke me just before dawn, nothing was any clearer than it had been. I seemed to be caught in some kind of endless relay race, in which parents handed heartbreak on to their children.

While I fed Girolamo, Mariam packed a small satchel for me with the remains of last night's bread, a pot of the salve she had given me for my breasts and, most particularly, Donna Lucrezia's gold, counting out the coins with great deliberation. Then she went to the shelf where she kept her simples and some bunches of dried herbs and took down what looked like a book. A book? Mariam?

"I kept this for you too," she said. The leather binding was salt stained and battered, what might once have been red morocco turned rusty brown with age and neglect.

"What is it?"

"Your mother's recipe book. It was among your things when you came here. I don't expect you remember. There never seemed to be a good time to hand it over, but now you're a grown woman with a family of your own, you should have it."

The book felt both strange and familiar in my hands, the leather as warm to the touch as my lover's skin. When I unwound the thong from the toggle which held it closed, a few loose leaves drifted to the floor, carrying with them old smells of our kitchen in Toledo, of fried almonds and orange oil, cinnamon and roast lamb, precious vanilla, like a silk lining for the nostrils, scents as frail and desiccated as pressed flowers. Uncertain what Mariam expected of me, I bent to pick up the loose pages, to hide my face. *Lokum*, I read, *a sweet made from rosewater by the Moors of Al-Andalus. I do not think there is a Spanish name for it.* Lokum. In exile, Cesare would teach me to make lokum, and we would be happy. Mariam had said, follow love, and now love had shown me a signpost.

"Thank you, Mariam. You should know men may come for me from Don Jofre Borgia. If they do, be sure and tell them I am going to the Vatican and will return the mule to San Clemente." The mule. I had forgotten it until now. If it had been stabled, or left in the courtyard, Eli must know I was still here. Perhaps Don Jofre's men had already come for me and Eli had sent them away. No, of course not; it was barely light, no hint of day yet but a faint paling of Mariam's square of wax-papered window.

"I think you had better forget the mule, Esther. I'll let you out by the back gate. If anyone asks, just say you are going to the market in Campo de' Fiori. You have to go early to get the best vegetables." I hardly heard her, so loudly did my impatience to be gone rage in my head. My father was dead and my brothers cared nothing for me. Now, at last, I was truly Violante, the *conversa*, the girl with no family name but the one my son gave me. Borgia.

⋙⋘

A silvery mist clung to the river, from which the figures of other early risers, bargees, and beggars, bowed women with great covered baskets, emerged with the silence of wraiths. The mist seemed to dampen sound as well as sight. I had to step smartly down the river embankment to make way for a raucous hunting party, young men and women in bright velvets and plumed hats riding skittish horses, with falcons balanced on their wrists. I thought I recognised one of the young men, an Orsini cousin who had accompanied Donna Lucrezia to Ferrara, but he showed no sign of having noticed me. Below the embankment was a different world, where the paupers who slept under the bridges lay caught in the mud like Adam awaiting the Creator's hand. A row of men in manacles and leg irons, chained together at the neck so their heads looked like beads strung

304

together on an ogre's necklace, clanked aboard a sailing barge, bound for Ostia and the galleys.

Yet, as I climbed the steps in the westernmost pier of the Sant'Angelo bridge, a ragged rim of sunlight began to show above the roofs and towers to the east. Gulls mewed as they curved across the sky above the mist and the undersides of their wings caught the gold of the sun. I smiled at them, my heart caught in a sudden bliss of pale aquamarine, oyster pink, primrose yellow. I thought of the gulls wheeling past the high windows of Cesare's apartments in the Vatican, of his valet opening the shutters to get the best light to shave him by, and the new sun catching the red lights in his beard. You follow love. Love is the most constant of constant things.

A crowd had gathered in Saint Peter's Square. This would not have been unusual except for the early hour. The parties of pilgrims and other foreign visitors who came to look at the palace of the ruler of Christendom would appear later, after Mass and breakfast and the customary haggling with the city guides. All heads were turned towards the north side of the square, in the direction of the Porta del Popolo. As I joined the throng I was jostled and carried forward in a sudden lurch.

"What's going on?" I asked, not being tall enough to see over the heads of several men in front of me.

"The duke's leaving," said one over his shoulder. Leaving? How could he be? Don Jofre had promised I would see him this morning. Something must have happened, but what? Tying Girolamo more securely into my shawl so I had both arms free, I fought my way to the front of the crowd, ignoring those who jostled and swore at me as I trod on toes and elbowed ribs. As I dodged a big pikeman in Cesare's livery who was struggling to keep a passage clear for his lord's cortege, the mass of people behind me fell suddenly still and silent. For a second it was as though the whole world had stopped; I half expected the birds to drop out of the sky, a thousand tiny Icaruses falling for the one who had truly flown too close to the sun.

Then the bells of the basilica began to toll the morning Angelus, the pikeman drew himself to attention, and a group of mounted soldiers rode out of the palace gates, their pace slow, their mien solemn. They were followed by eight men bearing a litter closed with curtains of crimson damask, and behind it a riderless, high-stepping war horse decked out in black velvet and bearing Cesare's ducal coronet and other insignia on a cushion strapped to its back. I saw people cross themselves and heard a woman burst into tears somewhere behind me.

I had to know. Not knowing is the worst thing. What you know, you can deal with. Eventually. I ran across the empty space between the crowd and the litter. The distance seemed interminable; as I reached out my hand towards the gold-fringed curtains the blood hissed and pounded in my ears as though I had run all the way from Ferrara. So I did not hear the shouting, the thud of galloping hooves, the rasp of a sword drawn from its scabbard. Then suddenly my feet were running on air, an unimaginable jumble of ridges and points was digging into my left side, and my nostrils were filled with the smells of horse and leather.

"Back off, Don Jofre!" shouted a familiar voice.

"Michelotto?" He could not have heard me; I could scarcely catch my breath for speech.

The men carrying the litter halted in consternation, though they did not set it down. Michelotto lowered me gently to the ground as the crowd oohed and aahed as if they were watching a display of acrobatics.

"What the devil...? She was...she might have..." Don Jofre, breathless, red in the face, his sword still raised, reined his horse in nose to nose with Michelotto's and glared at him. He was a head taller than his brother's henchman, and of higher rank, yet there was no doubting who was in command of the situation.

"She meant no harm," said Michelotto and Don Jofre's gaze slid away. He sheathed his sword, fiddled with his reins, then turned his horse and rode back down the column to wherever he had come from. Michelotto smiled at me, displaying a jagged array of worn, brown teeth. "Is the child unharmed?"

Girolamo was bawling lustily enough to reassure me he had come to no harm. I nodded. "Thank you. Cesare...?" I jiggled Girolamo in my arms to soothe him, to be able to hear Michelotto's response.

Michelotto's pomegranate face looked grave. "You helped Donna Lucrezia. You will help him."

"Michelotto, I'm not...she would have got well anyway, I suppose."

"That is not what he believes. Let him see you." Michelotto leaned from his saddle and lifted one of the curtains. His actions seemed interminable, his movements as slow as the sun crossing the sky, so the moment when I could peer into the dark interior of the litter came as suddenly as the sun's disappearance below the horizon.

The smell hit me first, a sickening stew of vomit and faeces and stale sweat. And old dog. He had his blind hound with him as always. It was hard to believe anything human or animal could breathe in such an atmosphere. A hand reached out of the gloom and grabbed my shawl, so emaciated the skin had taken on the colour of the bones beneath and I thought it must be the hand of an unquiet ghost. Pulling me close, into that closed, blood dark space, that abject stench, he whispered, "Lucia. You have come to save me. Like you did before. All will be well now." Then he was overcome by a violent bout of retching and spitting.

I caught a glimmer of his face as he sank back against his pillows, and he was smiling. His smile terrified me. I could not bear the burden of his trust. Then I realised that burden was not mine to bear. "Who is Lucia?" I asked Michelotto as he escorted me to the back of the procession where, he said, he would find me a place in a carriage.

"Oh, just a name. He gets confused. Torella has bled him so much I doubt there's enough blood left in him to keep his mind sharp. You know Cesare and...women." He looked sheepish, which made me uncomfortable.

"Michelotto, why are you being so good to me all of a sudden?"

He nodded at Girolamo, now thoroughly absorbed by sunlight flashing off harness and weaponry. "His son, my son," he said, and I could have hugged him; if Michelotto did not doubt Girolamo's parentage, then surely neither did Cesare. "Here," he went on, drawing rein beside a closed carriage drawn by a matched six of very fine greys, "you climb up here."

As I opened the door a woman's voice asked, "What's happening? Why have we stopped?" It was a strong voice, almost as deep as a man's, and accustomed to answers.

"Don Cesar wishes this lady to join you, Monna Vannozza, if you please."

"Whether I please or not is clearly immaterial to my son as the lady is already getting into my carriage. Has his brush with death taught him no humility?"

"I must get us moving again, madama. Don Prospero Colonna will not wait for us forever. My respects, Monna Violante." He bowed and rode away, shouting commands as he went.

So I was to travel with my lover's mother, the redoubtable Vannozza dei Cattanei, the spirit of whose absence from the life of Santa Maria in Portico had always seemed to me stronger than her presence in it would have been. What mother simply hands over the care of her only daughter to another woman and takes no part in her upbringing? She was a frequent visitor to her sons' homes, and they to hers, but she had never set foot in Santa Maria while I lived there. Thinking these thoughts, it was not difficult for me to keep my eyes down and my expression suitably grave as I seated myself opposite Monna Vannozza.

"Hey, Violante!" A boy's treble, slightly wheezy.

"Giovanni!" Although I had never especially liked the child, I turned and embraced the Infant of Rome with such passion I almost knocked the breath out of him.

"I say," he said, pulling away from me and stroking the feather in his cap, "have you broken my feather? Where's Lucrezia?"

"Holy Jesus, Mary, and Joseph," said Monna Vannozza, "you are the Jewess. It's true what they say."

"I was born Jewish, but I have converted, madonna," I said. Her tone was not friendly, and I wondered if she was one of those who mistrusted *conversi*. She was said to be a pious woman.

"Lucrezia is her godmother, Nonna," explained Giovanni.

"Yes, dear," said Monna Vannozza, but continued to stare at me as if she dared not look away. The carriage lurched into motion, stopped again, then settled into a slow walk. The rumble of its wheels vibrated through the floor; the murmurs of the crowd came muffled through the dustblinds, which admitted a blurry, underwater light. "Look, Dorotea, look. Is she not the very spit of my illustrious daughter?"

"I have never had the honour of seeing the Duchess of Ferrara, madonna." It was a gentle voice, meek, with an uncertain, wavering quality as though speech were something its owner rarely experimented with.

Dorotea? Was this, then, the mysterious Dorotea Caracciolo, the woman Cesare was supposed to have kidnapped? I stole a look, and saw she was doing likewise, though not so much at me as at Girolamo, on whom her sad, dark eyes rested with a kind of saintly resignation. She shifted the weight of a bundle she carried in her lap from her left knee to her right. The bundle gave a small cry. A baby. She had a baby.

"Well, she is, you may take my word for it. It is uncanny."

I thought Monna Vannozza was labouring the point, but perhaps she could not really remember what her daughter looked like. Dorotea's child began to grizzle.

"Is she hungry?" demanded Monna Vannozza.

"I hope she's not going to start crying again," said Giovanni, puffing air down his nose and folding his arms in a parody of a vexed adult.

"She shouldn't be. She was fed just before we left."

"Here, give her to me." Monna Vannozza held out her gloved and heavily jewelled hands. Rings glistened on every finger, even her thumbs, and three or four bracelets hung from each wrist. She must have been wearing most of her portable wealth. Dorotea handed over the baby. She looked to be close in age to Girolamo.

"How old is she?" I asked, wishing I had not felt compelled to do so, hoping my enquiry sounded merely friendly.

Dorotea smiled. She had a beautiful mouth, the lips full and shapely and the same dark rose colour as a November olive. "She was born just after Easter." Not more than six weeks before Girolamo. I felt jealousy settle behind my ribs like an incubus and hoped it would not sour my milk.

"And your child?" enquired Monna Vannozza.

"In May, madonna." Monna Vannozza looked proud; Dorotea shifted her gaze from me to the top of her baby's head and I fancied I saw a slight blush tinge the saint-like pallor of her cheeks. I found myself wondering if he had kept her indoors these two years, like a toy in a cupboard, to be fetched out on his whim. Her skin looked too thin for wind and sunlight. At least that had not been my fate. I felt better. Then I felt like a peasant, and hid my hands among Girolamo's wrappings, and was glad my hair was loose so I could shake it close around my chapped cheeks.

"Is it a boy or a girl?"

"A boy, madama."

"Splendid."

"Good," said Giovanni, "he can be my friend. There's only Camilla and she's a girl. Where's your husband, Violante? Did he die of the fever too, like my papa?"

I felt the two women's eyes on me, felt them waiting to hear what I would say. So, if Dorotea did not know who Girolamo's father was, she had guessed. "He has been very sick, sweetheart, but he is getting well now."

"Good. You're nice. Cesare always said you were the most fun of Lucrezia's ladies. He said you could make jokes in Greek."

"Only one, and it wasn't mine; it was something I had to memorise from Aristophanes when I was a little girl. I expect Don Cesare saw through it very quickly." All the same, I stole a glance at Dorotea to see how she would take Giovanni's remark. She busied herself arranging her child in Monna Vannozza's lap and appeared not to have heard him. My gaze met not hers but Monna Vannozza's and, for a second, Cesare's eyes looked back at me, hooded and dark, full of watchful intelligence.

"Girls don't usually learn Greek, though, do they?" said Giovanni.

"Well, I just used to sit in with my brothers, really." I thought of the little tutor with the burning eyes and the tubercular bloom in his cheeks, and how it would have broken his heart to know all he had taught me came down to being able to flirt in a dead language.

"I bet Dorotea can't speak Greek." Giovanni made her lack sound unforgivable. I took his hand and squeezed it.

"Oh really," said Monna Vannozza. "You are too precocious, child, be silent."

"Sorry, Nonna." He looked contrite, but when he thought Monna Vannozza wasn't looking, he winked at me. I wondered how old he was now. Six, perhaps? Seven?

We seemed to reach the Porta del Popolo quickly, considering the crowds lining the narrow streets and the size of our party with its horse soldiers and foot soldiers, its baggage carts and mule trains and, no doubt, the special wheeled cages in which Cesare would have his leopards transported to hunts. There we stopped, presumably to meet Don Prospero who, Monna Vannozza explained, had been forbidden to enter the city because he was at the head of a troop of Spanish infantry. Don Prospero had placed his villa at Tivoli at Cesare's disposal to aid his recovery and that, Monna Vannozza told me, was where we were now headed.

As she was explaining this to me, the carriage door was wrenched open and Don Jofre's face appeared, the diamond in his cap winking fiercely in the mid-morning sun.

"You're to come with me," he said, jerking his chin in Dorotea's direction. A puzzled frown briefly drew her fine brows together, but she turned without question to take her daughter from Monna Vannozza. After two years with Cesare, I supposed she must have become used to mysterious commands and sudden changes of plan; though everything he did made perfect sense to Cesare, he tried to ensure it made no sense at all to anyone else.

"Not the child," said Don Jofre. His voice was harsher than his brother's, not so carefully tutored. Don Jofre, I decided, was a lazy man.

"But..?" Dorotea's pale, tapered fingers tensed around her child. Monna Vannozza's jewelled hands did likewise. In this Judgement of Solomon, there was no doubting which mother would win; the backing of superior force can transform any travesty into a just cause.

"The child will be well cared for by my illustrious mother and her wet nurse. Your husband wants you, woman, doting old fool that he is. But he most certainly does not want any reminders of your sojourn with the duke. Don't worry, I'm sure he'll get plenty more babies on you, if he still has ink in his quill." Don Jofre and his mother exchanged identical, spiteful smiles. Tears welled up in Dorotea's disbelieving eyes; she blinked, and they spilled over, running unchecked into the corners of her beautiful mouth. I clung so hard to Girolamo he began to squirm and whimper, and thanked my Creator for making me stubborn and manipulative and for giving Donna Lucrezia a good conscience. They could not do this to me. Girolamo had no wet nurse.

"Oh do get a move on, Dotti," snapped Don Jofre. "There are some men from Venice waiting for you, and they look none too comfortable around my brother." He gave a bark of laughter. "I'm afraid they believe he has risen from the dead."

"Jofre!" Monna Vannozza raised one hand from baby Camilla to cross herself. When Cesare was a baby, it was said, she had posed with him for a Madonna and Child, but had later forbidden the statue to be displayed because she felt it to be sacrilegious. Remembering this, I felt a stab of pity for her, trying to appease whatever malign fortune had put her child in the shadow of death.

Dorotea hesitated. Her hands fluttered, her gaze wandered as though she could not bear to look at her daughter. The baby, perhaps catching the mood from her mother or my fractious son, began to cry. With an animal howl, Dorotea threw herself out of the carriage door and against Don Jofre as though she planned to wrestle him to the ground but, though tall, she was not a strong woman. Don Jofre, caught off guard, staggered a little but quickly recovered himself and seized Dorotea by her wrists. She struggled against him until I thought her wrists would break then suddenly all the fight seemed to go out of her and she slumped, head hanging, knees buckled, held upright only by Don Jofre's grip on her.

"Good girl," he said, "that's better. Off we go." He turned her towards the head of our train and marched her away, the flat of one hand against the small of her back, her narrow feet dragging and stumbling in the dust.

I bent to kiss my son's head. Never, my heart told him, never will anybody do that to us.

❧

"I will speak to you in Latin," said Monna Vannozza. Giovanni, bored and whiny, had been despatched up top to sit with the coachman and Camilla's nurse had taken his place in the carriage. I wondered what Monna Vannozza had to say that must not be understood by the nurse and if, indeed, I would understand it for I had had little practice at spoken Latin.

"Let us understand one another. As you are the mother of my grandson, I will tolerate you. The child cannot be blamed for whatever duplicity you and my daughter concocted between you to get him, so you may stay and care for him until better arrangements can be made." She paused, her mouth a puckered line of distaste, her hands folded in her lap. Her jewellery flashed from time to time as chinks of sunlight found their way around the window blinds. I thought I must have misunderstood her, for I had no idea what she was talking about.

"Yes, domina."

"But you cannot expect to win my good opinion."

"No, domina."

"Yes, domina, no, domina. Pretending the innocent won't wash with me, young lady."

This unjustified onslaught was making me angry. "Domina, forgive me, but I have no idea what you are talking about. I hope I have served your illustrious daughter loyally and well, and I am…I love the duke very much and long for his recovery. I am here only because he asked for me, as Michelotto will bear witness." The mention of Michelotto seemed to give her pause; whatever his shortcomings, Michelotto's devotion to his master was not in doubt; if I had his support, I could not be all bad.

"Perhaps you do love him. Perhaps, after all, Lucrezia has deceived you too, but it is complicated and I'm afraid my Latin doesn't run to it." She turned to the nurse. "You, girl, shut your ears. If you repeat a word I say to Monna Violante here, be sure I will know of it and I will tell the Duke and he will have your tongue ripped from your head. Do I make myself clear?"

The girl nodded. I wondered if she too remembered the fate of the man who had spread word of the Savelli letter.

"Good." Monna Vannozza settled herself as if she were about to tell me a bedtime story. The tale she told me was a strange one, and like all good tales, it began with a castle. "All my children, that is, the children I bore Rodrigo, were born at his castle of Subiaco, up in the hills. His ambition made him discreet then, you see. The children would all be born in the country and only brought to Rome when he could pass them off as his nephews, or protégés. The house has been refurbished since, but then it was a proper castle with tall towers and crenellations. None of these ugly squat walls you see nowadays for resisting cannon fire.

"The afternoon I went into labour with Cesare was lovely, just what you expect of mid-September, the sun golden, the grapes ripening, the second cut of hay just finished. But in the night, the devil breathed on Subiaco. By morning there was frost on the ground. Even through my travail I could feel the cold, chilling my sweat and the midwife's hands when she examined me to see how I was progressing. When Cesare came, she cut the cord and blew in his face to make him cry and I knew, I just knew, the way a mother does, that with that cry he had breathed in the devil's frost. I could see it lying in his lungs, shrivelling them as it shrivelled the grapes on the vines. I fancied when he breathed I could hear the rattle of icicles in a wind. He fed poorly, his lips and fingernails were blue, his skin as clammy as the grave. The midwife herself baptised him because we did not think he would live. That is why he is called Cesare, you know, and not one of those Borgia names, Juan or Pedro Luis or Rodrigo. It was the midwife's brother's name.

"But we had underestimated his stubbornness. He lived. Juan was born and quickly outgrew his brother. Rodrigo treated them both the same, gave them swords and ponies and little suits of armour, but Cesare hadn't the strength for riding and learning the knightly skills, though you could see how he envied Juan with every bone in his body when Juan showed off on his pony or with his sword. But he had the kind of mind that couldn't help learning. He learned to read very young, and he watched and listened. He once told me that what he remembers most clearly from that time is lying on his daybed in the garden of my husband's house and being able to hear a cockroach crossing the terrace and the cat stalking it. He was a remarkable child.

"When Lucrezia was born, he was five. Rodrigo was so thrilled to have a daughter, he insisted on bringing both boys up to Subiaco to see her. I didn't want Cesare to come. I had a bad feeling about it. I was sure the journey would kill him. There I lay in bed, with the new baby in her crib beside me. Juan came bounding into the room and leapt on me, covering my face with kisses, prattling on and on about how he had learned to jump his pony now and Papa had promised him a kestrel for his birthday. So I scarcely noticed Rodrigo, who was carrying Cesare, put the boy down beside the crib and say, look, here is your new sister. But I remember what happened next with every breath I draw.

"Cesare peered down into the crib, and she looked straight back at him. She didn't blink, she just stared, and her eyes looked as old as eternity, and Cesare said, clear as a bell, not a wheeze or a cough to be heard, that changes everything. That changes everything. What sort of thing is that for a five-year-old child to say, even one like Cesare? It made my flesh crawl. Juan stopped his chatter and even Rodrigo looked slightly doubtful. That was when I knew. They had taken my baby away and put a changeling in her place.

"I tried to tell Rodrigo, but he just patted my hand and gave me a diamond ring. New mothers were prone to strange fancies, he said, and told the midwife to give me something to help shrink my womb and dry up my milk. Let's get you back to normal, he said, with an unmistakable glint in his eye. Time passed, and I learned to keep my suspicions to myself. Cesare grew stronger. By the time Lucrezia's first birthday came around he was taller than Juan and could outdo him at most sports, though Juan competed with him fiercely, not least over Lucrezia. Even then she could charm the birds out of the trees and her father and brothers spoiled her rotten. Rodrigo said her effect on Cesare had been a miracle, but I didn't trust her then, and I don't trust her now. She's a witch, and whatever purpose she had in saving Cesare's life is evil, I'm sure of it.

"I'm afraid of you, Violante. You have been sent here by witchcraft, and I will do everything I can to keep you away from my son."

I wondered if she truly believed what she had said. If she did not, she insulted my intelligence by thinking she could make me think it was true. I glanced at the nurse, but she remained absorbed in feeding Camilla, her head bowed over the baby whose tiny sucking sounds fell like small pebbles into the chasm of silence which had opened up between Monna Vannozza and myself as I thought about her tale.

True, Cesare and his sister were close, far closer, I thought, with a twist of regret in my gut, than my brothers and I. But if the relationship was not equal, it was Cesare who had the upper hand, not Donna Lucrezia. She had been the one reduced to impotent rage by his action at Urbino, who had waited in a terror of ignorance for the outcome of Senigallia, not the other way around. Did Monna Vannozza know her son so little? If there was magic involved in his survival, it was his own, not Donna Lucrezia's. She was no more a changeling than I was.

And then I remembered something else, a scene from far back in my childhood. Rachel Abravanel pulling my hair, dancing around me with a hank of my hair in her hand, my neck twisting and twisting till I was forced to turn myself, and Rachel chanting, "Esther's a *dybbuk*, Esther's a *dybbuk*." Round and round. Over and over. What exactly had Donna

Lucrezia seen in me that pleased her? I closed my eyes and hoped Monna Vannozza would think I had fallen asleep. Perhaps I did sleep. Perhaps the images of Cesare and his sister which converged and floated apart and converged again inside my eyelids were the manifestations of a dream.

# CHAPTER 4

*You always held it against me that I left Nepi without saying goodbye. Didn't you realise goodbye had already been said?*

I knew immediately we were not at Tivoli. I had been there often with Donna Lucrezia, who loved the town and used to say she would emulate the Emperor Hadrian and build herself a villa there one day. We climbed out of the carriage and stretched our stiff limbs in the courtyard of a fortress, not a house built for pleasure. We were surrounded by the same kind of squat, anti-artillery walls Monna Vannozza had complained of when describing Subiaco, and the living quarters appeared to be a series of round towers with only arrow slits for windows. The curtain walls might have been the latest thing in military science, but the buildings inside them must have been hundreds of years old, with moss sprouting from the mortar and old water stains streaking them like tears.

"Nepi," said Monna Vannozza, reaching her arms towards the deep, afternoon blue of the sky, her gems winking in the mellow sunlight. "That boy never does anything he says he's going to do. I doubt I will have any warm enough gowns."

Nepi. My heart seemed to somersault behind my ribs as I saw madonna once again at Belfiore, her bare, bloody feet crunching over shards of glass and pottery, shrieking as though Cesare would hear her all the way from Urbino, *You promised. At Nepi. You swore you wouldn't interfere.* I looked around, at the blind towers casting their deep shadows over the melee of men and animals, carts and carriages in the courtyard. What were they hiding? I wondered, as my gaze came to rest on Cesare's litter, lying enigmatically at the centre of all this activity, surrounded by his guards, its curtains still drawn. What words were trapped in their stones, what actions had been done in the thin bands of light falling through the arrow slits and the shadows beyond their reach?

Monna Vannozza, perhaps noting the direction of my gaze, swept past me, so close I felt the swish of her skirts against my bare ankles, calling instructions to the guards, who shifted about uncomfortably but made no move to obey her. Michelotto came to the rescue, detaching himself from a group of men who were rolling a small gun into position in front of the tallest of the castle's four towers. He pulled back the curtains on the litter.

To teach us life drawing at the convent, Sister Arcangelo used to use an articulated wooden figure. One day, the boy who kept the ink wells filled loosened all its pins, so that every time Sister Arcangelo attempted to pose it, it flopped uncontrollably. This was what Cesare reminded me of as two of his guards linked their hands in a lift and two others hauled him from the litter. As they hoisted him beneath his armpits, his limbs dangled and his head lolled. His poor, shorn head, the mass of curls patchily replaced by dark, dull stubble.

I heard a cry of pain, then a sudden, shocked silence. Everyone stopped what they were doing. Everyone turned towards me, open-mouthed laundresses clutching bundles to their bosoms, mules with baleful eyes and flicking ears, strapping Swiss infantrymen, and a couple of dwarfs wearing caps with bells on them and brandishing pigs bladders on sticks, just as though they were about to perform for their master. Camilla's nurse placed a comforting hand on my arm. Was it me, then, who had cried out? I had thought it was him.

"Oh Lord, Violante," whispered Giovanni, slipping his hand in mine, "what's going to happen to us? Will I still be Duke of Camerino?"

Though all I did was give the little boy's hand a reassuring squeeze, I thought, what ever is going to happen is happening now. History isn't despatches from new worlds or the dry observations of Herodotus or Plutarch or Livy I once studied with my brothers, it's this small, sad chaos, this directionless muddle of bewildered women and children and dogs, and leopards in cages. "Don't worry," I said, because there was no point in worrying.

Cesare was installed in the Governor's Tower, guarded not only by his Swiss lancers but by his mother and her priests. She surrounded herself with them, peering out from between their black-clad or lace-bedecked shoulders like a soldier watching his enemy from behind a barricade. I, meanwhile, bided my time, exploring the ancient castle and its grounds, pacing its squat ramparts and peering into its little stone caves of rooms, looking for clues as to what had happened here, what promise Cesare had made to his sister and then so catastrophically broken by invading Urbino.

Then one morning I encountered Michelotto on the well-trodden path to the latrine. Whatever privy arrangements there might have been in the Governor's Tower, which had been refurbished for Donna Lucrezia when she was appointed governor of Nepi, the rest of us had to make do with the communal latrine just beyond the castle walls, at the head of the ravine; a precarious perch, but hygienic as a steep waterfall rushed and bounced from there into the gorge many feet below. As we bade one another good morning, Monna Vannozza swept past us with a jangle of keys and a swish of the heavy, damascene silk she favoured. Her bevy of priests scurried in her wake, heads down against a sharp breeze, leaving traces of incense and camphor on air that tasted of cold stone and dying leaves.

"Autumn's coming," remarked Michelotto, squinting at the sky, which was full of fast-moving cloud.

"How is your lord this morning?"

"He needs rest, but with only Don Jofre to safeguard his affairs, well..." Michelotto shrugged.

"I wish I could see him."

"I wish you could." He cast a dark look at Monna Vannozza's back then suddenly grinned at me, giving a fantastic display of his ruined teeth. "We all have feet of clay, you see."

"It is proper for a man to respect his mother."

"If he was well enough he'd be showing his respect with the toe of his boot," said Michelotto with feeling. "Come today. I'll be damned if she's going to get all her own way. And now my bowels are telling me they will not wait, if you will excuse me."

I was not afraid of Monna Vannozza. I told myself she had more cause to be afraid of me if she believed I was a witch. Leaving Girolamo in the care of Camilla's nurse, with whom I now shared a bed in a room crowded with all kinds of women in the tower which also housed the castle's kitchens and scullery, I made my way to Cesare's rooms. Two guards were posted outside his bed chamber as usual, but the door was half open and I could hear low, urgent murmurings coming from inside. A grave-faced physician emerged bearing a covered bowl, followed by a maid carrying a bundle of dirty linen, her cheeks blotched with tears. I felt cold. As the girl hurried past me, wiping her nose on her sleeve, I wanted to ask her what had happened but my heart seemed to block my throat, as though it did not want to know. Suddenly I heard a great shout, almost a scream, tailing off into a querulous whine.

"Lucia? Lucia, where are you? Someone find her for me, I can't…"

I did not wait to hear what he could not, but darted through the half open door before the guards could bar my way. "It is me he wants," I said, making straight for the bed, scattering a flock of priests and doctors and another little maid who was struggling all alone to pull a clean sheet beneath the writhing, thrashing patient.

"Get that woman out of here. She means him harm."

I heard the rasp of swords being drawn behind me, but I did not care. If I had to die, then at least it would be because I had tried to help him. As my flesh cooled, it would quench the fever in his. For he was almost too hot to touch; he radiated heat like a devil in Gehenna. I gripped his shoulders and tried to push him back against his pillows. He screamed again, and the old dog crouched at the end of the bed growled. I sprang back, my hands clammy with Cesare's sweat. And blood. His nightshirt was soaked through, his back and chest oozing patches of pale, brownish blood and yellow pus. Sweat pooled above his naked upper lip and sparkled in his cropped hair. His eyes had a blind stare, the pupils dilated, nothing in them but tiny reflections of my own face, of this Lucia, whoever she was.

"*Vamos,*" said Michelotto, somewhere behind me. I was not sure whether he was speaking to the guards, or Monna Vannozza, or any of the rest of the people crowded around the bed. I did not care.

"He needs air to cool his fever," I said, willing myself not to retch. "All of you, step back. Look, he is calmer already." He had stopped fighting me and lay still, his eyes half closed, hands plucking at the bedclothes in small, futile convulsions. I saw now that his skin, where it was visible, was covered in blisters and open sores where other blisters had burst. His wrists and knuckles were swollen like those of a rheumatic. His breaths came short and harsh and foul through his open mouth. He would have stopped thrashing about soon enough anyway, I thought, for he was utterly exhausted, but the priests crossed themselves, the doctors hawed and harrumphed and rubbed the backs of their necks, and the little maid exclaimed, "It's a miracle."

Monna Vannozza gathered up her entourage and swept out of the room with her chin in the air and a vengeful expression on her face. Soon we were alone, except for Michelotto.

"What do you need?" he asked, and I could hear him asking the same of Cesare, in different circumstances.

"Water and some clean cloths. And a sponge if you can find one, and watered wine, sweet if there is any." What might Cesare have answered? A spy, a sword, a man's head on a plate, a clean whore?

When Michelotto had gone, snapping some order at the guards in his barbarous Navarrese, I stretched out beside Cesare on the bed. His hound shuffled sideways in response to the toe of my shoe, leaving a smudge of white hairs on the purple silk coverlet embroidered with the arms of Bisceglie. The bed curtains were the same, all made, I supposed, for Donna Lucrezia's mourning, shrouds for her broken heart. Stroking his head, I told him tomorrow I would find merrier bed furniture to aid his recovery. I was careful to keep my voice cheerful, though I wasn't sure if he could hear me. Feeling the frail bones of his skull under my palm, I wondered if he was already beyond the realm of human hearing. For what the little maid had called a miracle seemed to me to be more like dying.

Then suddenly the rhythm of his breathing changed, deepened, and he turned his head towards me and nuzzled my waist.

"The gown is very pretty," he said, though his eyes remained closed. He spoke softly, intimately. Obviously it was not my gown he was remarking on, for I was still wearing the old day dress Mariam had found for me, plain, high-necked, too short in the skirt, and far too tight at the breast. "You will make a beautiful bride, but you know I cannot be there."

"Why not?" I thought it wisest to humour him.

"You know why not." Now he sounded impatient and I immediately regretted my decision. I began stroking his head again and tried to shush him but this time my "magic" failed me. Shaking me off, he sat up, his eyes once more blank and staring, his mouth twisted in agitation. A crack opened in his bottom lip and began to bleed. "Give me your shoes."

"What?" He was speaking in Catalan; perhaps I had misunderstood.

"Your shoes. The ones you will be wearing. Come on, come on, quickly. We haven't got all day."

I took off my shoes and handed them to him. Placing one in his lap and holding on to the other, he began to rummage under the bedclothes with his free hand. "Knife," he said, "where's my knife? Lend me yours, sweetheart."

I had misgivings, but untied my eating knife from the plaited leather thong which fastened it to my girdle and offered it to him. It was not very sharp; I might do less harm in giving it to him than by withholding it. I watched in astonishment as he set to work on the soles of my shoes, carefully scoring the leather diagonally from heel to toe one way, then the other, the way boar are prepared for roasting.

"There," he said, passing the shoes back to me, "now you will not slip when the oaf dances with you. For they've been polishing the floors for days, and he can't be trusted to hold you properly." As I was putting the shoes back on, for though the soles were ruined, they were better than nothing on the old castle's cold stone floors, he grabbed my shoulders, his fingers grinding against my bones with unexpected strength. "I am always with you, you see, always watching over you. Never forget."

And then he kissed me, a harsh, hungry, furious kiss, his teeth jarring against mine, his tongue scouring my mouth, his heartbeat shuddering against my breastbone. "I'm going now. But don't worry. We are not like the calf at Caprarola. We won't die." He released me, lay down again, turned on his side away from me, and seemed to fall asleep, leaving the taste of his blood on my lips. I was still shaking when Michelotto returned.

"Here you are." He put down a jug and basin and a small pile of folded napkins on top of the linen chest at the foot of the bed. "Is everything all right? You look a bit feverish yourself."

I told him what had happened. "What can it mean?" I asked.

Michelotto shrugged. "No idea." I was sure he was lying, but he was so confident in his lie I knew there was nothing to be gained by challenging it. Later, in the dungeons of the Castel Sant'Angelo, even under torture he never said a word; you might almost have believed, they said, that he had never heard of Cesare Borgia. "He looks peaceful now at any rate."

"Yes. I think he's asleep. Perhaps the fever has broken." I touched the back of my hand to his forehead. It felt cooler, less clammy. "Will you stay with him? I have to feed Girolamo." I would not risk the wet nurse taking my place, not after witnessing the way Dorotea Carracciolo had been separated from her daughter. That was not going to happen to me.

"I will." He smiled at me, the weathered skin crinkling around his currant eyes. What did this Lucia matter anyway? She was not here, I was.

"You've done well, girl."

"I'll be back as soon as I can."

❦

As it turned out, I did not return that day, or the next, for Girolamo developed a fever and I dared not leave him. On the third day, Monna Vannozza came in person to enquire after him and to ask if there was anything I needed.

"How is the duke, madama?" I asked, ignoring her request. I was the woman with the healing hands, was I not? What could I possibly need to treat my son? Besides, I was certain Girolamo's hot cheeks and grizzling discontent were no more than his teeth coming through. Camilla's nurse, who had brought up five children of her own and nursed three more, had given him a little bone ring to chew, which seemed to soothe him.

"He is sitting in a chair receiving a deputation from Cardinal Carafa," she admitted. "I imagine they are discussing the election." She looked about the packed room for somewhere to sit. The young priest who was attending her finally took the hint and carried a low, three-legged stool across the room, stumbling over bundles of clothing and tangles of bedding. She brushed at it vigorously with her hand before lowering herself and smoothing her skirts over her knees. It crossed my mind she must keep the inns she had bought in Rome with Pope Alexander's money to a very high standard, and woe betide any maid who left a corner undusted or a bed unmade.

Girolamo turned his head towards his grandmother and levelled his dark, unblinking gaze on her. Did I imagine she shivered a little? A sharp breeze was banging the shutters and billowing among petticoats hanging from a wall hook near one of the slit windows.

"He ate two bowls of chicken broth with almond milk at breakfast, and tried to demand ham. Ser Torella said he feared it would be unwise," she continued. "Violante, let me tell you something." She leaned towards me, elbows resting on her knees, and spoke in a low voice so as not to be overheard by the priest. "I wish he had died in his infancy, as God surely intended. I wish he had not lived to disappoint all my hopes for him."

I could not imagine a more terrible and unnatural thing for a mother to say, yet I heard it with something approaching relief because now I knew beyond doubt that she was mad, that whatever she thought of Donna Lucrezia and whatever they used to say about me in the synagogue in Toledo, we were neither of us witches. If Cesare had flattered the fates into doing his will, he had done it alone.

"I thought he might be pope too, one day, but oh no, he must have other ideas, ideas that were bound to bring him into conflict with his father eventually. And he has always needed Rodrigo's protection, whatever he thinks."

"Surely you cannot believe he was suited to the Church, madama?"

"He would have been safe there, safe from…her."

"Really, Monna Vannozza, I cannot hear more of this. Your illustrious daughter has been kind and generous towards me. She is my godmother and it behoves me to turn my face from what you allege about her. Please…"

"Very well, I am going, but you are a stupid, naïve girl and you cannot see what is under your nose. The very walls of this place sweat it on wet days. Or perhaps you are merely wilful." She swept out, almost colliding with Fatima, the swarthy girl who wore earrings made of cascades of tiny gold coins and whose sweat smelled of cumin. The young priest scurried after her, the back of his neck turning red in response to Fatima's carmined lips and bare arms.

Later that day Michelotto sought me out in the scullery where I was washing Girolamo's clothes. "He's asking for you," he told me, propped against the low, arched doorway, a flock of scudding clouds behind his head, steam billowing out where the land fell away in rock and scrub to the stream which fed the castle's well.

"I can't..." I straightened up from the stone sink, pushing damp strands of hair out of my eyes with a hand reddened and pruned as a laundress's. "I'll come as soon as I've finished here."

"Actually, he's summoned you." Michelotto sounded almost apologetic. It was a measure of how everything had changed.

"But..."

"Well he's hardly looking his best either."

I unwound the sheet I had wrapped around myself to protect my dress and followed him.

Cesare was seated in a high-backed chair facing the window of his bed chamber. The governor's apartments had proper windows, partially glazed and overlooking a small garden and the muddle of roofs, terracotta and moss yellow, of the town of Nepi at the foot of the hill. The oblique honey glow of the autumn sun fell on the back of Cesare's right hand where it rested on the arm of his chair, on the powder burn and a gleam of red gold hair and the sapphire in his wedding ring. The ring was loose and had slipped up towards his knuckle. A small table was drawn up beside the chair, piled with documents whose seals hung from their ribbons like clusters of strange fruit, crimson and purple, yew green and gold, one in Donna Lucrezia's favourite shade of deep mulberry brown.

I crossed the room and dropped a curtsey, aware that Michelotto had withdrawn, closing the door behind him.

"Well, Violante, should I change your name? Should I call you Panaceia, perhaps, or Egeria? They tell me you saved my life."

"I think only He who gives life and takes it away could do that, my lord, and I would not presume to say I was His instrument. You are strong, and you have been well cared for."

"Oh for God's sake let's not have any of this my lording and sparring.

Are we not a little beyond that? Did you bring the boy with you? I should like to see him. My mother says he is the very spit of me."

Did she indeed? "Now I see you are well enough I will bring him. I was not sure…you never replied to my letter."

I felt him willing me to look at him, the way some lepers do when you pass them in the street with your face averted and a kerchief held to your nose and, as with the lepers, I could not.

"Letter?" He sounded puzzled.

"I wrote, to tell you I was pregnant. Perhaps it never reached you. I sent…a verse by Pietro Bembo."

Silence. I felt utterly foolish. How many girls, I wondered, had written, or paid a scribe to write, or dreamed of writing, such a letter to a man like Cesare? What right had I to think he would remember mine?

"Oh yes," he said slowly, then cleared his throat, pleated folds of the loose brocaded gown he was wearing between his fingers, smoothed its sable cuffs. "The verse is not by Bembo." As if he knew how I had come by it, as if he had found me out. "You should not have sent it. That is why I did not reply."

I stared at his hands, opened my mouth to ask why not, saw his fingers curl suddenly into white-knuckled fists, grasping the fabric of his gown as though he would tear it. The words died on my tongue. "I'm sorry," I whispered and tried to swallow, but my mouth was dry.

Then he raised his hands in a gesture of dismissal, palms facing out. Pushing me away. "No matter. It's all water under the bridge now. I should like to see my son."

"Now?"

"Why? Do you think me too ugly? Are you afraid I'll frighten him?" He gave a harsh laugh. "I notice you will not look at me when not so long since you couldn't take your great moonstruck eyes off me."

I stared at my ruined shoes. Perhaps I was infected by Monna Vannozza's strange superstitions, but somehow I felt this shrunken, haggard figure, almost swallowed by the high, dark chair in which he was sitting, was not Cesare at all. And if I looked at his face I would know this; I could no longer pretend otherwise, and all my dreams and memories would flee before his dead man's stare.

"So you are a latterday Delilah. I am weak, my head is shaved, and you will run to your Philistines."

"And at the moment, my lord, I think you are lame in both feet." For the joints of his feet and ankles, resting on a footstool, were as swollen as his wrists and hands.

"I cannot follow you."

"Only if I go very slowly."

"I am in no mood for punning." Truth to tell, nor was I.

"Pardon. In Jewish legend, Samson is lame."

"Makes you wonder what she saw in him, doesn't it?" He turned the joke on himself like a torch.

Now I looked at him, drawn by the sudden return of his old, wry humour, echoes of a time when I did not know I was happy, caught up in the marriage fever at Santa Maria in Portico. The bones of his face were sharp as knives and sometimes, even now, when I am tired, I close my eyes and feel the scars he left there on the undersides of my eyelids. The look he returned me was that of a brave child, determined, uncertain of the future, scared, and defiant. With each unmasking, each layer of glamour stripped away, I seemed to understand him less.

"Sit down, Violante," he said. I found a stool and dragged it into the window embrasure where his chair had been placed. I sat down and waited. He fiddled with his ring, smoothed his cuffs, and said, finally, "The children are important to me."

"Of course they are. You must have heirs."

"True, but that's not what I meant." He paused, as though he was unsure what he meant, then began again. "When Juan was made gonfalonier, my father commissioned a new setting of the *Beatus Vir* for the service. After Juan died, and the honour fell to me, he had the same piece performed at my investiture. And now he's dead and I could never make him love me enough; I was always just Juan's substitute. Less good looking, less charming, less easy to love. I didn't matter enough to have new music written for me. The things I was better at—strategy, tactics, politics, government, diplomacy—they only mattered in my father's mind, not in his heart. He never sent for me when he knew he was dying. All the time I lay sick, just one floor above him, and he never sent to find out how I was.

I couldn't make a place for myself in his heart and now it's too late. He's gone. Dust. Do you see?" Stone words, too perfectly sculpted.

Something inside me clenched, made a hard knot in my belly. "Do you know why I'm here, Cesare?"

He shook his head. "I hadn't thought about it, to be honest."

"Donna Lucrezia sent me back to my father. Because of Girolamo."

"Girolamo? That is the boy's name?"

"Girolamo Giulio Cesare. Don Giulio d'Este is his godfather."

"Good. Giulio is an honest man. So why are you not at your father's house?"

"Because when I arrived there I found my father had died, and my brother would not receive me. Because of you."

"Me?"

"My father suffered a seizure after your men came to…" I paused, breathed, tried to steady my voice, "…collect taxes, as I believe they put it. They even took the *menorah* we brought from Spain, my mother and I. To pay for your soldiers. I travelled through the Romagna to get to Rome, of course. I saw soldiers, though I tried to keep out of their way. They were not behaving like men who had been well paid, Cesare."

"It's artillery that costs," he commented sulkily.

"Shut up and listen to me. I wanted to kill you. Then a good woman reminded me that love matters more than duty. Though as far as I know, she has done her duty all her life so I don't know where this wisdom came from. So I have brought you your son. He is your only son, and we must think about him now. There will be time enough to mourn our fathers later." My heart had set up such a tattoo in my chest I was afraid I would faint. My sight blurred and my head felt like a bladder full of air; I half expected it to lift from my shoulders and float out of the open window.

"What do you think it would be best to do for him?" he asked. He spoke with tenderness, almost humility, but he could not disarm me that easily.

"You're asking me? You are the great Valentino, the victor of Senigallia, the…"

"Spare me your sarcasm, woman. It does rather take the shine off your last pretty speech. I could hand him a fistful of titles but frankly, keeping him alive, keeping all this…" He waved his arm at the window, the room, the castle. His sleeve caught the pile of parchments and scattered them over the floor, "...circus going is my top priority at the moment. How many people do you suppose are here? What are they all to eat come winter? I have nothing but what Michelotto managed to seize before the buzzards started flocking round the Vatican, and that little I must use to keep Della Rovere's arse off Saint Peter's throne or I am finished. I can scarcely get out of this chair, let alone ride at the head of an army. You know, I had thought of everything. Everything, Violante, except that when my father died I would also be laid low with the fever.

"And now I am so tired. Sometimes I feel as though I have a dark daemon clinging to my shoulders like the Princess Sherezade's old man of the sea, and he wraps his legs and arms around me so tight I can scarcely breathe, let alone move, or think, or do anything."

*I am sick,* he had written. *Sickness smoulders in me like fire at the heart of a damp haystack; it ticks in the night like a death clock in the rafters.* Now I understood.

"You should make your peace with your God, Cesare."

"Why? Have you changed your mind about me, my lady physician? Am I dying after all?"

"If there is a disjunction between man and his Maker, that is where the melancholy enters in."

"Torella tells me it is an imbalance of black bile and makes me eat white food to counteract it. I dare say we Christians must take a more circuitous route to God, not being His chosen people."

"I am trying to help, and you must be flippant!"

Suddenly he raised his hands, backs facing me. A gesture of surrender? The wide sleeves of his gown slipped up his arms, exposing their thinness and the raw and blistered skin. But that was not what he wished to show me.

"See the scars?" he asked, twisting his hands this way and that. There were, perhaps, six scars on the back of each hand, fine bridges of raised skin across his veins, left by the physicians' bleeding fleams. "They set me thinking about my sister's nun. I have realised that her prophecy was right."

"How right?" I filled my voice with brisk common sense, but I remembered, and I could see he did, the shocked whiteness of his face, the way he had stumbled, almost as though Sister Osanna's words had physically struck him.

"She gave me the number twenty. I believed then she referred to my age. As I had already passed my twenty-sixth birthday, I dismissed her as a charlatan who wished merely to flatter me. If Lucrezia wanted to give her to Ercole d'Este, all well and good, I thought. But recently I realised, if you count the months from the date of her prophecy to my father's death, it is twenty. And so, every time I see a possible way out of this mess, I look at the backs of my hands and am reminded there is no point, no plan I can contrive, no action worth taking."

"Oh Cesare." I rose and crossed the short space between us, impelled by some vague idea of comforting him, and tried to put my arms around him, but he flinched and hissed with pain as my hands came into contact with his shoulders. I backed off, apologising. He gave a grim laugh.

"Stay away from me, Violante, for I am the emperor of the kingdom of pain, encased in ice."

"Cesare, you're not raving again, are you?"

He shook his head. "Merely misquoting Dante. At the height of my fever the physicians had me plunged in a barrel full of ice to stop my blood from boiling. The ice ripped most of the skin from my body. *I did not die, nor yet remain alive.*"

"But you did remain alive. Dante didn't give up and neither must you."

"Dante had faith. Dante had Beatrice."

"And you have only me. Is that what you're thinking?"

"Don't flatter yourself. I've told you what I'm thinking. I have been honest with you. Can you not take that as the compliment it is intended to be?"

"It is a burden, a responsibility. Do you expect me to do nothing with the knowledge you have given me? I might as well take a knife and stick it between your ribs."

He took my hands. I stared at my skin, rough and reddened by laundry soap and the pox, and at his, swollen and scarred. "You don't give up, do you?"

"If I were inclined to give up, I would have died when my mother died, and never met you, and you would not have a son. And before you start up again about how you can't be of any use to him, consider what you said to me about Juan and your father. Even if you have no cities or guns or diamond rings, you can give him your love and that will mean more to him than anything."

"Bring him to me, and we shall see. Tomorrow. I am tired now. I think I shall sleep for a while."

"Let me help you to your bed."

"I can walk that far unaided, for Christ's sake. Leave me."

As I turned to go, the heel of my shoe, which had come loose as a result of Cesare's delirious attack, caught in a gap between two floorboards and I stumbled.

"Here," he said, "catch." But I turned too slowly and the key clattered to the ground. As I stooped to pick it up, he went on, "There's a room on the floor below here where my sister left some clothes and things. I suppose you are her size. Help yourself." It was impossible to know whether he remembered what he had done. Or that he had kissed me.

I had no intention of taking him up on his offer. It seemed to me somehow improper to pick over madonna's clothes in her absence, like going through her private letters or eavesdropping on her conversations. But once the idea of a new dress which would fit me properly, of clean linen and darn-free stockings and waterproof shoes had taken hold, I could not let it go. I found myself drifting towards the Governor's Tower, the key pressed to my palm, pictures of gowns both remembered and imagined flicking through my mind as though it were nothing more than a dressmaker's design book. I knew I was watched, by Michelotto and Monna Vannozza, by Don Jofre as he crossed the courtyard in consultation with his secretary. A messenger from Don Prospero Colonna had recently brought Don Jofre word that his wife intended to accompany Don Prospero to Naples, to console him for Cesare's deception, and Don Jofre was working hard on his reply. I felt I must at least unlock the room, if only to show them all I was not merely mooning after Cesare, to wipe the various, complicated smiles off their faces.

Two rooms shared the floor below Cesare's apartments, the one to which I had the key and the strongroom, guarded by four of Cesare's Swiss infantry with their tall pikes and gaudy uniforms. I held the key out in front of me like a safe conduct as I advanced on the door and the cold eyes of the montagnards watched me.

The door was stiff. No, it was obstructed. I had to put my shoulder to it to open it, and even then sidle, crabwise, through the narrow gap. I will take nothing, I told myself, just look. There might be things madonna would like back, things I could pack up and send with the next messenger who came from Ferrara. It was the lightning that changed my mind. I had not noticed the weather closing in while I had been talking to Cesare, then rushing to feed Girolamo, singing him distractedly to sleep while thoughts of skirts and bodices and embroidered chemises whirled about my mind. But the sudden explosion of light drew my attention to the window slit, to the slap of rain on the stone sill, a brown, twisted leaf dancing across the narrow bar of steel-coloured sky. Winter was coming. I had to have stout shoes and a decent cloak. I owed it to my son not to risk my health.

Thunder growled as I closed the door behind me. At first the room was full of shadows, strange, cloudy shapes that only gradually resolved themselves into bound chests, and piles of clothing. But these were not madonna's clothes, I realised as I clambered among them. Doublets decorated with rosettes and ribbons like the costumes of a mountebank, sleeves and breeches slashed with coloured silks and cloth of gold, caps set with stones and pearls the size of birds' eggs, fur-lined cloaks with clasps of filigree, soft boots and gold spurs were scattered about like dismembered bodies on a battlefield, everything thrown together in utter abandon. With the next lightning strike I was nearly blinded by the brightness of the gems.

I waded through this fabulous sea, picking up articles at random as if I were a beachcomber on the shores of some fairy-tale kingdom. Here a cap of violet-coloured velvet, so encrusted with precious stones it weighed as heavy as a crown, there a spur pointed with diamonds. There were shirts so fine they slipped through my fingers like air, a dancing slipper with a gilded leather sole which looked as though it had never been worn paired with a green kid boot whose chased shin was caked with mud. I held the boot up to my nose, as though the smell of the earth might tell me what journey it had been on, but the earth was old and dry and crumbled away under my touch, and smelled of nothing. A peacock feather shivered in the storm's draught, a fountain of dark sea blue sprang from a turban of gold satin pinned with a chunk of polished coral. I imagined the ghost of Prince Djem, chuckling like an indulgent uncle over the follies of young men, and wondered if Cesare had ever worn it, or if it was just some memento mori. Here were all the skins he had sloughed off, and now the last decorative sheath had gone, the beard, the river of red hair, the upholstery of muscle, even the skin he had been born in, so all that remained was blood and bone, the fire in his heart and the stone in his will.

I put down the boot, trailed my fingers over the fringe of the peacock feather, stepped over dressing cases and jewellery boxes to reach the far side of the room where a row of skirts and bodices swung austerely from a rail. Mourning clothes, I realised as the next bolt of lightning picked out the rich, dull gleam of black satin, a thin froth of lace at a neck or cuff or the edging of a skirt. That was why madonna had left them behind.

I chose a dark violet skirt and a bodice striped in black and white which I thought must have been designed for the period of half mourning. They were a little old-fashioned, and far too grand for me, but well made, and with enough stuff in the skirt for me to cut it down and make a second dress if I needed to. A chest with a broken padlock yielded undergarments made of Egyptian cotton and beautifully embroidered in black silk with trails of ivy and tiny figures of Orpheus looking over his shoulder. I unpacked violet and mulberry silk stockings with black garter ribbons, neatly folded, cedar perfumed. I changed quickly, with a sense of trespass, almost as though Donna Lucrezia were watching me step into her skirts, tie her stockings, fasten her bodice across my own full breasts just as she must have done, alone behind these thick walls with her own infant son.

Shoes, I thought, or did she put the word in my mind, a practical nugget of a word trailing wisps of soft laughter and dance tunes playing in neighbouring rooms? As many as a dozen pairs were lined up beneath the rail of gowns, velvet slippers, kidskin boots with gilded heels and pearl buttons, tall Venetian pattens for rain. One after another I picked them up, looking for the stoutest, examining the soles for signs of wear. I found a suitable pair quite quickly, morocco riding boots which looked as though they had never been worn and scarcely pinched my feet at all. But as I sat down on the lid of a chest to put them on, another pair caught my eye.

These were not black, but made of rose-coloured satin and scattered with tiny pearls and emeralds. I picked them up, just to examine the workmanship, I told myself, just out of idle curiosity. They were worn, these shoes, the heels scuffed, the toes crumpled and one darkened at its point with what looked like an old bloodstain. I felt a tug at my heart as I remembered how often we had all danced till our feet bled, then spent the daylight hours gossiping with our toes poulticed and ankles raised, ready to do it all again the next night. As though the cycle would go on forever, as though it had the certainty of sunrise and sunset. Lightning caught the tears in my eyes and blinded me. Clutching the shoes, I counted the space between lightning and thunder and waited for my sight to return, traced the pattern of embroidery on the shoes, the sharpness of their toes, the curve of the heels. Something else. The soles of these shoes were cracked, no, cut, scored crosswise.

I flung them away from me as if they had burned my hands. In the sudden silence left by the thunder I heard myself gasp, mutter some denial. I fancy I even heard the small grind of the bones in my neck as I shook my head. Gathering up my old clothes, I fled. I did not even pause to lock the door, was only half aware of the wolf whistles of the Swiss guards cutting through the drumming of my blood, the thud of the heels of madonna's boots on the stone flagged floor.

❧

"Who is she?" There were no guards on his door, nothing and no one to stop me crashing into the room with this question swelling inside me until it felt as though it would burst out of my chest. "Who is Lucia?"

The shutters were closed. The thunder prowled outside, rattling them with the power of its voice. Monna Vannozza sat in a wavering circle of candlelight, her embroidery frame in her lap. The face she turned on me, pale, deepset beneath her voluminous wired hood, the large eyes full of calm enquiry, was like an owl's.

"He is asleep," she said, as though there were no possibility of his having been awakened by the thunder and lightning, or my shouting, or the door banging against the wall. As though he might not be lying behind his closed bed curtains listening to the storm, the fizz and crackle of the guttering candle, the rasp of thread through canvas, his own heartbeat, the daemon chattering in his ear. She professed herself so proud of his skill at listening. She looked me up and down, pushed a contemptuous breath down her long nose. "So you have added thieving to your impertinences now, have you?"

"His grace said I might. He gave me the key. My shoes…you saw the condition of my dress before. Winter is coming. And Donna Lucrezia will not be wanting these things, not now she is married again."

Monna Vannozza chose to ignore my last remark. "You talk of practicalities, but I know your game. You will put those things back where you found them. I forbid you to allow yourself to be seen by my son in the changeling's clothes. The shock would kill him."

I straightened my back, squared my shoulders, clenched my fists at my side to stop my hands shaking. "Your son commands this household, madama, not you. I will change my clothes if he orders it, not otherwise." I did not wait for her reply. I wanted Cesare to sleep; I wanted him to wake up tomorrow and be himself again, to be strong and funny and in charge of things. I feared the wraith with his hands frail as fallen moths and his bleak talk of daemons far more than I had ever feared the terrible duke who used to wink at me during dreary theatrical pageants and make me laugh. I wanted to be able to ask him about Lucia in the certainty I would be answered with some smooth and entertaining lie.

❧

Two days of cold and rain were followed by a last, soft breath of summer. Grape picking began on the terraces below the castle, and in the castle's own orchard we were all suddenly busy gathering pears and early apples and fat, golden apricots that basked against walls as warm as flesh. After the storms, and an apathy induced by low cloud and grey light and smoking fires, we were imbued with a sense of urgency, a sense we could not stay here forever.

In Rome the conclave had begun to elect a successor to Cesare's father and among those anxiously awaiting its outcome were no doubt many of the men dispossessed by Cesare in his conquest of the Romagna. Yet as we cleaned and bottled the fruit, we women and children laughing and singing and gossiping around the great trestle table in the kitchen, with its knife scars and the smooth dents made by years of kneading, we knew we were also at the centre of something here. A web of information spun out from Nepi and back again, embassies arriving daily, sometimes hourly, from all over Italy and beyond, messengers coming and going, sometimes in Cesare's livery and bearing sealed letters, sometimes anonymously dressed and carrying nothing.

I thought he had forgotten Girolamo, and for now I was content to leave it that way because I knew when I saw him again I would have to find out the truth about Lucia and I was not sure I had the courage for it. Despite Monna Vannozza's hostility, I enjoyed special status among the women in the castle as the mother of the duke's son. They treated me as if I were, indeed, his mistress, and I was content to prolong the make-believe. Perhaps, if we all pretended hard enough, it would, somehow, become true. So, when I unexpectedly found myself face to face with him in the garden, my heart did something complicated which had as much to do with dread as desire.

"You see, Violante," he said, waving an ebony cane in my direction, "I defy the riddle of the Sphinx by walking on three legs at midday." Clearly his joints were still plaguing him, though he had put on a little flesh and had some colour in his cheeks, and his smile, fringed by the rough regrowth of his beard, had the fierce merriment of a pirate's. I had come outside to find somewhere peaceful to feed Girolamo, to rest my back against warm stones after hours stooped over the kitchen table. He was accompanied by a whole retinue of people. His secretary, Agapito, recently returned from Rome, and Torella, conferred together as they walked like a pair of black crows. One small page was almost hidden behind a pile of cushions while another staggered beneath a load of books and a guitar. A demure girl with bony wrists balanced a wine jug and goblet on a tray while managing to keep a long-handled fan tucked beneath one arm.

I curtseyed. "I am glad to see you on your feet, my lord."

"I am feeling a good deal stronger. Come and sit with me. Introduce me to your son."

A daybed had been set up for him in a lemon grove overlooking terraces of olive trees knotted like dark fists against the red earth. The leaves of the lemon trees gleamed against a creamy blue sky, though we were too high up here for good lemons and the fruit was still green, its scent acerbic and cleansing. We waited while his servants arranged the bed with cushions and blankets. Girolamo began to grizzle. I tried to soothe him, stroking his downy head and whispering to him, but I was tense, anxious Cesare would lose patience with a crying baby and dismiss us, and my hungry son could smell milk.

"I shall sing to him," said Cesare, and cleared his throat. He tried a few words of some nursery song but quickly gave up. "I cannot. My voice is weak since my illness."

"It will recover. You sing pleasantly, my lord, as I recall."

"Well more pleasantly than that child of yours at any rate. No, two behind my back, boy," he snapped at the page arranging the cushions. "And put the wine there, where I can reach it," he added, exchanging a look with the demure girl which I wished I had not seen.

"I'm sorry. He's hungry," I said.

"Then feed him."

I felt myself beginning to blush.

"Here. If I sit a little further back, there is room for you at the end of the bed. What is it? You think I have never seen a mother nursing a baby before? By God's merciful ears, woman, stop up his mouth before he deafens me." He said this as though he was rather proud of the fact that Girolamo was capable of deafening him. "The rest of you, leave us. Master Agapito, prepare the letters we were speaking of and bring them here to me for signature."

With a flurry of bows his retinue departed, melted away among the lemon trees as though they had never been there, as though the tree sprites had arranged this bower for us, with its cedar-scented cushions, the books in their jewelled bindings, the silver wine jug, the slender-waisted Spanish guitar leaning beside the bed.

Cesare watched me with almost the same hungry intensity as Girolamo as I unfastened my bodice and put my son to my breast, and I knew what he was concealing by the self-conscious way he took a book from the pile beside him and opened it in his lap. But all he said was, "My sister's clothes suit you."

"Thank you." I gave him a smile, yet the look he returned me seemed curiously full of pain. I reached out and touched his foot, and perhaps because of the warmth of his skin through the fine stocking, or because of the scent of lemons, or a bird singing somewhere as if it was spring, or the delicious sensation of my baby's mouth tugging at my nipple, instead of asking him about Lucia and the cut dancing shoes, I said, "I still love you." Almost as though he had told me he was no longer fit to be loved, with his disintegrating state, his wasted body and flayed skin and the way his skull showed so white and bony when he pulled off his cap and raked his fingers through the stubble of dark red hair.

And once the words were out, it was as though all the words that had been knotted up so tight inside me began to unravel, and I could not stop. "Let me stay with you. I wouldn't ask much, just to see you sometimes. We could have more sons. I'd be discreet; I'd never embarrass you or your wife. I'd marry myself, if that's what you wanted, someone older, and respectable. I wouldn't expect you to be faithful, or even to love me, particularly. But I'd like to sleep the night with you sometimes, and wake up next to you in the morning. All I want is to be allowed to love you or I might...I don't know...stop breathing or something."

Girolamo's mouth slackened around my nipple, his eyes closed, and he began a sweet, soft snoring. Instead of covering myself, I turned towards Cesare, offering him my body, my breasts no longer the shallow pads of rebellious flesh he had caressed in his sister's orange garden but swollen with purpose, the nipples tender and erect under the teasing touch of the breeze. I was as beautiful as Helen, or as Eve when Adam's eyes were first filled with her. The memory of Cesare's touch illuminated my skin; I felt the warm weight of his belly on mine, the sharpness of hip against hip, the sweet pain of him inside me, his tongue in my mouth tasting of rosemary as though it were all as real as it had been then.

For a moment he was still; everything was still except my heart banging in my chest and the light dancing among the lemon leaves. Then he whispered, "No," and held up his hands to ward me off. "Do you really think this is what she had in mind, the woman who did her duty but spoke to you of love?" His eyes held mine with the fastidiousness of a monk.

He learned to listen, his mother had said, to the click of a beetle crossing a paving stone, to the thin screech of my shame crawling across my skin.

I turned my back on him, hunched over my nakedness as I attempted to rearrange my clothing, but my hands were shaking so badly I fumbled all the hooks and laces. "Forgive me."

"Give me the child," said Cesare, not without kindness. He imagined, I suppose, that it was his forgiveness I was asking.

I turned just far enough for him to be able to take Girolamo from me, but I kept my face averted. "I usually..."

"I will unwrap him," Cesare announced. "I wish to be sure his limbs are straight."

"...unwrap him," I finished, and the coincidence made us laugh. "Shall I do it?"

"I can manage."

This I doubted, and watched anxiously as he pulled one of the cushions from behind his back, smoothed it over his lap, and lay the baby on it, then began to unwind his swaddling clothes. He completed the task with great assurance, and never a murmur from Girolamo who kept his eyes fixed on his father's face then, free of his bindings, gave a little shriek of delight and pissed all over the cushion.

"Oh no."

"It's all right, he has a true aim. He managed to miss my clothes and his," said Cesare, lifting Girolamo's testicles with the tip of his finger then running a hand down his legs as if testing the soundness of a horse. "Nothing like a good piss in the open air, eh, Girolamo?"

"You are very patient with him, my lord."

"Oh well, there were always a lot of babies around. You get used to it."

"It is not the way in which you are generally seen, my lord, as a great patriarch."

"I was not head of my family until recently," he replied quietly. Then he gave a brittle laugh and scrubbed at his chin with the knuckle of his free hand. "And now I really need it, my doctors have even deprived me of my patriarchal beard."

"I think it was a little neater than Moses'. And it is growing again. By the time Girolamo has his front teeth, I'm sure your beard will be the envy of Italy."

"Just my beard, you think? This election worries me, Violante. Della

Rovere must be a contender and he is the one man whose wit I fear. And he will never be my ally. What he wants is too close to what I want."

"Whoever is pope needs a good gonfalonier. There is none better than you."

"But alas, I have shown my hand. Everyone knows my ambitions extend well beyond collecting the vicars' taxes to fill Saint Peter's coffers. Della Rovere would as soon put a scorpion in his shoe as give me an army. Besides, he'd probably rather do the job himself. Aside from Ippolito, he's the only cardinal I know who is more comfortable in armour than scarlet silk."

"Ippolito?" I could not conjure an image of Ippolito in armour.

"Don't be deceived by his smooth manners. He loves the machinery of war as much as Alfonso; he's just better at hiding it. Young men must dissemble to get on in the world."

"As you dissemble with me?"

"I have dealt with you as straight as I know how." He sounded hurt.

Girolamo whimpered.

"I think he may be getting cold. Give him to me and I'll dress him." Cesare handed him back to me, and as I dressed him, I bent over to kiss his forehead, breathing him in, his scent of sour milk and vanilla and linen dried over smoky fires. "Then who is Lucia?"

"She is no one, a figment." His answer was too quick, too pat. He was not even attempting to disguise his lie. It made me angry to think I did not deserve even a pretence of truthfulness, a pantomime of puzzlement and casting about in his memory for the name of some half-forgotten paramour.

"A figment you called on in your delirium. I found the shoes, Cesare, hidden among Donna Lucrezia's things. The soles were cut just the way you cut mine."

Now he did look confused. "What?"

"You took my shoes, when you were in a fever, and cut the soles to ribbons. Like this." I carved the air in front of me into diamonds with the edge of my palm. "And there is a pair in the wardrobe just the same, with Donna Lucrezia's things."

"Well I'm not surprised. It's a trick of hers to stop her losing her footing when she dances. It helps the shoes to grip the floor. Surely you have seen others of hers cut that way, or are you such an inattentive lady in waiting?"

"But you…" Kissed me, I was going to say, but the words stuck on my tongue. If I spoke of his kiss, it would dissolve in the air the way perfume does, or morning mist in sunlight.

"No wonder she sent you away."

"She didn't send me away, she…"

"Yes?" He linked his hands across his belly and waited. What could I say? What was the point of saying anything as he already knew the answer? I rose. I was going to leave. I would take a horse and leave Nepi this very day. I would return to Rome and cast myself on Eli's mercy, renounce my conversion, and never again set foot among Christians. Cesare might be thrown into the Tiber like his brother Juan, or be elected Holy Roman Emperor, it would make no difference to me. They could live and die as they pleased, him, his sister, his mother, Angela, all of them with their cold glitter and their fatal charm.

Suddenly there were footsteps running towards us, thudding along the packed sand path. A voice shouting for Cesare.

"Where are you, brother? It's over. *Habemus Papam.*" Don Jofre, flushed and out of breath, wiping the sweat from his upper lip with the back of his hand. A messenger, whose face was a mask of white dust, skidded to a halt behind him and bowed.

"Who is it?" asked Cesare. His tone was calm, but a tic started up in his left eye and his fingers tightened their grip on one another. I suppose it must only have been seconds before Don Jofre replied, yet I stared at Cesare's hands and thought of all they knew, of how to excite pleasure or tighten a garota, coax a horse, write a sonnet or sign a warrant of execution, and it seemed as though hours had passed before Don Jofre said, "Piccolomini," and I realised I had been holding my breath.

We all looked to Cesare, awaiting his reaction, but he hesitated, seemed uncertain.

"What do you think, Jofre?" he asked finally.

"Me?" Jofre's cheeks turned as pale as they had been scarlet. "Well, I…"

"Cardinal Piccolomini is a scholar," I said quickly. I remembered him as a frail, serious man who had taken an interest in my conversion because my father's agents had on occasion negotiated for him in the purchase of rare polyglot Bibles. "I do not think he will be concerned to change things on the temporal side as long as they run smoothly. I believe he will reinstate you, your grace."

Cesare looked relieved; I might almost have imagined grateful. "Yes. And his uncle, Pius II, was indebted to my father for his election and preferred him in many things. What name will he take?"

"Pius also," said Jofre.

"Good, good. Then I will write and remind him that he can emulate his uncle in more practical ways than merely by taking his name. How did the vote go?"

Jofre clicked his fingers impatiently at the messenger, who produced a letter from his satchel and handed it to Jofre. Jofre broke the seal and scanned the contents. "Della Rovere came out ahead on the first ballot." Cesare snarled. Jofre hurried on. "So D'Amboise and Ascanio Sforza joined forces on the second to propose Piccolomini."

"Then Agapito made a felicitous blend of my directions and his own initiative and advised them well," said Cesare. "No one can object to Piccolomini. He has no political interests, no family looking for advancement. But we need to act fast. My enemies will be whispering in his ear in no time, trying to persuade him I threw them out of their vicariates illegally. I must make sure of his heart before others gain sway over it."

"He's not in good health either, by all accounts," added Jofre happily. The possible implications of a short papacy held no threats for him if Cesare had rediscovered his characteristic decisiveness. "He suffers terribly with the gout."

"Then," said Cesare, picking his way cautiously through his words, "he will look sympathetically on my own predicament. Come, Jofre, give me your arm, there is much to be done." Jofre helped him to his feet, but he set off ahead of his brother at an energetic limp which reminded me of his father. Then suddenly he stopped, so abruptly Jofre had to take a smart step aside to avoid colliding with him. "Oh, I almost forgot," he said to me, fishing in a pocket concealed among the quilted panels of his doublet. "Here." He tossed me a small box, and nodded his appreciation as I managed to catch it in my one free hand. It was the gold and enamel pill box given him by Ser Torella for his lozenges against the pox. "I noticed...a little scarring when you..." He sought for discreet words to use in front of his brother and the messenger from Rome, but finished by resorting to a vague gesture of his cupped hands in front of his chest. "You must be sure to guard my son's health."

Don Jofre sniggered and shifted slightly away from me. He'd be poxed himself, I thought, a furious blush coming to my cheeks, if that Neapolitan whore he was married to ever deigned to share his bed.

"But do you not have need of them?" I asked Cesare.

"Oh, I am cured. The French disease cannot live alongside the tertian fever. Torella tells me they make poor neighbours and the tertian fever always drives the other out. Take them, and I will have Torella make you more."

"Thank you," I said, though gratitude was not what I felt.

❧

The new pope quickly confirmed Cesare in all his titles, but balked, it seemed, at granting permission for him to return to Rome. He regretted he could not guarantee the duke's safety, and would never forgive himself if he thought his actions had put his holy predecessor's beloved son at risk.

"Yet I am hardly safe here," raved Cesare, sending the lesser kitchen staff running for cover. He was showing Giovanni how to kill a crayfish, and it was the man who had brought the crayfish, one of a dozen in a barrel of water from the lake at Bracciano, who had told him of the rumour that Guidobaldo of Urbino was trying to raise an army to march on Nepi. He stabbed his knife into the crayfish's head then turned the creature deftly through the angle of Pythagoras until the knife blade was aligned with the middle of its back. Its claws waved feebly. Giovanni watched with his mouth open and eyes as round as chestnuts. "You have to be quick, you see, or you'll make a mess of it."

"Maybe you should go to Romagna," I said, picking up on his double meaning.

He brought the knife down through the back of the fish. "There," he said to Giovanni, "you clean it. Stomach and any dark bits from the tail. That would be the coward's way," he answered me.

"Or the way of common sense. Build up your powerbase there again, then go to Rome."

"Women understand nothing. No, Giovanni, that's the roe. You're going to have to learn the difference, boy, or you'll never get far with your wooing." He looked at me and chuckled, and something seemed to melt just below my ribs, and I loved his cool head and the way he could always make me laugh, and I knew I was not going to leave him.

❦

Pope Pius changed his mind quite quickly in fact, though for us, watching Cesare chafe at Nepi, the wait seemed interminable. He was our sun and moon, and his foul temper affected us all like a change in the weather. The autumn remained golden and fair, yet my bones ached with anxiety as though afflicted with a winter ague. I grew impatient with Girolamo, who was teething, and resentful of my attempts to wean him. His crying sliced me so thin I snapped at him then, full of remorse, weakened and let him have the breast. Monna Vannozza told me I should hand him over to Camilla's nurse. She told me I had become addicted to my child the way some people grow dependant on poppy. I will not repeat the things I said to her in reply for they shame me.

Then one afternoon when I had been walking in the hills behind the castle, trying to soothe my nerves and distract my mind from my aching breasts, I met Don Jofre at the gate with a bundle of letters. He was always the first to greet the messengers who arrived almost daily from Rome or Ferrara or the court of France, ever hopeful of a letter from the errant Princess Sancia, ever destined for disappointment. But today a grin cracked his narrow face from side to side, revealing his three remaining canine teeth and the gap where the fourth used to be until he lost it in a fight.

"He's done it at last," shouted Jofre, waving a parchment which bore the papal seal. "Cesare's persuaded the old goat to let us go home."

"I wish you wouldn't read my letters, little brother." Cesare, naked to the waist and trailing an old, blunted broadsword in the rutted dust of the yard, spoke mildly but fixed Don Jofre with a stare as blank as a snake's.

"I...I thought you were probably resting. I didn't want you to be disturbed with anything unimportant."

"I've been sparring with Michelotto. Got to get my strength up, now I'm to be gonfalonier again." His chest still bore the scars of the ice bath, patches of dead white and puckered skin where no hair grew, as though the goblet I had once traced with my fingertips had been smashed and poorly mended. "Give me the letter, Jof." Jofre handed it to him. He shook out the rolled parchment and skimmed it with his eyes, and a thin smile stretched his lips.

"He wrote and told old Piccolomini he was dying, you know," Jofre told me. "Begged to be allowed to go home and die in peace. And the daft old sod believed him. Apparently he told the Ferrarese ambassador that he had never thought to feel any pity for the duke, but that he now found himself pitying him most deeply." Jofre gave his irritating snigger.

"Hold your tongue, Jofre. You're blathering nonsense like a girl."

"His Holiness will be very surprised when he sees you, my lord," I said. "Pleasantly surprised, I am sure."

"Ah, but there are many ways to die, Violante."

# CHAPTER 5

*I have been remembering the place we used to hide among the fruit canes, where I crushed the ladybird because I was sure I would never need its tiny store of luck.*

And for every way of dying, there is a way to protect yourself from death. Rome was full of Cesare's enemies, vultures, he said, come to pick over his carcass and more dangerous than ever now they were condemned to go hungry. Once we had returned to the palace of San Clemente, Cesare rarely left it, and never after dark. The main gates remained locked and barricaded and despite objections from the Vatican, and all the major Roman families, a row of small cannon were ranged across the square outside, causing carters to have to take alternative routes through the cacophonous maze of the Borgo. Cesare had makeshift wooden firesteps slung up around his garden walls, which his guards accessed by means of rope ladders so the walls took on the aspect of the high sides of a ship ready for boarding. The towpath which ran between the palace grounds and the Tiber was patrolled by men with dogs, and several complaints were received from bargemen whose horses had been savaged. In the garden itself, he allowed his pet leopards free rein, and they were irritable after the journey from Nepi, bouncing over pitted roads on the back of a cart.

Cesare himself went armed at all times, even, said those who might or might not know, sleeping with his sword on his pillow. He began to wear a ring I had never seen before whose cameo setting formed the hinged lid to a tiny compartment which, it was rumoured, contained the legendary poison called cantarella. We used to laugh about cantarella, which was supposed to have been devised by Donna Lucrezia for disposing of her first husband, Giovanni Sforza.

"Well," Cesare would say, punning on the poison's name, "a milksop like Sforza might well be killed by a blow from a mushroom." But now, thinking back, I could not recall he had ever actually denied its existence.

And looking at him, I wondered whether he kept it about him to use on his enemies or himself. The fine skin beneath his eyes had begun to resemble ink-stained parchment and his eyelids were pleated with weariness like those of a much older man. Lines like deep scars ran from his nose to the corners of his mouth. I doubt he slept, even when he did finally retire to bed as dawn was beginning to overpower the magic of candlelight and the city's bells struck up the call to Prime. His imagination was too agile; even an unsheathed sword on his pillow and armed guards at his doors and windows could not ward off all the terrible possibilities that must have been whirling around his mind, the spectres of failure lurking in unlit corners, the loneliness, the temptation of death. I suppose there were women for the loneliness, but now I can see they would only have made it worse.

Yet to the outside world he kept up the smiling mask of optimism. The builders who had erected the firesteps and checked for weak spots in the palace walls were kept on to resume the work of modernisation which had been abandoned on the death of his father. Wherever Cesare went, he was shadowed by his clerk of works cradling a stack of thumbed and dog-eared plans, trailing a flow of questions and observations about stable buildings with hypocausts, flushing systems for privies, windows for the library and whether or not a revolving studiolo could be constructed with mechanics to keep pace with the daily transit of the sun. The palace itself seemed to be infected with the same sense of shifting impermanence as the household it sheltered. You might walk into a room one day, only to find yourself teetering on the edge of a cliff of brick rubble the next. Walls appeared and disappeared and reappeared in new formations as though performing a strange, slow, dusty dance. Candelabra of Venetian glass hung from the ceilings in linen shrouds, like the chrysalises of giant moths. Figures in half-painted frescoes seemed in one light to have the energy of Adam struggling out of the mud, yet in another were ghosts fading back into the pale plaster. The house breathed fumes of quicklime, catching in our throats and making our eyes stream.

As the builders and painters and carpenters remodelled his palace, Cesare worked to rebuild his wasted body. He wrestled daily with the African giant he kept for the purpose and spent hours at target practice with bow and arquebus or fencing with his master-at-arms. He organised *calcio* matches among his guards and the men of the household, with himself as one team captain and Don Jofre, wheezing and grumbling and stopping frequently to drink from a flask of grappa, at the head of the other. Then he decided the players should toughen their feet by playing without shoes, because as soon as the new pope's coronation had taken place they would be marching back to the Romagna under the banner of the papal gonfalonier. He had already dispatched Michelotto with an advance guard to Rocca Soriana.

What salves we had for cuts and blisters were quickly used up and every spare chemise or worn-out shirt had been torn into strips for bandages, and the master of horse was doubtful he could acquire enough mules or ox-carts to transport the lame north when the time came. Besides, what sort of army journeyed on carts with feet bound like the courtesans of Cathay? The men's health also suffered from the amount of betting that went on, resulting in accusations of match fixing and fights which led to an array of cracked ribs and broken noses, and one man who almost died of a stab wound to the lung.

Eventually his serjeant-at-arms, with much muttering and head shaking about the duke's state of mind, asked me if I could persuade Cesare to put a stop to the games as he, it seemed, could not. The one constant in the makeshift world enclosed by the high, blind walls of San Clemente was my strange non-relationship with Cesare, the circle of questions unasked and unanswered which to those outside it looked like a love affair.

"You speak to him; he'll listen to you," people said, and I wanted to believe them.

He was in his garden. I could not see him as I peered through the sunlit crack in one of the three doors opening from the ground floor salon on to the garden, but I knew he was there because of the number of men at arms standing watchfully among the statues and the topiary. He had many shadows, as though he needed them to prove his substance. I pushed the door cautiously a little wider, telling myself not to be stupid. If Cesare's guards were unconcerned, the leopards must be safely chained for once. One of the men turned sharply as I stepped out under the cloisters, his hand shifting to the pommel of his sword. The hand was bandaged, I noticed, with dark stripes of blood soaking through.

"It's Violante," I said, hoping I spoke loud enough, for my throat was still dry at the prospect of the leopards.

"He's in the rose garden," the man replied, and looked as though he was going to say more but then thought better of it and turned away from me to watch in the direction of the kitchen garden with its wall of espaliered peach trees whose fruit lay for the most part rotten and crawling with wasps. Stepping cautiously to avoid the dung from the leopards, whose stink was sharp and persistent, I made my way to the rose garden.

Cesare was sitting on the ground, his back propped against the plinth of a marble bust of Cicero. A late mosquito perched on the orator's noble forehead, and his blind eyes stared out over Cesare's head, lips pressed together in stoic disapproval. As he might well have looked on the Caesar of his own day. Drawing closer, I saw the long, thin blade of a Biscayan knife hanging from Cesare's fingers. It was dark with blood. His hands and his Flemish lace cuffs were caked with a rust of the stuff. I felt the breath leave my body as though I had been hit in the chest. I may even have staggered a little. I thought he was dead, that his daemon had returned and taken the Visayan knife and plunged it into his belly.

I could not move. Should I call the guards? Would they think I had murdered him? Had one of them done it? They were not all men who had been with us in Nepi. Those who had stayed behind might easily have been bought by their master's enemies while his back was turned and his death from the fever expected daily. Footprints. I must hunt for footprints in the soil scattered with dead rose petals.

As I stood transfixed by my indecision, Cesare turned his head and looked at me.

"Violante." His tone was dull and disinterested, as though I were inevitable. I shook with relief. Unaware of how I came to be there, I found myself on my knees at his side, plucking at his sleeve with futile, shaky fingers.

"I thought you were dead. I came out to talk to you about the *calcio* and…Where did all the blood come from? Are you hurt? What happened?" Questions tumbling out of my mouth as inane as the braying of an ass.

"Tiresias." He gestured with his chin towards a point in front of his feet. A heap of white fur and bloody flesh lay there, the soil around it stained crimson.

"Tiresias?" I repeated.

"He must have wandered out here, poor old boy. The leopards got him. There was nothing else for it by the time I found him. I had to…" He slid the knife across his throat, the blade almost grazing his beard. I looked at the dead dog, saw the cut, clean and beautiful, among the tatters of flesh and fur left by the leopards' claws.

"You didn't let him suffer. And he was very old."

"Born the same month my father was made pope." There was a catch in his voice, as though he was trying not to cry. His eyes, I noticed now, were bloodshot, but then, everybody's were on account of the builders' limekiln. "I should have had him drowned, but I thought a blind dog might make a good truffle hound. More acute sense of smell, you know? So I kept him. And he did."

"You gave him a good life. The old pass. We live on. It's the way of things."

"Yes." He sighed, and the new air in his lungs seemed to bring him to his senses. He wiped his knifeblade on his sleeve and leaned forward to return it to the sheath attached to the back of his belt, then examined his blood-caked hands and stained cuffs with an air of mild vexation. "I am going to Vespers with my mother this afternoon," he said. "I had better change. I shall ask Bernardino to design him a tomb," he added as he got to his feet and pulled me up after him, leaving tiny flakes of the old dog's blood on my sleeve. "He's in one of Bernardino's paintings, you know, in the big fresco he did over the door in the Sala dei Santi, the one with me as the emperor and Lucrezia as Saint Catherine. Tiresias is at the feet of Juan's horse, looking up at Juan adoringly, which only a blind dog would do." He laughed. I responded with a cautious smile, never sure what Cesare's feelings were towards his murdered brother.

He had taken to attending Mass regularly, most often in the company of his mother, in her family chapel at Santa Maria del Popolo, where Juan was buried. The *avvisi* opined that his own brush with death had sharpened his conscience; Cesare's men tore them down from the Pasquino and set them alight in front of the crowds who gathered around the statue each day to discuss the latest gossip. It was impossible to know whether this was done at Cesare's command, or without his knowledge.

One morning, as I was sitting in the garden with Girolamo, watching his efforts to roll himself over on to his front, I overheard raised voices coming from the house.

"But if I leave the gesso now it will dry and the whole wall will have to be re-plastered before I can start again." I recognised the Mantuan accent of the little painter, Bernardino, summoned back to Rome by Monna Vannozza to decorate the walls of Cesare's chapel.

"God's work must come first."

"Painting is God's work. How else are your congregations to understand what you prattle on about in Latin if they have no pictures to look at?"

"Wonderful though your frescoes are, Ser Bernardino, you must admit that the duke's desire to make confession is little short of miraculous."

"I'd be careful what you say, priest."

"And you want to be careful what you hear, painter, for you are not protected by the confessional and I dare say there are some in Rome who would go to very…creative lengths to find out what the duke might have to confess. A wall of spoiled gesso would be of less consequence to you than a set of smashed fingers."

Then, with a string of triumphant gurgles, Girolamo finally flopped over on to his belly and lay beaming up at me, one cheek squashed against the blanket on which he lay, and by the time I returned my attention to the argument, the speakers had moved out of my hearing. But their words stayed with me, and the silences between them, and I could not help wondering how Cesare would break the silence, what he would choose to confess.

Certainly, in the coming days, he behaved like a man from whom a burden had been lifted, though privately I believed it was the resumption of a responsibility which had cheered him rather than being relieved of one. The new pope was crowned, and, as he had promised, he returned to Cesare the white lance of gonfalonier and captain general of his army. Though the Orsini and their partisans still prowled outside the Borgo like wolves around the edges of a fire, Cesare announced that he would give a party to celebrate, and to thank those who had supported him through his difficulties. The builders and decorators now worked around the clock, hammers pounding like massive heartbeats, new-laid marble floors flushed and shimmering with torchlight, dust everywhere, dulling the stars and choking the moon.

Whole carcasses of beef and boar, shoals of fish of all kinds, and flocks of fowls were swallowed up in the maw of the kitchens. A papal tiara materialised, made from almond paste set with jewels made from tiny pieces of crystallised fruits, and a giant pyramid of gilded duck eggs containing spice *bottifacci,* which had to be constructed in the dining hall, despite the presence of carpenters working on the ceiling bosses. I dare say as many woodshavings as leaves of gold found their way into the confection, though in the end, as things turned out, it was probably eaten by the kitchen staff, who would not have complained.

A chef who suggested oil flavoured with truffles in which to stew hares was summarily dismissed, as Cesare had declared he would never eat truffles again since the death of Tiresias. A new chef was hired who brought with him a small wooden spice box which he never let out of his sight; the spitboy who took his fancy said he even slept with it fastened across his chest by a leather thong, "just like a Jew with his boxes of spells on his head and arms." A rumour began to spread that it contained the beans of the cocoa plant, much prized by the savages of the New World and used by them in their religious ceremonies. This was followed by a darker rumour that Cesare aimed to conceal a poison in the beans, for as no one would know how they should taste, no one would be able to say they tasted strange.

Cesare had never looked less like poisoning anybody. He directed the operations of his household with gusto and good humour, mediating with all his old diplomatic skill between bickering chefs and quarrelsome painters. He auditioned musicians and inspected new recruits to the papal army, and spent hours cooped up with Don Jofre and a jug of the strong wine from Avignon that was his particular favourite, devising spectacles to entertain and astonish his guests.

Suddenly we were all sent for to witness one of these. We assembled in the dining hall, crammed in awkwardly around scaffolding poles, work benches, and paint pots, while Cesare and his brother mounted a platform suspended by pulleys from the ceiling which was then winched up a little way so everyone had a clear view. They had with them a shallow dish set over a brazier and several rabbit carcasses, already gutted and stuffed. Girolamo, caught by the buzz of excitement in the room, squealed and wriggled in my arms like a little piglet; I had by now given up trying to swaddle him for he would simply scream until he was unbound. Monna Vannozza, who might easily have returned to her own house now Cesare had been confirmed as gonfalonier but had chosen to stay at San Clemente, frowned in our direction before her own sons' antics captured her attention.

Jofre laid one rabbit in the dish. The onlookers fell silent. The rabbit began to sizzle and a smell of frying meat mingled with odours of paint and sawdust and unwashed bodies. A murmur of conversation resumed and grew louder, like a tide coming in. Jofre turned to Cesare, who looked puzzled, then vexed, passing a hand repeatedly across the dense, dark cap of hair which now covered his head. He muttered something to Jofre, who took up a pair of tongs and was about to lift the rabbit from the dish when gasps from the front of the crowd made the rest of us jostle and crane our necks for a better view. Clutching my baby firmly under one arm, I used the other to steady myself as I stepped up on to a low cross pole and looked out over the others' heads.

The rabbit flipped in the dish like a landed fish, its belly convulsed with ripples and tremors which increased in vigour until the legs were lifting and falling in a mad parody of running. Jofre let out a great whoop of laughter and did a little jig which set the platform swinging and spilled a few embers into the crowd. Cesare, hanging on to the pulley rope to steady himself, wore a grin like that of a small boy absorbed in pulling the wings off a fly.

Then there was a loud bang. A woman screamed and Girolamo began to cry. Both men leapt backwards and Cesare's free hand flew to the pommel of his sword. Jofre lost his footing and fell into the arms of the buxom woman who had charge of the laundry, and then looked happily inclined to stay in her embrace as he watched Cesare regain his footing and peer cautiously into the now empty dish.

"What happened?" called Jofre.

"Damned if I know."

"Well I do," called a voice from the floor. "The rabbit exploded. I've got half-cooked meat all over me and...silver rain drops?"

"Mercury," said Cesare. "You put mercury in the belly of the rabbit, then cook it, and it leaps as if it's still alive. I wanted to see if it worked before trying it out on my guests."

"Oh really," said Monna Vannozza, turning to leave, the throng parting before her. I looked at my baby's tear-stained face and wondered how long it would be before he was contriving jokes and I was failing to see the humour of them because all I could see was the danger, the awful fragility of his life.

"Is he all right? I'm sorry if he was frightened." Cesare's voice, close now. I looked down from my vantage point at his upturned face, both remorseful and amused. He held out his hand and steadied me as I jumped down. "I had no idea mercury did that when it got hot. I've only come across it warmed before, in the baths Torella prescribed for me." He cleared his throat. "The pills...? They are working?"

"I am quite well, thank you."

"Good. Yes, I remember Sandro Farnese, you know, Giulia's brother, telling me he'd seen this trick done with chickens and I'd always fancied trying it." He grinned his boy's grin, and kept hold of my hand so I had no option but to go with him as he left the dining hall. I felt the eyes of the household on my back, jostling me with their speculations, and wrestled against the temptation to whirl around and shout at them. *This means nothing*, I would say. *I am no different from any of you. Leave me alone. Stop giving me hope.*

But I said nothing. I loved the warmth of his hand and its firm grip, and the whisper of my shoulder brushing his upper arm, and how I matched my steps to his as we walked. At the foot of the stairs leading up to his private apartments he paused and said, "I have work to do now, but I was wondering. After the party, will you have supper with me? Privately?" He nodded in the direction of the upstairs rooms. My throat squeezed shut with excitement. Unable to speak, I tried to smile, uncertain if my body would obey me even that far.

Cesare gave me a quizzical look, eyebrows raised. "Is that a yes?"

"Yes," I managed, in a strangled squawk, and fled before I would be obliged to say anything else.

⟨☙⟩

There were to be no women guests at Cesare's party, in deference to the cardinals he had invited he said, wearing his new piety on his sleeve like a lady's favour. *Because there is hard business to be done*, was what he meant. *Because Pius is old and feeble and Della Rovere still prowls around my house like a hungry wolf.* My own preparations, however, were as intense and frenetic as though I were to be the guest of honour.

A suitable gown was my most pressing requirement. The skirt and bodice I had taken from Donna Lucrezia's discarded wardrobe at Nepi were showing signs of wear, the skirt hem frayed and dusty, the bodice milk-stained. But I had neither time nor money to acquire anything new. The memory of all the dresses and jewels I had left in Ferrara nagged at me, made me ache for a while with impotent frustration before I shook myself free of my inertia and set about begging and borrowing what I could from the other women in the household. I pretended it was simply a matter of needing a change of clothes while I cleaned and mended those I had brought from Nepi, but no one was fooled; they had all seen Cesare holding my hand; they had all seen us talking at the foot of his private stairs.

Some sulked and refused to help; others caught my excitement and together we set to work with needle and thread and what we could scrounge from our own resources, barter for in the markets, or steal from owners sunk in self-pity. Since the death of Tiresias, Cesare had ordered his leopards confined to their cages once more, so on fine days a group of us would sit in the garden, with Camilla and Girolamo, and sometimes Giovanni, playing on a rug in the centre of our circle as we stitched and gossiped. A taut, singing thread of possibility bound us. It was easy to tell what the others were thinking from the fever in their eyes and the flights of fancy in their conversation. I might have my turn this time, but what about the next, and the time after that? Their sultan had signified his intent to visit the harem, and they had begun jostling for position like pigeons in an overcrowded loft.

I did not mind. I could afford to be generous. One afternoon, Fatima offered to read my fortune from the *tarocchi*. As everyone else then began to clamour for their own reading, she kept it simple, using only the Major Arcana in a three-card spread. She turned up first The High Priestess, with her Torah in her lap, second The Lovers, and finally The Emperor; you did not need to be an expert to see what was signified. So I scarcely listened to her interpretation; I refused to see the look in her eyes as she spoke of choices and dualities and the fine line between wisdom and madness, and how power cannot always be controlled.

On the day before the party, I scrounged a lemon from the kitchens, squeezed its juice into a basin of water, and washed my hair with a sliver of rose-scented soap I had been hoarding because it was of a make favoured by Angela and reminded me of her. I braided my hair while it was still wet to put a little curl into it, then sat before the brazier in the little room Girolamo and I had to ourselves and rubbed the lemon shells over my skin to whiten it while my hair dried. My face and forearms were unacceptably brown from all the riding and walking I had done since leaving Medelana.

On the afternoon of the party itself, while Cesare's guests arrived in a chaos of shouting grooms, jangling harness, and the thud of litters banged down on the flagstones, I stripped and washed my body carefully with the remainder of the soap. Its musky perfume made me yearn for Angela. How much more fun this would be if she were here with her outspoken advice on the arts of love, her long, strong fingers whose tips were always slightly calloused from her guitar playing riffling through my jewellery box, her way of whirling around the room with different combinations of skirts and bodices, chemises and fichus held up against her while she decided what looked best. I glanced down at the untidy triangle of dark hair masking my woman's parts and the down on my calves. It was as bad under my arms. I needed hot wax and scissors, but had neither. Besides, if I waxed myself now I would end up looking like a fresh plucked chicken.

"He'd probably make me swallow mercury and put a light under me," I said to my uncomprehending son, who continued to be engrossed in his efforts to push himself up on his arms.

I managed to tidy my garden a little with the aid of a comb and my meat knife, and consoled myself with the thought that darkness would have fallen by the time he...by the time we... And besides, he would probably be a little drunk. I dressed slowly, to eke out the long afternoon, straightening all the tiny bows on my clean linen, smoothing my silk hose, only slightly worn about at the knees. As I tightened my corset, I paid special attention to the way it pushed up my breasts to show them to their best advantage. Although Girolamo was mostly weaned now, I still fed him myself occasionally at night so my breasts remained full and firm and the nipples nicely defined, carrying in their nerve ends the memory of my lover's tongue and fingertips and his strange knowledge of the personal letters of Don Cristoforo Colon.

Finally I stepped into my skirt of primrose satin skimped with gold lace panels, fastened my bodice of apple green brocade, front laced so I could manage it myself, put on the peach silk shoes which pinched my toes only a little, and sat down to wait. For what? What would happen next? Would one of his slaves be sent for me? Did Cesare even know where my room was located in this warren of a palace whose shape seemed to shift day by day? How long would his party last? I tried to estimate the number of courses, and how long each would take, and the entertainments between them, and then how long Cesare would have to spend talking to each of these men, thanking his friends and flattering his enemies. Surely it would all take most of the night and then he would be too exhausted to entertain me to supper. Or he would simply forget he had asked me.

I wished I had some distraction, some needlework or a book to read. I had, for once, allowed Girolamo into the care of Camilla's nurse so I did not even have him to play with or sing to or soothe to sleep as the square of light from my small window dimmed, then flared orange as torches were lit in the courtyard. I got up to light my own candle, pausing by my washing bowl to look at my reflection in the surface of the water as I had no mirror. The water was clouded with a scum of soap so it was like looking at myself through a fog, but even so, even in the flattering glow of my candle and the torchlight from my window, I could see how my features had sharpened and aged in the past few months, how I had come to resemble my mother.

I reared back as though a fist had emerged from the water and punched me. What would my mother think of me, dressed in my low-cut gown and cheap jewellery like a streetwalker. Eli had been right to bar me entry to his house and keep his wife hidden from me. But then again, if my family had not been so eager to exploit my prettiness, I would be a good Jewish wife by now, observing *kashrut*, teaching my children their Torah, lighting my candles on Shabbat. And I was not a whore. I had but one lover, had never so much as glanced at another man, and had given him his only son. To all intents and purposes, and despite his French princess, I was Cesare's wife.

So there was nothing to stop me making my own way to his apartments. I had no need to wait for a summons as if I were some slave girl he might look to for necessary relief. I would simply make my way to his rooms and wait for him, and if he kept me waiting too long I might even send a slave myself to remind him of his obligation.

"Well, no need to ask where you're going in your finery with your hair all crimped." Monna Vannozza. She stood at the foot of the private staircase flanked by two of the Swiss guards like a small crow courted by a brace of parrots. As she looked me up and down in contemptuous silence, I could hear the muffled hubbub of conversation from the dining hall and delicate scents of vanilla and beeswax reached my nose, a combination which to this day makes me think of chestnuts. "I dare say he'll keep you waiting," she went on. "There is more at stake here than your fluttering heart."

"Of course I know that, madama; I am not stupid."

"Yet you put on a good pretence of it. Violante, walk with me a moment." She took my arm, not too firmly but with a demeanour that made it plain she did not expect me to resist, and led me out of earshot of the guards, into an alcove which housed a classical Venus without arms.

"I have spoken to you of the danger I believe you present to my son," she began, "and you have chosen to pursue your own selfish course despite me. Perhaps, then, you will listen if I tell you I believe you and your son are at risk from him." She paused, scratching at the dust caught in the folds of the Venus' draperies with a slightly yellowed nail. "My son is a passionate man, Violante."

I wanted to say, I know, but then I realised. I had seen Cesare angry and wilful; I had known him flirtatious and seductive, and helpless with laughter, but not passionate, never that. He had, it seemed to me now, something cold, detached, and analytical at his core, a kind of personal Dis where all passion would freeze. If he were capable of it, I wanted to find out for myself, not stand beneath a marble Venus and be told by his mother. "I must go," I said.

"Wait, let me finish. This…passion of his, there is no other word for it. It is something very particular, and very deep. Hidden, perhaps, where you do not see it. But I do, and I see it sucking you in. You are like a small boat in the vortex of a sinking ship. Take heed of me. Go back to your own room, I beg you."

If she had spoken as plainly about Cesare's passion as it was her custom to speak about most things, perhaps I would have done as she asked. Perhaps not. This pleading without substance merely aroused my spite. "Did you think taking him off to Mass every morning was going to make him change his ways?" I snapped. "Did you imagine he would be asking Pope Pius to restore his red hat rather than the white lance?"

To my astonishment, she gave a snort of laughter. "I am not a fool, girl, and I understand Cesare a good deal better than you do. He goes to church not to be seen by God but by the men close to our new Holy Father. Pius is as pious does and he surrounds himself with devout servants. I believe Cesare even took Holy Communion with him just before the coronation. I'll wager there was some merriment in Hades that day. I believe it is a measure of Our Lord's compassion my son did not choke on the sacrament."

A measure more, I thought, of Cesare's lack of belief, for anyone who paused to reflect on the notion that the bread and wine were miraculously transformed into a man's flesh and blood when the priest said his words over them was bound to choke. But I was in no mood for theology. "Well, you know how Cesare loves his food. And so I must not keep him waiting for his supper. Excuse me, madama." I pushed past her out of the alcove. Wrong footed by my rudeness, she let me pass.

I need not have worried about keeping Cesare from his supper. Apart from the guard on his door, who recognised what I was there for even if he did not know who I was, and stood aside for me with an unmistakable leer, the private apartments were deserted. A fire burned in the reception room, by whose light I saw a low table spread for two with delicate porcelain and gold cutlery. There were even forks, I noted with some misgivings, for I was not very adept in the use of forks. Don Alfonso had brought some from Venice shortly before I left Ferrara, and though we had all tried them at private dinners in Donna Lucrezia's apartments, most of us had made a pretty poor fist of it and ended up dropping our food in our laps.

I took a spill from an alabaster vase standing on the hearth and lit the candles, trimmed and pristine in an ornate silver-gilt stand. The clean, sweet scent of beeswax mingled with pine resin from the smouldering spill and a wraith of jasmine which set up a starved tingling in my women's parts. I sat down on one of the divans arranged along two sides of the table, my hands squeezed between my thighs to stop them shaking. Desire fluttered in my belly like a trapped moth. Never mind the forks, I thought, for I would have no appetite for food. Wine shimmered honey gold in a crystal jug, but I dared not pour myself a goblet in case I spilled any. I looked around the room in the hope of finding something to distract me.

It was richly furnished, the wall panels decorated with scenes from the life of Caesar, the ceiling studded with gilded bosses which featured bulls and lilies and Saint Peter's keys. A set of ebony chairs inlaid with ivory and mother-of-pearl stood sentinel around the walls, and the divan where I was seated and its companion were upholstered in Alexandrine velvet. A motto was carved into a marble panel set above the fireplace: *Aut Caesar, aut nihil.* Caesar or nothing. Nothing, I thought, casting my eyes once more around the elegant, empty room, a stage awaiting its principle actor.

A log collapsed in the fireplace in a shower of sparks. I raked the embers and tossed in another from the copper log box on the hearth. As the heat intensified and the candles burned down, my eyelids grew heavy, but I had to stay awake. What would Cesare think if he found me asleep? Taking one of the candles from the massive candelabrum I determined to explore. After all, it was only a small set of rooms, and I would easily hear his tread on the stairs, the clatter of arms as his guard came to attention. I would have plenty of time to return to the reception room and arrange myself on the divan as though I had never stirred from it.

The rooms were linked by doors of walnut, first a small bureau containing a work table set with writing materials. A magnifying lens lay on top of an open book, a Euclid by the looks of it, or perhaps a Vitruvius, for it was filled with annotated diagrams and only sparse lines of Latin text. Vitruvius, Donna Lucrezia used to say, was her brother's Bible and guns his Holy Apostles preaching their gospel of power and destruction. There was also a locked book case, its contents chained behind ornate brass grilles, their jewelled bindings giving off a sullen glint in the light of my candle. Such valuable texts had perhaps come from the library at Urbino. The thought sent a frisson of unease through me as I pushed open the next door and found myself on the threshold of my lover's bedroom.

And there I stayed, held fast by an overwhelming sense of intrusion. I felt like a child who has inadvertently stumbled on her parents making love. Why? Was this not where I wanted to be, where Cesare intended me to be? I stared at the bed, its curtains tied back to reveal perfectly plumped pillows, silk sheets and a brocade coverlet turned down at one corner. I longed to lie on it, to lift the sheets and slide under them, to rest my head on the pillows just as he did each night, yet I was barred by its complete impersonality. Not a single crease or indentation betrayed the fact that anyone had ever slept in this bed, dreamed or made love in it, or simply stared into the dark and waited for the night to end. It might almost have been put there along with the gold forks and the new candles, to set the stage for a seduction.

Yet the jasmine scent was stronger here, drawing me into the room. A fire was lit here too, and by its uncertain, flickering light I saw faces gazing down at me from the walls, mocking, impassive, eyeless. They flashed sudden, toothless grins, made soundless screams, pouted at me enigmatically with ruby lips. Though I knew they were hanging from the walls, they seemed nevertheless to be hovering just in front of them, challenging my sense of the possible and bringing to mind Monna Vannozza and her stories of spells and changelings.

But Monna Vannozza was as mad as Don Sigismondo and I knew what they were, these glowing faces. They were masks, gold masks. No doubt they were the masks made by Fidelma's brother and given to Cesare by Donna Isabella. I smiled to imagine her expression if she knew he had used them to decorate his bedroom, that den of mysterious vices. I walked slowly around the walls, holding my candle up to each of them, admiring the wit and delicacy of the worksmanship, the tiny quirks of expression which had made them spring to life in the firelight.

Hanging right beside his bed, where a pious man might hang a crucifix, was a mask shaped like a skull, the jaw articulated with tiny gold pins and set with mother of pearl teeth. A diamond was mounted in one of the canines, giving the skull's grin a certain roguish charm. This death's head had the sort of smile which forced you to smile back. Tomorrow morning, I asked it, reaching up to touch the fine sweep of the cheekbone, will I wake up looking at you? If not tomorrow, one day, you may be sure, the skull replied. The fire popped and spat, the wax in my candle sizzled softly before spilling over on to my hand where it stiffened and dried. The silence left by Cesare's absence blanketed everything as I made my way back to the reception room, carefully closing each door behind me.

How much longer? I crossed to the window and pushed the shutters ajar, but there was nothing to see, nothing to hear except the restless conversation of leaves in a rising wind and beyond them the river slapping against its banks. These rooms overlooked the palace garden, but the entertainment was all indoors this evening due to the lateness of the season. A sudden animal scream pierced the darkness, just a rabbit perhaps, or a water rat, and I thought of the leopards, their lithe, silent bodies, the secret glint of their eyes, the bloody strings of flesh in their teeth. No rest, not in this house. Closing the shutters, replacing my candle in the stand on the table, I sat back down to wait.

☙❧

A taste overshadowed the place between sleeping and waking, something dry and dark and bitter on the tip of my tongue, the inside of my lower lip. I opened my eyes to find the darkness sculpted by candlelight into the shape of a face, Cesare's face, so close to mine it was little more than an abstraction of light and shade. But my body recognised him, drawing itself around him like a closing fist.

"The powder of the cocoa beans," he whispered, "a peace offering."

I licked my lip, discovering with my tongue the tip of the finger which had opened my mouth, tasting salt now, mingled with the strangeness of the cocoa grains. "What hour is it?" I mumbled, still half asleep.

"No idea. The fifth or sixth maybe? It's the middle of the night in any case. I could not get away sooner. The Florentine ambassador arrived very late with some story about an amorous adventure that had gone wrong, and there is much fence mending to be done between me and Florence. Besides," he added, straightening up from where he had been squatting in front of me, stretching and yawning, "I like Messer Niccolo. He has a quick wit."

I sat up, smoothing my hair and skirt, dabbing the remains of the cocoa from my lips with a fingertip.

"What do you think of it?"

"Strange. Bitter. It tastes like…tree bark. What do you do with it?"

"Apparently there was some in the wine sauce for the hare, but I could not taste it. That is why I had this ground separately." He tapped the lid of a small spice box lying on the table next to the salt.

"You know what they will say? That you have brought it up here to mix with poisons. The career of the cocoa bean will be over before it has begun." We laughed and he sat down beside me, his long legs stretched out in front of him and crossed at the ankles.

"The cocoa bean as metaphor. Are you hungry?" I shook my head. He poured two cups of wine. "Drink then. You were sleeping with your mouth open. It must be dry." I felt myself beginning to blush, and he caressed my burning cheek with one finger, tracing a line like a duelling scar from my temple to the corner of my mouth. "Don't worry," he said, "you looked gorgeous. I almost didn't want to wake you, but I did really. Music?" His mouth was so close to mine I could feel his breath on my lips, smell wine and cardamom and jasmine. I could see nothing but his eyes, huge and black with a mote of quicksilver somewhere at their heart, but there must have been a musician in the room with us because a lute began to play, a fountain of notes pouring into the hot spring of desire which was dissolving me.

We kissed, first with artifice and then with greed. Something fell off the table and crashed to the floor, then there was more knocking, shouting, scuffling, a thud like the sound of a body hitting the door. The lutenist stopped playing. Cesare was on his feet, dagger drawn. "Back me up," he ordered the lutenist, waiting with his free hand on the door catch until the man had put down his lute, drawn a short sword, and stepped up beside his master. Then Cesare hauled open the door and sprang through it just as Don Jofre fell across the threshold into the room. A kind of lunatic mirth rose up inside me and I began to laugh uncontrollably, though neither of the brothers could see the joke. Cesare looked murderous. He kicked Jofre over on to his back and pinned him there with one foot planted on his breastbone while the lutenist held the point of his sword to Jofre's throat and several men at arms with pikes at the ready blocked off the head of the stairs.

"What is this, brother?" Cesare spat the word brother as though it were the worst insult he could contrive. But what most condemned Jofre was that Cesare spoke to him in Italian rather than the Valencian patois the family reserved to themselves.

"Let me up, Cesare. I mean no harm. It's the pope."

"The pope?" Cesare removed his foot from Jofre's chest and the lutenist lifted his sword point, though he remained on guard and made it clear Don Jofre would be unwise to make any sudden moves. Jofre got cautiously to his feet, rubbing his bruised bones.

"He has been seized with vomiting and a high fever. They say he is dying, Cesare."

Cesare rammed his dagger back into its sheath. "Oh Christ's blood and bones," he bellowed and picked up one of the ebony chairs and hurled it out of the door. The pikemen at the head of the stairs scattered as the chair bounced and whirled down the steps sending out showers of splinters as it went. "Could he not have waited a week?" A second chair followed the first.

"Calm down," said Jofre.

"Calm down?" Cesare seized his brother's beard and twisted it until Jofre was forced to cock his head so sharply he looked almost as though his neck had been broken. "Calm down?" Cesare repeated. "I am mocked and thwarted at every turn and all you can say is calm down. What in God's name have I done to deserve such ill fortune?"

"Where would you like me to begin?" his brother replied with, I thought, scant regard for his own safety. But Cesare's anger had passed, or perhaps he realised he was in danger of making himself hostage to his own rhetoric.

"Send Sassatelli to me, and find me a messenger who can ride fast."

"Last time I saw Sassatelli he was unconscious in the dining hall."

"Then throw a bucket of well water over him and tell him the pope is dying. That should cure his hangover." Turning his back on Jofre his gaze came to rest on me. He looked bewildered, surprised, as though he had entirely forgotten me. "Ah, Violante," he said, passing a hand across his eyes as if trying to wipe me out of his vision.

"You're tired," I said, astonished by my own boldness. "Nothing's going to happen tonight. You can't send out messengers in the dark. Leave it till morning."

To my further amazement, he seemed to listen. Taking both my hands he pulled me to my feet and stared at me hard. "What do you want?" he demanded. "Do you want a quick fuck from a man with more pressing matters on his mind? To be treated like some slave girl or back street whore? Or would you like to leave this until better times, when I can give you my full attention? I made you a promise, I seem to remember, in my sister's orange garden. The least you can do is allow me to keep it. Now go, look to my son. I rely on you to keep him out of danger."

❧

I was chasing a beast, something leonine with a dark red mane and flanks dappled with the strange underwater light of a deep forest. I was afraid, but wanted the beast to know I was there so I called out to it. For a time it made no response; I heard nothing but the rasp of my own breath and the rhythmic thud of the beast's paws on the earth floor of the forest. Then suddenly it turned to reveal the face of a golden skull. I walked into one cavernous eye-socket, following a pinpoint of firelight that glimmered at its heart, but it was not a fire; it was the beast's face, grinning a pearly grin. I knew I should run but I was held fast by creeping vines with leaves like sweating palms and tiny suckers which prickled my skin. The beast clenched its jaws around my shoulder and began to shake me.

"You're a mask," I told it.

"I am blind Tiresias," it replied.

"Violante, wake up."

I opened my eyes. A tall figure without a face held my son to its chest, his head cupped in its hand, his orange curls licking its clawed fingers like newly ignited flames.

"It's a dream," I said, though my heart tolled like a warning bell.

"Wake up, girl."

I wanted to stay in my dream and follow the will of the beast, but I could not leave Girolamo in the clutches of something with burning hands and no face. "Give me my son," I screamed. "Give me my son!"

"Here you are." Monna Vannozza held the child out to me, leaning forward so the afternoon light caught her face, all patches of gaunt shadow within the recesses of her stiff hood.

I sat up, pushing my hair out of my eyes, smoothing my tangled skirts.

"We are to go to my house," said Monna Vannozza.

"We? Your house? " I repeated, my mind still torpid with sleep. "Is that the afternoon Angelus? What hour is it?"

"About the twentieth." Too early for the Angelus. "He says he will leave Rome for the Romagna in the morning. He wants us to take the children before he goes, while he still has troops here to protect us."

A sense of dread dropped on me like a wet mantle. "Has the pope died then?" Rome's laws require all soldiers to withdraw from the city in *sede vacante*.

"Not yet, but it is sure to be soon. He can no longer protect Cesare from his enemies. His best hope is to join with Michelotto and wait out the interregnum in his own power base."

I rose, pushed my feet into my shoes, felt a tightness in my breasts that told me Girolamo must be hungry and a pressure on my bladder that made me think I must have been asleep for several hours. I remembered the conversation I had had with him in Nepi, when he had condemned such a move as the coward's way out and teased me for my lack of understanding. "I want to go with him," I said. "Surely Girolamo would be safer out of Rome."

Girolamo grizzled and butted his head impatiently against my chest until I sat down again on the edge of the bed and put him to my breast.

"There will be fighting," she said, looking with a tight, wistful smile at her grandson's plump cheeks and the vigorous working of his jaw as he suckled. "He tells me he has got wind of a meeting at the Venetian ambassador's house last night. Annibale Bentivoglio was there, and Giovanni Sforza, and some people of the Manfredis. With his customary irony he says he thinks it unlikely they were there to draft a paeon of support for him."

So that was why he had come so late. "I remember Lord Annibale," I said stupidly, "from our journey to Ferrara." Hard to imagine that bluff, gallant man plotting an assassination. Yet our brief stay there, where Giulio and Angela first met, and Donna Lucrezia played the guileless inamorata to her new husband, seemed just as unreal.

"A pity my daughter could not do more to win him over."

The bell still tolled, a thin, mournful clang. "What is that?" I asked again.

"Pay it no mind," Monna Vannozza commanded. "It is none of our business," she added, as much to convince herself as me, I felt.

It quickly became clear there were many others who were not to be so easily deterred. As I gathered together Girolamo's and my few possessions, the sound of raised voices and running feet swelled on the other side of the door. When we stepped out into the narrow passage, we found ourselves swept along with the rest.

Everyone rushed towards the main courtyard. We joined a throng of bakers and secretaries, priests and snivelling laundrymaids, all elbowing and jostling one another in the narrow passages and old, low doorways that lurked behind the modern façade. As we drew closer, the clanging of the bell grew louder, until I realised it must be the bell in San Clemente's own campanile.

Which meant the palace was under attack.

We burst out into the cloister bordering the courtyard on the crest of a wave of small boys, choristers and drummers and spit boys. Cesare stood on the parapet of the well, surrounded by a mill of hostile, shouting armed men. A thicket of blades glittered above their heads in the midday sun which shone straight down into the courtyard and re-ignited the fires in Cesare's close-cropped curls. I felt my stomach tighten with a mixture of terror and longing.

"You want to kill me?" He did not seem to be shouting, yet his voice was clearly audible above the grumbling discontent of his mutinous troops. "Come on, then. I am alone and unarmed. Now's your chance." What he said was not strictly true. As my mind began to sort out what my eyes were seeing, I realised the well was ringed by a cordon of the gigantic Swiss lancers who formed Cesare's personal bodyguard. But the way he put one hand to his throat and loosened his shirt collar challenged all of us who were watching him with his vulnerability. No one saw the lancers; no one noticed the way they bunched around their leader and lowered the points of their lances. All any of us would remember from that moment was the triangle of fragile skin at the base of his throat.

I heard Monna Vannozza suck in her breath. She crossed herself, jabbing at her forehead and breast and shoulders with rigid, fervent fingers. "What is he thinking?" she muttered. "They'll cut him to pieces."

The air whistled. As if Monna Vannozza's words had conjured it, a long knife carved a slender arc across the square of sky bounded by the palace walls. Sunlight poured over it, bounced off it like water from hot iron. I thought it would hang in the air forever, while the eyes of the now silent mutineers were raised towards it in a parody of prayer and Cesare flung his arms out to his sides with a cry that sounded almost exultant. I closed my eyes, smelled sweat and cooking fat, the sharp stink of Monna Vannozza's fear and the milk souring my bodice. I seemed to fall forwards, hunched over my son, my hand cupping his soft skull, his fingers tangled in my hair, pulling, pulling me down...

When I opened my eyes again, I found myself kneeling, Monna Vannozza's hand gripping my sleeve. "It's a miracle," she breathed, "a miracle."

The courtyard was empty except for Cesare, now sitting on the well parapet, his elbows resting on his knees, hands clasped at the back of his bowed neck, and two of his Swiss lancers who were engaged in sliding the great iron bars across the main gate. A glint of steel showed me the knife resting on the parapet beside him. The body of a man lay face down, no more than two arms' lengths from the well, with the blade of an axe half buried in his spine.

"What happened?"

"The knife fell short, then the gate was opened somehow and the Swiss chased them all out into the street."

As we got to our feet, a man shouldered his way past us and our crowd of little boys struck dumb and stone still as a flock of grubby marble Cupids. Calling out to Cesare, he raced across the courtyard.

"Now what?" asked Monna Vannozza. Cesare leapt to his feet, as the man gesticulated urgently in the direction of Saint Peter's Square. Although most of what he said was inaudible to me, I did hear the word Orsini, then Cesare let out a string of oaths that caused Monna Vannozza to hiss with disapproval, and called for armour and a horse. Once again the courtyard filled up with soldiers, more of the Swiss this time, and a contingent led by Don Jofre, wearing no protection but a breastplate and looking nervous on a skittish horse. After some altercation between the brothers, Cesare took the horse and spurred it at the palace gate as the men who had just barred it opened it again. Sword drawn, he rode out into the street at the head of what looked more like a rabble than an army. The gate was already closed again by the time Cesare's squire, Juanito, who was an elderly man, though loyal and fastidious, arrived in the courtyard with his armour.

It was the man who had been ringing the tocsin in the campanile, and had seen everything, who eventually explained to us what had happened. The guards who had driven the mutineers out into the Piazza San Clemente had discovered that, at almost the same moment, a hostile contingent of the Orsini and their followers had broken through the gates of the Borgo and were advancing on the palace. Many of the mutineers had been cut down, and some had gone over to the Orsini, but others had swung back to Cesare's side when he appeared among them, swinging his sword above his head, yelling that he had never intended to die in his bed anyway.

No, I thought, with the image of his bared throat and the knife spinning across the blue sky fresh in my mind, but he would not mind dying out there, in the great square where he had once danced with bulls, under the golden eye of Caesar. I was angry. How could he be so reckless and self-indulgent? Clearly his sentimental feelings towards his children at Nepi had been inspired by nothing more than his weakness and now he was strong again he was content to strike any bargain he liked with his daemon and to hell with the lot of us.

"He's a child himself," I told Girolamo furiously, but Girolamo merely turned his cool, black gaze on me for a few seconds then fell asleep.

I could not bear to dwell on what might be happening beyond the palace gates, so I went out to the garden and walked down towards the river, as far from the street side of the building as I could go. I found myself in the rose garden, though even there the din of the fighting infiltrated the air to compete with the drowsy fizzing of late bees and the cries of the bargemen for whom it mattered not one whit who was pope as long as Romans still needed wheat and olives, cheese and sausages and cork stoppers for their wine bottles. Somebody had raked over the spot where Tiresias's blood had soaked into the soil, leaving a patch of earth bare of weeds and fallen petals. After the bullfights they used to scatter sawdust over the square to soak up the blood, then sweep the pale pink clumps into barrows and cart them off to be burned in the refuse dumps outside the walls. I hoped there was somebody who would do as much for Cesare when he fell.

❧

"Dry your tears, girl."

I was unaware I had been crying, though now Monna Vannozza drew attention to the fact, I could feel the moisture cooling on my cheeks in the breeze coming up from the river.

"They are safe." Her face, framed by the severe, dark hood, looked old, the skin falling in fine, dry pleats around her mouth and nose. "They are in Sant'Angelo."

I felt suddenly weak and shaky with relief, and almost dropped Girolamo before I collected myself. "What happened?"

"They were forced to retreat, but they managed to get into the Vatican by the door in the basilica and then through the underground passage to the castle. I dare say Pius wouldn't have known they were there until they were already out the other side." We exchanged guarded smiles, each no doubt shielding our personal memories of hidden doors and secret passages, cold air saturated with ancient fears and romances. I wondered, briefly, what La Fiammetta was doing now, to whom she had transferred her favours when Valentino fell. "He has negotiated a safe conduct for his family. For us. We are to join him in Sant'Angelo immediately."

The pope died two days later, but already life in the old castle was almost unbearable. Despite improvements made by Cesare's father, the quarters were still as cramped as Cesare had described them to me in the orange garden in Ferrara, and the cries of the prisoners in the dungeons reached our hearing through the thick walls with an eerie persistence, both distant and immediate. So we allowed ourselves to be infected by the optimism with which Cesare initially greeted the prospect of a new election. He recalled Michelotto from Rocca Soriana, and other troops who had been in service with the French, and the cardinals graciously allowed him to keep them. He had made the last election from his sickbed in Nepi. Now he was fit again, and back at the centre of things, he would make the next one too. The round of embassies began again, with formal processions of retinues across the Sant'Angelo bridge, and hard negotiations in the dank underground passage between the castle and the Vatican.

Then news began to drift in from the Romagna, messengers apologetic and ragged who begged the duke to understand their position. They had been told he was imprisoned in Sant'Angelo. Della Rovere was bound to win the election; they had heard he had the support of both France and Spain. How could they hold out? What guarantees were there that the duke could protect them? They had to think of their citizens' welfare. Of course their old vicars were greedy and capricious tyrants, but you remember the old saying: better the devil you know... They beseeched the duke to be merciful. The duke had them thrown into the dungeons or, if he thought the right people were watching, had them garotted and flung into the river.

When no one was watching, he would sit for long periods sunk in an untouchable stillness, his eyes unfocused, his hands empty in his lap, and I knew his daemon weighed heavy on him then and longed to be able to exorcise it. I hoped he might renew his invitation to a private supper, but privacy was a commodity in short supply in Sant'Angelo except, I suppose, for certain of the prisoners in the dungeons below us. He seemed to take more solace in the company of Giovanni than that of anybody else. His patience with his little brother's whining boredom made me envious, but also hopeful that when Girolamo was older he would be as happy to teach him card tricks, answer questions about training dogs and what stars are made of and how long it takes to travel to the kingdom of Prester John.

He even took Giovanni with him to a meeting in the Vatican with Della Rovere and some other cardinals. A change of scene would do the boy good, he said. He was seven years old now, and it was time he started to put his education to some practical use, he said. I watched them ride back over the bridge, Giovanni sitting up in front of Cesare while Cesare led his brother's pony. Giovanni appeared to be asleep, his cheek lolling against Cesare's chest. While he waited in the courtyard for a groom to lift the little boy down from the saddle, I saw him bend to kiss the top of the child's head in a gesture of naked tenderness that made me look away, as though I had caught him out in something secret and shameful.

Two days later, Della Rovere was elected pope and, with an irony which was lost on none of us, took the name Julius. His predecessor, Cesare seemed to remember from his theological studies at Pisa, had been a saint revered for his role in the resolution of the Arian controversy, but he doubted that was what had moved Della Rovere to take a name most famously paired with that of Caesar. Then, with a thin, hard smile, he disappeared into the little dressing room he used for private audiences, followed by Agapito, sharpening a pen as he went.

It was after dark when Cesare emerged. I had settled Girolamo for the night and was setting out platters and cups for the evening meal. There was a curious egalitarianism about our household. Cramped as we were in our few thick-walled, low-ceilinged rooms, we all ate together, men and women, children, soldiers and their officers, and the few servants who had accompanied us from San Clemente. Most of us even shared our sleeping quarters, with blankets hanging from lines strung across the largest room to divide the men from the women and children. Only Cesare and Monna Vannozza had bed chambers to themselves.

Yet until Cesare came into the hall, I was alone. Camilla's nurse was watching the babies and Monna Vannozza had gone to collect bread from the kitchen. He said nothing, merely nodded then stood watching me until I felt a hot flush creeping up my neck and cheeks and down to the tops of my breasts. I fumbled my work and dropped a drinking horn on the floor. Stepping forward, he bent to pick it up and placed it in a bracket on the long table. "Leave the rest," he said, "and come up to the roof. I want to talk to you."

Discarding my pile of cups and dishes, I wiped my sweating palms on my skirt and followed him as he ducked through a deep, recessed door and ran up the staircase which wound like a twisted spine through the centre of the old keep. As I struggled with my skirts on the narrow steps, worn ice-smooth by centuries of footfalls, I loved him for his surefootedness. A soldier to his bones, he was at home here, whatever he might say, in this grizzled old fortress whose walls were mortared with stories of heroes.

He crossed the roof, strewn with rubble and bird droppings, to a firestep facing out over the river and the city, and the Vatican.

"I come up here to breathe," he said, resting his arms on the parapet of the wall. As I stepped up to join him, the guards who had been patrolling that sector, seeing their lord was keeping company with a woman, melted away into the darkness. A few lights still glimmered below us, the links of those reckless or desperate enough to be abroad after dark, the spill of lamplight from tavern doorways, the small fires of the people who lived under the bridges, and the braziers of the bargees hove to for the night. The Vatican itself was in darkness.

The moon shone in fits and starts, between deep furrows of cloud seeded with small, distant stars. There was a thin, penetrating cold to the wind which made me wish I had brought my cloak. Or dared press my body up against his for warmth.

"I am moving back to the Vatican in the morning," he told me, fiddling with his cameo ring.

"Is that your own wish? Or the pope's?"

"I am his gonfalonier. His wish is mine."

"So you gave him your support in the end."

"Did I have any choice? The college rejected D'Amboise and there was no chance of getting another Spaniard elected." He paused for a second. Perhaps he was hoping I would respond with some flattering platitude about his father. "You will return to the Vatican as my guest," he went on. "That's what Della Rovere said. I am to be his guest, he assures me, yet he does not request my company, he commands it. Guest is a word with many interpretations. Context is everything."

"You might turn it around," I said, trying to sound confident. "In Latin, the emphasis comes at the end of a phrase, not the beginning."

He gave a grim laugh. "Julius Caesar. How do you think he felt on the Ides? Did he know what he was walking into, or did he trust Brutus? Della Rovere has a reputation for being a man of his word."

"So did Brutus." I wish now I had said something different, but at the time it seemed right, and we both laughed, and he praised my wit, saying it was as well honed as a man's.

"Well we must hope Della Rovere is a better man than Brutus, or at least more fearful of ending up in Satan's maw. But Violante..." He turned to face me, just as the moon emerged from behind the clouds, casting his features in marble. "Though we hope for the best we must plan for the worst."

I felt a shrinking in my chest.

"The children will go to my mother's country house at Caprarola. When I am re-established in Cesena, I will send for them."

"Your mother and I have been getting on better," I said, and immediately I was ashamed of my words, the utter untruthfulness of them, their false, brittle hopefulness.

"You will not be going with them."

The impossibility of this began to well up in me like a hot tide of nausea. How could he continue talking in that calm, decisive tone, as though he were ordering a disposition of troops or planning the details of a carnival prank?

"There is something else I want you to do for me. You will return to Ferrara, and give my sister this." As he pulled the cameo ring off his finger, the scream broke from me, a blast of noise which made him step back, lose his footing, and almost fall over the parapet. In a pinpoint of calm at the heart of my fury, I thought of pushing him. Perhaps I did lay hands on him, for the next thing I knew, he was holding me, one arm across my back, the other hand cupping my head, pressing my cheek against his chest so I could feel his heart beating and the gold threads decorating his doublet cutting into my flesh. Like a hawk newly hooded, in the darkness of his embrace I was suddenly docile, helpless, bound to him by blind trust.

Except that I was not a hawk; I was a woman threatened with the loss of her child. The image of Monna Vannozza with Girolamo in her arms, her face buried in the shadow of her hood, his fiery curls caught between her clawed fingers, rose up between Cesare and I, forcing me out of his grasp.

"No!" I shouted, ducking under his arm. He grabbed my wrist, but I twisted free and began to run. A guard barred my path with his pike. I heard Cesare, somewhere behind me and a little out of breath, order the man back to his post. The door to the stairs was in sight, still ajar as we had left it. If I could slip through and shut it behind me that would give me just enough time to grab my baby and run. I would go to the river, find a boat bound for Ostia. I would go home to Spain, for there was nothing to keep me here. Better to have my faith tested by the Inquisition than to give up my son. Perhaps I might even steal a barge horse and get out of the city tonight.

Then a sudden gust of wind banged the door shut. I hurled myself at it, but the moon disappeared among the clouds and I could not find the catch. I scrabbled and pushed, but my fingers were weak and out of control, my weight too slight to make any impression on a hand's thickness of oak.

"All right." He was whispering in my ear, his breath hot on my neck, his hands braced across my ribs. He would break them, I thought, if need be, and think no more of it than of cracking open the carcass of a bird at dinner. Then I realised, with a mutinous sense of pleasure, that he had slid one hand upwards until it cupped my breast. "You win. Your baby is safe. Now, come to bed."

Almost as though he had ordered it thus, the moon slid out from behind the clouds and shone on the door latch. Still holding me with one arm, he lifted it with his free hand, kicked open the door, then hoisted me off my feet and carried me down the stairs. Did we pass through the hall that way, under the various gazes of the people dining there? I do not think so. I have an impression still of some narrow, dank passage, unlit and unevenly floored. I feel the magical brush of cobwebs and smell cold stone, and remember opening my eyes on a room as snug and richly decorated as a chamber of the heart of love.

He laid me gently on the bed, then sat beside me and tugged off his boots. "Do you," he asked, as he unlaced my bodice and kissed the warm place between my breasts, "still take Torella's pills?"

I nodded, unable to speak.

"Good."

⁂

His lovemaking that night was leisurely and generous, as though nothing awaited him in the morning but a late breakfast. His mouth and hands were so sweetly inquisitive, I felt as though I was the first woman whose body he had ever explored, and his touch so wise and responsive it seemed somehow to peel away the ordinary layer of the senses, exposing the raw nerve, the heart of pleasure. And when, finally, I fell asleep, his arms were still around me and his dark eyes still smiling into mine.

⁂

I awoke with the sense that my sleep had been disturbed. As my mind swam into consciousness, I was aware of the shutters banging and rain gusting through the narrow, unglazed window. I rose, shivering, and cast about the room for something to cover myself with. And realised what else was wrong. Cesare was gone. Not recently risen to visit the privy or shout down the stairs for his valet but utterly vanished, as though he had never been there. Looking at the smooth sheets and plumped pillows on his side of the bed, I began to wonder if I had dreamed the whole of the previous night, though touching my fingers to my bruised lips and feeling the slight, delicious strain in my thigh muscles as I walked, I knew I had not.

Then I noticed the cameo ring, lying on the nightstand where he had left it, saying it hindered him in the delicate work his hands were engaged in. I picked it up. The gold must have been of a high purity, for it was soft and had moulded itself to the shape of his finger, but the setting was plain, decorated with nothing more than an engraved motto. The cameo itself depicted the suicide of Lucretia. What motto, I wondered, had he chosen to accompany that? I read, turning the ring slowly as I spelled out the letters: *Age debendo quidquid accidet.* Then I saw there were more words written inside, this time in Catalan. *Un cor, una via.* I sat on the edge of the bed, drawing the silk coverlet around myself, and stared at the image of the woman pointing a knife at her breast. What did it mean? My thoughts flew to Nepi. Had they made some pact there, some sad and sinister plan for a future catastrophe that must then have seemed like no more than a dangerous game? And what was my role in all this? Why had he chosen me to carry his bleak instructions to his sister? I wanted none of it. I wanted my son, and the normal round of our day, and to see if any new teeth had broken through his hard little gums during the night.

But first, if there was poison in the ring, I had to get rid of it. Donna Lucrezia was the godmother who had given me new life and however shaky my belief in her religion, I was certain it would be a travesty to carry her the means of her death. What if the Lord of Vengeance chose to avenge Himself for such an act of betrayal on my son? We were not all Abraham; we could not all rely upon a goat in a thicket. I tried to prise the ring open with a fingernail, but it would not budge. I felt around its edge for some catch or pressure point which would spring it, all to no avail. Perhaps I could find some tool to help me. Cesare's dressing room would be the place to look. There I might find combs, nail files, razor blades, brooch pins.

With the ring closed in my fist, I cautiously opened the door to the dressing room. It too was empty, the clothes chests gone, leaving dustless squares on the floor, the table where he had worked swept free of everything except a broken quill and a stub of candle stuck in its own wax. A cobweb strung across one corner of the ceiling shivered in the wind; even that had no spider dwelling in it. The air of dereliction clung to my skin like a succubus, smelling of dust and stone and jasmine. I scarcely dared open the next door, for fear of what I would not find.

"You're awake, then." Michelotto. A smile of relief spread itself over my face. If Michelotto was here, his master could not be far away. I was tired, over-stimulated. One banging shutter and a cobweb and there I was, imagining I had been deserted.

"I fear I've slept late. His lordship must have risen very quietly."

Michelotto made a non-committal noise in the back of his throat.

"Well, I had better dress and go and find my son." The ring pressed into the flesh of my palm; even though Cesare had entrusted it to me, I was reluctant to let Michelotto know I had it. I needed to get away from him, to some private corner where I could examine it at my leisure.

Michelotto rose from the stool where he had been perched beside the door and stepped in front of me. He was not a great deal taller than me, but his body was broad and powerful, and his demeanour made it clear he was not yet ready to let me go.

"What is it?" I asked.

"He's gone."

"Who? Cesare? To the Vatican?" I felt foolish, discarded, like a soiled shirt or a pair of torn hose.

Michelotto shook his head, then seemed to change his mind and gave a curt nod. "Yes. I mean, no. Yes, he has gone, but that's not what I meant."

"Why are you not with him?" I tried to take refuge in a commanding tone, but sounded merely peevish and strident.

"Because he ordered me to stay here with you."

"Did he?" Somehow I could not think of a greater honour.

"Monna Violante…" He placed a hand on my arm. This seemed over-familiar to me, not an action his lord would sanction were he present, and I shifted my arm. He took the hint and dropped his hand with a sigh. "They have all gone," he said. "Don Cesar, Monna Vannozza, the children…"

"No, you're mistaken. He said…"

"I am not mistaken. I lifted your son into the carriage myself. They left last night. They will be well on their way to Caprarola by now."

"Then we must take fast horses and catch them up."

"Violante…"

"Do not be familiar with me."

"Oh for God's sake, listen to yourself, you silly little strumpet. No, on second thought, listen to me." He patted the stool. "Sit there, don't move, and listen to what I have to say. You are going to Ferrara. I am to escort you. You are to deliver…"

I knew what he was going to say, and opened my fist to reveal the ring.

"That's it," he affirmed. "You are to deliver it to Donna Lucrezia. When she sees it, she will take you back. Your son is to be brought up by his grandmother. It is unlikely you will see him again. Do you understand?"

My legs began to tremble. I slumped down on the stool, was vaguely aware of Michelotto gripping my elbow to steady me, of wishing he would just let me fall and keep on falling, away from this empty castle, away from Cesare's betrayal and my humiliation, and the aching emptiness that was forming inside me where my joy in my baby used to be. "Last night, you say?"

"I'm sorry."

"Are you? Somehow I doubt that. I do not matter to him, so why would I matter to you?"

He had no reply to this. "Cover yourself," he said, pulling at the coverlet which had slipped down my shoulder. "Go and dress. And don't try anything stupid. I shall be at this door, and the other is bolted from the outside. And the drop from the window is very long. And perhaps you'd better let me look after the ring." He held out his hand and I placed the ring on the flat of his palm.

I thought of the long drop to the river, of course I did, then I remembered that, however bereft I felt, my son was not dead. What if he came looking for me one day, only to be told I had given up so easily I had thrown myself out of a window when he was taken from me? What kind of puny love would that be? Love charged me with the duty of staying alive and believing we could be reunited. You follow love, Mariam had said; she had never told me it would be easy.

I dressed briskly. I wanted to cover my body as quickly as possible, to conceal its shame and imprison its rebelliousness in whalebone and laces and layers of cloth. It was time to grow up now, I told myself, yanking my corset tight across my bruised breasts and pulling up the neck of my chemise to conceal the place where my lover's teeth had grazed my flesh. As I picked up my bodice from the floor and began to straighten its ties, I noticed a fine, gingery hair caught in one of the eyelets. I remembered how Cesare had appreciated the changes wrought on my body by childbirth, as he ran his deceiver's hands over my breasts and belly and between my thighs. Permanent changes, that would not fade like bites and bruises or turn to lies like my lover's endearments.

I recalled the mottoes on his ring. *Do what you must, come what may,* I told myself. *One heart, one way.*

# THE BOOK OF GIDEON

*Who is the third who walks always beside you?*
*When I count, there are only you and I together*
*But when I look ahead up the white road*
*There is always another one walking beside you*

T. S. Eliot, *The Wasteland*

# CHAPTER 1

*Send me something you wore. Send me stockings you have danced in or a chemise you slept in on a hot night. Send me your pillowcase or your hairbrush. Reassure me I am still alive.*

M adonna's in a gay mood this morning."

"Perhaps the baby is a little stronger."

"I don't know. I think it's more to do with some letters that got through from her brother."

Only now, despite myself, did I start to pay attention to the conversation, to sort out in my mind one speaker from another and make sense of what they were saying. A bevy of new girls had joined madonna's household since the old duke's death the previous winter. They were all the same, all impossibly young and hopeful, as concerned with necklines, hair ornaments and the shapes of shoe heels as if their lives depended on such things. Which, I suppose, in a manner of speaking, they did. I had no wish to differentiate between them. Though Angela chided me, and reminded me I had been just the same, I believed her memory faulty; I had never been so frivolous; I had never had the chance.

"Oh I do wish I'd met him," said the first speaker. "They say he was terribly good looking."

"Well I don't suppose he is any more, not after a year and a half in a Spanish dungeon. Violante, you must remember him? Was he very handsome?"

I was aware of Fidelma pausing in her work, her needle poised in the air like an antenna.

"Well?" prompted the curious girl.

"Nose like a hawk," I heard myself saying, "and his eyes were too close together." Then I laid my work aside and muttered something about needing the privy, because I did not want to talk about him any more.

I went to fetch my cloak, and found a slave to escort me to the house where Angela and Giulio were staying. I had to get out of the *rocca* before Donna Lucrezia sent for me, as I knew she would if she had received letters from Cesare. She refused absolutely to countenance any notion that I might find it painful to hear news of him, or even that I might have simply lost interest.

When I had remonstrated with her, told her how he had deceived me over Girolamo, and how uniquely cruelly he had done it, she had responded with a chilly smile and said, "It is the basic rule of deception, Violante, to employ your victim's susceptibilities against himself. And besides, what harm has he really done you? The child is safe; he made sure you were brought here unscathed. Surely you did not expect to keep your son with you forever. It is not the way of things. Look at my own Rodrigo."

And look at yourself, I wanted to say, at the presents you choose for him, the letters you write to him your husband knows nothing about, how you are distracted when there are rumours of plague in Naples, or the summers are too hot and the winters too cold. "You had time to say goodbye to him, madonna." *You were not lying in your lover's lying arms while your son was whisked away into the dark, into memory with all its tricks.*

❧

Angela herself answered my knock at the street door. With her hair bundled under a broad-brimmed straw hat, her skirt kilted up above her ankles and her feet encased in scuffed old riding boots, she looked like a beautiful peasant.

"We're gardening," she said, and I hoped the owner of the house who had been displaced by the arrival of the duke's brother would not mind the consequences of Giulio's passion. "Come and join us. You look pale."

"And you look as brown as a farm girl."

Angela and Giulio were openly living together as man and wife, and it was accepted they would marry in due course, once Duke Alfonso had won over his brother, the cardinal, who was now his chief adviser. In the weeks since the birth of madonna's son, they had grown even more confident of their happiness. By proving herself capable of bearing a living boy, madonna had surely swept away the last possible stain on her name. And the latest falling out between Ippolito and Giulio, over the *cappellano* Rainaldo, had been conveniently terminated by the musician's sudden disappearance. Giulio thought him dead; Angela said he was probably sick of being fought over and had gone to someone else's court. Ippolito said nothing.

"Look who's here," she called as she led me through the arched colonnade to the garden. Giulio emerged like a dusty faun from a bed of fuschia bushes, shaking the pink fairy flowers out of his hair.

"Violante." He stepped out of the bed and gathered me into his arms, into his scent of earth and sweat and greenery, his wooden trowel scraping my back.

"Really, dear," Angela remonstrated, taking it from him, wiping the earth from the blade with a hand whose nails, I thought, probably contained enough dirt to make a new flowerbed.

"Are you all alone?"

"I brought a slave. He's gone to the kitchen."

"You should have let us know you were coming. As you see, we're unprepared for guests."

"That doesn't matter."

"Violante is hardly a guest, Giulio."

"I came on the spur. Had to get away for a while." Addressing myself to Angela, I added, "There has been news..."

"Of Cesare," said Angela, relieving me of the need to say his name. "So Sancho must have got to see him finally. Do you know how he is?"

I wanted to retort I neither knew nor cared, but I bit my tongue. He was her cousin after all. I shook my head. "I left before Lucrezia could send for me."

"Well, I expect she will let me know if there's any news of note."

"I expect so."

"Leave it there, Angela. Violante hasn't come here to talk about Cesare. Quite the opposite, I suspect. We'll go round to the west terrace, get the last of the sun, and have a cup of something." Clapping his hands for a slave, Giulio led us around the house to the balustraded terrace, enjoining us to step on the cushions of thyme sprouting between the paving stones. "It will cheer your heart, Violante. All the day's sunshine trapped in those tiny leaves. A miracle."

"You cheer my heart, Giulio."

He handed us into the old, comfortable chairs, covered with rugs, which mouldered contentedly in the evening light the way I liked to think he and Angela would, when they were full of years and the bare parterres below us were stuffed with mature plants. A house slave came out with a jug of sweetened lime juice.

"We had ice this morning," said Angela, "but it's all melted now. The cart should really come round twice a day."

We sipped our drinks and contemplated the long, blue shadows cast by the fruit trees at the bottom of the garden, the fiery face of the setting sun cross-hatched by their branches. In silence, we listened to the earth breathe, to the last flurry of birdsong in the cooling air, the whisper of mist creeping up from the river and along the narrow streets of the town.

"October already," said Angela, pulling a stole around her shoulders.

"Thank God," said Giulio with feeling. It had been a terrible summer, hot and plague ridden, and as the old duke had sold off most of the previous year's grain surplus to pay his architect, many people in Ferrara had gone hungry. Madonna was forever telling us, had it not been for the generosity of Francesco Gonzaga in providing transport through his territories for grain ordered from Piemonte, more would have died of starvation than from the plague.

"All the same, an early cold won't help Alessandro." The new heir was sickly and underweight, and reluctant to take the breast. Like his uncle Ferrante, joked the wags, though I thought of another of his uncles, and watched to see how much determination there was in the set of his pale lips or the curl of his tiny fists.

"He'll live if he wants to," I said.

"How can anyone not want to live?" asked Giulio.

"Surely a child cannot have any say in the matter."

"Oh he can," I said, and as Giulio reached out his hand to Angela, wished I had not. She was afraid she had damaged herself by procuring her miscarriage, and that she would never be able to give Giulio children, and clearly she believed I was showing myself privy to some kind of knowledge only vouchsafed mothers. I thought I should go; there was no place for my calloused and embittered spirit in their paradise. I rose and made my excuses.

"When we all get back to Ferrara, you must come on a proper visit and dine with us, you and Ferrante," said Angela. It was part of the life Angela and Giulio were planning for themselves that Ferrante and I would marry.

"He is kind," Angela had told me. "He will be a consolation, and when you find another lover, well, he's hardly going to be consumed by jealousy, is he?" Simple.

⟡

"Where have you been?" Fidelma, looking more severe than she sounded, in her plain, dark gown and a hood which entirely concealed her hair. "She's been calling for you." Since I had been away, and Angela had withdrawn from her cousin's household to live with Giulio, Fidelma had become one of madonna's longest serving ladies, and seemed to feel this entitled her to adopt a proprietory tone. It was a measure of her standing with our mistress that Fra Raffaello had been asked to preach in her chapel three times during the previous Lent.

"I went to see Angela. Give me five minutes to change my shoes and tidy my hair."

"She shouldn't do this. It's God's will, what happened to Duke Valentino, and there's no gainsaying it. If she thinks he will ever be allowed back in Italy, she deludes herself—and you."

"Not me, Fidelma. Nor him, I suspect."

Almost as though she meant to confirm my supposition about Cesare's state of mind, the first thing madonna said to me as I entered her room was, "Good news. They have moved him to La Mota."

La Mota was the great royal fortress of Medina del Campo, the impregnable heart of Spain. I could not see how this was good news.

"He says he is visited there often by emissaries of Philip of Flanders, who works for his release. He says Philip wishes to entrust him with the task of bringing Don Carlos to Castile, now that his mother is queen."

"Is she to be allowed to rule, then?" Philip's wife, Juana, Queen of Castile in name since the death of Isabella the previous winter, was generally held to be insane and was kept under virtual house arrest by her father, King Ferdinand.

Donna Lucrezia shrugged. "She is not my brother's concern."

"Where is Don Carlos now?"

"In Flanders, I believe."

"Cesare will not return to Italy, then."

Madonna laid a hand over mine. "I am sorry. Not yet. He must rebuild his position before he can come back and confront Pope Julius."

I was not sorry; my concern was for Girolamo. Donna Lucrezia had been gracious enough to keep me informed about him, though sometimes I believed it would have been easier if she had not.

Cesare had managed to negotiate his freedom from Pope Julius on condition he went into exile in Naples. The three children, Girolamo, Giovanni, and Camilla, had gone there with him, to the house of Don Jofre and Princess Sancia. The pope, however, had double-crossed him. Or perhaps it was the other way round. Between Julius and Cesare it was impossible to know who was cheating whom. Cesare had been arrested again, this time at the behest of Queen Isabella, who wanted him to stand trial in Spain for the murders of Don Juan and Alfonso of Bisceglie. If Cesare did ever return to Italy, I was certain it would put the life of his son and heir in greater danger than ever.

"But Sancho has seen him," Donna Lucrezia went on, in the same bright, brisk tone she used when handling petitions for which she had no easy response, "and says he is well. A little thin, but in good spirits. And these letters," she waved a fan of travel-stained parchments at me, "are full of how much more comfortable his quarters are than at Chinchilla. And how King Ferdinand shows him favour since the queen's death. Ferdinand is our kinsman, after all."

"The duke will have a warmer winter, at any rate."

"He will be in Flanders by the winter," replied madonna, as if she would brook no opposition to her assertion. "Free."

"How is Don Alessandro today?" I asked, peering into the lace-shrouded crib which stood beside madonna's bed. Though she was dressed, she was still confined to her chamber, unable to wear shoes because of the swelling in her feet and ankles left over from the fever she had suffered after the birth. The baby looked serene, his little face between his cap and his swaddling bands as pale and still as a child saint's. With a sharp stab of loss, I recalled Girolamo at the same age, his cheeks a weathered red, his features scrunched with all the frustrations of being bound and helpless and dependent.

"He has taken a little milk," said madonna, "but he is too quiet."

"I expect he is listening."

I had never spoken to Donna Lucrezia about my conversations with her mother. On my return, I had simply witnessed Michelotto handing her the ring, then left him to deliver whatever news of her brother he saw fit. I had done what I was charged with; he would never be able to say I had deceived him as he had deceived me. I went back to the room I had once shared with Angela, to her outmoded gowns and a stale wraith of her tuberose perfume, and resumed my household duties as though I had never been away.

But now madonna said, "So you know, then? About Cesare? I am hopeful. Alessandro shares his birth sign, you know."

I knew. *Hope,* he had said to me once, trying, I think, to be kind, *is the thing we should be most afraid of.* I stretched my hand towards the crib, intending to stroke the baby's face, but I could not bring myself to touch that soft skin. I rocked the crib once or twice and murmured some of that soothing nonsense that seems to enter a woman's head as soon as a man's seed takes root in her. His features twisted a little. He opened his eyes. I thought he was going to cry, then noticed his irises had swivelled up into his head so only the whites of his eyes showed. A bubble of saliva appeared at the corner of his mouth.

"Madonna, I think..."

"Holy Mary, it's another fit, isn't it? Quickly, run for Castello and the *comatre.*"

Doctor and nurse were not far away. Alessandro had suffered several fits in the night, and I could tell from the expressions on their faces, the encouraging smiles they donned like masks before going into madonna's chamber, that his life was despaired of. I made to retire, but madonna pleaded with me to stay. I drew a stool up to her bedside and sat holding her hand while the doctor and the *comatre* did what they could.

When death entered the room, the doctor stood back with his head bowed. The *comatre* lifted the rigid little body from the crib and laid him in his mother's arms. Donna Lucrezia kissed his forehead and whispered to him in her own, old language, "*Adeu, nen petit.*" Then she meekly handed him to the priest, who said what he had to say and bore the body away for laying out.

Castello packed up his equipment and departed with no more than a brisk, mute bow. The *comatre* tried to give some advice about breast binding and an ointment of rose oil and pomegranate pills for shrinking the womb before I shooed her away. Given her profession, she should have learned more tact in dealing with mothers bereaved of their babies, but she had come to Reggio on the recommendation of Donna Isabella, whose liking for her sister-in-law had not increased during the months I was away. And now, no doubt, she would rush back, for Donna Isabella was also pregnant. For the fourth time.

"And no doubt as healthy as a brood mare," madonna had remarked when the *comatre* arrived, with a condescending letter from Donna Isabella. As though being as healthy as a brood mare set her at some social disadvantage.

I called for a slave to carry the crib from the room, but madonna clung to the lace hood and refused to be parted from it. She took out the pillow on which Alessandro had lain and cradled it in her lap, pushing her face into the fine white cotton slip as though she wished to smother herself. Yet she breathed greedily through her nose, inhaling the scent of milk and new skin which was all that remained of her son, then straightened up, smoothing the pillow over and over with her plump fingers, nipping its pleats and corners between her perfectly manicured nails.

"My husband must be told." Though her cheeks glistened with tears, her voice was firm. Duke Alfonso was at Belriguardo. He had spent the summer there overseeing the renovations he had set in train since his father's death. "And, there is another letter I must write. You will help me with it."

"No, madonna, I…"

"Not to my brother, Violante. To Francesco Gonzaga." Something in the way she said Francesco Gonzaga's name made me wonder, for a moment, about Alessandro's parentage, but I pushed the thought away as quickly as it came. I could find myself hanging in a cage from the Torre Leone for less. But a bitter echo remained, a mean little voice which told me madonna, at least, had the consolation of a new love to lessen the grief of losing her child.

She wrote the letter in her own hand, and I took it, as instructed, to a place near the main city gate, where there was a stall selling poultry set up just below a plaque in the city wall commemorating those who died in the Battle of Legnano. Ercole Strozzi hobbled out from behind a tottering pile of wooden cages full of angry chickens and bewildered partridges. He bowed and greeted me as though we met this way every day. He asked after madonna's health, and hoped Don Cesare was comfortable in his new surroundings, and I began to wonder if the last year and a half had been no more than a bad dream from which I had now awakened to find all was as it had been before Pope Alexander died. I replied that I had had no word from Don Cesare, but madonna was making a good recovery, but as I handed Strozzi the letter and turned to go, he placed a hand on my shoulder.

"Life takes no prisoners, you know, little mistress. Your lady duchess knows that and you could do worse than learn from her example."

"Thank you, Ser Ercole, you are wise."

"Merely practical, my dear, merely practical."

⚜

Duke Alfonso's response to the loss of his son was to summon his wife to Belriguardo.

"He expresses the hope I will be distracted by seeing all the changes he is making there," said Donna Lucrezia as she directed our packing. "Dossi is exhausted, he says, so he is bringing in a painter from Carpi to finish the main *salone* in time for a concert with that singer...what is his name...honestly, my memory...that's what pregnancy does for you, ladies, be warned..." and on she prattled, as gay and brittle as a butterfly.

"Stay a moment," she commanded me, once all the clothes chests had been carried down to the carts waiting in the courtyard, and the jewellery boxes entrusted to her majordomo. "I have one more errand for you before we leave." Her expression was a mixture of exhaustion and indominability which reminded me, in spite of myself, of her brother, that last night on the battlements of Sant'Angelo. "You are to meet Ser Ercole as before. He will have something for me."

⬥

Strozzi was not there when I arrived at the poultry stall. I waited, impatiently at first, in a wind from the mountains, sharp with the first snows, which whipped sawdust from the chicken coops into my eyes. Then, as the poultry seller began to mutter about people who hung about his wares without buying anything, in rising anxiety, I shifted a little, and pretended to examine a pyramid of yellow apples at a neighbouring stall. I had just picked out the least bruised, and handed over some coins to the stallholder, when I noticed another figure loitering near the poultry seller. A man I had never seen before, tall, bony, dressed with unremarkable shabbiness as though to compensate for his striking height and thinness. He must be a spy, I thought, madonna's subterfuge had been discovered. Pulling my hood close around my face, I set off in the opposite direction, willing myself not to run, not to do anything to draw attention to myself. I was just a girl buying an apple. What could be more ordinary?

But a creeping stickiness on my fingers made me realise I had dug my nails right through the skin of the apple. Then I felt the weight of a hand on my shoulder. The breath left my body in a little shriek. Somewhere, I heard the rasp of a sword pulled from its scabbard. A voice began to mumble the prayers we make in childbirth and other dangers, a woman's voice, breathless and shaky. My voice.

Now someone else was speaking, a man. The spy. "Put up your sword, I mean her no harm."

My legs gave way and I sank to my knees in the dust and cabbage leaves and dog shit of the street.

"I'm sorry, I didn't mean to frighten you," said the spy. Placing a hand beneath my elbow, he raised me to my feet and began to dust down my skirt.

"Who are you?"

"Messer Ercole sent me."

My relief was so overwhelming my legs almost gave out a second time, which irritated me. "Well why didn't you say so instead of skulking around like a…a…"

"Poultry chef? Pigeon fancier?"

"There were no pigeons," I snapped, but I could hear the smile in my voice and so, it seemed, could Ser Ercole's deputy because his long, bony face was suddenly split by a huge grin. His teeth, I noticed, were large and somewhat crooked; a man of more delicate breeding might have ensured he kept them covered when he smiled.

"I think you are expecting something from me?"

It could still be a trick. "You mistake me, sir."

"Surely you are Monna Violante?"

"How do you know?"

"I didn't, until I heard you saying the *Birchat-Hagomel.* Then I was sure. Ser Ercole told me you were a *conversa.* The other *conversa,* he said." He made a shallow bow. "I am Gideon da Quieto d'Arzenta of Mantua, the brother of the woman I believe you know as Fidelma."

"The goldsmith," I exclaimed.

"The very same."

"If you had been wearing your star, I would have realised." As I looked at him now, it was obvious. He had Fidelma's gangling build, the same bony face, and fine, prominent eyes. He looked, I thought, rather like a hare.

"You think so? In my experience, *conversos* are the worst anti-Semites. Besides, I am wearing it." He opened the homespun coat he wore over his doublet to reveal a star of yellow cloth sewn inside it. "It would hardly do to get arrested on one of Ser Ercole's clandestine missions. Now, shall I give you the letter?"

"Why did Ser Ercole send you? Why did he not come in person?"

"Stop clutching your cloak like that, it makes you look like a cutpurse. He didn't send me, I asked to come." He laughed, and pulled me to the side of the road, out of the path of a mule laden with wide panniers. "Don't flatter yourself, my fine lady. It was not the beauty of your face that inspired me, though it is very beautiful and if I had seen it before, perhaps I would have spoken to Ser Ercole sooner. It was your influence with the duchess. My sister tells me she reposes great confidence in you, and I am anxious to win a commission from her. Her brother is aware of my work and…"

"I know." I wondered what had happened to those masks now. San Clemente had been thoroughly looted by the Orsini after the battle in Saint Peter's Square. I wondered which of them might have the *huspa* to hang a gold death's head beside his bed and concluded, with a sense of fierce pride, there was none. "But my mistress is not inclined to make much play of her closeness to her brother in the present circumstances. You might," I went on, choosing my words with care, "make more capital from her rivalry with Donna Isabella Gonzaga."

"So this is from Don Francesco?"

"Shhh. Keep your eyes open when the duchess leaves Reggio, that is all."

≈≋≈

It was reasonable to travel to Borgoforte, from where I expected we would go on by river to Belriguardo, but when Don Francesco met us there, he and Donna Lucrezia soon made other plans. He was adamant Donna Isabella wished to see her sister-in-law, to condole with her about the child, but, with her own pregnancy now so advanced, she was unable to leave Mantua. So, after a night at Borgoforte, we moved on to Mantua. While I thought it quite plausible Donna Isabella would wish to flaunt her fertility in front of my poor lady, it was obvious from her demeanour as I dressed her for the journey that she and Don Francesco had snatched some opportunity to exchange private words the previous evening. If Donna Isabella had planned a triumph, I suspected she was in for a disappointment.

I wished Angela was with us, but she and Giulio were returning to Ferrara. They had no desire to go to Belriguardo, where they were bound to encounter Ippolito. I could not have confided my suspicions to Fidelma, even if I had wanted to, as I did not want to give away her brother's role in the affair. Or my own, for that matter. So I kept my counsel, and if there was gossip, I did not hear it. My presence usually had the effect of striking madonna's new girls dumb. Angela used to say it was because I had come from Rome; there was about all of us, she joked, the odour of Borgia sanctity. But I knew it was more than that. Though none of them were even aware of Girolamo's existence, I wore his loss like a shroud; I was a ghost, unwelcome in their vivacious round of fashions, flirtations, and parties.

I was not present when madonna was received by Donna Isabella, but once we were embarked on Don Francesco's bucentaur, the enforced intimacy of shipboard life made gossip redundant. Madonna made sure only those she felt she could trust travelled with her and Don Francesco, with everyone else following on a second boat. So I was surprised when, leaning over the prow our second morning out, I found myself standing next to Gideon d'Arzenta. The creak and splash of the oars mingled with snatches of music from Don Francesco's string players, creating a curtain of sound between us and the lovers who were seated in a makeshift bower at the stern of the boat. The smell of fresh tar and smoke from their brazier stung my nostrils.

"I think we can expect rain," remarked Gideon, squinting up at the cloud which hung low and yellowish over the brown waters of the river. "I'll wager you didn't expect to see me again, did you?" he went on when I made no reply.

"I have not thought of you one way or the other, Ser d'Arzenta."

"And there I was thinking you would have wasted no opportunity to recommend me to your lady."

"Had there been an opportunity, I would not have wasted it."

He laughed then, tilting his chin to expose the brown skin and jutting bones of his throat. Turning his back to the deck rail and leaning his elbows on it, he said, "You're a sharp one, Violante. I don't envy your husband. I think your embrace must be pricklier than the iron maiden's."

"How exactly do you come to be here, messer?"

"Ah, I am Donna Isabella's eyes and ears." My alarm must have shown in my face, for he laughed again, touched the inside of my elbow with his fingertips and said, "You're an easy target for a joke, mistress."

"There are some things you should not joke about."

"And the amours of people such as your duchess and our upstanding Marquis of Mantua are to be taken seriously?"

"Love is a very serious matter."

"Were we talking of love, I would agree with you. But that," he nodded towards the stern of the boat, "that is merely a game. I would take *calcio* more seriously."

Part of me knew he was right, that Don Francesco's hand lying in Donna Lucrezia's lap hurt nothing and nobody. Yet if I did not believe in the sincerity of their kind of loving, how cheaply had my own heart been broken? "All the same," I said, "I believe my lady's conscience is sufficiently sensitive for her to resist the presence of Donna Isabella's eyes and ears."

"In exchange for my admittedly vague promise to report to her about her husband and her sister-in-law, Donna Isabella gave me a letter of recommendation to Donna Lucrezia. I will send her something non-committal. After all, what have I seen? A lady and a gentleman taking their ease on a boat. A grieving mother seeking the consolation of a friend. I sleep on deck among the galley slaves and all that disturbs my sleep is the clank of their chains when they get up for a piss. Excuse my bluntness."

"I am getting used to it."

"I am glad, because I hope to have much more conversation with you once I am installed at Ferrara. I think there are deep seams in you to be mined."

"I suppose that is a compliment. From a goldsmith."

At Sermide, on the border between the states of Mantua and Ferrara, Don Francesco took his leave of us, and those who had been travelling on the second boat joined ours so Don Francesco had a means of transport home. Among the gaggle of Donna Lucrezia's girls hemming me in with their questions and speculations, only Fidelma kept silent, whether through disapproval or an altogether more subtle kind of curiosity I could not be sure. I expected her at least to raise the subject of her brother, but she did not, and I only once saw them talking together, when I was taking Fonsi for his daily walk around the deck. They seemed ill at ease in one another's company, the sharp angles of their bodies cutting the air between them into awkward shapes, their big feet shuffling around one another in a clumsy dance.

I remembered how the Holy Father used to like to watch Cesare and Donna Lucrezia dance together, how their shared blood flowed in unison when they led the Catalan *sardanas* and the haunting voice of the *flaviol* made their father weep. I saw again in my mind's eye Donna Lucrezia's old dancing shoes with their scored soles, and Cesare in his delirium, hacking at my shoes with my meat knife. And perhaps I would have seen further, except that at that very moment our boat slid past the jetty at the bottom of Ser Taddeo di Occhiobello's garden, and I turned away and went below decks.

I had thought madonna was resting, but as I climbed down the companionway, she called out to me from her cabin. As I entered, and made an awkward curtsey in the cramped space, she patted the bed beside her and commanded me to sit. There was no room for a chair, or even a stool; all the available floor space was taken up by madonna's clothes chests. I found myself thinking how out of place Don Francesco must have looked among the spillage of silk and lace. I put down the little dog on his satin cushion and balanced myself on the side of the bed.

"What do you know of the young man Fidelma says is her brother?" madonna demanded.

"I believe he is her brother. They certainly look alike. Ser Strozzi trusts him."

"Strozzi?"

"The last time you asked me to meet Ser Strozzi in Reggio, madonna, he sent Ser d'Arzenta in his place."

"You mean..?"

"I was circumspect, madonna. I accepted nothing from him until I was certain of him."

"Certain? How could you be certain, foolish girl? He might have been sent by anyone. Donna Isabella, my husband..." She paused, then went on in a softer voice, as though talking to herself, "no, not him. Isabella, it must be. Did Fidelma not say he had worked for her?"

"Madonna, I have spoken with him a little. I really do not think he is interested in..."

"He will be interested in what he is paid to be interested in. That is the way the world works. Fonsi, bad dog." The dog, tired of not being the centre of attention, had jumped into madonna's lap and was on his stout hind legs, trying to lick her face. Usually this would make her laugh, but now she swatted him impatiently on the nose. "Get him down here, Violante," she went on, raising her voice over the dog's whimpers. "Let's find out what he's up to."

I found him still on deck with Fidelma.

"Donna Lucrezia wants to see you," I said.

His face lit up in that crooked grin of his. "Really?"

Even Fidelma looked less solemn than usual, and began to fuss around him, tucking a loose thread into his frayed cuff, telling him to smooth his hair, hide his star, and not to look so...well, so Jewish. "And have you got your drawings?" she demanded finally.

He patted the battered leather scrip hanging from his belt. "Always," he said.

"I wouldn't get your hopes up too much," I warned him, but he was striding ahead of me towards the companion hatch, and the wind snatched my words out of his hearing.

⁂

I wondered what he saw as he stood in the cabin doorway and bowed. Did he perhaps see wealth and influence, the focus of his ambition? Did he see power and majesty, or some last residue of the magnificent decadence of her father's court? Or did he see what I saw? A woman lying on her bed, clad in deep mourning, with her hair unbound and the ash cross on her forehead which we refreshed every morning from the flask of holy dust she kept among her pots of carmine paste and white lead. Had he noticed the steel in her grey eyes, or was she going to take him by surprise?

"Ser d'Arzenta," she said.

"Duchesa. You do me great honour."

"On the contrary, it is I who should be flattered by your attention. You must forgive me for not having noticed you before." She waved one deceptively flaccid hand. "So many men, you see...It was ever thus."

He walked straight into the trap. "Your great beauty, duchesa..."

Donna Lucrezia sat bolt upright, dislodging one of her pillows, which hit Fonsi on the nose as it fell. He set up a frenzied yapping in response. I saw Gideon wince as the sound sliced the musty air.

"My beauty is none of your concern, boy," said madonna and her voice, though low with menace, was perfectly audible above the dog's cacophony. Gideon was staring at her now, and I pleaded with him silently to look away. Ambitious he might be, but he had clearly taken no trouble to school himself in the ways of the court.

"So you will avert your eyes from me, and tell me just exactly what concern it is that brings you aboard my boat."

I picked up the dog and pressed my hand over his nose to silence him, though I never managed this trick as effectively as Cesare had been able to. I fancied Gideon's shoulders relaxed a little as the thud and splash of the oars became the dominant sound in the room.

"My concern is only to serve you, duchesa." He shifted his gaze to the deck, but I did not think he sounded as contrite as madonna would have wished.

"A pretty phrase, but I had heard many prettier before I was out of the nursery. I have been surrounded by flatterers all my life."

"Then you will know I do not flatter you. I am no courtier, duchesa..."

"That you are not."

"...but I do have skills I believe would be pleasing to you."

"And these are what, exactly? Trickery? Subterfuge? Spying? Reading other people's private letters? I could have stones tied to your feet and have you tossed into the river like so much kitchen waste for less."

His hand moved to his scrip, which was fastened to his belt next to his knife. Donna Lucrezia flinched. "Violante, what is he doing? Where are my guards?"

"I do not think he means any harm, madonna."

"I wish only to show you some demonstration of my skill, duchesa." He was teasing her, I realised, with a mixture of shock and admiration. No one teased madonna, not even Duke Alfonso. Well, almost no one.

He withdrew a sheaf of papers from the scrip, and handed them to me. "If you would do me the honour of looking at these, duchesa. They are sketches for a commission I undertook for the Marchesa of Mantua in the last year of your illustrious father's pontificate."

I glanced at each sheet before placing them, one by one, in madonna's lap. I saw faces, strangely familiar, despite the fact that each was scarred with ruled lines and scribbled over with jottings of angles and lengths of measurement. Here was a turbaned potentate and here a whiskered cat. A curly-haired cherub followed a slant-eyed mandarin. The final sketch showed a skull with a roguish grin and a diamond set into one of its teeth.

"I think I know these," said madonna in a tone of suppressed excitement which let me hope the danger was past. She had recognised talent in Gideon's work, and scented the possibility of wresting him from Donna Isabella. "These are some of the masks made for my brother, are they not? As a gift from the marchesa?"

"Yes, duchesa. She commissioned twenty-five masks in gold and twenty-five in silver. I was to do the silver, but then my master got sick and could not afford to delay. The cost of the gold, you understand. So I did the designs and the casting myself under his supervision."

"They are cast, not beaten?" asked madonna, shrewd as a housewife testing the quality of bedlinen or the freshness of fish.

"These are all cast, duchesa. Some were beaten, as the design demanded."

"And who was your master, boy?"

"Sperandio, duchesa."

"Ah yes, I know him, I think. He once cast a medal of my noble father-in-law, I believe. And is knowledgeable on gunmetal."

"He died last year, duchesa. He had attained nearly eighty years."

"May God have mercy on his soul." Donna Lucrezia crossed herself, and Gideon looked at me to see if I would do likewise.

"So you are now your own master?"

"I hope one day to have my own workshop. For now, I will take work where I can get it."

"And you do not fear making images of men?"

"The masks do not represent the living, duchesa. They are only masks."

"Well, perhaps we will make a Christian of you, Ser d'Arzenta. Your sister is a most pious woman."

At that he made a small bow, but there was a mutinous set to his mouth which made me think it unlikely he would ever follow Fidelma's path to Christ.

"I have a challenge for you, then. You will cast a medal, with my image on the face and a design of your choosing on the reverse, to commemorate my first full year as Duchess of Ferrara. So it must be ready before the beginning of Lent next year."

"Thank you, duchesa. You will not regret your confidence in me."

"Do you know for what purpose the marchesa commissioned the masks?"

"Everyone knows it, duchesa."

"Then I would remind you what happened to those men who conspired against my brother at Senigallia. In case you are ever tempted to do anything to make me regret my confidence in you."

"I understand, duchesa." He bowed and backed out of the cabin, and winked at me as he turned to set foot on the companionway.

# CHAPTER 2

FERRARA, NOVEMBER 1505

*This morning a mirror was brought to me, good polished silver, and I saw my face for the first time in I don't know how many months. What kind of gift was that meant to be, I wonder?*

By the time we returned to Ferrara, at the end of Strozzi's hunting party at Ostellato, madonna had been churched, and there was no doubt in my mind she and Don Francesco had somehow contrived to consummate their passion, even though both Duke Alfonso and Ippolito had been among the guests at Strozzi's country villa. While it was more than possible the duke was too taken up by the competition to take the biggest bag to notice what his wife was up to, I marvelled that they had been able to deceive Ippolito. To me, it was so obvious, though Don Francesco could not have shared her bed, nor she his, and I supposed they must have seized whatever opportunities were offered by the grottoes in Ser Ercole's gardens, or his woodland rides, or the boathouse where he kept his sumptuously appointed river barge. But there was a hectic animation about Donna Lucrezia which I had not seen since before her father's death, and Don Francesco, whose sexual appetites were notorious and indiscriminate, was recklessly attentive towards her. They exuded lust like horse sweat, and I felt like a starving woman standing down wind of a bakery.

So although madonna became peevish and intolerant once we returned to Ferrara for the winter, and Don Francesco went back to Mantua to await his wife's confinement, I was relieved to be back. I looked forward to the quiet weeks of Advent, the firelit evenings when we sewed vestments for the cathedral and our own Christmas party gowns, entertaining ourselves with low gossip and exalted readings both equally aimed at preparing us for the coming season. I found serenity in the fact that neither faith nor flirtation mattered to me, and cherished the little things, the scent of burning applewood, the sound of rain on window shutters in the middle of the night, a spider's web sparkling with dew. This was the compass of my thought and I wanted nothing more.

Visits to Sister Osanna were also a feature of Donna Lucrezia's Advent preparations, though conditions at Santa Caterina were less spartan than they had been. Rumours had begun shortly after the old duke's death that Sister Lucia da Narni was a fraud, who had inflicted the stigmata on herself and kept the wounds open by poking at them with a sharpened stick in the secrecy of her cell at night. Within weeks she had been confined to that cell permanently, not even allowed out to attend services in the chapel, and Sister Osanna's stock had soared as the only authentic bearer of Christ's wounds in Ferrara. She quickly revealed a hitherto well-hidden liking for sweet food and upholstered furniture, and a capacity like that of a tyrannical child for getting her own way.

A visit was planned one late November morning of still cold, the river's breath hanging over the city in a low mist and condensing on the castle walls behind the tapestries which had been hung up for the winter. But madonna awoke complaining of a headache and chills in her limbs, so she sent me to Santa Caterina in her place, bearing scented beeswax candles and morellos in syrup as gifts of contrition. The candles, she told me, were to be used to make prayers for Cesare's liberation, and I smiled, and nodded my assent, and felt as though I were a rich tapestry with the cold sweat of winter running behind it.

My journey took me past Giulio's palace and I decided on a whim to stop and pay a call on Angela. I had scarcely seen her since our return, and a break in even my short ride to the convent was welcome for my joints were aching cruelly in the damp air. I was sure the apothecary who had taken on the responsibility of manufacturing Ser Torella's pills for me must have got the recipe wrong.

There were already several horses in the courtyard, and a mule whose scarlet caparison told me he was a cardinal's mount. A shiver went through me which had nothing to do with the cold weather. Since the Rainaldo affair, Ippolito and Giulio had not exchanged a civil word; Ippolito's presence in Giulio's house could not bode anything but ill. Even before the house slave threw open the great double doors of the piano nobile, I could hear raised voices.

"Where is he?" demanded Ippolito. "You might as well tell me. I have men searching the house and grounds. They'll find him."

"Take your hands off me," Angela shouted. "Giulio isn't here and I know nothing about your wretched singer one way or the other. And care less." Though her words were defiant, her voice sounded strained and fearful.

The slave hesitated, his white-gloved hands hovering over the silver-gilt door handles. I urged him on with a nod.

"Monna Violante," he announced with a perfunctory bow, and scurried away. Ippolito had hold of one of Angela's wrists. He dropped it like a firebrand as soon as he saw me. She rushed to embrace me, and I felt her body shaking against mine, her lips parched against my cheek. She remained at my side, gripping my hand, while Ippolito stood with his back to the fire, fists clenched, his scarlet silk strained across his chest. He had begun to gain weight, to grow as compact and powerful as a good fighting bull, and his anger seemed to fill the room.

"I was on my way to Santa Caterina," I said, my voice sounding small and muffled. "I thought I'd..." Just then the door opened once more. I felt Angela relax, then tense again as she realised it was not Giulio but one of Ippolito's men at arms.

"Nothing, excellency," he said, clicking his heels together smartly. "We have looked everywhere, even the ice house."

"All the domestic offices? The cave behind the waterfall? The Temple of the Graces?"

"Yes, excellency."

Forcing the breath down his nose in vexation, Ippolito strode to stand in front of us, so close I could smell wine and clove oil on his breath and a whiff of camphor from his clothing. Staring at Angela as though I were invisible, he asked, "Why do you suppose the little bastard wants everything that's mine?"

"I am not yours, and nor is Rainaldo. God gave each of us free will."

"You dare to speak to me of God, hussy?" He raised his hand as though to hit her, but she stood her ground, her neat chin tilted up at him in defiance, and he lowered his hand. "What can he give you that I cannot, Angela? I have greater wealth, I have power, and you cannot pretend I do not know how to please you."

"You cannot define love by wealth, power, and expertise in the bedroom, Ippolito," she said, not unkindly but with the weary patience of an adult talking to a persistent child. "I love him. One look from his eyes means more to me than anything you could give me. I'm sorry."

"Sorry?" he repeated. "You don't know the meaning of the word." He paused, breathing heavily. "But you will."

Shouting for his men at arms, he left us, and Angela sank into a window seat, leaning her back against the open shutter. I sat beside her and waited in silence while she looked out over the garden, her gaze mirroring the restlessness of the fountain below us, whipping about in the breeze. Then she recollected herself, smiled at me, and seized both my hands.

"I'm pregnant," she announced. "I think I must have been for ages, but I thought it was just, you know…since the abortion. But the other evening I felt the baby move. I mean, I thought it was indigestion. There had been a particularly rich macaroni at dinner, but Giulio said he'd rub my belly for me, and he realised." She pressed one of my hands against her midriff. "There. Feel." Though her belly was not very large, it was quite rigid, and after a few seconds I felt the flutter of a new life under my palm.

"How many months, do you think?" I asked, making my voice sound pleased and excited.

"Five, six maybe. Isn't it wonderful? They must let us marry now."

"I hope you didn't tell Ippolito."

"You're the very first person I've told. If you hadn't come today, I would have sought you out even before Lucrezia. Be happy for me, Violante."

I smiled, and hoped my smile placed a convincing poultice over the wound in my heart. I wanted to share in her joy; I could not cure myself of the loss of my own child by resenting her happiness. And after a while, its warmth began to thaw me. We moved from the window seat to an upholstered settle beside the hearth. A slave stoked the fire and brought a tray of *crostini* and little salads, and some deep fried rabbits' ears which

Angela refused for fear of giving her baby a hare-lip. We talked of the need to eat hot, bright foods to make a boy child, of rest and exercise and names, and how Angela would furnish her lying-in room. She hoped I would be able to stay with her during her confinement and told me Giulio was already composing songs to soothe her in her labour. The door to the birthing chamber would be open, she explained, with only a curtain across it for decency, and Giulio would sit just outside with his beautiful voice and his musicians. We gossiped about Donna Lucrezia and Don Francesco Gonzaga, and the frequency of their correspondence. Madonna said Don Francesco was helping her in her efforts to secure Cesare's release from prison, and perhaps he was. It would be the surest way to her heart.

By this time evening was closing in, and when a slave came in to light the candles, I suddenly remembered my errand to Sister Osanna. Angela walked down to the courtyard with me. I mounted my mule and she stood rubbing its nose as we said our farewells and promised to meet again next day when Angela intended to bring news of her pregnancy to her cousin at the castle. Suddenly the street gate crashed open and Ferrante galloped into the courtyard, scattering cats and chickens and almost flattening a kitchen boy who was fetching water from the well. Mourning was still being observed by the family for Duke Ercole, and Ferrante's untrimmed hair and beard framed his anguished face like wild, sandy snakes. His horse's heaving flanks were sweat darkened and flecked with spittle.

"Angela, you must come. Thank God you're here, Violante," he gasped, flinging himself out of the saddle.

"What's happened?" My first instinct was to resent his abrupt intrusion on our intimacy, but there was something deadly serious underlying the drama that frightened me. Glancing at Angela, I could see she felt it too. I wished I could take Ferrante aside and find out what he had to report out of her hearing, but it was too late for that.

"It's Giulio," he said. "He's been attacked."

"Attacked?" Angela's voice was a strangled squeak. She swayed and clutched at the mule's bridle to steady herself. The mule tossed its head and skittered, and while I struggled to control it, Ferrante took Angela's arm and sat her down on the mounting block. Her terror seemed to calm him.

"He was ambushed on the Belriguardo road."

"He went that way this morning," said Angela. "Hawking in the meadows, he said. I would have gone but…"

"I know," said Ferrante. "you're with child. He told me earlier. I was with them for a while."

"Is he…?"

Ferrante shook his head, and I found I had been holding my breath. The sudden rush of air into my lungs made me dizzy.

"They've taken him to the castle. I think you should come back with me."

"He is badly hurt?"

Ferrante paused, and I fancied I could almost see his mind putting words together then rejecting them. In the end, you cannot dress up either the best of news or the worst, only the compromises and equivocations in between. "It's his eyes," he said, putting an arm around Angela and gripping her shoulder as though he was afraid she would fall to pieces. "Whoever did this tried to put out his eyes."

"Then I know who is responsible."

"You do?"

"It's Ippolito."

"Ippolito? Don't be absurd."

"You must believe me, Ferrante. Don't ask me how I know, but I do."

Ferrante looked up at me in a mute appeal for reason.

"I'm afraid Angela might be right. But never mind that now. Surely we had better go to him."

"I can't," said Angela.

"But he needs you; he's been asking for you. Come on." Ferrante tried to lift her to her feet but she refused to budge. He heaved at her as though her body was as heavy as the mounting block itself, then gave up, shaking his head in puzzlement. "Why?"

"I won't be able to look at him. What if he's blind? What if it makes the baby blind?"

❧

For two weeks Giulio lay in a darkened room, and though it was clear he would live, his wounds being clean and clear of infection, his sight was despaired of. He was attended not only by his own physicians but by two doctors sent from Mantua by Donna Isabella. Giulio was her favourite brother and she reported herself prostrate with grief at the attack on him. Duke Alfonso and Donna Lucrezia visited him daily, and Ferrante scarcely left his bedside, putting his own eyesight at risk, I feared, by reading to Giulio for hours by the light of a single shaded candle. Even Don Sigismondo came to see him. He blamed the rats for Giulio's injuries and assured him he was scaling up his offensive against them and would exact retribution. Giulio's doctors indulged him because he seemed to be the only one who could make their patient smile. Fra Raffaello, on the other hand, who came once at Donna Lucrezia's bidding, they forbade to come again because his moralising seemed to aggravate Giulio's distress.

Two people were conspicuous by their absence: Ippolito, and Angela. Though it was officially put about that Giulio had been set upon by bandits, everyone knew of the bad blood between him and Ippolito, and when rumours began to circulate that those responsible had fled to Hungary, where Ippolito held an archbishopric, two and two were put together with more than the usual accuracy. Yet Duke Alfonso showed no signs of taking action against the cardinal, and even gave him leave to visit Mantua, where Donna Isabella apparently received him kindly despite her grief over Giulio. The court lay under a cloud of disgruntlement and unease which made it a relief even to visit Angela, who remained shut up like an anchoress in Giulio's palace.

I went there nearly every day, often at Ferrante's prompting, to try to persuade her to visit her lover. He asked for her constantly, and her absence made him weep, and the salt in his wounds made his suffering almost unbearable. Ferrante could not understand her heartlessness. I repeated her concern about her baby, in the hope this would blunt Giulio's pain, but what I knew to be the truth was dark and hopeless, and deeply rooted in Angela's Borgia blood. She would not see him because she could not bear to look at him. She had loved him for his beauty, for the full, golden plumage of his youth, and there was no compassion in her heart for a scarred, blind wreck of a man. Listening to her increasingly thin excuses for her failure to go to him, I began to understand something about Donna Lucrezia also, about the way in which the murder of Don Alfonso of Bisceglie seemed to have sunk to the bottom of her heart's ocean. What they loved, these Borgia women, what they clung to for their own survival, was success. By allowing themselves to fall foul of their attackers, both Giulio and the Duke of Bisceglie had failed.

❧❧

Donna Lucrezia had offered my services to the doctors, saying I had knowledge of healing and was unflinching in situations which might defeat a less robust temperament. She did not know the half of it, I thought, as I modestly bowed my head and the doctors in their black robes smiled like jackdaws stealing trinkets. One morning, when I had removed Giulio's dressings so the doctors could inspect the progress of his wounds, Ser Andrea, the senior of the two physicians from Mantua, said he wanted to try a treatment on the right eye he had once witnessed in Florence, and despatched me to the market by the cathedral to purchase two white doves. Giulio himself, though hazy from the effects of the poppy juice I had given him before taking off his bandages, whispered to me to light a candle for him to Saint Lucy and to ask her to bless the doctors' endeavours. He gave me a smile full of sweet mischief.

"If you think she will listen to my entreaties," I said.

"Oh, I think she is kindly disposed towards me. I can see you this morning. With this eye." He pointed at his left eye, keeping his finger well away from the ragged and roughly stitched cut which followed the line of the eye socket but had miraculously missed the eye itself.

"What can you see?" demanded Ser Andrea, opening the window shutter a fraction.

"An angel in a halo of light."

Ser Andrea crossed himself and Giulio laughed. His laughter blurred my own sight with tears; it was so long since I had heard it. "Fear not, doctor, I'm not dying. The light falling on Monna Violante's hair is doing something quite extraordinary. As if I were looking at her through a prism. This earth we live on, you know, is full of miracles."

I left quickly, before I began to weep in earnest. He was a miracle himself, it seemed to me, with his stoical and forgiving temperament. As my slave and I fought our way through the market, she with her basket and I with my elbows, I grew angry, half on Giulio's account and half with him, for his failure to rail against Angela or vow vengeance on Ippolito, or even to complain about the cruelty of his fate.

"He might as well become a monk," I muttered, shoving my way to the front of the crowd around the best poultry seller. He had a stall right beside the cathedral's main doors and proudly flaunted the arms of both the Este and the archepiscopate on the little flags that snapped above his rows of plump, trussed fowls.

"Who should?" A man's voice, full of laconic amusement, too close to my ear. I was in no mood for familiarity. A thin, greasy rain had begun to fall, which did nothing to improve my humour. Rather than answering the question, I stepped back hard on my inquisitor's foot. He gave a hiss of pain, and I focused my attention on beating a large woman in a high, turbaned headdress to the last pair of pigeons.

I sent the slave back to the castle with my purchases and went into the cathedral to keep my promise to Giulio. I took my candle from the store in the side chapel where my Madonna of Strangers gazed out at the priests and altar boys, the nuns visiting from the country, the shoppers and businessmen, and the girls stealing glances at boys from behind their veils and chaperones. Giulio had given me a gold *scudo* to pay for my prayers, so I thought I could afford a second candle for Catherinella. I lit my two small lights and added them to the bank of jaunty flames and smoking stubs beside the altar, then leaned against a misericord set into one of the pillars flanking the chapel and let my thoughts carry me where they would. I thought of Giulio, and of Ferrante's unsung bravery, and Ippolito's charm and the close, gruff duke and what must be in his mind, having lost his father, his son and the loyalty of his brothers in the space of a single year. Briefly, I remembered my own brothers, before my mind revolted from its last memory of Eli, raging among the tangles of fallen wisteria in our courtyard. And shifted, inevitably, to Donna Lucrezia's brother, to Cesare, unimaginable in prison, and our son, now more than two years old, whom I probably would not recognise, even if I ever saw him again.

"Good day, mistress." Gideon d'Arzenta was straightening up from his bow as I came to myself and realised someone was speaking to me.

"Ser d'Arzenta. What are you doing here?"

"Praying for my foot," he answered with a rueful smile. "Somebody stamped on it at the poultry seller's. I am afraid it might be broken."

My embarrassment made me short with him. "It serves you right for speaking to a lady without making yourself properly known."

"You're right, my manners are appalling. My sister is forever telling me so. Please forgive me." He dumped down his basket of vegetables and a trussed goose which lay on its back with its tied feet in the air and flapped furious wings.

"How is your work progressing? I hope you are settled in here and beginning to feel at home."

He shrugged. "One thing about the Jews, they belong nowhere so the whole world is their home."

The goose honked, drawing a hostile stare from a priest who had begun fussing about the black Madonna's altar.

"Perhaps we had better go outside," said Gideon. "I fear my goose might give me away however well I keep my star hidden."

"It looks as though you're planning quite a party."

"It's Hanukkah. Had you forgotten?"

Hanukkah, when I was allowed to stay up late to help my mother, and later, Mariam, light the candles. Mariam and I would always have the same conversation. I would watch her dipping sweet cheese in batter for *bimuelos* and ask her why we always ate cheese at Hanukkah.

"To remember how Judith tricked Holofernes," she would reply.

"Why did she trick him?"

"Because she was a brave woman who did what she had to."

I shook my head, but I could not look at Gideon and I knew he must realise my denial was a lie.

"Why don't you join us?" he asked. "Come to the house where I'm staying tonight for the candle lighting. And dinner, of course," he added, waving the indignant goose at me, "if your husband will permit it."

We were standing in the shelter of one of the cathedral's two west doors, from where I could see the Torre Marchesana, and the walkway leading to the Torre Leone, and Duchess Eleanora's orange garden, where the rain was making the braziers smoke.

"I have to attend Don Giulio."

"Even at night? Is he so sick? The word in the city is that he will live."

"Oh, he will live, in his body at least. Though the light has gone out of his heart as it has from his eyes. He is the best, sweetest man alive and how she can treat him so…well, she doesn't know how lucky she is, that's all."

"You are clearly very fond of him. I hope you don't make your husband jealous."

"I'm sorry, I spoke out of turn. Forget what I said. These are family matters. And why," I added after a short pause during which my better judgement should have prevailed, "do you keep talking about my husband? What makes you think I am married?"

Gideon cleared his throat and suddenly seemed absorbed by the vegetables in his basket. "I just assumed…I mean, you *seem* married."

"I am not."

"But you wish you were. There is someone, isn't there?"

"There is no one, I assure you, Ser d'Arzenta."

"Good, that's settled, then. I will meet you at the San Romano gate at sunset."

"I cannot promise," I said. "I must have leave from Donna Lucrezia." It was unthinkable that she would permit me to attend a Jewish festival, yet as I hurried across the square, head down against the rain, I was already devising means of escaping from court for the evening.

I used Angela as an excuse. She would lie for me if need be, if only to make herself feel better about Giulio. Choosing a slave for whom I had once successfully recommended a coltsfoot poultice for his piles, I sent him to her with a message and told him not to return until well after the household had retired for the night. The sun had already set by the time I left the castle; madonna had changed her mind several times about her dress for the evening, even though, or perhaps because, she was to dine alone with the duke. Then Fidelma accosted me with a request that I read the sermon Fra Raffaello proposed to give on the last Sunday of Advent; if I found it persuasive, she reasoned, then it would surely move even the least pious of his congregation.

Shining his light on my face, the officer of the watch recognised me and let me pass. Though the evening was overcast, the clouds seemed to hold the last light of the day just long enough for me to cross to the gate at the corner of the cathedral square which led into the Jewish quarter. It was high and blind, and I had no knowledge, yet every knowledge, of what lay behind it. As Gideon stepped out of the shadow of the wall, holding aloft a torch whose light stuttered over the bumpy, irregular landscape of his face, I was so full of apprehension I almost turned and ran back to the castle. But he had placed his hand under my elbow to guide me, and the guard had pushed open the wicket with an admonition to Gideon not to cut it so fine next time, and it was too late.

The streets were empty, yet the jumble of tall, old houses seemed to pulse with life, as though their flaking walls and slipshod roofs could scarcely contain the press of humanity within them. All the ground-floor shutters were open and the window spaces filled with little constellations of lights. Snatches of conversation, sudden shouts of laughter, or the shrieks of excited children spilled out into the gloom of the evening, and as we passed one house we heard men singing to the jolly clatter of a zither. The damp air was laden with cooking smells; whenever I breathed in, rich scents of hot oil and caramel, roast goose and fried onions gathered in the back of my throat, making me salivate.

I almost missed the narrow entrance to the alley where Gideon lived, so as he turned to his right, I attempted to walk straight on and we collided. For a second our bodies brushed together, and it was as though the lights and laughter and music had formed a tight little ball in the pit of my stomach, a *bimuelo* of joy soaked in a delicate syrup of desire. I broke away and walked ahead of him down the alley, heedless of his warnings to tread carefully because it was muddy and there might be rats and next door had a vicious cockerel which kept odd hours for a chicken. I could not possibly desire him; I was not even sure I liked him. Then, out of the dancing shadows cast by Gideon's torch, by some magic Cesare's features appeared to me, the red river of his hair, the dazzle of his smile, the sharp, savage bones of his face. Was that what he had made me into, a woman stricken with lust for any man who accidentally touched her?

"This is it," said Gideon, pushing open a street door and standing aside for me to enter.

The door was warped, and the sound of it scraping on flagstones set a dog barking and brought the family out to greet us. Perhaps it was the fact that the courtyard was tiny, and almost completely filled by a broken fountain whose cracked tiles flashed blue as a summer sea in the torchlight, but there seemed to be at least twenty people jostling and smiling and welcoming me into their home for Zot Hanukkah. Several children pushed to the front of the crowd and stared at me out of round, solemn owl eyes and I remembered, with a pang of guilt, that I should have brought gifts. Yet here I was, empty-handed and with nothing in my heart but the bitter echoes of an aborted love. A man whom I took to be the head of the household scolded the children and they darted away, weaving like fish between the women's skirts and the long, dark robes of the men.

They had delayed the lighting of the lamps until our arrival, and now led us into a room which was unlit except for the *shamash* candle, the *menorah* behind it like a small tree glowing in the dark. We gathered around it, the adults shuffling politely, pushing the children to the front, passing babies from hand to hand until everyone was settled. I stood at the outer edge of the circle, with my eyes cast down to avoid looking at Gideon, who kept gesturing to me to move closer. At the lighting of the first candle, I flinched, but perhaps it was more a recoil of the soul than the body because no one seemed to notice, not even Gideon whose gaze I could feel upon me, insistent and concerned. So I found myself relaxing a little as the ceremony proceeded. I discovered I could remember all the words of the blessings, could even note the places where the customs of this household varied from those of my father's house.

When all the candles had been lit and the *menorah* taken to stand in the open street doorway, the lamps were lighted in the main room and the women began to bring food to the long table which sparkled with silver and bronze and coloured glass. I knew these people, I thought, as an elderly woman in black handed me a wide majolica dish of buttered cabbage and told me to set it on the table. They were the same people I had shared the festivals with as a child in Rome, living unnoticed in small, plain houses with everything they owned of value or beauty packed in boxes, ready to leave. But if you went into their houses at Purim or Hanukkah or Yom Kippur, you would see how they could blossom, as suddenly as flowers in the desert when it rains. The older girls and their mothers would exchange their modest, even drab, clothes for striped silks and slashed velvets, and headscarves tinkling with tiny gold coins. Tableware of wood and horn would be replaced with silver and glass, and there would be dishes coloured with saffron and turmeric, fragrant with cinnamon and nutmeg and the distillation of orange flowers. My father, with his expansive self-confidence and his broad network of roots in the city, kept a very different house. It looked like the country villas of the *goyim* to whom he lent money to build them, and it was right on the edge of the Jewish quarter so if my brothers and I climbed the tallest of the plum trees in our orchard, we could see right into the upstairs windows of the Christians.

After the meal, the children were made to clear the table and then Gideon stood up and began to delve theatrically in his pockets. As the children crowded around him, he began to pull out, one by one, beautifully carved and decorated *sevivot*, one for each child and all unique.

"He has been making them for weeks," a young woman told me, in a proud, proprietory tone which made me take particular notice of her. I thought her beautiful, in the same frail, ethereal way as Dorotea Caracciolo. I saw she wore no wedding ring, and watched Gideon to see how often he looked in her direction. But he was wholly absorbed in handing out the little spinning tops and explaining the rules of the game to his over-excited audience, one of whom had now clambered on to the table and was trying to dislodge Gideon's skull cap. I had a fleeting, uncanny sense that I was looking down some kind of magical telescope into the future, seeing him as he would be in ten or twenty years, a benevolent patriarch presiding over his family. The prospect warmed me for a moment, and then I wished I had never come, because what was his future was my past, and the past is a place you can never go back to.

I rose abruptly.

"Are you unwell?" asked the young woman, with perhaps a little more hope than concern.

"I should leave," I said, addressing myself to Gideon. "If I stay too late I will not be able to get past the guards at the gate."

"Oh, don't worry about them. They're used to me going in and out at strange times." He grinned. "I tell them the duchess has summoned me to talk about her commission." A hum of nervous laughter ran around the table, eyes flicked in my direction then dropped away again. The children, sensing tension among the adults, fell silent.

"Well," I said, forcing a smile, "it is true we often keep late hours. I suppose you might be believed."

"So you will stay a little longer?"

"No, really, I…you have all been very kind and the meal was delicious but…"

"I will fetch your cloak," said the young woman, rising from the table.

"Then I will escort you home," said Gideon.

"You will miss the Cordoban," warned an older man who wore a full beard and ear curls.

"I shan't be long. Go to my room as usual when he arrives. Everything is ready."

The night had cleared and grown colder, and a hazy moon silvered the wet roofs. Most of the Hanukkah lights had gone out now, and the old streets harboured nothing but slinking cats and the faint residual odours of roast goose and burnt sugar. And us. Gideon and I, listening awkwardly to the loud crunch of our footsteps.

"Who is the Cordoban?" I asked, to make conversation. "I am sorry you will miss him on my account."

"Best you don't ask," he replied, his matter-of-fact tone at odds with his words. The gulf between our worlds yawned and secrets seethed in it.

"It was kind of you, Gideon," I said, "but do not ask me here again."

"You used my name." He sounded triumphant. "You used my given name. Of course I shall ask you again. Didn't you enjoy yourself? Wasn't the food wonderful? Weren't you made welcome?"

"Your hosts behaved exactly as they should when a guest enters their house on a festival, but they didn't warm to me. They were curious about me, that's all. A *conversa* at court. They would probably have stuck pins in me if they dared, to see if my blood runs the same colour as theirs."

"No, there is a prohibition against it in the *Torah*." He spoke so earnestly I did not immediately understand he was joking, so he pinched my arm to make me laugh. But my laughter was false and I longed to be back in my own room.

"I don't belong here, that's all. I am no longer a Jew." I had no place but that room, where Angela's old gowns gathered dust and Leonardo's drawing had begun to fade, and Cesare's letter had cracked along its folds in the bottom of my travelling chest. No family but Girolamo, and Girolamo was a Borgia. "I am Violante; I break promises."

"You are always a Jew. Even my sister is still a Jew. We didn't ask to be Jews, we were chosen. We promised Him nothing; the promising is all on His side."

We had passed through the gate and were almost across the cathedral square. The sight of the great old fortress looming out of its moat made me feel homesick, as though I had been away for a long time. I wanted to be back inside its walls, cocooned in its intrigues like a fly wrapped in spider silk. "You may leave me here," I told Gideon.

"If you're sure. Well…" He offered me his torch. "I'm sure I shall see you when I come to court to show the duchess my designs."

I closed my hand around the stem of the torch, but he did not immediately let it go, and we stood there, hands touching, locked in a wordless, decorous battle for the light. "Do not seek me out," I warned him. "You know nothing about me. Nothing."

"All the more reason to look for your company. I am a curious man, Monna Violante." He bowed and left me, loping back across the square with his hands in his pockets. The brim of his felt hat was frilled like a lettuce by the damp in the air.

When I reached my room and made myself ready for bed, I could not sleep. The fire had gone out, and the bed-clothes felt damp, and the Hanukkah meal lay heavy on my stomach. Perhaps that was why my mother's recipe book came to mind. It lay now in the bottom of my travelling case, along with the rest of my meagre history. I had put it there on my return to Ferrara and had not looked at it since. I lit the candle on my nightstand, removed the book from the case, then climbed back into bed and, with my bent knees for a lectern, opened it at the first page.

*Leah Sarfati*, she had written, with more confidence in her hand when she wrote her given name than when adding my father's. The date beneath I took to be the date of their wedding, since it fell about a year before Eli was born. *In this book I will keep a record of everything I have learned and will learn about keeping a good Jewish home and raising children in the sight of Our Father. By His Grace I may one day have a daughter to hand it to on her wedding day, but I pray first for sons.* Below this, in my father's hand, were written some words in Hebrew which I took to be prayers and blessings for the home and family.

The pages that followed contained recipes for festival dishes and daily meals, remedies for cuts and bruises and common agues, charms against plague and small pox, compounds for cleaning silver and bronze and mending broken pots. She had recorded her timetable for Shabbat preparations, in what order the cooking and cleaning should be done, how the boys' clothes should be laid out and my hair braided last thing before sundown on Friday to give me the best chance of looking tidy until the Shabbat ended. Her cooking utensils were meticulously listed so there could be no mistaking which were for meat and which for milk.

Her entries began in the same neat, self-conscious hand that had written her newly-married name but as the years passed and her family grew, and Spain became an ever more frightening place for Jews to live, they became more hurried and untidy, the ink smudged and blotted, the writing leaning further and further forward as though straining towards its end. How happy she must have been, I thought, with a fierce pang of loss, when she did eventually have a daughter to whom she could hand on all this accumulated wisdom. There was a clutch of childbirth charms and remedies for pain in labour, sore nipples and stretch marks on the belly around the time of Eli's birth. These were followed by potions to make babies sleep, unguents to ease their gums during teething, tips for keeping children's limbs straight and making their hair curl. Each of our histories was there to be read between the lines of recipes for weaning foods, remedies for colic, unguents for the chicken pox, and poultices for grazed knees; yet none of us was mentioned by name, as if her love for us was a dangerous force which had to be bound by the careful listing of ingredients and proportions, methods and doses, the way spirits can be bound by charms.

My mother's domestic life seemed to end abruptly with a recipe for beeswax furniture polish given her, she noted, by Yasmin Abravanel during the month of Elul in the year 5251. A whole year before we left Toledo.

Slowly, I flicked through the empty pages, until I chanced on another one, near the back of the book, on which she had begun to write again. *Charms to Rekindle Passion,* she had inscribed at the head of the page. *You must take a good wax candle and anoint it with oil of cinnamon. Burn in its flame a bay leaf on which you have written the name of your beloved. Put a pillow stuffed with cloves and vanilla flowers upon his side of the bed. Keep one seed from a lemon you have consumed and plant it, and give the plant to your beloved to keep your love fresh and true. You must make a poppet with hair or nail clippings of your rival within and surround it with angelica leaves and that way you will ban her from your house.*

*I got these from Señora da Souza, the Portuguese laundress on Cal' Ebraico,* she had added beneath the charms. *I expect they are nonsense but what can I do against a woman so strong in magic she can draw him all the way to Rome? He has left again this morning, saying it is unavoidable business, but he has clerks in Rome. Why must he go there himself barely six months from his last visit? Last night he said her name in his sleep, so today I went to Señora da Souza, who has a reputation for discretion, or so I have been told. The woman's name is Mariam.*

I closed the book abruptly, as though by not seeing what my mother had written I could erase it. So that was why he had left us behind. It had nothing to do with my fair hair and blue eyes, though, of course, he had made good use of them since. Like any successful man of business, he exploited what he had and did not regret what he lost. I was smitten with a dizzying sense of dislocation, a sudden notion that the person I had believed myself to be, and the place I had believed I occupied in the world, had never existed and I was someone else entirely. It was not until I realised I was not to blame for my mother's ill-conceived, panic-stricken departure from Toledo, and her wretched death, that I understood how weighed down I had been by my guilt. I could simply off-load it now, as I had so many things, from housework to loving my family, on to Mariam.

*You follow love,* she had said. But where had love led her, or my father? They had not married, even when he knew he was free to do so. I searched my memory but could not bring to mind a single instance when I had seen them demonstrate affection toward one another. Had my mother been following love when she took me from Toledo, even though we might safely have stayed and passed as Christian, or was she driven by something else entirely? And where had love led Angela, or poor, scarred Giulio? Or me. By the time I finished pondering these questions it was dawn and I was no nearer finding any answers. I had just closed my eyes, thinking I would attempt to sleep for an hour, when the cathedral bell began to toll and I remembered it was Christmas Eve and I would be obliged to accompany Donna Lucrezia to morning Mass.

My head pounded with a dull ache all through the service, which seemed interminable, and my knees protested at the cold striking through the marble floor of madonna's chapel. I hoped I had taken a chill, but thought it more likely it was my other ailment flaring up again, and made a mental note to have words with the incompetent apothecary. Fra Raffaello did not preach, the Lord be praised, his style being better suited to the less joyful dates in the Church calendar. Madonna's own head chaplain, a man as sleek and plump as a seal, did not detain us long with his reflections on the impending birth of Christ. At the end of the service I asked madonna if I might be excused to lie down for a while, but she forbade it.

She made me go with her to her room, to put aside her prayer book and rosary, she said, but I was afraid she wanted to talk to me about Cesare. Her majordomo, Sancho, had returned from Spain some days earlier. He had seen Cesare at Medina del Campo and had brought letters from him. Could there be one for me? I wondered, then dismissed the thought; even if he had written to me I did not want to know what he had to say, to set eyes on that familiar hand with its loops and sweeps, to read his beautiful lies.

So I will tell you I was relieved when she said, "I wish you to accompany me to the duke's rooms, Violante. He has arranged to bring the cardinal and Don Giulio together. He wishes to make peace between them before the festivities begin tomorrow. Then we shall go to Angela. I have a proposition for her also."

∞

It was a horrible interview. Giulio, wearing a patch over his right eye and with the left still very swollen and discoloured despite the treatment with pigeon's blood, stood in a shadowy corner of the duke's private salon, outside the light cast by the lamps. Ippolito, who had been ordered back from Mantua by the duke, looked like a sulky bulldog. He stood as far from Giulio as possible in the intimate room, and refused to accept the challenge of his brother's ruined beauty. Apart from the three Este brothers and madonna and myself, only the duke's aide, the poet Niccolo da Corregio was present. I wondered if he was intended to compose a eulogy on the event.

The duke looked to Ippolito to open proceedings, but he refused to speak, so the duke told Giulio how sorry Ippolito was for the wrong he had done him. Then Giulio, shaking off the servant who had him by the elbow to guide him, stepped into the light. I sensed Donna Lucrezia, at my side, wince and look away. I kept my own eyes down because my position required me to do so, and saw Ippolito's scarlet-shod feet shuffle a little beneath his soutane.

"My lord," said Giulio, addressing himself to the duke as though they were alone together, "you see how I am. Yet," turning to Ippolito, "I must thank God and Our Blessed Lady who have granted me my sight. And although my case has been most cruel and inhuman and done to me with no fault of mine, nonetheless I pardon your lordship and will not cease to be to you the same good brother I have always been."

Duke Alfonso, who appeared unaware of the irony in Giulio's tone, which, perhaps, I had picked up because I had only my ears to rely on, mumbled something then gave up and burst into tears, whereupon Correggio prayed the brothers to love one another and enjoy their state or the duke would be forced to act against his natural inclination to forgiveness.

"You will exchange a kiss of peace," said Duke Alfonso, recovering himself. No one moved. I held my breath and I am certain Donna Lucrezia did likewise. Finally, Giulio took a step towards Ippolito.

"Your grace?" prompted the duke, and Ippolito also stepped forward. I fancied I heard no kiss, merely the rasp of beard on beard.

***

"I have laid my plans in the nick of time," said Donna Lucrezia as soon as Giulio's house slave had closed the door behind us and we were alone with Angela in the small day room overlooking the garden where she now passed most of her days. Though she had no idea when her baby was due, it was clearly a matter of weeks rather than months. She lay, huge and inert, on a daybed beside the room's single, tall window. Her thin wrap revealed not merely the swell of her belly and breasts, but the fat which mounded her thighs and shoulders and upper arms. On a table at her side stood a dish of sweetmeats and candied fruits, and a jug of sweet, yellow wine. She neither looked at us nor offered us refreshment but continued to stare out of the open window over the wet, brown garden while her hand moved mechanically between her mouth and the dish of sweets. There was no fire lit and the room was freezing. In the silence which followed Donna Lucrezia's remark I heard nothing but the thin chirping of a winter robin, and realised even the fountains in the garden had stopped working.

Donna Lucrezia gave a sigh of exasperation. Signalling me to pull a chair up beside Angela's daybed, she sat, leaning forward, her forearms resting along her thighs. It was a masculine pose; it reminded me of her brother. "Well if you won't speak to me, at least you can listen. This morning my husband effected a reconciliation between his brothers. If you will care for him, Giulio is free to leave the Corte and come home."

Another silence. It was to be a day of eloquent silences, it seemed.

"In that case," madonna continued, " he must stay where he is until he…grows accustomed to his condition. You must marry, clearly. I have spoken to the lord of Sassuolo, Alessandro Pio, to this end and he will gladly have you. He is most generous, for I fear your dowry cannot be much. What I have I must spend for Cesare's release. I wrote to your brother. Suffice it to say if he were as rich in ducats as he is in excuses, there would be no problem. Still, we shall manage. Don Alessandro complimented your beauty," she cast her cousin a sceptical, unheeded look, "and your accomplishments and told me he counted himself most fortunate. Make sure you do not disappoint him.

"We will have the wedding at Carnival. In the meantime, you will go to Medelana for the birth. It is far enough away to be discreet. The duke has most generously offered his bucentaur for your journey. Violante will help you pack." At this, Angela turned her head in our direction and fixed her cousin with a bovine stare. Her eyes were dull, her complexion pasty, and she had spots on her forehead. Her hair was untidily bound, and tendrils like tarnished copper wires clung to her temples. I wanted to weep. I wanted to gather her in my arms and tell her nothing had changed; it was still we two together with our jokes and schemes, and the men could all go fry in Gehenna.

"I cannot go today. I need to rest," she said. When she opened her mouth to speak I noticed her diet of sweets was beginning to discolour her teeth.

"You will be on board the barge before dark," said Donna Lucrezia. "Violante will go with you. I have retained a midwife and *comatre* who will also travel with you. You have nothing to fear. The country air will do you good. Now, up off that bed and let us see to your packing."

As madonna and I each took one of Angela's arms and heaved her up off the daybed, my first thought was that I was glad to be going with her. My second was of the ugly, charming face of Gideon d'Arzenta.

❧

By the time Angela and I boarded the duke's bucentaur, the light had drained from the low clouds and the river slapped against the jetty as thick and black as molasses. Looking back towards the city I could see the Corte and the castle ablaze with lights for the Christmas Eve festivities, and searched my heart for some sense of envy or exclusion. Yet I was content, happy to be alone with my friend even in these circumstances, about to set out on the river in the winter dark, into what was, however temporary, a kind of exile. The ducal barge was as luxurious as a small palace, with the walls of its staterooms velvet padded and hung with tapestries to keep out the cold and the thud of the oars. As well as the midwife and *comatre*, we had slaves to attend us and a cook, and madonna had lent us La Fertella to keep us entertained. Perhaps neither she nor Angela remembered the clown had been given to her by Ippolito.

But though all these things contributed to my contentment, if they had been taken away, they could not have lessened it. As we had waited for madonna's litter to be brought round to Giulio's palace to carry us to the dock, she had taken me aside.

"I have some news which will please you," she announced. "You know Sancho came back via Naples? He stayed one night with my brother Don Jofre."

"And is my son well?" I should not have interrupted her but I could not help myself, and she seemed content to let the matter go.

"Very well," she said, her expression alight with a very charitable joy, "as you will soon see for yourself. He will travel to Ferrara with his sister Camilla and the Duke of Camerino in the new year." Perhaps I asked her how this had come about, perhaps she simply chose to honour me with an explanation, I cannot remember. At the time, I hardly took it in, it seemed to matter so little why he was coming in comparison with the wonderful fact that he was coming, that in a few, brief weeks we would be reunited and I would be whole again. The reason, it seemed, was that Don Jofre, who had been widowed the year Cesare was sent to Spain by the sudden death of Princess Sancia, wished to marry again and his new bride was reluctant to take on the care of the three little Borgia bastards. Under certain conditions, Duke Alfonso had agreed to their coming to Ferrara. I did not ask what those conditions were, and madonna did not tell me. Not then.

# CHAPTER 3

*I was so young then, and confused lust with love as the young do.*

Looking over Angela's naked shoulder, at her candle-lit reflection in the long mirror, I thought how our lives move forward in tiny increments. Like a spring tide, we take great sweeps back and forth, yet each high water creeps only a little higher than the last.

On Christmas Day, as we sailed to Medelana, she had given birth to a baby girl aboard the bucentaur. The child was small, brought on early perhaps by the upheaval of travel, but she was strong. Angela was decisive in choosing the name Giulia for her daughter, but then handed her straight to the wet nurse and seemed to take no further interest in her. All the time we stayed in Medelana she bewailed the ravages of pregnancy on her body and set about trying to restore it to its former glory. She bound her breasts with bandages soaked in a paste of ground fig kernels to restore their firmness and had me rub her belly with sweet almond oil and lavender to banish stretch marks. Even before she had stopped bleeding she took to walking and riding on the estate, which I feared would bring on a falling of the womb but she was convinced would help to tighten her women's parts so her new husband would take pleasure in her. At least, she said, in the only reference I heard her make to her daughter, the child had been a girl, and small, so did not stretch the quim like a boy.

Donna Lucrezia had chosen the *comatre* wisely. She had attended a great many women who, for one reason or another, desired to return to a man's bed as soon as possible after childbirth. Make a game of it, she suggested with a laugh not altogether respectful. Mix a little rosewater in with olive oil and let him massage you. Well, Angela and I had not a lover or a husband between us, but we had each other, and we whiled away our time in the country with games the *comatre* had probably never dreamed of.

But now, with her wedding scarcely an hour away, she was still not happy with her appearance. "God!" she exclaimed, twisting this way and that as tongues of candlelight flickered across her skin, "I look an utter hag. My belly sags like a sow's and my tits are flat as pancakes. He will run screaming back to his mother and she will feel perfectly vindicated." The bridegroom's mother was less than happy with the match, which was why Angela had not travelled to Sassuolo for her wedding but was to be married secretly in Donna Lucrezia's chapel and would stay on at court afterwards. Angela had greeted this plan with relief; she had no wish to be buried in the country with only her dairy and her fruit orchards to occupy her.

"He will love you just as we all do," I said.

"Really?" She turned towards me. Unsoftened by the polished silver of the mirror, her face looked tired, the skin below her eyes fragile and puffy and a deepening of the lines at the corners of her mouth once caused by laughter. Whatever the artists may say, it is the flaws which make human beauty. Perhaps that is why the Creator did not abandon Adam when he ate of the fruit.

"Really."

I was right. Don Alessandro, attended by a cousin from Carpi, could not take his eyes off his bride throughout either the brief service or the longer supper which followed. I thought he would burst with glee when madonna finally took mercy on him and, rising from the table, ordered Perro and Gatto to escort the happy couple to the bridal bower. In the lull that followed, while we waited for a space to be cleared for the actors and musicians who were to entertain us while Don Alessandro and Angela made good their promises to one another in the neighbouring room, it seemed to me there were more absences in the room than just theirs. I thought of Giulio, still staying in the Corte Vecchio, of his baby daughter in Medelana, of his closed house and the silent fountains in his garden. I wondered about Girolamo, on the road from Naples, as I did a thousand times a day, pleading in silent desperation for his safety to whatever deity might hear me. I tried to imagine what he looked like now, but all my mind ever showed me was his father's face, and that was the greatest absence of all.

"Do you miss him?" Angela had asked me one evening at Medelana, when we lay together in front of the fire drinking wine mulled with honey and cloves.

"Who? Here, eat." I threw a handful of raisins at her.

She threw them back. "I'm dieting. You know that and you know who."

Perhaps because I had drunk more wine than was good for me, I found myself striving to give an honest reply. "In here," I said, tapping my fingers against my temple, "I can never forgive him for the way he tricked me. But the rest of me…yes, I miss him."

"Does he know?"

"Would he care?"

She shrugged, causing her shift to slip off one golden shoulder. "Write to him and see if he writes back. Some of his letters seem to get through."

"No." I sat up, suddenly uncomfortable with my body, aware of the cold breath of the empty summer palace on my back. I shivered, hugged my knees. "There is nothing in my heart which makes me feel inclined to do him any kindness. He doesn't deserve it and he wouldn't thank me for treating him as a charitable case."

Angela broke into slow applause. "Oh what a pretty speech." She knelt behind me and wrapped my gown about my shoulders like a cloak. "What you really mean is, you're afraid he wouldn't write back. You're still running from the truth about my cousin, aren't you, Violante? Just because he is free with his favours doesn't mean he can be cheaply bought."

"I know that. I'm just not sure any more that he's worth the price."

Her hands froze on my shoulders then, and I knew I had touched on more of a truth than I had intended. I had given voice to what was in her own heart concerning Giulio.

After the wedding, Don Alessandro returned home alone to his mother, while Angela hurled herself into Carnival like a parched man jumping into a river. She danced all night, frequently with Don Alessandro's cousin from Carpi, and accompanied Donna Lucrezia every day on masked rides around the town in the company of certain of the duke's favourites. In the front row at every spectacle, she attracted several champions for the Battle of the Eggs and blew a kiss to a man who succeeded in sticking a pig while blindfolded. Hers were the most extravagant gasps of admiration for il Cingano, the duke's gipsy, when he walked a tightrope strung across the piazza with iron bars chained to his ankles.

The court held its breath when Ippolito, extravagantly masked in a confection of pearls and peacock feathers, but Ippolito nonetheless, asked her to partner him in a chaconne. We sighed when she accepted, and danced with matchless grace behind her own mask of white satin trimmed with tulle ribbons that floated around her head like angels' breath. Duke Alfonso and Donna Lucrezia were as energetic and splendid as it was possible to be, their very presence at the heart of the festivities a mask to cover the grieving stones of our castle of ghosts.

On Shrove Tuesday I went to visit Giulio. I took him pancakes and a dish of *pane perso* from madonna's own kitchen; I did not like to think of him embarking on the long privation of Lent without a little of the holiday fare to cheer him. When I arrived, however, he already had company. Ferrante and Don Alessandro's cousin, Don Alberto Pio da Carpi, were with him. An empty wine jug stood on a low table between them, and they were well on their way to finishing a second. Don Alberto's presence surprised me. Ashamed of his scarred face and the clumsiness brought on by his damaged sight, Giulio had stayed away from Carnival altogether, and received scarcely any visitors. Ferrante called on him daily. He would, he said, have gladly admitted his brothers the duke and the cardinal but neither had seen fit to interrupt his revels to while away dull hours with an invalid. Of Angela, and his daughter, he said nothing, though his readiness to spend time in my company, to listen to me read, or even sit in silence, was eloquent enough. The odour of Donna Lucrezia's court clung to me. I was Angela's friend and had been with her at the birth of her baby. For him, perhaps, I embodied hope, possibility.

So although I set down the food and begged to be excused, Giulio insisted I stay and his companions, mellowed by the wine, put forward their own enthusiastic, if somewhat muddled, arguments in my favour. I sat, and answered their enquiries about my health, how I had enjoyed Carnival, what had been my favourite masques and spectacles, but all the time I had the feeling I had interrupted something. Our polite conversation skimmed the surface of a deeper, darker exchange, and I was uneasy. When madonna's Dalmation slave appeared in the doorway to Giulio's gloomy sitting room and told me, in her still scarcely comprehensible Italian, that madonna required me to come to the Camera di Paravento, I could have hugged her.

The Camera di Paravento was a new addition to her apartments, a room divided by a trellised screen behind which madonna would sit with her ladies while gentlemen danced on the other side. It was a device she used to allow the unmarried girls in her care to observe the young men she had in mind for them without compromising their modesty. I was sure either the slave had misunderstood her orders, or I had misunderstood her. There had been no talk of finding me a husband since my return from Rome; at my age, and with my history, I was pretty well unmarriageable. Nor had I much modesty left to compromise. But the Dalmatian made her way decisively enough along the adjoining walk between the Corte Vecchio and the Torre Marchesana, so I followed without question, picking my way through the thicket of scaffolding poles like a fairy-tale child lost in a forest. After the holiday, work was to begin on raising a roof over the walk, and not before time, I thought, as I stepped through a crust of ice into a puddle.

Madonna was attended only by Fidelma, which was also strange, as admiring the turn of a young man's calf or giggling at the sinuousness of his hips when performing the moresca was not her favourite pastime. Fidelma's heart was devoted to Fra Raffaello with his saintly pallor and the silvery glow of sanctity in his black eyes, though she believed she had given herself to the god of the Christians and petitioned madonna to allow her to enter a convent at every end and turn. She had fulfilled her promise to her father; her brother had his commission from the duchess; surely now her life might be her own. I found her naivete touching when I did not find it irritating.

"Look," said madonna as I entered, and the slave busied herself pouring wine and handing a plate of dates wrapped in marzipan. She held up a rough-edged silver disk. "The design for my medal. Ser d'Arzenta presented it yesterday." He had come to court yesterday and had not sought me out? Well, I had told him not to. "What do you think?" Madonna handed me the disk. On the face was a very true likeness of Donna Lucrezia in profile. I feared she would not think it flattered her enough, for it did not spare her her receding chin or a tendency to plumpness in her cheeks. On the other hand, he had captured the wry, determined set of her mouth as if he had known her all his life.

"I find the image very pleasing, madonna."

"Good. So do I. It is honest, as Fidelma observed." She would; her feet were as big metaphorically as they were in life. "Honesty is a trait I should admire, as duchess."

"Yes, madonna." What could I say? Perhaps, as the chosen conduit of her love letters, and the woman who, she believed, loved her brother as much as she did, I was the only person in the world with whom she could be honest.

"And I would not wish to be portrayed as some slip of a girl. That would not inspire confidence in my subjects. It is right I should look a little…matriarchal. Now," she continued, before any of us had a chance to dwell on the frightening irony of the word matriarchal, "turn it over. Look at the reverse."

The reverse was decorated with a blindfold Cupid bound to a laurel tree, and beside the tree a violin with its bow and a music stand, its voluptuous outline brushed by the tips of Cupid's wing feathers.

"It is very well executed, madonna." The composition was perfect, the tree arching over the figure of the god and its curve reflected in the angle of his body as he pulled at his bonds. All was fluid, windblown, captured on the edge of change, so you felt that if you closed your eyes for a second, the next time you looked, the image would be different. I could not equate its grace with Gideon's huge, bony hands, his flat-tipped fingers and scuffed knuckles.

"How do you read it?" madonna demanded.

"I must defer to you in that, madonna. You have the benefit of a superior education."

"Absolute nonsense. When we first met you matched me quote for quote from Dante, and your Greek is…quite subtle."

I thought of Giovanni, and my one Greek joke, and how he and my son and Camilla would be here any day now. "Well," I began, "Cupid bound to the laurel cautions us against loving unwisely."

Madonna smiled and nodded, though in the winter light which reached us only through the screen it was hard to tell whether or not her smile reached her eyes. "Go on," she said.

"The violin, perhaps, represents your illustrious husband as he plays it so well, and the bow his...virility." I heard Fidelma gasp. "And...the bow points to Cupid, and his wings touch the violin, so he blesses your union, madonna."

"Good, but I will go further. I will postulate that Ser d'Arzenta intends us to see the violin as hewn from the wood of the laurel, which symbolises Daphne's chastity. And Cupid's blindness enjoins me to concentrate on what my other senses tell me, to rely not upon what I can see, but upon what I hear. My husband tells me he is chaste and all is well with Ferrara. And that is what I must believe."

"He gives you the secret of marital harmony, madonna."

She laughed. "You see how clever he is. His work has inspired such discussion I had almost forgotten why I sent for you. Fidelma, you may leave us. Seek out your brother and tell him we are pleased, and he can go ahead and cast twelve medals in gold for the twelve months of my husband's reign, and thirty—no, let us say twenty-nine—in silver. Sancho will arrange payment with him if he will come to his office tomorrow."

As Fidelma left, I became aware from a sudden draft and a change in the light that the door to the main part of the room, on the other side of the screen, had opened. Some muttered conversation reached our ears, and a scuffling of feet, as though someone were being pushed or dragged across the threshold. Then a high-pitched cry of, "Shan't," followed by rapid thuds on the sprung dance floor. Footsteps, light and rapid. A child's steps. Pressing myself against the screen I called, "Girolamo!" Then realised the runner was a little girl, then was unsure. After all, Girolamo was still several years away from being breeched or having his hair cut. Red ringlets, a hot temper, and a dislike for authority, it might equally well be Camilla as Girolamo, or any other child born to Cesare.

"Shhh," commanded madonna. "Do not let them know we are here."

All the children had entered the room now, with a bevy of weary-looking nursemaids and a travel-stained man bearing a hobby horse, an armful of dolls, and a hoop and stick. Giovanni, I noticed, had grown taller and thinner, though his resemblance to Donna Lucrezia and their father remained strong. Turning my attention to the other two, I realised, in a whirl of guilt and panic, that I could hardly tell one from the other as they danced about in front of the man with the toys and tugged at his sleeves to release his burden. Both wore woollen gowns, plain but of fine quality, and soft caps pulled well over their heads to ward off the cold, both had long, unruly red hair.

"Girolamo?" But they were making too much noise to hear me. One of them grabbed a doll, which the other immediately wanted, and a tug of war ensued. Inevitably, the doll's head was sundered from its body and the child holding the head lost its balance and sat down abruptly. The other gave a crow of triumph, waving the decapitated body in the air, and trotted a lap of honour around the room, showing a glimpse of stout legs in wool stockings. To add to the mayhem, Fonsi, who had had his nose pressed to the trellis throughout, now escaped underneath it and flounced, yapping, in among the children. The child holding the doll's head glanced towards the trellis and, though he was unaware of it, for a second our eyes met. His were very dark, with an old, cool spirit in their depths I knew very well. Then he turned his attention to the dog, and tossed it the doll's head. That was Girolamo.

"Madonna, please may I go to my son?"

"No, Violante." She placed a restraining hand on my arm. "Best not to."

"I don't understand," I said, a sense of dread trickling into my veins, not certain I wanted to understand.

"I wanted to give you this opportunity to see he is well, but I will not be giving him back into your care. He is to go to Carpi under the tutelage of Don Alberto Pio. Don Alberto is of good standing and has some talented men in his household. He can ensure Girolamo grows up with all the accomplishments proper to his station."

"But…"

"There can be no argument. Were you married, it might be different, but you were unlucky there and we must ride our luck, as my brother would no doubt be the first to tell you."

"I am willing to marry, madonna. When have I ever said I was not?"

She gave me a sad smile. "There is a gulf between willingness and ability that I cannot afford to bridge. I would have to pay any man a high price for you, and I simply do not have it. Pope Julius sequestered everything of Cesar's, you know. You will be able to see your son. I will make sure he is brought to Ferrara sometimes. But you must promise not to make yourself known to him." After a pause she went on, "This is Cesar's will also, Violante."

*The children are important to me,* he had said, and had proved it, had done me the courtesy of an entire night in his bed to prove it. The thought of resistence flashed across my mind and disintegrated, like a shooting star, but I could see very clearly in the ensuing darkness. Resisting their plans would only separate me further from my son; at least, if I abided by madonna's terms, I would see him sometimes, and have news of him. I would know how he grew, and what he learned, when he passed through his childhood ailments, had his first pony, fell in love for the first time. I would know more about him than my own mother ever had the chance to know about me. *You follow love.* It is not a straight path, nor, perhaps, a very moral one.

❧

I found myself increasingly drawn to Giulio. Although Angela moved back into our shared room and carried on as though nothing had changed since we had come to Ferrara four years ago, I could not confide in her my deepening sense of betrayal over Girolamo. Her daughter, still at Medelana in the care of her nurse, seemed to have made less of a mark on her mother's heart than she had on her beautifully restored body. She would simply have told me that this was the way of things, that I had had my fun, paid the price, and it was time to move on. The festering air of nostalgia in Giulio's apartments suited my inclinations better.

Even as Easter drew closer and the days lengthened, Giulio remained indoors, behind closed shutters, saying the light hurt his eyes. His rooms stayed in the grip of perpetual winter, though spring was advancing everywhere else. Sometimes I read to him and sometimes we would entertain ourselves by reciting from memory or singing together, though my musical accomplishments were very poor compared with his, and it was a relief to me when Ferrante was there, or the singer from Artigianova whom the duke favoured and had lent to his brother to hasten his recovery.

"A bloody singer," said Giulio, with uncharacteristic ill grace, when Gian Cantore first arrived in his rooms, "and one I procured for him myself in the first place. What I need is money. Christ's balls, I cannot even hunt for my own table any more nor see to sign a bill for the very cloth to make my eye patches. How am I to live?" He was exaggerating, of course, and the singer knew it as well as I did, and it took little more than a new *barzelletta* from Tromboncino to restore his equilibrium. Music could always cheer him because he did not need his eyes for it; on the contrary, he discovered his ear was truer, his fingers more responsive to the tremor of strings without the distraction of sight. He joked, once, bitterly, that if Angela were ever to return to him she would find his touch could give greater pleasure than before. At night, he had added, with all the candles snuffed. He apologised immediately for his coarseness and never mentioned her again. Often it fell to me to fill the silences, which I did by talking about Girolamo. Though we never spoke of Giulia, somehow I knew Giulio understood my pain and that listening to me helped to ease his own.

Shortly after Easter, Duke Alfonso left for a visit to Venice and made madonna governor in his absence. He sent word to Giulio that he should return to his own palace, as he wished the duchess, his wife, to occupy his rooms in the Corte while he was away, and the rooms in use by Giulio would be needed for her household. He garrisoned the castle with a levy of Swiss mercenaries, though there seemed to be no reason for it, which sent a frisson of unease through the court. It reminded me of San Clemente during my last days in Rome. Whenever I went into the castle, it sounded like San Clemente, full of the guttural rumblings of the Swiss, the clank of spurs and armour, the click of dice cups. It smelled like San Clemente too, of leather and grease and steel, stale wine and men's sweat.

I believed this to be the source of my unease, until, while helping Giulio to settle himself back into his home, I dropped one of his books and a letter fell out from between its pages. I would not have looked at it, except that I saw the name of Alberto Pio written there, and could not resist. Giulio himself was in his garden with Ferrante; I could hear their voices through the open window, Giulio complaining about the light and Ferrante telling him he needed air and exercise and would have to get used to it.

The letter was from Francesco Gonzaga, though not written in his own hand, which I would have recognised immediately. He thanked Giulio for his expressions of friendship and assured him his love for his brother-in-law and grief at his treatment were no less. *Don Alberto Pio,* he had written, *will have conveyed to you in person, I trust, my sympathies for the action you and Don Ferrante propose to avenge the misuse of Your Excellency's person by the most reverend cardinal...* I dared not read on. What did it mean? It sounded to me like treason, for any revenge Giulio was proposing on Ippolito would be as much an attack on the duke himself, so close were they. Yet if they were planning revenge, how could Giulio and Ferrante and their associates be so inept as to commit themselves in writing? Perhaps it was just some joke after all, or an old letter, long past its relevance, tucked inside the book and forgotten. I looked at the book: some newly printed verses of Ariosto's from which I had been reading to Giulio only days before. I looked at the letter again to see if it was dated; it had been written during Holy Week. Pushing the letter into my bodice, I called down to the men in the garden through the open window that I had to leave, as the duchess would be looking for me to help her dress for her evening audiences.

"Apparently a lady from Cento wishes to petition her to allow a tournament of ladies to take place in the Barco on Corpus Christi," I told them, astonished at my own calmness.

"I hope she agrees," Ferrante called back. "That would be a sight for sore eyes." At which Giulio dug him in the ribs and they fell to scuffling like a couple of children. They had no inkling of what I had found nor what I intended to do with it.

What could I do with it? And how soon before Giulio realised it was missing and suspicion fell on me? I thought of taking it straight to Donna Lucrezia; she would do anything in her power to avert the distress of further discord between the brothers. But therein lay the difficulty. During her Holy Week retreat to the convent of Corpus Domini she had suffered a bout of tertian fever and was still weak. I feared a relapse if I showed her the letter. Walking back down the Via degli Angeli towards the Corte, however, I passed a man carrying bundles of trussed fowls suspended from a pole across his shoulder, and that gave me an idea.

After hearing the petition from the lady of Cento, which she declined, and others on the more usual matters of property disputes, marriage dispensations, pension claims, and requests for patronage, madonna went to rest and I was able to slip away. Donna Lucrezia's influence had enabled Gideon to set himself up in the workshop of a popular silversmith who had his business under the arcades bordering the piazza, so I did not have far to go. The early evening was fine, and people were still spending enthusiastically after the privations of Lent, so the old town was thronged with shoppers and porters, fishmongers with the smell of the river clinging to their clothes, *campesini* with earth under their fingernails wheeling barrows of squashes still capped with their little yellow flowers. A swordsmith and a knife grinder were fighting a duel of words about the quality of their wares which almost deafened me as I ducked into a tiny alley beside the apothecary's shop, where the scent of ground nutmeg mingled with the reek of pig. At the end of this, past the pigpen and a woodstore, and a rack of saltpans spread with drying olive pits, stood the silversmith's workshop where I hoped to find Gideon.

As I entered, pushing aside the thick leather door curtain, I heard whistling, and bursts of tiny percussions from somebody working with small tools. No lamps were lit, but blades of light struck through the gloom from gaps in the plank walls and the roof, forming a bright grid in which motes of gold and silver dust drifted and turned with the draught. As my eyes adjusted, this prison of light seemed to dissolve and I caught sight of Gideon, stooped over the workbench, chipping away at something with a chisel no bigger than the tweezers I used to pluck madonna's eyebrows. He had a magnifying lens in some kind of wire support strapped to his forehead and a plate of bread with slices of smoked eel lay untouched beside him. The food glittered with a dusting of gold powder. I cleared my throat, suddenly shy of interrupting him. He jerked upright, almost hitting his head on a roof beam. The lens bounced then slipped over one eye and would have fallen had he not thrust up a hand to catch it. Unravelling the leather strapping which had bound it to his head, he put the whole contraption down on the bench. The back of his hand, I noticed, also glinted gold, and gold scored the lines in his face when he smiled at me as though all the pores of his skin were filled with it.

"Ah," he said, as though he had been expecting me.

"I need your help," I told him, feeling it was important not to waste his time.

He rested his buttocks against the workbench and folded his arms. "I see. In what way can I help you?" He made no attempt to avert his gaze as I rummaged in my bodice for the letter which had slipped further inside my gown as I walked. As my hand brushed my breast, I had a sudden sense of his hand lying there, patterning my skin with gold dust, and a slow fire ignited in the pit of my stomach.

"Can I do anything?" he asked, with laughter in his voice. I turned away from him. I should not have come. I should have gone straight to Donna Lucrezia.

"I found this," I said, at last laying hold of a corner of the letter and drawing it out of the neck of my gown. As I handed it to him I was aware how warm it was to the touch, and how the vellum had bent to the shape of my body. Holding it in one of the shafts of light, fading now and more oblique as evening drew on, he scanned the letter quickly, his mouth tightening and a frown scoring itself between his brows as he did so.

"Where did you find it?"

"It fell out of one of Giulio's books. I didn't mean...it's just that..." But how could I explain? This was not the time to tell him my story.

"You would have done better to put it straight back."

"But if Giulio is planning to..." I could not bring myself to say it. "And Ferrante. They must be stopped. Don Francesco is clearly using them, perhaps because of madonna, perhaps on account of some new argument he has with the duke. And if they are caught, do you think he will protect them?"

"They are his brothers-in-law also," he said, but he did not sound convinced. "But anyway, what has this to do with me?"

"I remembered what you said on the boat. About being Donna Isabella's spy. I know it was said lightly, but all the same, if you have her ear, you could tip her off and she could tell Don Francesco and..."

"She'd be more likely to go straight to the duke or the cardinal. And she'd want proof; she'd want to know how I came by it."

I had not thought of that. I wondered if I had thought of anything, except that the man with the fowls had reminded me of Gideon with his Hanukkah goose.

"Why not go to Donna Lucrezia? She clearly favours you, and she strikes me as the kind of woman who would be adept at smoothing over a feud."

"She has been ill. I did not wish to upset her."

"Well perhaps you could blame the messenger, this..." He scanned the letter to remind himself of the name. "...Pio. Just say you're sure he got the wrong end of the stick but..."

"No!" I shrieked.

Gideon looked momentarily alarmed, but then an expression of understanding spread over his features. "Aha," he said. "So you do have a sweetheart. I knew it."

"No...no, you have it all wrong, Gideon. I have no sweetheart but...I would not wish to impugn Don Alberto falsely." My explanation was lame, but how could I begin to justify my concern for Don Alberto's good name? I suddenly, passionately did not want Gideon to know I was the cast off mistress of the disgraced Valentino, the mother of a son I was not thought competent to raise. I wished he could melt me down in his furnace as he might a poorly cast ornament and turn me into something new. I struggled, I blinked, I swallowed and gritted my teeth but I could not prevent the sobs that overwhelmed me.

Gideon pushed himself up from the workbench and gathered me into his arms. "I'm so sorry," he said, "whatever I've said or done I didn't mean to. I'm really, really sorry."

He must, I thought, be a similar height to Cesare, because his collarbone pressed against my temple in just the same way as Cesare's used to, but the fabric next to my cheek was homespun, not velvet, and spattered with wax. He smelled of woodsmoke and wool and rough wine, not the dark and dangerous seductiveness of jasmine and other men's fears. A good man, I thought, with a mixture of disappointment and relief.

"It's all right," I said, lifting my face free of the folds of his tunic. I sniffed. He pulled a threadbare kerchief from his sleeve and offered it to me. I blew my nose and he laughed.

"Now you have a golden nose," he said, which made me laugh too.

"Tell me, do you get your clothes laundered for free, so long as the laundress can pan the washing water for gold?"

"They are queuing up to wash my shirts. Can't you tell?"

I plucked at the crumpled sleeve of his shirt which had, I supposed, once been white. Beneath it his arm was warm, its muscles hard and sinewy. Standing on tiptoe, I placed a kiss on his wide mouth with its lopsided smile. He started back with a baffled expression, making me feel ashamed.

"I should go," I said. "You're right, I should simply go to Donna Lucrezia and let her sort it out." Our conversation had gone far enough, perhaps too far; I did not want to risk any further mention of Don Alberto Pio. I turned to leave.

"Wait," he said, putting a hand on my arm. I stiffened; the fleeting bond forged by my tears was broken now, and his familiarity was unseemly. He withdrew his hand as though from a fire. "Do you fish?"

"What?" His question was so bizarre I turned back to face him, to see what might have prompted him to ask it.

"Fishing," he said again, as though it was the most normal thing in the world. Which, of course, it was, in some people's worlds. "Come fishing with me on Sunday."

"I have to go to Mass on Sunday."

"Not all day, surely."

"Twice."

"Good, then you can come."

"I doubt madonna would permit it." Though even as I said this, I knew madonna would not mind. I would make some formal excuse, plead illness perhaps, to explain my absence from the day's round of needlework and readings from the lives of the saints, and she would wish me a speedy recovery. We would both know the other was lying and that, though she liked me, and sometimes confided in me, as I no longer had any currency in her marriage market, I was free to do as I pleased.

"She wants to see the finished medals. I will bring them tomorrow and we can persuade her together."

"Why fishing? A lady would usually expect an invitation to admire a garden or listen to music."

"So fishing will be something new and original for you. I'll wager Ser Pio doesn't take you fishing, or I would if I were a betting man."

"I scarcely know Don Alberto Pio, honestly."

Gideon gave a sceptical snort. "Now," he said, "go, before it's dark. I will see you tomorrow. And good luck."

"Good luck?"

"With the letter."

I had almost forgotten it. I had been thinking about fish.

As I turned out of the alley towards the Corte, a figure emerged from the shadow of the arcade and stepped in front of me. With his cap pulled over his eyes and his cape swathing the bottom half of his face, I did not immediately recognise Ferrante.

"Violante."

I flinched. My hand flew involuntarily to my breast where I had replaced the letter.

"It's me, Ferrante. Nothing to fear." Lowering his cloak, he revealed an ironic smile which did nothing to dispel the anxiety in his eyes. "I will escort you back."

"That is most courteous of you." My skin prickled with sweat; perhaps the ink would run and Don Francesco's dangerous words would become no more than a black smear on my skin. Ferrante offered me his arm. I took it.

"Thank you for helping Giulio. He has so little confidence and you have been very kind to him."

"I count myself his friend."

"In all company?"

"I would like to think so."

"Then you should return to him what you have taken."

"Me? I have taken nothing." My voice sounded forced and unnatural. I felt the pressure of the letter like a stone on my chest.

"Oh well, perhaps I was mistaken." His tone was light, conversational, but he pulled his elbow in to his side, trapping my hand against his ribs. "As you profess yourself to be Giulio's friend, doubtless there is nothing to worry about."

"I hope not, Ferrante, I really do."

We had almost reached the Corte by this time, but at the gate Ferrante steered me away and we continued walking along the palace wall. Dusk thickened in the piazza and the crowds of evening shoppers thinned out as the merchants put up their shutters and prepared to count their money. Ferrante and I, shrouded in the half-light, might have been the only people in the world, and it crossed my mind to wonder if he intended to kill me, to slip his knife between my ribs or snap my neck. The thought calmed me, because, if that was his intention, there was nothing I could do about it. Like all the Este brothers, Ferrante was a big man.

He stopped then and turned to face me as though he had come to some decision. I thought of Gideon and wondered how long he would wait for me on Sunday before giving up. I wondered about pain, and praying, and whether, in any deep recess of his heart, Girolamo would ever remember me.

"You could join us," said Ferrante. Interpreting my dazed silence as permission to continue, he said, "help us get access to Alfonso and Ippolito and we will give you your son back."

My heart lurched. "How?"

"Once they are...out of the way, I will be duke. We could marry. I would have to have a wife, I suppose, for form's sake, and what better for me than a woman who already has a son? I would make Girolamo my heir. He could be the next Duke of Ferrara, think of it."

I tried to think of it, but my mind seemed to be a whirl of dust in which shapes and possibilities loomed but never became clear. Then, to my astonishment, Girolamo's father came to my rescue. I thought how he had taken my son from me, how he and Donna Lucrezia had packed him off to Carpi as though he were no more than a gift of carriage mules or sugared *cedri*. If I agreed to Ferrante's proposal, I was surely no better. I, too, would be using Girolamo for my own ends. *You follow love,* said Mariam, and sometimes it takes you in the opposite direction to the one on the signpost.

"No, Ferrante, I'm not getting involved."

"Do you have the letter?"

"I've told you, I'm not getting involved, and you and Giulio should stop now before any more harm is done. You merely add a bruise to a wound."

Abruptly Ferrante dropped my arm and slumped against the wall beneath one of the Corte's high, barred street windows. "God I'm tired of this," he said. "I don't want to be duke. Can you imagine it? I just wanted to help Giulio and now…well, the whole thing is out of hand."

"Go away for a while. Go to the baths at Porretta. They have entertainments to your taste there, do they not?"

"I never cease to be amazed by you, Violante. How would a young lady like you know what goes on at Porretta?"

"Don Francesco has spoken of it."

"In front of ladies?"

"For the duchess's…elucidation."

He sniggered. "I tell you, Violante, you and I would make an altogether more upright duke and duchess than Alfonso and his lady, one all day in the whorehouse and the other being titillated by stories from the baths at Porretta."

"Never speak of it again, Ferrante. Go away, and tell Giulio to go too." I turned and walked away from him.

"What will you do?" I heard him call after me, but pretended I had not.

❧❧❧

Donna Lucrezia was silent for a long time while she read the letter, then turned back the page and read it again. Though she was pale, I did not fear for her health because at the same time her features settled into an expression of shrewd and determined calculation, one of those expressions that thinned and honed her face until it reminded me of her brother's.

"Leave us," she commanded her ladies. Angela hesitated. "You too," said madonna, and Angela slammed down her hand of cards on the table. She cast me a venomous glance over her shoulder as she left.

"Look out of the window," madonna ordered me. "Look for open shutters anywhere in hearing distance and make sure no one is on the moat. They were dredging earlier." The moat was dredged every spring to keep its depth constant and the water clean so it did not smell too much in the hot weather; every spring my heart remembered the shuttered, blank-eyed mask Cesare had turned on me as he stepped on to the ravelin and emptied Ser Torella's basin, and I feared the discovery of the dead child's tiny bones. An irrational conceit; how many bones had sunk into the silt of the moat over the years, what was there to distinguish hers from those of a dead pet or the remains of a meal cast out from the kitchens?

"You must tell me everything you know about this," said madonna as I drew the shutters close behind me as a precaution, though I had not spotted any evidence of spies. But spies are everywhere in courts; they are the essence of courts as wood is the essence of a tree and without them courts would be something different.

I told her how I had discovered the letter, and about the time I had visited Giulio and found Alberto Pio in his company, and as much else as I could think of, although I did not mention my visit to Gideon d'Arzenta. And I did not mention my conversation with Ferrante.

"Well Pio is easy to deal with," she said as I completed my account. "Find a slave and have him sent for." Although Girolamo had been dispatched to Carpi with his nurse, a valet and a gaggle of tutors, Don Alberto had remained in Ferrara; his reasons were now obvious. "Then go and fetch my brother's letters. You know where I keep them." She unfastened the key to her bureau from her girdle and handed it to me. I think she had always believed it would comfort me to know where the letters were; sometimes I wondered if she intended me to read them, though I never did.

By the time I had returned with the leather case, so slim you would never notice it beneath the bureau's false bottom unless you knew it was there, Don Alberto was standing before madonna looking a little like a rabbit caught in a bright light. Don Francesco's letter lay on her card table, tossed casually among the discarded hands of *cacho* and heaps of small coins. Every time she glanced at it, she pulled Don Alberto's gaze in the same direction, towards his own name inscribed there as if on a warrant.

"Ah, Violante, thank you," she said as I handed her the folder and she made a great play of opening it. "I thought you would wish to know, Don Alberto, that I have excellent news of my brother." She withdrew a parchment and waved it in his direction. Cesare's monogram, his personal signature, was in plain view. The letter's date was not. Don Alberto nodded, swallowed hard, turned, I fancied, a shade of green. His experiment with a smile failed.

"Yes," madonna continued. "He writes that he believes the charges against him will be dropped, for there is no evidence, you know, and that

King Ferdinand will release him. He says," she added, perhaps believing that by saying it she could make it true, "that he hopes to spend Christmas with his family in Ferrara. He attaches great importance to his family, Don Alberto, and to those who do us loyal service."

"I am honoured to be of service to your noble brother, duchesa."

"Are you, though, Don Alberto? Are you, do you think, setting Don Girolamo the best example? Will my brother approve your care of him when he next sees his son?"

Don Girolamo, I thought, my baby, made out of two very different sets of dreams.

"You yourself chose his tutors, madonna." Clearly Don Alberto thought he could take refuge behind a screen of righteous indignation.

"Yes," said Donna Lucrezia, in that voice which made you believe it could etch a pattern on a sword blade, "and I chose you. And just because I favoured you, and your cousin is now married to mine, do not think that gives you license to meddle in my affairs."

"Madonna, I…"

"Do not interrupt me, Don Alberto. And if you value that not unpleasant head of yours, use the brains God put in it to work out which side your bread is buttered. Do I make myself plain enough for you?"

He made a gesture that was a combination of a nod and a bow.

"Good. Then I suggest you return to Carpi posthaste and attend to my nephew, or I will have to discuss his future further with my brother. And my husband of course."

Don Alberto bowed again and backed unsteadily out of the room.

"Wine," madonna said to me, "and have a cup yourself. I do not suppose that was easy for you. Still," she went on before I could respond, "perhaps we have killed two birds with one stone and he will go to Giulio and Ferrante and warn them they are discovered. I would rather not have to drag Alfonso into it." I thought I would rather she did not either, and prayed Giulio and Ferrante would listen to Don Alberto if not to me. We drank our wine in silence for a few moments, then she heaved a deep sigh.

"Oh God I miss him."

"He will be back soon, surely, madonna. He has only gone to Venice." And you have Don Francesco, I added silently.

"Cesar, Violante. Would to God he were only in Venice. Would to God what I told Don Alberto was true. You know, if I did not have you to talk to, I think I would go mad with the worry."

"You honour me, madonna."

"No I do not. It is merely that we…share a concern."

I thought of Gideon and his invitation, and of Cesare and invitations, of my brother's broken eye glasses glinting in the mud and a chair shattering against stone stairs. My heart banged about in my chest like some creature maddened by captivity and would not let me speak, but madonna seemed content with my silence.

"When we were children, of course we did not live together. I was with Aunt Adriana as you know, and the boys had their own household under Cardinal Vera. But we used to spend the hottest weeks of summer all together at my mother's farm at Caprarola. One year, a calf was born that had two heads and six legs. Amazingly, neither it nor the mother died straight way, so the man who managed the farm just left it."

Reason prompted me to wonder why she had begun to tell me this, but instinct told me to keep quiet and listen.

"It was in a field near the house to begin with, but Juan used to throw stones at it, so the cowherd moved it into a byre some way away from the village. It was just as well because it made people nervous, six being the number of the devil. They blamed it for a series of bad storms we had that summer, and when the Jewish tinker came as he did every year, the villagers stoned him down the main street and refused to buy from him."

I thought perhaps she had forgotten me, but with a sudden, mischievous smile, she said, "Cesar tried to stop them. He said he didn't think the devil would choose a Jewish tinker to represent him, as it was too close to God choosing a Jewish carpenter. He thought the devil would be more original. Of course no one understood the joke and for a while it looked as though they'd start stoning him too. His career as the devil's right hand man began early, you see."

"How old were you then?" I ventured.

"Let me think…he would have been twelve, because it was the second to last summer before he went to Perugia. So I must have been seven."

"And what happened to the calf?"

"Eventually it died. The cowherd became more and more convinced it was growing into two calves. So one day he decided he would cut it in half. We went to watch. That is, Cesar and Juan were permitted to go. Jofre and I were not, but I got Cesar to smuggle me out of the house during siesta, while Mama and my nurse were asleep. We did it all the time, out of a window and down the back stairs from the loggia."

Where was she now, I wondered, the barefoot hoyden who scrambled out of windows to go adventuring with her brothers, skirts kilted up to her skinny knees and grass seeds in her hair? If I stripped away the layers of pomp and fine costumes, the white lead and carmine, the scars on the heart and the lines on her face that made her look older than her twenty-five years, would that girl still be there?

"There was quite an audience, but we were recognised and allowed to the front, though I got some disapproving looks I can tell you. I expect they were meant for the boys, for bringing me, but Juan would have disarmed them all with his smile and Cesar could always stop people looking at him somehow, as if he had shields around him. The calf was slung in a harness from the byre roof. It was lowing out of one mouth and one set of eyes was wide and rolling. The other head hadn't really grown properly. Its eyes were blue and filmy. It was more like a kind of big, complicated carbuncle. The cowherd had a little mallet to stun the calf. Juan tried to object to him using it. I began by agreeing with him, but then Cesar said two things. First he said the mallet showed the cowherd's thinking. If he believed the animal should be stunned before the separating began, then he knew it was going to suffer and probably die. Then he told me to look in the calf's eyes, and that if I did that, carefully, I would have seen all I needed to see. Finally, since he was sent to Spain, I have understood what he meant."

*We are not like the calf at Caprarola. We won't die.*

"It's another of the clues he's been leaving me. All my life." I was sure, now, she had forgotten I was there and was talking to herself, holding up to the light something which had gone unexamined for a long time. "I feel there were thoughts in my mind when I was born that he had put there, left in the womb for me to find." A changeling, her mother believed. A *dybbuk.* Like me.

Madonna's interview with Don Alberto seemed to have succeeded in its purpose. He returned to Carpi the following day. The duke did come back unexpectedly from Venice on the Saturday, but seemed relaxed, and left again on Sunday morning for the annual fair at Lanciano. He enjoyed the fair season, and the excuse it gave him to indulge his enjoyment of whoring, drinking, and brawling in taverns.

In the uproar of his departure, it was an easy thing for me to slip away to keep my assignation with Gideon, who met me at the Porta Mare, which I had last passed through with Angela on our way to Medelana. A terrific argument was under way between a carter carrying a load of building materials and a man standing before a smashed cheese lying in the middle of the street. It was one of the enormous, salty cheeses they make in Parma which are nearly as hard as marble. Ferrante used to joke a splinter of it would make the perfect murder weapon, for you could get the mice to eat the evidence. Quite a crowd had gathered to support one side or the other or merely scavenge pieces of cheese before the street dogs had them all. As I looked about for Gideon, I noticed one enterprising urchin slip a handful of scaffolding ties off the back of the cart, and wondered how much he would ask to sell them back to the duke's builders next day.

Gideon's height made him easy to spot. He wore a soft, broad brimmed hat which bobbed above the crowd as he fought his way towards me. His hatband was stuck about with a lot of tiny, bright-coloured feathers; it reminded me of pictures I had seen of the natives of New Spain, or is that just what I think now? His rods were slung over his shoulder, but he seemed to keep forgetting they were there, so they were endlessly catching on people's clothing, or the backs of their legs, and his progress was accompanied by a chorus of indignant shouts. By the time he reached me, I was almost helpless with laughter.

"What a circus," he said by way of greeting, using the bulky basket he was carrying to swipe at a tiny child who had been about to cut my purse. He missed, but the child ran off anyway to try his luck elsewhere.

"It's always like this down here."

"I would have liked to have taken you north of the city. The fishing is better there, but that's all the duke's land. I'm afraid we shall have to walk a bit." He took me by the elbow and steered me around the quarrelling men and the broken cheese, through the gate, and on to the public dock with its clamour of bells and raised voices, the slap of rigging against masts and coin against the table tops of the wholesalers and tax collectors. The air smarted with the smell of fish and tar. Gulls screamed over our heads, and, looking up at them, I suddenly felt the vastness of the sky, how it spread from here, over Carpi and Nepi, over Nettuno and Rome, to Spain and Jerusalem and the New World and the Kingdom of Prester John. Everything I knew was in it, and everything I was yet to know. It seemed to sway, like an awning buffeted by wind, but it must have been me because Gideon tightened his grip on my elbow and asked me if I was quite well.

"The crowds," I said, "and it's rather warm."

"Perfect for the fish. No wind, and the warm weather brings out mayflies at this time of year."

I laughed. "You might as well be speaking Turkish."

"Your ignorance is shocking. Did your father not think to educate you?"

"I'm a city girl, Gideon. I grew up in Rome."

"Rome has a river, doesn't it?"

"Not one you'd want to eat the fish from."

"Well Mantua is a very small city with a lot of lakes around it."

"So did you do all your courting on riverbanks?" I teased.

"Boats mostly," he replied, and it was impossible to tell whether or not he was serious.

As we passed the duke's private jetty, deserted now he had taken the bucentaur to Venice, all the mooring ropes neatly coiled and the Este standard hanging limp from its pole in the humid air, Gideon said, "Tell me about Giulio d'Este."

"Why?"

"He has sent for me. Says he's seen the medal I did for the duchess and would like to give me a commission."

"So that is why I am here." I twisted my arm out of his grasp and walked up the bank a little to increase the distance between us. He made no move to close it again, just raised his voice a little so he sounded like a poor actor trying to project to the back of a large room.

"A moment's thought before you climb on your high horse, Violante. When I asked you to fish with me, no one had seen the finished medals, not even the duchess. This all happened only yesterday."

Of course. What was the matter with me? Had my wits gone to Carpi with my son? Or further afield, with my old lover.

"Here. Here's a good spot." He stopped where the river began to narrow and was overhung with willows newly in leaf, all white bark and spears of silvery green trailing on the water's surface. He put down his basket and lay his rods beside it on a sliver of grey beach curved like a giant's nail paring while I hovered on the grassy ridge above wondering whether grass stains or river silt would be harder to clean off my skirt. I was wearing silk, the weather being too warm for a woollen gown, and though it was only my second best, I loved its deep blue colour and the embroidered panels of *mille fiori* I had done myself. Taking his cue as perfectly as a shepherd in an eclogue, Gideon produced a blanket from his basket and spread it at my feet.

"Sit," he said, as he delved in the depths of the basket, taking out first an array of mysterious small boxes, then enough food to feed the entire crew of a fishing smack. Fine white rolls, fresh cheeses, fruits, and salads followed one another on to the rug as though he had emptied a cornucopia. "I didn't know what you liked to eat," he said, "so I brought everything."

"So I see." I tried to sound appreciative, but I felt guilty. Such a spread must have cost him far more than he could afford, even with the promise of a commission from Giulio.

"You must work for your meal, though." Squatting on his haunches, he opened one of the boxes and took out a ball of lead shot. From another box he withdrew a tiny feathered hook similar to the ones decorating his hat. These he tied to one of the fishing lines then repeated the performance with the other. Then, stepping to the water's edge, he told me to watch carefully while he demonstrated casting. "First, look behind you. There is nothing more foolish than a fisherman—or woman—with his line caught in a tree. Then you must think of your rod as a spring. You load it with the weight of the line and shoot it out into the water."

I tried to watch as he instructed me, paying attention to the angle of the rod on the back cast, the straightness of the line, and a thousand other technical details, but all my wayward senses would take in was him, his gangling silhouette haloed by the river's sparkle, the unexpected grace of his movements, the concentrated set of his head, his ridiculous, unabashed delight at every catch, however small. So I proved a poor student. I let my line become tangled, my casts fell short, and then, when I thought I had a bite, it turned out to be an old boot.

"Not much use," observed Gideon, "unless we can find its mate."

By this time I was flushed and hot and far too cross to appreciate his humour. Flinging my rod on the bank, I climbed up to sit on the rug and sulk. My corset chafed and my scalp prickled with sweat under my cap. Looking at the river carving its lazy, sinuous path between its banks, the silver fish jumping after turquoise dragonflies, the low, wide arcs of swallows and swifts, I longed to swim, to be part of heedless nature with its simple necessities. Perhaps I might at least remove my cap, and take off my shoes and hose and cool my feet in the water. Thinking Gideon was absorbed in his fishing, I was careless, lifting my skirts to the knee to make it easier to unlace my hose. A sudden stillness, a sense of breath caught and held, made me look up and realise he was watching me. For all my loosened hair and bare calves, I felt hotter as my body struggled with its constrictions.

Gideon lay his rod aside and climbed the bank towards me. He had removed his doublet. His shirt was so worn I could clearly see the dark circles of his nipples and a smudge of chest hair through the fabric. A gold ornament on a chain swung free of his loosened collar as he climbed. I thought of covering myself but my arms seemed too heavy to lift in the sultry heat. As he knelt in front of me, his face in its frame of dark curls was that of a slightly battered angel, but men's bodies are not subtle, and the humanity of his intent was obvious. Reaching forward, he brushed the inside of my knee with the tips of his fingers, then took hold of the hem of my skirt and pulled it down to my ankles.

"You never know," he said, "who might be passing."

I felt dirty and ashamed, and seemed to catch a glimpse of Cesare laughing at me from his castle in Spain. You made me, my heart snapped back, knowing in the same instant that he would have said we make ourselves.

"It's so hot."

Gideon had the grace to ignore my lame apology. "Let's eat," he said, "before it gets any hotter." He knelt on the rug, rolled up his sleeves, and handed me a hunk of bread piled with cheese and olives. "Not as elegant as the duke's dinner table, I'm afraid." His hand was trembling.

<hr>

When the meal was over, we lay side by side on the crumb-strewn blanket, eyes closed, listening to the murmur of the river and the occasional splash of the fish in Gideon's keepnet. The birds had stopped singing in the noon heat, and the docks downstream had fallen silent. The broken glitter of sunlight through the willow branches flickered red through my closed eyelids. Except for Gideon's breathing beside me, I might have been alone in the universe. After a little while, I felt the back of Gideon's hand brush my own, a cautious pressure more of air than muscle and bone.

"Violante?"

"Mmm?"

"What is your given name?"

Cocooned in my sense of solitude, I had no objection to telling him because, somehow, it would only feel like telling myself. But as I brought my old name to consciousness, I suddenly doubted my ability to say it.

"I'd like to know," he persisted, sensing my hesitation.

"Why?"

"Because Violante is a cruel nickname. It pains me to use it."

"It's just an irony, Gideon." But it was not; it had been true then, and my inconsequential investment, my flirtatious failure to reply to an invitation to the races, had paid me interest many times over. I was not going to break any more promises. "It's Esther," I said. "My name is Esther Sarfati."

"You see?" He curled his fingers around my palm. "That wasn't so difficult, was it?"

A sudden dimming of the light made me open my eyes. Gideon had turned on to his side and lay facing me, his cheek propped against his left fist. The dappled light spilled around him, making it hard for me to see his face clearly. "Will you marry me, Esther Sarfati?" he asked.

I laughed at the absurdity of his question. "You do not want to marry me, Gideon." I could not even go through the motions of thanking him or telling him he honoured me. "You do not know me."

"I know you are clever and beautiful and it gladdens my heart to be in your company."

"I have no money, you know, no family."

"If I had been concerned about a dowry, I would have gone to the duchess first." He would too, I thought, squinting up at him against the sun. There could not have been a man in Italy more oblivious to the workings of a court. He probably needed a woman like me to protect him from himself. "I can earn my living, and yours," he went on. "You are not one of those frivolous girls, are you?"

I shook my head. "I am not a girl at all." I was twenty years old then. I might as well have been ninety.

"At least do me the courtesy of thinking about my proposal."

"I must do you the greater courtesy of declining it. Believe me, Gideon, I am not what you want."

"You say these things, but you show me no evidence. Without evidence, how am I to believe marriage to you would be such a terrible mistake? We live in a scientific age, Esther. It is knowledge that matters. Tell me something about yourself. Justify your assertion."

If I told him about Cesare and Girolamo, that would be sure to put an end to his interest in me. I opened my eyes and looked at him, as if I might read in his face the kind of knowledge that would satisfy him. A cloud drifted past the back of his head. Its shape reminded me of a woman's breast. "All right," I said, "here is something I know. Don Cristoforo Colon once wrote to Isabella the Catholic that his travels had led him to conclude that the earth is shaped like a woman's breast."

Gideon was not impressed. "That is either no secret at all, or not yours to tell."

"I assure you it is a secret. I do not think the Inquisition would like such a thing to be widely known or believed. And I had it from a source who is very good at finding out secrets. As the source was mine, then the secret is mine."

"An argument, I grant you, though perhaps not irrefutable."

"Is any argument? Now it's your turn. What will you tell me about yourself?"

He sat up, removed the gold chain from his neck and placed it in my hand, the ornament warm as a living thing in my cupped palm. It was made of three concentric circles with a triangle at their centre and linked by figures I recognised as Hebrew characters. "That is my secret," he said, in a tone which made it clear he was showing me something of great importance to him.

"What is it?" I felt stupid, and somewhat guilty at having palmed him off with Cesare's pretty, and probably untrue, seduction.

"It is a symbol of knowledge. Special knowledge, vouchsafed only to those who have ears to hear and eyes to see."

A lock was unfastening, a door sliding open in my memory, of serious men who used to visit my father in our house in Toledo in the months before he left for Rome. I fancied I had seen some of them again there. My father never kept a very strict house, but when these men visited, I was always banished from the public rooms. One of them, I seemed to recall, came from Cordoba.

"Is it something to do with the Cordoban?"

"Shhh." He replaced the chain around his neck. "Do not mention him. Perhaps it would be best if you forgot altogether that I had shown you the symbol."

"Then why did you show it to me?"

"Because I thought…wondered if it might be familiar to you."

I shook my head. "The characters are Hebrew, aren't they? How many women do you know who can read Hebrew? My father was an enlightened man, but there are limits."

"The characters themselves matter less than how they are placed, what they represent. They show the universe. The letters at the centre name the Unnameable, that's why I keep the ornament hidden."

"Yet you would uncover it for me?"

"I want you to understand. That I'm not just who I appear to be."

That was something I understood very well.

"Because you aren't either, I don't think," he went on. "But what this does," he lifted the ornament clear of his throat and held it towards me, "is teach us that a time is coming when we can be ourselves. When we'll no longer have to disguise ourselves to realise our true potential."

I sat up, suddenly alarmed. "Gideon, are you talking about rebellion?

Because if you are I must warn you I can't hear of it. Whatever you think of my position, Donna Lucrezia has been good to me. Besides, I do not know how things are in Mantua, but in Ferrara the Jews are treated well. Why upset the apple cart?"

"Well, Esther? You think the Jews are treated well? Even in our own land of Israel we are outcasts. We have to bow the knee to the Christian pope on one hand and the Sultan on the other. We are harried from pillar to post, crammed into the oldest and worst housing, excluded from public office, blamed for everything from the plague to crop failures." And malformed calves, I thought, though I kept silent and let him exhaust his theme. "You call that being well treated? I tell you, when we are ready in the Lord's sight and the Messiah comes, you'll see some changes."

"Oh, I shall probably go up in flames with the Christians and the Musselmen."

"Don't be flippant," he said gently. "I haven't expressed myself well. Of course I know messianic talk is ridiculous. The Messiah is not a man, not even a god dressed in a man's clothes. Messiah is a state of mind, a readiness, an openness. What the Cordoban teaches us is to look for opportunities and take them when and where we find them. That's what I'm offering you, Esther, an opportunity."

"For what? To marry you and be a good Jewish wife with two sets of cooking pots and a *mezuzah* on every doorpost? Or to turn against my duchess? For all her sins, she is my mother in Christ, Gideon, and she and her family have given me more than my own ever did." I rose to my knees and began cramming the remains of our picnic into the basket, squashing cheeses and bruising fruit instead of hitting Gideon, which was what I felt like doing. "Now I should like to go home."

"Your wish is my command, madam," he said, rocking onto his haunches then springing to his feet and making me a deep bow.

"Stop it!" I tried to fasten the basket, but I could not push down the lid. Yanking on the toggle, I succeeded only in snapping it off. I shook as though I had an ague, and wondered if I were indeed coming down with a fever. Gideon took the basket from me and, with a few deft twists, managed to re-attach the toggle. He offered me his arm, but I rose unaided and set off towards the city without even waiting for him to gather up his rods or haul in his keep net. We strode in silence towards the deserted docks, past the duke's jetty, past gulls roosting on bollards and stevedores sleeping away the afternoon in the shade of the warehouses. A series of grunts and squeals drew my attention to a jade entertaining a customer up against a tree trunk, her grey, pitted thighs locked around his waist, his plump buttocks flexing and shuddering. My skin crawled with a thousand emotions, as though I had been flayed in an ice bath like Cesare.

It was not until we were almost in sight of the Porta Mare I realised Gideon was not carrying any fish, and broke the volcanic silence between us to ask him what had happened to them.

He shrugged. "I had to leave them. You didn't leave me time to stun them all and pack them up."

"What a waste."

"I don't think so."

# Chapter 4

*We have never hidden things from one another. That is our unique strength, for we have both had to be adept at hiding truths from others.*

I did not see Gideon again for some months. Our life continued serenely enough in the duke's apartments in the Corte, but now I look back, I can see our peaceful routine was like the smooth surface of a sea concealing fierce currents.

Madonna had become inseparable from Ippolito, with whom she shared the governance of the state while the duke was away. A frequent, if improbable, third member of their regency was little Giovanni, who had been allowed to stay in Ferrara. I consoled myself with the thought that the duke must think madonna's little brother less of a threat than Cesare's son. Madonna took a close interest in his education and believed he could learn much from witnessing the day-to-day management of the duchy, though he usually looked very bored and often distracted proceedings by dropping his toys or asking how much longer he must sit there. Madonna was all smiling patience with him. Whatever Ippolito thought, he kept it to himself.

Not only did he and Donna Lucrezia work together, receiving embassies, holding courts, reviewing the city's defences, but often dined together as well, laughing at the duke's letters, which recounted in robust detail his adventures in the Adriatic with a couple of Venetian sea captains he had picked up at Lanciano, and planning the entertainments for Corpus Christi. Angela was never far from Ippolito's side either, with her husband safely in his mother's house at Sassuolo and her daughter still in the country.

My own part in court life was a less prominent one, of necessity, since I still carried letters to and from Don Francesco between madonna and Ercole Strozzi. I was still expected to listen, when no one else would, to her schemes for obtaining Cesare's release, to read over and approve the pathetic appeals she made to King Ferdinand, relying on a kinship which everyone but the Borgias themselves knew to be an invention. She even wrote to Pope Julius, who no doubt prayed daily that imprisonment would take its toll on Valentino and speed him to an early grave. He had been in prison for two years now, and still no date had been set to try him for the crimes with which he was charged. Since the letters brought by Sancho, we had heard nothing of him, or, if madonna had news, she did not share it with me.

She was punctilious, however, in letting me know how my son progressed at Carpi. He had shown himself precociously intelligent, she said, and could already identify the letters of his name written on a slate. Don Alberto had acquired a pony for him, and had led him over some small jumps without mishap. Don Alberto's wife and her ladies were enchanted with him though the servants less so.

"He sounds more like Juan than Cesare," she remarked, knitting her brows in a brief, troubled frown. Or Little Haim, I thought, who used to drive Mariam to distraction with his disorderliness and the variety of tricks he could devise involving slimy creatures or large insects.

Ferrante came to court irregularly, and was not much company when he did. His Vittorio seemed to have evaporated along with everything else of Cesare's except his place in his sister's heart, which had plunged Ferrante into a febrile irritability I recognised only too well. I suppose he had other boys, but they were not Vittorio. He remained quietly mutinous at the way everybody seemed to ignore Giulio, watching Ippolito and Donna Lucrezia with a cynical twist to his mouth which disfigured his broad, pleasant face almost as much as Ippolito's assassins had disfigured Giulio. Eventually, he tried to talk to her. If Ippolito had not been there, if she had been able to speak freely, many things might have turned out differently.

Madonna held her daily audiences in the castle, in the Sala Grande. She and Ippolito sat on a dais at the far end of the room, madonna dwarfed by the duke's high-backed throne, her feet resting on a gilt and crimson footstool because they could not reach the floor. Ippolito's clerks stood behind him; Giovanni and those of us who were in attendance on madonna sat on cushions before the throne, just as she used to do when she attended her father's audiences as a girl. Guards were posted on the main doors and the smaller ones behind us which led to the room used by the Savi as a robing room. The times being as uncertain as they were, we also had soldiers stationed at intervals along the walls.

That morning, Ferrante waited at the back of the hall until all the other petitioners had been heard. Once the room had emptied he walked forward, the thud of his boots against the floorboards echoing from the frescoed walls and vaulted ceiling. Snatching off the voluminous cap which had given him a semblance of anonymity, he made a deep bow. Ippolito shifted in his chair like a man suffering from piles, but madonna bestowed her most charming smile on Ferrante. "Brother," she said, "we welcome you."

Ferrante stepped on to the dais and knelt to kiss her hand, but she stood up, raised him to his feet, and kissed both his cheeks, standing on tiptoe to reach them. He flicked a glance in my direction.

"How can I help you, Ferrante?" enquired madonna. "It distresses me you feel you must wait your turn among all those people complaining about their stolen goats and the state of the city middens. You know you have my ear at any time. Isn't that so, cardinal?"

Ippolito made a non-committal sound in the back of his throat that could have been interpreted as assent. Ferrante did not so much as glance at him.

"I am here on behalf of Don Giulio," he began.

"Could he not come himself? Is he ill again?" Before he left, the duke had made it clear Giulio was free to come and go as he pleased. Duke Alfonso did not, he had made plain, attach any credence to rumours of plots against him. He trusted his brothers as was proper. The strengthening of the garrison was a natural precaution during his absence.

"He will not leave his palace, madonna. He prefers to spend his time with his horses or among his plants than at court where he is afraid people will look at him. I fear his pride is slower to heal than his body."

"Poor Giulio."

"You could do much to alleviate his suffering by visiting him, sister."

"Can we go? It's boring here," said Giovanni. He was always an insensitive child, lacking the instinct for adult moods most children seem to develop in order to survive. I shushed him and tried to distract him with a little wooden knight on horseback he had with him.

Madonna's gaze flicked uncertainly in Ippolito's direction. "Yes...yes, I must do that soon."

"He feels much aggrieved that so little has been done for him. He has, like myself and Sigismondo, only the house and pension left him by our father and now no means of augmenting it with spoils of war or an advantageous marriage."

"Neither does Sigismondo," Ippolito responded.

"With respect, your grace, his case is somewhat different. He has no obligation to maintain the same standard of household as Giulio. His needs are as simple as he is, if you will. Perhaps...a benefice or two? Our brother feels he might well take holy orders. He is a devout man as you know, and his love of music would stand him in good stead in the Church. With the right level of income he might become a considerable patron of devotional music."

"You expect me to share my living with him?"

"Some might say there is some justice in that. Others might say Christ's servants on earth have a duty to emulate Him."

"You speak wisely, Ferrante," said madonna. "I will write to my husband on the matter."

"With respect, duchesa," said Ippolito, "you will find he is of the same mind as I am in this matter. Don Giulio and I have mended our differences. I have apologised for my rash and unfraternal behaviour. Don Giulio is taken care of. And while he may not soldier again, I believe there is nothing to stop him marrying. A man does not need his eyes to get heirs. In some cases, I'll wager, he is better off without them."

Madonna greeted Ippolito's joke with a faint smile. "If that is your word, cardinal, then I am afraid I can do no more. Ferrante; please tell Giulio I...grieve for him."

"And his daughter, madonna? Can he at least see her?"

"I am afraid that decision must rest with Don Alessandro Pio, brother, for he is now her legal guardian. Donna Angela...Donna Angela might fear the effect of her father's injuries on the child's health. I am sorry."

Ferrante turned very pale; the freckles scattered over the bridge of his nose seemed almost blue. He looked at us all, so prettily arranged on our dais, with an expression of such contempt it made me blush, then bowed and stalked off.

"Do not turn your back on me," Ippolito shouted after him, but he did not appear to hear.

"What a pity," Giovanni whispered. "I hoped there was going to be a fight."

"There might still," one of the new girls whispered back. She looked barely out of childhood herself.

As soon as the doors were closed, Donna Lucrezia turned on Ippolito. "Everything you have said might have been calculated to make things worse. Was that your intention? If so, I doubt Alfonso will be very impressed."

"You think not? He knows as well as I do the pair of them are up to something. The sooner they're flushed out the better."

My cheeks burned. I busied myself with Giovanni and hoped Ippolito would not notice.

"You don't think, perhaps, the most effective way to win them over would be to do something for Giulio?" said madonna. "What about the archbishopric here? That would be a nice gesture."

Ippolito glared at the top of Giovanni's head. "As long as you are duchess here, I doubt the Holy Father will listen to any entreaties from this family."

"Is that a threat, your grace?"

"Of course not."

They eyed one another up for a moment like a couple of prizefighters, then madonna said, "Well, if we have no more business for this morning I shall ride out to the Barco to look at the condition of the race course. My ladies will want to know which way to bet on the Corpus Christi races. And you too eh, Gi'anni?" She patted her brother's head, smiled at us, then rose, gathered her skirts, and swept past Ippolito to the small door at the back of the dais which gave on to the robing room.

❦

As soon as we had returned to the privacy of her apartments, and Giovanni had been sent to his mathematics tutor, she gave vent to her fury. She paced the floor, raking a hand through her hair until I thought we would be more likely to spend the afternoon re-dressing it than riding in the Barco.

"Why must I be plagued by quarrelling brothers?" She shook her head and sighed and muttered to herself, and finally came to a halt in front of me. Drawing me out of earshot of the rest of her ladies she commanded me to go to Giulio. "Ask him, no, tell him from me that he must leave the city as soon as he can. He should go to Mantua. Donna Isabella will look after him and I will put in a word for him with Don Francesco."

"Is that wise, madonna, given the letter I showed you?"

"I will speak frankly with you, Violante, as there is no point in doing otherwise. I have addressed that business in my correspondence with Don Francesco, and he assures me he has no intention of scheming any further against my husband. He appreciates it puts me in an impossible position and says he was motivated merely by a jealousy which, though flattering to me, is unworthy of him. I have his word as a man of honour."

"Will you give me a note for Don Giulio, madonna?"

"I think not. We must have nothing in writing if we can avoid it. Show him this as a signal of my good intent." She removed a large pearl from her bodice which had been a wedding gift from Giulio and handed it to me.

"I will be back within the hour, madonna, before anyone can notice I am gone."

❧

I arrived at Giulio's palace to be told he was in the Temple of the Graces. This was a summer house he had built at the foot of a stepped water feature that cascaded the length of his garden. A fountain of spewing bronze dolphins screened it from the house, and it stood at the centre of a box knot garden in the English style. Its entrance, pillared and porticoed in pink-veined marble, faced away from the palace over rolling parkland where Giulio kept deer and miniature horses, and a giraffe in a sort of giant aviary made of silver wire. I knew Giulio's garden well, so I made my way to the temple unaccompanied.

As I approached the entrance I thought I could hear the murmur of voices, but Giulio's majordomo had not mentioned other visitors so I thought it must be a trick of the water splashing from the fountain.

Stepping under the portico, I called out to him. There was no reply, but I could definitely hear voices now, and as I followed the sound across the atrium where Giulio kept his collection of classical sculpture, an eerie, guttural growling joined them, as though someone were strangling a dog. I hesitated, then quickened my pace.

I found Giulio in the long, bright room which would have been the sanctuary had his temple been a real one. He was stooped intently over the "altar." A rough-looking mongrel lay there on its side, surrounded by an array of jars and basins and a large stone pestle and mortar such as you might find in an apothecary's shop. The dog's head rested in a pool of drying vomit; its eyes were fixed open and had the dull glaze of those glass pebbles you sometimes find on beaches, scratched by the salt of the sea. Giulio did not notice me immediately, for he was engrossed in conversation with Gideon d'Arzenta.

I walked forward slowly, taking in the details of my surroundings. As well as the dead dog, there were several other mangy animals, dogs, cats, pigeons, and a large lizard, in cages scattered about the floor. The room stank of animal fear and puddles of urine and faeces stained its marble floor. Blank-eyed nymphs and satyrs surveyed the scene from their plinths. Bonny, bucolic Graces, all with features like Angela's, revelled in woods and meadows and beside the banks of streams all over the walls and ceiling. I looked at Gideon, levelling a spoonful of some whiteish powder with a little wooden spatula before tipping it into an alabaster basin, and at Giulio with his seamed and puckered face, his right eye patched with black velvet, and felt sick.

I should have left then, but I had Donna Lucrezia's mission to discharge. And besides, the light falling over Gideon's shoulders picked out an attractive, raven-blue glint in his hair.

"Good day, gentlemen," I said, raising my voice to ensure it could be heard above the various mewings and cooings and flappings of wings. They both looked up, quickly and guiltily as small boys caught out in some prank.

"Violante," said Giulio, his tone apprehensive.

"Madonna." Gideon bowed with a formality I thought ironical.

"To what do we owe the pleasure?" asked Giulio.

Taking my cue from his abruptness, I wasted no time on the niceties. "Can we speak alone?"

"I have nothing to hide from Ser d'Arzenta," he replied, as though he very well knew that I had.

"My mistress charged me with bringing you a message."

"Go on."

"She says you should leave Ferrara. She suggests you go to your sister in Mantua."

"Why? Does she think a change of air might restore my eyes?"

"Giulio, can I speak frankly?" I glanced at Gideon, who busied himself with his powders as though he was not listening to a word we said.

"I have said so."

"Very well. Ferrante came to madonna's audience this morning. Ippolito was there as usual. Ferrante came to ask for more to be done for you. Ippolito was having none of it. He said...well, he said he believed you and Ferrante were plotting something and it needed flushing out."

Gideon dropped a jar, which set one of the caged dogs to a frenzied barking. A viscous purple liquid fizzed among the shards of blue glass as though the marble floor were dissolving in it like salts. Giulio laughed. "If she is so concerned for me, why not come herself?"

"You know she cannot be seen to act against her husband."

"Other than by sleeping with his brother-in-law, you mean?"

"I'm certain I do not know what you mean."

"Oh Violante, get off your moral high horse; it doesn't suit you. You've been her go-between all along."

I could almost hear Angela's voice, her tinkling, insinuating laughter as she gossiped about me, her head beside his on the pillow, or chatting over her shoulder as her maid laced her corset and he lounged in the doorway. If he could, he showed no sign of it. A man's face is difficult to read if his eyes hold no expression.

"The letters I carry are all to do with madonna's campaign to secure Duke Valentino's release. Don Francesco is supporting her."

"Don Francesco is as anxious as the rest of us that the former duke should never darken Italy's shores again. Dear girl, your old lover is for the hangman's noose; resign yourself to it."

For a second that was as long as a lifetime, the scene around me took on the frozen aspect of the wall frescoes. The cages of animals, the dead dog lying in its vomit, Giulio's sneer like another scar disfiguring his face, Gideon on his knees with a brush, clearing up the broken glass, we were all like figures in a fairy tale, struck by the sudden casting of a spell.

Then Gideon spoke. "Excuse me," he said, "I'll just get rid of this." And waved the shovel of glass shards, and fled. We watched his back, Giulio and I, until it disappeared around the edge of the door.

"I've done something, haven't I? What have I done?" said Giulio, sounding stricken, just the way he used to when Angela had quarrelled with him and he would come to me because he could not understand what he had done to upset her.

His tone softened me. "Since we are speaking frankly, I'll tell you. He asked me to marry him a few weeks ago. I tried to warn him he knew nothing about me. Well, now he does, I suppose."

"Were you considering his proposal?"

"No, of course not. He's a Jew and a goldsmith. Hardly a fitting husband for me."

"Well then, no harm done."

"No. Giulio?"

"Yes?"

"Please go to Mantua. Even if Ippolito is wrong, he has already proved he can be dangerous to you."

"I'll think about it. Now, I must go and retrieve Ser d'Arzenta. We still have work to do."

"Of course." I glanced once more at the dead dog and the caged animals, and decided I did not want to know what work they were engaged in.

I saw Gideon as I left, a blurred silhouette on the far side of the fountain with the lowering sun at his back. I had the impression he saw me, so I took another route back to the palace gates, along the cypress walk and past the little amphitheatre where Giulio had once liked to stage entertainments on summer evenings.

❦

Two days later, the first victim was sucked under by the current running beneath our calm sea. A servant of Giulio's, a man I did not know but whom they said was employed in the kitchens to keep flies away from the food, was arrested on Via San Romano carrying a basket of stray cats. We were puzzled to begin with, as we could think of no reason why catching cats might be considered a crime. Then the news came that, on being shown the strapado, he had confessed Don Giulio wanted the cats for his experiments. Experiments? asked his inquisitor. With poisons, the man replied. They put him in the castle dungeons; at least, I thought, if he had the strength to haul himself up by the window bars, he would have a swan's eye view of the boat races on the moat at Corpus Christi.

There were no boat races, however, only the customary horse races in the Barco, and these were a subdued affair, with no one in the ducal box but madonna, Ippolito, and Giovanni. He, at least, seemed to enjoy himself, betting enthusiastically against his riding master with a box of old coins and beads madonna had given him. I had hoped Don Alberto might bring Girolamo to the city for the festival, but madonna had advised against it during the present uncertainties. I told myself her concern was a good thing. I told myself seeing him would only re-open the wound in my heart and thought of Donna Dorotea, and wondered how often she thought of Camilla. Camilla did not come to the races either for she had been given to the nuns at Corpus Domini.

The only excitement of the festival was occasioned by Sigismondo who, in a rare moment of lucidity, remembered being told that sleeping with a virgin would cure him of the pox. Never one to do things by halves, he was caught trying to break into the Convent of Corpus Domini. He was halfway up a ladder, stark naked, when Mother Abbess saw him and raised the alarm. His doctors came and returned him to his palace, wrapped in a rough blanket and with a sack over his head. Much like one of his rats, I thought, while Angela made predictable jokes about the likelihood of finding a virgin in a nunnery.

A week after Corpus Christi, Ippolito's men arrested two of Ferrante's household in the Romagna. Though they were released without any charge, Ippolito's action had an effect like that of an earth tremor. No buildings collapsed, no cracks appeared in the roads, but everything shifted slightly, felt darker, less dependable. We stayed in the Corte, walking sometimes in the duke's garden, though he was making many changes to it at that time, and it seemed to me to be not much more than earthworks and little sticks marking the promise of thyme cushions or box mazes or matted pinks in seasons to come. Fonsi enjoyed himself, digging a great many holes and spattering his white coat with clods.

Ferrante took to keeping us company, like a man who wears his coat open to show the world he has no weapon concealed in it. Giulio did, at last, depart for Mantua, and Fidelma happened to remark that her brother had gone with him. I decided I was relieved about that.

Others were arrested or disappeared, leaving behind them the echoes of rumours. One had planned to poison the duke in Venice, another to stab him while off his guard in a favourite brothel. Don Giulio, it was said, plotted to make Don Ferrante duke for Don Ferrante had promised to double his pension and knew of doctors in the east who could mend Don Giulio's eyes and make him even better looking than before. Ippolito and Donna Lucrezia laughed at all this in public as though it was just another of Ser Niccolo da Correggio's comedies, but the slightest creak of a floorboard or the banging of a shutter in the night would startle madonna awake, and Angela said Ippolito had the humour of a chained and hungry bear.

One night, hearing madonna cry out, I went to her chamber to find her sitting up in bed, her candle lit and Cesare's ring clutched in her hand. Hardly thinking what I was doing, I made a lunge for it. With a look full of shock and disapproval, she clutched it to her breast.

"Madonna, you mustn't..."

"Mustn't what, girl?"

"The ring...nothing can be that bad. Think of the duke. Think of... your son." I had often asked myself if her attachment to Giovanni had something to do with her separation from Rodrigo and her continuing failure to produce an heir for Duke Alfonso.

She looked momentarily puzzled then burst into laughter. Looking at her, her face bare of makeup, her hair escaping from her sleeping cap, I realised I had forgotten how young she still was.

"Did you think it had poison in it?" she asked. "I am surprised you have never looked inside it."

"I couldn't find out how to open it," I confessed with miserable honesty.

"It is one of my brother's more ingenious devices, true," she admitted, "but I promise you there is nothing dangerous in it. Just..." By some sleight of hand I could not see properly in the poor light of our candles she flipped open the top of the ring and held it out to me. "...this."

Holding my light close, I peered into the compartment, which was lined with mother-of-pearl. Coiled at its heart was a little, untidy plait of hair, much faded, though with still enough of its original colour for me to see that the strands were mixed, a silvery blond and dark red.

"I made it years ago, on a summer afternoon in a secret place we had among my mother's soft fruit bushes. Cesare was supposed to be studying Greek but he and Juan had dosed their tutor's midday wine with fig syrup and escaped while the poor man dealt with the consequences. Would you believe it used to fit around his wrist?" She continued to gaze at it, as though seeing again the boy's wrist, thin and brown, with its knobs of bones and the delta of veins under the skin. "So strong, human hair, and very elastic."

"Do you think that is why he sent it to you?"

She shook her head. "I don't know. Perhaps, on one level." She smiled. "I shall ask him as soon as I see him again. I shall say Violante wants to know."

"I doubt that would sway him, madonna." But I felt myself flush with pleasure nonetheless.

"I have not said this to you before because...well anyway. He is grateful for your care and friendship at a difficult time."

Emboldened by the intimacy of the small circle of light which bound us, I said, "So that is why he took my child from me and sent me back here like...like some horse he had tried out and found wanting?"

"Oh Violante, if you do not yet understand his actions, I cannot help you." She replaced the ring on her nightstand. "Leave me. I shall sleep now, and so must you." She blew out her candle and I returned to bed, though I did not sleep much. My mind boiled with shame and the sense that something important lay just beyond my reach, that one more candle would illuminate the clue I sought, yet I had no flint with which to strike the light. Everything would be clearer in the morning, I told myself, it was just a matter of waiting.

The morning brought a posthaste messenger from Duke Alfonso, saying he was returning to Ferrara. The Venetians had had his sea captain friends arrested as spies and had refused to hear the duke's entreaties on their behalf, so he was coming home to consider how best to respond to La Serenissima's arrogance. This, at least, was what madonna told Ippolito and Ferrante. Later, it became clear he had other reasons as well. By the time Ippolito and Ferrante had returned from Monastirolo, where they had gone expecting to meet him, he had already arrived in Ferrara and was deep in private discussions with madonna, and a man called Capilupo who often carried letters between the courts of Mantua and Ferrara.

Of course I was privy to none of this, but piecing it together later, this is what I think happened. When he heard of Giulio's flight to Mantua, the duke became more convinced than ever his brother was plotting against him, so cut short his travels using the incident with the sea captains as an excuse. He also wrote to Giulio, summoning him home, but Giulio refused. According to Niccolo da Correggio, Giulio believed he had as good cause to fear returning to Ferrara as he had for leaving in the first place. More arrests were made of men close to Ferrante and Giulio. Ferrante went to the duke to intercede for them, but instead told his brother everything, about Giulio's experiments with poisons and their plans to take over the duchy. I waited, feeling sick to my stomach, for him to confess the proposal he had made to me. No one would believe I had rejected it, not if it had meant getting my son back, not once they found out I had witnessed the goings on in Giulio's Temple of the Graces and had said nothing.

There were many who said Ferrante was a coward, but I have never believed it. In his own way, Ferrante was the bravest of men. He was no longer prepared to be dishonest, to pursue justice for Giulio by unjust means. Like me, I expect he saw the white bones of Catherinella in his dreams. Unlike me, he would also have been able to recall the expression on her face when he opened her cage and dropped in the rope.

Ferrante was confined in a room below madonna's apartments in the Torre Marchesana, on the same floor as her kitchens. When one of her chefs reported seeing him looking out of the window, across the moat and on to the piazza where there had been a popular hanging that day, of a man accused of having sexual relations with a donkey, the duke ordered the window to be bricked up. We heard the singer, Gian Cantore, had been arrested in Rome and was giving the performance of his life for the pope's interrogators in the Castel Sant'Angelo. His Holiness, it was said, looked forward to each new development in the saga of the Este *Coniurga* with the eagerness of a child waiting for the next episode of a bedtime story. For myself, each new revelation seemed to come with searching looks in my direction, expressions and tones of voice laden with insinuation. I wore a grave face, made noises of shock and sympathy in the right places, and seemed to feel the fine edge of the axe grazing the hairs on the back of my neck.

In one, irrational sense, I was content to suffer this way because it gave me common cause with Cesare, himself at the whim of powers beyond his control. It put us in the same skin.

At the beginning of August, a trial of the conspirators began in Sigismondo's palace. Schifanoia, it was called, the palace of forgetfulness. I think the name had been Giulio's idea. Giulio himself remained in Mantua. Don Francesco and Donna Isabella had agreed he should be confined to his room, but they would not send him back to Ferrara, even when the duke sent a posse of crossbowmen to fetch him.

The trial opened with a grim parody of the pageantry which marked the year's progress from one festival to the next. One of the conspirators, a man called Gherardo from Carpi, was paraded through the piazza seated backwards on his horse and shackled by his wrists and ankles. He was preceded by priests as well as soldiers, and prominent among them was Fra Raffaello, whom the people cheered as enthusiastically as they booed Gherardo. We watched from the balcony over the main gate to the Corte, flanked by the duke's ancestors, Borso, and Niccolo, the man who had executed Ugo and Parisina.

Gherardo glanced up at us as he was led past, and I found myself looking straight into his eyes. Did he know my son? I wondered. Would it be possible to see, behind the glaze of terror, the blinking bewilderment, an image of my little red-haired boy as he was now, riding his pony, forming his letters, wielding his wooden sword against straw men in Don Alberto's tilting yard? Womanly foolishness, I know, but as the cathedral bell tolled what might have been a death knell for the House of Este, each of us needed something to cling to. When we had dressed Donna Lucrezia that morning, she had chosen to wear, among her jewels, Cesare's cameo ring. It was too big, of course, and fastened to her finger with a bent gold hairpin.

Later that day all the court and the nobility of the city attended a solemn Mass in the cathedral. As we processed down the aisle, led by Ippolito and his clergy, and the singers from the duke's own chapel, with whom Gian Cantore used to sing like an angel, I shifted my gaze from the flagstones in front of my feet just enough to take in, out of the corner of my eye, the black Madonna. As we stood and knelt, bowed our heads in silence or muttered our responses, her face in its frame of beaten gold consoled me with its featureless flatness, the smile that was just paint, the eyes shaped like plump almonds which saw nothing. She had not seen the tense set of Ferrante's shoulders the day after Catherinella's death, nor Gideon's merriment as he invited me to the Hanukkah feast, nor the feathers left by his goose, floating among the dust motes in the dim, cold air. She knew nothing of us, our loves and jealousies, our fears and disappointments. She had no heart to be broken. I wondered how long she had been there, and what else she had not seen, and what she would not see in times to come, and the thought of her not seeing had for me the consolation of prayer.

Next morning, early to avoid the August heat, Donna Lucrezia's household rode out to Belriguardo, passing on our way the spot where Ippolito's men had ambushed Giulio and set the whole sorry mess in train. I played a bleak game with myself. If we were not stopped there, by the duke's men sent to arrest me, then I would be safe, Ferrante would not have mentioned my name. As the road crossed the meadow where Giulio had been hawking, I kept my eyes fixed on a spot somewhere between my horse's ears and tried to ignore the sense of my flesh creeping up my spine. But I could not ignore the message of my ears as we neared the edge of the meadow and the drumming of hooves grew louder behind us. My legs began to shake. I clung to the pommel of my saddle to stop myself falling and tried to fix my thoughts on Cesare. How had he conducted himself when Gonsalvo da Cordoba's men came for him in Naples? Was he gracious, abject, enraged? Did he laugh, or weep, or curse Fortune, or himself for having trusted her? What should I do? Surely the duke must understand, have compassion. I just wanted my son back, that was all. What could be more natural?

The riders were upon us now, two men, breathing hard, their horses' coats foam-flecked and dark with sweat.

"Message for the duchess," panted one as the other rode up abreast of her litter and spoke briefly with one of the men at arms flanking it. The litter halted. A gloved hand reached out of it to hold back the curtain as the messenger dismounted, knelt, and spoke briefly through the chink.

"What is it?" I asked the other man. My voice trembled but he did not seem to notice.

"They've brought in a verdict on Don Ferrante," he said.

❦

The duke came out to meet his wife in person when we arrived back. Standing at the foot of the long staircase in the courtyard of the Corte, he looked old and broken. With head bowed and shoulders sloped, he seemed much smaller and frailer than the guards surrounding him. Giovanni, flinging himself off his pony and racing towards madonna as she dropped the duke a curtsey, fixed round, curious eyes on him and said, loud enough for us all to hear, "Have you been crying?"

"Don Giovanni!" I fetched him a good clout across the ear and handed Fonsi to him. "Here, take him to the garden. He wants to run about after the journey."

For a moment he looked as though he was going to complain to his sister about his treatment, but thought better of it and ran off with the dog in his arms. I am afraid I made a great play of arranging madonna's train so she would not trip climbing the stairs, in order to be able to overhear some of the duke's conversation with her.

"Giulio is on his way back. I sent two hundred men this time, including some of those Albanian cavalry. That put the wind up Francesco, I can tell you. After that, I fear it's just a formality. The evidence is overwhelming. Had some Jew making poisons for him by all accounts."

"Has he been caught also?" asked madonna, almost as if she had felt my grip on her train intensify. How much did she really know, I wondered, about what Giulio had been up to in his Temple of the Graces?

The duke shook his head. "Francesco has men out looking for him, of course. But he's a Mantuan apparently and has most likely gone to ground among his own sort. I'm not worried. I dare say it was Giulio's money he was interested in and now that's gone he'll find himself some other master."

"You're right, my lord. You have enough on your plate with your brothers, without going looking for some inconsequential Jew."

I finished my work and stepped back with a bow. So Gideon was free and Ferrante had made no mention of our conversation in the piazza. The day was windy, so no doubt it was a trick of the shadows of blowing clothes, or horses' tails, or pennants snapping on the Corte's roof, or perhaps madonna had caught some dust in her eye, but I could have sworn she winked at me as she gave her husband her arm and went inside.

◦৵৵◦

The last time I saw Giulio was on another morning of bright sunshine and stiff breezes in early October. The previous day had been set aside for the execution of the other conspirators, and it shames me to say I had sat behind madonna and counted my blessings as they went to their deaths. A scaffold had been set up in the piazza, but it proved almost impossible to transport the guilty men the short distance from the castle dungeons as the furious crowd mobbed their waggon, kicking the spokes out of its wheels and terrifying the horses. A second waggon had to be brought, and the horses blindfolded, and while the prisoners waited, two of their guards and several spectators were injured. The mob did not calm down until the first of the conspirators was led up to the scaffold where he received grudging absolution from a priest of Ippolito's household, was blindfolded, knocked unconscious, beheaded, and quartered. All the rest suffered the same fate, despite the fact the crowd made it plain they would have preferred them to be conscious when they were taken to the executioner's block. Their heads and quartered bodies were placed on lances above the city gates.

I slept fitfully that night, and was aware of Angela tossing and turning in the bed beside me, though neither of us said anything; it was easier to pretend to be asleep. Sometimes I thought I was dreaming, sombre nightmares dominated by the dark shape of the scaffold squatting like a monster in the piazza. But they were not dreams, not really, and the scaffold was there, perhaps sheltering a few beggars from the chill of the night, waiting for morning, for Ferrante and Giulio. For me to learn the cost of my blessings.

We had all expected the duke to commute the sentence. There had been raised voices when Donna Lucrezia had tried to suggest it. Now, as the darkness thinned and gave way to pearl and lemon and pale green over the roofs and towers of the city, and the morning star faded, and the doves began to rustle and coo in Alberti's bell tower, the buzzards to wheel and screech around the heads and legs and torsos on the gates, I knew there was no longer any hope.

Angela and I dressed in the same silence, as though we were still pretending to be asleep. In silence we laced one another and dressed one another's hair and in silence we went to wake Donna Lucrezia with white rolls and oranges from her roof garden. We found her already up and dressed, though her hair had not been done and she wore no makeup or jewellery. She was kneeling at her prie dieu and Fra Raffaello and Fidelma were with her. Perhaps I saw only some reflection of my own state of mind, but it seemed to me her body, straight backed, head bowed, heels neatly together, was a battleground where her inner and outer selves, her past and her future, were tearing each other to pieces.

When she had finished her prayers, she dismissed Fidelma and the friar. I put her breakfast on a table in front of her window and Angela opened the shutters. She sat, but made no attempt to eat, and we stood in front of her, waiting for her instructions about her hair and jewels while the Dalmation slave went silently about the business of folding her nightclothes and tidying the bed. She had long outgrown the collar Cesare had put on her, but her neck was very long and very white, as though the collar had formed it. Finally madonna pushed the food away and indicated to the slave she might have it. She sidled across and took it with the shy haste of a wild animal, and squatted with it by the fireplace, where she began peeling the oranges with a sound like tearing flesh which seemed to fill the room.

"Do you remember when Juan died?" Donna Lucrezia asked Angela.

"Not really. I wasn't in Rome at the time."

"I had never lost anyone close to me before. I wondered how it was possible to bear such pain and still be alive and then...I realised. Pain proves we are alive. God sticks pins in us to keep us awake." She gave a wan laugh. "Remember that, whatever happens today. God gave you your life. Live it."

"I will try," said Angela gravely, but it was impossible to tell if she felt grave or if she had decided gravity was what the situation called for.

The piazza was already packed with onlookers by the time we took our seats on the balcony above the gate. People were crammed under the colonnades and hanging out of the upstairs windows of houses bordering the square whose owners were no doubt making good money out of their view today. Small boys swarmed over the statues of Borso and Niccolo; overloaded boats bobbed dangerously on the moat. Pie hawkers and miracle sellers jostled with tapsters and bonbonniers to feed the bodies and souls of the crowd. Bare-breasted whores lounged in shadowy doorways. Whole families had come in from the country and were now balanced on their handcarts with their children on their shoulders. The smell of boiled meat and unwashed bodies was trapped under the blue dome of the sky and the glitter of flags and birds' wings, trumpets and cheap jewels made my eyes ache.

As word went round that the duke's party had appeared, all those red-cheeked, open-mouthed faces turned towards us, a many-headed hydra of dumpy Padano peasants. A piece of cheap paper fluttered on to the balcony and landed at my feet. I picked it up and looked at it. It carried a crude, printed woodcut of Don Giulio and a hook-nosed Jew grinning hideously as they pored over a large bottle labelled "POISON." I screwed it up and pushed it into my sleeve, but it was too late. Madonna had caught sight of it. She spoke quietly to the duke, who flushed, clenched one fist, and banged it several times against his thigh. Madonna put her hand over his, but he shook her off and turned to speak to one of the officers of the guard standing behind us. The next thing I knew there was a brief scuffle in the square and a man with a leather satchel over his shoulder was hustled away in the direction of the castle.

Then someone detected movement at the castle gate and the crowd turned to watch, their babble giving way to silence as yesterday's cart, bearing today's victims, lurched across the drawbridge and out into the piazza. There was no kicking of wheels or jostling of horses this time as the crowd fell back like the Red Sea for the cart to pass. Many of those closest to it clutched their hats off their heads and bowed and the women dropped ungainly curtseys. Their faces expressed shame and embarrassment, as though the wrong done by their rulers somehow put them in the wrong too. A boy too old for tears burst into noisy sobs; I wondered if he had perhaps been one of Ferrante's lovers.

I was aware of Angela, seated next to me, drawing in her breath sharply. She had not set eyes on Giulio since Ippolito's attack on him. Was she shocked, I wondered, or regretful? For Giulio looked magnificent. He was bare headed and his golden hair, which had grown long during his captivity in Mantua, blew across his face so you could not see his scars. Unlike Ferrante, he held his head high, the clean, graceful line of his jaw clearly discernible despite the untidiness of his beard. Whether or not he could see us, he remained steadfastly facing our balcony, keeping his back to the scaffold as the waggon swayed through the crowd.

When the carter dropped the tailgate, he jumped down unaided, in spite of the shackles fastened round his wrists and ankles, then turned to help Ferrante as best he could. Ferrante looked frail, and moved as though the weight of the chains was almost more than he could bear. I dare say he had not been as well cared for in the Torre Marchesana as Giulio had been in Mantua. Giulio had almost to push him up the steps to the scaffold, and he staggered when he came face to face with the executioner so I was afraid he would faint.

We saw the executioner kneel and ask each man's forgiveness, and Giulio even seemed to share a joke with him. As the brothers knelt in their turn to receive absolution from the priest, Giulio once again doing his best to steady Ferrante, I realised he was doing it as much for himself as for Ferrante. *We are the same,* Ferrante had once told me, *both tolerated but not quite accepted.* I thought of madonna and her *conversas,* of Ferrante himself giving Catherinella back her human dignity, and understood how we all need outsiders to mark the boundaries of ourselves. Then I was distracted by Angela's fingers creeping into my palm, and curled my fist over them to stop them shaking.

"How much can he see?" she whispered urgently. "It's such a beautiful day. I want him to be able to see it."

A young deacon with an unsteady hand had just begun to swing his thurible, casting wraiths of incense on the air, when the duke rose to his feet. He tried to command silence but his voice failed him. A quick-witted trumpeter came to his rescue and blew an improvised fanfare. The duke nodded his thanks.

"Let not the mark of Cain be upon this house," he said, his voice strengthening as he warmed to his task. "I will not have my brothers' blood on my hands, even though they would not have hesitated to have mine on theirs. Executioner, put up your axe. There will be no more deaths today."

During this speech the brothers had risen and now stood facing the balcony with their hands linked, their chains entwined. I saw Ferrante begin to shake like a man with an ague and slump against Giulio, who staggered slightly but managed to keep them both upright. The executioner laid his axe on the block and a ragged cheer went up from some parts of the crowd, though others looked disappointed. Many had travelled a long way for the spectacle, and others had probably expected to make their year's earnings out of the day. Quickly attuning himself to the uncertain mood, the duke went on, "Let us celebrate instead, an end to discord and bloodshed between brothers and the beginning of a new age of peace and prosperity. We will have bonfires lit and there will be music and dancing and we will have oxen and suckling pigs roasted in the piazza." The duke sat down looking well pleased with himself. "Good," he said, with the brutal compassion of a surgeon drawing the skin over an amputation, "now to dinner." The cheering coalesced into a gleeful roar loud enough to scare up the buzzards from above the city gates. Smiles and murmurs of approval spread among the ducal party, though I noticed Donna Lucrezia neither smiled nor looked at her husband. Perhaps she had known all along what he intended.

⧉

Ferrante and Giulio were taken back into the castle, to separate rooms in the Torre Leone. The doors to these rooms were sealed and the windows bricked up until a space not much larger than one of the old duke's cat doors was left in each of them. There they were condemned to spend the rest of their natural lives and it was forbidden ever to speak their names in the Duchy of Ferrara or the County of Modena though sometimes, in her sleep, my friend Angela disobeyed that command.

In that year of the Christians 1506, Ferrante d'Este was twenty-nine years old and his brother Don Giulio was twenty-six. I never saw either of them again, so they have remained that age for me, caught like those who die young in an aspic of remembrance.

# THE BOOK OF LOVE

*A brother is in me*
*Whose letters*
*Were like water*
*When my heart was thirsty*

*Now, when others' come,*
*Not his,*
*The thought of him writing*
*Within me is fire.*

Shmu'el Hanagid, *On the Death of Isaac, His Brother*

*The Head of Jupiter, Mantua, Sixth Day of Teveth in the Year Five Thousand
Two Hundred and Sixty-Seven
To Esther Sarfati from Gideon da Quieto d'Arzenta, greetings.*

*I had promised myself I would not do this. I made myself a solemn vow never to
try to contact you, but now they tell me Valentino is free and will return to Italy
so there seems to be little to lose and everything to gain in writing you this letter.*

*I suppose you are very happy and I rejoice for you, truly, if you are. Yet I
remember some of the things Don Giulio said to me during his exile, about you,
and Valentino, and I wonder if you are happy, and then I feel the chink in my
armour, the temptation to reach out to you and see if what I thought I saw in
you was real or just the product of an imagination inflamed by loss and hunger
and fear and hopelessness.*

*I will have to begin at the beginning, at the very point when I saw you
hurrying away from me in Don Giulio's garden. I watched your back until you
came level with the glass houses, then suddenly the sun emerged from behind a
cloud and its light on the glass dazzled me. When I could see again, you were gone.*

*Don Giulio had the grace to apologise for his indiscretion. He was angry; he
was in pain and desperately worried for his future. He was so bound up in his
own concerns he had failed to give sufficient consideration to the effect his words
might have on others. And he did not blame me for having a weak spot for
you because you were a very pretty girl, accomplished and amusing and a loyal
friend to his beloved Donna Angela. He never stopped talking about Donna
Angela; even after her marriage to Alessandro Pio part of him believed she
would come round, and they would live happily ever after with their daughter.
While another part of him grew twisted and plotted against the duke and the*

cardinal and seemed honestly to believe Don Ferrante could make an effective ruler. I did not know Don Ferrante at all, of course, but what I saw of him was a charming, lazy fop, quite incapable of running a hen house, never mind a state. At that time, Don Giulio's powers of self-delusion seemed immeasurable.

I wonder now if that is why I continued to work for him, even after I became aware his interest lay not in my artistic abilities but in my knowledge of chemistry. I was attracted to the idea of self-delusion. I was living in a dream in which I was destined for the same kind of fame as Michelangelo or Leonardo or young Raffaele. I even thought I looked like Raffaele. I saw him once, when my master took me on a trip to Urbino, and he was thin, like me, with curly hair, though not so tall. Actually, his face was beautifully proportioned, which mine is not but, as I say, this part of my story is about self-delusion. You might also be interested to know our trip was fruitless because your Valentino had just taken the city and was not interested in commissioning artists. We could not gain access to the palace, so we stayed a night with Ser Santi, Raffaele's father, and went back to Mantua the next day. The roads, I remember, were crawling with soldiers.

Self-delusion can also give rise to extraordinary, some would say, reckless, courage. Looking back now, I can scarcely credit the fact that Don Giulio stayed in Ferrara as long as he did, and experimented as openly as he did with the poison that was going to—without, of course, being in any way detectable—kill the duke and the cardinal and avenge his eyes. Perhaps he should have asked the advice of your Valentino about that. Is he not a great man with poisons?

Eventually, however, Donna Isabella prevailed with her brother and he set out for Mantua. He graciously invited me to accompany him, pointing out that at least one person at court—you, of course—had come across us together in compromising circumstances and that I would be safer back in Mantua. Among my own kind, he said, as though one Jew is much the same as another and I might blend effortlessly in, a goldsmith indistinguishable from a butcher, a candle dipper or a knife grinder. I was content to go. I had no further work in Ferrara and nothing else to keep me there, and as Donna Isabella had patronised me before, I had no reason to suppose she might not do so again.

Are the Borgias so good at poisoning because they are themselves made not of flesh but of some poisonous substance? It quickly transpired that Don Giulio was not an honoured guest in his sister's house but a prisoner, albeit *a comfortable one. As for myself, hearing that I had been "taken on" as she put it by her sister-in-law, Donna Isabella wondered if I would not find her own humble requirements insufficiently challenging for my great talents. And so on and so forth. Reason dictates that she was distancing herself from me because she saw me as part of Don Giulio's conspiracy, but why not say so? Why couch it all in terms that made it sound as though I had been contaminated by association with Duchesa Lucrezia? Well, that has been the fashion, hasn't it, since Valentino's fall, and Donna Isabella was ever a slave of fashion.*

*So perhaps Valentino's release—or did he escape? This has not been made clear to us here in Mantua—will signal an improvement in my fortunes. Perhaps the great man himself may look generously on me, for by all accounts he was very pleased with his masks. Have you seen them? Donna Isabella reported to me that he was so delighted with my gold skull he had hung it beside his bed, so I dare say you have seen that one at least.*

*The All-Knowing knows I need a break in my luck. Until the soldiers came to fetch Don Giulio, I managed to find work on a small scale, among less scrupulous patrons than Donna Isabella. I made a salt cellar of fabulous vulgarity for a man who has done well out of the current craze here for perfumed gloves. Do they have it in Ferrara also, or does the rivalry between the duchess and the marquesa preclude any common ground on fashions? I worked some small pieces of enamel jewellery for a sea captain who has four wives among the Indians of New Spain. I will come back to him. Don Francesco himself commissioned me, through a discreet third party, to make a silver cap badge with a large citrine for a boy chorister who had taken his fancy, though he has yet to make the final payment on it. I wonder if your lady Lucrezia knows how incontinent he is with his affections, or if she is used to that kind of thing in her family.*

*Since the trial, however, I am persona non grata everywhere. I have moved away from my father's house because I am afraid my presence there might put my family in danger. I thought I might lodge in my old master's studio, which has stood empty since his death while his widow and sons quarrel over what is to be done with it, but everything was locked and barred and I was loathe to break in in case I drew attention to myself and got myself arrested. You ask why I too did not leave Mantua? Well, of course you don't, but you might. It would be a reasonable question. I will say this. If I had had to leave Mantua then, the only place I would have wanted to go would have been Ferrara. I would have* been drawn there as Plato says the soul is drawn to beauty, but I would have been less sure of my welcome.

Well, winter was coming and I was beginning to wonder if I would have to cast myself on the mercy of the Franciscans who run a hostel here. At least Duke Alfonso's men, if they came, would be unlikely to look for a Jew in a Franciscan hostel. Then I remembered the Jupiter. At the time of his death, old Sperandio was working on a bronze Jupiter so large it could not be cast all of a piece but was to be done in sections then dovetailed. A revolutionary technique, very difficult to achieve, but that will not interest you. What may interest you, given the address I have put at the head of this letter—oh, a fine pun, worthy of a courtier—is that at his death, Sperandio had completed only the head of the Jupiter and this was lying in his studio yard as it was too large to fit indoors. It had been cast using the lost wax method and was therefore hollow—and big enough to accommodate some kind of bed.

A new wife setting up her first home could not have been more delighted than I as I scrambled up Jupiter's beard and through his open mouth into the empty dome of his head. A casting of this sort is like a moral tale converted into an image—though it is beautiful outside, within it may be rough, with craters made by bubbles of gas from the heating of the metal and sharp jags where the bronze has cooled around the plaster core. So my first task was to hammer and chisel and file until I had a space where I could lay my bedding without tearing it, or my own flesh, to ribbons. I was very pleased, though, with one outcropping I found, in the space between Jupiter's nose and his left eye, which has made a very serviceable hook for my clothes.

I have been here two months now and I am quite cosy. I managed to scrounge some hides from the tanner to use as curtains to keep out the wind. They are heavy, which is excellent, though smell rather strongly of sheep's piss. I have rigged up a shelf in Jupiter's brow where I can light my Sabbath candles and a board across one side of his jaw where I eat, and where I am writing this letter. I remain undisturbed because when people see lights or movement inside the god's mouth or eye-sockets, they think the head is haunted and keep away. I could, I suppose, stay here for as long as Don Giulio stays in his prison—until I starve or go mad. But Valentino is free, and that changes everything.

I have decided to leave Mantua as soon as the weather improves. I shall go first to Rome and from there to Ostia where I am going to meet the sea captain

I have mentioned, the man with four Indian wives. Esther, I have decided to go to New Spain. There is no future for me here, no future for any of us I fear. You know, of course, of the massacre of the Jews in Lisbon.

I am a resourceful man, and though I still have ambitions to be a great artist, I now know they cannot be achieved quickly or straightforwardly. The skills I have learned in my craft are adaptable and can be put to good use anywhere—if it is His will I should be a blacksmith or a sword-maker, so be it. As I said to you once before, what my beliefs teach me is that I must hold myself ready, open to whatever plans He has for me.

The proposal I made you was no flirtation, though it surprised me at least as much as it surprised you. I love you, and there is nothing to be done about it. I have tried. Don Giulio and I both tried all those things men try when they want to forget women. We worked and drank and made love to strangers—and still found we talked about you and Donna Angela endlessly, and found the strangers we made love to just ended up looking like you.

Don Giulio told me something else about you during one of those long, maudlin, drunken conversations. I suppose he thought if I could not be put off by the thought of being the rival of the dangerous Valentino, then more drastic measures were called for. He told me you have a son, and that he is the boy's godfather.

I will not describe to you how sick that made me feel, the thought of that living, breathing confirmation of your love for another, the way a child binds you indissolubly together. It conjured images in my brain and sentiments in my heart that shame me. Valentino has red hair, they say. Does your son have red hair? No, I don't want to know. I shall find out soon enough.

Esther, will you come with me to New Spain? If not for your own sake, for your son's. Even if Valentino can take back all he has lost, what chance does the boy have in Ferrara, with Don Giulio for a godfather? With the help of the Father of us all, I am prepared to try to be a father to him, and in the new world he can grow up free of the past and all its dangers. And a child might bring us together, who knows?

Well, if I am wrong, I will perhaps hear news of you from time to time in the great house your lover will set you up in, and I will rue the day I did not stay in Italy so I might have you as a patron. But do me the honour of thinking carefully about my request, in case what you think you want is not what you really want, or if you are no longer in love with Valentino and do not rejoice *in his liberty. Though if I am honest, as I must be now, I realise this is more self-delusion for I always felt there was someone special in your life and chose to disregard my instincts.*

*I wish you had trusted me with the story of your life before, then I remind myself that everything you do is still you, even the lies you tell. Were you afraid to confide in me? Can you love a man who makes you afraid? No, that is not a fair question. It is late and my head aches with the cold. Did you celebrate Hanukkah this year, as we did last? Another unfair question. Write back. Ask me some unfair questions. I shall not leave Mantua for another month at least for my captain does not sail until the month of Adar. Tell me if you are a good sailor.*

*Your heart's bondsman,*
*Gideon d'Arzenta*

# Chapter 1

*These are the letters I will never send, the blood of my heart. The deed is planned for tomorrow. I am entrusting these to Juanito, with orders to bring them to you should I die in the attempt. From my words you will be able to reconstruct me, as Isis did Osiris.*

The rumours had been eddying around us for weeks. I am certain all of us had rehearsed what we would say and do, how we would think and feel, if they were confirmed. Yet when Juan Grasica arrived, and dismounted slowly in the castle courtyard, as if, by delaying the end of his journey he could also deny its purpose, we were not ready. We were like the city militia who drill every year for the spring floods, then stand amazed as the river races through the streets, carrying off their sandbags and leaving a trail of yellow mud, drowned pigs, and broken furniture in its wake.

Juanito had been well briefed for his task. He went first to Ippolito to deliver his news, but I suppose they were behind the times in Pamplona, in the wild country of Navarre. Relations between Ippolito and Donna Lucrezia had never quite recovered after the *Coniurga*; the unspoken names of Giulio and Ferrante hovered between them like the fairies who sour the milk. This was no time for Ippolito to pretend otherwise, so he charged Fra Raffaello with carrying Juanito's message to madonna.

Easter had come early that year, and madonna had been preoccupied during Carnival by a visit from Don Francesco, so some of the marriages she had negotiated for her young ladies were taking place in the weeks between Easter and Corpus Christi as Carnival had fallen in the dead of winter. Madonna had also suffered another miscarriage, which some attributed to too much dancing and going about on horseback and others, behind their hands, to too much activity of another sort in the company of Don Francesco Gonzaga who had come to Ferrara without Donna Isabella, who was about to give birth again herself.

We were in the Camera Dal Pozzolo, sewing a trousseau for a distant Gonzaga cousin who was to marry the Venetian ambassador's nephew the following Saturday. I remember these inconsequential details, even the fact that I had just re-charged my needle with the cream silk thread I was using to embroider bouquets of love-in-idleness around the neck of a nightgown. I remember Fra Raffaello's flushed cheeks and working mouth and the way self-satisfaction and terror warred in his eyes, and the calm way madonna laid her work in her lap as the slave scratched on the door and she said, "Enter."

What I do not remember, what I have since had to reconstruct in my imagination, is how I felt as Fra Raffaello bowed his head and said, "Madonna, you must brace yourself. I have news of great seriousness."

"Yes," she said. I am sure she knew, as I did, what he was going to say next.

"News from the King of Navarre," he went on, working himself up to his task. Madonna did nothing to help him; the gaze she levelled on him was as cool and grey as the oblong of unseasonal sky showing in the window behind her. Though she valued his spiritual counsel he was not, ultimately, in her confidence, merely in that of the Duchess of Ferrara. Watching her, it became clear to me that she was, in her way, as good at wearing masks as Cesare had been. Had been. I had thought of him in the past tense.

"His messenger brings word of the death in battle of the Duke of Valentinois, madonna."

"The Duke of Romagna," she corrected, but almost under her breath. Fra Raffaello showed no sign of having heard her.

"God granted him a brave end in a just cause," he continued.

Donna Lucrezia nodded as if in appreciation of a poem or a piece of music. "The messenger," she asked, "who is he?"

"A man called Juan Grasica, madonna. I believe he is..."

"I know who he is, brother. I will thank you to leave us now, and ask Juan Grasica to attend us."

"Will you not pray, madonna?"

"Of course I shall pray, but not here and now. I find myself a little at odds with God just now. The more I try to please him, it seems, the more He tries me."

The friar bowed and retreated.

"Fidelma," said madonna, "go and tell your little friar I will receive Juan Grasica in my own chamber. The rest of you, leave me. Not you, Violante," she added as we all laid aside our work and prepared to absent ourselves, "you will come with me." She rose from her chair and, on an impulse, I stepped forward and put my arms around her. After a brief hesitation, she returned my embrace. No matter how often I replay the scene in my memory, I cannot be certain what was in my mind. I do not know whether I sought to comfort her or myself, or whether I was trying to make contact through her with some emotion I could not feel.

Juanito was not admitted to her private chamber until I had dressed her in the mourning clothes so recently put aside after the deaths of her father-in-law and her baby son. She chose the deepest mourning, a skirt and bodice of plain black, a chemise without any lace or embroidery, black hose and shoes. I washed the makeup from her face, brushed her hair loose and adorned her with no jewellery but her wedding band and the cameo poison ring I had brought from Rome. Then she stooped to dip her finger in the ash of last night's fire, and made a cross with it on her forehead.

"Should have let the priest do it," she muttered, "but Cesar would like it this way. I am ready now, Violante. Please call Juanito to me. I will lie on my bed. I don't think I have the strength to sit."

"Perhaps you should delay seeing Juanito, madonna."

"No. I shall see him now."

"Yes, madonna."

Poor Juanito. He was not a young man; like Michelotto, he had joined Cesare's household when Cesare went away to school in Perugia and had kept company with every twist and turn of his fortunes. He looked grey when he entered the room, grey with exhaustion and misery and the dust of his wretched journey which rose around him in a cloud as he pulled off his cap and knelt to his lord's sister. His limbs were so stiffened by his long ride I had to help him up.

"Please sit, Juanito," madonna urged him but he refused. He stood to attention beside her bed, one hand clutching his cap over his breast, the other spread protectively over a bulging satchel which hung at his side.

"Very well, but I warn you, this will be a long interview. I require you to tell me everything."

"I expected you would, madonna."

"Begin please." Signalling me to sit beside her on the bed, she took my hand. By the time Juanito had finished his story my fingers were numb and my knuckles bruised from the pressure of her grip.

"My lord, as you know, was to escort his excellency Don Carlos from Flanders to Spain." We both nodded. Cesare's conviction that he had a part to play in upholding the infant Don Carlos's claim to the throne of Castile had not been shaken by the sudden death from influenza of the boy's father, Philip of Flanders. On the contrary, it was this which had made him decide on escape. As he had written to madonna on his arrival at his brother-in-law's court in Pamplona, he had no intention of sitting about like a hen in a coop waiting for that old fox Ferdinand of Aragon to get him.

"As part of his preparation, he and King Jean wished to strengthen Navarre's defences and they asked the Count de Beaumonte to hand back the fortress at Viana. He refused, saying he was a vassal of King Ferdinand and not of King Jean, so his grace the king put my lord at the head of an army and required him to take Viana by force. Madonna, you should have seen him the day we rode out of Pamplona. It was like the old days, men cheering and women weeping by the roadside, small boys hanging on to his stirrups and himself so big and handsome, *soro*, like a young falcon.

"We went to Larriaga first and besieged it."

I could see madonna was becoming impatient, but she let Juanito continue out of charity. By dwelling on the details of the campaign, he kept his beloved lord alive to his heart, and this gave him the courage to go on. After a great deal of arcane talk of bombasts and breastworks, culverins and ballistas and the calculation of firing trajectories and the digging of trenches, it transpired Cesare had lost patience with Larriaga, which refused to fall to him, and had raised the siege and gone to Viana.

"King Jean held the town," Juanito explained, "but Beaumonte's son was holed up in the castle. He was running out of food, though, and no supplies or reinforcements could get through without the King and Don Cesar hearing of it. So it looked like an easy job, a quick finish and off to Flanders. The weather up there was terrible. Flat, brown hills with nothing to stop the wind or keep off the rain. Nothing but sheep and ravines for them to fall into. My lord decided not to post sentinels at night as he said the storms were our best defence. We had a decent house, good stone walls, but even inside there it was freezing. King Jean had given Don Cesar a fine wolfskin cloak and I don't think he once took it off, not even to sleep unless, saving your presence, ladies, he found other means of keeping warm.

"Come dawn on March 12, a Tuesday it was, we were awakened by a great commotion, shouting, bells ringing, the guards on the city walls running about like scalded cats saying we were under attack. We found out later Beaumonte had managed to get supplies into the castle under cover of the storm, so the weather turned out to be his friend, not ours, and what the guards had seen was just his escort returning. But I'm getting ahead of myself.

"I heard Don Cesar shouting for his armour, but he was in one of his rages, stalking up and down like a leopard in a cage, cursing so even the trollop in his bed looked embarrassed, so I couldn't manage to get him into any more than his light armour and a corselet and I had to throw his helmet down the stairs after him because he forgot it."

Donna Lucrezia smiled while I thought about the "trollop" in Cesare's bed, unwrapping his body from the wolfskin cloak like a gift, and wondered if she had tried to stop him going.

"By the time I got to my own horse he was gone. Hadn't even stopped to check his girth the groom said, which was not like him as you know and was a measure of how impatient he was with the whole business of these little Navarrese and their domestic squabbles. He was so angry he rode like a madman even by his standards and of course none of the rest of us could keep up so..."

"Go on, Juanito. I wish to hear everything. I have said so."

"When he rode into Beaumonte's ambush he was completely alone. I didn't realise what had happened till I saw his horse galloping back towards us. Even then I thought…well, he was a great fighter and nearly twice the height of the little Navarrese." Juanito cleared his throat. He fiddled with the fastening of his satchel and cast a pleading glance at madonna but she gave him no quarter.

"By the time I got there they had made off. They'd taken everything, his armour, his weapons, even his clothes. One of them had had the decency to put a stone over his genitals, that was all." Tears spilled out of the squire's eyes and made tracks in the dust on his cheeks. Only the pressure of madonna's hand crushing mine kept my own tears back by giving me a simpler and more immediate pain on which to concentrate.

"It was still pouring with rain so his body looked quite clean, just the earth around it was red. The king came up then, and covered him with his cloak. He said a prayer, then had him carried back into the town. I did the laying out myself, madonna. I wasn't having strangers take care of him. I'd been his body servant since he was fourteen years old so it was only right."

"Thank you, Juanito. It was proper and considerate of you."

"He looked like a bridegroom when King Jean's six best knights carried him into the church of Santa Maria. I'd brushed his hair and trimmed his beard the way he liked it, and dressed him in his best armour, the black with the gold chasing on the breastplate. He always used to say it felt like a second skin, that armour. He had his wedding ring and his Order of Saint Michael that King Louis gave him, and King Jean gave a coronet in place of his ducal insignia which had got lost somehow in all that fuss in Naples."

"Tell me how his face looked."

"As I say, madonna, he looked most handsome and serene. The church was full of weeping women. They tell me there were twenty-five wounds on his poor body, though his face was unmarked. All I know is it was too many for me to count and he must have put up the very devil of a fight."

"Twenty-five. Good. That is five times the five wounds of Our Lord on the Cross. Were his eyes open or closed?"

"Closed with pennies, madonna, of course."

"When you found him."

I wished she would stop. I was not sure Juanito had the strength to continue, yet she did, so he and I must also.

"Open, madonna. Sort of…surprised looking."

"And could you see anything in them? They say the image of a man's killer will imprint itself upon the eye for a little while after death."

"Do they, madonna? Well perhaps I got there too late. I could see nothing in his eyes but the rain."

"The gods must weep for the death of such a one. Thank you, Juanito, you have spoken well and bravely. You know Sancho, my majordomo?"

"I met him in Medina del Campo, madonna."

"Go to him. He will give you money and find you lodgings. As soon as I am able, I will make more permanent arrangements for you. I would like you to stay in Ferrara, Juanito, so we can talk sometimes about the old days."

The squire bowed. "I have nowhere else to go, madonna."

As I saw Juanito out and told him where he might find Sancho, I also asked him to tell Sancho to send a messenger to Donna Angela in Sassuolo.

⊰❦⊱

Angela arrived the following evening, on horseback and accompanied only by a groom. One of her ladies-in-waiting was to follow on with her luggage, she explained, to fill the awkward space between us. The last time I had seen her had been the previous winter when, madonna having pawned some of her jewellery and sold a small parcel of land she had forgotten she still owned in Calabria, had managed to raise a dowry for her cousin sufficient to mollify Don Alessandro's mother. The whole Pio clan had come to Ferrara for a second, public wedding in the duke's newly decorated rooms in the Corte. We had feasted on platters of oysters with oranges and pears, on pike dressed with crystallised borage flowers and anchovy salads, and you would hardly have known it was Advent. For dessert there were nudes fashioned from liquorice biscuit, the eating of which occasioned a great many jokes suitable for a wedding, though Don Alessandro's mother did not seem to be amused. After dinner we had formed a noisy procession, headed by musicians and acrobats, and a fire eater produced from somewhere by La Fertella, to escort the bride and groom to their lodgings in the town. Our cheeks glowed with cold and wine; torchlight sparkled on jewels and danced along the snowy streets, threw wild shadows up the walls of buildings, picked out the gleam in the eyes of watchers behind their window shutters.

Only fleetingly had I felt the dark pull of the Torre Leone as we passed, glancing up as I always did to see if the food baskets were still hanging from the pulleys on the roof, for their daily journey up and down the sheer face of the tower was the only evidence we had that Ferrante and Giulio were still alive. From where I was in the procession I had been unable to tell whether Angela looked in that direction or not, and my thoughts had shifted quickly back to my own joy.

Don Alberto Pio had brought Girolamo with him to Ferrara for the wedding. Giovanni's attachment to me, which had begun with Cesare's commendation of my Greek joke, had deepened during our time at Nepi and in Rome. We were, I suppose, like soldiers who have campaigned together, bound by a common experience not shared by anyone around us. So, when he played with Girolamo, he often wanted to include me in their games. Elated and heartbroken, I had watched them race hoops through the Sala Grande or play at jousting with their hobbyhorses and broom handles. I had referreed their fights when Giovanni tried to dominate his nephew and Girolamo, small and wiry, tenacious and bold, had fought back. Though not as plump as he had been, Giovanni was still indolent and somewhat slow of wit. Girolamo, though, was much as I imagined his father would have been if he had not been so poorly at that age, as he had become after Donna Lucrezia was born and he decided to live.

We had also just heard that Cesare was free. He had broken his collar bone, some ribs, and an ankle jumping from the end of the rope he had hung from his window, having miscalculated the drop, and his journey to Pamplona had been a torture. But now he looked forward to celebrating Christmas there with his brother-in-law, and to the year of Our Lord fifteen hundred and seven which he knew would see a rise in his fortunes.

And now he was dead.

As Angela and I greeted one another in the castle courtyard, in the cool spring dusk, the contrast of present sorrow with past happiness seemed to reinforce the gulf that had opened up between us now she was a married woman with a good name and a substantial household.

"How is she?" asked Angela as we made our way to madonna's rooms.

"I can't describe it. You'll see for yourself."

Donna Lucrezia's mourning for her brother was as desperate and visceral as his dying must have been. There was no dignity to it, no restraint or self-consciousness or thought. Once Juanito had finished his tale and left us, she had utterly collapsed. She tore at her clothes, her hair, the skin of her face and arms, and howled as though possessed of a devil, unearthly, guttural moans and growls that made me think of fighting cats and the beggars who do not have the decency to die silently by roadsides. She took handfuls of ash and rubbed it all over her head and face and breast, and when the fire was re-lit she shovelled hot coals out of it and tried to walk on them, so I had to douse it with the first water that came to hand, the contents of a chamber pot. The Dalmatian slave fled in terror, crossing herself repeatedly, her long white fingers fluttering in front of her long white neck.

I thought Angela's presence would calm madonna, but she scarcely seemed to notice her cousin's arrival. When I tried to leave, however, she rose briefly to the surface of the pit she had fallen into and forbade me to go. "You are me," she said. "There is nowhere for you to go."

"Violante just wants to get some food and drink for me, cousin," said Angela, "and a broom to sweep up the ashes."

Donna Lucrezia stared at her as if she had no idea who she was or what she was talking about and shook her head. A hank of hair caught on her lip. She stuck out her tongue and hooked the hair into her mouth and sucked it. That seemed to distract her for a moment, and she allowed herself to be led back to her bed.

"Do you think we should restrain her?" Angela asked me. "At least until we can get her physician to see her."

But before I could reply she was up again, spitting out the hair, heading for her bedroom window, muttering about ropes and drops and how Cesare could have been a good mathematician if he had only had more patience. I ran in front of her, slammed the shutters closed, and used my girdle to make them fast while Angela once again wrestled madonna back on to her bed.

"I'm going for her doctor," said Angela. "This is much worse than I'd expected."

"What had you expected?" She gave me an odd look then, both calculating and troubled, but did not reply to my question.

When she returned with the physician, madonna smashed a perfume flask and yelled through the door that if anyone other than Angela were to come through it she would stab them with the broken glass. It was a floral perfume, with notes of jasmine, and its scent wreathed like a ghost around the bed furnishings and ceiling bosses, the chair legs and the jewelled crucifix on the prie dieu, and clung to our skins.

Donna Lucrezia had cut her hand, but when I tried to bind it she pulled away from me. "You think that matters?" she asked, her tone full of contempt.

Fra Raffaello received the same treatment, as did Ippolito and even the duke, who arrived on a lightning visit from Genoa, where he was helping the French king to crush a rebellion. No doubt he was glad to have a rebellion to go back to. For two weeks, madonna would let no one near her but Angela and myself. She raged and wept and called out Cesare's name, sometimes pleading with him in her rapid, incomprehensible Catalan as though she could persuade him to come back. She would not let us change her ragged clothes, so we tried to cover her with blankets which she would trail around the room after her, knocking over furniture, swiping books and cups, hairbrushes, jewellery, and powder pots off tables until the floor was sticky and treacherous with a porridge of spilt wine and makeup and broken glass. She soiled herself with the random wilfulness of a small child. On the rare occasions we could persuade her to eat and drink, she pushed food into her mouth with her fingers and lapped water from a basin, and a pappy crust formed on her lips and chin which cracked and irritated the skin.

When she slept, which was rarely and for short periods, Angela and I would sit slumped in half-conscious silence, without the energy to speak, let alone attempt to clean up the sad chaos of our surroundings. I waited, braced for my own sorrow which I was certain must come, but it did not, not then. It was as though madonna's grief, in all its savage grandeur, shamed mine into hiding itself. No one could mourn as she did; even the women of Troy seemed like faint pretenders compared with her. And I was so tired, too tired to muster the resources needed to properly grieve for my first love, my son's father, the man whose dark eyes and clever smile had defined the whole world for me.

Madonna tended to sleep on the floor, curled up like a child, with her knees to her chest and her thumb in her mouth. So when she awoke on the last morning, squinting into a bright bar of sunlight that fell through a gap in the shutters, the first thing she saw was the travel-stained satchel Juanito had left and I had stuffed under her bed and thought no more of.

"What's that?" she demanded, removing her thumb from her mouth and wiping it on the remains of her bodice. "What is it?" she repeated as Angela and I struggled into full consciousness and tried to discern where she was looking. "Under my bed? It wasn't there before."

"Ah." Realisation dawned. "Juanito left it. I don't know what's inside."

She sidled across the floor, still lying on her side, flexing her body like a snake, until she could reach her hand under the bed and seize hold of the satchel. As she pulled it clear, the flap fell open and some documents fell out. They were faded and battered, but the handwriting, with its loops and curves and tendency to slope towards the end of each line, was unmistakable. Donna Lucrezia sat up. She pushed her hair out of her eyes, then looked at her hand, the nails broken, the cuticles crescent moons of grime, as though it was something unfamiliar and rather horrible.

"Leave me," she said.

"But..." Angela began.

"You have nothing to fear. Go."

❧

I went to my room with the intention of trying to sleep. But though my body was leaden with exhaustion, my mind felt sharp and restless, expectant. Unable to settle, I dragged my travelling chest from under my bed and delved in the bottom of it for the letter Cesare had written me from Rome and the drawing done by Ser Leonardo. First I had to take out my mother's recipe book and the more recent letter I had received from Gideon. I had surprised myself by keeping it, in the uneasy peace following the *Coniurga*. I thought it odd and impudent and anyway, he would be long gone by now.

I laid all these items in a row on my bed and stared at them as though I expected them to tell me something. I picked up Cesare's letter and re-read it, but it remained as elegant and incomprehensible as it had always been. I laid it aside and my gaze shifted to the drawing, the hooded eyes, the expression of the mouth obscured by his beard and moustache. It was a wonderful drawing, the face true and human with the slight irregularity of the nose and the pouches under the eyes, but it was lifeless, a figment of burnt wood and lamb skin, a moment caught and pinned like a beautiful moth.

"I'm sorry," I said to it, and suddenly I was sorry, for everything we had not done together, for the torchlit skating parties I had once imagined, the summer walks in scented gardens, the songs not sung and the dances not danced, the verses we had never exchanged, the sweet nonsense we had failed to whisper to each other. I had always assumed there would be a future and now, abruptly, at the stroke of some anonymous Navarrese's sword, there was none. Crumpling the picture against my heart, I sank down on the bed among those other small relics of my time on earth, and wept until my eyes burned and my throat ached and I thought I must have wept all the tears that were mine to weep.

I was not aware of Angela's presence until she flung herself down on the bed at my side and put her arms around me.

"That's better," she said, stroking my hair and my back, pulling a kerchief out of her sleeve for me to blow my nose on. "It's important to cry." There was solace in her affection, her physical closeness. I managed a weak smile, but the look she returned was deeply serious. "After Giulio was attacked," she said, "I felt cold inside. As though I'd turned into a statue, or one of those mechanicals they put on carnival floats, just going on doing things automatically." She gave a sudden laugh. "And you were so disapproving."

"I wasn't." I thought of the time we had spent alone together at Medelana, after Giulia was born. Was that disapproving?

"Oh, you were, underneath. You thought I should have stuck by him in spite of everything. I know you, Violante, remember? You didn't have to say anything. And you were right. But I just couldn't. I kept thinking, what if I find him repulsive and he senses it? How much worse would that be than my just doing what everyone expects of us?"

"Us?"

"Me and Lucrezia. The Borgias. Ruthless. I was wrong, though. If I'd

500

been braver and more honest, Giulio wouldn't be locked in that room." She shuddered. "I tell you, Violante, there's not a day goes by I don't think about it. What if this, what if that. And Giulia looks so like him now, not a trace of me in her anywhere. As though God made her to test me."

"I think He is a great ironist. He tests you by your daughter's presence and me by my son's absence." I felt another tide of grief wash against my heart. "I shall never get him back now, shall I?"

Her silence told me all I needed to know. Eventually she patted my knee and said, "Cesare wasn't brought up by his mother. I wasn't. Most people aren't. It doesn't do us any harm."

"Most people are at least allowed to know who their mothers are."

"Oh, Lucrezia will relent on that. Now he's properly settled in Carpi and there's no longer...any likelihood of his circumstances changing again, there can be no harm in it. It will be fun. We can visit together when my husband and Don Alberto meet. I'll tell you what. We'll slip Alberto's wife a doubtful oyster, and when she dies you can marry him." She was beaming now, rocking back and forth like a child herself, full of the excitement of her plan. It was Ferrante and Giulio all over again, another impossible scheme to give her the illusion of control over her life. The domestic version, I thought, with wan amusement, of what her dead cousin had tried and failed with his armies and his politicking.

❧

Had it not been for Donna Lucrezia's black clothes, the ash cross on her forehead, the scabs on her face and hands, I could almost have believed I had dreamed everything, from Fra Raffaello's self-conscious solemnity to the abject, animal intensity of her suffering. I could almost believe she had sent for me to tell me Cesare would be returning to Italy in the spring. She had already spent some time alone with Angela that morning, and had received Agapito, now secretary to the papal legate in Bologna, but with whom she could share close memories of her brother. There were few at court who were willing to talk about him. The duke could not even see the point of official mourning, though he had agreed to Ippolito arranging a requiem Mass in the cathedral. I hoped there would be new music for it.

"I owe you my thanks," Donna Lucrezia said to me as I curtseyed. She was lying on her bed, which she did not yet feel strong enough to leave.

She had Juanito's satchel beside her, and also the empty filigree box she had once charged me with giving to Cesare if anything should happen to her.

"I have done no more than my duty, madonna."

"Violante, ever since I have known you, you have always done far more than your duty. And now I am going to ask one more favour of you."

I bowed.

"Later today I must speak to Giovanni. He knows Cesar is dead, of course, but I have not yet spoken to him directly nor ascertained his feelings on the subject. He was, as you know, very fond of Cesar. He is also very fond of you, and I would like you to keep me company during our interview. There is much he cannot understand, and I fear this will only serve to sharpen his grief."

"Of course, madonna. I will do my best to comfort him." I wondered who would comfort Girolamo, if he needed it.

"There is something you must know about Giovanni first." She paused. Some unaccustomed note in her voice made me look at her. The skin under her eyes was smudged with grey and her lids were puffy and pleated like those of a much older woman. The gaze she turned on me seemed nervous, partly guilty, partly defiant. With the air of someone who had made what might be a reckless decision she went on, "Giovanni is not my father's son, but Cesar's."

"I see." I realised I was not surprised. An image floated to the surface of my memory, of Cesare in the courtyard of the Castel Sant'Angelo, stooping to kiss the child's sleeping head before the groom lifted him out of the saddle. A tender action, the action of a fond parent. I supposed madonna had hesitated because she was afraid how I would react when I realised Girolamo was not Cesare's heir after all. I found I was not angry. What was there left for either of them to inherit? Perhaps I should be glad Girolamo had been put into Don Alberto's care rather than being left to drift aimlessly around Ferrara as Giovanni appeared to do.

"No, my dear, you do not see. Cesar is his father, and I am his mother."

I should have left then. I tell myself I stayed out of compassion for madonna, or out of the habit of waiting to be dismissed, but it was my own prurient fascination that kept me there.

*You are the Jewess. It's true what they say. Look Dorotea, is she not the very spit of my illustrious daughter.* "I have been a complete fool, haven't I?" Donata. The gift. They had seen their opportunity and grasped it.

"No, Violante, you have been deceived by people who are, perforce, very good at it. I realised my mistake almost immediately, as soon as I saw how genuinely attached you had become to Cesar. I tried to get him to stop it…"

Oh, so that made everything better; if madonna had tried to act on her conscience, she, at least, was exonerated. "You make it sound as though he and I were somehow deeper in the wrong than you were," I said, with a degree of wonder.

"I love him." Her voice rose to an hysterical quaver and I feared for a moment she was plunging back into the grief which had overtaken her after her interview with Juanito, but she took control of herself and went on, "just as you do. More than that. There has not been a day, a moment of my sentient life when I have not been tortured by guilt for him and me alike. And now…" She waved a hand at her room, "here I am with all my comforts and he is, he is…" Words failed her. She shuddered.

"You told him to write me that letter, didn't you?" I asked. Because I had to know, and because I, too, shrank from thinking about where Cesare was now. I had an irrational urge to pray he had been right, that religion was no more than story telling and he was nothing now, just flesh falling quietly from bone in the dry, red earth of Navarre.

She nodded miserably. "But he was unwilling to break off with you completely. Perhaps that flatters both of us. Cesar always prized honesty. Most people find that strange, and many have seen it as a weakness in him. He has, on occasion, relied more on a man's reputation for honesty than on the evidence of his own eyes. It is my belief he valued it as we always value things we cannot have. And he recognised it and valued it in you. I have convinced myself he would want me to tell you all this, but perhaps it is just that I cannot support all my memories, all my…love, on my own. If I am to continue to live, and care for my son and make plans for him, I have to know there is someone else in the world to help me bear the burden. And obviously I cannot tell Giovanni himself. Not yet. Probably never."

"Isn't what you have already said enough? You took me into your household to be a plaything for your brother. My son, whom I always believed to be his heir, is not. Am I the only one who didn't know what was going on? Angela?"

"Angela was completely opposed to my plan from the beginning. She befriended you to protect you. You have every right to be angry, and I have no defence. I merely ask you, out of your natural compassion, to hear me out."

But it was not her deceit that angered me, it was the fact that she had left me nothing to mourn. The man I grieved for had never existed. I could not trust myself to reply to her request so watched in fierce silence as she began to pull sheaves of documents out of Juanito's satchel. "You may read these," she said, spreading them around her on the bed. I shook my head, held up my hands as if to ward off a blow, but she pushed the pages at me with abrupt, insistent little thrusts of her hands.

Some were neatly written on good, clean parchments, some scrawled on dog-eared palimpsests. There were even a few frayed squares of linen which looked as though they had been cut from bed sheets, or even shirts. The ink was faded in places to a pale, yellowish rust, scarcely visible, let alone legible in the artificial dusk of madonna's shuttered room. As I had noticed before, all these documents were in Cesare's hand. I now saw that they were letters, and that all were addressed in the same way.

*Lucia, mi cor* he had written at the head of every one. Lucrezia, Lucia. It was so obvious I felt even more foolish, and angry with myself, that I had not realised it sooner. His faith in me to heal him, the cut shoes, the talk of the calf, his delirious kiss that had no artifice, merely the desperate hunger I had once known myself when I thought of him, all the clues were there and I had stumbled into the mess of it as blindly as Cupid.

❧

"You know the beginning of it," she said as I shuffled the letters around on the bed with the futility of someone trying to find a winning combination in a poor hand at cards. "My mother has told you."

"Your mother told me she believes you are a changeling and that you kept Cesare alive for some nefarious faery purpose."

"And you are inclined to agree with her." She gave a brief, stifled laugh. "My mother is only comfortable with things she can find an explanation for. Cesar and I are…were…perhaps, the same, but found ourselves with one foot on each side of the divide between this world and…somewhere else. Sometimes I feel as though I am living through a never-ending All Hallows' Eve."

"What did Cesare think?" I wanted to make her tell me.

"He remembered having the impression, when he saw me for the first time, that everything in the world had shifted a little to make room for me. And that when Juan pushed him out of the way so he could look at me, it didn't make him cross because he knew it was no longer important."

"You do not believe Cesare killed Don Juan, do you?" It was a time for plain speaking, for unimaginable truths.

"I know he didn't. Juan was murdered on the orders of the Orsini. The girl Juan was going to meet that night, the honey-trap if you will, belonged to an Orsini family. Cesar's only crime was to persuade Papa to call off the hunt for the murderers and let him arrange a proper revenge. It made him look guilty.

"And there's something else. At my son Rodrigo's baptism, he was given to Don Paolo Orsini to carry from the basilica back to Santa Maria. I was watching from a window as I hadn't yet been churched so couldn't attend the ceremony myself. The moment he was placed in Don Paolo's arms he began to scream, and he'd been good as gold up till then. Surely that was a sign of their guilt.

"Cesar was quite capable of murder, as I know to my cost—and his—but there was no reason for him to want Juan dead. On the contrary, Juan gave him a foot in the Spanish court, as long as he behaved himself. And he wasn't vicious, you know, just young for his years and rather silly."

I felt a kind of awe, listening to her cool analysis of Don Juan's murder. I began to understand what Monna Vannozza saw in her that made her fear her daughter.

"But I am getting ahead of myself. You must stop asking questions and let me tell my story as it unfolds. She gave no sign she was aware of the effect she was having on me. "I have virtually no memory of the time we all lived together at my mother's house. I was about six when I was sent to Aunt Adriana, and Cesar and Juan were long gone by then. We would meet at Santa Maria for visits from Papa, but, as you know, we only spent long periods together in the summer, at Caprarola." She pronounced the name with tenderness, and her expression softened. "On hot nights we used to sleep on the roof and sometimes, if I got frightened or felt lonely—the stars can make you feel lonely, can't they, so far away and not concerned with us at all—I would snuggle up with Cesar under his blankets. Never Juan because he would just make a fuss about being too hot, or me stealing all the bedclothes or something. And not Jofre, of course, because he was only a baby himself." She paused and rummaged among the letters strewn about the bed. Retrieving one, she handed it to me. "Here," she said, "read. Let him tell you in his own words."

"No. Please. Anyway, I cannot read your language."

"You can if you want to," she said.

It was as though I was trespassing on a place of the deepest secrecy and privacy, yet I was not; I had been invited in, and I had not refused the invitation. I began to read.

*The first night they allowed me above decks on the voyage to Villa Nueva del Grao there was a full moon. Do you remember—of course you do—how we all used to sleep on the roof at Caprarola, and you would creep under my blanket and ask me all the questions that were racing around your head and stopping you falling asleep? How could bats see in the dark? How did the planets know where to go? What would happen to the six-legged calf? Could you marry me when we grew up? I suppose we were about eleven and six then.*

*One night, when the moon was full, I explained to you about how the moon controls the tides, and you said I was like the moon and you were the sea, always following me about. And I said nothing, because I knew it was truly the other way around.*

I was entranced all over again. Looking up, I met her eyes and she knew the meaning of my look instantly. "They're all like that," she said. "Here." She handed me another.

*We started so young, you and I,* I read. *We were like soft clay for the moulding. Our bodies are what each made of the other, stroked and smoothed to fit one another perfectly. And then we were fired in life's kiln, set forever in a form to suit only each other.*

She began to speak again. "It all began to change about the time Cesar went away to school. The first summer we went to Caprarola and he came from Perugia, he was different. He was bigger, broader, his beard had begun to grow, and he just wanted to be off with Juan doing what he called men's things. They went hunting and fishing and fussed over their puppies and fought little bulls just as they had always done, but they also spent hours in corners giggling over some book Cesar had acquired which he told our mother's husband was a Platonic dialogue illustrating suitable conduct for young men. It was nothing of the sort, of course, but it was in Greek and Ser Giorgio's Greek wasn't very good.

"We would still sleep on the roof and I would still get in beside him, but sometimes he would turn his back on me and get impatient with my chatter. Then one night my hand brushed against…"

"Please, madonna, I am sure I need not hear all the details." But I could not stop her telling them, either as a way of reliving them or of seeking atonement, or perhaps something of both.

"I was shocked," she said, "but he grabbed my wrist and held my hand there, and then I was curious. I was always curious, you see. Not a very feminine attribute. And then I was content, because I realised whatever I was doing gave me some power over him. I didn't feel left out any more. It restored us to the way we had been, me and Cesar together and Juan and Jofre on the outside.

"And that's the way it stayed, despite the cost. Perotto, Pantasilea, Djem…"

The first two names meant nothing to me; they sounded like characters in a comedy, but Djem. I remembered Cesare doing impressions of Djem, of madonna begging him to stop because of the pain of laughing with her breasts engorged. "Djem?" I queried.

"You know my father inherited Prince Djem, as it were, when he became pope? And we children took to visiting him in his apartments. Oh Violante, it was like stepping into another world. Perhaps that is why Cesar and I felt so at home there, even though it was Juan Djem always wanted to see most. Even the air. He used to burn incense all the time, but it never had that cold, righteous smell it has in a church. It was spicy, hot, like breathing in the sun on the desert Djem came from. And he had no chairs, just cushions all over the floor, so we all sat together, the Sultan's brother and we three parvenu *marrano* bastards, eating sweets. Real gipsies we felt like there, in Djem's 'tent.'

"Before very long at all, Djem had seduced Juan. He used to dress him up in Turkish robes and turbans and…touch him. And because we would be full of wine mixed with poppy it seemed quite hilarious to us."

I wondered if this was why madonna, for all her piety, had always accepted Ferrante's inclinations with equanimity.

"So hilarious we would imitate them, with Cesar taking Djem's part and me Juan's. Well by then Cesar was about eighteen. He had been to university; he was a man of the world, even if he had just been admitted to the Sacred College and made to wear a tonsure." She burst into giggles. "God in heaven, how he hated that. He was forever letting it grow out and being given penances. Anyway, yes, for myself, there was much talk of betrothals, and Aunt Adriana had given me her little speech on the duties of wives. Though the duties of wives vary quite a lot, I think, from the duties of young women who are in love with their brothers.

"So I cannot say we did not know what we were doing, or that it did not mire us as deep in sin as it's possible to be, yet it felt…right. It was the inevitable end of the path we had embarked on from birth."

*Djem let us be ourselves,* he had said to me.

"But that is why he had Djem killed."

*I will never forgive the French for Djem.* "Cesare?" I queried.

"He didn't die of a fever, not Djem. He was never ill."

"But I thought Cesare was fond of Djem."

"Not so fond as he was of me or his own reputation."

I tried to console myself with the thought that at least his body had not lied, that his desire for me had been real. Then I remembered his unflawed skin, the clean grace of his bones and sinews, the beautiful deceit with which that body had contaminated mine with its disease.

"He saw to everything," said madonna, "but he could never control his jealousy."

*You used to be so jealous of Sancia,* he had written on another page. *You accused her of being my first love. Hah! You are my first and last and only love and you know it. You were just being disingenuous, weren't you?*

"He would not come to my wedding, you know, my first wedding to Giovanni Sforza."

*I was very young. I confused lust with love as the young do. There was perhaps a day when I believed I could not live without Sancia (probably the day she gave me the white velvet suit. Remember?)—a day of relief and despair. But I have always known I couldn't live without you. That is a constant, like the sun rising in the east or my having five fingers on each hand. That is love, Lucia, and it doesn't go in for showy swooning or pretty phrases or extravagant gifts. It is plain and deep, like the sea when no one is looking at it.*

"He came in the morning, to my room in Santa Maria where my maids were dressing me. I was so cruel. I wouldn't let him embrace me. I was all covered in lemon juice, you see, for whitening my skin, and I was sticky. I sat there in my shift, with it clinging to my body, and watched him suffer. He said he had brought me a gift." She picked up the filigree box, wearily, as though it was a great weight. "There was nothing inside but a rolled up vellum, tied with a plait of gold and copper wires. When I lifted it out, he said, 'There, now, inside that box is my heart, empty without you.' At that I burst into tears and stopped all my play-acting and coquettishness. I was terrified, of Giovanni, of going away, of losing Cesar. He comforted me." She gave a sad laugh. "Got his soutane covered in lemon…"

"He said you wouldn't be like the calf, didn't he, said you wouldn't die of the separation? And scored the soles of your shoes for dancing."

"How did you know that?"

"He spoke to me honestly once, when he was delirious."

"I am so sorry."

"What was written on the vellum?"

"Oh nothing much, just some verses from a Catalan poet we used to like."

She fell silent. I stared at the scattered letters, phrases emerging from the scrawled lines as images sometimes form themselves from clouds. *There is a gipsy girl…I would like to pluck her songs from the air and press them between cards for you, like flowers…I woke in the night with the taste of raspberries on my tongue…I had to tell you about the sunset…the earth burned with the sorrow of parting…always, when I dance, I am dancing with you.* I wondered if anyone else would ever read these words, and how they would know if they were true. I looked at madonna, clutching her empty box, her hands folded over it the way a pregnant woman's hands lie on the rise of her belly.

"Tell me about Giovanni," I said.

She blinked and looked bewildered, like someone woken suddenly from a deep sleep, then put the box aside. "When I realised I was pregnant I went to San Sisto. I knew it was Cesar's, and even a dolt like Sforza would have been able to work out it wasn't his if he could count to nine. He and I had been content enough in Pesaro, but once we came back to Rome things became difficult. Cesar had the perfect excuse to keep us apart, as it was obvious by this time the marriage was serving no useful political purpose and Papa was keen to arrange a divorce. I needed time to think, somewhere I could keep away from my family. I took one maid with me, my favourite, a girl called Pantasilea, and refused to communicate with the family except through messengers. Papa used to send Perotto Calderon because he knew I was fond of him.

"This made Cesar even angrier and eventually he burst in one day, scattering the sisters like a fox among the chickens, and accused me of having an affair with Perotto. I calmed him down and made him walk with me to a far corner of the convent garden where I knew we would not be overheard, and told him I was pregnant and that he was the father." A soft light came into her eyes. "He was so excited, and so ridiculously solicitous. It mortified him that he had shouted at me. He was worried I had walked too far, started fussing about the convent food and the hard beds and a thousand other silly things. The food and the beds at San Sisto were little different to what I was used to at Santa Maria." She flashed me a mischievous smile. "Sister Osanna would have felt at home there. You know I have sent her back to Mantua, the old fraud? Isabella is welcome to her. I have a mind to put Fidelma into Santa Caterina as abbess, and make Fra Raffaello their spiritual adviser. What do you think?"

But she went on without waiting for my reply. "For a brief moment, in that neglected corner full of nettles and white butterflies, Cesar and I were like any other couple who loved each other and had just discovered we were expecting our first child. I was happy all through that pregnancy, thinking about that scrap of love, that magical second of union growing into a whole life inside me. It was as though I was protected by a carapace of contentment, even when Juan died and Cesar cried when he told me and then was angry with himself and broke a stool. He always missed him, I think, because he had always measured himself against him. Even when I had to go before the College of Cardinals and lie to them about my marriage to Sforza, I kept my eyes locked on Cesar's and made myself believe there was no one else in the room, that my elegant little statement was really a hymn of love to my beautiful brother.

"I was about the same age you were when Girolamo was born, so you see, for me, watching your child grow in your belly, being with you at his birth, I was re-living that time. I measure all my subsequent joys by it. None has ever come close, and now none ever will."

I wondered about her second marriage, to the Duke of Bisceglie, but I held my peace because I knew she would come to that. She would have to. As I waited for her to continue with her story, I picked up another of Cesare's letters.

*I have been trying to think of a moment when I was truly happy,* I read, and had the uncanny sense he was guiding my actions from whatever place he now was, as a way of carrying on his lifelong conversation with his sister from the other side of death. *I expected to find it in my memories of you, but I didn't. Nothing was ever simple for us, was it?*

"Open the shutters," she said, "or you will damage your eyes."

As I obeyed her command, I looked out on to the segment of garden visible from her window, roses just coming into bud, silvery rosemary bushes starred with tiny blue flowers, the vine walk where I had once sat to read Cesare's only letter to me. Dusk was falling, soothing my strained eyes, wrapping the garden in a furze of forgetfulness. A pale sliver of moon fine as a nail paring, holding the ghost of its former fullness in its slender arms, hung just above the city walls in a sky the colour of aquamarine. Swallows looped and dived past our oblong of window, skimming the moat then soaring back up towards their roosts.

"It's going to be a lovely evening," I said.

"Is it?" She patted the bed. "Come and sit down again. I still have much to tell you before I send for Giovanni and I do not want to keep him up too late."

Making a space for myself once more among the letters, I resumed my place at her side and she resumed her story.

"Time passed and we still had not decided what we would do when the baby arrived. Cesar was all for going back to his old notion of my having had an affair with Perotto. I would have to 'confess' to Papa and Papa would see the child was taken care of. But I disagreed. For one thing, Perotto would have to be punished for something he hadn't done, but far worse was the fact that Papa would certainly have taken my baby away from me. He was heavily involved by then in negotiating for Alfonso of Bisceglie's hand for me, and I was to be presented once again as *virgo intacta*." She gave a laugh of bleak irony. "I couldn't bear the thought of losing my child, and I think Cesar felt the same way, underneath, which might explain why he hesitated, even though it seemed the only practical suggestion.

"Then Fate took a hand, almost as though the gods had despaired of us making our own minds up and felt they had to intervene to save us from disaster. The same day Giovanni was born, Giulia Farnese also gave birth to a little boy. There was our solution. Giulia was quite poorly and her baby had been given straight to the wet nurse. A sum of money and the co-operation of Perotto and Pantasilea were all that was needed to effect a swap, and Giulia would be none the wiser. Or so I thought. Cesar decided…more caution was needed.

"Giovanni was given to Giulia's nurse as planned, but Cesar thought it needed more than money to buy her silence. He had Pantasilea and Perotto killed, and made sure the bodies were found, in the river, close to the Sant'Angelo bridge. Our stretch, you might say. That way the woman would be sure to get the message."

"And the other baby?"

She paused before replying, then said, "I was told it died."

I saw again Cesare stepping on to the ravelin by the castle drawbridge, emptying the contents of Ser Torella's silver basin into the moat. I saw the face he had turned on me and finally understood its absence of expression. I went to the hearth, struck a flint on the hearthstone, and began to light the lamps.

"So there you have it, Violante. Will you go and fetch Giovanni now?" She began to gather together Cesare's letters and bundle them back into the satchel. As she did so, one slipped on to the floor and I stooped to pick it up.

*You always held it against me that I left Nepi without saying goodbye,* I read along the top line before handing it back to her.

"Madonna, I have listened with patience and not a little personal suffering to what you have told me. Perhaps you would permit me to ask you a question?"

She looked as though she would have preferred to refuse but, like her brother, she had a sense of honour, however peculiar. "Of course," she said.

"What happened at Nepi? Why were you so distressed by Cesare's action against Urbino?"

"That is two questions, but you are right to link them and I will answer. We will have to go back to the Jubilee year, when Cesar finally came back from France. He had been away for more than a year. We had written of course, almost daily, as we had always done, but much had happened to change us both during that time. I had discovered in myself, with the Duke of Bisceglie, a capacity for love and happiness outside my relationship with Cesar, and I had another son to dull the pain of being forced to watch Giovanni brought up as another woman's child. Cesar also had a wife in whom he had expressed himself well pleased, and now a daughter, though he had never seen her. But more than that, he had begun to build his state. And his reputation.

"When we met again, we tried to be as we had been before but it didn't work. I took no joy in him because I felt guilty about Alfonso, and then guilty about him because I had hurt him. After France, he found our ways silly and parochial, he said. He would sit among us like a raven in his black clothes and bore us all senseless with his plans for his court at Cesena once it was established and how it would all be French this and French that. And the more he extolled the virtues of France, the more convinced I became he loved his wife and the more I cleaved to my husband. What do you make of this?" She riffled through the satchel and pulled one of the letters back out of it; I marvelled at the sure way she had distinguished it from the rest, as though she knew every curlicue, every crease in the parchment the way a mother knows her child.

*I find myself thinking about Charlotte, though I can scarcely remember what she looks like. Do you know what won her to me? My knowing the names of wild flowers. By the time I left France, I had only to whisper in her ear the Italian name for coltsfoot or mallow and she would be all over me like a clambering rosa gallica. I never told her that I know wild flowers because their presence or absence can tell you the nature of the terrain you are marching into. A politician must read men's faces, a soldier must consider the lilies of the field.*

"It seems very…true, madonna."

"Yes. There is something about it that troubles me. Well, I have all the time in the world to wonder about it now, don't I? Where were we? Ah yes.

"You know, of course, how everything came to a head between our family and that of Aragon? It was not only Alfonso and Sancia who rankled with Cesar, but the fact that their sister, Carlotta, had refused to marry him and her father had done nothing to make her. His pride could not endure it, even after King Louis gave him Charlotte, who was just as well born and much prettier. He was inconsolable, and terribly lonely, everywhere surrounded by people who were getting on with their lives. He was getting on with his too, of course, but he had so much less patience than the rest of us. He could never wait for anything to take its course but must be hurrying it along.

"Suddenly he had decided my marriage to Alfonso was an obstacle to his alliance with the French because of their rival claim to Naples. Or so he said. I knew he was jealous, not just of Alfonso but of all of us and the cosy family party he believed we had become without him. He thought Sancia had seduced Papa and was trying to undermine his position with his own father.

"Then the roof fell in, literally."

I remembered this. During a particularly violent summer storm, a chimney on the Vatican roof had been blown through the ceiling of a room where the pope was sitting. For several hours, it was believed he had died, until his guards managed to dig him out of the rubble, unscathed except for a cut on his head.

"After that," madonna continued, "there was no longer any reasoning with Cesar. It was as though he had but one thought in his mind and that was of the need to secure his future while our father still lived. He was seventy years old by then. Anything might have happened. Cesar didn't even bother to discuss his plans with me any more. He never sought out my company for any reason. Slept with that whore of his, La Fiammetta, because he said it was easier to pay than to waste his effort charming women into bed. I wasn't surprised that he sent Michelotto to finish off Alfonso, but I was horrified by his callousness and scared witless by his brazenness.

"They say I went to Nepi to grieve for my husband, and I did, but it was more complicated than that. I was grieving for two loves, for Cesar as well as Alfonso. And I had to think. Clearly Cesar could not be trusted any more where my future was concerned because of this jealousy of his, yet my future was vital to his, and to our son's. Thinking of Giovanni, I had a sort of epiphany, you might call it. You know Heraclitus?"

I nodded. I had heard of him, of course, but knew little of his philosophy.

"He was a great favourite of Cesar's. 'Nature loves concealment,' he said, which might have been written for Cesar. He also speaks of a *logos* which gives order to chaos but is comprehensible only to a very few. Well, at Nepi, for a kind of philosophical second, I understood it. I saw what we had to do with absolute clarity. I wrote two letters, one to Cesar, begging him to come to me at Nepi and ask my forgiveness for I felt my grief so severely I feared I would not live. He was not the only one who could tell pretty lies, you see, or make them believed.

"The other letter was to Ercole d'Este, proposing myself as a wife for Don Alfonso. I know. Breathtaking boldness, but I knew my father had already opened tentative negotiations, and the stakes were very high for me. And Giovanni. My father was old and enfeebled by his accident and my brother apparently unhinged with jealousy where I was concerned even if the things he did in the rest of his life made sense. Who else had I to rely on but myself? And a marriage into a family as distinguished as the Este would make me safe, part of the establishment. Regardless of Cesar, that was the best way open to me of securing Giovanni's future."

We were interrupted by a discreet scratching on the door.

"What is it?" madonna snapped.

"The cardinal sends to know if you will dine with him tonight," replied a disembodied voice.

"Please thank the cardinal and tell him I do not yet feel well enough. I will dine in my room."

We waited in silence as soft footsteps padded away. "This is not a conversation I would wish overheard," said madonna.

"I should like to have seen Duke Ercole's face when he received your letter."

"His reply was very prompt and courteous. I had written to him at length about my religion, and my interest in the stigmata, as well as reminding him I had proved my ability to produce a healthy son," an ironic laugh here, "and to administer my property in my own name. Oh, and I might have touched on my brother's territorial ambitions and his recent military successes. He could not help but listen to what I had to say."

"And Cesare?"

"He came, as you know. He was on his way to join his troops for an autumn campaign, and stopped a night with me. Yes," she said, intercepting my glance, "a night.

"How strange it is that secretive people are often also histrionic. He entered the hall of my castle in full armour, with his head bare, looking for all the world like a figure from a novel of chivalry, and without saying a word, fell to his knees at my feet and kissed the hem of my dress. D'you know, Violante," her voice became remote, "I have asked myself over and over if that is the last sound he heard."

"What?"

"That clash of his armour as he fell from his horse. And if it reminded him, if he was thinking of…well, never mind, that is idle speculation. One part of me knew it was an act. Clearly he had not ridden all the way from Rome in full armour. He must have stopped just outside Nepi to put it on. But the other part, the part that was his, could think of nothing but that he was here, alone with me, with all his beautiful hair spread out around my feet like a lake of fire. I knelt and put my arms around him, and for a moment that could have cost us everything; I believed we could just stay that way forever, locked up in the old fort, hidden from the world, living on love."

I was suddenly, strangely, moved to take her hands in mine, to show her it was not just our looks we shared, but our wild dreams as well.

"I led him to my own chamber and helped him out of his armour myself so we wouldn't be disturbed. He thought…what men always think, but I told him no, I had important things to say to him. He prevaricated, insisted he wanted a bath, told me I could talk to him while he bathed, and I could wash his hair because I always washed it better than anyone else. The bath was filled. He undressed in front of me as if he were a whore and I his client, and his beauty there, in the firelight and the steam from the water, nearly broke my heart. As he knew it would.

"But he had underestimated me this time. So he bided his time and took his bath quite meekly and I washed his hair, and told him what I had brought him there to tell him. That he had gone too far by murdering Alfonso and that, however much we loved each other, we must never again allow ourselves to be driven by our passion. Because we had to think of Giovanni, always Giovanni.

"I told him I knew he and Papa had discussed the possibility of marrying me next to Alfonso d'Este, so I had written to the duke myself and assured him he would find in me an eager, pious, and loyal daughter-in-law who would always put her husband's will ahead of that of her father or her brother. I had hinted that my presence in Ferrara would curb any designs my brother might have upon that state, for surely Ferrara would become his ally in the circumstances. I told him he must carry on building his state and that my presence in Ferrara would secure his northern border and keep Venice out of his affairs until he was strong enough to take her on. One day, I said, our son would be King of Italy.

"Cesar began to shiver. I held a towel for him as he climbed out of the bath and wrapped it around him as if he were a child and told myself the feel of his body beneath the cloth meant nothing to me. I tried to make my heart as hard as the old stones sheltering us, but I failed. I had intended to make him leave straight away, but I couldn't resist him with his skin all scrubbed and smelling of soap. So we...and then I combed his hair while it dried by the fire and the night drew in.

"When I awoke next morning, he was gone, so I knew he had understood. That was our last time. From now on we could not think of ourselves, only of Giovanni and the state we would build him.

"Now do you understand why I was so furious about Urbino? It was a rash act; it jeopardised what we had given up so much for. It betrayed our love. It made a mockery of everything I had sacrificed for him."

I stared at her. I no longer knew what to think. There was something of the cosmic jest in the revelation that the great Valentino, scourge alike of Italy's tyrants and Italy's women, had given his heart and his obedience all along to his little sister. Yet at the same time, her power over him put me in awe of her. I fiddled with the letters, unsure if I should feel honoured by her confidence or hurt by her utter disregard for my own feelings.

And picked up a rough square of what appeared to be bed linen, on which were scrawled, in blotchy ink the colour of brick dust, the words which made up my mind: *Pio tells me Girolamo shows spirit and a sharp intelligence. Keep him close, Lucia, and do not let him forget Giovanni is my heir.* My son was all I had left now, all that was made of Cesare and me and what had been between us, just us, not mediated or manipulated by Donna Lucrezia. Why should he, like me, pass his life as second best? I would take him from Don Alberto and go away, far away, where the name of Borgia meant nothing. Angela would help me, and in the end Donna Lucrezia would see it was for the best. It would ensure Giovanni had no rival for his father's inheritance.

I found Angela in our old room with her maid, packing for her return to Sassuolo. As I came in she turned to me, holding the black and white striped bodice I had taken from Nepi up to her chest.

"Darling, can I take this? It would look so nice if..." Her words died away as she saw my face. Dismissing the maid, she said, "You know, don't you? She's told you. I wondered if she might...now. Come and sit down. This is terrible for you."

I shook off the hand which pawed at my sleeve. "I haven't time. She's waiting for me to fetch Giovanni, before his bedtime."

Angela looked aghast, her face pale and sharp in the candlelight which still shivered a little in the draught of my arrival. I looked away, at the open chests and boxes strewn about the room and the emptiness beneath.

"She's not going to tell him, is she?"

"Of course not. He's just another excuse for her to go on about Cesare."

"You're upset. Take a little time. I'm sure Giovanni's bedtime can wait, in the circumstances."

"Oh stop trying to be kind. It's a bit late for that now. You knew about... them, Cesare and...," but I could not bring myself to link their names out loud, "all the time. Why didn't you tell me? What sort of friend are you?" The image of Giulio, his bright hair blowing across his scarred face, seemed to give me my answer.

"I tried," she shouted, "I tried a thousand times but you would never listen. You were as blind as that revolting old dog of his where Cesare was concerned."

"Well I'm listening now. Help me get Girolamo back. Tell me how I do that and I'll never trouble any of you again."

I might as well have asked her to steal madonna's jewellery or seduce Duke Alfonso. "She'd kill you before she'd let you have him. It's impossible. You don't think just because Cesare's dead she's given up her ambitions for him? She'll keep those two boys closer than ever now. Your only hope of seeing Girolamo is to carry on here as if nothing had changed."

"No. How can I? I'll take him away. It's Giovanni she's interested in anyway. Girolamo and I can just…disappear." I thought of Gideon's letter, and suddenly knew why I had kept it despite its insolence, despite the risk. "I know how. I have a plan."

Angela made a great play of covering her ears with her hands. "Don't tell me. I really can't be part of this."

"No, of course you can't. You never could. Have a safe journey. I shall probably sleep in the nursery tonight so I don't expect I shall see you before you go."

You follow love. Even if the path leads to shoddy compromises, secrets, and lies. Yet how can you follow it beyond the point where you cease to be the person to whom that love means something? What Mariam had never understood, living meekly in her servant's room with its earth floor and poor furniture, was that love requires you to be true to yourself first.

# Epilogue

## Cachiquin, on the Day of Atonement, 5281

*This morning my captors finally decided it was safe to unchain me. I have been fastened to the wall by my wrists and ankles since being brought here—five or six days, I think. I have kept myself from going mad with pain and inertia by thinking about the Christmas I spent at Cesena, when I was most alive, touring around the mountain villages incognito, wrestling and dancing and drinking too much of their fearsome spirit and fucking their plump women. I was happy, Lucia, just plain, heedless happy. You know why? Because no one knew who I was.*

There is little more to tell now about the time and the ways in which I served Donna Lucrezia Borgia, the Duchess of Ferrara. My life since I left Italy is part of another story, one in which I am no one's mother or daughter, servant or concubine or double, but just myself. It has no place in this tale of masks and pretences, so I will not tell it here.

✧

A requiem Mass was sung for the most noble and illustrious Duke of Romagna and Valentinois, Seigneur of France, in the cathedral of Ferrara on a Wednesday in May. The Este family, preceded by their clergy and followed by their households, processed across the square in bright sunlight which already carried within itself the ferocity of summer. All wore deep mourning and black banners decked the house fronts; even old Borso and the cuckold Niccolo were swathed in black ribbons. The shops were shut and the bell tolled mournfully in Alberti's campanile and a few townspeople stood about in resigned and sceptical silence. Had it not been for his sister's deep distress, her scarred face and hands hidden by gloves and a thick veil, Cesare would have laughed his head off.

Donna Lucrezia had insisted his children attend the Mass, so Camilla was there with two sisters from Corpus Domini, her face a small, grave oval, her red hair hidden by a white novice's veil. Don Alberto Pio and his wife had brought Girolamo in person rather than entrusting him to his tutors, and he sat between them on a bench, a perfectly solemn expression on his face as all the while he tickled Don Alberto's elder daughter and she squirmed beside him in an agony of mirth. I had made sure of a place for myself where I could watch him and reflect, not on his father, who was my past, but on the future which would begin the moment this service ended and we emerged once more into the light.

As soon as madonna had told me Girolamo would be coming to Ferrara for the Mass I had laid my plans. I had discovered Gideon's whereabouts from Fidelma and had written to him, though I doubted he would receive my letter before my son and I reached the shores of New Spain ourselves. I had booked passage from Venice anonymously, through agents of my family's business. I had sent on what little luggage I proposed to take with me into my new life, and had arranged post horses for a speedy journey to Venice. All this had been done without drawing the least suspicion; not for nothing had I been Valentino's mistress. All that now remained was to watch for the opportunity to take possession of my son and get him away from Ferrara before anyone noticed he had gone. The Corte and castle were in the usual chaos caused by guests descending on us, jostling for space and precedence, losing themselves in our warren of rooms and passages. It was worse than ever now much of the Torre Leone was out of use and Duke Alfonso had given Don Giulio's spacious palace to his favourite, Niccolo da Correggio. I had no doubt my opportunity would quickly present itself as long as I remained alert.

Just as the congregation fell silent to listen to Ippolito's eulogy, Don Alberto's daughter retaliated and kicked Girolamo's shin. He let out a howl of pain and pulled her hair. As Ippolito cleared his throat and shuffled his papers, and the adults turned looks of varying amusement and disapproval on the two children, Don Alberto's wife leaned across and reproved them gently. I saw her smile at her daughter and stroke

Girolamo's curls. He shuffled closer to her and laid his head against her side, his cheek fitted into the curve of her waist. She continued smoothing his hair and in seconds his eyes closed and he was asleep, a soft little moue of contentment playing about his mouth.

Ippolito began to speak, and in his elegant, meaningless phrases, in the silence of listening but not hearing, in which his audience wondered how long he was likely to go on and what they would be having for dinner after the service, I heard my heart crack. It sounded loud to me, as loud as breaking ice or burning glass, so I thought it best to leave the cathedral before it broke completely and distracted the congregation. Or woke my child. I did not mean to run. I knew it was disrespectful but less so, surely, than splintering in pieces in front of the great ladies and gentlemen, the scholars and merchants, all the assembled ranks of society to which I did not belong, had never belonged, though Girolamo did. Donna Lucrezia had made sure of it.

☙

I sailed from Venice with nothing in my mind but a swirl of broken memories cast off from the sinking ship of my heart. For several days I lay sick of the sea, tortured by the perfume of oranges and the blind gaze of the Madonna of Strangers, by cages that turned into food baskets, black flesh and white bread, white bones silted in black mud, dark eyes and white teeth and red rivers of hair. I think I hoped to die.

But Death is perverse; he rarely comes when you court him. I recovered; I found my sea legs and began to set my mind to how I would live, a woman alone in the raw, new world whose very newness made everything possible. It had no rules; it had not yet learned its limitations. When we put in at the Azores on the voyage out, one of our junior officers received word his wife had given birth to their first child. He wanted to send her a letter but was not sufficiently schooled in writing to be able to express himself as he wished. He asked if I could help him; the only other women on board were the captain's wife, whom he dared not approach, and the women who lived below decks and did laundry and other services for the crew, though not of the kind that extended to writing letters to their wives. His sentiments, he felt, were too delicate to share with another man.

I helped him. I found in myself a certain skill in ordering and articulating other people's feelings, and one way or another, I knew a lot about letters and the power of written words. By the time we docked in Villa Rica, I had already acquired quite a reputation among my shipmates. I took a room in a bustling house, part tavern, part rooming house, part brothel, just back from the city's main square, and with the money I had left after paying a month's rent I bought quills and pen-knives, a sand caster, a quantity of ink, and some clean parchments. My landlady's brother made me a sign, a flamboyant quill painted on a piece of silvery driftwood, and hung it in a mesquite tree that shaded the patch of red dust she had fenced off and called her terrace. There I sat, mornings and evenings, at a rickety table propped up with stones, writing other people's letters for money. My landlady took her tithe and blossomed in the aura of respectability I conferred on her house like the strange, bright, blowsy flowers that grew in the bush all around us. As she learned what little I was prepared to divulge about my past, she had her brother add a rough approximation of the arms of Este to my sign.

I dare say that is how Gideon found me. Queues formed quickly. Sometimes I would have several clients waiting for me as I set out my tools in the benign, deceitful light of early morning, in the sharp, blue shade of the mesquite. They would ask me to fashion requests for money or news from home, marriage proposals, accounts of successes or setbacks, letters full of passion or frozen with rejection. Light fell on my clients' lives the way it fell through the tavern's palm roof, in spots and slices, surrounded by shadow. I wrote prayers on small parchments to be left, tightly rolled, in the crevasses of holy rocks or church doors which had cracked in the hot, salty air. I wrote in Spanish or Latin or Italian or French with equal ease, as though the freedom of the new world had unfettered my tongue.

Best of all, though, were my love letters. I acquired some fame for my ability to mould the inarticulate urges of people in love into elegant, passionate phrases. Of course, many of those phrases were not my own. *I have wept so much I look like a man with snow blindness. I beg you to kiss my eyes, to soothe them one last time with the balm of your lips.* If the phrase had been my own, I doubt I would have remembered it. As I added the final flourish to the tail of the "s," I looked up and smiled. Because I knew the man who had wept away the night at Nepi had had no one to kiss his eyes, and I hoped the young lover standing in front of me, with his future glowing in his ruddy cheeks, would fare better. My client bowed to me and there, behind him, towering over his short, sturdy frame was Gideon, dressed like an Indian in a white cotton tunic with a parrot-bright woven belt. I waited while my client put his mark on the letter and handed over his money. Gideon watched as I set aside the tithe and pocketed the rest.

"I expected to hear from you," he said, placing the letter I had sent him from Ferrara on my table, "then someone told me there was a public letter writer in Villa Rica who was a woman. Something to see, I thought. Have you noticed yet how you can come all the way to a brand new world and it's still dominated by the same repetitive round as the old? Me hoping and you giving me the slip?"

I was disappointed. This did not sound like the man who had written to me about the importance of waiting with an open heart. "My plans didn't work out," I told him.

He drew up a stool and sat down in front of me so I could not help but look at his face. Though he smiled and his eyes were warm, it was a tired warmth, an old flame. The backs of his hands were cross-hatched with burns in various stages of healing. "I waited a month for you at Ostia," he said, resting his elbows on the table, "after word started to get about that Valentino was dead. I thought that might change your mind." An Indian woman in Spanish dress, her broad face frilled by an elaborate mantilla, started to shuffle her feet and sigh impatiently over Gideon's shoulder.

"Closed till the twenty-third hour," I said, "until the sun is over there." I pointed to the bell tower of the Church of the True Cross. The woman left, muttering in her own language, something which made Gideon laugh.

"You understand their language, then."

"So might you if you tried. She speaks the language of the Totonac people. I live in Cachiquin now, where they come from."

"And what did she call me?"

"You don't want to know."

I shrugged. I had been working since dawn. My eyes smarted and my shoulders were sore from the hours hunched over other people's desires. I wanted to eat, then sleep away the heat of the afternoon without dreaming. I was in no mood for games.

"So I was right, anyway," said Gideon.

"Right?"

"Valentino died and you came here. In the end. Is your son with you?"

I shook my head. I feared the sad taste of Girolamo's name in my mouth. Gideon reached across the table and covered my hand with his scarred, bony paw. "Let me take you somewhere to eat."

"I can eat here. It's free."

"I have money," he said. "Quite a bit, actually." Seeing me raise my eyes at his dress, his Indian tunic and the battered straw hat which lay in his lap, he added, "I dress for the weather. Had I been sure I'd be meeting you today I'd have tidied myself up a bit."

I noticed he was no longer wearing the gold ornament he had shown me the day he took me fishing. "Something's changed, Gideon. Where is your neck chain? What has happened?"

He shrugged. "I discovered old values and new worlds don't mix."

He took me to a place near the docks which was rough and cheap but famed for its fish stew and the good wine the proprietor managed to liberate from the warehouse next door, which belonged to a Genoese who had made a fortune in vanilla. Gideon told me he too cultivated and traded the spice in a small way, though he made most of his living fabricating and repairing the wire racks on which the slender black pods were spread to dry.

"Hence the burns," I said.

"Hence the burns. When I first got here, I thought goldsmithing would be easy. After all, this land is quite literally paved, or at least veined, with gold and silver. But the Indians believe gold is a sacred metal. Only their priests are allowed to work it, or their goldsmiths are priests. I've never quite worked out which way round it is. And I...don't like the way the Spanish have gone about things." For a moment his expression was clouded with a sullen anger. "I took off my charm and melted it down. It ended up as part of some meaningless nonsense I made for a sailor's sweetheart. The amount of blood that's been shed here over gold doesn't make it precious; it makes it shameful." Then he brightened. "Vanilla is much better because you can't really cultivate it, just hope the vines will grow up the trees you happen to own. Xanat says God only gives the black flowers to people with true hearts."

"That's nice. Who's Xanat?" He did not have to reply; I could tell from the shifty look in his eyes, the way he swallowed as though the answer he had prepared was best not spoken.

"Ah," I said. "And does she have a true heart?"

"We rub along," he said.

❧

The next day he came back and waited again at the end of my line of clients, clutching his old hat to his chest.

"Marry me, Esther," he said as soon as the last one had left. "I couldn't sleep a wink last night. I discussed my situation at length with the moths and the mosquitoes and quite a big lizard and they all said my finding you again like this was a providence and urged me to press my suit."

I laughed. The muscles of my face felt stiff, and I wondered when I had last laughed. "Don't tease me," I ordered him. "It's serious."

"Too late then."

"What about Xanat?"

He shrugged. "She is a native woman. Their customs are different."

My memory showed me a picture then, a Judith with the Head of Holofernes in a basket carried by a black slave. "That's just the way people talk about the Jews, Gideon, as if we aren't people with feelings too. I thought you said you'd abandoned the old values. Xanat is a woman. There's no difference between her and me."

"Why are you here, then, if not to find me?"

I could not tell him. Even now Donna Lucrezia is dead I cannot tell him, or anybody. I pray the letters were destroyed. "When I was a girl, we had a housekeeper called Mariam. Once, when I had reached a kind of crossroads in my life, she told me her advice was to follow love. I wasn't sure she knew what she was talking about then, but later I found out she did. I've tried to follow her advice. I was trying when I came here and I'm trying now. I'm sorry, Gideon, that's the best explanation I can give you."

"So marry me. Follow my love."

"It doesn't work that way. I have to follow my own, and I really don't think you'd want to go where it's taking me." I picked up my pen, dipped the nib in a cup of water to clean it, then laid it aside. "There is one more thing you need to know about Cesare Borgia and me, one thing you didn't find out from Don Giulio. He gave me my son, but he also gave me the French pox." As long as Cesare had lived, I had gone on believing in Ser Torella's pills, but his death had severed all my connections with hope, that sentiment he had warned me against. He was right; it is delusory. Sooner or later, if I managed to avoid snakebite, or the fever that turns the skin yellow or the one that blackens the urine, I was going to die of the pox. "He was a very jealous man, you see. He liked to brand his mistresses as his own."

"It's you I love, Esther. The disease is not you."

⧼⊗⧽

He was right, but it is a mask I wear, a convenient way of hiding my feelings. I came to Cachiquin when my health began to fail, but not to marry Gideon. I have found a measure of peace watching he and Xanat grow older together, entwined like tree and vine. I told him I would live with him as a sister, and I do. I am a dutiful aunt to his children, spoiling and scolding by turns. I have delivered all of them into this world and buried two. I cook and clean, make and mend alongside Xanat and sometimes I still write letters for other people. There is no one left for me to write to on my own account, no one who knows exactly what the word "sister" means to me.

⧼⊗⧽

So, I have reached the end. I raise my strained eyes from the page and look out through the open door, at our yard of beaten earth, our chickens and goats and Gideon's workshop where he makes the drying racks out of Toledo steel wire. Wraiths of blue smoke drift across my view of the forest, the trees all stripped of their lower branches and laced with vines, and their exotic scent is mixed with the homely smell of hot steel. Gideon says love is a heavy burden. I think of my parents, of Mariam, and Angela and Giulio, and Cesare and his Lucia, and two young men growing up in Ferrara who do not know who their mothers are, and realise I shall be content to lay that burden aside.

My eye is drawn to the orange tree, with its two hopeful green oranges and its jaunty, glossy leaves glittering against the darkness of the vanilla forest. I wonder if my son ever walks in the orangery when he visits Ferrara, if he ever sits in the loggia where he was made. I believed, when

I began, I was writing this account for myself, but now I realise it was always for him, the boy with the black eyes and the clever smile, and the river of red hair, the boy I loved and left behind.

*Finis*

# AFTERWORD

This is a work of fiction, a weaving together of imaginary people and the imagined lives of real historical figures. It lays no claim to historical accuracy.

A converted Jewess called La Violante was among the women who accompanied Lucrezia Borgia to Ferrara. Cesare did have a son called Girolamo whose mother is unknown. The paternity of Giovanni Borgia, the Infans Romanus, was attributed first to Cesare and then to Pope Alexander. Again, his mother is not known. What evidence there is for Lucrezia being pregnant at the time of her divorce from Giovanni Sforza amounts to little more than gossip. There is nothing but circumstantial evidence that Camilla's mother was Dorotea Caracciolo, or that Angela's child was fathered by Giulio d'Este. On the other hand, neither is there anything to refute these suppositions.

Lucrezia was married to Alfonso d'Este for seventeen years and they had five children. Their second son, Cardinal Ippolito d'Este II, built the famous Villa d'Este at Tivoli. Lucrezia was sincerely mourned on her death in childbirth aged only thirty-nine, and is still fondly remembered by the Ferrarese for the sophistication of her court and the gallantry with which she helped defend the city against an army led by Pope Julius II during the War of the League of Cambrai. She kept up her correspondence with Pietro Bembo for the rest of her life, and her intimate friendship with Francesco Gonzaga right up to his death in March 1519, three months before her own. Isabella outlived them both by twenty years.

Ferrante d'Este died in prison in 1540. He was sixty-three and had spent thirty-four years without a visit from a single member of his family. Giulio was released on the accession of Lucrezia's grandson, Alfonso II. He was eighty-one years old and had spent fifty-three of those years locked up.

History does not record whether Angela Borgia was then still living. She disappears from the historical record around the time of Cesare's death, as does La Violante.

Both Giovanni and Girolamo Borgia remained at the court of Ferrara. Giovanni seems to have been an ineffectual man, tolerated by Alfonso d'Este out of affection for his wife. Girolamo married one of Alberto Pio's daughters and was a popular figure, but was overshadowed in later life by his association with several mysterious deaths. Cesare's daughters fared better. Camilla Borgia became abbess of the Convent of Corpus Domini and died there in 1573 with a reputation for saintliness and administrative ability. Luisa, through her second marriage to Philippe de Bourbon, founded the line of Counts of Bussett and Chalus which continues to this day. Luisa's mother, Charlotte d'Albret, never remarried and lived the rest of her life in deep mourning for her husband.

Vannozza outlived all her Borgia children except Lucrezia, Jofre having died suddenly in Naples in 1517. Her funeral was attended by the entire court of the then pope Leo X who, as Giovanni de' Medici, had been at university in Pisa with Cesare.

Michelotto da Corella is last heard of as a *condottiere* in the pay of Florence, a commission for which he was recommended by Niccolo Machiavelli, Florence's ambassador to the court of Cesare Borgia. Cesare was famously Machiavelli's model for chapter 7 of *The Prince,* on *New principalities acquired with the help of fortune and foreign arms.*

The constraints of this novel and the particular issues I wanted to explore in it have obliged me to simplify drastically the political and military background, especially relating to Cesare's invasion of Urbino and the Senigallia coup. My chosen viewpoint has also led to my underplaying the diplomatic skill and shrewdness of Pope Alexander VI, whose colourful personal life tends to have overshadowed the contribution he made to keeping foreign invaders out of Italy by consolidating the temporal power of the papacy. I have also conflated the two trips Cesare made to Ferrara during Lucrezia's illness of late summer 1502. I have also taken a small liberty with the game of *calcio fiorentino*, a form of football that is first recorded in Florence in the sixteenth century, so a little later than the setting of this book. I think it very likely, however, that Italians have always played football!

For readers who want to delve further into the history of the Borgias, I cannot recommend too highly as a starting point Sarah Bradford's elegant, insightful, and compassionate biographies of Cesare and Lucrezia, *Cesare Borgia, His Life and Times* and *Lucrezia Borgia: Life, Love and Death in Renaissance Italy.*

# ACKNOWLEDGMENTS

My thanks are due first and foremost to Emma Barnes and all at Snowbooks, to Shana Drehs and the team at Sourcebooks, and to Stephanie Thwaites. Love and gratitude, as always, to Mary Allen, Mary-Jane Cullen, and Sue Fletcher, to Bernardine Coverley and Ingrid Perrin, and to my fellow members of Writers Without Walls: Harriet Carter, Karen Cheung, Claire Hynes, Gary Kissick, Claire MacDonald, Michelle Remblance, Iain Robinson, and Barrie Sherwood. Great feeds, great feedback. Last but not least, love and thanks to Mark for sharing his life with the Borgias with such equanimity.

# ABOUT THE AUTHOR

S arah Bower has worked at an assortment of jobs, from call centres to market stalls. After many years working in the charitable sector, she became a professional writer and creative writing tutor after completing an MA in creative writing at the University of East Anglia. She lives in the country with her husband, two dogs, and a geriatric cat. She is the author of *The Needle in the Blood*.

# The Needle in the Blood

BY SARAH BOWER

AN ENTHRALLING NOVEL EXPLORING THE MANY MYSTERIES OF
A FAMOUS TAPESTRY—AND OF THE HUMAN HEART...

The charismatic Bishop Odo of Bayeux, brother to William the
Conqueror of Normandy, commissions a tapestry to record the
conquest of England. Gytha, previously handmaiden to the mistress
of Odo's enemy, is hired as an embroiderer. As Odo's life becomes
entangled with Gytha's, he comes into conflict with his king and
his God. Friends become enemies, enemies become lovers, nothing
in life or in the hanging is what it seems.

*"A story of love, war, and the tangled truth of Britain."*
—Sarah Bryant,
author of *Sand Daughter*

## Coming 2012

978-1-4022-6252-4